A SENSE OF IT

A SENSE OF DUTY

A SENSE OF DUTY

Sheelagh Kelly

HarperCollins*Publishers*

HarperCollins*Publishers*
77–85 Fulham Palace Road,
Hammersmith, London W6 8JB

Published by HarperCollins*Publishers* 1999
1 3 5 7 9 10 8 6 4 2

Reprinted 2000

A catalogue record for this book is
available from the British Library

ISBN 0 00 225739 4

Typeset in Ehrhardt by Palimpsest Book Production limited,
Polmont, Stirlingshire

Printed and bound in Great Britain by
Omnia Books Limited, Glasgow

For the Dead
in appreciation of their sufferings

PART 1

Childhood

1855–1861

I

Katherine Kilmaster weighed fourteen pounds at birth. She was her mother's last child.

This was not to say that her entry to the world caused maternal expiry, merely that the shock of it inspired firm decision: no more would Beata Kilmaster suffer thus. Alas, how could she or anyone else predict that in another way it was already too late, that Katherine's arrival would affect the lives of every member of this family?

The huge blood-smeared infant burst into the February night on an explosion of steam, inflicting a discomfort that would extend far beyond the immediate physical pain. After twenty years of marriage, a three-year gap since the entry of the last baptism in the family bible and all the indications of a dwindling fertility, Beata had dared to assume that her childbearing days were over and that the poverty which had dogged her could soon be remedied as first one and then another of her offspring started work. Hence her air of dread upon experiencing that familiar squirm of new life within, her abdominal skin stretching tauter and tauter until it appeared it might split – and little wonder, commented observers now at Katherine's dramatic entrance in the bedroom of the Kilmasters' tiny cottage.

'Lord a'mercy, she's a biggun!' came the gasp from one of the youngsters crammed into the solitary bedroom with their parents, all craning their necks for a look at the product of their mother's labour who had kept them from sleep and who now slithered from beneath the maternal nightgown on to a straw palliasse. 'There be more meat on her than Ashman's pig!'

Naturally, no one was aware of her exact weight as they all gathered round to gape at the bawling newcomer with fists like small hammers

3

and thighs like Christmas hams. This extraordinary fact was only to be revealed a few days later when Katherine, swathed in a ragged shawl, was bundled from the rickety stone hovel, along the frosty village street to the grocery, accompanied by an eager gaggle of spectators, carried through to the back of the shop amidst the sacks of flour and oats, and dumped with great ceremony on to the scales normally reserved for potatoes.

'A ztow-n!' A shriek of incredulity distorted the grocer's Somerset burr as he employed yet another brass weight to counterbalance the hefty babe. 'A full stone! Well, I nevurr seen the loike – you'm given birth to a sack o'taters, missus!'

'And to be sure that were what it felt like,' the sorely afflicted mother declared to an astonished, tittering crowd who had been laying wagers on the outcome. 'Never again!'

The latter phrase was to become commonly heard in the following months, during which Beata lost none of her sense of amazement, exemplified by a shake of head and a heavy sigh every time she laid eyes upon her seventh living child. If the climacteric could not be trusted to halt conception, then one look at the enormous Katherine most surely did the trick, as Beata was keen to inform anyone who had not yet heard. ''Twere like being delivered of an elephant. Never again!'

And her sigh was echoed more mournfully by her husband, Richard, who could not fail to interpret the unspoken message: his conjugal pleasures had been mercilessly docked.

From the outset the effort to feed and clothe Katherine was a constant battle for this unskilled labourer and his wife. Notwithstanding the contributions made by his two elder children and the allowance of flour from his employer the miller, the eleven shillings Richard earned were woefully insufficient to maintain nine in victuals, let alone pay the one and sixpence rent and the doctor's bills, and the incessant need to reclothe.

By her third birthday, Katherine – or Kit as she had become – was almost as large as her six-year-old sister, Amelia, whose outgrown dresses lasted barely a month on Kit before her sturdy knees were showing beneath the hem. Inheriting a deeper, richer version of her father's auburn hair, but alas his lofty stature too; her mother's clear blue gaze, but her propensity to accrue fat, Kit was someone to be pitied or teased, though never ignored. Yet, as the newest member of the Kilmaster family grew, so did a warm and amiable personality, and despite being the cause of extra

4

hardship she became a favourite with her father, who, denied any form of tenderness from his wife lest it lead to dangerous intimacy, turned his own limited affections to Kit, calling her his big, beautiful girl and donating a sweetmeat from the pocket of his coarse linen frock-smock on the rare occasions he had a half-farthing to spare.

This did not sit well with others: Montague, the eldest, condemned as a reprobate by his father for his inability to show deference to those in high office and thereby keep a job; fifteen-year-old Gwen who should have been allowed time to court a sweetheart after working so hard in the fields but instead was fettered to the home by yet another youngster, especially one of such proportions – 'Why, I do need a crane to lift her!'; Owen and Amelia, small enough still to need parental indulgence. There were few enough morsels of benevolence to go round as it was in this austere and overcrowded household – why, they asked, should this gurt lump of a child be the one to receive them?

Nor did Richard's wife approve of his acts of waste when she herself had been forced to take in laundry to eke out their income. Hence, when Kit's pretensions of daintiness caused her to lollop around the room in lively imitation of the dancing she had seen around the village maypole, she drew not compliment but ridicule from the children and rebuke from her mother, who whipped her soundly to discourage her from pagan ritual and the even greater sin of self-importance. To Beata, Kit was just an oddity to be paraded as testament to her own powers of endurance. Any display of fondness, which would usually only extend to a pat, was always accompanied by that distinctive shake of the head and that telling sigh of, 'Never again.'

Far from being warped by the combined disapproval, this happy child did not see herself through others' eyes and merely danced when no one was around to curb her, danced to the hymns learned at chapel, performing for her own delight or perhaps for Charity, the only one of her sisters not to mock. She yearned to be able to dance for her father too, but received stern warning that it ill behoved the child of a respectable Methodist family to occupy herself thus.

Seeking male approbation elsewhere, Kit decided one day to await her elder brother's homecoming from the coal mine, accustomed and unafraid now of Montague's devilish face, for out of the blackness shone kind blue eyes. It might have been a risk, for Monty, being such a disappointment

5

to his father, could have resented the subject of Richard's favours. True, he did harbour a grudge that every penny he earned was poured into the family coffer, receiving small thanks in exchange, but he was not so mean as some to direct it at this innocent child.

Disporting herself before him in twirling skirts, bare buttocks and all, Kit was thrilled when, instead of issuing outright condemnation, her brother gaped and stuttered, 'Very expert, Kit, but –', which she immediately grasped as praise and cavorted with even more abandon, robbing him of the heart to complete his reproach. Henceforth, whenever the opportunity arose she danced for him, eager for an audience and too young to decipher the hint of censure that accompanied his kindness.

Then, one evening after Kit had gone to bed, there came up through the floor the sound of angry voices that rose into a fiery exchange between mother and son. On the surface, Monty was a reserved and pensive individual like his father, but when confronted would display his mother's lack of self-control, and there was most definitely confrontation that night, for the next morning he had vanished.

Bereft, Kit risked censure from her mother to ask where he was, as the two of them were labouring over a steaming trough of laundry in the barren twiggy area behind the cottage where the only sign of greenery was in the late winter vegetables.

'He be gone to look for work!' Though parsimonious with affection, Beata always had time to answer queries, however young the interrogator. Besides, there was something in Kit's attitude that transformed her three years into thirty-three and often Beata genuinely forgot she was speaking to a child. 'The quarrelsome young varmint, he's lost himself another job – that's a score he's had since he left school! You'd think with times being so bad round 'ere and half the population gone from the village to the town to find work he'd think himself lucky, but do he ever?' Her voice lingered as a cloud on the cold morning air, her fists scarlet on the wooden handle of the posser as it rose and plunged. 'Tried everything from making buttons to digging coal, not expert at any of 'em, and he still thinks he can tell the master how to do the job. Don't know where he gets that temper from, his father's such a mild-mannered soul.' Under her violent thrashing water trickled over the sides of the tub, mingling with the stream of effluent from the nearby pigsty, plus that from the shallow excavations that held human waste. 'Wrong time o' year for the hiring fair – at any rate everybody round 'ere knows Monty Kilmaster too well to risk hiring him – so, he be gone to other parts, and there's your answer.'

'Is he comin' back?' asked her wistful assistant, with infantile attempts to attack the laundry in the trough using a sized-down version of her mother's posser.

'Better not if he don't get no job!' puffed an exerted Beata with nary a hint that she might be joking. The loss of Monty's wage had made a huge deficit in her housekeeping. 'I'd kick him out fer good.'

'Aw, don't do that, Mother!' appealed Kit, too young to realize she was about to let slip her secret. 'Who'd I have to dance for then?'

'Didn't I tell 'ee about that?' Beata delivered a clout that was laden with suds, knocking the infant off her feet to land in the surrounding quagmire. 'Sinful child! I don't know where you learn it – certainly not in this house. You'll dance for the Devil, indeed you will.'

And Kit wept, not at being deemed sinful, for she did not know what sin was, but for the supposed loss of her brother.

However, to Kit's great joy, a month later to coincide with bud burst, a newly matured Monty – one with grand gestures and a confident manner – was to burst through the door on a rain-lashed Saturday afternoon, presenting his mother with a fistful of coins that was sufficient advertisement of new-found labour.

'Had to travel 'cross watter to get it but it were well worth the journey! Yes, indeed, well worth it.' A glint of satisfaction in his eye, he bashed his cap over his palm, sending droplets of rain on to the stone floor, then hung this and his jacket on a hook near the fireplace, adding cheerfully to the passive figure who sat by the hearth. 'Good day to you, Father!'

Flour in his auburn hair and still dressed in his working smock and gaiters, Richard regarded him quizzically for a moment, then pointedly ignored him to attend to more important things than this lackadaisical youth who assumed the air of prodigal son but in truth was not worth a candle. Horny-nailed fingers grappled with an earthenware flagon, lifting it from a shelf and transferring a measure of the cider within to a mug already laced with ginger. A drink brewed from "God's good apples" could never be adjudged sinful. Kit watched as her father removed a red-hot iron from the grate and plunged it into the pot, the resultant frothing and hissing making her giggle and clap her hands.

'Zuppose you be wanting a drop too?'

'Why, thank 'ee kindly.' Monty knew the query to be directed at him; it could not be addressed at anyone else, such was the tone of its indifference.

With a sigh Richard temporarily raised his large body from the chair to reach for another mug, whilst instructing one of his daughters to bring more ginger, then with no great enthusiasm handed the steaming vessel to his son.

As yet unseated, his tall frame having to stoop in order to avoid impaling his head on the various hooks that dangled from the low-beamed ceiling, a grateful Monty tilted his mug, feeling the ginger hit the back of his throat. Then, after a lick of his lips, and with Kit at his side, he told the family how, with no work forthcoming in the local vicinity, he had taken the ferry across the Severn into Monmouthshire and had immediately gained employment in a small coal-mining community. 'So I reckon I'll bide there for a twelvemonth – or longer if my bond's renewed – if that's to yur likin'.' As was his lifelong habit he directed all queries at his mother. There might be friction between them but it sprang from a base of genuine affection. His father rarely argued with him – never argued with anyone – just held his opponent in contempt. In fact his father abhorred emotion of any kind; even his punishments were administered with calm deliberation.

'You think I mind if you take that filthy coal dust into somebody else's house?' Beata gave a sharp laugh and examined her son's clothes for a hint of grime, of which there was none, save for that lodged deep in his skin. 'So long as you're not paying too much for rent. But pray tell who's scrubbing your back now?'

Monty chose not to answer the latter query, replying confidently, 'Oh no! Just a few pence for a bed and a bite to eat.' He took a quick gulp of the cider, somewhat discomforted by his father's narrow-eyed stare. 'They're decent folk, very decent. I made a lot o' friends already.'

Beata was unconcerned with these new acquaintances, only that her son was contributing to the family's income again. 'Well, just make sure you don't let this job slip.'

8

'Oh, that I will! I learned my lesson, Mam. I don't want to lose such a good place.' And that's a fact, thought Monty, who had no intention of coming back here to slave his life away just for his mother to take every penny of his wage and his father to display such ingratitude. 'No, I'll do as I'm bidden from now on.'

A faint breath of scorn emerged from his father whose eyes remained fixed on the coals.

'Mm.' Beata sounded doubtful too, but as the coins chinked through her fingers she began to smile and even made a joke. 'Biss thee fetching this amount home every month? 'Pon my word, yur father an' me can soon retire! Bide thee here and take sup with us.'

Monty developed a sudden nervous tic. Beneath the facade of the homecoming hero, the more perspicacious amongst them glimpsed the callowness of a nineteen-year-old, unsure of his place in the world. He sat at the table, auburn head lowered whilst grace was said, and afterwards partook heartily of the special weekly ration of boiled bacon, bread and butter, with shortcake to follow, inwardly grateful that no conversation was permitted during meals.

The rest of the Kilmasters gathered round, only those who earned their living being allowed to have a chair. For Kit, bursting to speak to her favourite family member, the meal was a trial, especially as her father seemed to take much longer than usual to consume it, chewing his bacon in thoughtful examination of his elder son whose freckled cheeks reddened under the scrutiny and who wolfed down his own meal as if it would be his last.

After tea, the children were granted free rein to question Monty who, still pinioned by his father's gimlet eye, babbled uncontrollably until birdsong eventually gave way to the croak of amphibia from the pond on the common.

'Han't you better be on your way?' asked his mother, lighting candles and closing the curtains – two pieces of dimity nailed above the window and draped inelegantly on either side by means of hooks. 'Long road to travel if you want to be back in time for work on Monday, and best go while the rain's eased. Here, I'll get 'ee a lantern.'

Nostrils tingling with the scent of newly ignited candlewax, Monty shot to his feet and reached for his cap and jacket. 'Oh er, I suppose I better had be off.'

9

Kit, until now perched on a piece of sacking on the bare floor, sprang up with a wail.

'Hush! You'll see him again. Be making your visit once a month, will 'ee, Monty?' asked Beata, her mood buoyed by the donation of cash. 'Though, faith, you're welcome any time if you bring gurt handfuls o' silver like that.' She chuckled gaily and threw her shawl around her shoulders to ward off the nighttime chill that was trickling between the planks of the door, her action setting the candle flames guttering.

Her son shifted uncomfortably in his still-damp breeches, his blue eyes those of a man destined for execution. 'Well, er, I might not be seeing so much o' 'ee in future – I'm getting wed, you see!'

'I knowed it!' barked Richard, to whom the glint in his son's eye had been instantly recognizable, which is why he had been watching him so relentlessly, awaiting the confession. 'I knowed dang well he were hiding zommat!'

Beata was at first speechless, then furious, abandoning her search for the lantern. 'You selfish little – out! Get 'ee gone from this house!' She dealt her son a hefty shove towards the door, which was swiftly opened by one of the girls. 'Leading us on like that! All these years I been slaving after you, and another woman gets the benefit! How we goin' feed these children without yur wage? Tell me that!' She poked Monty in the chest, ignoring Kit's tears, as he backed through the doorway, his red cheeks clashing with his hair.

'I'll send you money when I can!' Hardly granted time to lower his head so as not to bang it on the lintel, the lanky youth stumbled over the threshold, a round-eyed audience gathering in the doorway behind their mother.

'Not once she gets her hands on it you won't!' yelled Beata, eyes like chips of jet. 'Turning yur head with her wicked ways – I know her sort! Well, go on! Back to your doxy!'

'Don't call her that, Mam!' begged Monty, on the street now, his face pleading earnestly through the dusk whilst the whites of his siblings' eyes shone in awe. 'Sarah's a lovely girl. It's not my money she's after, her father's deputy at the pit, she could wed anyone she fancies – so you see I'm marrying well.' He omitted the fact that his prospective in-laws shared Beata's antipathy for the match. 'I know you'll like her. Come to my wedding, 'tis two weeks from to –'

'And when's the child expected?' yelled his mother.

'Beata!' Richard deplored such scenes. 'There bain't no call for crudity.'

At his masterful tone Beata reined in her temper somewhat, wrapping her shawl tightly around her, but her chin remained jutted in obduracy. 'Ain't there? He's known her but four weeks; you're telling me she han't tricked him into marrying her? And ain't you forgetting something, my boy? You're not of age yet. What happens if your father and me don't give our consent?'

Peeking between a skirt and a gaitered leg, Kit's blue eyes were wide, studying first one opponent then the other, whose voices drowned out the frogs' lovesong.

Monty abandoned his pathetic air, adopting the look of determination that had got him into trouble with countless employers. 'She han't tricked me and she bain't having no child! I love her and we're goin' be wed, consent or no.' Mouth set, he planted his cap firmly on his head. 'I come here in good heart to invite you and Father –' He broke off and said hurriedly by way of explanation to his disappointed siblings, especially Kit who looked most fearful and hurt by the verbal aggression, 'We can't afford to have you all – we need every penny we got – but you'll all meet Sarah in time. The honour's still open to you, Mother, Father, if you care to come. You know where to find us.' He made as if to go. Bats, newly emerged from hibernation, swooped and veered around the cottage.

Beata made one last swoop herself, but this time used a different tactic. 'Please, please, don't do it, son! You haven't known her five minutes.'

'Long enough to know she's the girl I want to marry.' Monty altered his approach too, attempting to caress with his voice. 'I'm sorry, Mother, I can't go back on my word, I really can't. A man has a duty.'

His father's floury lungs wheezed in mirth, he threw up his hands and brought them smacking down upon his knees, his anger tempered by a sense of the ridiculous.

'Your duty is to this family!' Tears of frustration blurred the hardness in his mother's dark eyes but it was there in her voice. 'Call yourself a man? Well, in my book a man wouldn't come 'ere and slap his money on the table then take it away with his other hand! There's only one thing'd make you a man in my eyes and that'd be for you to repay all that's been invested in you!'

Guilt-ridden, for he knew what she said to be true, Monty retreated down the unlit, unpaved country road between the naked silhouettes of oak and elm, eager to be away as his mother shrilled after him, 'Well, don't you go 'specting to see us at this mockery you call a wedding! We ain't got money for luxuries, nor time to waste neither. If you've abandoned your duty others'll just have to do it for 'ee!' And she would have shouted more had her husband not commanded her to show some decency, at which she ordered her family to bed, slamming the door on her errant son as a mark of finality.

Whilst Mother and the older girls rushed back and forth from table to scullery in a furious rattling of crockery, a tearful Kit sobbed to her father, 'Ain't our Monty coming back?'

Though seething with contempt at his son's desertion, Richard administered words of balm whilst urging her to hurry into her nightgown. 'Don't 'ee worry about all this fuss, my beauty. You'll see your brother again. More's the pity,' came the muttered addition. 'Your mam don't mean half o' what she says. Give her a fortnight to get over it an' she'll be pestering to go to Monty's wedding – if only to have a look at the woman who stole her boy.' And God help that poor girl, came his bitter thought, having to rely on that idle ne'er-do-well as a husband. 'No, your mam won't give up her lad without a struggle. Mark my words.'

And sure enough within the week Beata was sewing ribbon on her bonnet and braid on the dress she normally wore only to chapel, and grumbling over the pay her husband would lose in order to travel the hundred miles or more to and from the wedding. Thus, Kit learned to rely on her father's word. If Father said such and such was going to happen, then so it surely would.

Caught up in the air of excitement on the morning of her parents' departure, she begged to be allowed to go to Monty's wedding with them, not simply in order to see her brother again, but because she hated being left in Gwen's charge, for her fifteen-year-old sister would be even bossier in their mother's absence and inflict more petty rules than usual.

'Couldn't I come?' Her large open face directed its plea to her father.

Richard, freshly shorn for the occasion, was barely listening as he

12

cleaned a last speck of flour from the wagon that his employer had lent him for this special trip. When he had casually mentioned his elder son's wedding to the miller, he had not expected so magnanimous a gesture as the loan of the vehicle and three days' release from his labours. Any argument that he had put up about his employer being discommoded by his absence fell flat when the miller said it would be easy enough to hire a temporary labourer in Richard's place. Even the objection that he was unable to manage without the pay was rendered invalid, for he was offered a loan, without interest, and the chance to repay it when harvest time brought extra work; no one should be deprived of attending their son's nuptials. Beata might have grumbled at the financial disablement, but had become doggedly intent on witnessing her son's marriage. Thus, Richard found himself pushed into a trip he would rather not make.

Now he stood back to inspect the bay horse in its harness of polished leather and ornamental brass. 'What was that you said, my dear?'

'Can't I come?' repeated Kit. 'I'm only little, there be plenty of room in the cart for me.'

Whilst her siblings howled with laughter and made quips about her size, Richard smiled down at her and swept off his wide-awake hat, his red hair arguing violently with the bright yellow wagon. ''Tain't that there's no room, my dear, but your brother can't rightly be expected to feed all of us. He's only a young chap and he need all the money he got for his new life.' It was said not in defence of Monty but to cushion the little girl's feelings.

'But I want to see him,' Kit sulked.

'What makes you think you're more 'portant than us?' challenged eight-year-old Owen, his dark features set in the mould of adult disapproval. 'We all want to go but we can't. So stop behaving like a baby.'

Kit started to cry.

'Oh, now, now!' The impatience Richard felt at his wretch of a son for dragging him off to a wedding on the far side of nowhere was for a moment deflected on to Kit. 'You'll see Monty again 'ere too long. Don't make such a fuss, you know I can't abide it. Here, dry your eyes, your mother's a-coming.' He pulled his best, his one and only, handkerchief from the green second-hand tail coat he normally reserved for chapel and handed it to the child. Then, planting his hat on his auburn head he went to divest his wife of the basket of food she had prepared for the journey, lodging it in the wagon. The other children lined up to take their last orders from their mother.

Whilst they were thus engaged, Richard bent and murmured to the still-tearful Kit, 'Hush now, let there be an end to it. We'll not be gone too long if I have anything to say about the matter. Here, gimme that 'kerchief a minute.' Snatching it, he proceeded to tie a loose knot in each corner, then waggled the handkerchief under her nose. 'Now each morn when 'ee get out o' bed I want you to unfasten one o' those knots – just one a day mind – and when you've untied the last one you must count to five, turn around, then run outside and you'll see me and Mother coming down that road there, I promise.'

'Richard Kilmaster, what heathen nonsense are you spouting to that child?' demanded his wife, but in pleasant mood at the thought of the big adventure ahead.

'Nuthin!'

'I heard it all! And what're you gonna do if you need to wipe your nose, pray tell?'

'I got two sleeves, ain't I?'

'Fie!' Beata gathered her knitted shawl around her, laughing. 'He looks like a dandy till he opens his mouth. Don't bend over that far, my boy, they kerseys won't take the strain.' The buff kerseymere pantaloons bought for a few pence had been expertly mended but their fragility bespoke the fact that there had been several wearers before Richard. 'A good job you're wearing a tail coat to cover your shortcomings.'

By way of answer Richard extended a hand round his rear to act as reinforcement, but remained crouched over his daughter. 'Now, you understand what I tell 'ee, Kit?'

Kit gazed into his brown eyes, her tear-stained face creasing as she tried to memorize his instructions, fingers playing with the knots.

'Don't 'ee untie them yet!' Richard warned. 'Or 'twon't work.'

Others watched the interplay, wondering resentfully why their father, usually such an undemonstrative man, chose to lavish so much attention on one who contributed nothing. Kit's tears seemed to affect him where theirs could not.

The lofty figure straightened his back, tugged the edges of his bottle-green coat, assisted his wife into the yellow wagon, then grabbed the reins and clambered up next to her. Sensing departure, the horse snorted and shifted from leg to leg, jingling its harness.

Clutching the important handkerchief, Kit stood and waved with the others as the cart bearing their parents rumbled down the village street, over the bridge and out of sight, her father's instructions already a blur in her three-year-old mind.

The next day Kit woke early, roused by a feeling that there was something crucial to be done. Screwing her knuckles into her eyes, she suddenly remembered her father's handkerchief downstairs and kicked herself free of the blankets, making contact with her bedfellows in the process. Groans of censure emerged from the warm mounds in the patchwork quilt. The culprit bit her lip and looked innocent, waiting for the cross faces to retreat under the covers before padding across the floorboards. Carefully negotiating the decrepit staircase, she went downstairs to retrieve the handkerchief, then out into the half-light where fumbling fingers undid every knot, the child totally forgetting the rest of her father's instructions.

Though the sun was attempting to emerge, appearing as a golden haze on the dark horizon, it was a cold and unpromising start to the day. Kit hugged the handkerchief against her nightgowned chest and peered down the road, then beyond to the north-west where the bluish rise of the Mendip Hills could be seen in the distance. She concentrated her eyes on the route into the village. There was no sign of her parents, just the stark, eerie outline of a leafless tree bent almost double by centuries of wind, clawing at the air like an arthritic hand. Perching on the damp step she waited, sang a hymn, then fell silent, chewing a corner of the handkerchief and shivering. Nearby, a blackbird began to trill, cheering her somewhat. In time others joined the chorus. Smoke began to curl from chimneys, faint grunting emerged from the pigsty, a dog yapped, and soon besmocked labourers emerged from neighbouring cottages to start the day's toil.

There were sounds of life from within her own cottage too and shortly Gwen came out to draw water from the well, simultaneously ordering Kit inside for breakfast. To disobey would be inviting wrath, and so after a last lingering look down the road the subject responded. Inside, a cast-iron pot squatted over the fire, a row of empty bowls awaiting its bubbling grey contents – a mixture of flour, butter and water. The loaf that would serve as lunch sat as yet unbaked upon the hearth. Kit stood up to the table to say prayers between Flora and Charity. Amelia had needed a box in order to be able to reach her bowl at Kit's age, but not this strapping infant.

In their parents' absence the rule of silence at mealtimes was ignored. 'What you been a-doing out there?' demanded her eldest sister after grace was said – with Gwen it was always a demand, never a query – and when Kit told her she uttered a scold. 'Ninny! They won't be coming back this soon.'

'They will,' retorted Kit, through a mouthful of gruel. 'Father said when there weren't no more knots in the hanky he and Mother'd be coming back.' And what Father said was always true.

'You weren't meant to untie 'em all at once!' Jealousy had caused Owen to eavesdrop on the conversation between his father and Kit. 'And I bet you ain't done anything else right. He told you to count to five and turn round before you went outside.'

Kit's blue eyes widened and the hand holding her spoon paused in mid-air.

'Oh, you gone and done it now, Kit,' teased Flora. 'They won't be a-coming back at all.'

Kit's lips trembled. Amelia looked concerned too. Eleven-year-old Charity gave a comforting laugh and as usual sprang to the little one's aid. 'She's pulling your leg! Of course they'll be back.'

The youngest child turned to Gwen, but was told sternly, 'They won't if you don't do as yur bidden – an' if you spill aught on that tablecloth you'll get a good whipping! I'm sick o' you making extra work for me.' As eldest girl she had always felt close to her father and had until recent years rather enjoyed the role of little wife, looking after his other children, but now come to womanhood she resented being held back from her true adult role, especially when the one who kept her prisoner was a rival for her father's attentions. He never so much as looked at her these days. 'Wish I could escape like our Monty.' A heavy sigh. 'But I suppose one of us has to behave responsibly. Come on now, all of you, eat up, I ain't got time to bide here all day, I got work to go to.'

Kit inserted the spoon between trembling lips, worrying throughout breakfast over her parents. Whilst the table was being cleared, she got dressed, stood in line to have the tangles brushed out of her hair by the impatient Gwen, then, trailing the handkerchief behind her like a pennant, she ran outside again to sit and wait. The elder girls left for work on the farm, placing her in the kinder hands of Charity who, in response to Kit's anxious enquiry, explained that of course their parents would be home but not for three or four days. Having no inkling of time, Kit maintained her optimistic vigil until the sun went down and it was time for bed, clutching the handkerchief to her breast. But still her father and mother did not come.

Monty was overjoyed to have his parents attend his nuptials, though he did wish his mother wouldn't harp on so to his in-laws throughout the wedding breakfast about how much she would miss his financial contributions: it would cause him eternal guilt.

Thankfully her nagging seemed not to affect his bride, Sarah, who remained as sweet as the day he had fallen for her, invited the groom's parents to stay the night and replenished their basket with food for the long journey home, including slivers of wedding cake for the children. Despite which, Beata could not resist giving her daughter-in-law a last warning before making ready to leave – a warning that held a touch of reproach.

'Well, you are indeed very fair, my dear, and very obliging too. Thank 'ee for the victuals. I can see why my son's so smitten he's run off and left us.' Beata's eyes retained that look of suspicion as they toured the figure in the white dress and bonnet. 'But I do hope you know what you're taking on. Monty has a rotten temper on him. I dare say we'll see him come a-storming home if he don't like what you're giving him for dinner.'

Sarah's dark-eyed gaze remained level, though her sentence held as many undulations as the Welsh landscape of her birth. 'Then I'll just have to come over and drag him back, won't I?'

Staring back into the friendly but unyielding face, Beata was given the first evidence of her daughter-in-law's iron will, and knew finally that her son was lost to her. A nod of understanding passed between the two women. Monty felt a twinge of pity for his mother as she turned to climb up into the wagon, helped by her husband, who was obviously keen to be away. Out of conscience, he grabbed her hand and

17

pressed a coin into it. 'Sorry I can't afford more, Mam, but it'll pay for the ferry.'

Beata surprised him with her warmth that extended beyond her voice to her eyes. 'Why, thank you, my dear! That's most welcome. And hark' – she gripped his fingers with uncommon tenderness – 'forget that nonsense I talked about 'ee not doing your duty. You're a good lad.' Loath to agree, her husband hung his head and said naught, his fingers impatient upon the reins. 'And she be a fine young woman you've chosen. You'll both be welcome any time you want to visit. I hope that'll be soon or we won't hear the last of it from Kit! She been going on an' on – ain't that right, Father?'

Wearing the falsely patient smile he always employed with his elder son, Richard Kilmaster confirmed this, telling the young groom of his instructions about the knots to Kit. 'Well, giddup, horse!' He flicked the reins. 'Let's see if 'ee can get us to that ferry before nightfall.'

'Oh, I'm dreading it!' Still holding on to her son with her eyes, Beata groaned and clutched her breast as the wagon wheels jolted into movement. 'All the way across I be thinking we're going to sink at any minute – goodbye, my zonner! Goodbye!'

And her waving hand was swallowed up into the morning mist.

As fate would have it, they arrived at the coast too late to catch the last ferry of daylight and, unwilling to travel over water in darkness Beata said they should camp by the shore until morning.

Aching from the bumpy ride, Richard was not averse to this suggestion and, after making the horse comfortable, saw to his own needs. 'Leastwise we got plenty o' grub.' Big face smiling in anticipation, he lifted the edge of the cloth that covered the basket.

Beata slapped his hand. 'That's got to last till we get home! Small chance o' that with you troughing every five minutes. No, you go collect some o' them mussels like them folk're doing.' She indicated a group of people who were levering shellfish from the hull of a boat that had been dragged from the water for repairs. 'No point throwing away the chance of free food.'

'No indeed,' muttered Richard, reluctantly abandoning the basket and loping off towards the boat. ''Twould never do to spoil ourselves once in a while.'

Later, having collected a hatful of the blue–black shellfish, he was still not greatly impressed. 'Why we have to put up with these when there's good victuals going stale in that basket . . .' He sighed and shook his head. 'I'll wager that ne'er-do-well son of ours is getting better fare, and him so undeserving. Sarah's a good cook for one so young, ain't she? No wonder he left home.' Catching sight of his wife's scowl, he realized his blunder. 'Oh, I didn't intend no slander! She nor anyone else could ever compare with you, my dear, but . . . well, you know what I mean.' He offered a lame grin.

It was too late. Nostrils flared, Beata did not speak to him for the rest of the night.

Some days later, his brief honeymoon over, Monty had braved the teeming rain to join the mass migration from village to colliery when, above the ring of miners' boots upon the cobblestones, he heard his name called and turned, narrow-eyed, to see his wife running after him. Hunched against the torrent, he stopped at the top of the long terraced street, allowing a breathless Sarah to catch up with him and lean upon his arm. Notwithstanding the usual bank of surliness that precursored their dangerous descent, and the odd grumble from a superstitious collier at the appearance of a female before the day's work, the cloudburst failed to deter the odd joker amongst them.

'Oh see, she can't let him out of her sight for five minutes!' It was impossible to tell who the lilting Welsh accent belonged to as, in their sodden dozens, the miners veered around the young couple and continued heads down on their way to the pit shaft. 'It's very frail the poor boy's looking, isn't it? I don't think he's got it in him.'

Monty blushed, but his wife ignored the taunts and spoke worriedly to him, still grasping his arm with one hand whilst the other clutched her shawl under her chin, the icy rain drizzling down her cheeks. 'A boy just brought a message from your father. That horse and cart they came in, you're to go at once and collect it from Bristol and take it to its rightful own –'

'Bristol! What's it doing there?' Drenched now, he showed irritation with the passers-by who jostled him. 'I gotta go to work! How can I –'

'Monty!' Sarah tightened her grip and enunciated clearly. 'Your parents are in hospital.'

'Oh my good Lord! The ferry –'

'No! No, 'twasn't that. Seems they ate something poisonous – it can't have been anything I gave them!' A defensive tone edged her tongue. 'That food was perfectly fresh. Anyway, they obviously didn't feel the ill effects till after they'd made the ferry crossing.' Calmed by the absence of blame from her husband, she turned thoughtful. 'I wonder what –'

'Are they bad?' Face aghast, Monty interrupted her. 'Lord, they must be if they're in hospital.' People only went there to die – oh no, he couldn't allow himself to think of it. 'I have to go! Sorry, it'll mean losing pay –'

'Ach, don't fret about that!' she urged him genuinely, blinking the raindrops from her lashes. 'We've got cash put by.' Her overwhelming infatuation with this flame-haired youth that had precipitated such a hasty marriage now extended to compassion. She longed to take him in her arms and comfort him, but in this public place words must suffice. 'Come, I'll get you some food to take with you – and don't worry, *cariad*, they might be recovered by the time you get there.'

Hurrying back with her down the rain-lashed street, Monty nodded, but a pool of ice had begun to settle upon his stomach.

At his forlornness, his bedraggled bride clung to his arm and offered softly, 'I'll go with you if you like.'

Too immature to realize how his refusal would hurt her, Monty issued vaguely, 'No, I'd as lief go alone.' And never had he felt so alone.

In the time it took him to get to Bristol, Monty clung desperately to that thread of optimism provided by his wife; envisioned his arrival at the hospital to find his parents hail and hearty and laughing with relief as they sent him on his way home to his lovely Sarah.

His previous visits to this city had been fleeting and, worried and disorientated, clothes still sodden, the country lad was forced to ask for directions many times in the bustling streets before locating the hospital.

His footsteps clip-clopping upon a tiled floor, his nostrils inhaling the stench of sickness, he approached the enquiry desk, braced himself and issued self-consciously, 'My name's Kilmaster. I were told to come here 'bout my parents. They ate somethin' poisonous.'

'Let me see,' uttered the slow-witted man behind the desk, consulting a list. 'Ah, you be come to claim their bodies for burial.' The flash of shock on the other's face told him that he had made a gross error. Unable to think how to rectify this he bit his lip and said nothing, the poignancy of that interval and the mixture of nervousness and pity in his eye confirming to Monty that everything he had feared was come to reality.

Hope expunged, Monty staggered and grasped at the desk. The dullard jumped to his feet and aided the bereaved son to a chair, then, averse to his dumb grief, rushed off to fetch someone more able to cope with this.

Eviscerated by shock, Monty barely heard a word of the doctor's explanation that a large number of people had been admitted suffering from a most virulent affliction, though he nodded constantly, feeling that it were expected of him, as if he were taking in every word. Even when told that his parents had finally succumbed to the toxic attack on their hearts only a few hours before his arrival he wagged his head automatically like some wretched clockwork toy, and allowed himself to be led to the mortuary for the purpose of identification, feeling that it was he himself who had died, for the ground beneath his boots seemed insubstantial as a cloud.

As if the demise of his parents were not hard enough to suffer, the mortuary attendant led him to a place that could only be described as a charnel house which took his breath away with its awfulness, where, amongst the other naked victims of the contaminated shellfish he saw two that, despite the grotesqueness of their demeanour, were most familiar to him. Upon laying eyes on them, he escaped quickly and made for fresh air. Only when he had taken several lungfuls did Monty entertain the pitiful thought: he had not even been in time to make peace with his father.

The ensuing two days were a blur: first an inquest, then hurried interment in a paupers' grave. Yet there was perhaps worse trial to bear during the journey to his old village for it was then that Monty had time to think, to digest the awful truth that his parents were indeed gone and that he was the one who must shoulder the dreadful responsibility of breaking the news to his siblings. With each grinding jolt of the wagon – so incongruous in its cheerful yellow hue – the image jumped into his mind of six young faces puckered in grief. It was the worst thing he had ever had to do in his life – but he would do it. Never again would Montague Kilmaster be accused of relinquishing his duty.

None the less, wanting to delay the moment for as long as possible, his first act was to return the horse and cart. The miller was shocked and sympathetic, told the distraught young fellow that if he needed to borrow the vehicle again it was at his disposal. Monty loitered at the flour mill for a while, accepting other commiserations, but there came a point when there could be no further avoidance.

For days Kit had endured all the bossing and teasing from her brother and sisters, and on each of those days had sat patiently upon the step, clear blue eyes searching for her parents. This was how Monty saw her as he plodded dolefully up the village street that late afternoon carrying his awful burden.

Kit saw her elder brother and yelped in joy. He faltered, agonizing, as she ran to meet him, then with cursory greeting he took her hand and allowed himself to be dragged into the cottage where Gwen and the others were laying the table and speculating whether their parents might be home that night. All smiled upon him. The time had come at last for Monty to inform them that their parents were dead.

Shock postponed tears for a moment. The children just stood there looking at him in disbelief. But with the eventual digestion of the news, faces crumpled, sorrow began to flow. Kit did not understand the concept of death at all, just knew that something terrible had happened and because others cried, she wept too.

Monty could think of naught to say, simply donated a rag and administered awkward pats though his heart felt leaden, and he wished that he could change gender so that he could be allowed to weep too, but he was a man, upon whom they were all depending for support.

In between the bouts of tears, Gwen wrung her hands and searched her elder brother's face, no hint of her normal rivalry, an unspoken question on her lips: what would become of them?

The newly wed youth, desperate to assuage his guilt over the selfish abandonment of his mother, decreed without a second thought, 'Don't 'ee worry about who's taking care of 'ee. You shall all come and live with me and Sarah! 'Tis my duty to keep the family together now.'

And they howled again, for they were no longer a family, but a collection of orphans.

2

Sarah Kilmaster gaped at the host of young strangers and the cartload of household goods that accompanied her husband upon his return after a five-day absence, listened in disbelief as he confirmed his parents' death then went on to tell her that Gwen and Flora, Charity and Owen, Amelia and Kit would be joining them in their two-bedroomed cottage.

'They're all willing and able,' he announced rather grandly for his siblings' benefit, then bent his face to confide in his wife, 'Poor Kit's taken to pissin' the bed, but I don't reckon it'll last.'

All this before they were even over the threshold! A moment ago, Sarah had been sweeping the pavement outside her new abode, anticipating her husband's homecoming and imbibing the springtime air. Now, the besom lay redundant in her hands, her initial joy at seeing him eclipsed by shock.

With her lack of response Monty called for the youngsters to start unloading the cart and take their beds into the house. 'Come now, look sharp! This young chap's got to get the wagon back to his master. Be you coming in for a bite and a sup, John, to set you on your way?'

Having eaten not so long ago, the miller's boy refused the offer. 'No, I'll jest stretch my legs and water the horse, then be off, thank 'ee. Don't want the master to think I been idlin'.'

Monty nodded and spoke again to his wife. 'Thought the miller were most charitable to lend us the cart and a boy to drive us! Otherwise I'd ha' been travelling back an' forth till kingdom come.' His tone was brusque, though his inner pain was evident in the starkness of his brow. Trying to dispel the image of his parents racked by pain, he told Sarah, 'Sorry we ain't seen as much of each other as we should, my dear, but there were a lot to sort out back home. I mean, where I used to live. But when I leave you again tomorrow – if I still got a job to go to – you'll have all these willing helpers to keep you company while I'm gone.'

Sarah looked on still dumbfounded as the children lifted items from the cart, two redheaded like Monty, the rest of them of sombre hue. Did it never once occur to him that his eighteen-year-old bride might like her new home to herself, that she might not wish to share it with five 'willing helpers' aged from fifteen downwards and a three-year-old who had reverted to wetting the bed at the ordeal?

After issuing a subdued greeting, she continued to stare, wondering how he could heap this huge responsibility upon her, her dream of wedded bliss slowly disintegrating, whilst the bereaved children returned her scrutiny with grim faces.

Kit examined the pretty young woman before her who, with unconscious effort had begun to drag the twigs of the besom across the pavement again, though from her expression her mind was less intent on her task than on the newcomers. She was very dark and foreign-looking, her eyes almost black. Her hair with its centre parting was held fetchingly in a bunch of ringlets over each ear. Her figure was slight, the top of her head barely reached Monty's shoulder, yet there was no hint of frailty in her bearing . . . nor one of welcome either. Aware of the cool observation that had fallen upon her, the youngest child cast her desolate gaze further along the street, looking beyond the neat rows of stone and slate terraced housing that nestled at the foot of green hills, to the colliery with its slag heaps and its black towers that housed the winding gear, presiding over the village like ogres and bringing a chill of fear to the infant breast.

'Come on, get a move on!' called Monty upon noticing that he was the only one actually working. Neighbouring women, interested in the proceedings, had gathered on the footpath to watch, making him feel conspicuous. Kit was given the large leather-bound bible to carry and traipsed after her brother into the house.

Annoyance rose in Sarah's breast as the two elder girls almost elbowed her out of the way and manhandled a table over her threshold, gouging plaster as they went. The dark and suspicious-looking Owen and the younger ones formed the rear of the procession, trooping past Sarah with more belongings. Only consideration for their recent loss prevented her from voicing objection. Tight-lipped, she was eventually allowed inside her own home, simmering with resentment as they cluttered up the rooms into which she had put so much elbow grease.

Her grip becoming tighter and tighter on the shaft of the besom, she was finally unable to constrain herself, and blurted, 'Stop! Don't put that there, it's in the way, put it here.'

Flora, grappling a chair, looked uncertainly to her sister for advice. 'Gwen told me to put it over here.'

'Oh, and it's Gwen's place to tell you where to put things in my house, is it?' Sarah's voice was not raised, her Welsh intonation lilting gently over the sentence, yet it informed all present in no uncertain terms as to who was to be obeyed.

Gwen's dark features were quick to shrug off the air of bereavement and challenge her sister-in-law. 'Hadn't 'ee better ask Mont –'

'Doesn't matter what Monty, the Queen of Sheba or anyone else says, I'm telling you to put it here.' Sarah held the other's gaze.

A confused Kit stared from one antagonist to the other.

Gwen set her mouth, puffed out her rather matronly bosom and looked to her brother for confirmation, but Monty merely shrugged. Though angry that his wife had dared to undermine his authority he made as if this was of no consequence and muttered, 'The house is Sarah's domain. You must do as you're bidden.'

Nevertheless, half an hour later, after the installation of furniture was completed and his wife went out to get water from a pump, he followed her to remonstrate. 'Don't reckon you ought to have talked about me like that in front o' the young uns.'

'Oh, don't you!' Her smouldering mood evolving into anger, Sarah abandoned the pump handle to confront him, hands on hips. She had changed from her pretty dress into one more fitted to mourning, but there was no obvious respect in her stance.

Never having been faced with her temper, Monty was surprised and backed off. 'What I meant was, it makes me look a fool, you telling 'em what I say don't matter.'

'And what kind of a fool have you taken me for?' With her black garb and black hair she resembled a furious little raven. ''Twas but a week ago you promised to endow me with all your worldly goods – no mention of six extra mouths to feed!'

25

Monty hit back. 'Didst expect me to put them in an orphanage? I didn't ask for my parents to die!' His voice caught with emotion.

His wife felt sympathy, but that did not solve her own dilemma. 'I'm not saying you did, and I'm sorry for you all, but, Monty, this isn't what I expected married life to be!' She imagined her parents' derision – what of your romantic notions now? 'I thought it would be just you and me and babies of our own.' Heaving a sigh, she implored him with those black eyes that set his groin a-throb.

Immediately he grasped her in his arms, pressing himself against her. 'We will have babies of our own! And you'll have plenty of hands to help with them, so you got all the time in the world for me.' Though heaven knew, the last thing he wanted was a host of invaders who might threaten his libidinous rompings. He tried to kiss her.

She extricated herself with a gasp and turned back to the pump, the cut of her shoulders communicating her feelings.

Frustrated at her rejection and unable to understand her attitude, the young man heaved a sigh. 'It's my duty to look after 'em.'

Water splashed into Sarah's bucket and on to her boots. She ceased pumping. 'Is there no one else? Aunts, uncles?'

'No! I dunno, I think we got kin in Gloucester – but even if we have, they're my responsibility, no one else's.' He brought the altercation to an abrupt end by going inside. To Monty there was a duty to be done and that was that.

Grim-faced, Sarah heaved the pail of water into the kitchen and began to prepare the evening meal. Monty barked at the elder girls to go and help her, whilst he remained in the parlour and sat brooding by the fire. With the lack of any rival, Owen seized possession of the spindle-backed chair opposite his brother. Kit had put the family bible down by the slate hearth and was sitting upon it, too close for his liking.

'Shift yourself, mousy bum,' commanded Owen.

Kit resisted. 'Aw, don't call me that!'

'Why? 'Tis true. You're allus pissing yourself and your clothes do stink like they're full o' mice. I can't abide it – now shift 'ee.'

Kit looked to her elder brother for assistance but received just an impatient gesture for her to comply with Owen's wishes. Dutifully, she manoeuvred the bible so that it lay between the two fireside chairs, then sat upon it once again, twisting her father's handkerchief around her hands, her blue eyes watching every twitch of Monty's face, every play of feature.

Owen rested his elbows on the wooden arms and laced his fingers over his abdomen in the attitude of lord of the manor, asking, 'You know how you've had to take this time off work, do you still get paid, bain't your fault, so to speak?'

Monty gave a bitter laugh. 'Noo! What master's gonna pay good money for coal left in the ground? Far as he's concerned I've broken my bond and I'll have to take my chance with the day men. Probably have to get down on my knees to be taken back on.'

'Don't seem jestly right to me,' objected Owen. 'When it weren't of your making.'

'Master don't care 'bout that.' Monty had forced himself to ignore the injustice of his position, would in future just accept his lot in life. The need to provide for his family superseded any thought of pride. Never again would a Kilmaster be buried in a pauper's grave.

'Why, he should be made to care!' The dark-featured urchin glowered. 'How you going to buy food for us all if you've no money?'

'I may have to feed one to the other.' Monty was unsmiling.

After staring for a moment, Kit's eyes turned back to the younger brother, awaiting his contribution.

Owen, renowned for quoting adults, fumbled to recall his father's explanation, then announced in businesslike manner, 'You can't rightly be expected to feed all of us, you're only a young chap. I'll go down the mine too!'

The other showed slight irritation. 'You're too little.'

'I saw a boy my age covered in coal dust when we were on the way here!'

Monty himself had started work when not much older than Owen but he was unwilling to inflict that on his eight-year-old brother. Somebody had to get the education that would lift the family out of this trap. 'True, but I want you to get some proper schooling fir –'

'Don't need schooling to dig coal!' Enthusiasm made Owen rash. 'I reckon I could do as good a job as thee.'

Monty was already annoyed that his wife had managed to usurp his authority and was not about to permit this brat to do likewise. 'Owen, you might think you know everything but you don't. If you're going to bide here with us remember this: I'm the man of the house.'

Such dismissal of his noble offer wounded the youngster, who responded by lamely mumbling into his chest, 'Don't seem jestly right to me, them not paying you.'

'That's the way of it,' snapped Monty, after which there was a long hiatus. Kit did not like the expression on his face and struggled to think of some way to alleviate it.

At the flash of inspiration she beamed, jumped up and prepared for action. 'I got a new dance, our Monty!'

Her brother stared at the eager, grinning face that was in size more fitted to adult shoulders than an infant's, the stout limbs like the branches of a tree, extended in anticipation of praise. What a lot of bad luck this child had brought with her. Before Kit's unwelcome birth the Kilmasters had been poor but not destitute. Her arrival had changed everyone's life. Every sibling had some pertinent grievance about Kit. His parents had been forced to struggle to accommodate the extra burden, he himself had had to contribute money for which he had worked hard and which could have been better spent on himself, which was why he had left home, which was why his parents had had to travel so far to his wedding, which is how they had come to eat the thing that had killed them. Ergo, in his quest to find a scapegoat for his present dilemma, he saw not a little child but the cause of all his ills, and his response was issued with a scowl of disapproval. 'Shame on you, girl! Our mother and father are dead. Just sit 'ee down and behave yourself! There bain't time for your nonsense now.'

Kit's face fell. Deflated, she sank back to her seat on the bible and chewed on a portion of the handkerchief. If this was a sample of what it was going to be like to live here, she was not sure she wanted to remain.

A moment passed.

'How long we gotta stay here, Monty?' When he glared at Kit she shrank, but put her question another way. 'When are Mother and Father coming back?'

'I *told* 'ee.' Monty fought to keep his voice even. 'They're never coming back.' At the sight of her juddering lips, he buried his face in his hands.

'Stupid! It's all your fault!' Eyes bright with tears, Owen turned on Kit and made a grab for the precious handkerchief; his sister shrieked and hung on to it, forcing Owen to curse her again.

Monty lifted his head with a roar. 'Stop that! There'll be no more arguing or fighting – ever! We are a family! Not animals but human beings, and you'll behave as such! If you've got grievances you'll keep them to yourselves. I haven't sacrificed my own happiness to listen to 'ee at each other's throats and this is the last time I expect to have to raise my voice in my own house – and that goes for all of 'ee!' Shocked by the intensity of his anger, he swore to himself that this was indeed the last time he would lose control. After a final trembling glare, he wrenched his eyes back to the fire.

Leaving Kit too dazed for tears, Owen slunk from the room.

In the tiny kitchen, fearful looks were exchanged between the children. An apprehensive Sarah carved great wedges of bread from a loaf and set to buttering them as the sullen little boy elbowed his way in. Gwen, only three years younger than her sister-in-law, continued in her attempts to imprint her own authority. Arms folded under her corseted bosom, she examined a cake that sagged in the middle and pointed it out to Flora and Charity. 'Must've been taken out o' the oven too soon.'

Sarah clenched her jaw. Missing her new husband, she had spent his absence making this treat for his return, had tried to mask its deficiencies with icing sugar but had only succeeded in making it worse by lifting it and the icing had crazed.

Flora knew what it was like to be the butt of Gwen's criticism. Indeed, she had always regarded herself as the filling in the sandwich between her domineering elder sister and the more popular Charity. Everyone else seemed so much more confident of themselves. Desperate to make an ally of her sister-in-law, she offered enthusiastically, 'I'm sure it'll taste nice though.'

Gwen was furious with her. 'Presentation's as important as taste, so Mother taught me. Course, you wouldn't know that. Her never wasted much breath on you, did her?' Tears came to her victim's eyes. It had always been very easy to make this one cry.

To deter lachrymosity, a crimson Flora edged nearer to Sarah, wearing an eager-to-please expression. 'Should I lay the table?' At the other's curt nod she bustled between kitchen and parlour looking for the tablecloth, opening doors and cupboards, appearing to be industrious, but in the end having to ask where it was. After this, she fussed and rushed about getting nowhere and having to seek constant instruction, trying so hard to please that Sarah found her earnestness overpowering and was forced to tell her she had done enough and to sit down.

'Please! You'll do me more service in there. It doesn't do to have too many in the kitchen.'

'Ah, it is a bit poky, ain't it?' mused Gwen.

'How old are you?' enquired Owen.

Sarah did not care for his familiar edge, and the tone of her voice was set accordingly. 'I don't think that's any of a little boy's business, do you?'

Owen sought to punish her for this denigration. 'You don't look as old as our Gwen.'

Charity, a lover of food, complimented Monty's wife on the offering and said in bright tone, 'Would 'ee mind if I take a slice of bread with me? I'm ravenous after that journey.' Nothing much perturbed Charity, or if it did she hid it well.

'Take what you like but all of you get out of my way!' Overwhelmed, Sarah waved her hand at the others to shoo them out of the kitchen.

Only Gwen lingered, turning her attention to Sarah's lack of dexterity in carving the bread. 'You could get another four slices out o' that loaf. Mother always used to –'

'I like my slices thick!' For a young bride trying to make her mark the criticism had twice the impact.

'Oh, I'm not saying anything untoward.' Gwen presented a shrug of innocence. ''Tis your kitchen, you may do as you please. Well . . . there must be zommat you want me to do?'

Sarah instructed her to get down the best china teapot and was upset again when Gwen said, 'D'you mean this?' – whilst beholding the wedding gift disparagingly.

Under more pretence of helping, Gwen hovered, as if testing her sister-in-law's competence, and from time to time would sniff and, after a heavy pause, murmur, 'Course, Mother wouldn't do it like that – but then you must do it how you like, 'tis your house.'

Goaded to the brink of fury, by the time they were seated around the put-together tables Sarah could eat nothing, her disrelish exacerbated by Flora who, anxious over the manner of her parents' death, sniffed suspiciously at every morsel before putting it into her mouth. Jumping to her feet, Sarah announced that she was not hungry and would go instead to ask if her mother could lend them some fresh bed linen.

Monty showed surprise as she hurried to the door. 'We brung some with us.'

'It's filthy!' In a childish effort to get back at Gwen, Sarah threw an accusing look at her sister-in-law. 'My mother'd have a fit if she saw me putting that on the bed. Anyway, I want to see my father too. One of us has to do something about getting your job back – won't be long!'

There was no chance of walking out her anger, for her parents lived quite nearby, though in a much smarter house. Neither was there much sympathy when she had finished her outpourings. Her father, akin to management, had not wanted her to marry beneath her station, but had been wise enough to see that it was no good trying to dissuade a woman in love from the path she had chosen. Sarah's humiliation was all the greater in that her elder sisters were part of the audience, each barely able to conceal her glee at the downfall of one who had lorded it over them at being the first to marry.

'Well, you've made your bed, madam, and now you can lie on it,' Probyn Rogers told her flatly, which was rather ironic, thought Sarah, for encumbered by the ready-made family it was unlikely that she would ever have the time to lie down again.

'What bed?' she retorted. 'I'll have none to lie on if my husband loses his job.'

There was a lack of compassion from her mother. 'Won't be wanting these sheets then, will you?' A stack of linen over her arm, Mary Rogers made as if to return it to the cupboard.

Sarah grabbed it, the anger at her husband still fermenting. 'I was just speaking figuratively! I thought you'd be interested in your daughter's troubles.'

'You mean you're expecting me to do something about it,' corrected Probyn, tilting his chin at her. It was easy to see where Sarah inherited her own recalcitrance from.

'Well, you are the deputy – and you are my father.' Even granted this opening there was little subservience.

'And I'll give you a damned good whipping if you don't alter your tone, married or no! How's it going to look to the men who beg me for work every morn and I have to turn them away? What are they going to say about me if I let my son-in-law have a week off whenever he chooses and then give him precedence over them?'

Her mother showed similar harshness. 'We warned you, didn't we? Said once you were a married woman you couldn't expect us to look after you.'

Recognizing that it was useless to go on, Sarah gave a cool nod of understanding. Trying to hang on to her dignity as tightly as she held the sheets, she bustled towards the door and had almost got to it before her father spoke again.

'Have I said I wouldn't help?'

'If you want Monty to beg for it –' guessed Sarah.

Probyn was terse. 'No, I just want my daughter to show me a little respect if she demands a favour of me! I am right in thinking you want me to give your husband his job back?'

Sarah considered her situation carefully. Without her father's assistance there was no chance of Monty being reinstated. After the battle she had had to obtain consent to marry him it galled her to have to grovel, especially so soon afterwards, made her appear weak and dependent in her own eyes.

'Well, do you or don't you, girl?' demanded Probyn.

The words stuck in Sarah's throat, but it was not really her father with whom she was angry, it was Monty for placing her in this position. 'If you please, Father.'

'That's better. Right, I'll see Monty gets his job back – but just this once, mind. You'll have to go down on bended knee before I show another such favour.'

'Thank you, Father, I shan't ask again.' Thinking bitterly that the sea would dry up before ever she resumed such a humiliating position, Sarah went home, but the short journey was given to much angry thought and later, after the children had gone to bed in their overcrowded room, she decided that she must confront Monty about their future.

'Right!' She handed him a cup of cocoa and sat opposite him, nursing her own cup, only the glow from the fire to light her face which shone pale and serious from its dim surroundings. 'Now we've got rid of that lot you can tell me. How do you propose to look after the eight of us?

Just because I've managed to get you your job back doesn't mean we'll have money to burn.'

He took a tentative sip of the hot beverage and, more out of awkwardness than discomfort, shifted position, the embers casting golden lights in the flaming red hair she had so recently found attractive. 'Well . . .'

'Hadn't even thought about it, had you?' The expression of faint disgust descended into her cocoa cup.

'Yes, I have!' His tone was indignant. 'Gwen and Flora are no strangers to work. They could get a position round here and pay their way – and they'd do their own washing if that's what concerns you.'

'No.' Sarah's voice was firm. Sitting ramrod straight, she rested the cup on her aproned lap, both hands curled around it. 'They'll go into service. At least that way they won't be under my feet.'

'Send them away? That's harsh after we just lost our parents. I know Gwen can be a bit bossy –'

'Monty, it may have escaped your notice, but apart from our bedroom there's one other; the six of them can't stay in it indefinitely.'

'Oh, they're used to it, we only had the one room at ho –'

'Well, I'm not used to it! 'Tisn't decent for boys to sleep alongside girls – and don't say Owen can come in with us 'cause I'm not having it, see! No, I'll tell you what we're going to do. We're going to stick a partition up in that room, Owen can go on one side and the younger girls can have the other. Gwen and Flora can get a job at the mansion and live in, so can Charity.'

Alarmed by this revelation of his wife's dominant streak Monty attempted to regain control. 'She's barely finished her eddication!'

'She's old enough to work, and so is Owen come to that.' Sarah forestalled any argument about this by making her own concession. 'But there's not enough weight on him, the pit ponies would take him for a wisp of hay, so we might as well have him educated – even if the clever little devil thinks he already knows it all. With him and Amelia at school all day there's only whatsername to cope with.' She had taken an inexplicable dislike to the youngest child who had done nothing at all to provoke this, apart from the irritating way she kept staring with those big blue eyes. 'Though we might have to rethink the arrangement when we have our own family.' She noticed the change in his expression and in response said, 'Oh yes, I still intend to have

33

children,' but her attitude was composed more of determination than warm enthusiasm.

Misreading the strength of her obstinacy, Monty put down his cup on the slate hearth in order to kneel before her, taking one of her hands and kissing it. As ever, the contact with her flesh spawned tumescence. 'I beg humble pardon for not consulting you first, my dear – but you must see I couldn't abandon them.' He nuzzled her seductively.

'I understand that.' Her voice was level and she allowed him to hold on to her hand though she remained aloof and craned her neck to deter anything further. 'You feel you have a duty to your brother and sisters. You made your decision to put their welfare above that of your wife – well, that's all right, I married you for better or worse and I'll stand by you . . .'

The tone of her voice led Monty to believe that this statement was about to be qualified, and duly it was.

'But just as you've let me know where I stand,' Sarah continued in even tone, though her proud heart was broken, 'it's only fair that I tell you where you stand with me. I have a duty too and that's to my own children when I have them. No one shall ever come before them. Not even you.'

Rejected, Monty leaned back on his heels, stared into her unyielding expression, saw a hardness in the Celtic eyes that had not been there a week ago. How could he, not yet out of his teens, have forecast that his unselfish act would have different connotations to others? But he knew now. His marriage was doomed before it had begun.

3

After a bitter struggle, in which Gwen fought to maintain the responsibility that had always been hers – and lost – the three elder girls were sent to live and work at the mine owner's mansion two miles away, at least one of them harbouring a deep grudge.

'Just let her see how long she can boss our Monty around,' Gwen declared to her younger sisters. 'A month, that's all I'll give her before our brother gets sick of it and takes us all back home.'

'But it ain't home now, is it?' whimpered Flora.

'You know what I mean, you daft biddy!'

The youngest of the trio decided it was time to assert herself. 'Well, I like her.'

Hostile astonishment. 'What, even though she's throwed you out?'

'Ain't of her making,' retorted Charity. 'She just got herself this nice little house and a husband and gets lumbered with us – how'd we all fit in there? And it don't behove 'ee to talk about her being a bully when your most favourite occipation is to shove folk around.'

Far from retaliating, Gwen was deeply hurt at being labelled thus and was hard-pressed not to cry. 'I do not! If I offer advice 'tis only for the good of others whose welfare I have at heart.'

'Well, I like her,' came the firm repetition. 'And I reckon we must all do what we can to help.'

'I suppose so,' sighed her eldest sister, though she did not yield completely. 'Reckon her do need all the help she can get.'

Never was a truer word spoken. At first Sarah coped admirably with the younger ones' material and physical needs, instilled cleanliness and manners, continued the religious instruction laid down by their mother, though was not so rigid in her teachings, found a school for Owen and

35

Amelia who were at least off her hands for most of the day – but that still left Kit, great lolloping Kit who was forever showing off and trying to grab her attention – and inevitably fate would have it that within two months of being wed Sarah found herself with child.

By the end of that year a daughter was born, and only fourteen months later another, leaving Sarah no time for those who were not of her flesh. Kit suffered from the lack of attention but not for long, for she was packed off to school where to draw attention to oneself usually invoked punishment and Kit couldn't wait to get home to her elder little niece, Beata, whom she regarded more as a sister and was the only one to give her the kisses and affection she craved.

She had never danced for Monty since that day they had arrived here. Though she still felt deep affection for him, and her feet itched unbearably from lack of practice, she had no wish to incur her surrogate father's wrath.

However, today was different. Kit felt that her sixth birthday was an auspicious enough occasion for her to be allowed some favour. Catching sight of her brother on his way home from the pit, she grabbed her little niece's hand and the pair of them trotted up the street to meet him. There had been something very odd about Monty for the last couple of weeks. Instead of being coated in black dust he came home looking as freshly scrubbed as he had done upon leaving for work in the morning, and some days he had not come home at all. There had been lots of other men hanging around the streets too. Kit had asked him about this but had received no satisfactory answer. From the number of glowering looks that had passed between the man and his wife – and some of them directed at her – Kit deemed it unwise to keep asking. She only knew that Monty had become more glum by the hour and this afternoon showed no improvement. He barely paid her and little Beata any heed at all as they scurried back down the street alongside him. It wasn't as if he had forgotten that it was Kit's birthday, for he had been the one to raise the issue with his wife this morning, though it had been said with a mutter as if there were some secret involved. Perhaps they were going to allow her special request! Now was the time to ask.

Kit attempted to phrase her desire as sweetly as possible. 'Monty, my dear . . . being that it's my special day, might I be permitted to dance for 'ee this eve?'

Her brother did not reply, merely grunted and continued to pound the pavement, his empty belly teased by the scent of cooking.

They reached the house. Kit jumped on to the doormat and stood smiling eagerly in Monty's way, repeating her question. 'Can I?'

Face uncompromising, he brushed past her. 'No, you may not. I got better things to do than to watch you cavort like a cart horse. You're old enough now to be more dignified.'

Cut to the quick by his remark, Kit blushed and hovered there looking foolish for a second, before wandering lamely into the house.

It became obvious that the aroma of cooking came from somewhere else. All that lay on the table was a loaf of bread sliced thinner than had been the custom. Just in from school, Owen and Amelia were washing their hands in an enamel bowl, each trying to nudge the other out of the way, but when their brother entered they immediately desisted. Another tiny girl was crouched upon the home-made rug, playing with dolly pegs. Her mother was checking the dampness of some clothes hanging on the brass rail attached to the mantel when she heard Monty's entry.

The moment she laid eyes on his face, Sarah clapped a hand to her brow. 'You haven't found anything?'

For answer, he sank into a chair and shook his head. 'Travelled right over into the next valley, naught to be had. My feet are killing me and my belly's growling like a bear.'

There was no sympathy. 'Better get used to it then, hadn't you!'

Her husband felt too tired to respond. There had been a drastic reduction in wages. Monty could not possibly support his extended family on less than he had previously received and, along with others, had objected. A lock-out had followed. Evictions were threatened unless the men returned to work and accepted the reduction.

'Nothing else for it, then,' came Sarah's brusque addition. 'Get round to my father's house and tell him you'll be back at work tomorrow.'

'But how will we manage on less money?' he entreated.

'And how will we manage on no money at all?' came her retort. She noted the look on his face. 'I hope you're not expecting me to go begging to him?'

'I don't need anyone to beg for me.'

Good! Then get round there – now!'

Reluctantly, Monty dragged himself from the chair and went to visit his father-in-law.

He was gone barely ten minutes.

Sarah's heart fell. 'He wouldn't help you?'

'Oh, he wasn't completely without mercy,' said Monty, with undisguised bitterness. 'He did gimme this.'

Sarah took hold of the newspaper clipping that advertised for miners in the coalfields of Yorkshire.

Monty gave the cryptic addition: 'Couldn't he think of anywhere further to send me?' Sarah screwed the piece of newspaper into a ball. 'Yes, well, he's probably had a bellyful of you – and so have I!'

Wondering what on earth was going on, Kit looked from one to the other. From the pocket of her pinafore she drew out the man's handkerchief that was her constant companion and began to twist it nervously around her fingers. Never being allowed out of her possession, it was extremely grubby.

'Well, that's it then, we're out on the street!' The glint of anger and despair pricked Sarah's eyes.

Monty looked away, his fingers resting across his mouth as if to prevent some rash utterance that would bring his wife's wrath down upon him. He had been putting off making a disclosure to the children about their impending eviction in case something came up, but now with Sarah's declaration the fear that he himself was experiencing grew evident in their faces. In a desperate attempt to lessen the blow, he made a lame request to his wife. 'Maybe if you talk to your mother she could put us up for a while?'

'Where do you suggest she puts us, in the linen press?' Sarah's four unmarried sisters were still at home. 'Don't be stupid!' She looked deeply worried, rubbing her swollen abdomen – three years of marriage and a child born in each! 'God knows I've done my best . . .' Lately she had been taking in sewing and mending over which she toiled until midnight, but for such poor reward that it was hardly worth the effort.

Monty did not care for the way she laid emphasis on the word *my*, as if he hadn't been doing everything he could. Did his wife think it made him proud knowing that it was only her skill as a seamstress that stood between him and starvation? But he offered no retaliation. How could he?

'Why do we have to leave here?' Owen was the only one of his siblings who dared ask. He hated the way his big brother allowed this shrew to belittle him. What had happened to that famous temper?

Sarah turned on the boy, her bark making Amelia jump. 'Because your brother has lost his job!'

'Don't make out as if it's my fault!' Hurt by her disloyalty, Monty explained to the wide-eyed children, 'The master wanted to reduce our wage, I couldn't manage on less and so I sided with the union –'

'What's the union?' interrupted Owen.

'A group of men who don't think it right that the master has so much power,' explained his brother.

Owen affiliated himself with this noble cause. 'Hurrah for you, Monty!'

'Rubbish!' put in Sarah. 'A bunch of troublemakers, they are.'

'But if the master's cut wages –'

'There are too few of them to make a difference!'

Keeping his tone reasonable, for no one was allowed to raise their voice here except his brother's wife, a helpful Owen supplied what he saw as the answer. 'But if you all band together –'

'No one can beat the masters!' snapped Sarah. 'And it's a waste of time even trying. For all your brother's high-minded ideals he's only succeeded in getting himself blackballed. Union – pff! All they do is ruin other people's livelihoods. The master has always done as he likes and he always will.'

'But that ain't fair!' opined Owen.

'No, it ain't,' agreed Monty. 'But Sarah's right, he's the one with the power, and wages bain't the only thing he can take away. The company owns this house so being as I don't work there any more, well, I'm afraid we gotta get out.'

'See what you've reduced us to!' yelled Sarah.

'I can't win!' Monty gritted his teeth, barely hanging on to the temper he had so successfully curbed. 'You'd have complained just as loudly if I'd given up without a fight.'

'I'm not just talking about that!' Her security threatened, Sarah grew cruel, old resentments spilling out. 'I'm on about wasting what little money we do have on others instead of using it for your own children.'

'That's unjust – and plain silly.' Monty could not be more frugal if he tried, only partook of an occasional drink and did not smoke. 'The girls give as much as they can, and it's not as if they live here.' Gwen and her sisters brought money home every quarter. Nevertheless, with so many to support, there had never been any spare cash to put by for such an emergency, and with his sisters' latest contribution having served to cover his own lost wages it was doubtful the family could last until the next payment.

'No, but what about the other three?' demanded Sarah.

Young as she was, Kit felt the incrimination was directed at her, that Sarah had never really wanted her here. It was obvious that Owen felt that way too for he announced evenly, 'I'm old enough to work for my keep now.'

'And what use would a sprat like you be to any master?' At the look on the youngster's face Sarah regretted being so harsh but it was the truth. As from the outset it was she who made the decision. 'Right! Well, there's no point standing here prevaricating. We'll waste no more time but go straight to Yorkshire.'

'Mining's not the only thing I can do you know!' Monty resented the infringement of his free will.

'What else then?' demanded Sarah, folding her arms over the bulging apron.

'Well, any old job, I dunno –'

'Exactly! If there was "any old job" available you'd have found it by now. Now it's either Yorkshire or parish relief.'

Monty, averse to this emasculation, voiced what he saw as a problem. 'We'd have to take the children out of school.'

'I heard it rumoured they have schools in Yorkshire.'

'And what about Gwen and the others?'

'They're grown women! They've got a roof over their heads and a job.'

Monty showed a hint of his old spirit. 'I'm not leaving them behind with no husbands to look after them!'

'Well, if they want to come with us I expect Yorkshire folk need servants to cater for their whims too. 'Tis said they pay better money up north.' Sarah grew tired of this exchange. 'Right, that's settled! Owen, go up to the big house and tell your sisters they're to come home at once.'

'They'll have to give notice,' pointed out Monty.

'For pity's sake!' bawled his wife. 'Do you have to keep putting all these idiotic obstacles in our way?' She shoved Owen towards the door. 'What on earth is their employer going to do if they don't give notice – sack them?'

'I only meant they'll need references to get another job. They won't fare very well if they leave their master in the lurch.'

Loyal to his brother, Owen hovered in the doorway awaiting Monty's sanction.

Relinquishing the fight and, in his younger brother's eyes losing face, Monty gave a nod.

'Thank you – Owen, if you're not gone this minute I'll give you such a thrashing!' Sarah covered her face to stifle an explosion of fury, but still it burgeoned in her breast and when she uncovered her eyes the first to fall under her angry glare was poor watchful Kit, who immediately began to twist the handkerchief more nervously than ever.

Emotions roused by the combination of her delicate state and frustration over her own lost youth, Sarah lunged for the scapegoat, wrenched the tattered rag from Kit's hands. 'Well, wherever we're going, to hell or Timbuktu, you can leave that filthy thing behind. I'm sick to death of seeing you fidget with it!' And she cast it into the fire.

Kit shrieked and tried to rescue her father's handkerchief, but the heat from the coal was too fierce, compelling her to watch it singe then disintegrate into flames.

Acute silence followed. Mouth slack with disbelief, Owen lingered in the doorway, he and everyone else awaiting tears from Kit – they knew how she treasured her comforter. But no tears came, for the victim was too shocked. Never, even in sleep, had she been parted from this last reminder of her father; without its magical properties how could she survive?

Though not immediately contrite – it was only an old rag after all – Sarah was the first to break the awkward atmosphere. 'Ach, come on now, Kit, you can go with your brother to the big house. You'd like to see Charity and Flora, wouldn't you?' She steered the youngster firmly towards the door. Pitying his sister, Owen held out his hand. Monty caressed her as she drew even with him.

The stunned child allowed herself to be piloted only so far before she balked and protested that she could not leave without her father's handkerchief.

Sarah tried to coax her. '''Tis only a wretched bit of rag. Anyone would think it was the crown jewels with all the fuss you're making.'

But Kit struggled and fought against her exit, voice cracking hysterically. 'I can't go through!'

And so wildly did she kick and wriggle that Sarah abandoned her efforts. 'Oh, for heaven's sake! Owen can go on his own then.' With a dismissive flick of her wrist she turned her attention to other matters.

Breast rising and falling, Kit stared feverishly at the door, searching for the invisible barrier that prevented her from following her brother, wondering at the reason for this strange handicap. With no handkerchief to twist, her hands strayed to her pinafore, mangling the cheap cotton with tortured fingers, thoughts racing towards madness.

And somewhere from the back of her mind came the notion that it was she who had caused all these terrible things to happen, because of some failure on her part to carry out vital instructions, some fateful omission that could never be put right.

PART 2

Girlhood
1873–1879

4

The journey to her brother's home involved a six-mile trek, but the young woman's vigorous pace belied this. Long of limb and proud of breast, she strode out with a confident air, presenting an impressive sight. Kit's birth-weight had been a portent of things to come. Now, eighteen years later, she had donned the best part of a stone for every birthday, but on such a lofty frame – a mere wafer under six foot – it was excellently proportioned. Perhaps it was Sunday that lent buoyancy to her step, for Kit was never quite so energetic in her actions during working hours, or so her current employer and all previous ones had complained. But with only half a day off per week she was eager to spend as much of it as possible with her brother's family. Kit loved children.

She had come to love the West Riding countryside too – could remember no other place as home – for despite the wounds inflicted by man in his greed for coal there remained pockets of beauty where Kit had spent many a happy interval frolicking with her nieces until adulthood had forced her into employment. Today was a day for frolicking, thought Kit, delighting in the bright blue ceiling overhead, what few clouds there were having the appearance of wispy feathers raked by some giant comb across the brilliant plain. Summer was most definitely in command. Beside hedgerows that were weighed down beneath a creamy shawl of elderflower, swayed an abundance of thistle, teasel and dandelion. The shorn, ungainly creatures in the pasture were already beginning to sprout next year's crop of wool, all intent upon devouring their verdant carpet and paying not the slightest heed to this passer-by.

Following the skein of polluted sludge that was the River Aire, Kit descended the eastern slopes of the Pennines, passing through a conglomeration of sandstone mills and factories – hidden gold beneath the grime –

before finally emerging into coal-mining territory. Her pace undaunted, she strode on along a road grey with coal dust, taking note of various landmarks: a wayside cross from a bygone age, a church spire peeping from a group of trees, grotesque constructions of black wheels and pulleys like devices of torture looming up from every point to mar the landscape, the sward defaced by railway line and excavation, and numerous colliery villages – Rothwell, Robin Hood, Methley and Mickletown – the deeply furrowed course of the river alternately swerving away then curving back, its banks rich not only in mineral wealth but in history, for relieving the grim industrial scars were oases of woodland and pasture where the aristocracy dwelled in their numerous ancient mansions.

Leaving the Aire to meander on its way, Kit veered south and headed towards the Calder, for her destination lay almost at the confluence of the two rivers. The undulations of the landscape became gentler now, the city of Leeds behind her a smudged outline of towering chimneys on the distant horizon.

The land here was low-lying and fertile. Kit left the main road, climbed over a stile and, avoiding the foetid bristles of hogweed, took a short cut across a field, leaving a trail of footprints in the boggy ground to her wake. The meadow was of a purplish hue, spangled with clumps of buttercup and tendrils of purple vetch that curled around the traveller's feet. Quaking spikelets of flowering grass clung to her skirts as, at times, she waded knee-deep in foliage, making for the village in the distance.

At the other side of the meadow she rejoined the road that would eventually lead her into the heart of the pit village, but as yet there was a mile to go.

Ralph Royd was a small and ancient hamlet with a church, two chapels, several shops, a post office, an inn and a row of almshouses, whose once pretty view over the wooded valley had been devalued by the ugly pit headgear, the pumping shaft and its great Cornish beam engine, the slag heaps, locomotive sheds and the accompanying network of railway lines that connected to the Aire and Calder Navigation. But the optimistic Kit preferred to focus on the brighter aspects of her route, occasionally calling a greeting to a familiar face.

After the group of farmworkers' cottages stood a whitewashed public house, the Robin Hood's Well, and from its open door came the gentle waft of malted hops. Now, only a few hundred yards lay between Kit and the place she called home. Turning off Main Street between the post office and the church graveyard, she travelled up an incline, the fronts of her thighs beginning to feel the strain. On her left, smelling of sun-warmed greenery and manure, was a stretch of allotment gardens where pigsty, chicken coop and pigeon loft nestled amongst a veritable forest of rhubarb, their occupants clucking, cooing and grunting in contentment. Crossing the road, her pace much slower now, she followed the grimy wall of the churchyard, heading for the sequence of houses erected by the colliery owner for its workforce – Fenton Row at the very top of the incline which overlooked a moor, Charlesworth Street in the middle and, thankfully before these, at the very bottom, Savile Row where her brother lived. Perspiring and tired now, she rounded a corner, almost barging into a knot of men in flat caps and coloured neckerchiefs who waited to use the communal privy.

'Eh up, Kit!' Pipe in hand, one grizzled miner hailed her. 'That's a grand hat tha's wearin'.'

Involuntarily, Kit touched her new apparel, a huge straw bonnet trimmed with loops of blue ribbon and white heather, and was about to thank him when another made droll contribution: 'Nay, that's not a hat it's a roof.' Succeeding in drawing a chuckle from his companions, the culprit grinned at her to show his humour was not malicious. 'Eh, I can get thee a cheap quote on guttering if tha's interested.'

'Cheeky monkey!' Kit summoned a not entirely genuine laugh and marched on along the final stretch.

The bricks of the thirty-six houses had been made from fire clay dug from the mine, their roofs constructed of thin grey slate and every one of them belonged to the mine-owner, yet the majority of tenants took pride in their homes. Each step and sill gleamed with freshly applied donkey-stone, its effect almost blinding, and Kit was forced to squint to block out the glare. On their way back from an outing, a young couple came towards her, arrayed in their Sunday best. The woman carried a baby swathed in a shawl.

Forgetting the insult over her hat, Kit greeted the two and stopped to probe eagerly between the crocheted layers around the infant's face. 'Come out, we've seen thee!' The West Country accent was long gone, replaced by local dialect. 'Aw, there you are – isn't he a grand little chap!' She offered a digit which the babe immediately grasped, apologizing upon being told that the child was female. 'Ooh, sorry! What do you call her?' Babbling over her mistake, Kit heaped undue praise upon the infant, before finally tearing herself away.

Envying the new parents, she continued thoughtfully, imagining herself in the maternal role – for a family was the thing she desired most in all the world. The vague thought occurred that she already had a family, but was just as quickly dismissed. Kit had never really felt part of it, forever isolated because of something she had done. Fantasizing about the children she would one day have, their names and fortunes, Kit wished that she could remember her own parents, but they were a distant memory now.

Suddenly realizing that her daydreaming had taken her two doors beyond her intended terminus, she laughed at herself and retraced her steps.

Even before she entered she could hear snatches of conversation through the open window, most of it conducted in flat West Riding vowels. Of the family, only Monty and Gwen retained any trace of their Somerset burr. The younger ones, teased unmercifully on their arrival here twelve years ago, had been quick to adopt the local vernacular.

Kit was not surprised to find all her siblings here. Traditionally they had always gathered on the first Sabbath of every month, travelling from their homes in nearby townships. Only Owen had not so far to come, living only a few streets away. On these occasions spouses and children were left behind, not simply because the dimensions of the house forbade such mass invasion, but because this was the Kilmasters' special day to commemorate the time when their parents had been killed and their newly wed brother Monty had vowed that he would fight to keep the family together – and to his credit he had. Hence, once a month they would gather here to bicker and snipe and chide over misunderstandings as families were wont to do. They were adults now, but the childhood pecking order remained.

A beaming Kit poked her head round the door, opening it with care lest anyone were seated behind it. The living room was large but had many people to accommodate. The draught of her entry billowed the green curtains, which in turn panicked the canary into fluttering about in its cage. Kit edged her way in, the scent of fresh air clinging to her clothes. Taking prominence in the room was the Yorkshire range, black and gleaming like some living beast, its iron face cast with garlands and wreaths and roses. The fire in the grate had been allowed to burn low without actually going out, but still it brought a glow to the cheeks on such a hot day. There was a large oven on one side of the fire and a boiler on the other and before the hearth was a rug made from clippings by every member of the family. Kit knew exactly which section she had done, as did everyone else. It was the only covering upon the stone floor.

Indeed there were few trappings in her brother's house. Those that existed had been with him a long time and came not from his own endeavours, for every penny had been spent on his extended family: the bible on the sideboard in which was listed every Kilmaster birth, death and marriage in the past fifty years; a print of John Wesley, and a painting – an amateurish attempt to depict the Welsh landscape by one of Sarah's sisters. Over the fireplace was a mirror which reflected the clock on the opposite wall. Kit had become adept at reading the time back to front whilst brushing her hair. It was not actually an entire clock, just the face and workings of an old timepiece found in a junk shop, secured to the whitewashed wall by a nail. The only other adornment was a map of the world on the wall opposite the window. Apart from the scullery with its shallow stone sink, a pantry, and a cylindrical copper for boiling clothes with a fireplace underneath it, this was the extent of the downstairs living area.

The conversation stopped with Kit's entry, Owen first to remark on his sister's appearance. 'Good Lord! If tha can't fight, wear a big hat.'

'A big hat for a big girl.' Gwen made critical observation of Kit. 'Every time I come here you seem to have got fatter.'

Before the subject could utter displeasure, Amelia jumped in, brimming with importance. 'That's what I've told her! She'll never get wed if she doesn't stop stuffing her face.'

Kit finally managed to insert her objection. 'I hardly eat a thing!' It seemed grossly unfair that whilst Owen's appetite would put a gannet to shame he remained as thin as a lat. In further self-defence – a lifelong stance for poor Kit – she reminded her female detractors, 'Neither of you are exactly whippet-like. And I'm a lot taller than any of you.'

'You can't kid me an extra six inches in height justifies an extra six stones,' teased Amelia.

'Well, at least mine's in all the right places,' retorted Kit, thrusting out her enormous bosom whilst looking disparagingly upon Gwen's barrel shape and Amelia's disproportionate rear.

An objective observer would agree, Kit's flesh was evenly distributed. In all she was a striking figure with beautiful copper tones to her hair, whilst Amelia's pale skin was framed by an insipid carroty frizz which, along with her wide blue eyes, gave the impression that she was in a state of permanent fright. The premature death of their mother and father was etched in both sets of blue eyes, yet in Kit's there was a certain calmness, a knowledge that death could come at any time and there was no point worrying over it.

'These're childbearing hips,' came Amelia's attempt at having the last word.

'So are mine,' volleyed Kit.

'I can't see you putting 'em to much use.' Owen, a black-haired billy goat with a pale high forehead, tiny pointed chin and eyebrows like strips of astrakhan, was in one of his acerbic moods today, needled by the reminder that Kit was taller than himself. 'The bloke who'll take you on 'ud need to throw up some scaffolding first.'

Kit levelled a derogatory eye at the wad of Socialist pamphlets on his lap. 'The man *I* take on will have better things to do on his day off than shove bumfodder through people's letter boxes.'

'I can't think of owt better to do on me day off than helping my fellow man.' At Kit's dubious smile Owen wagged the pamphlets at her. 'We all have our ways of serving the Lord and this is mine. What's thine – wearing big hats?'

Monty, seated in one of the fireside chairs, sighed at the way the afternoon was turning out. He rubbed a knee that was swollen with fluid and callused from kneeling at the coalface. Sixteen years down the pit had taken its toll on his body. But there would be no let-up until he dropped dead. He worked alongside men who were in their seventies – one of them eighty. There was even no let-up at home. 'If it's an argument you want 'ee can do it in your own homes.'

He might as well not have spoken, for the days were gone when one word from their brother could silence them and Gwen carried on as if there had been no interjection. 'Men have no respect for women who draw too much attention to themselves, you know.' An observant eye could discern that she was Kit's sister, though with her rather waxen features it was as if Gwen's face had melted round the edges, presenting an air of misery. Creeping towards middle age, she had still not learned to curb her bossiness and frowned on her youngest sibling's habit of always trying to gain an audience by these outlandish displays. 'Lord help us, every time I come here you're sporting a new hat! Couldn't 'ee fit any more ornaments on it? 'Tis a wonder you know whether to wear it or prune it.'

The tone of the banter was in the most part good-natured, but that didn't prevent it being hurtful.

Sensing this, Beata tried to help. With only four years between them, she and Kit were more like sisters than aunt and niece. 'Heather's very lucky.'

'She'll need more than a cartload of heather on her hat to conjure up the bloke who'll take her on,' scoffed Owen.

Kit wondered why it was that she was meant to accept these indignities with composure, when the perpetrators would take umbrage were she to turn the tables. She'd given Owen short shrift once and had cut him to the quick. He had looked so bewildered and hurt that she had not done it again. Gwen too could be destroyed with one harsh word, yet even knowing how it felt, the two of them remained quick to judge Kit. Amelia was just thoughtless. Often, the idea had occurred to Kit that she had been born into the wrong family – why was it a sin to want nice things, or to enjoy oneself?

As usual it was the amiable Charity who sprang to her aid. 'Leave the lass alone!' Now twenty-seven, she had developed into a large-boned, capable-looking woman – though nowhere near as tall as Kit – her dark hair and eyes accompanied by sallow skin lending her an almost exotic look.

'She dun't mind! quipped Owen in genuine fondness. 'She knows we don't mean owt. Skin like a pachyderm has our Kit.'

'What's one o' them when it's at home?' obliged Amelia as he had known she would, thereby allowing him to donate the benefits of his knowledge.

He feigned surprise as if expecting everyone else to know this. 'Why, it's an animal with a thick skin like an elephant or rhino.' These little snippets of information were a sop to his own self-esteem, for despite all hopes being pinned upon him Owen had failed the examinations that would have elevated him to college and thus from the pit.

Kit objected to the comparison.

'We're only saying it for your own good,' provided Gwen, as she saw it quite truthfully.

'Well, I think she looks grand,' smiled Charity. 'How are you, Kit?'

'I were fine till I came in here!' Adept at hiding her wounds, Kit gave her tormentors a theatrical glare, then turned her smiling attention to the little red-headed girls who crowded round her in greeting, each of them pulling at her skirts to attract notice and telling her to sit by them. 'Oh, now then, now then!' She bent to receive their hugs.

'They never welcome me like that,' muttered Gwen.

Kit could have made a nasty response, saying that there was no wonder that Gwen was unpopular when she was always speaking her mind, but it was not in her nature. 'It's only cupboard love.' Smiling down at the girls she withdrew a bag of locusts from her skirt pocket and warned the children not to squabble as their fingers tussled over the pods. All were wearing ribbons in their hair and freshly laundered pinafore smocks which always started out white for chapel and Sunday school but after a couple of days would be creased and grubby.

'She's trying to make thee as fat as she is,' Owen jokingly warned the girls.

Anticipating more insults from her sisters, Kit ordered, 'Oh, shut tha gob, there's a train coming!'

Monty pointed a finger at her, his meaning made clear by the expression in his bright blue eyes.

Beata, by nature the antithesis of the grandmother whose name she carried, thought the others unfair and, in gently compassionate manner, advised, 'Don't pay no heed, Kit, they're only jealous.'

Owen cackled. 'Oh, aye! I've been saving up for ages to get meself a bonnet like that. Just the job for t'pit. We could all shelter under it if t'roof caves in.'

'Do you all mind if I manage to sit down first before you cast any more slurs?' Kit looked for a place to accommodate her bottom. The benches on which the younger ones usually sat up to the table had been taken by the visitors, so the children were seated on the hearth and on the mat. There were two wooden armchairs for their parents and two more basic rush-bottomed ones which were regularly fought over if the parents weren't around.

Beata was admiring her aunt's hat. 'Shall you be wearing it for Amelia's wedding?'

Amelia's blue eyes turned icy, mainly at the lack of deference from her niece. She had always clung defiantly to the fact that she was not the youngest in the family, preferring to group herself with her married sisters – as she would soon be able do quite legitimately – and her attitude showed that she resented this familiarity from one so young. Just because Kit allowed the girl to drop the suffix *Aunt*, did not mean that all should comply. However, out of fear of alienating her elder brother, she chose not to voice her resentment openly – nothing was aired openly in this household, but made apparent in more furtive ways, usually via Kit's expense. 'Anyone appears at my wedding in an abomination like that'll find themselves barred.'

Unaware of her own wrongdoing, Beata objected. 'Aw, I think it's lovely!'

Kit took the hat off, then pulled a sheet of paper from her pocket and, inserting her hips into the space that had been made available to her, leaned towards the tall but underdeveloped figure with the translucent skin, blue eyes and large nose, the latter being a family characteristic. 'Just look at this one then, Beat! I tore it out of Mrs Larder's magazine.' The two dark auburn heads came together. There followed an animated discussion about the latest in millinery – an even more ostentatious example than that which she wore today. 'Look it's got bird wings on! And there's instructions on how to make a cheaper version using a domestic fowl.' As the other little girls gathered round to marvel at the pictured hat, Kit voiced her determination to acquire one. 'I've got a plain straw bonnet just lying there begging for decoration.'

'Eh up, our Monty,' warned Owen, 'she'll be after thy banties. I'd keep me eye on poor Sammy, an' all.' This was the canary.

Kit made an uncomplimentary reply, then, faced with disapproval from her elder sisters, sat quietly for a time, pondering her hat.

Owen resurrected the conversation he had been having with Monty before Kit entered. 'So are you coming to our meeting on Thursday or what, then?' The other shook his head, drawing forth a complaint. 'Well, it's a fine thing when a man can't rely on his own brother! I've fought tooth and nail to get this union recognized. What point has there been if the majority don't join? We've got to get the numbers up otherwise

53

we'll have no clout.' The Ralph Royd Coal Company was known as one of the most uncompromising in West Yorkshire.

Monty was unmoved. 'I've told you there's no point anyway. The masters will always win.'

Owen detested such short-sightedness, not just in his brother but in the majority of miners. 'Not if we all stand together! All of us, not just a handful. This is the perfect time to make a stand, while they're getting a good price for their coil – so's we who dig that coil get the benefit!'

'It's no good ranting on at me. I just can't afford to pay out any more a week,' Monty finished his say.

With a sound of exasperation, Owen gave up.

'Shouldn't be long now.' Flora's reedy voice came somewhat out of the blue. Her presence was often overlooked.

'What shouldn't?' Kit barely glanced up from the page.

'Our Sarah's started.'

'Aw, when?' Only now, Kit noticed that Gwen was in her sister-in-law's chair, and upon being alerted she detected groans from above that she recognized as the signs of labour – though after six children it could hardly be called labour, the last babe had arrived within ten minutes of the initial pain.

'About five minutes ago,' simpered Flora.

'Tut! Nobody tells me anything!' Kit looked miffed.

'Maybe you'd get to learn more if 'ee weren't always so full of yourself.' Monty felt instant remorse, for his youngest sister's face fell. But it was too late to retract the words now. He hoped Kit would understand they had been provoked by the worry of another mouth to feed and the extra penny he would have to find to insure the life of this new child, taking the total to sevenpence a week – not to mention another lot of school fees. It wasn't as if this penurious existence had been brought about by frivolity. That's what he found so irritating about Kit. She didn't earn very much, and one would think she'd spend what little she had on sensible attire but no, she'd arrive on her day off wearing another new hat or the next Sunday she'd be disporting herself in useless little gossamer gloves. Why did she not appreciate that he had struggled to bring her up? It wasn't that he expected her to give him her entire wage, simply not to squander her own allowance on fripperies and to flaunt them so much. He really liked Kit's obliging nature – notwithstanding the thoughtlessness of

54

youth, if asked to help she would do so immediately without grumbling – but he was often harried to dementia by her dreamy self-indulgence. Please God, the years ahead would instil more responsibility.

Gwen was more concerned about the instant. 'She were just putting the kettle on for tea an' all. Us'll have to wait now.'

Eager as ever, Flora offered to do it.

The elder refused. 'I want tea, not coloured watter.'

The mild-mannered Flora blinked and retreated into her bonnet like a tortoise.

'I'll mash it.' To cover her own hurt, Kit rose and put the kettle on the hob. Monty's displays of exasperation always upset her, for of all her siblings he was the one she most respected. The thing of greatest upset was that his ire was usually deserved. How could she be so full of her own ideas that she hadn't noticed Sarah's absence? She turned apologetic eyes on her brother.

It was remarkable how he always managed to look so clean and youthful despite his tribulations. Many in his profession had deeply lined faces but once Monty was scrubbed up his skin was smooth as a babe's. Kit's thoughts came round again to Sarah. Normally at this time of day she would have had the children doing bible readings. Kit suggested this now to Beata, who took up the scuffed leather volume and began to recite as her aunt stirred the teapot and in due time passed out the cups.

'What're you going to call this'n?' asked Kit during an interval between the bible readings, trying her best not to spill her tea, with one child draped fondly around her shoulder and another on her lap.

Listening to the groans from above, Monty tried to make amends for his previous harshness. 'If I get to choose I might name her Katherine, for you.' After six daughters he had ceased to waste his time pondering over boys' names.

Kit beamed, her pleasured glance embracing her sisters who did not seem to share this emotion. She hoped their jealousy would not extend to her little namesake. Barring the easy-going Charity they were even jealous of each other's offspring. Owen was jealous that his brother had six children and he, not long married, only had one, offering the defensive retort that at least his firstborn was a lad – 'It takes a man to get a man.' Gwen was jealous of Flora and Charity because they had girls and she had only boys. Kit was glad Gwen hadn't brought them today. She adored the company of children but Brian and Donald were pampered little tykes. Thank goodness there would only ever be two of them. Since the second one's birth there was the whispered suggestion that Gwen might have some sort of trouble with her works.

The bible reading was having no effect in taking the children's minds off their mother's travails. Kit struck up a jolly conversation to mask the sound of the groans. The older girls were used to the sound of their mother giving birth but six-year-old Wyn and two-year-old Meredith were wide-eyed and anxious. Kit favoured the youngest, who was a large child like she herself had been, with big stocky limbs, and she wanted to protect her from any hurtful comments – though oddly there were few; everyone seemed to like Merry's merry nature.

Kit reassured them. 'Sithee! I've got a new face.' She contorted her attractive features into a horrible mask, making the little girls cross their legs in laughter. Pleased with their reaction, the natural entertainer provided more. Again the girls brayed aloud.

The jocularity was interrupted by a summons from the midwife. Monty looked alarmed – this was unusual. After each previous delivery she had made Sarah comfortable before sending him up as she herself left. There must be something wrong. Running a palm over his thinning, bright red hair – an act that bespoke his concern – he made for the staircase that led off the scullery, leaving his anxiety to infect the children. Again, Kit tried to jolly everyone but they chose not to heed her, waiting apprehensively for their father to return.

Monty was absent barely two minutes. They heard his tread upon the stairs, then his stunned face appeared in the kitchen doorway, one hand clutching the jamb for support. His skin, always pale from working underground, was completely drained.

A jolt of alarm flipped Kit's stomach and she folded the two-year-old into a protective hug on her lap.

'It's a lad.' Monty's jaw hung open in disbelief.

There arose a combined sigh of relief and amusement – 'You soft aporth, you had us all going!' said someone – and he was pulled into their midst, his skin turning the colour it adopted after a Bank Holiday outing.

'Let your poor father sit down!' Gwen ordered young Alice from the chair she had jumped into when Monty had previously vacated it. 'He looks ready to pass out.'

Monty flopped on to the warm polished timber, still stunned, though with delight spreading over his face now.

Kit laughed her own pleasure and reached over to grasp his hand, no trace of disappointment that the child would not now be named after her. She knew how much this must mean to her brother.

'Can we see 'im?' Alice jumped up and down. 'Can we, Father?' She pronounced it feather.

'Give your poor mother a chance to get her breath back,' warbled her Aunt Flora.

'Why no, she be sitting up as bright as a button,' laughed Monty, growing brighter himself by the second. 'raring to show him off – but don't all go at once, you'll suffocate the poor mite.'

'We'll go in shifts,' decided Gwen, carrying a cup of tea for her sister-in-law and leading the way.

Kit let others go before her, content to smile upon her brother's face.

A grinning Owen put the wad of Socialist pamphlets from his lap in order to rise and deliver a congratulatory slap. 'Well done, me old love, tha's a man at last!'

Monty rarely issued a foul word, but now in his head he damned his brother as a mean little shit who wouldn't even permit him to relish this moment of joy. Owen had never enjoyed a special position in the family. Neither eldest nor youngest, he resented both Monty and Kit their privilege – resented everyone in the family come to that. The lack of a father had caused other complications; for Owen, in addition to the normal sibling rivalry, Monty represented the father figure to be constantly challenged. Tragic circumstance had thrust an uncharacteristic patience upon the elder brother, but at this moment it was becoming dangerously stretched.

Kit watched the interplay between her brothers, wondering if the younger man was aware of the offensiveness of his remark. She thought not. Owen seemed to live his life back to front. It was somewhat anomalous that he who had been like a little man when he was a child grew more childish with every year.

Under the barely concealed look of contempt from his brother, Owen swallowed his congratulations and gave an inner sigh, rubbing thought-fully at the gap on his left hand where two fingers had been severed in

57

a pit accident. Whatever he said and however enthusiastically, it would not find favour with the dour Monty, who had always resented him. It was as if by being born he, Owen, had usurped Monty's position as only son. He didn't want to usurp his brother – he loved him, not that he would ever utter it.

Fortunately, to ease his discomposure, the first shift came down from admiring the baby, allowing others to go up.

Upon returning, the younger man announced appeasingly, 'By, he's a grand lad,' though the dialogue between him and his brother remained stilted.

Waiting her turn, Kit had succumbed to dreaming about her own babies and so lost had she become within her imagination that she failed to notice her siblings' return. Gwen had to speak twice. 'Wake up, dopey!'

Excited children scampering before her, Kit ascended the staircase. On the landing was a doorway that led to two bedrooms, the first of which belonged to Monty and his wife, the other, reached only through the marital room, having to accommodate six girls – and previously more, until the last of Monty's siblings had left home to enter domestic service. Coming from such overcrowded circumstances Kit had thought herself in heaven to receive a room of her own.

Today, on this late afternoon in summer, the parental room was ripe with the smell of birth fluids. Fingers of sunlight pierced the front window and trickled through the dividing doorway to infiltrate the normally gloomy back room. Particles of dust floated and danced upon the sunbeams which crept over the floorboards and up on to the counterpane, illuminating a happy scene. Eyes glittering like the black nuggets hewn from the mine, Sarah was propped up on pillows, the new arrival in her arms, an anxious two-year-old Merry cuddled up beside her mother and a host of other admiring little faces.

'Make way for your Aunt Kit, there's good girls.' At their mother's Welsh lilt the collection of small bodies parted and drew back allowing Kit to approach the bed, but when she perched on the edge of the mattress the sea of red heads closed around her again, one child resting her chin on Kit's shoulder to gaze upon the babe, another little girl crawling under Kit's arm with her head laid upon the plump breast, yet another sprawled across her lap. They loved this young woman almost as much as they did their mother – more in some ways, for besides having a naughty streak

58

their aunt always had time to play with them and listen, at least she had until she'd gone into service. How they cherished the days when she was allowed to come home to be with them again.

Using a gentle finger to explore, Kit laughed softly at the dark red fuzz on the babe's pulsating fontanelle. 'Another copper-knob.' Every one of her nieces had auburn hair of varying shades.

'Some things never change,' smiled Sarah, who wished that just one of her children might have inherited her own dark looks.

The poker-faced midwife beheld the collection of redheads and shook her head in sympathy. 'Must be like living in a box of blinkin' matches.' Everyone laughed, even though Mrs Feather said the exact same thing every time a new Kilmaster child was born.

After all these years and all these births, the Kilmasters had only recently been truly accepted by Mrs Feather and other residents of the village. It took patience to get to know these strange Yorkshire folk, for although the mining village housed Welsh and Irish and Scots and incomers from all over England, there was a wall of nepotism to break through. However, once Monty had gained a foothold and had shown that he was prepared to risk his life to rescue an injured collier, or sacrifice a great portion of his earnings to help a miner's widow, acceptance had gradually come. Some of them might speak with foreign accents, but it was felt now that the Kilmasters were as Yorkshire as anybody.

'Here, have a hold of your brother.' Sarah passed the new-born to Beata, at which all the girls clamoured to be allowed to hold him and the snuffling bundle was passed from one to another before his aunt was finally allowed to cradle him in her arms.

'Oh, isn't he gorgeous!' Kit almost wept.

Sarah agreed, but wished she had more privacy to enjoy this long-awaited son. The house was never empty it seemed. Life had been very difficult. Over the years she had seen each of her extra burdens married off. Only Amelia and Kit retained their spinsterhood and the elder had found herself a nice young man so would soon be away to make her own home like the others. How Sarah would love to sit in an empty house. Yet they all imagined they were doing her a favour by congregating in her parlour once a month! Monty thought it wonderful that he had kept his family united. He had such lofty ideals, especially about duty, and was almost fanatical about keeping the family together, when in her opinion most of them would have been happier kept apart. But then he had never asked for her opinion. Sarah felt that she had never had a youth, that her husband only saw her as a mother to his children and someone to cook his meals.

Kit gazed upon the latest creation adoringly, her senses acute with the newness of him, the piglet-like snuffling, his featherweight warmth in her arms, and her mind was filled with thoughts of the baby she would have one day. 'None of us could believe he's a lad. Our Monty's still in shock downstairs.'

'He ain't, you know.' Monty grinned from the doorway then came forward to take the precious bundle which Kit reluctantly surrendered. She retained her position on the edge of the bed, smiling, not a little envious of her brother's wonderful brood – but she would have all this herself one day. She surely would.

'Have you recovered enough to think what to call him?' Kit asked eventually.

Monty looked bemused, although truthfully downstairs he had been giving it careful thought and had come to the decision that there was only one name he could bestow – his own father's. Some might deem this odd for one who had been at such cross purposes with his sire, but perhaps it was for this very reason that Monty chose to make belated amends. 'Well, I been waiting for this moment all of fifteen years . . .'

Kit maintained her smile but felt sorry for his daughters whose existence was somehow demeaned by this statement. Monty's sense of nonfulfilment over the lack of a son, hidden so well all this time, was now clearly evident in that one remark. Yet, in a trice her sympathy was transferred to her brother as his wife jumped in with her own announcement.

'Probyn!' Though Sarah beamed, her tone brooked no discussion. 'He'll be named after his grandfather – and Montague, of course, after his father.'

Alice demanded to know why this child had a grandfather and she didn't. Her mother said she had, but he was down in Wales and it was too far away to visit.

Monty hid his disappointment well. Time had shown that there was no point in trying to change his wife's mind. For a moment his downcast eyes took in the new-born's cherubic face. Then he smiled and asked himself if it really mattered. He had a son – was so full of pride that he felt his chest might explode. 'Probyn Montague Kilmaster.' His voice cracked as he spoke it.

Kit issued compliment, but privately thought that it was far too grand a name for a poor little boy whose only role in life was to follow his father down the pit.

5

In those first waking moments, when a persistent tapping infiltrated her dream, Kit had no idea where she was until the realization came: she had stayed the night at home. Normally, after she had spent the afternoon and most of the evening with her family she would leave at nine thirty and return to her workplace near Leeds. Yesterday, however, she had been unable to tear herself away from the happy atmosphere. After her sisters and Owen had said their goodbyes and gone home, she voiced her intention of remaining until morning. So long as she rose at four o'clock with Monty she would be there in time to light the fires and clean the sitting room before waking Cook with her morning cup of tea.

Automatically, she reached an arm across her bedfellows and used her knuckle to return the tap as indication that she had heard. For the last few years the Kilmasters had been spared from having to pay tuppence to the knocker-up by old Mrs Allen, their neighbour, who, since her husband's death in a pit explosion, had been unable to slumber past the hour that he had normally risen and so had transferred the benefits of her insomnia to them.

Lack of bed space notwithstanding, Kit rolled on to her back, yawned, then commenced her morning ritual. Extending her warm, marshmallow body to its full length, she wriggled her toes to bring them awake – issuing soft apology to Ethel who slept with her head at the foot of the bed and now received Kit's toe in her ear – stretched calf and thigh muscles, buttocks, shoulders, neck . . . then relaxed into the mattress again to lie for another few seconds, trying to postpone the release of accumulated bodily gases out of compassion for her roommates.

The figure directly beside her was stirring too. Since Kit's departure it had fallen to Beata to heed Mrs Allen's tap and consequently go and rouse her parents. Feeling her start to rise Kit murmured, 'Stay there a while, I'll see to your dad.' Then, as was her usual habit, she rolled out of bed feet first, toes slipping expertly into boots placed at a strategic point the night before and, whilst lacing them, made use of a chamber pot.

Standing in her chemise and drawers, a tousled plait dangling over one shoulder, Kit moved through the darkness between the beds crammed with slumbering bodies to the bowl of cold water on the dresser where she sponged her face and voluptuous upper body, dried herself, then put on her stays, her petticoat and her dress. The room smelled faintly of last night's urine. Carrying a full chamber pot before her, her arm trembling under the weight, she opened the door and crept through the other bedroom on her way to the stairs, whispering into Monty's ear so as not to wake his wife. Unable to pass the crib without smiling fondly into it, she lingered for a moment, then went downstairs.

At her arrival, the beetles that came out at night to feed on kitchen debris scuttled back behind the skirting boards. Kit barely noticed them and proceeded outside, first having to count to five in order to make her exit. She did not know why this was, it had always been so. If she tried to go through an outer doorway without counting to five an invisible wall confronted her. It was not essential to do this when entering a house, just upon leaving. Kit was hardly conscious of her habit now, just did it instinctively. Once outside she tipped the slops over the grate, rinsed out the chamber pot and went back inside.

The fire had been banked up overnight with slack and only needed the tease of a poker to get it going. Yet, its flame was insufficient to light the room, for the sun had not yet risen, and Kit was forced to grope about in the dinge for an oil lamp. The room was suffused with the smell of bacon. Contrary to this indication there would be none for breakfast, the aroma merely came from the lamp which had been fed with the dregs from the frying pan in order to save money. Still not fully conscious, acting merely from custom, Kit put the kettle on, shoved a communal toothbrush up the chimney and transferred the sooty bristles to her mouth.

Last night, before leaving, Gwen had taken over Sarah's kitchen in her usual bossy fashion and prepared the dough for a new supply of bread. All Kit had to do now was to put it in the oven. It would not be baked in time for Monty's departure, though. Taking yesterday's loaf from the bread bin, she carved numerous slices and spread them with dripping.

At this point the fragile-looking Beata appeared.

'Eh, I thought I told you to have a lie-in!' Kit was softly accusing. 'You don't start for hours.'

'I've got used to getting up early since you left.' Her niece also used the brush on her teeth, then seeing that the kettle was boiling, made a pot of tea. 'Anyroad, I have to get our Ethel's and Rhoda's snap ready.'

Kit frowned. The last time she had come home Rhoda had still been at school. Then she remembered. 'Oh aye, she's twelve now!' Monty and Sarah refused to let any of their girls go to work before this age. 'So what's she doing then?'

Beata said she was at the same glass works in Castleford where she herself and Ethel were clerks. She coughed several times to clear her throat, her pale features always appearing more delicate than ever first thing on a morning. 'She's in t'factory, but just half-time, 'cause she's still struggling with her sums. Some weeks she goes mornings and t'next she goes afternoons . . . sorry for this here beffing.' She thumped her chest.

'That's all right. Who's looking after your mam if you're at work then?'

'Alice is having time off school and Rhoda's coming home at dinner time, and Mrs Allen'll be popping in. Is there enough o' that bread left for us?'

Kit checked the loaf. 'Aye, I think so. I'll do it for thee. You pour us a cup o' tea – oh, here's your lord and master, best get him one first.'

Monty hawked to clear his lungs, expectorated upon the fire, then sat at the table waiting to be served. The tea emerged like treacle, which was the way he liked it. After lacing her father's mug with sugar, Beata spread a large handkerchief to receive the slices of bread and dripping prepared by her aunt, knotted it, then made a similar parcel for her sisters. Alongside these she placed three billycans, each with a twist of tea and sugar. Kit packed her brother's wedges into his snap tin and filled his bottle with water. All would be consumed later at work; it was far too early for breakfast at this hour.

Only now did Kit sit down to enjoy her tea. After the cups were drained Beata took them away to wash whilst Kit did her hair. Standing before the small mirror over the fireplace – which was set too high for children; it didn't do to encourage vanity and the mirror was purely for practical purposes – she unravelled her braided tresses and swept them into a chignon. The insertion of several hairpins lent time for appraisal. The reflected gaze displayed a fundamental honesty, which was a great asset to one who, in moments of crisis, was not averse to resorting to untruth. With sleep not fully banished from the heavy-lidded eyes it was an attractive and sensual reflection. Beneath the residue of baby fat lay good foundations. Far from being rounded like her body, the head in the mirror was quite long with large dramatic features. Too large? Kit stared at herself. Was she truly as bad as everyone seemed to think?

Monty glanced at his sister, thinking how vain she was, always checking her appearance. To discourage this display he stood abruptly. 'Come on then, 'ee don't wanna be late.'

Kit turned away from her reflection and helped him into his jacket, Beata handed him his cap and then his snap tin which he affixed to his belt and was ready to go. There were few kisses exchanged in this household. Fondness did not have to be demonstrated.

'Should I take Sarah a cup o' tea?' Kit's offer was not completely altruistic. She hoped to sneak a last cuddle of the darling baby Probyn before leaving.

'No, you get off,' said Beata, bending her willowy frame to open the oven and check the bread, the smell of which had begun to permeate the house. 'I'll take her one. I have to go and empty t'potties.'

'I've done 'em,' replied Kit. 'Leastwise one of 'em in our room. I left t'other; it had nowt in.'

'Aye, I noticed but Father's will be almost overflowing –'

'Cheeky cat,' interjected Monty.

Beata laughed. 'Anyroad I have to get our lasses up.'

Thwarted, Kit reached for her bonnet.

Monty groaned. 'Do I have to be seen with 'ee wearing that?'

'I'll walk six paces behind you if you like, maungy.' Kit fingered him playfully in the back, counted to five, and the two tall figures set off. Before reaching the end of the row Monty cautioned his sister to keep a low profile for, although he was not superstitious himself, some of the men with whom he worked would turn around and go home if they encountered a woman on their way to the pit. However, such characters were not in evidence at the moment.

By now the sun was almost risen, which was a mixed blessing for as

65

they were passing the allotments Monty noticed that one of his bantams had died overnight. Through the half-light he could make out the gleam of white feathers in the cleft of the lower branches of a lilac tree.

Kit saw it too. 'Aw, the poor thing.'

'Poor thing?' Monty looked accusingly at her. 'It seems like an awful coincidence, you just mentioning yesterday that 'ee wanted a bird for your new hat.'

She gasped in outrage. 'I haven't touched it! Look, there isn't a mark on it!'

'I wouldn't put it past 'ee to've made a little clay effigy and been sticking pins in it overnight!' Monty relaxed his scowl and nudged her. 'I'm kidding 'ee, daft clot. I reckon it's that flaming dog o' Kelly's been chasing 'em again, scared the poor bird to death!' He reached up into the tree and dislodged the corpse.

Kit watched him examine it. 'Well, you won't be able to eat it, will you? I mean, it might've died from some disease.'

'If this be your way of asking if you can have it for your hat, then no you can't. That bird were fit as a lop yesterday. She's died o' fright, I tell 'ee. Bain't no way I'm throwing good food away.' A slight note of relent entered his voice. 'But you can have the feathers once it's been plucked if you want.'

'I don't want 'em wi' blood and muck all over 'em! I need the skin in one piece. Aw, go on, Mont! I'll go back and do it this minute and the meat'll be there for your tea. I won't make a mess of it.'

'Well, zee you don't!' Monty handed over the limp-necked fowl and, saying that he was going to be late if he dallied here any longer, headed for the grim silhouette of the pit headgear – for although it was only half a mile away he would have two more miles to walk underground before he reached his workplace. Kit hurried back to the house.

By this time Ethel and Rhoda had risen and were poised in the scullery amidst a heap of bedding whilst getting the copper fired up. Both they and their elder sister gawked as their aunt rushed in, placed the dead bantam on the table, snatched off her bonnet and began to rattle the contents of a drawer. 'Knife, knife – I need a sharp knife!' Successful in her search, Kit rummaged in her pocket for the instructions, following them stage by stage, first making a neat incision down the bird's breast, shallow enough to avoid drawing blood, then began a tedious peeling of

66

skin and feathers. Thankfully the sun was donating more light now. 'I have to get it off all in one piece,' came her explanation to the watchers. 'So's it'll look like a real bird on me hat.'

'Are you gonna keep t'head an' all?' enquired Rhoda, grinding a knuckle into her eye corner.

'You daft aporth, who wants a chicken's head on her hat?'

'I were only asking.' Rhoda turned her back and rammed the dirty sheets into the copper.

At the offended tone, Kit said, 'Well, maybe I'd leave it on if it were summat pretty like a dove. Don't talk to me for a minute, I have to be right careful.'

Fascinated, the red-headed sisters stood watching for as long as they could before having to leave for work.

'Kit, you should be off too or you're going to be late!' Ethel, who had the strict air of a school mistress, was never irresponsible like her aunt.

Kit was too immersed in her delicate operation. 'I can't rush it, it'll be spoiled. It's got to go in t'oven yet – is that bread out?' She dared not lift her eyes.

'Aye.' Beata pulled a shawl around her tall but slender frame. 'We really have to go. Good luck with your thingy!' The three sisters left.

Without lifting her head, Kit returned their farewell and continued with her task, too involved to heed the faint summons of bell and whistle calling people to their labours at various manufactories across the Aire valley. Finally, after much biting of lips and facial contortions, the bird's plumage came off in one clean piece, along with its wings. Another consultation of the instructions told her to apply salt and pepper to the underside of the skin, which she did, though could see no earthly reason why if no one was going to eat it. Then, leaving a grotesque pink carcass lying on the table, Kit transported its overcoat to the oven, handling it like precious china.

Once it was installed there was time to relax and to share a congratulatory grin with herself in the mirror – until she caught sight of the clock's reflection and balked at the time. If she left now and walked briskly she might still make her destination. Perhaps she should leave a note for someone to take the feathers out of the oven – but what if they got scorched? She dared not risk it. The new hat must come before all else. Putting her waiting time to good use she tried to make the carcass look presentable. It was at this point that Sarah came in looking like a wild Welsh mare, her black locks all tousled.

Caught out, Kit tried to conceal her own guilt with a look of reproach. 'What're you doing out of bed?'

'Never mind what I'm doing! What are you doing still here?' Sarah wore a perpetual frown of anxiety that would only be smoothed by the safe appearance of the breadwinner home from the pit each night. To the onlooker she had always been middle-aged, had never been young and fancy free. Her dark eyes fell on the carcass. 'And what's that mangled mess?'

'Kellys' dog killed one of our Monty's banties so I said I'd dress it so's it'd be ready for your tea.'

'Dress it? It looks as if it's been undressed to me – and very violently.' Sarah looked with some revulsion upon the flesh which Kit was frantically trying to make into something more attractive. 'And I don't know about it being safe to eat. If a dog's had it in its mouth –'

'Oh no, its teeth didn't pierce the skin, it was just a bit knocked around, you see. I had to do the best I could with it. Do you want me to cut it into pieces, and you can use it in a stew?'

Sarah tossed her head. 'What I want is for you to go to work!'

'Let me get you a cup o' tea before –'

'Kit, just go!'

Kit wondered if the precious feathers were sufficiently dried and how she could get them out of the oven without her sister-in-law catching her. 'I'll just put this in t'pantry. You really shouldn't be up, you know. I thought Alice was meant to be looking after you?'

'I don't need looking after.' Hand pressed to the small of her back, Sarah wrinkled her nose and began to sniff the air. Above the fresh soapy scent of boiling linen was a less pleasant odour. 'Has something crept into my oven and died?'

Kit winced as her sister-in-law flung open the cast-iron door. 'Ah, well, you see,' she explained under the other's responding glare, 'I didn't want to put the feathers to waste so I thought I might as well use them to decorate a hat.' She bustled forward in an attempt to rescue her prize. 'They needed to be dried in the oven so –'

'Just get out of this house!' Brooding Welsh eyes gave weight to the order. 'I'll take care of them.'

'Well, you really shouldn't –'

'Be gone!'

'You will look after them till next time I come? Oh thanks, Sarah!' Kit thought it expedient to leave. 'Oh, well then – I bid thee farewell!' Counting to five, she grabbed her bonnet and fled.

Across the meadow, along the road, down valley and up hill Kit ran, the urban sprawl of Leeds and its smoking chimneys looking deceptively close but the ache in her legs telling otherwise as she paused for breath, then ran, jogged, stumbled, ran again the entire six miles and finally arrived in the basement of the large sandstone villa at seven thirty clutching her side, dripping with sweat and barely able to issue an apology to the furious and dishevelled cook.

'Mrs Atkinson, I'm really so –'

'I'll give you sorry!' Cook was dour at the best of times but now looked ready to throw the breakfast tray she was carrying. 'Where've you been? Never mind! Put your cap and apron on and take this up at once. The master and mistress are waiting!'

Beads of perspiration on her brow, and heaving with exhaustion, Kit had already thrown off her shawl and rushed to snatch a clean apron from a drawer.

'Come on, frame yourself!'

Mob cap askew, Kit grabbed the tray and hurried for the stairs.

'And when you come down you'd better be able to give an explanation!' spat Mrs Atkinson before collapsing into a chair.

Staggering up to the drawing room, Kit prepared herself for retribution, but this manifested itself only in the form of arctic expressions from her employer's family, the master registering his own disapproval by a theatrical look at his watch.

Downstairs, however, was a different matter. Mrs Atkinson's anger was unabated by the conciliatory cup of tea that Kit poured for her. Though she did not rise from her seat, the authoritative tone of her voice was sufficient to convey her superiority.

'I am not a housemaid, Katherine, I am Cook! I do not clean fireplaces, do not light fires. I cook. That is why, strange as it might seem, my title is Cook!'

'I'm really –'

'If we were employed by Lord Bountiful there'd be other maids who could do the work when you failed in your duty, but we're not, we're working for a skinflint who can hardly afford the two of us, so when you decide you want to slonk in bed –'

'I did set off in time!' pleaded Kit, but was cut off by a glare.

'When you give in to your idle nature it's me who cops all the extra work!' Cook lifted her teacup to her lips but stopped halfway. 'Up to me armpits in black lead, looking like a nigger minstrel and the master wants to know where his kippers are!'

Kit gave earnest apology, wringing her hands afore her buxom chest. 'I'm *truly* sorry, I *swear* I did set off on time but you see, our Sarah had another bairn last night and –'

'And you're the one doing the lying in?' Cook remained waspish.

'No! I mean –'

'You mean you're using others as an excuse for your shortcomings!' Mrs Atkinson took a last angry sip of tea. 'I'm not having it, Katherine! There've been too many of these incidents. You started off competently enough but you've been very slack of late. This is the last straw.'

Sensing disaster Kit sought desperate and shameful action. 'We had a death in the family!' It was only stretching the truth a little – Monty loved those banties as if they were his children.

There was stunned silence, a look of horror, then an exclamation. 'Eh no – the babby, was it?'

Kit hesitated, then shook her head.

'Oh no, not your sister-in-law?' Cook pressed a hand to her mouth and spoke through fingers that still bore a hint of black lead. 'Eh, that's dreadful!' She had no personal knowledge of Sarah but both were acquainted with Mrs Feather, the midwife, who had been responsible for Kit being offered this job.

The look of shocked sympathy on the woman's face sent a wave of guilt flooding through Kit, who was about to correct Mrs Atkinson's assumption but was not given time, for the other was issuing profuse commiserations. Covering her eyes as if to stem tears she wondered how to rectify her rash proclamation. Perhaps later when Mrs Atkinson had cooled down Kit could explain that it was all a misunderstanding.

'I'm sorry, it won't happen again – my being late.'

'What? Oh, well,' Cook shook her head miserably. 'I suppose you've got a good excuse. Eh dear, how tragic, those poor motherless children.

There must be summat I can do.' She racked her brains, then made a beeline for the mistress's pantry. 'Here look, have this bit of ham for the funeral.'

Kit thanked her and took possession of it, feeling more dreadful by the minute.

'You'll be wanting time off to attend, I suppose? I'll talk to the mis –'

'Oh, don't go to the trouble now! We'll talk about it later.' Eager to change the subject, Kit made keen gesticulations at the stove. 'Can I get you some breakfast?'

'Well, I must say you're being very stoical about it. But then I suppose we all have to soldier on.' Mrs Atkinson's temper had been completely deflated. 'And yes, thank you, dear, I'd appreciate some breakfast. Oh, deary me, how dreadful.'

'And after that I'll make up for all the work you had to do!' promised Kit, launching into action. 'I'll do luncheon and everything.'

'Aye well, I won't say no.' Mrs Atkinson slumped pensively in her chair. 'I don't feel as though I could do another stroke all day.'

True to her word, she remained in her seat, leaving Kit to rush round with uncharacteristic industry, getting Cook's breakfast whilst grabbing only a quick bite for herself, clearing the master's table, dusting and cleaning and washing.

Cook did rise briefly after lunch, but it was not to help with the work. Putting on her coat she announced that she was going for a trip to the market in Leeds, and left sufficient orders to keep the housemaid busy for the next two hours.

Kit blurted, 'Are you going anywhere near the library? I wonder if you'd be so kind as to take my book back. It'll be overdue otherwise.'

'Can you ever accomplish anything on time?' Mrs Atkinson looked sour, then remembering the girl's bereavement, relented with a flick of her hand. 'Go on then – but look sharp!'

Kit ran to fetch the book from her room, wiping her hands on her apron as she pounded up the stairs, great bosoms bouncing, and wishing it were she who were off into Leeds. If ever she were given time off through the week she would spend most of it in the library, not because she thought to better her position but because she loved to read and learn about other countries and peoples. Even with the aid of a dictionary some books were beyond her capabilities – as was the tome she retrieved now. Kit wished she were more learned, could understand all the text that accompanied the pictures. But there was no chance of that for one who had left school at twelve.

After delivering the book into Mrs Atkinson's hands she bent purposefully into her work until all the tasks on Cook's list had been completed, when she was able to relax a little and finally seek out a remedy for her indigestion brought on by the hurried meal, wondering what was keeping her superior so long in Leeds.

She was not to discover the reason for Cook's extended outing until eight o'clock that night after the master and mistress had received their supper and the pots had been washed and everything got ready for morning.

'Right!' said Mrs Atkinson with a grim expression – she had been in an odd mood ever since she'd come back from Leeds, Kit had noticed. 'You can go pack your box and make arrangements to have it carted home.'

Kit was perplexed. 'Home?'

'Well, you might as well be there for all the amount of work you do here.'

'You're giving me t'sack? Oh, that's not fair!' Kit felt qualified to apply for a job as a pit pony after all the work she had done today, though she was not brave enough to offer this impudent observation to Cook.

'It wasn't fair that I had to do your work as well as my own this morning! And it's certainly not the first time you've let me down – and when you are here your mind isn't on your work. Besides, you'll be sadly needed at home what with all the arrangements for your sister-in-law's funeral.'

The cryptic manner in which these words were issued caused Kit's heart to sink.

At the look of guilt that flooded her subordinate's cheeks, Mrs Atkinson launched into a full attack. 'Aye, you do right hang your head! I happened to see Mrs Feather when I were in Leeds and guess what she told me? You lying toad! What a dreadful thing to say about anyone, let alone the woman who's been a mother to you.'

'I didn't actually say our Sarah was dead!' Kit remained flushed.

'No, but you let me think it!'

'You didn't give me a chan –'

'You ought to be ashamed of yourself. Anyway, it's no good wasting time arguing!' Cook smote the air dismissively and turned away. 'I've got someone else starting in the morning. The mistress knows all about it. She says you're to come back tomorrow when she'll pay you what's owed.'

That wouldn't be much, thought Kit dismally, imagining Sarah's volatile reaction to the news of yet another dismissal, though her concern was mostly for herself.

Cook brought the shameful affair to a conclusion. 'Mrs Larder says she'll consider overnight whether or not to give you a reference – which is a damned sight more consideration than you deserve. And I'll have that lump of ham back, thank you!'

And so at nine o'clock that night Kit found herself making hurried arrangements with a local carrier to have her large box of belongings transported to the village the next morning, whilst she had to plod home on foot through the country lanes. When she arrived, weary and despondent, the kitchen was in darkness and swathed with pristine linen that smelled of fresh air. The household was abed, yet it was no comfort, for now the confession would have to wait until morning and Sarah would be in an even worse mood to receive it. After plaiting her hair, Kit gazed forlornly into the banked-up fire, before creeping aloft, using the very edge of the staircase to avoid creaks. For one awful moment whilst inching her way through her brother's and sister-in-law's room she feared she was about to be discovered as baby Probyn stirred in his crib, grunting and snuffling like a piglet. But all remained still as she grasped the knob of the inner door, twisted it gingerly and finally reached her goal.

Gently rousing Beata, she whispered for her to move over. Unquestioning, the semi-conscious girl in turn nudged Ethel, and their grateful aunt rolled into the warm space provided, murmuring apologies for robbing them of elbow room.

She had just made herself comfortable when one of the little girls in the other bed piped up. 'Beata, there's a fly.'

'Ssh! Don't disturb everyone.' Kit groaned and snuggled down. After sampling the luxury of her own room, it would be hard to cope with being thrust back into this sardine tin.

'Is that you, Aunty Kit?' came the anxious voice in the dark.

'Yes – now shush, there can't be a fly. You're just dreaming.'

73

'I can hear it! It keeps coming round me 'ead. Please, dear Aunt Kit . . .'

With an inward groan, Kit dragged her body from the bed and groped for a candle and matches on the dresser, for she knew from past experience that there would be no peace until she reassured Alice. 'All right, all right, don't wake the pizzocking house.'

'Aw, you swore!' giggled another child.

'It's not swearing.' There came the abrasive zip of a match against sandpaper, then the tang of sulphur. After a frustrated search Kit finally glimpsed, in the light from the candle, a gnat hovering right before her face, attempting to settle on her nose. With a deft swipe she grasped the insect in her free fist, then examined it closely. 'You can hardly see the blessed thing it's so small!'

'It were buzzing in me lug 'oile.'

'You must have good ears, that's all I can say,' hissed Kit.

Demanding that the pest be exterminated, eight-year-old Alice could only be satisfied by the presentation of its corpse on Kit's palm before settling down to sleep, thus allowing her aunt to squeeze back into bed. Imagining the scene that would greet her tomorrow, Kit lay awake for ages.

In the morning, at Mrs Allen's knock, she allowed Beata to rise before her, explaining that she had been dismissed and whispering, 'Don't tell your dad!'

'He already knows.' Beata looked woeful.

Kit groaned and shoved her head under the sheets. She continued to lay in bed until she heard the clatter of miners' clogs fade into the distance and knew that her brother would have set off for work. Ethel and Rhoda were stirring. Kit rose then to dress, with the intention of creeping past Sarah and preparing breakfast in bed for her and so perhaps reduce the vilification.

However, when she peeped round the doorway there was no one in the other room apart from the red-headed baby. Heart sinking, Kit went downstairs to meet her fate.

Mrs Feather had obviously wasted no time in conveying the report of Sarah's death to the corpse herself. 'Dead, is it? Funny, that – I feel as right as rain!'

'It wasn't me that told her!' blurted Kit as Beata tried to make her willowy frame unobtrusive by crouching over her sandwich-making. 'She just assumed –'

'What a lovely excuse to give for your being late. Ought to be ashamed of yourself, you should.'

'It were a misunderstanding! She thought I were late because –'

'Because you told her I'd inconveniently died and made you late!' The nightgowned figure was furious. 'Dozy, wretched creature! Messing around with your stupid hats –'

Kit had an awful premonition. 'You haven't thrown me wings away have you?'

'What do you think that is, the archangel Gabriel?' Sarah stabbed a finger at the sideboard where the bantam's plumage was displayed in all its glory. 'But if you don't get it shifted you'll be seeing angels, my girl.'

Kit hurried to protect her prize. 'Oh, thanks! I'm really sorry, I didn't know it was going to take that long and once I got started on it I couldn't leave it.'

'So you sacrificed your job to vanity!'

Kit looked chastened, stroking the white feathers. 'I didn't mean for her to think owt had happened to you, she just got wrong end o' t'stick. Does our Monty know?'

'You think I want to tell my husband about his sister's wicked lies? He's taken it hard enough that you lost your job.'

'What did he say?' Kit glanced at a watery-eyed Beata who was creeping around the kitchen as best she could, not even daring to clear her throat for fear of attracting a stream of Welsh invective.

'You don't want to know! Well, you can get yourself right out and find yourself another job this morning. Did you get a reference?'

Shamefaced, Kit shook her head. 'I have to go back today to see if she's going to give me one.'

'Kit, you really are the limit! Useless, you are!'

Kit lifted her head at a frail cry from upstairs. 'Probyn's crying. Shall I fetch him down for you?'

'That won't be necessary.' Carrying a laundered napkin, Sarah half marched, half limped for the stairs. 'I'm quite capable – strange, that, for someone who's meant to be dead!'

*   *   *

75

After breakfast, Kit left the house saying she would go and collect her reference early so as to be better equipped in her consequent search for employment, but in reality spurred by an eagerness to keep out of her sister-in-law's way.

Alas, there was further admonishment in store that day, not the least of it from Mrs Larder, her former mistress.

After tramping six miles, Kit was made to stand in the hall for a full hour in retaliation for making her employer wait for breakfast. Swaying in her boots, calves and feet throbbing, she was further tormented by the sight of her successor flitting back and forth with a tea tray until Mrs Larder deemed herself ready for an audience.

'Well, Katherine, and what have you to say for yourself?' The middle-aged woman in the lace cap and fichu, and silver-grey dress with voluminous skirts, rested her hands in her lap, her hooded eyes projecting anything but welcome.

Kit hated grovelling to one who hardly registered on the social scale, but had no choice. 'I do apologize for being late yesterday, ma'am.'

The response bore a hint of sadness. 'Ah, if that were only the extent of your trespasses upon my good nature, Katherine. I understand that you told Mrs Atkinson your sister-in-law had died?'

'No, I said we'd –'

'It is quite unacceptable behaviour.' Pathos gave way to stricture. 'Your laxity toward your work has been hard enough to tolerate, but I will not countenance downright lies. I think your master and I have been most patient with you, wouldn't you agree? And I'm certain Mrs Atkinson deserves more support than you are willing to give her.'

'Yes'm. Sorry, ma'am.'

'Well, that is all I have to say. Here are your wages.' At Kit's show of gratitude Mrs Larder inclined her head. 'However, after great consideration I regret that I am unable to grant you a recommendation.'

Kit was genuinely shocked. Who would employ her without a reference? There was no position lower than domestic service, which had been her last resort after being sacked from various factories and local shops.

'You might think me harsh, that your misdemeanour was not serious enough to warrant this decision, but consider it from my point of view. Any prospective employer would need to know that you are trustworthy

76

and in telling them that you are I would have to resort to untruth. That I cannot do.'

Feeling bilious, Kit acceded to Mrs Larder's smile of dismissal, and trudged the six miles back to her village.

Averse to another tongue-lashing from her sister-in-law, Kit stopped short of going all the way home and instead spent the afternoon lolling in the sun on farmland that overlooked the colliery, wading through the bag of buns she had purchased from her wages and afterwards making daisy chains whilst contemplating her future. If she were to receive condemnation from both Monty and his wife she might as well wait until they were in the house together and have it over in one go, hence she delayed going home until a trickle of colliers from the shaft indicated that their working day was at an end.

Her journey coinciding with that of the miners, she greeted each in cheery and unselfconscious fashion, whilst keeping an eye out for her brother. Once, she had been unable to decipher the clean men who went into the colliery in the morning from the grimy ones who emerged on an afternoon, but over the last decade she had come to tell who was who under the coal dust from their individual mannerisms. All returned her greeting with a laconic but warm acknowledgement, some having known Kit from their schooldays before following their fathers down the pit.

Undecided whether to enter by the front door and face Sarah's wrath first, or sneak through the back way and hide upstairs for a while until her brother came home, Kit chose the latter.

But when, with gritted teeth, she gingerly lifted the sneck on the gate to the yard and peeped around the splintery timber, she found that Monty had somehow beaten her to it. Fortunately he had his back to her, and was stooped over an enamel bowl on an old table. In the act of sluicing water upon his blackened face, head and neck, he was unaware of her arrival and she put a finger over her lips to Ethel who stood by with a jug of fresh water and a towel, waiting to scrub her father's back. Unlike others in the village, Monty never entered the house before ridding himself of coal dust, despising those who not only sat in their muck until bedtime but crowded the public saloon before tea. His fastidiousness was treated as eccentricity by some of his ilk, but Monty shrugged off their jibes.

This was a well-worn ritual which Kit now observed cautiously, waiting for the chance to sneak past and in the meantime listening to the trill of the canary who was evidently enjoying the benefit of this spell of fresh air whilst his master bathed. In colder weather strict concessions were made, her brother would unhook his braces, leaving them to dangle whilst taking off his shirt to wash the upper half first, and at the last minute whipping off his trousers and stockings to stand in the bowl and wash his legs, only a piece of sacking to guard the soles of his feet from the icy yard. Today though was warm and he had stripped off to his shorts immediately, lathering soap into his skin until the black layer was removed, save for that embedded deep in scar tissue. His hands plunged again and again into the water that was fast assuming a layer of black scum. This leisurely pace gave Kit time to sidle past, taking the opportunity whilst his face was buried in the towel and Ethel had started to scrub his back.

Inside, tea bubbled on the hob, ready and waiting for the master's arrival. Normally this meal would be the focus of attention whilst the hungry children awaited their father, but today there was a more interesting topic to hold them. Kit slipped into the scullery unnoticed to find them all crowded goggle-eyed around the table where baby Probyn was having his napkin changed by his mother. Even the older ones wore looks of intense curiosity over the unfamiliar appendage on the youngest member of the family. Whilst it was hard in this overcrowded house for a maiden to be kept innocent from activity between the sexes, their parents' room being in such close proximity to their own, few of the girls equated those animal grunts with the tiny protuberance before them.

'What exactly is that?' asked Wyn, pointing.

'I told you yesterday,' returned her mother brusquely. 'It's what a boy has and a girl doesn't.' At hearing the creak of a boot upon the stair, she glanced up sharply, foiling Kit's evasion. Attempting a conciliatory smile, Kit abandoned her plan and came into the living room, ducking under the sleeves of laundered linen that hung from the pulley over the fireplace, and put her wages on the mantelpiece.

'But what do you call it?' Alice, too, wanted to know.

Sarah gave a sound of exasperation and was overzealous in her task, drawing forth a mew of protest from the baby as she gathered his tiny ankles in one hand and almost yanked him off the table to shove a fresh napkin underneath. 'It's just part of his body!'

'But –'

'Kit, you're expert at changing the subject,' muttered her sister-in-law, covering the offending object with a corner of the flannel. 'Think of something.'

Kit pondered over the scrawny new-born legs that barely protruded from the napkin, reminding her of a plucked fowl. 'What did that chicken taste like?'

A gasp of ingratitude. 'Good at rubbing it in, aren't you?'

'Well, you said change the subject!' Kit hooked her forefinger over her lip, trying to think of some way to ingratiate herself. 'Here, let me help you – you shouldn't be out of bed.'

'When have I got time to lie in bed? I've got to go down for my churching later.' Sarah gathered little Probyn in her arms. 'Anyway, I haven't been up long. Rhoda cooked the tea. A very good job she made of it too by the look of it. There, get it on the table now, Rhoda, your father will be in in a moment.' At her further instruction the soiled napkin was whisked off the table by another daughter and a cloth laid in its place, plates and cutlery carried in by a smaller girl. 'She cooked that chicken yesterday too, which, as it happens, was very tasty – but I'll still be having words with that Mrs Kelly about her wretched dog when I'm out and about – though much good it will probably do. She doesn't even look after her children, let alone the dog. Dirty little arabs. Vulgar creatures, all of them. But what can you expect when the father's a drunkard?'

Two of her little girls exchanged secret smiles. They loved their mother's Welsh accent, the way she said words like *der*-tee and *vol*-gar and *cree*-tures, which Aunt Kit often imitated for their entertainment – though not in Mother's presence, of course.

Indifferent to their amusement, Sarah went on, 'They might live in the same street, and the same sort of house but their morals leave a lot to be desired – shame the whole village, they do. Water costs nothing. They must roll on the ground to get that filthy.'

Forbidden to associate with the Catholic family, the young Kilmasters had adopted their mother's prejudice. 'Teacher made me sit next to Cissie Kelly last week,' said Rhoda, adding hurriedly. 'I didn't talk to her, though.'

'I should think not.' Sarah winced and put a hand to her aching back.

'Didn't talk to who?'

At Monty's voice Kit assumed a guilty posture and awaited his admonishment.

'Kellys,' provided Sarah.

'Huh! They'd populate the world if we let 'em.' Monty examined the youngest child in his wife's arms, speaking to the babe. 'But we won't, will we, little chap? Noo, indeed. For every one o' theirs we'll provide a good Wesleyan child.'

Kit and Beata shared a glance as if to express an opinion that it was not Monty who had to do all the running about after these children.

Unfortunately he lifted his eyes in time to catch it. 'Got zommat to say for yourself, have 'ee?' His query was directed at Kit, who hung her head. Others in the room, sensing a bad atmosphere, made themselves scarce.

'No! Nothing you can zay, is there? Get another job did 'ee?'

Still mute, Kit shook her head.

Sarah made a noise and turned a keen eye on her. 'What sort of reference did Mrs Larder give you?' The ensuing look of guilt was enough.

'God a' mercy on us!' Face pink with suppressed anger, Monty told Kit, 'Well, you can do some work afore you get fed! Ethel's been at it all day like the rest of us. Go on!'

Kit rushed outside. Enveloped in a black cloud of dust, Ethel had almost finished beating her father's trousers and jacket, but was happy to let another clean his boots and rinse his socks. Kit hung the latter on the line before daring finally to come in.

Monty was seated at the head of the table, his harassed wife indicating for others to join him whilst she herself laid the baby in the sideboard drawer that had been lined with a blanket. He was still annoyed.

'I can't understand you, Kit. I really can't. You've no man to look after 'ee and like as not never will, yet you seem to think you can chuck a good job up whenever you feel like it – Lord, we humbly thank Thee for the meal Thou has provided, amen.' After this perfunctory grace he delved a spoon into various bowls of vegetables, finally transferring a large portion of mashed potato to his plate.

Kit lifted her head from prayer to accept the spoon thrust at her rather rudely by her brother. 'I didn't chuck it up, I got the sack.'

'Through your own daft fault.' Monty's knife and fork were poised to eat, the criticism he had received from his father over similar transgressions long forgotten. 'Who's going to give 'ee a job with no reference –

by the way, I hope I got a clean shirt for class meeting tonight?' This was directed at his wife. A grim Sarah replied that he had.

'I thought I might try a new direction,' mused Kit, heaping more vegetables upon her plate.

'You've exhausted every direction there is!' complained Sarah. 'Unless it's your intent to be a lady of leisure.'

'You should try the stage,' said Rhoda, her sisters chorusing agreement that their aunt was a wonderful entertainer.

Monty was shocked by the very suggestion. 'An actress? They're little better than – you know what!'

'What?' Kit frowned.

'Babylon,' replied her brother. 'And we're having none of that here. You're not in a position to pick and choose.'

Sorry for Kit, and ill at ease with the friction at the tea table, Beata made a tentative contribution. 'Maybe Amelia can put in a good word for you at the hall.'

The condemnation came to an abrupt stop. 'Oh, thank heaven someone can talk sense!' Sarah lowered herself gingerly on to a chair, dealt her daughter a congratulatory pat, then picked up her own cutlery. Amelia had been at the same workplace since she was twelve years old and was highly thought of by her employer. 'They'll want someone to replace her when she gets married.'

'They won't know what they're letting themselves in for,' grunted her husband.

Kit knew that Amelia would be none too keen to work alongside her sister, and she herself shared this view. 'I'm not sure –'

'Be told!' Monty directed his knife at her. 'First thing tomorrow, you're off to Cragthorpe Hall, and woe betide 'ee if you come home without a job.'

Sarah, who despaired of ever being rid of Kit, manufactured a beam. 'Right! Now that's all settled perhaps we can eat our meal without getting indigestion – oh, and whatever you wear tomorrow, Kit, just make sure it's not one of your ridiculous hats!'

6

Cragthorpe Hall was only half the distance to travel from home as her last place of work had been, and at a different point on the compass, being nearer to Castleford than to Leeds. Leaving her box behind, an act of pessimism in Sarah's opinion, Kit promised she would not come home without some kind of employment, but declared there was little point in lugging heavy cargo three miles if they did not want her to start immediately.

Kit had always assumed that Amelia was indulging in the usual showing off when she had spoken about Cragthorpe Hall resembling a castle and the folk who owned it dripping in money. That assumption was quickly expunged upon arrival outside the massive wrought-iron gates gilded with what appeared to be a coat of arms – although the family had no title, to Kit's knowledge. A skilled landscape artist had granted protection for its occupants from any glimpse of evil done to the countryside; the mansion was entirely secluded from the surrounding coal mines by undulating pasture and groups of trees. Kit stood there mesmerized, her gaze moving along the driveway to the rambling Gothic house with its towers and turrets, flying buttresses and vine-laced cloisters, and the innumerable chimney stacks, her first thought being to wonder what it would be like to have to light all those fires alone – but of course there would be lots of servants here, she would be just a cog in the wheel. Amelia had told her there were about twenty-five staff. Only now did Kit believe her, revising her intended approach to whoever should open the door. Indeed, she first had to find that door.

Apprehension tweaking her breast, she followed the line of the iron railings, searching for a servants' gate, and finally came to the appropriate entrance. Once through and embarked upon the correct route, she found herself separated from the rest of the grounds by shrubbery but still with an intermittent view of the house. There was some sort of repair work being done to its numerous windows. A series of ladders reduced the dignity of the east wing, where glaziers struggled to install a huge sheet of plate glass – or were they removing it? Yes, Kit decided they were, for the rest of the windows had small leaded lights. She watched their precarious operation for a while, then, heart thumping at such an adventure, she turned her head, allowing her eyes to roam over the vast park that flanked the east wing of the house, where red and fallow deer grazed in the dappled shade of lime trees. Enthralled, even by the kitchen gardens, by the time Kit found the door to the servants' quarters she was desperate to reside here and when her knock was answered she donned her most enthusiastic smile and introduced herself.

'Good morning! I'm Amelia Kilmaster's sister, Katherine. I wonder if I might speak to her, if that would be no inconvenience?'

The maid expressed amazement, her eyes taking in the caller's remarkable height, before inviting her into an enormous kitchen that was three times as large as Monty's entire house, and informing her companions in a gruff voice that matched her appearance, 'There's a giant here to see Amelia – says she's her sister!'

Contrary to Kit's expectations, there was little industry in the kitchen, the staff having time to stand and stare open-mouthed at this monumental girl who became rather awkward under their inspection and hoped her sister would not be too long in coming.

To divert their attention, she tried to recall what Amelia had said on Sunday. 'My sister tells me your master's coming up from his London house shortly.'

Once distracted, the staff were quite friendly, going about their leisurely business. 'Aye, we won't be stood round gossiping like this then,' laughed Lily, the maid who had let her in, a strong-looking girl with the protruding jaw of a bulldog, its misalignment causing the lower front teeth to be constantly bared, more of a snarl than a smile. The only pretty thing about Lily was the broderie anglaise trim on her cap. 'The family's arriving tomorrow. Most of the servants are coming on ahead this afternoon, Cook amongst 'em. That's why we're making the most of it now. Would you like a cup o' tea?' At Kit's grateful acceptance she picked up a china pot, another maid providing a plate of biscuits. 'Your sister might be a while in coming. It's not so bad for us with no one to cook for, but the upper servants are run off their feet getting all the dust sheets off and the house in order.'

Kit smiled and said, 'That must take a pretty while. I've never seen a house as big as this.' Her gaze rose twenty feet to a ceiling that was louvred to let steam escape, then descended again to examine the oak cupboards and shelves lined with countless utensils, copper and brass pans, gleaming fish kettles, huge sinks, the great kitchen range that almost took up a whole wall, the massive table where all the preparation was done. She pointed to an unfamiliar contraption. 'Is that one of them gas ovens? I've only ever seen a picture of one in a book. What's it like to cook on?'

Her query drew a combined groan from the others and a mysterious comment from Lily. 'It hasn't seen much cooking – I don't think that's what the mistress bought it for. Here's your tea. Sorry, I can't invite you into the sitting room to have it but we daren't let Cook catch us sat doing nowt.' An air of polite curiosity took over. 'Was it summat important you wanted to see your sister about?'

'Well,' Kit looked for somewhere to sit but there was not even a stool, forcing her to drink her tea standing up like the others. 'As our Amelia's getting married soon,' she knew she was not revealing any secret, Amelia had told everyone who would listen about her coming nuptials, 'I was hoping to fill her shoes when she leaves.'

The cordiality evaporated, a bellow of protest arising from Lily and her peers. 'Eh, there's others in line before you, you know! You can't just walk in and get a parlourmaid's job just like that, you have to work your way up. I've been here three year.'

Kit was trying to make amends when Amelia entered wearing her perpetual look of harassment, the carroty frizz exploding from a white beribboned cap. 'What's happened?' The impromptu appearance of a relative conjured images of a pit disaster, though she did not voice it for fear of tempting fate, asking instead, 'Is something wrong at home?'

The vociferous Lily jumped in. 'No, she's after my bloody job!'

Kit immediately sought to allay both women's anxiety. 'No! I just came to see if you'd put in a good word for me. I was forced to leave Mrs Larder's residence because they've had to go abroad suddenly. They wanted me to go with them but I couldn't leave Yorkshire –'

'Nor me neither, love,' agreed a different maid.

'– I don't want to steal anybody's job. I don't mind what I do,' finished Kit.

Guessing the truth beneath her sister's fabrication, Amelia was annoyed at being put in such an importunate position, did not want to be around when Kit's indolent nature was discovered, as surely it would. Pale lips set in a line, she told her, 'I don't have any influence here, you know. There's no saying they'll employ you.'

'Cook's here!' As the yelp went up, issued by one who had been posted as lookout, the maids scattered and tried to make themselves look busy in time for the entrance of an extremely corpulent figure who was accompanied by half a dozen men and women bearing hampers.

With nowhere to run, Amelia stood pale-faced as the cook's entourage took over the kitchen, swarming around unpacking hampers. Kit was fixed to the spot too, overwhelmed by the turbulence that had overcome this hitherto peaceful place.

'Amelia, shouldn't you be upstairs?' A high-pitched voice for one so fat.

'Sorry for getting in your way, Mrs Hellawell,' whined Amelia, 'But my sister here came looking for a job.'

From out of the mound of lard that was Cook jutted a tiny pointed chin, a button nose and surprisingly youthful eyes that were the most beautiful shade of green Kit had ever seen. Though her figure looked middle-aged she was probably not ten years older than the girls she dominated. 'Now, that's what I like to see, a big strong lass!' A nod of approval as she took off her hat and shoved it into waiting hands. 'I'll have her.'

Amelia cringed, fully aware of how deceptive her sister's looks were, but glad at least that she would not have to work alongside her. However, unwilling to be relegated to the kitchen, Kit prompted her with a hefty nudge. Amelia refused to come to her aid, remaining mute, but at that point the housekeeper entered, demanding to know why one of her parlourmaids was neglecting her duties and in an effort to save herself Amelia blurted, 'My sister wanted to apply as my replacement when I leave, Mrs Grunter!'

'Er, hold your hosses, I want her in my kitchen!' objected Mrs Hellawell, palms resting on heavily corseted hips, but one look from the housekeeper silenced her. With amazing force of character for one so tiny, Mrs Grunter had this effect on everyone, save the steward who was up in London ensuring the smooth transition of his master's move to the North. Delivering a petulant shrug, Cook went about her business, bawling at her own staff, 'Come along, get this stuff unpacked – as soon as these people get out of our way, that is!'

The diminutive figure in black with a white-frilled cap of lace and ribbons, a chatelaine at her waist, hands like delicate porcelain, and the eye of a pike, reverted her gaze to assess the applicant. 'Your name is?'

'Katherine – Kit, ma'am.'

'And what previous position did you hold, Katherine Kit?' There was no twinkle to show if Mrs Grunter was making fun or not.

'Parlourmaid, ma'am.'

Amelia blushed at her sister's lie.

'Very well, come with me – Amelia, back to your duties!' The formidable Mrs Grunter led the way out of the kitchen, along a corridor with several turnings and into her own territory which consisted of the still room, a store cupboard, and her own parlour that was lined with china cupboards, linen presses and jars of preserves and, to Kit, was a miniature palace in itself. Though there were several comfortable armchairs draped with lacy antimacassars and plump cushions, Kit was directed to a hard wooden one where she was forced to perch ramrod straight whilst awaiting further interview, hoping her plainness of dress and her pose were sufficiently demure.

'And who was your employer, Katherine – or would you prefer to be called Kit?'

'Whatever pleases you, ma'am.' Kit tried to pierce the woman's reserve with a friendly but polite response. 'I worked for Mrs Larder. She lives near Leeds.'

'Never heard of her. Allow me to see your references.' A dainty hand was outstretched, but was to be unrewarded.

'I haven't got them yet, ma'am. You see, I only left yesterday. Mr and Mrs Larder had to leave the country rather suddenly and –'

'Not wanted by the police were they?'

'Oh no, ma'am!'

'It was a joke.'

Discountenanced by the lack of animation in the grey eyes, Kit gave a rather exaggerated laugh. 'Oh, very funny, ma'am! Well, as I said they had to leave suddenly for America – I think it was family business. Anyway, they wanted me to go with them, but I prefer to bide here. What with all the rush they didn't have my reference ready when it was time for me to leave, so the master very kindly promised to drop it in the evening post to my brother's house. It wasn't there when I left this morning but I should have it by tomorrow.'

'Have you no recommendation from previous employers?'

'No, I worked for the same lady since I left school,' lied Kit.

Mrs Grunter's eyes narrowed, scrutinizing the open face that smiled eagerly back at her, before eventually coming to a decision. 'Very well, Kit, I will take you on trust. Presumably the letter will have arrived by tomorrow, you can fetch it with you when you start. Don't bother coming until later in the morning, you'll only get in the way. I'll speak to the master about your appointment when he arrives from his London residence.'

'Oh, thank you, ma'am! Would that be as parlourmaid I'm hired? Only I don't want to rob anyone of their rightful position. Lily was saying it's her turn to –'

'Lily does not make the appointments. Besides which, she is kitchen material. A fine-looking girl like you would be wasted downstairs.' Mrs Grunter knew her employer's taste in parlourmaids. 'Very different to your sister, aren't you? Not much to look at, Amelia. If it weren't for her efficiency she'd never have made it upstairs.'

Kit enjoyed an inward laugh and wished she could throw this at Amelia when next she chose to lob insults. She never would, of course. Kit was rarely vindictive.

'The mistress thinks very highly of her, I hope you'll live up to her standards. We'll start you on sixteen pounds a year and see how you perform, then maybe we'll consider giving you the same wage as your sister. Your caps will be provided. I assume your work attire is as presentable as the dress you are wearing?' Kit said she was sure it was and listed the items in her possession, most thankful that she had the regulation black dress befitting her upper house duties. Mrs Grunter seemed satisfied. 'In addition to your wage you will receive eightpence per day in lieu of beer and one half-day off per week, or perhaps an extra half-day at my discretion. You will be expected to attend prayers each morning. Apart from the necessary comings and goings demanded by your

employment, the garden is out of bounds to servants – and although I am
lenient in matters of the heart whilst a servant is away from the Hall, I
will not permit followers to enter the grounds, nor will I countenance
any hanky-panky between members of staff. That rule must be strictly
observed. Well, Kit, I expect to see you here at mid-morning tomorrow.
Good day.' A cool smile and Kit found herself outside the door.

Trying to remember the route by which she had come along the drab
corridor, Kit turned to her right and hoped it led back to the kitchen.
She was issuing mental congratulations when someone grabbed her and
she blurted a surprisingly girlish shriek for one of such proportions.

But it was only her sister. 'What did you say you were a parlourmaid
for?' hissed Amelia, snatching furtive looks over her shoulder.

''Cause I'm sick of being a dogsbody,' came the retort.

'Making me look a fool –'

'You might be a fool, I'm not.' Kit looked smug. 'I start tomorrow.'

Amelia groaned. 'You don't know the first thing about the job!'

'Well, it can't be that hard if you're doing it. You can teach me.'

'Huh! Insult to injury.' The dumpy girl tutted and steered her companion to the right, past the maids' sitting room. 'Whose idea was it to
send you here?'

Kit chose not to blame her niece. 'Our Monty's. I'll tell him you put
in a good word for me, he'll be right glad.' She continued to move along
the corridor at a jaunty walk.

'If you make a muck of this I'll kill you! God, I wish it wa' September.'
This was when Amelia would leave to be married.

'I don't know why you're getting so het up. I'm really looking forward
to working here. I thought you were having me on when you said how
big it were.'

'We're not all natural liars. What really happened at Mrs Larder's?
Suppose you got the sack again, didn't you?'

'Aye, mean old ewe wouldn't gimme a reference neither.'

'Ssh!' Amelia came to a halt, grabbed the taller girl's arm and pushed her
towards a nearby exit that would save her from going through the kitchen.
'If Mrs Grunter hears you you'll cop it, and me too for recommending
you.' She opened the door. 'How on earth did you manage to get this
job with no reference?'

'Told her I'd bring it with me when I come tomorrow.' Kit counted to five before taking a step over the threshold, her smile as bright as the sunshine. 'Well, I'd better be on me way – have to practise Mrs Larder's handwriting for tomorrow.'

On reflection, Kit, never an accomplished scribe, abandoned any attempt at forgery and turned up at Cragthorpe Hall with her box the next morning with the excuse that the post had not arrived before she had set off, and adding to Mrs Grunter, 'But I'll go home on my afternoon off if you like, it must have arrived by then.'

The housekeeper said she would take Kit on trial. 'Your sister is most trustworthy, I am sure you are similarly disposed. As for your afternoon off, I shall expect a good month's work out of you first, my girl.'

'Naturally, ma'am,' came the dignified response.

Mrs Grunter, head back, was peering rather disapprovingly at the new maid's hat that was bedecked with all manner of decoration. Unwilling to crush her latest creation into her box, Kit had transported the heather-laden bonnet on her head, even in the knowledge that it was bound to invoke adverse reaction. Folk did not want their inferiors dressed more finely than themselves. 'And I trust that we will not witness you in that attire for church?' She received the promise that it would be reserved for more fitting occasions.

'I can't for the life of me imagine what that would be fitted to,' murmured Mrs Grunter, rubbing the back of her neck which ached from straining to look up at her much taller companion. Summoning Amelia, whose pale face reddened at the sight of Kit's ostentatious headgear, she handed the newcomer over to her care. 'Five minutes to show your sister to her room and then back to work.'

Amelia helped Kit to lug her heavy box along the corridor, asking what assistance she had had in getting here. Kit said it was lucky that she had been given a lift on a vegetable cart or her knuckles would be trailing on the floor by now. It had been bad enough dragging the box from the road to the house. Amelia grumbled that it felt as if she had the horse and cart still in it but, despite all the puffing exertion, managed to point out various landmarks along the way – pastryroom, Cook's room, pantry, servants' hall – until they reached a narrow flight of stairs.

'This is our staircase. That one at the other end of the passage is the men's. They'll try to get you up it if they can. One particular footman,

Algy they call him, he tries his luck with all the new maids – but you should be safe enough.' Oblivious to her own implied insult, she huffed under the weight of the box and sighed thankfully as they reached a landing, which, like the staircase, was composed of bare boards. 'Here we are, this is thine.'

Kit was forced to duck her bonneted head to avoid collision with the lintel, but was otherwise quite pleased with the small room and its bed, washstand and one chest of drawers, and pleasantly surprised that she would not have to share. Amelia explained that their employer did not wish to encourage close relationships of any kind lest it be detrimental to the servants' standard of work.

Whilst Kit took off her bonnet and shawl, Amelia opened the box with the intention of helping her unpack but shrank at the sight of a pair of white wings. 'What the . . . ?'

'It's for me new hat.' Kit explained how she had Kelly's dog to thank for her prize, stroking the white feathers before storing them carefully in a top drawer. Next from the box she took the plain straw hat that awaited the decoration, having to punch it into shape before laying it on the top of the chest. After Amelia had helped Kit to unpack the rest of the contents – a bible, one spare chemise, a change of drawers, another hat, one flannel petticoat, two nightdresses, two print dresses, one stuff dress, four coarse aprons, four white aprons, a spare pair of black stockings, another hat, a pair of slippers and various lacy fripperies that should never be part of a maid's inventory – she exclaimed that it was like Aladdin's cave, ordered Kit to put one of her white aprons over the formal black dress and provided her with a lawn cap that had lain in one of the drawers.

At this juncture a smiling face of another parlourmaid appeared in the doorway. 'Hello! Is this your sister?'

Obviously embarrassed, Amelia was forced to introduce the two girls. 'Oh, er, Kit, this is my best friend, Ivy.'

A pleasant girl with a broad smile and a rather strong-willed gleam to her brown eye, Ivy gave Kit's hand a firm shake then cocked her head and asked, 'Has she shown you her wedding dress material? It's lovely!'

Kit looked perplexed, feeling rather hurt that this stranger knew more about her sister's wedding than she did.

'We only bought it the other day,' stuttered Amelia. 'On t'market.

Mrs Grunter gave us an hour off to go buy it – come on, I'll give you a quick look.'

The three hurried to Amelia's room which was virtually the same as Kit's, and Ivy pulled a box from under the bed, displaying the heavy, stamped velvet which had already been cut out though not yet stitched together. 'Have a geg at that then!' She held it to her own bosom. 'It cost seven pounds!'

'That's almost half a year's wages!' exclaimed Kit. 'It is to me anyway.' She asked Amelia how on earth she could afford it. All their other sisters had paid for their own weddings; they couldn't expect Monty to provide.

Amelia explained that her fiancé's parents were contributing to the wedding as they had lots of relatives, plus the fact that Albert was their only child and they wanted to give him a good send-off. Albert worked as a footman in another grand household. The pair had met when assisting their respective employers at a charitable party for the inmates of the workhouse at Christmas. Upon his wedding he would leave domestic service and take up something more suited to a married man.

Kit nodded. 'Oh, you're so lucky! Have you got a sweetheart, Ivy?'

A grinning Amelia answered for her friend, who had turned coy. 'She's just met someone!' The two tittered as if over some big secret.

Feeling excluded, Kit continued to admire the beautiful russet material, saying it would suit Amelia admirably.

'Well, I thought as it was an autumn wedding I'd get something more practical – not that I could afford silk anyway,' laughed Amelia. 'But it can double as my going-away dress, and I'll get plenty of wear out of it afterwards.'

Kit eyed the collection of buttons, hoops and bones that were also in the box, lying like a dismantled skeleton. 'You're going to need help to get it finished in time.'

'I'm helping her,' jumped in Ivy.

Amelia saw Kit's face drop. 'But you can help too if you like. She's a really neat sewer, is our Kit,' she told her friend, before turning back to her sister. 'Best go and change your boots. I'll just put this away and then I'll meet you back in your room.' She began to fold up the material as Kit left.

Once there were just the two of them, Amelia lowered her voice.

'See what I mean? She's like a house-end! How could I ask her to be a bridesmaid?' She had wanted so much to have her best friend as attendant but in doing so had felt that she would have to ask Kit too, as they were closer in age than her other sisters, and to leave her out in favour of a stranger might cause offence. Similarly averse to having any of her nieces without the others, and unable to afford dresses for everyone, she had decided not to have anyone at all. 'You know I'd love to have you if I could, but to have Kit too would ruin things.'

'Oh, I know that!' Ivy was forgiving, and sympathized with Amelia for being encumbered by such a relation.

'It's going to look like a pinchfist wedding with no bridesmaids though.' Amelia looked sad as she replaced the box under the bed. 'But we just can't afford it. Anyway, I'd better go and sherrick our Kit or she'll be sitting doing nowt. Do you know, she's gone and told Mrs Grunter that she's used to being a parlourmaid – when she's only ever been a skivvy! The cat.'

Leaving Ivy, Amelia returned to Kit's room and poked her head in. 'Right, are you ready? We've got a few things to do before we lay the table for luncheon. You wouldn't normally get to do it but the footmen are still in London – or rather they'll be on the train back up here by now I should think. Master and mistress are due back any time.'

Kit was bending over, changing from her outdoor boots into black, low-heeled slippers. Having paid little attention to her sister's gossip in the past, she now had to ask her employer's name.

'I've told you! Honestly, you never listen.' Amelia gave the information whilst chivvying her sister downstairs and along a further substantial length of dingy corridor. 'The master is Mr Geoffrey Dolphin, the mistress is Mrs Zenobia Dolphin, their eldest son is Master Eustace – everybody calls him Tish because when he was small he pronounced his name Eushtish.' Amelia checked to see they were unobserved before divulging, 'He's a simpleton. He's nineteen but not in the head, if you know what I mean. He's harmless but he's not much to look at. Then there's Miss Agnes, who's seventeen, Master Wyndham who's fifteen – he's at Rugby, that's a posh school down south, he'll be coming up for the holidays too – Miss Frances is twelve and Master Everard, eleven.'

'What're they like?'

'The mistress is kind, a bit highly strung, but I wouldn't trouble

92

yourself, you'll hardly have any dealings with them. They don't like the servants to be visible, so if you meet them in the corridor make yourself scarce.'

They came to a green baize door studded with brass nails. Upon reaching the other side Kit gasped, for they were now in the main house and instead of bare linoleum there were patterned runners underfoot, gilt-framed oil paintings on the walls, mahogany side-tables and Chinese vases, niches with precious porcelain and all manner of objets d'art. There were also huge mirrors that captured Kit's reflection from every angle. She just could not avoid staring back.

Nagging her sister to stop dawdling, Amelia directed her to the dining room, which was in the east wing overlooking the front of the house. Here, the door lintel and jambs were elaborately carved with mythical characters, and the doors themselves great slabs of panelled oak. The ceiling was like the icing on a wedding cake. Dizzy with delight, Kit wandered after her sister.

Upon entry Amelia gasped at the sight of a man's face at the vast window. 'Aw, haven't they finished yet? They were supposed to have that glass put in before the master got back – been at it for months. Tut! We'll have them ogling us while we're laying the table.' Asked what they were doing, Amelia explained, 'The master wants every plate-glass window in the building to be replaced by leaded lights.'

Kit offered a frowning opinion. 'What's he want that rubbish for? They look really old-fashioned.'

'I think that's the idea – I know it's barmy! The house was only built about twenty years ago. All those tiny panes'll be a demon to clean. Anyway, stop making cow's eyes at that fella and grab the end of this cloth!'

Amelia bustled around from one side of the twenty-foot table to the other, giving orders which Kit followed reverently, smoothing the pristine linen, following her sister's example, laying numerous pieces of silver cutlery and a cruet at each place, juggling with crystal goblets. Last to be put in place was a huge vase of flowers – lilac, roses, chrysanthemums and arching stems of foliage, fresh from the garden, their scent invading the entire room.

Amelia bobbed behind a Hepplewhite chair, giving critical direction whilst Kit set the vase down. 'A bit to your right.'

Careful not to spill any water, Kit shifted the heavy vase an inch or two but was told to go over to her right. 'If I move it any further it won't be in the middle.'

'Doesn't matter about that.' Amelia still squatted behind the chair. 'It's got to be set just right so that the mistress doesn't have to look at Master Tish. Mr Dolphin insists that the lad dines with them like a normal person – except if they have guests, of course – but his wife can't bear to watch him eating.'

Kit took offence and contrarily placed the vase off-side. 'He's her child! How can she treat him like that? Doesn't want to look at him indeed!'

'You haven't seen him.' Pursing her lips, Amelia came around the table and deliberately moved the vase to the required position, going all the way back round the table to check the effect. 'I'm surprised she doesn't keep him in the attic. Lots would.'

'That's wicked. He's their heir, isn't he? How's he going to be able to take charge of all this when his father dies if they don't teach him?'

Amelia gave a tight laugh. 'How can he be the heir? He doesn't even know how to tie his shoelaces – mindst neither does the mistress, by all accounts. It's not hard to see who he inherited his slow wits from.' Satisfied with the vase, she checked that everything else was in place. 'I feel sorry for her really, she's not very happy with the master – married for money, both of them. It's taken years for them to get a suitable heir. If Miss Agnes'd been a boy they would've been all right, but what with being forced to keep having children with someone you don't love until you fulfil your duty, well, it's left its mark.'

'I could never marry if not for love,' announced Kit wistfully.

Amelia snorted. 'Well, it's nowt to do with us, so don't you go causing trouble.'

At the sound of carriage wheels both girls glanced out of the window. The man on the ladder grinned. Amelia tutted and craned her neck to show she was not interested in his attention, showing disapproval when Kit returned the friendly gesture.

'Is this them?' The taller sister watched the carriage approach.

'No, it's the servants come on ahead – which means the master won't be far behind and that cheeky devil on the ladder'll get his comeuppance.' Amelia turned and flounced towards the door. 'Come on, we'll have to put water in their rooms!'

Kit was about to follow when her eye caught the table decoration again and, overcome by the injustice of its purpose, she grasped the vase, moving it almost a foot to the right, before racing gleefully after her sister who was totally oblivious to the misdemeanour.

On their way to the upper floor they encountered a young fellow whom Kit had little difficulty in identifying as Master Eustace. No amount of fine tailoring nor grooming could equip this unfortunate chap for the role of master. The vacant expression on his pimpled face displayed to all that for the rest of his life he would need instruction on everything that normal folk took for granted.

Seeing the new maid with Amelia, he faltered, smoothed his hair – though it was already flattened heavily by grease – then continued to walk towards them, though in a reserved and apprehensive manner, chin tucked into his chest. Kit issued a cheery hello as he passed, incurring censure from Amelia who told her she must only speak when spoken to.

'Poor thing.' Kit looked over her shoulder and was surprised to see that the young man had turned and was now walking in the same direction as she, though still with his eyes fixed shyly to the carpet.

Amelia snatched a backwards glance too. 'Aw no, you've done it now! He's taken a shine to you. We'll have him following us round all day.'

'Don't they take him to London with them?'

'Would you put a gargoyle on a Christmas tree?' demanded Amelia. 'Now, this is one of the bathrooms, there's another on the next landing, and here's the master's room.' She went in and took a jug from the dresser. 'This is usually the housemaid's job but we help out if they're busy.' She carried it to the bathroom to fill with hot water whilst Kit merely goggled at her luxurious surroundings – the willow-patterned toilet bowl and sink, the mahogany seat, the brass fittings – casting the occasional nervous glance at Master Tish, who hovered in the doorway.

As had been predicted, he followed the young women everywhere, watching furtively, waiting for them to finish in one room and then rushing on ahead so as to beat them to the next, all the while saying absolutely nothing. Amelia ignored him, though Kit began to find his presence unsettling.

When each sumptuous bedroom had been supplied with water, Amelia gave more instruction, evidently enjoying her role now. 'While the family's at luncheon you sneak back up here and empty the jugs, then later this afternoon you can put a hip bath in each of the rooms.'

Having been greatly impressed by the plumbing, Kit frowned. 'But if they've got two bathrooms why don't they use them?'

''Cause they're too bloomin' nithering – at least they are in winter. Come to that, nobody seems keen to use them now it's summer either. I think they're just for show. Don't ask me, I'm only the lackey.' Abruptly, she changed the subject. 'I like the way you've done your hair.'

Kit smiled at this rare compliment. 'I had more time this morning. Normally I just scrag it up. There's some wonderful styles I've seen in books but you need to be an octopus to do them – or hire a lady's maid, and there's not much chance of that for thee or me.'

'Would you help me do mine like that for my wedding?' asked Amelia, and donated a broad smile when Kit said that of course she would – although, looking at her sister's frizz, she was privately not sure how to achieve a similar result with such poor foundations.

'I can think of a lovely way to do it, with flowers in it and everything!'

Alarmed that Kit might go overboard, Amelia said hurriedly, 'Well, nowt too fancy –'

'Master's here!' A breathless Ivy appeared at the top of the staircase. 'Mrs Grunter wants everyone in the hall!' Without waiting for an answer she ran down again.

Thus summoned, Amelia snatched a quick inspection of her sister, pulling the other's clothes into place as if she were organizing a child, then the two of them went towards the back staircase. Tish had overtaken them. His face brimming with anticipation, he was careering down the main route to the hall.

Once assembled at the centre of the house with the rest of the servants, mostly unfamiliar to her, who stood on either side of the wide staircase and Mrs Grunter taking senior position on the landing, Kit waited nervously, head and shoulders above anyone to right or left. The master and mistress were as yet outside, lending time for further appraisal. The hall was more like a cathedral, with thick timber rafters arching overhead, pilasters and corbels, an iron chandelier suspended by a chain that must be thirty or forty feet long, an enormous stone fireplace carved with Latin inscriptions, above which was a tapestry depicting knights in armour and above that a great arched window with elaborate segments of stained glass the colours of which were reflected on the wall, plus oriels and nooks and a plethora of ancient weaponry.

There was a ripple of apprehension through the ranks as Geoffrey Dolphin and other members of his family appeared in the vestibule and finally entered the great hall, preceded by Tish, who had run out to meet them and was now behaving like an excited infant, the young man's boisterous antics obviously an embarrassment to his mother.

Apart from a few nods and smiles there was no other greeting from their employers who, along with their daughter and two of their sons, went directly up the staircase to be received by Mrs Grunter, who waited to accompany them to their rooms. After a brief glimpse of a smartly dressed but rather unattractive man with dark hair and whiskers above a starched collar, and a very plain and ill-at-ease mistress, Kit's lasting impression was the rustle of Mrs Dolphin's silken bustle as it ascended the staircase, before she and the other servants were sent about their business.

Luncheon followed, though Kit was uninvolved in the serving of it. She became, however, privy to the servant hierarchy when the lower orders were about to take their own lunch at one o'clock, a meal consisting of a roast and vegetables to be followed by apple pie. Mr Todd, the steward, she discovered, was even more of an authoritarian than Mrs Grunter, and she was glad to hear that she would not have to share a table with these tartars, for they and Cook ate their meals in the steward's room along with the head gardener, the two lady's maids and the coachman. As yet, Cook had not joined them but was still in the kitchen where Kit stood feeling ill at ease whilst people swarmed around her with pans and plates. Her discomfort came from the fact that there were more males around now and all seemed taken with her appearance – grooms of the chamber, an under butler, footmen – all remarking on the new girl's stature. Luckily the instruction was given for them to move to the servants' hall at that point, so deflecting their attention.

Before they had exited, however, a tall good-looking footman rushed in, tugged off his boots and, to female screams, ripped off his pantaloons and was about to drape them in front of the fire when the obese Mrs Hellawell bellowed at him.

'What do you think you're playing at, Algernon Boggs?' Whilst others tut-tutted she seized the offending garment and flung it back at him. 'I'm not having them dangling in my way.'

'Aw, take pity, Mrs H!' the good looking man beseeched her. 'There's no fire in our room.' Being the height of summer the only grate alight was in the kitchen. 'I've spilled wine all over 'em and I need them dry for this afternoon.' He tugged distastefully at the red stain on his underpants.

'And do you think these respectable girls want to eat their dinner alongside a man with no breeches?' Mrs Hellawell kicked his boots out of her way. 'Haven't you got another pair?'

'Aye, but I've ripped the arse out –'

'Language!'

'– and nobody'll mend them for me! These are the only ones I've got.'

'I don't care, you are not hanging them in my kitchen!'

Still half-clothed, Algernon strode briskly to his room; this being nearby he reappeared mere seconds later with his other pair of trousers. 'There! I've hung 'em in me room but they won't be dry for ages. How do you expect me to do my job in these?' He stuck his finger through a ripped seam, and waggled it beseechingly at the other women in the room. 'Aw, won't one of you lasses help me?'

'Don't think you're taking any of my girls away from their work!' chastised Mrs Hellawell, whilst others tittered over his rather obscene gesture. 'And pick up those boots!'

Clamping the boots under his arm, Algernon continued to beseech every female in turn; all refused. Then his eyes fell on the new girl. 'You look as if you've got more about you than this cruel lot. I'm going to get into awful ructions if somebody doesn't help me.'

'Tell him to sew them himself,' advised Amelia.

'I can't sew! What d'you take me for?'

Kit ignored his half-dressed state, concentrating on his smart upper half with its dark blue tail coat, starched collar and white bow tie, the brown hair immaculately groomed and parted in the middle around a face that could almost have been termed patrician, had it not been adopting such a contorted look. Appraising the worried expression, she took pity and, in bluff manner, grabbed the pantaloons.

'Let's have a look at 'em. Oh, that's nowt of a job – I'll do it after we've eaten.'

Mrs Hellawell was scathing as she went off to eat her luncheon. 'And here's me thinking you've got an ounce of intelligence. If you're daft enough to let Algy get round you on this score, there'll be no stopping him when it comes to you know what.'

'Ooh, the things she says!' Upon assistance, Algernon had immediately turned genial and, still in his wine-stained underwear and stockinged feet, joined the exodus to the servants' hall, putting his arm around Kit's waist as they went. 'You're a good looker, if I might make so bold. What's your name again?'

The recipient of his praise turned coquettish and provided her name, enjoying the contact and not the least disconcerted by his state of undress for her brothers often walked around thus.

'Have you met my little twinny?' He drew her attention to a man of similar proportions with whom he linked his other arm, adopting a coy and mincing walk. 'Allow me to introduce you. Kit, this is Charles, my twin – almost as handsome as me, is he not?'

Kit studied the pair, both striking in looks. 'You're very alike.'

Amelia tutted. 'He's having you on, dopey, they're not twins. They were only chosen because they match each other – both got big heads.'

'Ooh! Listen to her, twinny,' scolded Algy, still affecting his effeminate manner in a parody of his accuser. 'Leastwise we were chosen for our beauty.'

In the servants' hall, his masculinity restored, he insisted that Kit sit between him and Charles, and was most attentive, telling the youth who served them to give her the best portions, thereby helping to make Kit more unpopular than she already was with the other females over the way she had jumped the queue for the position of parlourmaid.

Lily in particular harboured resentment, muttering gruffly, 'Isn't it enough that you've taken my job without hogging all the food as well?'

Kit, desperately wanting to be accepted into this new family, prevented the youth from overloading her plate and said earnestly, 'I did mention to Mrs Grunter that you were first in line, Lily, but she said you were such a tremendous help in the kitchen that she knew Cook wouldn't want to spare you. I can't cook for love nor money. This is a wonderful roast! I really admire Mrs Hellawell.'

'I cooked it,' said the pug-jawed Lily, bridling. 'Mrs Hellawell was too busy doing the master's luncheon.'

'Truly?' Kit looked amazed, though she had known all along. 'Well, I don't know why you wanted to be a parlourmaid with skills like this. I think you're marvellous.'

'Well, I don't know about that.' But the look on Lily's face showed that the rift was on the way to being healed.

Kit shared a conspiratorial glance with her sister. Then, whilst lifting another forkful to her mouth, she noticed someone watching her from across the room, an elderly woman she had not encountered before who ate her luncheon from a tray on her knee. She voiced a greeting.

The woman, clad from head to toe in black, merely issued a smiling nod and continued with her meal.

Amelia turned her head to inspect the old retainer. 'You won't get much out of Mrs Garbutt. Poor old soul – she's almost ninety, you know.'

'No, she isn't, she's ninety already,' interrupted Lily.

Ivy supported her friend. 'No, she's not ninety till next month.'

The three took to squabbling as if the subject of their argument were not even present.

Kit adopted the same attitude, speaking not to Mrs Garbutt but to the self-appointed spokeswomen. 'What does she do?'

'Nowt,' answered Ivy. 'They just keep her on to save her from the workhouse. Mr Dolphin inherited her from his parents – she were ancient then. Never shifts from that chair, apart from to do the obvious. Just sits and watches the world go by. Listens to all our grumbles and groans.'

Kit chewed thoughtfully. 'It must be awful to be so old, mustn't it?'

Pondering on the battered face and its network of lines, the chin studded with polyps, the neck hanging loose like a turkey's, the young women agreed, all oblivious to the great beauty and experience that shone from Beth Garbutt's eyes.

'I sometimes feel a hundred, working under Mrs Hellawell,' sighed Lily.

Kit sympathized. 'At least we don't have to eat with her.'

'Not our main course, no,' said Amelia. 'but we always take our dessert together in Mrs Grunter's room.' She laughed at Kit's groan.

'So better look sharp with your needle and thread,' inserted Algy, indicating his undressed state. 'I don't want Mrs Grunter ogling me bag of goodies.'

*   *   *

After rushing the last of her meal, Kit found needle and thread and swiftly inserted a number of stitches into Algy's ripped pantaloons in time for the upper-house servants to move to the housekeeper's room for their pudding. Having been coached by Sarah, who was herself an expert seamstress, it took under a minute for the repair to be made.

'By, that didn't take you long!' Algy looked delighted as he slipped into his pantaloons.

'It's easy when you know how,' smiled Kit.

'Oh, an expert on men's breeches, are you?' The man bent to ram his feet into his boots, grinning up at her. 'Well, I'll take mine off for you any time.'

Taken aback by this indecency, Kit blushed, but was secretly pleased at the attentiveness of such a handsome man as she and everyone else, barring old Beth Garbutt, moved to the housekeeper's parlour. Here, under Mrs Grunter's fish-like eye, the atmosphere was more constrained and there was no opportunity for further liaison between Kit and her admirer – though she hoped there would be later.

What came later, however, was a reprimand. The plates had been cleared and the upper servants were preparing to go about their business when a query was relayed to the servants' zone: who was responsible for the laying of the table at luncheon? In particular, who had taken charge of the flower vase? Whoever it was, the mistress wanted to see them – immediately.

At the ominous note, Amelia and Kit exchanged glances, the latter wearing a guilty expression that told her sister exactly what she had done. 'You moved that vase!' the elder hissed. 'After I told you how important it was!'

Kit prepared to own up. 'I'll go and apolo –'

'No!' Amelia's tone was censorious. 'You'll only get the sack and our Monty'll have to put up with you again! I'll go tell the mistress it was my mistake. It doesn't matter if she sacks me, I'm leaving soon anyway.'

'You mean she'd dismiss you for such a paltry thing?' Kit looked shocked.

'It isn't paltry in her eyes! That what I was trying to tell you, if only you'd listen.' Highly annoyed, Amelia turned on her heel. 'Anyway, just stay where you are and try to do as you're told in future. Get those baths ready to take upstairs.'

Kit went to find the hip baths, opening and closing cupboard doors. It was as she was investigating another that she was pushed inside, the door was slammed, but she was not alone.

'Ooh, Kit, I think you're lovely!' murmured Algy, his breath warm on her neck, his hands kneading her buttocks, lifting her skirts. 'So cuddlesome and generous. I've never met anybody like you before, you're so different to the other girls. Will you let me kiss you? Go on, let me, just a little kiss.'

Overcome by shock and prone to his flattery, Kit scarcely had time to say no before his lips closed on hers. Robbed of breath, she was forced to inhale rapidly through her nose, taking in a combination of smells – tobacco, hair grease, polish and a tang of masculinity – whilst her hands scrabbled to prevent his from wandering all over her ample dimensions.

Aroused, he spoke into her mouth, the words muffled by passion whilst his victim half-heartedly struggled to free herself. 'Oh, you're so sweet, my darling, so desirable . . .'

Panic increased her heartbeat, caused both by wrongdoing and passion – he was a very appealing man. But the housekeeper's warning was fresh in her mind. She could not lose this job so soon. 'Algy, Mrs Grunter might find us!'

Encouraged by her lack of struggle, Algy grew bolder. 'That dried-up old stick'll never know what this feels like!'

Kit squeaked in horror and tried to withdraw her hand that Algy had pinioned against his groin. Inexperienced in the ways of men, she was thrown into confusion. 'Oh, don't! What are you doing?'

He gave a triumphant little laugh. 'Feel it – that's for you!' Then his mouth closed on hers again.

The warm dry lips now oozed saliva. Repelled, Kit writhed to be free. Algy let go of her hand then, but only in order to pull up her skirts, and continued to press his ardour, breathing lascivious encouragement, layering her with wet kisses, inching her petticoats higher and higher, telling her how gorgeous she was.

Kit fought and struggled in earnest then, trying to squirm her face away from his slobbering mouth, not fully understanding what he wanted but knowing it was dangerous and wrong. 'Algy, please don't, it's not right!'

'Come on, Kitty! You wouldn't have led me on so if you didn't want it.' Algy coaxed her with more frantic kisses – and before she could do anything about it one of his hands was investigating her drawers.

Kit almost fainted – what on earth would happen next if she did not stop him? She intensified her valiant struggle against the unknown, but her protestations fell on deaf ears, and she turned instead to the Lord, praying for him to save her.

Then, somebody banged violently on the cupboard – both occupants yelled – and Algy dropped her like a hot ember. In the ensuing panic Kit was able to free herself, unlatch the door and flee.

Whilst Algy threw a punch at the laughing culprit, Charles, who had disturbed him, a frightened Kit made good her escape, running for all she was worth along the corridor as far from Algy as possible.

Her heart had barely stopped thumping ten minutes later when a rather vexed Amelia found her upstairs on the servants' landing. 'There you are! I got a real lecture because of you!'

Alert to the reprimand, a nervous Kit pulled herself into order, whilst Amelia ploughed on.

'She wants to see you later – oh, don't worry, I didn't say you were to blame! She just wants to talk to you because you're new.' Her expression remained stern. 'And can I ask why you're up here? I told you to get the baths ready – and what on earth have you been doing? You're all flushed.'

Kit's blush intensified and, to hide it, she told a half-truth. 'I've just run all the way up the stairs – I can't find the baths anywhere!' However desperately she wanted to unburden herself of the terrifying incident it was not the sort of thing she could discuss with Amelia – especially as her sister had warned her about Algy. Oh, if only Beata were here to confide in!

'Well, you won't find them up here!' Amelia led the brisk march downstairs, annoyed at Kit's lie – she had obviously been slacking.

'Sorry! I did look high and low, honestly.' Following her sister, Kit retained a wary eye for her would-be seducer, for she was sure he had not done with her yet.

'Obviously not far enough,' complained Amelia, going straight to the place where the baths were kept.

Kit was too watchful of Algy to pay heed to Amelia's complaint, and felt her face burn as the footman offered her a crafty wink in passing, seemingly oblivious to how much he had frightened her. Dreading a confrontation, particularly in front of Amelia, she was vastly relieved when he offered no further interference for now – though the promise was there in his eyes, and she resolved to steer clear of him as much as she was able.

Carrying a bath between them, the two sisters hurried up the back stairs until there was no other way of avoiding the main house. They were struggling along a corridor when Amelia groaned and whispered, 'Oh no, it's the master! He doesn't like to meet servants on this side of the door.' Downing the bath, she flattened herself against a wall, indicating for her sister to do likewise, but it was impossible for one so well-endowed as Kit not be noticed and the master, in passing, dealt her an irritated glance, his eyes briefly resting on the shelf of her bosom that rose and fell from its exertions. Whilst Amelia lowered her gaze Kit stared directly at him until given a nudge by her sister.

'Haven't you caused enough upset for one day?' Amelia muttered at her when it was safe to do so. 'The mistress is one thing, he's another. If he thinks you're getting too big for your boots you'll be down that road.'

After having travelled up and down stairs several times in the emptying of baths, Kit harboured the private thought that perhaps it might be a blessing if she were dismissed, for to walk from one room to another in this house could seem like miles. But there was much more to concern her than this. Oh, she had been flattered by the attention of such a well-positioned man, and would gladly have allowed Algy to court her in a fitting manner, but she had not bargained for such overwhelming advances.

Having avoided her would-be seducer all afternoon, Kit was dismayed to find that she was expected to assist Algy in the serving of afternoon tea in the drawing room. Fortunately, encumbered by a fully laden tray he was ill-equipped to pounce on her – though the look in his eye told that he would love to do so, and as they made their way through the green baize doors he whispered a seductive apology for their being disturbed earlier but he would make up for it later tonight. Kit almost dropped the silver cake-stand in fright.

A clock chimed four as they entered the lavish drawing room. Neither the master, the mistress nor their son Wyndham paid them any heed, though the elder daughter of the house gave a faint smile when Kit happened to catch her eye. The younger children were upstairs taking tea with their nanny, but Master Tish was here, showing an avid interest in Kit's movements as, by her mistress's chair, she rested a stand arrayed with thin slices of bread and butter and small cakes, and on another stand a dainty kettle.

Whilst Algy was setting down his own tray that contained a silver teapot, milk jug and sugar basin, and porcelain cups, his counterpart, Charles, entered with news that a friend of the family had come to call.

'Show our guest in,' ordered the mistress. 'Tish, my darling, run along to your room, there's a dear.'

Familiar with such commands, Tish asked if he could take a cake with him, and on being granted permission, left by a side door.

When, hat in hand, the male guest entered, Kit tried to show that she was up to the job by approaching him with a polite query. 'Can I take your hat, sir?'

Handing it over on his way to greet his host and hostess he did not seem at all perturbed by this, though when Kit happened to catch the mistress's eye she saw annoyance in them and there was an edge to the voice that told her, 'That will be all!'

When, downstairs, Amelia enquired how her sister had coped, Kit frowned. 'I think I might have upset her, but I can't imagine how.'

She was not to be enlightened immediately, either. With countless jobs to be performed right up until the end of her working day, Kit had almost forgotten the mistress's displeasure until bedtime cocoa had been imbibed and she was sent to collect the empty cups from upstairs.

Only the mistress was present in the drawing room now, her attitude rather cool. Kit had placed the cups on the tray and was about to leave, when she was ordered to remain.

'Your name is Kit, I believe?'

'Yes, ma'am!' Kit laced her hands over her apron, adopting a subservient pose.

'I understand from Mrs Grunter that you have been chosen as a replacement for your sister when she marries. I have always thought very highly of Amelia's work.' Mrs Dolphin had obviously forgotten today's incident with the vase. 'That being so, you must pay the utmost attention to her instruction and to the rules of etiquette which I am now about to bestow upon you.'

Kit's clear blue eyes held the other's face. Her mistress's eyes slanted downwards, she had a long nose and a jaw that appeared wider than her brow, with brown hair parted in the middle and scraped back into a chignon which had the effect of dragging her face down even further and making her a picture of misery, though her voice was quite youthful.

'Clearly you have not worked in such a household as this before and that is why I am going to make allowances for your earlier faux pas.'

Though not conversant with the latter phrase, Kit knew by the tone that she had erred. 'I'm sorry if I did anything wrong, ma'am!'

'Kit, you must learn to attend your betters and then you will have no need to apologize.' Zenobia Dolphin showed no sign of haughtiness, was obviously genuine in her desire for Kit to do well, but it was most apparent that she felt she knew best. 'You must now heed what I say very carefully. Your approach to our guest earlier breached several rules. First you said, "Can I take your hat, sir?" It is not *can* I but *may* I. Secondly, it was a grave error that you approached him at all. You must never do so again. A gentleman always carries his hat until he has shaken hands with his hostess. He will then lay it down himself, at which point you may take it.'

'I beg your pardon, ma'am.' Kit was contrite.

'You are forgiven.' Zenobia Dolphin bestowed a kind smile.

'Thank you, ma'am.' About to go, Kit was recalled.

'Oh, by the way! I feel there is another matter I should mention. It may not fall to you to lay the table very often but should it do so I must warn you that I insist on strict adherence to my standards. I was forced to take issue with your sister about it today.'

Kit gave an inward sigh. Obviously the incident had not been forgotten after all. 'If it's about the vase, ma'am, Amelia told me you like it put in a special position.'

'Then I am surprised she was so remiss with its placement.'

Kit knew she should have owned up, but felt she had been chastised enough for one day. However she made token apology, adding, 'She did have a lot to think of, ma'am, what with having to teach me her duties.'

The tolerant smile was displaced by affront. 'That is totally irrelevant, Kit! Neither you nor your sister must presume to disregard your mistress's orders.'

For a second Kit was flabbergasted by the mispronunciation, then blurted, 'Oh, I'd never do that ma'm! I just meant –'

'Kit!' Mrs Dolphin interrupted in stern but serene manner. 'You must learn not to answer back.' At the other's apology, she inclined her head. 'You may go.'

Back in the company of her peers, Kit remained stunned. 'I can't believe it! I can't believe she said *irrevelant*. And her having just given me a lecture on how to speak! If she were a real lady she'd know how to say it – why, even I know that.'

Whilst others went about their business, making preparations for the morning, Amelia covered her face and groaned through her fingers. 'Oh, you didn't correct her?'

'What do you take me for? No, but I felt like it. Making me stand there, improving my speech when her own credentials aren't what she'd have others believe.' Oblivious to the stony expressions of the other servants, Kit continued to pour aspersions on her employer.

'Well, if you don't like it here you know what you can do!' snapped Ivy before going up to bed, others voicing similar sentiments.

Turning astonished eyes to watch the procession of candle flames that filtered from the room, Kit was immediately chastened. Looking to her sister for clarification, she saw that Amelia obviously shared the others' indignation.

'Those cocoa cups need washing – if it isn't beneath you,' said Amelia, making her own way to the stairs.

Ignoring Beth Garbutt, the only other person left in the room, Kit gave a perplexed sigh, then beheld the sinkful of pots with dismay, muttering, mainly to herself, 'How was I to know they were all so fond of Mrs Dolphin?'

The frail old woman pushed herself slowly from her chair and shuffled towards Kit, her face portraying great kindness. 'It's not so much that, lass. Can you not see? It's you going on about her being stupid – what does that make them as works for her?'

Astonished primarily that the crone could even speak, Kit had no reply.

'Yes, I can string two words together, should anybody bother to consult me,' came the sardonic response.

'Oh, I meant no disrespect!' stammered Kit who, even though she dwarfed the other, was awed by Mrs Garbutt's aura of experience. 'I just thought –'

'Just because others behave as if I wasn't here doesn't actually make me invisible.' At Kit's chastened attitude she relented. 'It's partly my own fault, I suppose. I gave up wasting my breath years ago on people who don't listen – but they'd learn a great deal if they did, you know!'

'I'm sure they would.' Kit was sincere. 'I beg your pardon, if I were rude.'

This was granted with dignity, the mottled, withered hand squeezing hers.

Kit's large breast heaved. 'I seem to have done nowt but upset folk since I got here. First Lily –'

'Oh, don't bother your head about her!' The look of kindness on the ancient face was replaced by one of dismissal. 'She's nobbut a kitchen drudge and thick as pig muck. Besides, as parlourmaid you won't be mixing much with the lower orders.'

Kit was surprised at the sudden lack of magnanimity. 'What position did you hold, Mrs Garbutt?'

The ancient retainer grasped this rare opportunity of an audience to state proudly, 'I was housekeeper to Mr Dolphin's father most of my life. But that's not to say that washing pots is beneath me – away, I'll give you a hand with these cups.'

'Nay, I'll do it!'

At the third voice, both women turned. Feeling sorry for her crestfallen sibling, Amelia had come back. Wearing a look of barely restrained impatience, she put down her candle. 'Off you go to bed, Mrs Garbutt. I'd better not leave this one to her own devices. That Algy might be lurking in the stairwell.'

Kit flinched.

Relapsing into her usual docile mode, old Beth delivered a final pat to Kit and hobbled to her room. But passing Amelia, she sought to donate the benefit of her experience. 'She'll learn.'

'She'd better,' announced Amelia, at which Kit offered an apology which was accepted.

Grateful for the support, Kit waded into the dirty crockery. 'Aw, thanks for coming back! I reckon you might be right about that Algy.' She hesitated, but was unable to voice her true reason for coming to this conclusion, and added simply, 'He's been looking at me in a funny way. I'm going to lock me door tonight.'

'You'll have a job.' Amelia dried each cup as her sister put it down. 'Didn't you notice? There's no locks.'

'I'll make a barricade with me box then.'

Remembering the difficulty she had had in lifting Kit's belongings, Amelia looked approving. 'The weight of that'd keep an army out.'

Kit giggled nervously. 'Algy – I thought that were summat that grows in ponds.'

Amelia had never been quick to spot a joke, and merely shrugged.

When the washing up was done, the girls left the deserted kitchen and, candles aloft, made for the stairs, encountering only the steward, who was always last to bed. Upon being escorted to her room by Amelia, who told her they would rise at seven, Kit did as promised and hauled her box against the door. Then, not completely satisfied that she was safe, she undressed nervously, pulled on her nightgown, said a quick prayer and hopped into bed. Hauling the covers under her chin, she lay there in the candlelight, pondering Algy's vow to 'make it up to her later' – when a faint noise caused her face to turn quickly toward the door.

The candle flame danced as she sat bolt upright. Her skin crawled. Knees up to her chin under the sheets, teeth nibbling the linen, a wide-eyed Kit watched the handle turn, saw the door come open an inch, heard it make abrupt contact with the barricade.

An urgent whisper through the gap. 'Kitty!'

Heart thudding, she waited, knowing who it was, not daring to breathe for fear that he would take it as a sign to force an entry, her distended pupils glued to the door for long, nerve-racking seconds.

But nothing happened. After that agonizing pause, the latch clicked back into place and all was silent.

Allowing her trapped breath to escape, Kit fell sideways in relief. Then, after a few more apprehensive moments, she leaned over, blew out the candle, and lay there pondering her day and all its excitement, rehearsing what she was going to say to Algy tomorrow morning to cool his ardour, wondering would she ever get used to life in such a vast household, and would she manage to keep this job long enough to make any friends.

7

The next morning, Kit awoke much earlier than the allotted hour, disturbed by the lower orders who were forced to start work at six. Keen to impress, she was already up and assisting a harassed-looking scullerymaid to mop up a pool of milk from the stone-paved floor of the kitchen when her sister came looking for her.

A bleary-eyed Amelia stood on the perimeter of the white puddle, observing her actions. 'Does Mrs Grunter know you're doing that?' There were strict demarcation lines amongst the servants.

'No, I haven't seen her, but she wouldn't expect me to let poor Myrtle struggle on her own, would she?'

'I wouldn't bank on it,' said Amelia.

'Well, the poor lass was just taking Cook her cup of tea and this happened.'

'And if Mrs Hellawell doesn't get her morning tea on time she's a devil to work for,' lisped Myrtle, mopping and wringing for all she was worth.

Amelia was unsympathetic. 'Well, you'll just have to leave her to it now, Kit, because we've the table to set in the breakfast room.'

Rising from her knees, Kit apologized to her partner for having to desert her, at which, Myrtle, an uncomplicated, rosy-cheeked girl, bestowed a grateful smile.

'You're making a rod for your own back helping her,' warned Amelia as they made their way through the dim corridor.

'I just felt sorry for her. She seems a bit dim.'

'A bit? I should say so. She hasn't been here a fortnight and I doubt she'll be here much longer. Give her anything more important to do than scrubbing floors and she'll always muck it up. You'll be forever covering for her if you're daft enough. There's enough work of your own to do without that.'

This was true. In the hour before breakfast Kit and Amelia had to perform several chores besides laying the breakfast-room table. Then just before eight, whilst the housemaids transported water for bathing, the sisters carried trays of tea for their employer and his family.

'You take Master Wyndham, Tish and the master,' ordered Amelia. 'I'll deliver these to the lady's maids.'

Thanking her sister for this dubious honour, Kit delivered the morning tea to the master first. Recalling yesterday's instruction that on no account must she speak unless spoken to, she felt that such intrusion warranted at least a polite cough. But there was no reaction. In fact Mr Dolphin did not even pay her the courtesy of opening his eyes, his blubbery visage, puffed and bloated from sleep, looking more unattractive than ever. Far from being insulted over the lack of acknowledgement, Kit was grateful to experience no further discomfort – unlike that which she received from Master Tish who, in the ten seconds that she was in his room, managed to instil her with extreme disquiet by sitting bolt upright and never taking his eyes off her, so much so that in her desire to escape she slopped tea over the sides of the last cup on the tray.

Distancing herself from Tish's room before dribbling the tea from saucer back to cup, Kit relaxed a little now that the worst was over and proceeded to Wyndham's room. The youth, with similar countenance to his father, stretched and yawned as the maid approached him with a polite greeting. Kit put the tea tray on the bedside table and handed the somewhat depleted cup to the recumbent youth. Still drowsy, his eyes barely open, Wyndham reached out but in his gropings found, instead of china, a voluptuous breast. Kit jumped back, spilling tea into the saucer yet again, for which she quickly apologized and tipped it back into the cup. Seeming not to have noticed the accidental contact, young Wyndham barely reacted and taking a nonchalant sip of the beverage, gazed blearily at the wall as an embarrassed Kit hurried from the room.

Amelia seemed oblivious to her sister's rather excited mood as they met upon the landing, and Kit found the incident too delicate to mention. Chores completed for now, the parlourmaids returned to the servants' hall where a meal of bread and butter and slices of cold meat from yesterday's roast awaited them.

Still flustered from her encounter, Kit breezed up to the table and sat between Algy and Charles as she had done yesterday, issuing an excitable, 'Good morning!'

Completely ignoring her, Algy reached across the table for a cruet.

Blushing furiously at this obvious snub, plus the knowing looks that passed between other members of staff, Kit lowered her eyes to the table and played with her knife. Hence, breakfast was a very uncomfortable affair and she was glad when, after forty minutes, it was over.

Amelia was all knowing. 'He tried it on last night, didn't he?' she asked as she and Kit left the hall to resume work.

Kit did not mention the previous day's close call when Algy had almost succeeded in overpowering her. 'Somebody turned my door handle but I had it barricaded. It must have been him.'

Amelia gave a sage nod, though in truth she was as ignorant as Kit over what actually took place when a man got his way. 'It would have been. I doubt he'll bother you any more now he knows you're not that type.'

Kit gave a lame, 'Oh.' However relieved she might be not to suffer a fate worse than death she had hoped that Algy's interest in her might be genuine. It was rather unflattering.

'Eh, you're not that desperate for a husband are you?' demanded her sister with a note of concern.

'Don't be so rude!' Kit was offended. 'I just meant, is that all he wants?' Whatever 'that' was.

'Well of course! He tries it with every person in a skirt, whatever they look like.'

Kit wondered how her sister could be so thoughtless. 'Has he pestered you much?'

'He wouldn't dare! At any rate, he's hardly going to waste his time when he can get what he wants more easily elsewhere. Didn't you notice Rosalind's expression when he were paying such attention to you yesterday?'

Kit could not put a face to the name, but upon being given a description of a ruddy-faced blonde girl with 'enough dirt under her nails to grow taties', she responded, 'Yes, I noticed she had a miserable gob on her, but I thought it was because of me getting the parlourmaid's position.'

'Well, that too – but she regards Algy as her property. Stupid girl, he'll never marry her, she's been with almost every man in the house, so I'm told.'

Kit was scandalized and, encouraged by Amelia's seeming authority on the matter, was compelled to ask what exactly Rosalind's behaviour involved.

Amelia bluffed her way out of this quickly, saying she wouldn't dream of repeating such filth, then returned to the subject of Algy. 'He'll never marry anybody, that one, just takes what's on offer – and it's always on offer from Rosalind. So don't worry, you're safe now he knows where he stands.'

Relief mingled with disappointment – he was after all so very good-looking – Kit hoped the latter sentiment would not show on her face as she was piloted to the great hall.

Here, Amelia instructed her to beat a gong and thus summon everyone to prayers.

After morning worship in the great hall, with Mrs Dolphin playing the piano, the family enjoyed a leisurely breakfast, during which Kit was slaving alongside housemaids in the bedrooms, carrying hip baths away, picking up clothes that had been carelessly discarded on the floor, helping to make beds which, with three mattresses to each, was a strenuous task, dusting, and all manner of other chores – though she left the more distasteful emptying of chamberpots to those of lower station. It was, she declared, bad enough emptying one's own, never mind those of strangers.

At eleven there was a brief pause for a cup of tea, and then it was back to work until luncheon, an extravagant affair with several courses, at which she was required to wait at table. Encountering icy detachment from Algy, she decided that to ignore him too would be the best strategy, which was easy enough when they were upstairs but made the atmosphere in the servants' hall unbearable – and it was all so incomprehensible. Kit was deeply hurt at his treatment, especially after having done him such a favour yesterday. Any sensible girl would have been thankful to be left alone, but Kit was too immature to know when she was well off, and she had never been one to endure injustice. So, when the time came for the upper servants to take their pudding alongside their superiors, she decided to bring matters into the open, using Mrs Grunter's presence as a shield.

'How long are you going to sulk just because I wouldn't let you into my bedroom?' Her abrupt demand stalled the clinking of spoons upon dishes.

Whilst others blurted scandalized laughter over the chocolate pudding, the housekeeper displayed indignance. 'Kit! That is not the type of conversation for the dinner table – nor, come to that, in any kind of polite society.'

Kit was respectful but firm. 'I beg your pardon, Mrs Grunter, but if I'm prevented from doing my job –'

'Who's stopping you?' Though deeply unnerved, Algy proceeded to cram pudding into his mouth.

'You are! With your hoity-toity attitude – after I were good enough to sew thy breeches yesterday!' Kit displayed hurt. 'Is this how you treat everybody who does you a favour?'

At her tone Algy's hard edge dissolved somewhat, though he still countered her accusation, for the glares of his superiors were upon him. 'I don't know what she's going on about!' His expression beseeched everyone at the table. 'I said thank you, didn't I?'

'Is it true you attempted impropriety with this young woman?' demanded the steward, Mr Todd.

'No!' Algy reacted as if the very suggestion were anathema.

This attitude upset Kit even more. 'Well, somebody tried to get into my room last night!'

'What makes you think it were me?' volleyed Algy.

His derogatory tone provoked more rash words. 'Because you didn't get what you wanted yesterday afternoon when you shoved me in the cupboard and you thought you'd try again!'

Crouched over her bowl, Amelia wanted to disappear beneath the table. Didn't Kit mind how much embarrassment she caused to others? A tight-lipped Ivy clutched her friend's arm in support.

'Mr Todd!' Spoon aloft, the housekeeper upbraided the steward. 'I would be grateful if you would keep your men under stricter control!'

The steward was furious at being told how to do his job. 'You can be assured, Mrs Grunter, Algernon will be suitably reprimanded.'

'I haven't done owt!' objected Algy, not just to his superiors but to Rosalind, whose grey eyes were like flints. 'It's wishful thinking on Kit's behalf. Why, she were acting like a –'

'Silence!' ordered the steward. 'I'll deal with you later.'

Frustrated, Algy plunged his spoon into his dessert and crammed his mouth to bursting point, though the glare of pure hatred directed at his accuser was sufficient to communicate his feelings.

Others were looking at Kit none too kindly too, her sister amongst them. By trying to acquaint Algy with the injustice of his actions she had only succeeded in making herself unpopular. In between the spoonfuls of pudding came hostile murmurs. A harsh rebuke from Mrs Grunter brought them to an end, but not before Kit heard the damning epithet – 'Troublemaker!'

Following habit, Mrs Grunter and Mr Todd went visiting that Friday afternoon. Instantaneous to their departure, Kit was pounced up on by various colleagues, all eager to pour disgruntlement upon her. Algernon was not amongst them, being otherwise engaged in mending fences with Rosalind, his frantic overtures being performed in the housekeeper's parlour, the risk of being discovered adding zest to the liaison.

Siding with Kit's detractors, Amelia clutched her frizzy ginger head between her palms. 'I've never been so embarrassed! How could you demean yourself like that – especially after I made a point of warning you about him!'

Kit was stunned by the furore, and deeply hurt by her sister's disloyalty. 'It wasn't me who started all this! I was only defending my honour. I'm sure none of you would stay quiet if Algernon'd treated you like that.'

'None of us are that stupid as to lead him on,' retorted Ivy, to nods from the others.

'I can't see how being nice to folk can be classed as leading them on,' protested Kit.

'There's being nice to someone and there's flirting,' scolded Cook. 'You need to learn the difference.'

In the pregnant silence that followed, Kit tried to deflect attention from herself by asking, 'What on earth is that ghastly noise?' It sounded like an infant in distress, and had been puzzling her since she arrived.

A grim-faced Amelia was sparing with the explanation. 'It's Algy.'

Thinking the man was under some kind of assault, Kit looked askance until, through the window, a brilliant flash of colour caught her eye and she spotted a peacock balanced on top of a high wall. His preening stance made it obvious why he had been named after the footman. 'Oh, isn't he a beauty!'

Irked by the bird's cries, Cook feigned agreement. 'Yes, the only thing that would improve him is sage and onion stuffing. A handful wouldn't go amiss with his namesake neither.'

Nettled at having the conversation brought back to her seducer, Kit complained, 'I only mended his trousers, I didn't expect the dirty dog to –'

'You still telling lies about him?' It was Rosalind, pink and dishevelled from her amorous entanglement. Algy's cajolery had obviously paid off, for he entered the servants' hall not far behind her wearing a smug grin, although he too pointed an accusing finger at Kit over Rosalind's shoulder.

Rosalind's face contorted in meanness – whoever had named her 'pretty rose' had a vivid imagination. 'Imagine he'd look at summat like you!'

There was a hardness about the other that prevented Kit from further objection. Without ally, she stared dolefully at the floor. Satisfied at having put the new girl in her place, Kit's blowsy rival gave Algy a possessive kiss and went off to the privy. The footman, now at liberty to take issue with the one who had caused him so much trouble, was just about to do so when a bell jingled.

'That'll be the master wanting his tea,' said Amelia, who previously to berating Kit had been in the throes of preparing a tray.

'I'll take it!' Seizing the opportunity to escape, Kit grabbed the loaded tray and hurried off.

Upstairs, his wife gone visiting, Mr Dolphin was preparing to entertain the Board of Guardians, of whom he was a respected member. Accepting the tea, he sat back and stared so long at Kit that she grew unsettled. Did everyone in this house find the need to examine her so closely?

Wriggling uncomfortably in her slippers, she felt herself turning pink and at the risk of causing annoyance eventually blurted, 'Will there be anything else, sir?'

Mr Dolphin appeared to emerge from his trance. 'What? Ah yes. The members of the Board will be arriving in half an hour. Convey to Algernon that you are to assist him in their reception. It has passed my notice that you and he are of similar height – indeed,' he displayed incredulity, 'you are of a most unusual stature for a woman. I think my guests will be intrigued by the pairing, some may even contend that you make a handsome match.'

Trying to glean some compliment out of these rude observations, Kit said, 'Thank you very much, sir. I'll pass on your instructions to Algernon.'

Apprehensive over the reception these orders would receive when issued by her unpopular lips, she left the room. In the corridor a huge looking-glass mirrored her movements. There were so many reflective surfaces here that Kit could not possibly resist their lure and paused before this one, examining her body this way and that for some hint of beauty. Handsome match? Chance would be a fine thing. As she turned away from the mirror to proceed along the corridor she almost bumped into Tish, who had been lurking quietly nearby watching her. Stifling a yelp, and embarrassed at being caught out thus, she attempted to hurry on her way towards the back staircase. But Tish decided to follow her, indeed, he stuck intimately close even when Kit increased her pace. Unnerved by his breath on her cheek, Kit stopped abruptly in her tracks, balanced the tray on her arm, delved into her apron pocket for one of the sugar lumps she had filched from the bowl to take home as a treat for her little nieces, and with a tentative smile handed it over to the nuisance.

Tish regarded the offering blankly for a moment, then turned his dull gaze to Kit's face. 'I'm not a horse.'

Feeling utterly foolish, Kit blushed and dropped the segment of sugar back into her apron pocket. 'I just thought you might like – well, if you'll excuse me, Master Eustace.' She put one foot forward.

'What's your name?' came the abrupt demand.

'Kit.' She remained wary. He had begun to walk alongside her again and was uncomfortably close. Simpleton or no, he was a man and she was now all too aware what they were capable of.

'I'm Tish.' His formerly expressionless face broke into a wide grin, then just as quickly returned to its impassive state.

Kit managed to return the smile. 'Pleased to make your acquaintance – but I'd better be about my business.'

Not easily put off, Tish hurried alongside her to the staircase. 'I like you.'

'That's very kind of you, Master Tish.' Thinking she would never be rid of him Kit paused at the top of the staircase and looked firm. 'I go this way now.'

Her hint unrecognized, Kit gave an inward sigh and proceeded down the back staircase, her admirer in tow.

Their entrance to the servants' domain caused more unrest. 'What've you brought him down here for?' demanded Amelia.

Kit hissed back. 'I couldn't get rid of him!'

'Now, Master Tish, you know you shouldn't be down here!' Ivy delivered a gentle scold at the young man who was wandering around paying close examination to objects and people.

Tish was a man of few words. 'She made me come.'

Finding herself the object of his abstracted gesture, Kit gasped. 'The cheeky –!'

'Ssh!' Amelia silenced her. 'Remember who you're speaking of. He might be daft but he can still repeat things.' Then she and her friend lurched after Tish who, in a sudden flash of adventure, had gone to explore the kitchen. 'Aw, catch him, Mrs Hellawell'll go mad!'

Mrs Hellawell did portray a degree of madness, demanding to know who had brought the youth down here, and when all fingers pointed at Kit, turned on her.

'I didn't encourage him, Mrs Hellawell!' Kit beseeched the persona of quivering corpulence. 'I can't help it if he's taken a shine to me.'

'Taken a shine to you?' The cook offered a scoffing high-pitched laugh. 'You think too highly of yourself, my girl! It's my baking he's after. Now, Master Tish, you be a good lad and get back up where you belong – yes, before you ask you *can* take a bun with you! And Kit can escort you safely on your way.' She made gesticulations for Kit to undertake this. 'And just make sure you take him all the way and see he gets to where he's going without anymore mishap,' came the hissed addition.

Inwardly cursing her employer's son for adding to her unpopularity, Kit ushered the intruder to the top of the back staircase, ascertaining he was on his own territory before returning to hers.

Before reaching the kitchen she was intercepted by Myrtle who, bucket and mop in hand, approached her in grovelling manner. 'Begging your pardon, miss . . .'

At Kit's smile she felt able to proceed. 'I just wanted to say sorry for getting you into trouble – I mean you getting the blame for Master Tish coming down to the kitchen.'

Kit gave a puzzled laugh. 'I don't see as how it's your fault.'

Myrtle continued to fawn. 'Well, it is in a way 'cause he came to see me.'

Whilst thinking it wrong that the other parlourmaids snubbed those lower in rank, Kit felt superior enough to Myrtle to offer a patronizing smile. 'I hardly think so.'

Myrtle stood her ground. 'Begging your pardon, miss, but he did.' With the other rendered speechless, she babbled on. 'He was down here on the first day I started and he's been coming down quite regular ever since.'

Kit found her voice, which bore the vaguest hint of contempt. 'Yes, well, apparently it's Mrs Hellawell's baking that lures –'

'No, she just thinks that! And Master Tish lets her. But when I'm on me own he comes and talks to me, using –'

'Talks to you? I've never heard him say much.'

Myrtle looked crafty. 'He does when there's only me and him about. He uses any old excuse to get down here.'

Kit was annoyed but couldn't quite reason why. 'If you want me to help stop him pestering you –'

'Oh no! He's lovely. Well, I mean –' Myrtle blushed and broke off.

Kit was glad no one was around to witness her humiliation – even the imbecile fancied somebody else!

She turned her wrath on Myrtle. 'Well, just you be careful who you tell it to! There's others who are not so understanding as me. They'll say you're showing off!'

So consumed with annoyance was she over this that she forgot all about the master's original instructions.

In the absence of authority an air of indolence prevailed downstairs. Many of the servants sat gossiping, though this was sharply curtailed when Kit entered, verifying the fact that she was an outsider. 'Fancy a game of cards before old Turd gets back?' Algy asked the others, at which a pack was brought out and shuffled, no one asking if Kit would like to join in. Only old Beth Garbutt, reclining serenely in her rocking chair, offered any support in the form of a smile.

Whilst the game of cards ensued, punctuated by oaths and cries of triumph, Kit was regretting her spiteful words to Myrtle, the only one apart from Beth to be nice to her. She determined to make it up to the girl later. It was ridiculous to be jealous of such a relationship. If Myrtle were lucky enough to attract a paramour then she was to be congratulated. At a loose end, Kit sat and pondered for a while, until a chain of thoughts finally jolted her into relaying the master's orders. 'Oh! Algy, Mr Dolphin says his members –' She broke off and frowned, trying to remember, 'What was it now?'

'His member's not as big as mine,' Algy muttered this helpful suggestion to Charles, who sniggered, causing Mrs Hellawell to demand suspiciously: 'What was that?'

Algy lifted an innocent face from the cards in his hand. 'I think what the newest employee is trying to say is that the members of the Board of Guardians will be arriving in . . .' he cast a quick glance at the clock – 'half an hour.'

Kit exclaimed, 'That's it!'

Algy ignored the ejaculation, a superior edge to his address as he prepared to lay his cards on the table. 'Mrs Hellawell, would you be so kind as to inform our newest employee that Charles and myself are fully conversant with the master's requirements and as I have now won this game –' with great theatrics he displayed the winning hand to groans of dismay – 'I shall attend to them forthwith. Come along, Charles.'

Kit blurted, 'He doesn't want Charles!'

The latter's haughty mien turned to interrogate her.

'No, I'm to go with Algy instead,' explained Kit with a sinking feeling at Algy's obvious disdain.

'And who d'you think you are when you're at home – Lady Effingham?' Charles's contempt was almost as great as Rosalind's when Kit protested innocently:

'It's not my fault the master wants me!'

Mrs Hellawell gasped at the audacity, setting her jowls aquiver.

'Now she's even got the master after her!' scoffed Lily, tossing her losing hand on to the table in disgust.

'I haven't! He just said me and Algy make a handsome couple.'

Rosalind almost upset the card table in her violent elevation from her chair. 'How long have you been here – two days? And already you've got every man in the house throwing himself at you – that's if we believe anything you say!' Out of frustration she punched Algy

– looked as if she might punch Kit too – then fled the room in order to hide her tears.

His afternoon's repair work undone, Algy beheld the culprit darkly, then grabbed a silver tray and strode off, leaving Kit to dither a moment before rushing after him.

Trying to keep up with him along the back corridor, she protested that she had not meant to cause any trouble for him, that in truth it was all of his doing, he really shouldn't have treated her with such low regard, but please could they start again and be friends? All fell on barren ground. Not one word did Algy utter.

One by one the members of the Board of Guardians arrived. Algy announced each, then when all were settled he and Kit retreated to the kitchen to fetch refreshments. Still not one word did he bestow upon her, and nor did anyone else, Charles deliberately turning his back on her

Whilst Kit and Algy were loading their trays the doorbell rang at the tradesman's entrance. In imitation of Algernon's announcement of the master's guests, a youth performed a deep bow and introduced the bookie's runner, here to collect the servants' weekly wagers. Even better, he brought winnings for Algy – ten pounds!

From being the most fiendish of sinners, Kit suddenly found herself elevated to the rank of angel as, being the nearest female to hand, she was seized, squeezed and whisked around the room in a frenetic waltz as Algy crowed of his good fortune.

Laughing, Kit begged to be put down – only half serious – and was eventually released but not until Algy had planted a resounding kiss upon her cheek.

'Now you know just how fickle he is,' muttered Amelia when rejoined by her breathless sister. 'A few quid and he's anybody's.'

'Good to tell you haven't won owt!' he goaded.

'I wouldn't waste me money.'

Algy pushed his face into hers, taunting her playfully with the ten-pound note. Kit tried to keep her face straight but could scarcely conceal her delight at being returned to favour. The bookie's runner collected the latest bets and Kit was asked if she would care to speculate.

'Ooh no! I don't think our Monty would approve of that. I'm pleased for your bit of luck, though!' she added just in case the others interpreted her comment as yet another aspersion.

Mrs Hellawell curtailed the celebrations. 'Hadn't you two better get those trays upstairs?'

With an eye on the clock that forecast the imminent return of the steward and housekeeper, Algy agreed. 'Aye, better not let old Turd catch us – nor Rosie neither, else I'll have to part with this.' He kissed the tenner and shoved it into his pocket.

'I'll tell her!' warned Mrs Hellawell, though Algy knew she wouldn't. However, he was not so certain of others' allegiance.

'Suppose I'll have to give you something to keep you quiet?'

The question was directed at Kit, who was slightly hurt at this cynicism, yet pleased enough at her new success in the popularity stakes to issue blithely: 'I'm not a big mouth! It's nothing to do with me if you don't want to share it with Rosalind. Though I think you're very mean to use her so.'

'I'm not using her!' Satisfied with Kit's reply, his own was more light-hearted now, almost playful. 'She'd do anything for me and I'd do anything for her – within reason.'

'Except marry her,' accused Amelia.

'I don't think you realize how many women would be heartbroken if I were to do that.' He embraced all the other maidservants in his cocky smile, being met by groans. 'But if you play your cards right, Kit, I'd give good odds on you being Mrs Bogg.'

There were guffaws. 'Who'd want to be called Mrs Bogg!'

Algy ignored this insult and drew Kit to him. 'The master's right, we do make an 'andsome couple, don't we, Mrs Hellawell?'

Cook regarded the evenly matched pair, a cynical gleam to her beautiful green eyes. 'Some might say.'

But Kit had learned her lesson. Wise to Algy's game now, she felt confident enough to play along, and gave a mischievous bump with her elbow before picking up her tray and accompanying him back to the drawing room. 'I'll stay Miss Kilmaster if that's all the same to you.'

Everyone went about their business, leaving only Amelia, Ivy and Beth Garbutt in the room. Amelia sagged and pressed a hand to her brow. 'Well, I, for one, am glad I won't be Miss Kilmaster for much longer. I don't know how I'll last till September. Our Kit, she's such an embarrassment.'

Ivy agreed, patting her friend sympathetically.

The elderly lady was more charitable and said, as she had done many times before, 'She'll learn.'

As ever, both young women looked surprised at the interjection from one whom they regarded as part of the furniture. Amelia sighed again. 'Happen she will, Mrs Garbutt, but I reckon she'll inflict me with as many wrinkles as you've got before she does.'

8

What Kit had assumed to have been an accident on Wyndham's part happened again the next morning. Just as she leaned over him with the cup of tea he 'accidentally' brushed her breast as he groped for the saucer. Alarmed, but too unsure of her position to take issue with the culprit, Kit hurried from the room and in shocked tone complained to her sister. Amelia showed little surprise, which to Kit illustrated that she had deliberately exposed her sister to Wyndham's advances in order to avoid them herself. Amelia argued that this were untrue, Master Wyndham had never touched her and if Kit were receiving this treatment then she must be flaunting herself, as was her wont. Recalling Algy's familiarity, Kit thought perhaps that it was her natural friendliness that had caused the wrong impression and so, the following morning when delivering Wyndham's tea she tried to convey an air of aloofness that might put him off. Alas, it did not. Moreover, due to her previous lack of censure, the youth had grown quite blatant about his fondling, not even bothering to disguise the assault as accidental.

Kit did not know what to do. It was one thing to complain to the housekeeper about a manservant's lewd attentions, quite another to accuse her employer's son. With no one else willing to take Wyndham's morning tea, and Kit of too junior a position to argue, she must either put up with the indecent behaviour or leave – and she simply could not lose another job.

Morning molestations, sedate luncheons, afternoon tea, evening dinner, bedtime cocoa; the rest of the week and indeed the rest of the month, was much the same, with Kit alternating between the two worlds, one sumptuous and genteel, the other unadorned chaos.

On the first Sunday of the month, she and Amelia travelled home together to Ralph Royd chiefly to attend little Probyn's baptism, and then it was back to her labours until the wedding. Any precious free time she might have was given to working on Amelia's dress, using a paper pattern cut from a magazine. The labour of love this might have been was somewhat spoiled by Ivy, who, in her senior position, delegated all the tedious jobs to Kit, such as sewing a covering around each of the three cane hoops that would form the bustle, stitching tapes to each end of them, making the bustle pad itself out of cotton wool, covering buttons, when Kit would much rather be working with the other two on the expanse of russet velvet. Night after night the three laboured, inserting bones into the bodice, stitching dozens of hooks and eyes, buttons and buttonholes, adding flounces, embroidery, underskirts, overskirts, until the finished creation hung in all its autumnal splendour from a rail in Amelia's room where she gazed upon it every night before going to sleep.

One would imagine that with her days so crammed with work the time to Amelia's wedding would fly past, but this was not the case for the bride who complained to her friend Ivy that it would be such a relief to get away from her sister's embarrassing behaviour – though she was made to regret this as, when her leaving day finally arrived, Kit presented her with the most splendid pair of silver-plated candlesticks that must have cost most of her quarterly wages.

'I'll really miss you,' Kit told her sister as they rode home together atop a local carrier's cart, Kit being granted an extra day off to help with last-minute preparations for tomorrow's wedding. 'You're the only friend I've got there.'

Amelia had the grace to blush. 'Ivy'll look after you.' Her friend would be travelling to the wedding tomorrow.

Kit chose not to say that she couldn't stand Ivy, her abhorrence reinforced by the girl's unflattering comparison of their two wedding gifts. Ivy had donated a more practical selection of linen, remarking that Amelia must have had enough of cleaning silver at the Hall.

'And the others aren't too bad if you don't try and get above yourself.'

'I don't!' At her sister's hesitation Kit asked, 'Is that what they say about me?'

Amelia showed a rare compassion and patted the larger girl's hand. 'No, I haven't heard owt. Anyway, don't let's talk about that lot, we're off to enjoy ourselves.' She hoisted her shoulders in excitement. 'I wonder what me cake's like . . .'

Sarah had made the wedding cake and a neighbour had iced it. In fact most of the neighbours had promised to make a contribution to Amelia's big day, some of them bringing flowers from their allotments, others providing ham, pork, home-made wine and confectionery for the feast and yet others attending to the serving of it. It would indeed be a village affair.

Kit cheered up. 'Oh, it's going to be a grand do! I wish it were me getting wed.'

Amelia said kindly, 'Your turn'll come.'

Kit bemoaned her unmarried status. 'It's rotten, being t'only one left.'

'Well, I won't be that far away.' Amelia and her husband-to-be had acquired a mortgage on a small terraced property in Castleford. 'I'm only over t'river. You can come and see me if ever you feel like a natter. Wait till I've got me house straight though. I want to get it just right before anybody sees it.'

Kit agreed that this would be lovely. 'It'll make a nice change to be working for yourself instead of somebody else.'

Amelia said she had little regret about leaving domestic service. 'But I will miss going to London.' In certain years she had been included in the retinue taken to the capital, and although her work forbade much sightseeing it had been an exciting change of venue.

Kit had heard from her sister before about all the noblemen and women who had visited the house, the luxurious parties, the opulent clothes, and she was eager for adventure. 'Ooh, I wonder if I'll be allowed to go. What's the house like?'

'A lot smaller than Cragthorpe, but grand all the same.' Amelia regretted the mention of it, dared not imagine what Kit would get up to if let loose in London. 'Anyway, it's not all it's cracked up to be down there, I'll be much happier having a husband and babies. You can take them out whenever you want – the babies, I mean.'

Kit tore her imagination away from London. 'Aw, thanks – I'm right glad for you. I'll still miss your company at work though.'

Swaying in her seat atop the cart, Amelia gave a warm nod. 'I'll miss you too.' And she meant it.

* * *

When the girls arrived at Ralph Royd late on Saturday afternoon a twittering mass of girls rushed out to meet the cart, begging to be allowed to see Amelia's dress, the gifts, and anything else pertaining to the wedding. Fighting a way through, a laughing Kit and a rather impatient Amelia carried the precious packages into the house, begging the youngsters to curb their curiosity. Beata came forth to greet her soulmate. Monty, too, looked in good spirits.

Though continuing with her work, Sarah tossed a greeting at her sisters-in-law. 'Thank goodness you're here. They've been driving me mad with their wittering – and that one . . . !' She gave a curt nod at baby Probyn, who grizzled and whined from his prison of cushions jammed around him on the floor to prevent injury. 'He's enough to test the patience of a saint. You can keep your boys, thank you very much. The girls were never half the trouble he is.'

'Aw!' Kit went straight to the baby, picked him up and cuddled him. 'That's all he wants, in't it, me little honey?'

'It's all very well for those with nothing else to do,' scolded the baby's mother, though there was light-heartedness in the accusation. She grabbed a cup. 'Here! If you've so much time on your hands you can get down to the Well and fetch a nip of brandy. There's threepence on the mantel.'

Still cuddling Probyn, Kit feigned shock and turned to her brother. 'Has your wife become a drunkard in me absence?'

Monty looked grave. 'Ar, it's a turble thing when a woman gets a taste for it.'

'Less of your cheek!' Sarah pretended to swipe both of them as they shared a laugh. 'It's not for me, it's for his highness.'

Naturally, everyone looked at Monty whose Wesleyan beliefs normally forbade him to partake of strong liquor.

Sarah pretended derision. 'Oh no! You're crediting the wrong person with the title. It's not Monty who rules the roost now, nor him who the liquor's for.'

Kit jiggled the baby and laughed. 'Who, then – this little thing? He's taken it up early hasn't he?'

'I'm not having his demanding behaviour spoiling my enjoyment of the wedding. An ogre he is! A veritable ogre. Nag, nag, nag, all night long – well I'm not having it tomorrow, see!' She wagged a finger at Probyn, who grinned and squirmed with self-importance, looking delighted with all the attention he was getting.

All the girls laughed at his brazen display, Beata taking his cheek softly between her finger and thumb and telling him that he was, 'Fond brussen.'

Kissing him affectionately, Kit passed the baby to Amelia. 'Here, get some practice in. I'll go to t'Well – are you coming with me, Beat?' Her niece, eager to catch up with all the news about Algy, made to accompany her.

'Can I come?' Alice grabbed the cup and got to the door before them.

Not wanting to share Kit's company, Beata asked if Alice wouldn't prefer to inspect all Amelia's gifts, for their other sisters appeared to be engrossed in these, but the little girl insisted on coming with them, thereby spoiling any intimate conversation.

'You only want to have a laugh at Maid Marion,' teased her aunt, but gave a relenting groan. 'Oh, away then!'

Swinging Alice between the pair of them, Beata and Kit pranced gaily along the street, past the allotments and down the slope towards the whitewashed public house on the main road. Entering the rear lobby of the Robin Hood's Well, they waited at the counter, the elder girls sharing a private smirk at the barmaid.

'I wonder what sort of wedding dress she'll choose.' Kit hid a titter behind her hand, as did Beata in her reply.

Knowing whom they were discussing, Alice wanted to share the fun but even when standing on tiptoe could not see over the bar. 'Will you lift me up, Aunt?' Her request ignored, she repeated it again and again.

'Behave yourself!' Her sister grabbed the cup off her and continued to share the whispered joke with Kit, careful not to let the subject of their amusement witness their fun, for it was not their intention to be hurtful.

There was a strip of panelling along the lower half of the bar. Somehow Alice managed to achieve a foothold on its inch-wide platform, hauled her upper body over the counter and propped herself up on her elbows.

From here one could catch a narrow glimpse into each section of the public house – the taproom with its sawdust and spittoon, bare boards and iron tables, its ceiling brown with tobacco smoke; the best room to the left where sat the junior colliery officials in their suits, collars and ties, reading newspapers in leather-bound comfort; the snug to their immediate right where women – definitely not ladies, accused Sarah – sat gossiping and knitting over glasses of stout. And there was Maid Marion serving on! Alice grinned and fixed the barmaid with her fascinated gaze whilst her aunt and sister continued to share their private joke.

Marion was not the barmaid's chosen name, but folk being what they are and the pub being called Robin Hood's Well, it was a label that had stuck. Though not as tall as Kit, she lacked her feminine roundness. Her build was angular, with long arms and long knuckly fingers. The fact that she had wound her dark hair into a bun and arranged a dainty little fringe of curls upon her brow and around her ears could do nothing to convince folk that she was anything other than a man in a dress, for twixt the dainty curls and the frilly lace collar protruded a huge Adam's apple.

Far from inviting discrimination, Marion had been eagerly hired by the brewery officials, not from any altruistic motive but because they saw her as an attraction for the curious and hence good for custom. Marion recognized this – hated it but accepted it. With strangers her communication was limited to a nod and a fleeting smile, her eyes never meeting theirs, for to unleash one word was to confirm the newcomer's suspicions. Only amongst her own did Marion feel free to enjoy the conversation, no one batting an eyelid at her deep voice. The publican's wife accepted her at face value and even swapped knitting patterns with her. There was similar acceptance from the rest of this community. Strange as it might seem, despite the odd sly nudge, no one in this overtly masculine environment, not even the most hard-bitten, foulest-mouthed, ignorant labourer, had ever laid the accusation at Marion's size twelve feet that 'she' was a big fraudulent jessy. Indeed, the miners treated her with the same respect accorded to their wives. Only the young could not curb their fascination.

Alice continued to give vent to hers until the much rowdier bunch in the taproom erupted into bouts of swearing. Bright-eyed, the little girl exclaimed, 'Eh, they're having a spitting contest!'

Beata gave a sound of disgust and craned her head over the bar for a glimpse into the taproom, but drew back immediately at the shower of tobacco-coloured spittle that arched across the room in her direction. That it was not aimed at her but at the spittoon at the foot of the bar mattered not one jot. Beata yanked the straps of Alice's pinafore and pulled her back below counter-level.

'Mother'd have a fit if she thought you were learning such things!'

Alice pulled her clothes back into position and waited, hopefully to be served by Marion, but to her disappointment it was the publican who arrived to take their order. Jim Wilcox – Peggo, to close friends – had once been a miner until the loss of his right leg had elevated him to a brighter world. By aid of a crutch, he limped towards them. The artificial leg that had earned him his nickname was missing today, its chafing having caused great painful ulcers to appear on his stump and had subsequently been tossed out of the window in a moment of agonized rage. He would go and retrieve it in a week or so when the ulcers had subsided. Until then he was forced to rely on the wooden crutch that was tucked under his armpit.

'Nah then.' The voice was deep but quietly respectful, the blue eyes twinkling despite his pain. 'What can I get for you young ladies?'

Kit pushed the cup across the counter and said she would like a measure of brandy.

Peggo, aware of tomorrow's wedding, observed, 'Tha'll not have much of a celebration on that.'

Kit laughed and said it was not for the wedding but was purely medicinal.

Peggo winked knowingly. 'Oh yes, we've had a lot of folk in here wi' toothache today.'

A roar went up from the taproom as one of the contestants completely mis-aimed and defaced the whitewashed wall with tobacco juice. Peggo seemed oblivious, continuing to lean on the bar and chat to the young women. Like most people in the village, Peggo was friendly with Kit but she could not help noticing that he concentrated most of his attention on Beata, for whom he obviously had a particular fondness. Had he been a younger man Kit would have said he was in love with her, but that was mere fantasy for one could almost see one's reflection in the expanse of baldness between the two strips of dark hair, and the smiling creases upon his face gave him the air of an indulgent grandfather.

'I'll have a jar when you're ready, Peggo!'

Kit noticed the barest alteration in Peggo's calm expression, though he made no detour from his conversation.

'So, how's that baby brother of yours?' Momentarily, he tore his eyes away from Beata's pleasant face to address Alice, who once again was balanced atop the counter attempting to see into the taproom.

At her sister's lack of interest, Beata supplied the answer. 'He's grand – well, we think so, don't we, Kit? Me mam isn't so sure.'

Wincing at the pain in his stump, Peggo rolled his eyes and leaned on the counter. 'Ooh, a bit of a lad, is he? I saw him out with your mam t'other day. He doesn't look like collier material to me.'

Kit laughed and said, 'Perhaps not this week.'

Peggo explained. 'Nay, but he's such a dainty little –'

'Oy, Peggo! Is tha deef? I'm gaggin' o' thust here.'

With barely a hint that he had heard, Peggo nodded mildly and continued – 'dainty little thing. My lad had hands like shovels as soon as he were bor –'

'Oy!'

Peggo formed a most dignified apology. 'Would you young ladies please excuse me one moment?' Reaching for the crutch that leaned against the counter, he pivoted slowly and deliberately to face the taproom, fixed the oafish face across the bar with an artificial smile, then with one expert and frequently practised movement brought the wooden crosspiece of the crutch down on the other man's head like a mallet, felling him instantly and rendering him semi-conscious and bleeding into the spittoon.

Without losing one iota of equilibrium, Peggo turned back to the astonished girls and spoke as if without interruption, '– as soon as he were born. I can pick 'em straightaway. I doubt very much your Probyn'll make his way down t'pit.'

Not knowing quite how to react, Kit nodded and smiled and, paying for the brandy as quickly as she could, almost fell out of the public house whence she and Beata broke into peals of laughter.

Alice danced alongside of them, full of admiration for Peggo. 'That were right good, weren't it? Eh, is Mr Wilcox coming to Aunt Amelia's wedding? I hope he bashes somebody there – it'd be a right lark.'

Eyes watering, Kit spluttered. 'I could have done with his help in dealing with a few people at Cragthorpe Hall!'

Alice wanted to know who, but Beata ignored her to ask Kit, 'Are they still troubling you?'

'Who?' repeated Alice.

'Nobody you know,' Kit told the child and muttering to Beata that little pigs have big ears, said she would tell her all about it when they could grab a few moments alone.

There was no chance of such intimacy that day nor the next, for the wedding preparations took up every waking hour. There were baths to be taken, hair to be coiffed, flowers to be carried to the chapel, vegetables to be dug up, food to be cooked, baked, roasted and transported to the Sunday school room – all this to be undertaken in a buffeting September wind.

The guests, all dandified in their wedding attire and eager to escape from the elements, jostled their way through the entrance porch, only to discover as they filed down the aisle and slipped into their wooden pews beside the rest of the congregation that it was as cold within, the chill travelling up from the floor and permeating flimsy wedding slippers. Yet at least, Kit was glad to observe, the usual austerity was relieved by brilliant splashes of colour from rows of fruit and vegetables, deposited here for harvest thanksgiving, and the vases of gold and ivory chrysanthemums whose scent mingled with wax polish and Flora's liberally applied lavender water. Uplifted by the occasion – as much out of thought for her own wedding as out of happiness for her sister – Kit almost drowned out the piano with her rendition of 'Rock of Ages' and had to be nudged by a disapproving Gwen for trying to outshine everyone else.

There followed a prayer by the circuit minister, during which children fidgeted and others offered blunt comment.

'Nowt much of a preacher, is he? I'm glad I don't have to rely on him to get me a place in Heaven, he'd bore the Lord to tears.' Owen did not usually attend the same chapel as his brother, deeming its congregation of pit manager, deputies and tradespeople too bourgeois. His own primitive rantings taking place in a basic wooden mission hall, he held the opinion that Sarah only dragged her family here out of snobbery.

After a final hymn and a prayer, the congregation began to file out, some openly weeping their happiness, others stoical, but all smiling in approval of the band of singers who rendered the 'Wedding Anthem' – until it was realized that the choir sought payment of ten shillings for the performance and an argument ensued between the circuit minister and the groom, both of whom refused to cough up.

'I beg your pardon,' Albert said for the third time. 'but I didn't hire them.'

'And neither did I,' retorted the minister.

'Yes, but they're part of your congregation,' the groom reminded him.

'In the capacity of pledging their hearts to God,' said the minister. 'Not in the form of entertainment. These men are perfectly aware of my views on the subject.'

'But I weren't!' objected Albert.

'Thou enjoyed our singing, didn't tha?' demanded the spokesman for the choir.

'Thoroughly.' Albert turned to him calmly. 'I just didn't realize it was costing me two bob a verse.'

'Look, never mind that!' butted in a member of the choir. 'Who's gonna pay us?'

'Not I!' The minister and Albert spoke in unison.

There was angry grumbling. Amelia was growing flustered and embarrassed. Seeing this, an annoyed Kit delved into her purse and thrust a coin at the leader of the choir. 'Here, take it and clear off!' Then she herded the guests towards the Sunday school room, only to be chivvied by Sarah, who deemed her to have more money than sense.

Amelia, however, thanked Kit for saving the day and upon greeting her guests at the door of the schoolroom conducted them all to view the splendid gift that Kit had bought her, displayed amongst the sheets, towels, pillowcases, tablecloths, dusters, pots and pans. Not wishing folk to think she had bought the gift in order to outdo anyone, a modest Kit directed them instead to look at the canteen of cutlery donated by Mr and Mrs Dolphin.

'They must have a bob or two,' commented Charity in her leisurely drawl. 'Very generous with it, an' all.' She went on to ask for Kit's opinion on her employers.

'She's all right,' conceded Kit. 'I don't care for him, though – he's got slack lips.'

The female listeners gave murmured understanding. The men merely looked at each other quizzically, wondering if they too were in possession of this obviously repellent feature.

The guests' attention was drawn back to Amelia and her groom, who were posing for the photographer. 'Albert's parents have come from Lancashire,' said Flora, in a tone that conveyed admiration.

'Never mind, we won't hold that against them.' Peggo winked at Beata, who grinned back. Alice watched him closely, hoping that someone would provoke him into using his crutch as a weapon.

There were further quips from Owen about the groom's parents having the surname Groom and, now that Amelia had married into them, the bride was now a Groom. Charity deemed Albert to be a good-looking chap even if he did have short legs and his fair hair was rather thin. He had kind blue eyes, she said.

'Oh, don't our Amelia look splendid?' Gazing upon the bride in her head-dress of autumn flowers, Gwen's waxen features had become rather tearful. 'And she's awfully like Mother, don't you think? Apart from her ginger hair, that is.'

Whilst Monty, Flora and Charity agreed, Kit experienced a pang of jealousy that her elder siblings had enjoyed more time with their parents and thus knew more about them. To Kit they were simply shadows.

She glanced at Ivy, who was accompanied by her sweetheart. Kit thought it had been rather a nerve of her to ask if she might bring him. In the few months that the couple had known each other they had only met three or four times to Kit's knowledge, and it wasn't as if they were engaged. But the bride had not seemed to regard this as impudence. Indeed, Amelia had voiced much eagerness to help the relationship towards the path of happiness. Which was more than she had ever offered to do for Kit, came the sad thought.

Following Kit's gaze, Charity noticed that Ivy and her beau looked rather excluded, and sought to involve them in the conversation, asking when would their happy day be. Ivy looked coy and replied that he hadn't asked her yet, upon which Gwen tried to bully the poor boy into making a proposal, though he smilingly refused to buckle.

'Can I be your bridesmaid?' asked six-year-old Wyn.

Ivy, fearing that her beau would be scared off, stammered that she would like nothing more but she did not know if she would be able to afford the material for so many dresses, for to have one was to have all. Wyn bemoaned having so many sisters; she could never hope to be bridesmaid when every bride made the same complaint.

Fondling the child's bony shoulder, Kit made a promise. 'Come what may, you'll all be attendants at my wedding.'

Gwen quashed the child's hopes. 'Wyn'll probably be wed before you are.'

Beata thought it mean to single Kit out. 'Before me too.' Always a rather sickly individual, she felt it was unlikely that anyone would want her either. In this she and Kit shared a bond.

Peggo fought the nagging pain in his leg to portray chivalry. 'Nay, they'll be queuing up to court these two. If I wasn't spoken for meself I wouldn't know which of 'em to choose.' Both young women smiled their gratitude.

The photographer finished his business and went back to his studio in Castleford. The guests were summoned to the tables, being waited upon by Mrs Feather, who presided at every birth, marriage and funeral in the village, and her select band of helpers, amongst them Marion from the pub.

'Here, you can't enjoy yourself properly with that encumbrance.' Kit divested a grateful Sarah of the baby and made a joke at her own expense. 'With Probyn on one arm I won't be able to eat as much.'

She seated herself at the largest of the tables, which also accommodated the bride and groom, Albert's parents, Sarah, Monty, his siblings and their spouses. The score of chattersome children sat at a table of their own, as did other guests of lesser status. Squeezed between Owen and his wife, Meg, Kit eyed Flora, opposite, who was sniffing suspiciously at a forkful of ham. The bride noticed too and looked apprehensive – surely, today of all days her sister could withhold this bad habit. Nothing passed this fussy eater's lips without being examined for at least ten seconds.

Others had obviously noticed too. Amelia could bear it no longer. 'It's not manky, you know!'

Flora, realizing what she was doing, blushed and stuttered that of course it wasn't, and somewhat reluctantly inserted the forkful of ham between her lips, whilst her husband's expression told that he wished he were somewhere else.

Trying to divert Amelia's attention from the annoyance, Kit delved on to her own plate and made appetizing noises, chewing happily and smiling down at the sleeping Probyn. 'That brandy certainly did the trick.' A teaspoonful of milk laced with a drop of liquor had been dribbled on to

Probyn's tongue before the service, guaranteeing them an undisturbed afternoon.

Albert's mother looked shocked and asked if this was wise, which offended Sarah, but once again Kit smoothed things over by drawing notice to the brooch at Amelia's throat and gushing how pretty it was and how kind it had been of Sarah to lend it to her, as the 'something borrowed'.

Albert's father seemed to be enjoying his meal, his knife and fork in constant motion, though his brow wore a puzzled frown. Once again, Amelia showed anxiety. 'Is everything to your taste, Mr – I mean, Father-in-law?'

Mr Groom raised his eyebrows but lowered his voice, leaning confidentially towards Sarah on his right. 'I don't want to alarm anybody but that woman there, I don't think she's really a woman.'

Everyone automatically turned to look at Marion. Sarah explained to Mr Groom that all were acquainted with Marion's foibles and 'she' was accepted by everyone in the village. 'It's a crying shame really, she's a lovely man.'

Beata and Kit tittered at the slip.

Mrs Groom senior was aghast, hardly able to tear her eyes from the man in the dress. 'I wonder what his parents make of him.'

Sarah, calmly, said she wouldn't know. 'We don't even know where he comes from.'

Mr Groom gave a muttered aside to his son. 'Obviously not from Viking stock.'

Attention was turned on Peggo, Albert's mother expressing more surprise on learning that he was a publican. Monty, offended, would not have his friend maligned. 'There ain't a kinder man in this village – even if he do deal in drink.'

Throughout the meal Mrs Feather and her helpers constantly reappeared with more platters until they were satisfied the guests were replete. Only then were the impatient children allowed to leave their table with the warning that they must not get too wild – it was after all Sunday.

Owen waited until the plates were cleared before asking Albert. 'Does tha smoke, love?'

Unaware that the men of these colliery villages used this endearment to each other, Albert regarded this as an affront to his manhood and a blush of offence rose to his cheeks. Embarrassed, Amelia answered for her husband. 'No, he doesn't!'

'Aye, a bad habit.' Owen himself had only taken up smoking to be different from his brother. Unconcerned that he had caused offence, he went on to ask the other men at the table, some of whom accepted his offer of tobacco for their pipes.

The seating was less formal now, guests changing seats to chat beside one person before moving to talk to another. The conversation between the two families had become rather stilted but was saved by a bunch of children who thudded across the bare boards to besiege the adults. Owen's little boy clambered on to his mother's lap and sucked his thumb.

'What's a honeymoon, Mother?' asked Alice.

'No use asking me,' replied Sarah somewhat tartly, envisioning herself as a new bride lumbered by a ready-made family.

'I've just told her!' Ethel was stern. 'It's a holiday the bride and groom go on after they are married.'

'And do they have to eat honey?' Alice looked concerned. She was told that they probably did in the olden days. 'I don't want to get married then. I hate honey.'

'Tha can eat fish and chips if tha wants.' Owen puffed on his pipe.

Unaccustomed to such indulgence, the children made the most of it, each clamouring for attention. 'Where did you go on your honeymoon, Uncle Owen?'

'Timbukthree.' Owen remained serious. The children wanted to know where this was. 'It's near Timbuktu but just a bit further away – don't they teach you owt at that school?'

Six-year-old Wyn, who had been tugging at various sleeves, jumped in with a question of her own. 'Uncle Owen, what's a farleymelow?'

Owen frowned and looked around the assembly for an answer. 'Nay, you've got me stumped there.'

Kit asked the child to repeat herself.

'A farleymelow – it's in a song Miss Ellerker taught us at school.' Seeing her aunt's bafflement Wyn broke into song: '*Early one mo-orning, just as the sun was ri-ising, I heard a maiden si-ing in the far-ley-me-low –*'

Kit feigned a choking fit, blaming the bun she was eating, whilst trying desperately not to laugh and so humiliate the child.

'I thought it might be some kind of privy,' ventured Wyn, 'because Mrs Smith sings in the privy really loud.'

Kit continued to clear her throat for some seconds, then wiped her eyes and tried to deliver the answer in calm tone – which was difficult as adults in earshot were not so sparing of Wyn's feelings and were laughing quite openly. 'Oh, dear, sorry about that, Wyn. A crumb went down the wrong way.' She explained that Mrs Smith was a nervous sort of person and she sang to prevent anyone walking in on her, there being no bolt. 'I think if you listen carefully to the song you'll find it's "the valley below".'

Angry at being the butt of adult laughter, Wyn flounced off, allowing Kit to release her own mirth. She wiped her eyes. 'Aw, poor little thing. I'm almost wetting meself!'

Gwen was unusually jocular. 'Better get yourself along to the farley-melow quick sharp then.'

Kit agreed and made to leave the laughing group. Beata said she would accompany her.

Gwen, suddenly noticing that her sons were missing, called, 'Have a look for those boys o' mine while you're out, would you? I told them not to go outside. Their father'll skin them alive if they dirty their new suits.'

Kit acquiesced as she and Beata left the hall, though her consequent surveillance amounted to nothing and she had so much news to divulge that by the time the pair reached their destination they had put the boys from their mind.

The privy was one of the few places where the girls could enjoy leisurely conversations, sitting side by side on the wooden bench and letting nature take its course whilst mouthing their dreams and ambitions. There was something comforting about the dark interior despite its insalubrity and the buzzing flies

'So tell me, I'm dying to know,' begged her niece, 'how is that dreadful Algy?'

'Good-looking, and he knows it,' came the disdainful reply. Then Kit relented. 'Oh, he's not so bad once you get to know him – no, it's Master Wyndham that's my bugbear.'

'Aw, is he still at it?' Beata's cheeks burned with embarrassment, trying somewhat perversely to imagine what such an assault must feel like, for she herself had no breasts to speak of.

'Yes, and I can't do owt about it or I'll get the sack. Amelia's well out of it. She looks lovely, doesn't she? It's been a grand do.' She tutted. 'Apart from bloomin' Gwen! She can't even let me get through an afternoon without telling me I'll always be a spinster.'

Beata dismissed this. 'She's blinkin' puddled. I wish I were as bonny as you – anyroad, I'm not sure I want to get married. I mean, it's really only another form of slavery.' Asked what she would really like to do if she got the chance, she tilted her chin. 'I'd love to do something artistic. Be a painter – if I could paint. Or a musician – if I could musish. I wish me dad'd let you go on t'stage. You'd be right good.'

Kit's smile turned to wistfulness. 'All I really want is a family.'

'Haven't you had enough to put up with, looking after us lot?' asked Beata, considering it unfair the amount of childminding that fell to Kit. 'Mother's the one who gave birth to us all, yet it's you and me who get the responsibility of looking after them. Oh, I know it's mean but sometimes, just sometimes, I'd like to be able to have some time to myself. This is the only place I can come for any peace.'

'I promise that when I have enough money I'll take you to live with me.' Whilst harbouring every good intention of saving for a little house of her own, Kit just could not help spending her wages as soon as she got them, not just on herself but on others. 'It won't be anything like Cragthorpe Hall, though – my, the work in that place!' She went on to tell Beata all that had happened this month, unaware that whilst she sat gossiping a man hopped from foot to foot outside.

Inevitably, the conversation came back to the subject of marriage. Beata wondering what actually happened on one's wedding night. 'I mean, I know it's summat to do with *down there*,' she mouthed the last two words, 'but I just can't fathom what it could be.'

Kit said that it somehow involved a man's thing. She giggled. 'I wonder if you have to look at it?' Both girls squirmed in horrified laughter.

Each then listed the finer qualities they would look for in a husband, not really believing that anyone would ever want them. Kit wondered out loud what qualities a man looked for in a wife. In Mr Dolphin's case it was not education or intelligence, for his spouse's mispronunciation of words was an obvious embarrassment.

An eye appeared at the peephole and an urgent enquiry was hissed. 'How much longer are you lasses gonna sit there gasbagging?'

'Nearly finished, Mr Wrigglesworth!' Kit barely diverted her attention from the conversation with Beata and in seconds was rattling along again. 'So anyway, Mrs Dolphin says yet again, "That is not *revelant*" – can you believe it! In front of guests! So . . .'

Neither she nor Beata heard the trap door at the rear being shifted, nor the giggles. But when each pair of buttocks received a smart thwack with a stick, both leaped up with yells of protest.

'That pizzock Donald!' Hauling up her drawers, a furious Kit barged out of the closet almost flattening the poor man who had been hopping about outside, and raced around the corner just in time to see her two nephews tearing down the slope. Remarkably light on her feet, she immediately set off after them. Still giggling, the culprits threw a look over their shoulders and were amazed to see that their hefty victim was pursuing them. A look of horror crossed each face. They tried to increase their speed but Kit was gaining fast. She had almost caught up with them when the younger one tripped, fell heavily and began to bawl. Instantly, Kit bent to comfort him and tend his bloody knee, tying her handkerchief around the wound, all mischief forgotten.

'I should be saying that serves you right!' But her scolding was mild as she wiped his tears with a brisk palm.

'You won't tell me dad, will you, Aunty Kit?' Eight-year-old Brian, who remained uninjured, asked anxiously.

'We ought to!' Kit glanced up as her breathless niece arrived. 'Oughtn't we, Beat?'

The other agreed. 'I don't know what your parents'd say if they heard you were up to such disgusting behaviour.' Wheezing, she leaned against a wall for support.

Leaving the boys in suspense, Kit and Beata escorted them back to the reception where their mother made a fuss over their dishevelled appearance.

'Oh, deary me, let's have a look at 'ee – why, Donnie, you're bleeding!' Pulling away the handkerchief, Gwen winced at the graze on Donald's knee, then hugged and patted the sufferer, asking how he had done it.

'Running, I'll bet!' barked their father, Roy, less concerned about the injury than the state of his son's clothes. 'What did I tell thee before we set out? I want to see that suit as neat and tidy when you go home as when you put it on. Didn't I say that? Barely closed me wallet after paying for it and now look at the state of you!'

'Never mind, it'll wash,' calmed Charity, this response having become a personal catchphrase over the years.

'How? He looks as if he's been dragged through the midden!'

Dangerously close to a hiding, both boys sneaked a plaintive look at their Aunt Kit.

'It wasn't Donald's fault.' Although incompatible with her nephews, Kit chose not to betray them. 'He tripped over a loose flag. Didn't he, Beata?' The other nodded.

It cut no ice with Roy, who retorted that this did not explain Brian's disarray.

But his wife jumped in with loud accusation, 'Wretched Corporation, letting things go to rack and ruin. Why, the poor child, he could have broke his neck!'

All those in earshot agreed, even though they knew from experience that the boys must be guilty of some mischief, none of them wanting the wedding to be overshadowed by corporal punishment.

However, once the bride and groom had departed there was no such need for restraint. At the end of the day when Amelia and her groom embarked on their new life and shoes were thrown to wish them luck in their travels, Donald's over-enthusiastic participation resulted in Meredith suffering a gash to the head from one of his boots and finally Gwen's brat got the good hiding he deserved.

Later that evening, Kit packed her belongings, kissed each and every one of her nieces, gave baby Probyn an extra cuddle and, with a sense of anticlimax, returned to Cragthorpe Hall. With no prospect of a wedding, the only vision she received of her future was months, perhaps years, of drudgery.

9

Yearning for excitement, Kit was to suffer a similar routine for the rest of the year, attending at table, endeavouring to place the vase of flowers at the strategic point that would screen poor Tish from his mother, being coached by the mistress into more ladylike behaviour and in the next breath accused of assuming the airs of a lady in her mode of dress.

However, things were not all so dismal, for Master Wyndham had gone back to Rugby and the staff had become a little kinder to her, and once she was over her homesickness Kit was to discover that Christmas was a splendid time at Cragthorpe Hall. Mr Dolphin arranged a party for the servants in the great hall whence to her delight Kit was able to indulge her penchant for dancing – she even danced with the master! Never had she enjoyed such a celebration, for the Kilmasters set little store by Christmas, other than providing a good feed, a visit to chapel and a few nuts for the children. Her brother's house bore none of the gay trappings of the Dolphin residence and, after a trip home with her quarterly wages, Kit was for once quite glad to leave the spartan little house and return to the grand mansion bedecked with holly and mistletoe.

After the constant round of visitors, the trips to the workhouse with gifts for the inmates, the feasting and general merrymaking, the last days of January descended upon the house like a shroud. A mere irritation in summer, the ghastly cry of the peafowl became a macabre echo on the wintry air, heralding a distinct change in Mrs Dolphin's mood. There were more complaints, more nervous little pacings about the drawing room. Indeed, the mood was contagious and Kit found herself feeling increasingly glum as the month wore on.

The dark mornings were an extra inducement to stay in bed. Coming round to another pitch-black morn with no birdsong, no noise at all, Kit fought the impulse to turn over and instead forced her eyes to remain open even though there was naught to see. An unpleasant smell pervaded her room. It was gas – someone must have turned on a lamp and forgotten to light it! Leaping up, she threw on a shawl and rushed along the landing to the staircase, for there were no gas brackets up here.

The smell grew stronger. Impeded by her nightgown, her bare feet beginning to feel the cold, Kit padded along the corridor towards the kitchen, pausing only to check every wall bracket as she passed.

She reached the kitchen, opened the door and ran in – tripped over something on the ground and fell headlong to the hard stone floor, calling out in distress.

Others came running too, one of them hauling on a rope that worked the louvres in the ceiling and casting a modicum of light on the situation, enabling Kit to see that she was not the only person on the floor.

'Heaven preserve us, she's done it again,' muttered Mr Todd, and immediately went to the unconscious person's aid, lifting her head gently from its pillow in the gas oven and calling to Algy to turn off the gas and assist him. 'Mrs Grunter, for pity's sake, we'll all be blown to bits!' The housekeeper had been about to strike a match. 'Get all the doors and windows open!' Several maids complied. 'Ivy, wake the master! Algernon, take Mrs Dolphin's legs!'

Every vein in her body pulsating with shock, Kit spared no thought for her own bruises, concentrating instead on Mrs Dolphin's nightgowned form that was being lifted off the floor and carried into the servants' hall. With no one the least bit interested in her welfare, Kit jumped up and hurried after the procession, trying to solicit an answer as to what on earth was going on. Not until the mistress had been brought round with a few slaps to the face, the master had arrived to take charge and Mrs Dolphin had been carried upstairs to more comfortable quarters, was Kit granted an explanation.

'She always gets melancholy at this time of year,' explained Mrs Hellawell, as if the attempted suicide were commonplace, waddling over to shut the oven door and wafting the air distastefully at the residual smell of gas, the great rolls of fat trembling under her nightdress. 'Can only stand Yorkshire in small doses – well, there's nowt much for her to do, you see.'

'I could find her summat,' replied one of the overworked kitchenmaids to her companions. All were clad in their night attire, with tousled plaits and swollen eyes.

'How awful!' Kit marvelled that she seemed to be the only member of staff perturbed by the affair. 'I could never contemplate taking my own life. It's wicked.' Despite her agitation, she noticed that Algy was eyeing her own nightgowned form rather too closely and wrapped her arms across her breasts. Mr Todd noticed too and ordered everyone to go and get dressed.

Making her way from the kitchen, a shivering Kit understood now what Lily had meant with her cryptic comment about Mrs Dolphin not buying the gas stove to cook on. Recalling Mr Todd's exclamation upon finding the victim, she tendered, 'The mistress's done it before then?'

'Oh aye, dozens o' times,' came the casual reply. 'We'll have to keep an eagle eye on her now till the start of the Season.'

This prediction proved to be correct, for Kit was to smell gas twice more until, thankfully, spring arrived and the Dolphin family, minus Tish, drove off for their London residence.

Bitterly disappointed not be taken with the other servants, Kit nevertheless found compensation in the lessening of her workload, this in turn granting time for other more interesting pursuits. Though strictly out of bounds the wondrous garden, hitherto experienced only from the kitchen window, was too great a lure for one with adventurous heart and Kit discovered a way of sneaking out there on her afternoons off. Parts of the garden were sectioned into rooms by stone wall, hedge and trellis, shielding her from any superior's prying eye and allowing her to avoid the army of gardeners who lurked within the grounds – for they paraded their territory like soldiers. So often did Kit dally here amongst the milk-white drifts of snowdrop and narcissus that she began to imagine that it was her own, resenting any sudden interruption of her happiness by means of a gardener's voice or an approaching footfall, for then she would be reminded that the garden belonged to someone else, and would have to make a rapid escape.

Kit's success in this field provoked other liberties. With no steward in the house, and the rest of the staff reduced in number, she was able to sneak unobserved into Mr Dolphin's library and browse to her heart's content. Most of the tomes were far beyond her capabilities, but many were not, and Kit took to borrowing one occasionally, spiriting it up to her room for half an hour's enjoyment before she went to sleep. Even more daring, the absence of both lady's maids meant that she was free to rummage through Mrs Dolphin and Miss Agnes's wardrobes and, although she could find no dress to fit her, there were feathered hats and beaded bags and silken shawls and stockings to play with.

Kit was like a child let loose in a toyshop, preening gleefully before the mirror, experimenting with tortoiseshell combs and diamante tiaras. If only there were someone other than herself to admire her.

Gazing wistfully at her own reflection one afternoon in April, an idea began to form. It was her afternoon off tomorrow. She was not due to go to Monty's but would only be enjoying a stroll. What harm would it do if she were to borrow one or two items just for an hour? It wasn't like stealing, she would return them unharmed, as she had done the books. No one would be any the wiser, for she would wait until she were well away from the house before putting them on. After the briefest moment of indecision Kit ripped off her apron, laid it flat and piled upon it a shawl, a bag and a hat, then swiftly wrapped them up in a bundle and hurried from the room. There was the briefest flash of fear as, in her dash along the corridor she encountered Tish, and she prayed he wouldn't follow her today. But he seemed preoccupied with other thoughts, allowing her to proceed via the back stairs to her own room, where she stowed the contraband under her bed. Heart fluttering, Kit gave a little laugh at her own audacity, then rushed off before anyone came to see where she had got to.

The trouble about getting away with things, thought Kit upon returning to the Hall after her first audacious outing, was that it made one even bolder, willing to take bigger risks. Alas, instead of listening to that inner warning voice, the borrowing became a regular habit; each time a different combination of hat, gloves and shawl. She even had the nerve to wear Mrs Dolphin's attire on a trip home to Monty's – which turned out to be a total waste of time as she had never been granted any admiration here, apart from that of the children.

Owen took one look at her green feathered hat and warned the gathering, 'Eh up, it's Robin Hood.'

After the initial jocular insults about their sister coming to rob the rich, and the protestations from Beata that she looked lovely, Owen returned to his more important task of gaining his brother's co-operation, putting forth an intelligent argument as to why Monty should join the union. Coal prices were falling drastically, there was talk of cuts in wages. Owen's intention to fight this move would inevitably lead to a lockout, whence everyone would suffer. At least if Monty was in the union he would receive strike pay. This monetary element gained him an unlikely ally in Sarah. Bit by bit, Monty's resistance dwindled. By the time the afternoon ended Owen's union had a new member.

Triumphant, the younger brother tried to consolidate his gains by telling Beata she should form a union amongst her female co-workers.

She gave a chesty laugh. 'Us lasses aren't interested in that!'

'No, that's why you're so exploited! Too busy wasting time on yer fancy hats.' Owen's complaint was directed more at Kit. 'If you women seriously want to get the vote you'll have to band together.'

'I'm not right bothered about getting t'vote.' Kit picked at a hangnail. 'I'd just like folk to know I'm capable of more than skivvying.'

'I thought you wanted to get married?' Sarah projected cynicism.

'Well, I don't consider it being a skivvy to look after one's husband,' opined Amelia, to whom marriage was still a novelty.

'You can still have a husband and children and have a brain as well,' reasoned Kit.

'Not round these parts,' rallied Sarah.

Kit was impatient with their grumblings. 'Who said I have to marry a collier?'

Owen rebuked her for this – was militantly proud of his class. 'There's nowt wrong with a man who gets his hands mucky. Never forget, the Lord was a working man.'

'Well, I say good luck to you.' It was a very rare occasion when Sarah was on Kit's side. 'I've told my girls, don't marry the first man who comes along, pay heed to your school books and get yourself out of this filthy hole.'

Monty frowned upon his wife's insistence on teaching their children that they were better than they really were, but what hurt even more was her implication that the home he provided was a filthy hole. 'I'm all for getting a good education, but it don't do to get above your station.' Once more Kit was placed under surveillance. Of all the people in this room, she showed the most ingratitude. Having sacrificed everything, it galled him to have to sit in his own house and hear this flibbertigibbet belittling his status. 'And let me tell 'ee, Miss High and Mighty, you can do a lot worse for yourself than a collier – ask Mrs Allen, ask all they other widows who sacrificed their men so that you and they nobs you admire so much can warm their bodies and cook their food. Where would you be without the likes of them?'

Owen too was annoyed. Every other collier he knew except Monty could expect support from his wife. Sarah could never seem to forget that she was the daughter of a deputy, thought she was a cut above anyone else. But his main accusation was for Kit. 'As if we don't have enough chucked at us from them flamin' newspapers, calling us from pigs to dogs, making out we get our brass for doing nowt –'

'I didn't mean to denigrate!' Kit showed contrition. 'I know you do a rough job –'

'And for what reward?' asked Owen. 'There's me and our lad up before dawn, home after dusk, in winter never seeing daylight, not knowing whether we're going to come out alive – not even knowing whether we'll get the same pay this week as last. Doesta think I wouldn't like to buy my wife some of them fancy clothes you've got on?'

Kit tried to disguise her look of guilt, anticipating the inevitable question.

'How can you afford them anyway?'

All eyes were on Kit. 'I can't . . . I borrowed them.'

It did not take much to work out from whom. Amelia clamped a hand to her mouth.

'My God, you'll have us hanged!' cried Sarah, all amity evaporating. 'Get them off right away and go back to your mansion!'

'Preferably in reverse order.' Owen managed a laugh of exasperation as his sister was chivvied from the house. 'We don't want to scare the hosses.'

'And don't you dare come here dressed like that again!' came Sarah's final volley.

Why do I bother? Kit asked herself on her dispirited journey back to her place of work. I might have known it would be a waste of time. Robin Hood indeed!

*   *   *

Despite this upset, a defiant Kit continued to borrow her employer's clothes throughout the spring and early summer – though she was careful not to parade them in her brother's house. Such displays of ostentation would be even less appreciated now, for almost immediately following her notable visit Owen's union had resisted a proposed reduction in wages and had been locked out. Now, in July, at Kit's latest call, they had been out for almost three months, their action replayed throughout the whole country as the mine owners sought to alleviate their own losses from the drastic drop in coal prices by reducing wages.

Kit donated a portion of her quarterly wages, remarking on the lack of enthusiasm this received.

Sarah explained the long faces. 'They're going back tomorrow.'

'Well, that's good isn't it?' asked Kit.

Her sister-in-law snorted. 'They're going back on the master's terms. What a waste of time it all was.'

Owen was sicker than most. Union funds had been milked almost dry. Men were asking what was the point of making these contributions and were threatening to leave. His elder brother was similarly inclined.

'How can a handful of men be expected to fight the masters?' asked Monty.

'I agree.' Owen fought his despondency. 'What we really need to do is unite all our separate unions.' He brought his hands together to form one fist. 'It's no good having a hundred here and a hundred there scattered about all over t'place – we have to form a national body.'

Kit groaned to herself and, having no wish to listen to such a conversation on her day off, gave Beata a nudge and cocked her head towards the door.

Beata rose. Other children jumped up too and, not wanting to miss out, asked where the pair of them were going. 'We're only off to t'farleymelow – can I have some paper, Dad?'

Monty reached for the wad of cut-up newspaper down by the side of his chair, first inspecting the printed squares for dubious material before handing four pieces over. None of his offspring was permitted to read the paper, the only bits of news they heard were those which he deemed suitable to be read aloud to them.

Kit and Beata went off to the privy. Beata wanted to know if Kit still borrowed Mrs Dolphin's accoutrements, and if so had they helped to attract any male attention?

'Yea and nay,' replied Kit. 'Yes, I am still borrowing them – I hid her hat and shawl behind t'pub before I came to your house.' She sniggered. 'I hope Marion hasn't found 'em! As for male attention,' she shook her head sadly, 'I've had nowt worth speaking of – but I live in hope.'

That hope was to be rewarded, for on Kit's journey back through the village which verged on Cragthorpe Hall, she was to find herself subject to the scrutiny she so desired. Glancing towards an old coaching inn she saw, through a window, a well-dressed young man in open admiration of her. Caught out, he immediately looked away and pretended to be admiring the view, but as a smiling Kit feigned to look straight ahead she could tell that his eyes had been drawn back to her. A quick look back over her shoulder provoked disappointment, for the face at the window had gone, but in the next instant she felt his presence again. He was walking up the lane behind her, struggling into a blue frock coat as if his departure had been made in haste.

Realizing that she was almost to her destination, Kit slowed to a snail's pace, allowing him to catch up. Soon they were walking at a level, though the strip of lane lay between them, he on one side, she on the other. The young man raised his top hat, though no word passed his lips. *Speak to me*, urged Kit, for the gates of Cragthorpe loomed to rob her of his presence. As encouragement she gave him a desperate sideways smile and drew to a halt outside the elaborate gates as if to say, 'I go this way.' Seemingly about to approach her, instead he merely doffed his hat again in awkward fashion and hurried on. Spirits plummeting, Kit watched his retreating back for a moment – and was heartened to see that he looked back over his shoulder, donating something resembling a smile.

Still under scrutiny, Kit was loath to abandon her ladylike air – could not possibly enter through the servants' entrance. Good sense giving way to impulse, she began her lofty approach to the house along the main driveway.

Only yards into her journey she was dismayed to spot a great deal of activity around the front entrance. The Dolphins had arrived from London!

Regretting her foolhardiness and in her panic abandoning all thought of the young man, Kit dived behind the nearest tree, darting from this to another and thence to a clump of shrubbery, trying to cross the expanse of parkland without being seen, scattering deer and peafowl before her.

Once inside the garden at the rear of the house she felt a little less exposed for she was on familiar ground now and, under cover of a series of stone walls and privet hedges, was able to make her way to the servants' entrance without being spotted, eventually to be safely ensconced in her proper place.

Her self-congratulation was short-lived, for there was no evading her peers who all gawked and gesticulated at her, at which point Kit realized to her dismay that in her frantic dash she had forgotten to remove the paisley shawl and feathered hat.

'You're in for it!' Lily took great delight in telling her. 'Mrs Dolphin saw you coming in by the front gate. Mrs Grunter's waiting for you in her parlour.'

'God, look at her fancy hat! You didn't buy that on your wage,' said Rosalind.

'What are you implying?' demanded Kit, at which the gaggle of kitchenmaids responded by giving each other knowing looks.

Taking off the borrowed apparel, Kit went reluctantly to the house-keeper's room, contemplating her inevitable dismissal and wondering where on earth she would go for a job next. With Monty and Sarah just getting back to financial stability after the lockout it was the worst possible time for this to happen. Added to the economical implication, loomed the vision of a humiliating departure in front of her peers, some of whom would take great delight in it. Even worse, it appeared she was to receive her notice in front of the entire family, its members gathered in the drawing room enjoying a reunion with Tish, who jumped from one to the other like an excited child.

The celebration became more subdued as the parlourmaid was brought before her master and mistress, though Wyndham and Everard shared a smirk at the comical contrast between the giant Kit and the diminutive Mrs Grunter.

'Well, this is a fine situation to greet us upon our return,' announced Mrs Dolphin, clearly revived by her spell in the capital, for her eyes were bright and her cheeks pink.

Kit bit her lip and looked at the carpet. 'Yes, ma'am.'

'You are obviously aware of your misdemeanour.' Mrs Dolphin inclined her lace-capped head as if to draw Kit's eyes to hers. 'One assumes you can supply an explanation for such audacity.'

'I'm sorry, ma'am,' offered Kit, her eyes darting briefly from the carpet, but only as far as the ruched skirt of her mistress's deep blue silk gown.

'I am grateful for your apology, Kit, but that is not an explanation. Presumably you have none to give?'

Thoroughly disgraced, Kit shook her head.

'You are fully conversant with the rules of this house?'

Kit gave murmured affirmation. Everyone's eyes were upon her, especially Wyndham's. At least she would no longer have to put up with his assaults.

'And yet you have just brazenly flouted one of them. I could scarcely believe my eyes upon seeing you on the main drive wearing the most unsuitable apparel!'

It was all Kit could do to keep a straight face. The mistress obviously did not recognize her own clothes! But this was no laughing matter; she was about to lose yet another job.

'All my coaching, all my good advice, did it count for nothing? How many times must I repeat myself?' Mrs Dolphin's next sentence was given great emphasis. 'It does not befit a maid to get above her station. Repeat the words that I may know you understand them, Kit.'

'It does not befit a maid to get above her station,' parroted Kit.

'Again!'

Kit repeated the adage several times before the mistress appeared to be satisfied.

'And will you similarly adorn yourself again?'

'No, ma'am.'

'And will you commit further trespass upon zones which are forbidden to you?'

'No, ma'am.'

'Very well, that is an end to your chastisement.' Throughout, Mrs Dolphin's hands had remained folded upon her silken lap, but now she raised a finger as if reconsidering her last statement. 'Apart from to say that you will sacrifice your next two afternoons off. You may consider yourself very fortunate that I am not disposed to waste such a beautiful day on irrelevant issues.'

Glancing momentarily at Mr Dolphin in his tweed suit, Kit noticed a slight flare to his nostrils – why, his wife's inability to pronounce this word annoyed him too! Feeling his glare as he realized that a servant shared his observation of his wife's stupidity, Kit looked away.

Oblivious, Mrs Dolphin continued, 'Mrs Grunter, you may tell Cook that we shall take an early dinner, thank you. The master and I will be going out this evening.'

Given leave to remove her presence, Kit made a chastened exit, but could scarcely believe her luck. 'So, I'm not being dismissed?' she asked the housekeeper on their way back to the servants' quarters.

'Not today!' Little Mrs Grunter barged through the demarcation door, passing briskly from Persian carpet to linoleum. 'But you are very, very lucky, my girl, and if ever I catch you –'

'Oh, you won't, Mrs Grunter. I humbly beg your pardon!'

Mrs Grunter issued additional severe warning for Kit to let nothing like this happen again and to pack away the unsuitable clothes. With this she went into her own parlour and closed the door.

Applauding her own luck – not only did she keep her job but could keep the hat and shawl too, for she would be unable to return them without admitting borrowing them – Kit could not prevent a grin from forming as she returned to the servants' hall.

'Leaving today, are we?' smirked Rosalind, and when Kit retorted that she had not been dismissed, she added, 'Well, you soon will be.'

Kit looked enquiringly at other faces, her eyes falling on Mrs Dolphin's personal maid, who was holding out the hat and shawl accusingly.

'I'm certain the mistress wouldn't have been so charitable had she been aware that it was her clothes you were wearing!'

Kit's heart skipped a beat. 'Please don't tell her!'

The lady's maid pursed her lips, hesitating.

'Well, I would!' said Rosalind.

'Don't be so bloody mean,' accused Algy, and was reprimanded for his swearing.

Smarting under her paramour's scorn, Rosalind remained tight-lipped though her face adopted an angry flush.

After much deliberation the lady's maid said she would not give Kit away but if ever the parlourmaid dared to touch the mistress's clothes again she would have no hesitation in having her dismissed. So saying, she removed Kit's prizes to their rightful place.

'You've got the luck of the devil, you have!' Algy gave an admiring laugh after the lady's maid had gone. 'Any of us'd come waltzing down the front path wearing the mistress's clothes we'd've been a gonner.'

'You'd have been arrested,' corrected Rosalind, jealous at his veneration of Kit.

'We-ell!' Kit defended herself before her audience. 'if Mrs Dolphin didn't even realize I was wearing her clothes, she must have too many of 'em, that's all I can say.'

With her employer's family once again in situ, Kit re-embarked on a timetable of drudgery and, robbed of her next two free afternoons, there was no chance of meeting her young admirer again. It was so terribly disappointing. She did search for him, as she passed through the village on her next Sunday visit home – clad in her own decorous bonnet – eagerly craning her neck into every nook, but never once did she set eyes on him.

Kit held the fervent wish that the same could be said of Master Wyndham, whose lascivious attentions continued despite all protest. If anything, the attainment of his sixteenth birthday had made him bolder than ever. Unable to avoid him, for Ivy, as senior parlourmaid, gave the order as to who went where, and unable to complain to a higher office for she would be accused of lying, Kit was forced to lean on her own devices which, in effect, were few. To 'inadvertently' forget Wyndham's morning tea was to receive reprimand from the mistress and Kit had had too many of those to risk more. Besides, Wyndham had started to maul her at any time of day now. Her only solution was to keep out of his way as much as possible, the most trustworthy method being to get out of the house altogether.

If Kit had learned her lesson about borrowing her superior's clothes, this did not extend to her infringement of other rules and she proceeded to make her illicit jaunts into the garden, a heavenly place where an oppressed parlourmaid could find a moment's solace before returning to the treadmill.

The particular corner into which she had strayed this afternoon had been formed into a grotto using weathered stone from an ancient ruin.

Coated in moss and lichen, it appeared to have been standing here much longer than the house – had an almost magical quality about it, opined Kit, as her eyes roamed beyond the sun-dappled rambling roses and erect spires of pink foxgloves to its mysterious fern-filled crevasses. Under its spell, she allowed herself to be lured inside. Wandering across a spongy patch of grass she sat down upon a stone bench, cushioned from its hard surface by a blanket of greenery. Crushed beneath the weight of her body, the foliage emitted a pungent scent. Arranging the skirt of her lilac cotton print dress, Kit gazed dreamily around her, then gave a sudden sigh at the collection of grey weathered faces that peered at her through leafy tendrils – was there nowhere to escape surveillance? Under their combined stony glare, she began to feel uneasy. To linger in this sanctuary for too long, one could almost imagine the statues coming to life. Damning her imagination, Kit leaned back upon the moss-covered seat and closed her eyes, listening to the humming of bees, the trill of a robin from an ivy covered pillar. The air was very hot and still and heavy with the scent of roses. The August sun sat low in the sky, appearing to be balanced atop the wall of her hideaway, the heat of it burning her eyelids. For a long time Kit relaxed, enjoying the thoughts that wafted in and out of her brain, emerging from them occasionally to wonder what time it was.

In danger of falling asleep, she roused herself and made the decision to go back to her work. About to rise, she heard voices approaching, and their owners were quite close, it seemed, on the other side of the wall. The grotto had two entrances – or at least Kit had supposed, but when she ran up some steps and under the stone archway she discovered that that path actually led nowhere. She was trapped.

Protected to some extent by the shady interior and the copious filaments of ivy that draped the archway, she tried to draw the greenery across the gap like a curtain, and it partly obliged, although the disturbance of it evicted hundreds of insects, which began to crawl all over her and inside her clothes. The cool interior smelled of damp stone and earth.

There was boyish laughter. Kit recognized it immediately. Master Wyndham had invited two schoolfriends to stay for part of the holidays. There was also some kind of teasing afoot. Everard would be going away to Rugby at the end of the summer and Wyndham seemed determined to get him acclimatized in advance of the ordeal.

'Fag!'

Trying to rid herself of the pestering insects, swiping and scratching and brushing at her clothes, Kit heard the order barked several times, the running of feet, the stricture that the younger boy was not quick enough, then the order for him to do it again – and again, and again

'Fag!' The yell was accompanied by the sniggering laughter of the perpetrators. 'Fag!'

Still under onslaught from insects, Kit grew more and more annoyed. She had had little relationship with Everard but the sound of any child being tormented until he burst into tears and then to be mocked for being a cissy had the power to enrage her. Without concern for her own dilemma, she charged through the living curtain to confront the gang.

'You mean little devils!'

The youths screamed in girlish fashion at the huge figure that descended upon them and had begun to flee until Wyndham saw that it was only a servant and marched back to challenge her.

'You wouldn't say that if my parents were around!' His pudgy face was scarlet at being made to look a fool before his friends.

'And neither would you do the things you do if your parents were around!' retorted Kit, deference overridden by anger.

Wyndham knew exactly what Kit referred to. His face donned a sneer as he looked up at her – for she was a good head and shoulders taller. 'Playing with your bosoms? Father wouldn't mind at all. He probably sent you for me to practise on.' His two friends and Everard stood open-mouthed at Wyndham's offer. 'You can touch her up too, if you like. She can't say anything or she'll be sacked.'

Kit gasped with fury and humiliation. 'I don't care if you do get me sacked, I won't stand by and see a little boy treated so cruelly and I won't be treated like dirt!'

Wyndham's reply was arrogant. 'Why, you are dirt.'

'Pack it in, Dolphin!' One of the other boys came forward now, his initial shock overcome by an air of authority. 'That was inexcusably rude.'

'She's only a servant, Postgate!' Wyndham seemed taken aback. His brother Tish who had tagged along but was afraid of the angry shouting, had half hidden himself behind a wall.

'All the more reason to set a good example.' Postgate was relentless. Despite the habit he had of scrunching his eyes up from time to time, in the manner of a cat, it was obviously not an indication of nerves, for he was more of a lion than a tabby. 'Apologize at once or I'm afraid I'm going to have to thrash you.'

Wyndham had never understood his friend's attitude. Most of the other boys in his house at school treated the lower orders as an inferior race, drew great enjoyment from poking fun at the yokels, but not Postgate. Yet, there were many more important aspects to this young man which Wyndham did respect and, chary of losing his friendship, he backed down from his stance.

'I thought she liked it,' he mumbled as if Kit were not present. 'She didn't order me to stop.'

'How can I order you to do anything?' demanded a red-faced Kit, who had pulled out a handkerchief and was twisting it nervously through her hands. 'You're my employer's son, you just said yourself I'd lose my job if I kicked up a fuss – but seeing as you're probably gonna get me dismissed anyway, I might as well go the whole hog and tell you that I *don't* like it! I don't like it at all and I want it to stop, if you please!' She was close to tears. Alarmed, the half-hidden Tish hopped from foot to foot, moaning.

Once again Postgate stepped in. 'Do the decent thing, old chap.' His voice forbade argument. 'Show a little house spirit. I'm sure your father wouldn't really like it if he knew.'

Afraid of bringing retribution upon himself if the truth came out, and not wishing to jeopardize this important friendship, Wyndham muttered an apology and said he would not do it again, his eyes flickering only briefly to the parlourmaid's face as if it were abhorrent to him.

Still plucking at the handkerchief Kit thanked him, but sought to take advantage of the other boy's obvious influence. 'And could I impose upon you not to let on to anyone you found me in the garden?'

'Your secret is safe with us.' The young lion was first to respond, consulting Wyndham, who gave a sullen nod, then the other boy, who gave more eager affirmation. Kit noticed that the latter was much taller than the other two, though built like a beanpole and rather stooped, having the appearance of a sapling under assault from a breeze.

Last to be consulted was Everard, who refused to promise that he would not tell.

'You little sneak!' accused Postgate. 'After – what's your name?' He spun swiftly on Kit, who provided her name. 'After Kit risked her honour to save you!'

'I don't need a woman to save me!' Everard was furious at hearing himself dubbed a little boy by Kit. 'I may tell, I may not.' Before anyone could catch him he ran off. Infected by panic, Tish followed.

'Oh, leave the little squirt!' Wyndham fell into a heap on the mossy grass and pretended to be bored with the whole matter. 'He won't say anything. At least we've got rid of Tish.'

'Is he likely to rat?' enquired Postgate, one eye blinking.

Wyndham gave a sound of mirth. 'Nobody listens to the poor idiot anyway. God, it's hot!'

Disregarding their smart attire, Postgate and the beanpole fell down beside him. Kit was about to sneak away when she heard Wyndham's sly utterance, 'Of course I didn't promise not to tell about her borrowing father's books.'

Kit wheeled around, mouth agape, her trepidation resurrected.

'Beware the all-seeing one!' mocked Wyndham.

But Postgate knew his friend a lot better than Kit. 'He's having you on – Dolphin, you blighter!' and he fell on the other, landing playful punches to all parts of his body, the beanpole joining in and the three of them rolling around on the ground, not like gentlemen, thought an amazed Kit, but like street arabs. Unsure of her position, she hovered there for instruction.

After sating their high spirits, the three youths emerged from their tussle with laughing faces, starched collars smudged with dirt and all memory of previous antagonism wiped away.

'God knows what she wants with a book like that anyway!' It was not said spitefully, Wyndham was in better humour now. 'It's not likely she'll ever get to travel.'

'No, but I like to learn about other countries,' objected Kit. 'It's all right for you, sir, who probably learn all about it at your fine school –'

'Geography!' Wyndham was contemptuous. 'That's just for squirts in Prep.'

Kit wanted to retort what exactly did they learn, but was too in awe of the young gentlemen even though they were three years her junior. The Postgate one was rather nice – she wondered what on earth he found in common with Wyndham. Anxious to learn whether or not the latter was serious about betraying her, she hovered, twisting the handkerchief round and round one finger.

The boys studied her. What a sight I must look, thought Kit, insects and bits of greenery infesting her auburn hair. A fit of whispering and giggling ensued, drawing a crimson flush to her cheeks. Embarrassment, combined with the heat of the afternoon, occasioned damp patches to appear under the arms of her printed cotton dress.

'This is most impolite,' laughed Postgate and sought to spare Kit's discomfort by telling her, 'I do beg your pardon, but my friend Denaby seems most taken with you.'

'Postgate!' The blushing beanpole punched the other on the arm, sparking another bout of wrestling.

Kit too blushed, unravelling the handkerchief and twisting it round her finger again, raising her voice above the hullabaloo. 'If you please, sir, may I leave?'

'Of course, off you go!' The obvious leader of the trio grinned at her in friendly manner, his eyes performing their leisurely feline blink. 'And have no concern, we won't divulge your little secret.'

Kit showed gratitude. 'Thank you Master Po–, Po –'

For some reason Wyndham found her stammering reply incredibly funny and rolled around on the floor, amusing his colleagues. 'Po-po!'

Increasingly humiliated, Kit was forced to explain, 'I'm sorry, I didn't catch your name, sir!'

'Pay no heed to these jackasses, Kit.' The youth jumped to his feet and beheld her kindly. 'My name is Ossie Postgate – and may I suggest you make good your escape before my oafish friend blames you for giving him an apoplectic stroke?'

To another hoot of laughter from Wyndham, Kit fled, leaving behind the sounds of renewed wrestling.

Try as she might to compose herself, the episode had left Kit highly ruffled and her reappearance in the servants' quarters provoked interested comment.

'Where the devil have you been?' demanded a cross Ivy. 'You said you were going to fetch new linen and that was over half an hour ago!' Reaching up, she picked at a strand of greenery that Kit had overlooked in her auburn hair. 'Went to look for it in the hedge bottom, did you?'

'Sorry, I got waylaid by the mistress on my way down the corridor.

She told me to change the flowers in the drawing room so I had to go get some from the gardener.'

Ivy remained suspicious. Kit was always sloping off, trying to dodge work. 'That's not your job – and it didn't take you half an hour.'

'No, but I had to wait ages for him to cut some. You know what these gardeners're like, won't let you touch anything. Then on my way back I ran into Master Wyndham and his friends –'

'Oh, now it's all coming out!' jeered Rosalind. 'I thought there'd be a man involved.'

'You speak for yourself,' scolded Kit. 'Master Wyndham just asked me to fetch some cordial for him and Master Ossie and – the other one whatever his name is.'

'Master Ossie?' Cook gave a quizzical frown.

Having invented the elaborate lie Kit now had to follow through, and bustled about collecting tumblers. 'Yes, you know, that fair-haired boy with the rosy cheeks – not the tall one, the other one. Nice boy.'

Lily's bulldog jaw emitted a gasp of outraged laughter. 'She means Viscount Postgate!'

At the unified splutter of mirth Kit stopped in her tracks.

'Master Ossie indeed, nice boy indeed – his father's the Earl of Garborough, I'll have you know!' Whilst others guffawed, Cook performed a weary shake of head. 'What next? Is no man safe from her designs?'

Kit tried to explain that it had been merely an observation, he was a nice boy, how was she to know he was a viscount?

Rosalind sought to warn her. 'Well, don't think you can get your claws into this one. He's been earmarked for Miss Agnes.'

The next morning Kit delivered tea to the young guests' rooms, leaving Master Wyndham's until last, as was her usual habit. Both boys were drowsy, allowing her to make good her escape before they realized that it was the girl from the garden and thus place her in a humiliating position. Anticipating the usual assault, she finally delivered Wyndham's tea, but to her relief nothing happened. He did not even bother to open his eyes. Expecting some kind of trick – that he would leap up at her at the last minute – she could hardly believe that he had allowed her to escape unscathed.

Similarly, her forays into the house, which previously would have met with Wyndham's groping, today went unimpeded. Greatly unburdened, Kit would have liked to reissue thanks to Ossie Postgate – for in her eyes he would be for ever thus – but in the knowledge that he was a viscount, it was improbable that she would make social contact with him again.

The day went as had any other day before it. For the most part of it Kit evaded work as best she could, then went to bed.

The moment she entered her room she was aware of a presence hiding behind the door. Encountering Wyndham she gave a sharp inhalation and tried to run but he grabbed her, wrapping both arms around her and pinioning her own arms so that she could not strike out at him.

'Shut up!' Seeing she was about to scream he hissed at her, 'Shut up, you stupid bitch!'

'You shouldn't be in here!' Dancing around trying to dislodge him, Kit twisted this way and that, envisioning some horrible assault upon her person.

'I can go anywhere I like, it's my house!' Wyndham grimaced, trying to hang on to her but she was much bigger than he and in her struggles eventually toppled over, bringing his weight down on top of her and knocking the breath from both of them.

Eyes wide, Kit fought to inhale. Being the first to recover she tried to push him off and clamber to her feet but Wyndham struggled to remain on top of her, himself gasping for breath.

'Agh, you stupid slut, I think you've broken my arm!'

'You promised you'd never touch me again!' she tearfully accused, all the while trying to push him off. 'If this is what a gentleman's word is worth –'

'For pity's sake!' Wyndham staggered to his feet and closed the door, trapping her. 'Keep your voice down! I only came to deliver a message!'

Breast rising and falling, Kit jumped to her feet and pulled her clothes to order. 'What is it?'

'It might have been easier to ask that before you inflicted these injuries – my God, I'm certain you've broken my arm!' He grimaced and examined it.

'Please, Master Wyndham, you shouldn't be in here! I beg you go before anyone comes.' Kit's agitation gave way to a frown. 'How did you know it was my room anyway?'

'I make it my business to know.' Wyndham turned smug. 'Come here all the time, as a matter of fact, just to keep an eye on things, you know. Oh, if only Father could see the selection of books from his library that have made their way here.'

'I always put 'em back though! Anyway, what message is so important that you have to wait till this hour to deliver it?'

'I'll tell Denaby you have no wish to meet him then, shall I?'

Kit's heart fluttered even faster. Her mouth fell open. 'What does a gentleman want with me?'

'A question I have asked myself,' came Wyndham's rude reply.

Kit had an awful thought. 'If he's hoping to take liberties like you did –'

'Do you wish to meet Denaby or don't you?' Suddenly impatient, Wyndham pushed his hair straight with his uninjured arm.

'Yes, I do!' How could Kit miss such an opportunity, dangerous or no?

Wyndham turned on his heel. 'Very well, be in the grotto where you saw us last, at four tomorrow.'

'But I might not be able to sneak out!'

'Then hard luck! Heaven knows what he sees in you anyway.' Wyndham left.

Her bosom fizzing with excitement, Kit slumped on the bed. Could it really be that she had an admirer? The very thought made her breathless. Spirits dancing, she cast her mind back, remembering Ossie Postgate's teasing statement that Denaby seemed most taken with her. Apart from the vague impression of a dark-haired beanpole, it was hard to recall his looks in detail – but then it did not really matter what he looked like. This would be Kit's first romantic assignation! Oh, how she wanted to run and tell someone. But who would believe her?

Only after a long, imaginative interlude did she eventually change into her night attire, knowing as she climbed into bed that she would never sleep a wink.

10

The lack of sleep proved a terrible hindrance. Throughout the day Kit
received constant reprimand for her lackadaisical efforts, though it had
little effect on her performance, what energy she had being focused on
getting to her rendezvous on time.

Counting to five, she sneaked out through a door in the main house, and
pelted as light-footedly as possible across a narrow strip of gravel, leaping
for the cover of bushes before anyone detected so much as a crunch. The
day was fine and hot. Adhering to the labyrinth of honeysuckled walls
and laurel hedges she hurried to her trysting place, bundling up her
apron along the way and shoving it under a hedge, all the while casting
apprehensive glances about her, for to be caught today of all days would
be disaster.

The grotto was empty when she arrived – but not for long. No sooner
had Kit let out a sigh of disappointment than Denaby appeared as if by
magic, a blushing beanpole who whipped off his straw hat and extended
his hand to greet her. 'How do you do?'

'Mr Denaby!' It seemed inappropriate to call him master, for his
height made him appear older than he was. A gushing Kit accepted
his handshake, the contact with his bare flesh reminding her of her own
inelegance. She should have worn gloves.

Equal in height, the youth smiled into her face for long unsettling
moments, then indicated the bench and blurted, 'Do sit down!'

Kit sat beside him, hands folded demurely on her lap. After which, a
long silence ensued, the couple merely turning to snatch the occasional
smile. An invading bumble bee droned amongst the foxgloves, his buzzing
intermittent as he bumbled from one flower to the next. For a moment
there was complete hush as he landed to investigate the pink mottled

interior of a bell, only his furry rump protruding. Then once again the sound of his vibrating wings punctuated the silence. After a full five minutes had elapsed, Kit began to worry that she would be forced to return to work and nothing had yet been said. The concern showed on her face.

Though only sixteen, it was not lack of confidence that stilted Denaby's tongue but lack of practice. This he sought to explain to Kit, turning awkwardly towards her in his stiff collar, his straw hat balanced on his knee. 'I'm afraid you may find this very silly, but this is the first opportunity I've had to be alone with a female companion and I'm not quite sure how to entertain you. You may find my conversation very boring.'

'No, of course I won't!' Kit reassured him. 'I've been really looking forward to meeting you.'

'Have you?' Immediately, Denaby laid his hat to one side and showed great attentiveness. 'Why?'

This response unanticipated, Kit looked taken aback. She shrugged. 'Well, because – you being a gentleman, like –'

It was the wrong answer to give. Denaby looked somewhat crestfallen. 'Would I be unappealing if I were of a lesser station?'

'Oh, I didn't mean to offend you, Mr Denaby!' Kit was anxious to put things right. 'I just meant what could a gentleman possibly see in me?'

He seemed pacified. 'I beg you, don't demean yourself! You're the prettiest girl I've ever met.'

Kit's heart leaped, yet unaccustomed to such compliments she almost ruined it with a jest. 'I'm probably the only girl you've met that's been tall enough for you.'

Denaby was sensitive about his height and her comment brought a flush to his cheeks. Kit grew alarmed as the rendezvous came close to ending in disaster and tried to salve things with an explanation. 'My family are always making jokes at me!'

'Are they really?' Denaby looked relieved. 'Mine too – and the fellows at school.' In fact he had suffered greatly at their hands, which accounted for his stooped posture, a practice which in fact drew more attention to himself.

'But it's fine to be tall if you're a man.' cried Kit. 'The taller the better

– but girls are expected to be dainty and I'm afraid I've never been that, or so I'm told.'

'Oh, who cares what others think?' Denaby smiled.

Kit noticed that his teeth were somewhat crooked, and that his eyes were the same shade of brown as his hair. Enthralled by his enthusiastic grin she decided there and then that even if he were not the most handsome of men she was in love with him.

'That's what I always say!' she told him, and the two of them gazed into each other's eyes for a time, before Kit said she could not stay for very much longer as she must return to her work.

He entreated her to remain, grabbing hold of her hand as if to keep her here. Heart fluttering, Kit said she must go or she'd invoke another castigation – she had been getting them all day.

Reluctantly he released her. 'Go if you must. I should hate to get you into trouble.'

There was spluttered laughter. Immediately Denaby sprang up and called out, 'Who's there? Dolphin, you beast, show yourself!'

Found out, Wyndham, Tish and Ossie Postgate emerged from their hiding place behind the wall, only one of them shamefaced.

'Postgate, I'm surprised at you!' accused Kit's companion, whilst she too stood and glared at them.

'Sorry, old chap!' Ossie's apology was genuine. 'It was this one.' He indicated Wyndham. 'He's so ignorant of how to behave in female company that he sought to take an example from you. I shall drag him away forthwith. Do excuse this intrusion, Kit. We won't bother you again, I give you my word.' And he piloted the others away.

Kit felt her afternoon rather spoiled and it showed on her face. 'I really have to go too, Mr Denaby.'

He gave a heavy sigh. 'Very well – but we must arrange to spend a much longer period together.' Warming to this idea, he added, 'Every day if possible.'

Kit cheered up. 'Oh, I'd dearly love to, but I couldn't possibly get away at a regular hour. And I'm also not keen on Master Wyndham fetching messages to my room.'

'Nor am I,' agreed Denaby. 'I don't want any other man to come near you.' And he planted an impulsive kiss on her lips.

Taken by surprise, Kit experienced a sudden influx of warmth as if hot syrup surged into every vein of her body. More surprising was that he smelled no different from any working man.

It was over as unexpectedly as it had started. Denaby's lips were now drawn back in a grin, seemingly as pleased with himself as he was with her. 'Will I see you again tomorrow?' Told that Kit would probably be bringing his morning tea, he showed delight. 'Wonderful! I shall look forward to it so much.'

She beheld him cautiously, wondering if he sought to imitate Wyndham's example. 'But it wouldn't be proper for me to stay long.'

'Oh, I totally agree.' Then he sensed her true reservation. 'You don't seriously think I would treat you so badly as Wyndham? Oh, I beg you –'

'No! I know you're much more of a gentleman than Master Wyndham. I was merely telling you not to expect me to stay long, as my services'll be required in the dining room.'

'Then can we arrange to meet here again tomorrow, same time?' He begged. 'Oh, say you will!'

'But what if I can't get away? I'd hate to think of you standing here alone, thinking I've deserted you – and then how would I know when I'd see you again?' Kit's response showed him that it really mattered.

'I know! If you're not here I'll write you a letter and leave it tucked in one of these crannies – this one!' Denaby bent and inserted his fingers into a gap between two of the slabs that supported the bench. 'Then when you can escape you must come and collect it and leave your reply in its stead.'

Kit dubbed this a splendidly romantic idea. 'And I can definitely meet you on my afternoon off!' She held him with her excited gaze for a moment, her clear blue eyes reflecting the sky, before crying, 'Oh, Mr Denaby I really must go now – no, you must bide here a while!' He had been about to accompany her. 'It wouldn't do for anyone else to see us together.'

He nodded and went with her only as far as the ivy-clad entrance to the bower. 'I detest letting you go.'

'So do I!' Kit had one last question to ask, turning rather awkward again. 'If I have to send you a letter, who do I address it to?'

He looked perplexed, then realized that she was asking for his Christian name. 'Oh! How silly of me, it's so rarely used that I'd almost forgotten. It's Thomas.'

Satisfied, Kit held out her hand. 'That's a nice name. Goodbye then, Thomas. Ooh, it feels very strange addressing a gentleman like that!'

The youth was unwilling to relinquish his hold on her. 'Don't think of it like that, I beg you. We are just Tom and Kit.' Planting another brief kiss on her cheek he finally allowed her to leave.

Kit scurried back to work, wondering if anyone would comment upon the heightened colour she could feel in her face.

As luck would have it, she did manage to keep their next tryst, rushing to it as eagerly as did Thomas. This time, the conversation not so hesitant, she was to find out much more about him. Whilst Kit would have preferred to spend the whole time hugging and kissing, it was not the done thing for a girl to initiate proceedings, and she must content herself with being fed snippets of information, which were in fact very interesting. Not only did he and Wyndham go to the same school, but Thomas's father was a very important man in the commercial world, being the owner of the famous pickle company where Kit had once worked, though she did not tell him this, and in addition was friends with Mr Dolphin – which meant that the future between Thomas and Kit looked promising, for he had every excuse to make a visit.

Kit expressed pleasure, then asked were both men acquainted with Ossie's father too?

Thomas seemed put out. 'Ossie?'

She blushed, assuming she was being censured for the lack of respect. 'I mean Viscount Postgate.'

'I know who you mean! What's your interest in him?'

Kit was alarmed at his response. 'Well, only that he saved my bacon from Wyndham –'

'I wouldn't have allowed Dolphin to harm you, you know!'

'I'm sure you wouldn't!'

'Just because his father is an earl . . .'

Ah, so that was it! Understanding that Thomas thought she was using him as a stepping stone, she tried to appease. 'I don't care who his father is, you're the one I love.'

This was sufficient to mend the fracture. 'Do you really?'

'Yes!' She wrapped tender arms about him. 'Don't let's fall out.'

Fighting his inhibited emotions, he embraced her awkwardly. 'We won't! I was just being an ass. Forgive me!'

With Kit's forgiveness came another kiss, then an even more encouraging event.

'I love you too – desperately!' His face was earnest. 'Will you marry me?'

Even whilst recognizing that his impulsiveness was sparked by youth, Kit was not about to spurn such an offer, could already picture herself with his babies. 'Oh yes, Tom! But are you old enough?'

Again her thoughtlessness over the difference in their ages upset him. 'I soon will be!'

'Then I will!' What would her family have to say now, thought a gleeful Kit!

Denaby looked rather overwhelmed. 'Oh gosh, isn't it exciting! Does this mean we're betrothed?'

Kit said it must do, and pressed his thin body to her bosom, hardly able to believe that in the space of two days she had embarked upon the path to realizing her dream. 'Of course, we can't tell anyone yet – there'd be such trouble!'

'I don't care!' Learning from her example, Thomas returned the hug with enthusiasm.

'Neither do I! But your parents might want you to finish your education.'

'I rather think they might – though I shall refuse to go on to university.'

Kit sighed and told him how clever he was. 'It would be such a shame to waste such good schooling. I wish I were brainy.' She told him, though he knew already, about the books she borrowed from Mr Dolphin's library. 'I so love reading but I've had no proper education, you see, and I can't understand a lot of what's in them. A couple of bits especially I want to know more about. If I bring them out with me next time, could you help me with them? I did think about taking them home to ask our Owen to explain, but he's such a know-all he'd end up making me feel more stupid than ever and anyway, I might get caught sneaking them out.'

Thomas said he would be happy to assist. 'Now, enough talk of education! I've got two months before I go back, and two whole weeks here to spend with you! Here I am offering marriage and all you want is to talk about books!'

Assuring him she didn't, Kit displaced further conversation with a lengthy kiss.

There was to be bitter disappointment at their next arranged rendezvous, for with Kit unavoidably detained a good hour in the servants' quarters, Thomas had grown tired of waiting and had gone. He had, however, left her a note. Kit prised the scrap of paper from its dark cranny and read it excitedly – her first love letter! In actual fact its main purpose was to tell her that Thomas would wait here at the same time next day, but as it was signed 'Your passionate admirer', Kit felt entitled to adjudge it a billet-doux and thus held it between her mountainous breasts, yearning for tomorrow to come quickly.

Over the next fortnight the sweethearts continued to meet sporadically, countless letters passing between them, each more florid than the last, both writers hopelessly infatuated. Up until now, Kit's enquiries over Mr Dolphin's books had gone unanswered, but today, as it was her afternoon off, she felt less compelled to rush and was able to bring the chosen books along.

After their initial passionate embrace, she sat down on the bench close to Thomas, pulling a small brown leather volume from the side pocket of her dress. 'This is one of the books I'd like you to look at and tell me – oh, don't snatch!'

'What are we wasting time with this for?' Thomas riffled the pages. 'Anyway, we hardly touch on English History. If it were Greece or Rome you wanted to know about –'

'Oh, tell me about that then!' begged Kit, eager for a glimpse of foreign parts. 'I'd love to go to either of those places.'

'I'll take you one day, but I'm afraid my knowledge is limited to the ancient world, and that's rather a dry topic for a sunny afternoon.' He put the book aside and lunged for her.

'Hang on!' Avoiding him, Kit pulled out the second book and, opening it at a marker, pointed at the page. 'This is a really good story but there's a few bits I don't understand – such as this line here.'

Thomas pretended to study the page, and made an effort to enlighten her, but it was evident from his manner that he would rather concentrate on Kit's voluptuous curves. 'Your guess is as good as mine. I'm afraid we do very little English Literature either.'

Irked by his obvious lack of interest, Kit grabbed the book off him, wanting to know, 'What exactly *do* you do at that swanky school?'

Thomas ceased his attempts to nuzzle her neck and reflected her annoyance. 'You wouldn't be any the wiser if I told you. What's the matter with you today? I thought you loved me.'

'I do! And I love to kiss and cuddle too, but nice though that is it isn't all I want to do.'

Thomas was about to demand what more could there be, but the look on Kit's face told him he had better show some respect. Trying to explain an exclusively intellectual education to someone of her humble station was virtually impossible, but in order to find common ground the young scholar tried to bring himself down to her level. 'Very well, you want to know what I do all day? Classics, Classics, Classics – and I'm hopeless at that too. There, see what a dunce you've chosen? I would have had to drop out last year, were I not in the team.'

'Team?'

'Football,' came his succinct reply. 'I'm not bad at cricket too, though I say so myself.'

Kit displayed astonishment. 'Do you mean to tell me your father pays good money for you to play games all day?'

Thomas had the grace to laugh at himself. 'That's what it sounds like, I know.'

His companion continued to be amazed. 'You *must* do Mathematics?'

'Mm, yes, and a few foreign languages. Or rather, I do French but not German any more. I opted to do Science instead – the last refuge of an incompetent!' The latter part was delivered in brilliant imitation of his housemaster, but as Kit didn't know the man concerned this fell flat.

'Oh, say something to me in French!' she begged.

'I couldn't possibly!' Thomas said that it was never spoken, only taught by means of grammar and translation.

Frustrated, Kit asked, 'What exactly is Classics?'

He tried not to sound too stuffy. 'Well, Latin and Greek, the translation and grammar of such texts, composition – you know, all that sort of thing relating to the ancient world.'

Kit thought she knew. 'Oh, you mean like the Cyclops and the Golden Fleece? Why, we read that when we were seven!'

Thomas gave a rather patronizing smile. 'Though not in its original form, I doubt.'

Kit shrugged. 'What about music?' This was another of her loves.

'We're only allowed to do that in our free time and I don't care to.'

Kit regarded this as a wasted privilege. 'You must have bags of free time from what you've told me! Are your friends similarly disposed?'

'Postgate manages to find time for piano lessons in between football practices – but then he needs so little practice. He's a magnificent sportsman, that's why he's Head of House even though he isn't in the Sixth yet. And he can lick anyone in the school. I wish I were as popular.'

Kit didn't understand the terms he used. 'I can't see Master Wyndham being that popular.'

Thomas gave an oblique smile. 'I'll grant he does fancy himself as a bit of a swell, but he's good fun.'

'Usually at someone else's expense,' muttered Kit.

Thomas regarded this as an opportunity to mention something. Reaching an arm over the back of the bench he took the velvety grey leaf of a foxglove between finger and thumb and began to caress it thoughtfully. 'By the by, he's got his hackles up about me seeing so much of you.' In actual fact Wyndham had told him that he hadn't brought his friend here to be Kit's companion and if all he wanted to do was canoodle with the maids he may as well go home. 'He says . . .' there was hesitation in Thomas's voice '. . .if I don't spend my last day here with him and Postgate he won't invite me again.'

Kit started. 'You mean this'll be our last meeting?'

'Only until I come at Christmas!' The abrupt removal of his grip on the leaf quaked the entire plant, releasing a shower of pollen. 'If I do as he wants now we stand a good chance of being able to see each other in the holidays. We don't want to funk it. I'm afraid I won't even be able to get away to leave a letter or he'll accuse me of letting the house down.'

'But you'll write while you're away?' entreated Kit.

'I fancy not, our letters are occasionally vetted – but be assured I'll be thinking of you all the time and the moment I'm able I'll arrange to see you. In the meantime,' Thomas added, taking her in his arms, 'we must make the most of this afternoon.'

Kit could not recall such pain as that experienced after Thomas's departure, the worst of it being that there was no one with whom she could share it. A Sunday visit home provided some relief in the form of dear Beata, who would listen and, at the right moment, congratulate or sympathize. But their get-togethers were few and far between, and besides, it was not Beata Kit wanted to see.

The summer dragged by, made worse by Master Wyndham's presence, for each time Kit set eyes upon him she was reminded of his friend. Apart from the delivery of morning tea there was scant contact between them now. Unlike his classmate, Wyndham found no interest in Kit other than to use at whim. Fortunately this did not mean a repeat of his molestation of her. He had obviously been warned off by Thomas.

At long last the time came for her employer's son to return to school, but alas this still left three months until Christmas – and even when the blessed season eventually loomed Kit was yet uncertain whether she would get to see her admirer, for there had been no word at all.

Then, a wonderful surprise! Along with the letters addressed to the house came one for Kit. All a-twitter, she declined to open it in front of her fellow servants, and slipped it into her pocket to read later, thereby confirming their suspicions that it was from a man and invoking the comment that she would cop it if Mrs Grunter found out, all trying to goad her into divulging his identity. Kit wondered what the housekeeper would have to say if she knew that her parlourmaid's admirer was none other than a friend of the Dolphins. But instead of rising to the bait, she remained silent, waiting until she was alone before ripping open the envelope.

There was instant reward. In his first sentence Thomas informed her that he would be coming home for Christmas and would also enjoy a sojourn at the Dolphin residence. Barely able to withhold a yell, Kit pored avidly over the rest. According to its author there was so much festive mail that the masters had little time to censor it, this being so he had dared to include a few lines of poetry that would more ably illustrate his feelings for her than anything he might try to compose himself.

Kit was to read those lines over and over again, delighting in the knowledge that she and Thomas would soon be reunited – might even get to dance together, for once again Mr Dolphin had arranged festivities for his domestic staff on Boxing Day.

It felt almost a duty to have to make a yuletide visit to her brother's house. Hardly before she had arrived there, Kit had an urgent desire to get back to Cragthorpe and the arranged dance. Even Beata, her normal harbour in times of turbulence, was less agreeable company, for her habitual winter cough had descended, proving such an irritation when one was trying to divulge intimate gossip.

Kit first sighted her niece's willowy form on Main Street, travelling from the opposite direction. Hunched into her shawl, her skin like tallow, she walked like a middle-aged woman, thought Kit, not a young girl. Running, she came to meet Beata. At once the face lit up, eager for Kit's news on Thomas, which the other was as keen to bestow.

'Come to t'farleymelow!' she urged her niece as they set off up the incline. 'I've got a birthday present for you. Where've you been?'

Beata replied that she had visited Dr Ibbetson with her cough. 'I'll give you three guesses what he said.'

Kit grinned and quoted the physician. '"There's a lot of it about – I've had it myself!"' Beata echoed the words, laughing breathlessly as they reached the top of the incline. The privies had obviously been recently cleaned out, for the whole village stank. Voicing distaste, Kit put her eye to the peephole in the door, then both went inside and sat next to each other. Prior to anything else, Kit handed over the roll of thick edging lace she had bought for her niece's sixteenth birthday. Beata displayed ecstasy and said that the lacework was so fine it must have cost a fortune. Kit admitted it had – that was why she could not afford to buy Christmas gifts for anyone else, though she had managed to plunder the larder at Cragthorpe. Removing the cover from her basket, she revealed a dozen oranges and a selection of confectionery. After bestowing sufficient praise upon her own gift, Beata shoved it up the leg of her drawers, saying she would save it for her wedding trousseau, then asked for the latest news on Thomas.

For a while Kit took the stage, but with the cold air savaging Beata's lungs, it was hard to relate one's hopes and dreams. Her voice drowned out beneath another bout of coughing, she signalled that perhaps they should go home where it was warmer.

Warmth was in the greeting Kit received too. Little Probyn was now sixteen months old. His hair was a pale sandy red and had developed a little curl at the front. Toddling over, arms upstretched, he squealed as his aunt swept him high into the air then squashed him against her breast to deliver a kiss. Almost immediately he struggled to be down again, eager to be on his newly shod feet and show off his prowess. Rhoda was in the throes of handing over her pay packet, receiving a penny in return. Kit remarked on how she had grown lately. Like her elder sisters she was now taller than her mother. Trapped by their rug-making, the rest of the girls made no move to break their fireside circle, though they called out in gladness to Aunt Kit, who came to inspect their work.

'We're trying to get it finished for tomorrow,' Ethel told her, the hook weaving in and out. 'And we will if everyone pulls their weight,' This strict addition was for the younger ones, towards whom Ethel was wont to be rather oppressive. 'You can help us if you want, Aunt.'

Kit said perhaps afterwards, when she had warmed her fingers, then accepted a cup of tea from her sister-in-law, greeted her brother, and sat down to enjoy the company.

Sarah was not so rigid in her Wesleyanism as some, and apart from carols the girls were allowed to sing songs to make their work lighter. Wyn broke into tune with 'The First Day of Christmas' and inevitably got the wrong words. There was much sniggering as each sang their own line – three French hens, two turtle doves – all awaiting Wyn's repeated mistake, the glee building into an explosion of laughter as they chorused the final line – 'And a parsnip in a pear treeee!'

Otherwise, Christmas at Ralph Royd was an unedifying affair: a trip to chapel and dinner at Owen's house. Having performed a morning address he was still all fired up by midday, which meant, thought Kit dismally, they were to be treated to an after-dinner sermon on the union. The return of two miners' candidates to Parliament, both without Liberal opposition, said Owen, showed that the working man was beginning to have his voice heard. Kit wished it was not heard quite so vociferously and tried to shut her mind to it, choosing instead to watch Monty's little boy play with the rest of the children, all the while thinking of Thomas.

'Well, our Kit obviously finds my conversation scintillating!' Owen's jocular comment shook her from her thoughts. 'Just 'cause nobody's taking any notice of thee – away then, maungy mug, let's hear all thy news.'

173

Sharing the briefest conspiratorial glance with Beata, Kit blushingly admitted she did not have much to tell. With most of her activities centred on Thomas she dared not voice them for fear of revealing her lover too soon. She said only that she was looking forward to dancing at the servants' ball.

'A dance?' said Owen, beholding his well-built sister. 'Is Mr Dolphin sure the foundations can take it?'

As Kit lashed out playfully, Monty looked despairing of the example she set for his daughters. How could he explain to them it was an ungodly pursuit when their aunt defied all propriety? 'You and your dancing.'

'What about that Master Tish?' asked Owen. 'Is he still following you round?'

Kit frowned and said she had seen very little of him lately. 'I feel really sorry for him, especially when his family goes off to London and leaves him behind. I doubt they'll ever let him marry, being such a simpleton.'

Owen agreed that it was unjust. He should be allowed to be a man. Sarah and Monty told Kit to mind her own business.

Owen said it was obvious the young man wouldn't have enjoyed the same education as his brother, then. Kit said that was of little significance. 'They don't teach them much to say it's a fancy school.' She told them about the narrow curriculum, explaining that they seemed to learn only about the ancient world.

Owen scrutinized her. 'You seem to know an awful lot about it. I hope you're not secretly hobnobbing with the gentry?'

Kit blustered, sharing another quick glance with Beata. 'I've just sneaked a look at the young master's books that's all. D'you know, that Wyndham is a filthy little devil, leaving his drawers all over the place for me to pick up – and you should see the colour of them. They're blacker than our Monty's!'

Their father's mock outrage caused a titter amongst the children. Having veered the subject away from its dangerous course, Kit was glad when the conversation returned to the miners, and she was able to spend the rest of the afternoon dreaming about Thomas.

How swiftly could a realized dream evaporate. The Boxing Day ball fulfilled all its promise, only to be over in the blink of an eyelid. Allowed one ecstatic waltz with her secret paramour, trying not to gaze into his eyes for fear of giving herself away, Kit was then forced to watch him depart into the drawing room with his hosts, permitting the servants to 'enjoy their treat without further interference from their superiors', in Mr Dolphin's words. Hitherto bereft, she must perforce depend on the kisses snatched when delivering his morning tea – kisses, oh so brief – for once again the jealous, spiteful Wyndham had forbidden his friend to have any dalliance with the parlourmaid, even to the extent of bursting into Thomas's bedroom in the hope of catching them out.

All too soon, Thomas was gone, leaving Kit to rely on the whispered promise that he would write when he could, and would make a gargantuan effort to see her in the summer.

I I

Perhaps this year, thought Kit, returning to her life of drudgery after Christmas, perhaps this year they'll take me down to London. At least it would help to break up the awful hiatus that yawned between now and her summer liaison. To this end, she spent the next dark months making herself appear far more industrious than was real, ensuring that such diligence was observed by her employer.

Paradoxically, rather than ingratiate, her efforts simply grated on Mr Dolphin's patience. Her constant appearances in the corridors when he happened to be passing, her perpetual bustling and dusting and humming – could he never find a place that was unsullied by her over-endowed presence? Was it not enough that he had to control his wife's suicidal urges, without this one ruining his peace too? Inevitably, Kit was to draw her master's wrath.

'Get out! Get out, you stupid trollop!' Faced with her looming presence once again, just as he was settling into a nook to read his newspaper, he hurled it into an untidy pile and railed at Kit. 'If I should be offended by that fat backside once more, you will regret it!'

Kit recoiled. How anomalous that in this great baronial hall, which epitomized chivalry, its master treated this maiden with utter contempt!

Barging a retreat through the brass-studded door, the angry young woman stormed along twenty-five yards of dimly lit corridor towards the servants' quarters, muttering oaths, blinded by fury and the fact that her eyes had not yet acclimatized to the sudden drop in light. It was in this state that she almost tripped over a badly placed bucket. Her boot made noisy contact, sending soapy water slopping over the sides and across the floor.

She emitted a bellow, demanding to know who had left it in such a stupid place.

In response, a meek figure emerged from a gloomy corner and began to mop the floor. 'I'm ever so sorry, miss!'

'Myrtle!' Kit took out her frustration on the underling. 'You blinkin' dimwit – I could've broken me neck!' It constantly amazed her how one so incompetent managed to keep her job. Contrary to Amelia's prediction that she would last only a few weeks, Myrtle was still here almost two years later. Kit was about to say much more when another figure came to stand at the girl's side, issuing disapproval.

'I'll thank you not to be rude to Myrtle.'

'Master Tish!' After only a moment staring from the scullerymaid's disarrayed hair to the master's son, Kit quickly deduced the situation and put a hand to her mouth. 'Aw, what are you thinking of –'

'Oh, please don't tell anyone!' Myrtle put down the mop to lisp tearfully. 'We've only had a little kiss.'

Her own secret love affair in mind, Kit immediately swore affiliation. 'Be calm! I'd never give you away.' Intrigued, she looked at Tish, at the possessive arm he laid around Myrtle's waist and the determined glint in his eye. It was as if she had never seen him before. 'But how long have you two – '

'We've been friends since the day I arrived,' gushed Myrtle. 'I told you before, didn't I? Got on like a house on fire.'

Kit recalled their conversation. 'You're a bit more than friends, though,' came her observation.

Myrtle blushed and looked adoringly at her companion. 'We love each other.'

Tish found his voice. 'Myrtle's my sweetheart. I'm going to marry her.'

'Are you, Master Tish?' Kit smiled, forgetting all about her previous contretemps. 'Then I'm very pleased for you.' The tone of her voice said she was not treating this seriously.

Myrtle reddened further but this time with annoyance. Turning to her young man, she advised him tenderly that she had been here a long time and had better go before someone came looking for her. They would see each other again tomorrow.

Once he had departed in the opposite direction she picked up her mop and bucket and set off towards the kitchen with Kit, telling her. 'He's not as loony as people think, you know!'

'Obviously not, but –'

'We do love each other and we want to be married, but we're hardly ever able to be alone together!'

Kit felt desperately sorry for the couple, but reminded Myrtle that this was the master's son. It was unlikely he would give his consent to the marriage.

Myrtle was still indignant. 'I don't see any good reason why they won't allow Tish some happiness. It's not as if they've got somebody picked out for him like they have for Miss Agnes and Master Wynd –'

'Who?' Kit frowned. This was the first she knew of it and it had to come from someone like Myrtle. 'And how do you know?'

'I just heard folk talking. Miss Agnes –'

'I know about her! Who've they got for Wyndham?'

'You know Viscount Postgate? Well, he's got a sister –'

Kit nodded as Myrtle proceeded, achieving a little more understanding of the situation. Reiterating her long-held opinion, she spoke to Myrtle with more equanimity now. 'I can't understand anyone marrying for power or money, can you?'

'No. Even if Tish were heir to a fortune I wouldn't be interested in his money. I just love him. I know he's a little bit slow and has trouble doing certain things but if we were allowed to marry I could look after him. It's just not fair.'

Kit thoughtfully agreed, her romantic nature coming to the fore.

They had almost reached the kitchen. 'Promise you won't give us away?' lisped Myrtle.

'I'm going to do better than that!' Kit turned mischievous. 'I'm going to help you see more of each other.'

Myrtle was overwhelmed by such kindness but asked how this could be achieved.

'For a start I can take messages between the pair of you! Don't you see? I'm allowed in the main house, I can reach Tish at any time, tell him when the coast is clear – or I can help you sneak out into the garden!'

Spurred on by the enthusiasm on Myrtle's face, Kit divulged her own illicit love affair, listing the wonderful things about Thomas, saying they were hoping to be married too, telling the startled girl that it would be so much nicer for her and Tish to meet amongst the daffodils and crocuses than in this dingy old passageway that stunk of cabbage. Yearning to be with her own lover, Kit derived almost as much pleasure from this substitute, excitedly conjuring all manner of plans for the scullerymaid's first proper tryst, much of it inspired by the derogation she had just suffered at the hands of her employer.

Final words were exchanged before they entered the kitchen. Told that it was Myrtle's afternoon off tomorrow, Kit arranged to take word to Master Tish and then help both of them sneak out into the garden. 'And see how old blubberlips likes that!' came her triumphant whisper.

Not so bold as her co-conspirator, Myrtle would only agree to meet Tish in her own free time, thereby reducing the risk. If Cook wasn't expecting her to be in the kitchen, said Myrtle, there would be no one sent to look for her. For a time, the arrangement served to take Kit's mind off Thomas, as she gleefully skipped from one end of the house to the other, delivering the secret messages. She had grown fond of this most unfortunate couple and her efforts to help them were genuinely motivated – though admittedly a measure of her enjoyment came from the knowledge that she was cocking a snook at her employer, and doing it under his very nose.

However, there was little danger of being caught out, for Mr Dolphin's attention was devoted to his wife, who had succumbed yet again to her usual depression, a mood that was not to lift until the Lenten roses began to force their creamy heads through a black layer of leaf mould, heralding the family's departure for London.

Kit had had no word as to when she could next expect to see Thomas – though certainly it would not now be at Easter, for with the family away there could be no excuse for him to visit Cragthorpe Hall.

More relaxed in his parents' absence, Tish could now enjoy a new freedom with his sweetheart, whilst for poor envious Kit the only consolation was a trip home to Ralph Royd.

Acquiring a lift from a carter who had arrived with a delivery from Castleford in the afternoon and had stayed for tea in the servants' hall, Kit decided to travel home that evening and so be able to enjoy a full day's holiday at home tomorrow. Her escort was not a great conversationalist and the journey was passed mostly in silence. Feeling under no obligation to talk, Kit was quite happy to sit there in the dark, swaying in response to the movement of the cartwheels, occasionally bumping against the man beside her. Only when they began to descend a ridge did she find something to interest her.

'What's that?' She pointed to a distant flickering light that appeared to hang in the heavens.

'Fair at Pomfret,' her companion murmured.

Soliciting a fuller answer, Kit learned that the assumed heavenly comet was in fact a naphtha flare hanging on a tall pole at the top of the helter-skelter. That it could be seen from six miles away was thanks to the ingenuity of a showman trying to attract custom. His tactic had certainly worked on Kit. With growing excitement she pestered the man for more information until they came to the bridge which led to Castleford, whence she thanked him for the ride, alighted from his cart and travelled the last segment of her journey on foot, feet moving like pistons in her haste to be home and organize an outing.

Though the younger ones were on school holidays, Beata and the older girls were compelled to work the next day and complained about being left out. Kit saw no problem. The carter had told her that the fair had only just set up and would be here for a week. If she could arrange to have next Saturday off would Monty allow the children to go with her then? With his consent came a unified yell from his offspring who gathered round their aunt begging to hear what the fair had to offer. Kit waded into glorious detail and enjoyed a secret smile at their obvious excitement, for she was keeping the most enjoyable part to herself – she was going to take Master Tish and Myrtle!

Upon returning to Cragthorpe Hall, Kit went first to Myrtle to convey the plan, then approached the housekeeper and explained that her brother's children had been so disappointed at being deprived of a trip to the fair yesterday that she wondered if Mrs Grunter would be so kind as to allow her to take next Saturday off and she would make up the time in the following week. The housekeeper was most obliging, and this being so, Kit took the opportunity to lay her cards on the table.

'I wonder,' she tried to look demure, 'do you think the mistress would have any objection if I were to ask Master Tish to accompany us? He gets so little enjoyment when the family's in London that I thought it might be a nice treat for him.'

Little Mrs Grunter tilted her head and held the parlourmaid with piscine eyes, looking for subterfuge. There was just something about Kit, pleasant a girl though she might be, that the housekeeper did not completely trust. Yet what subversive motive could there be? Intellectually Master Eustace was a child and it was not as if he hadn't been entrusted to a servant's care before. Kit had nothing to gain by her invitation, more the opposite. After a period of cautious thought, Mrs Grunter agreed, but with a reservation. 'I shall ask Algernon to take you in the carriage. We can't have Master Eustace walking all that way, besides which, he's in need of male supervision.'

Thwarted, Kit grappled for an answer, and as usual resorted to lies. 'Oh, there's no need to take Algy from his work, Mrs Grunter! Leastwise, I'm sure we'd all be obliged for a ride to the fair but there's no call for him to stay. My brother will be there to watch over us. Algy could just come and collect us at the end of the afternoon.'

This receiving the housekeeper's approval, Kit went straight to Myrtle, telling her that she would have to make her own way to the fair and to meet them at a prescribed time and place.

Thus it was that Kit rolled up at her brother's house in an open carriage driven by a footman in full dress livery with white gloves and a cocked hat, astounding the villagers who gathered to stand and stare at the glossy black landau, its matching pair of horses and its haughty driver.

Algy, piqued at having to go all the way to Pontefract and back again at night and not even be allowed a ride on the prancers, hoisted one girl after another into the landau, treating them like sacks of flour. 'That's seven already! Thank goodness they're not all built like you.' He scratched his head over the number of bodies jammed into the leather seats. 'We've still got to fit you and Master Tish in – where's Mr Kilmaster going to sit?'

'Oh, I'm not comin',' replied Monty.

Algy looked enquiringly at Kit, who blustered, 'I thought he would be!'

The footman didn't believe her. 'You just told Mrs Grunter that so I wouldn't be allowed to come with you.'

'I didn't, honestly!' The spring breeze caught the brim of her bonnet, causing her to hold it in place. 'You can come if you want, I won't tell.' She hoped he would not call her bluff, for then he would be privy to the secret liaison between Tish and Myrtle.

Luck prevailed. Algy said huffily that he had no wish to go where he wasn't wanted – besides he had arranged to go to the fair himself with Rosalind on his day off. He ordered Kit to climb in the back. This she did, clasping Probyn on her knee. With Tish sitting alongside the driver, and the carriage loaded to capacity, they set off. Beribboned auburn hair streaming in the wind, the girls waved merrily at their parents and neighbours until they were out of Savile Row, thence breaking into jaunty song which persisted all along the way.

Across the dirty river and onwards they sang, towards the pottery kilns that stood like giant beehives, the joyous expectation in each heart overruling the sordidness of their destination. Castleford had once been an important Roman town, but its antiquity was lost amongst the belching smoke of glass kilns where bottles were churned out by the million, its waterways sullied by coal-laden barges, oil slicks and debris. Through the dismal industrial town rolled the carriage and out the other side, along the arrow-like stretch of the old Roman route towards the ancient castle of Pontefract and its fields of liquorice.

Once Algy had dropped off his load and departed, still grumbling about having to come all the way back tonight, Myrtle emerged from hiding, Tish running to meet her like one of the excited children who accompanied him. Then, with the lovers walking hand in hand ahead where Kit could keep an eye on them, all descended on the fair.

The site had been decorated with flags and bunting, striped awnings that rippled in the breeze, which also bore the scent of liquorice from the town's numerous factories. Amongst the many fruit and vegetable stalls were ones selling bibles, religious zealots exhorting folk to come and be saved. But Kit joked to Beata that she and her charges had already given their hearts to God and were in need of more worldly pleasures. Childish eyes widened at the sight of the big wheel and helter-skelter, swing boats and gallopers with red flared nostrils and golden bridles. Somewhat out of keeping with his new-found responsibilities, Tish was first on board the roundabout, pushing others out of the way, though he did urge Myrtle to climb up on the brightly painted horse beside him. Naturally, the children wished to follow suit, jumping up and down to emphasize their pleas. Kit, muttering that apparently she was the only one with any money, took out her purse and counted out several coins, handing them to the man in charge. Beata offered to contribute. Rhoda too handed over the penny that she had been granted from her wage packet, but Kit smilingly refused, as was her habit, saying it was her treat, though she would have expected the housekeeper to have provided Master Dolphin with cash.

'I want to go on Dapple!' cried Wyn, pointing to a spirited-looking grey, whom everyone else wanted to ride. This occasioned a squabble, even little Probyn straining to climb aboard.

In the end Kit said that as she was the one paying she would have first turn and, sitting astride Dapple, took Probyn on her knee.

There was a united cry over their brother being so favoured: 'That's not fair.'

'Oh wisht! He's only little.' Beata said if the fighting continued she would take them all home and on top of that they would have to walk.

After each had enjoyed two goes on the gallopers Kit said they must move on or at this rate she would run out of money within five minutes. Still, there were more demands on her purse as they came upon a sideshow where dogs and monkeys, dressed like humans, performed tricks and acrobatics. Upon emergence from here they were summoned by a showman to yet another tent with the promise that they would see the fattest lady on earth.

Young Alice was unimpressed, telling her sisters. 'I didn't reckon much to her. She's not even as fat as Aunt Kit.'

Though hurt, Kit shared a laugh with Beata, guessing from the tone of Alice's voice it had been meant as a compliment. Their amusement was cut short by Ethel, who pointed out that Tish had run ahead with Myrtle and the lovebirds were in danger of being swallowed by the crowd. Gathering her smaller nieces, Kit hoisted Probyn into her arms and rushed to catch up.

Myrtle reacted to Kit's censure with an apology and the promise that she would try to keep Tish in check but he was just so excited. 'I wanted to go and visit that fortune-teller but he only wants to ride the gallopers!'

Kit eyed the master's son, who was sitting on such a roundabout now. 'Master Tish, you'll have to get off, I haven't got enough money.'

Myrtle apologized again, this time for her lack of contribution, and said she would pay for Kit to have her palm read.

'Me dad wouldn't like that,' came Ethel's stern warning. 'He says people shouldn't try to find out the future.'

Kit agreed, but when the other confessed that she dared not go on her own, she announced that she would go along just to keep Myrtle company. Having managed to unseat Tish from his garish nag, the assorted group made their way to the fortune-teller's tent where a leathery-skinned crone in a colourful headscarf and festooned in gold ushered Myrtle inside. Knowing Tish would be fidgety, Kit gave Beata half a crown and told her to buy toffee apples for everyone. Then she followed Myrtle into the tent and the gypsy dropped the flap behind them.

In the eerie glow of an oil lamp the three sat down at a table. For long moments the tanned face gazed at Myrtle's palm, her customers perched nervously on the edge of their chairs. When she eventually spoke it was of mundane facts, telling Myrtle what kind of work she did, which could easily be deduced from one look at her broken fingernails and rough red hands, and that she came from a large family who had endured many struggles, which could safely apply to a large percentage of families around these parts.

Then, she came to the future. 'I see much resistance to certain plans you've made.'

Myrtle glanced excitedly at Kit, both knowing that this could only mean the love affair with Tish and the desire to marry. 'But will I overcome it?' She yearned to know.

The gypsy did not raise her eyes from the girl's palm, murmuring thoughtfully, 'Someone who says they're a friend will help you achieve your aim, but you'll come to wish they hadn't.' She glanced up at Myrtle, saw the deep concern and, reverting to the lines on her hand, gave an addendum. 'I see a union –'

'You mean I'll marry?' Myrtle was desperate to receive confirmation.

'You'll marry.' The gravity on the gypsy's face belied that this would be a happy occurrence. 'A man of a higher station than yourself, if I'm not mistaken.'

Myrtle let out an excited gasp. 'When, when?'

'Before the year is out.'

'Will there be children?' Myrtle was on the edge of her chair.

'One.' Her information apparently completed, the gypsy dropped Myrtle's hand and held out her own palm.

Delighted, Myrtle placed a silver coin upon it and the two girls made to rise but a hand shot out and grabbed Kit's wrist, pulling her back into her seat. 'Your turn!'

Kit balked and tried to pull her hand away. 'I don't believe in hocus pocus.'

Myrtle offered again to pay and urged her to remain. 'She was right about me!'

'You don't know that!' scoffed Kit. 'It could be coincidence – she might have made a lucky guess.'

Annoyed at this slander, and determined to earn more money, the gypsy made a concerted struggle to decipher the lines on Kit's palm. 'I see a man – no, many men!' she began, and with that one utterance Kit's curiosity got the better of her. She settled herself more comfortably on the chair, an eager Myrtle in attendance.

Relaxing, the old woman traced a nutbrown digit over Kit's palm. 'You'll have a very long life, very long indeed, with many changes of direction. Oh, this is a very complicated hand to be sure . . .'

'When will I marry?' came the urgent interjection.

'All in good time,' was the stern reply. 'You'd do well to curb that impulsive nature. It's going to get you into trouble more than once.'

Kit didn't care to be told how to behave by a gypsy, and muttered to Myrtle, 'Huh! As if it isn't bad enough being told how to behave by your betters.'

This did not pass unheard by the gypsy, but for the moment she concentrated on trying to decipher Kit's marital fortunes, over which she appeared to be having trouble. 'The signs are very confusing here, very weak . . . Indeed, I can't see you marrying at all.'

Kit glowered. 'That's rubbish! I'm as good as engaged already.'

Insulted, the gypsy's leathery face turned hard. She thrust Kit's hand aside and crossed her arms. 'You know best, then.'

There was such authority in the woman's manner that Kit, who had been about to jump up and leave, now became desperate to have the matter rectified – the gypsy had, after all, given Myrtle an accurate assessment. Trying to assume a mocking air, but underneath very perturbed, she extended her hand again, knowing as she did that it was not in her best interests – Monty would have a fit if he knew.

The gypsy reverted to poring over the young woman's hand, for the moment saying nothing. She was still annoyed that her talents had been dismissed as rubbish, had taken a dislike to the fat girl's arrogant face, and was determined to take her down a peg or two.

185

'You must have been mistaken.' Kit's tone was not so rude now, but she was insistent on hearing a brighter prognosis. 'You did say you saw many men –'

'I didn't say they'd all be queuing up to marry you, though.' The gypsy stared hard at Kit's palm. Usually so certain of her ability, she was, in truth, having difficulty in predicting this young woman's chances – but as matrimony was obviously of such great importance to Kit, she acted on a spiteful whim, and denied her a happy forecast. 'I see no marriage, I see no children.'

Kit was so alarmed and disappointed that before the woman could tell her any more she pulled her hand away and jumped up.

'You haven't paid!' The gypsy was quicker to the exit.

Afraid of her, Myrtle delved in her purse, but a red-faced Kit exclaimed, 'We're not paying for lies!'

'What reason have I to lie?' Undaunted by Kit's size, the gypsy barred the way. 'If you don't like the truth you're welcome to leave, but not before I get my dues!'

'I did say I'd pay for you!' Anxious to escape, Myrtle proffered a coin, which the gypsy was quick to seize, only then stepping aside to let the girls pass.

'Absolute rubbish!' repeated Kit for the benefit of others who might fall for the crone's trickery and also for the group of girls who clamoured round to hear what was amiss. 'I knew it were a waste of money.'

Myrtle tried to justify the expense. 'She did tell me when I'm going to wed though.'

'That remains to be seen,' said Kit, which in retrospect she decided was rather cruel and thus tempered her tone. 'Oh well, I suppose it serves me right – our Monty always said no good came of such things.'

Finding herself trembling, she surveyed the group before her and, to cover her upset, started to laugh. Each was clutching the remnants of a toffee apple and had a scarlet circle around the mouth. Probyn had red goo all over his cheeks and even in his sandy hair. 'Oh my goodness, you look like a collection of clowns. Whatever is your mother going to say? And, Master Tish, we'll have to get you cleaned up before we take you back!'

One by one the chavelled cores on sticks were hurled away, only Wyn and Probyn having anything left, Wyn because she liked to spend time savouring such treats. Kit, Beata and Ethel spat on their handkerchiefs and began to attend to small faces, when there was a sudden wail. Probyn's apple had parted company with the stick and fallen into the dust. Kit did her best to comfort him, but how could one explain to a toddler that one had only sufficient funds to purchase tea and could not buy him another?

Sensing disaster, Wyn began to gnaw ferociously at her own apple, but it did her no good.

'Here!' Beata grabbed it and held it before Probyn's bawling face. 'Wyn'll share hers with you, won't you, Wyn?'

The latter watched with great resentment as a row of milk teeth mangled the apple and gave a subsequent beam that was laden with red toffee. 'Just because everyone else was greedy and ate theirs first, why should I have to have his spit all over my apple? It's always me who has to share. When I grow up I'm going to marry a rich man and I'm not going to share anything with anybody!'

Aside from incidents like this, and the unpleasantness with the gypsy, the afternoon had generally been a huge success, at least this appeared to be Myrtle and Tish's opinion, the latter saying he had never had such a lovely time in all his life and begging Kit to come to his and Myrtle's aid again. She promised she would, so long as he brought some money with him next time. If he was going to be a married man he would have to take responsibility for his own expenses.

The afternoon was rounded off by a visit to a cake shop where Kit had just enough to buy each a meringue for tea, these being consumed as they waited for Algy to come and take them home.

The footman showed mild repugnance at the collection of sticky-fingered children that he was expected to transport in his shining vehicle and also voiced surprise at the extra body.

Kit explained. 'Fancy us meeting Myrtle here! I said she might as well travel back with us.' This said, she orchestrated the seating, making sure that the scullerymaid was beside her swain, whilst she herself clambered next to the driver.

Algy flicked the reins, sympathizing with the horses, who had an awful effort to set the landau in motion, and was even grumpier when Kit decided to while away the homewards journey by reciting everyone's name backwards, starting with his.

'You are Nonregla Ggob!'

The children howled with laughter and begged to know their names backwards.

'You are Ecila Retsamlik, you are Htiderem Retsamlik . . .' Each was listed in turn, right down to the youngest. 'He is Nyborp Retsamlik!'

Thoroughly enjoying the game Tish demanded to know what his name was. Quick as a flash, if slightly inaccurate, thirteen-year-old Rhoda cried, 'Shit Nihplod!' and immediately covered her mouth, which threw everyone into hysterical laugher, including Algy, and even the strait-laced Ethel.

After receiving her children home safe and sound, Sarah invited the remaining occupants of the carriage to stay for tea but, to her relief, by reason of duty they were forced to decline.

When they arrived at Cragthorpe Hall the servants' sitting room was empty except for Beth Garbutt, everyone else at their labours.

Kit sank into a chair and swore she had never felt so tired. 'You'd better go tell Mrs Grunter you're back, Tish.' Being so involved in his love affair she felt entitled to treat him as an equal.

First he took his leave of Myrtle, saying he had had such a lovely time. It was the best day of his life. Myrtle told him it was really Kit he had to thank for that, and he did so.

Kit had gained a degree of affinity with him by now. 'There'll be lots more, Tish,' she promised. 'I'll see to that.'

He was about to go, then turned to ask wistfully, 'Do you think they'll let us get married, Kit?'

She dismissed his concern with a gay little laugh. 'You're almost twenty-one and can make up your own mind! You won't need to ask anyone's permission. Just keep it secret for a few months and you'll be dandy.'

Issuing more thanks, he left. Myrtle accompanied him as far as she dared. Kit smiled to herself, feeling rather self-satisfied until a voice from the direction of the fireplace threatened her attitude.

'You won't do the lad any favours by telling him he can lead a normal life,' came Beth Garbutt's grave warning.

Whilst at odds with this antiquated view, Kit maintained a polite silence, and humoured Mrs Garbutt by offering a cup of tea. What could this old lady possibly know of today's youth?

* * *

All the way up to summer, Kit continued to assist Myrtle's love life, which often extended into the occasional outing. Whilst none of these were so stimulating as the fair, any opportunity for the lovers to meet was gratefully seized, both waiting on the day when Tish would come of age and their union would reach fruition. Although genuinely concerned for them both, Kit now had other things on her mind, for the blooming of the lilac proclaimed that the family would soon be returning and with them, hopefully, her own beloved.

With no letter from Thomas at all since Christmas, Kit was forced to live on optimism, but this emotion was to be cruelly dashed when the Dolphin family returned unaccompanied.

How Kit railed at the injustice! Yet who was there to listen apart from Beata? The rest of the Kilmaster household remained ignorant of her plight. Even had they known, Kit would have expected little sympathy for mere romance, for again this year the miners had suffered a costly strike over reductions in wages. Faced with similar threat, other pits around Yorkshire had followed suit. Their various union leaders, predicting disaster, had tried to negotiate a sliding scale, whereby the miners did not lose out if the price of coal fell, but this was refused by the Ralph Royd Coal Company. With such divisiveness amongst the separate unions, the strike accomplished little. Yet again, Owen and his ilk had been forced to slink back to work with their tails between their legs.

His union beginning to lose what few members it had acquired, even the staunch Owen had been so dejected that he had contemplated severing his link with the lodge, although Kit was to find on her latest visit that he had somewhat recovered his ideals and was now trying desperately to persuade his brother to maintain his union dues.

Monty asked what benefit had he enjoyed. None. It was a total waste of money.

'It isn't! They've granted us our check weighman, haven't they?' This was one concession to which the company had agreed. Now the colliers could be assured that they would be paid correctly for what they had hewn. 'For us to be able to pay him we need to keep membership steady.'

Bouncing his son upon his knee, Monty was grudging. 'Well, if it's to protect our interests, I'll reconsider. At least I'll see something tangible for my union fees, I zuppose.'

Owen clarified the situation. 'Nay, his wages won't be coming out of them. This is a separate issue. You'd still have to pay your union dues.'

Monty balked. 'As well as contributing to this fellow's wage? Well, how can that be right? I thought you meant we'd be getting zommat to show for our money.'

'You will be!' Owen leaned forward. 'Tell me, if you stop paying union dues, where's your pay going to come from if we have to go on strike?' Seeing this was ineffective, he dangled a carrot before Monty's nose. 'Think about this: it could be you who's elected as weighman. You're always going on about your aches and pains, wouldn't you prefer a job on the surface? There's plenty who'd support thee.' His brother was known as a man who could be trusted.

Monty was dubious. Would it mean he had to suffer the intimidation from the management that had put Owen in court for his beliefs last year? 'I can't afford that, I got a family to think of.'

Owen dismissed this idea. 'It would be the men who pay your wages. The master can't sack you.'

Monty showed his brother he was not that naive. 'Why're you not offering to do it?'

Owen asked how could he propose himself. The discussion went on.

Too preoccupied with thoughts of Thomas, Kit drifted off to another place, paying no further heed to union rubbish.

How the summer dragged for this lovesick parlourmaid! Indeed it was almost at an end, and the time was approaching for Master Wyndham to return to school, when quite unexpectedly, upon return from her afternoon off, Kit learned from kitchen gossip that two extra rooms must be prepared by Thursday: Viscount Postgate and Master Denaby were coming to stay for the last few days of the holiday!

Standing behind the master's chair at luncheon, with three days yet to go until Thomas's arrival, Kit wished the family would not dally so long over their meal, for her enforced inactivity appeared to make the clock stand still. Never a glutton for work, this was one time when she would have preferred to be kept busy. Tortured by the thought of Thomas as yet so far away, she forced herself to concentrate on the meal, which in itself was torment. Oh, to be partaking of her own luncheon, instead of having to stand here watching others consume one course after another.

The tinkle of silver cutlery against bone china, the delicate crunch of puff pastry as a knife sliced into it, the rich gravy oozing out between succulent pieces of steak, fragrant juices dribbling off a fork – so well did she focus all her senses that she began to salivate, her tongue experiencing every mouthful of wine. Kit had in fact never tasted anything stronger than shandy, but imagined now that sweet viscosity against the back of her throat, the image so sensuous that it made her close her eyes . . .

'My name is Shit Nihplod!'

No one could believe what they had heard – Kit least of all. After all these weeks Tish had remembered! Eyes well and truly open now she watched a look of horror pass across the face of ever member of the family. Only Algy seemed to find it the slightest bit amusing, though the solemn atmosphere soon persuaded him to conceal his smirk.

Mrs Dolphin was staring, dumbfounded, at the huge vase of flowers in front of her, from whence the voice had come. Having hoped to impress, Tish found himself the subject of accusing faces, and consequently shrank.

Mr Dolphin mopped his thick, mustachioed lips on a linen napkin. 'Eustace, I demand to know where you heard such language!'

Frightened by the tone of voice, Tish said nothing but looked straight over his father's shoulder at the person behind. A furious Mr Dolphin abandoned his meal and rose to confront Kit. 'I demand to know the meaning of this!'

Kit tried to explain. 'It was just a silly game, sir!'

'Game?'

'When I took Master Tish for an outing to the fair and I were telling my nieces what their names were backwards and –'

'Who gave permission for you to take my son to the fair?' Mrs Dolphin found her voice.

Kit whispered that it was the housekeeper, who was duly summoned to explain herself whilst Mr Dolphin tapped an impatient foot.

Mrs Grunter was unaccustomed to being subjected to such ire. 'If you please, ma'am,' she replied with dignity, 'I merely thought it would be a nice treat for Master Eustace. You have permitted him to be in the company of servants before.'

'But not one of such low standards!' snapped Mrs Dolphin. 'Are you aware of the crude speech she has taught him? Suffice to say I have no wish to repeat it. What if there had been guests present? Well, we shall certainly ensure it never happens again.' She looked coldly at the miscreant. 'Kit, you have imposed upon my charitable nature too long. This time your crime is too serious to be forgiven. You will leave the house immed –'

'No!' Tish jumped out from behind the shield of foliage, knocking his chair clean over and rushing around to join the argument. 'She's my friend, you can't send her away!'

'Eustace, she is not a friend, she is a servant!' barked his father.

Automatically, Kit had reached into her pocket and was now twisting a handkerchief through her fingers, a sure sign that she was petrified. They couldn't sack her – she would never see Thomas again!

'She is my friend, she helps me!' Tish took hold of Kit's arm. 'I won't let you!'

'Eustace!' His father gave stern command. 'Go to your room!'

'I won't! You talk to me as if I'm a boy but I'm a man. Kit told me when I'm twenty-one I can be married! And I am twenty-one now so you can't tell me what to do any more!'

Kit's stomach lurched in terror – was he also about to reveal her involvement in his relationship with Myrtle?

But no, Mr Dolphin could never even contemplate such a farcical idea as Tish being married, though his son's vehemence did unsettle him and he sought to make his order less officious. 'Eustace, old chap, stop making an ass of yourself. I'm afraid, that despite what others may have told you, I *can* tell you what to do and I am ordering you to go to your room. You've just displayed quite ably that you're not cut out for marriage – why, who indeed would take you on, seeing you behave like this?'

Tish threw an anguished look at Kit, who silently urged him with all her might not to divulge anything further. However, he was not so dim-witted as to do that, being quite aware that his parents would not approve of his choice and having been sworn to secrecy time and again by both Myrtle and Kit. His only recourse was to repeat his claim. 'I am going to be married! I'm twenty-one now and I'm going to be married.'

'Yes, yes,' his mother sought to humour him. 'Now do as Father tells you.'

'No, you're going to send Kit away and I won't let you!'

'Tish, darling, please calm down!' Alarmed, Mrs Dolphin came forth and made timorous attempts to pacify him but he lurched away from her, working himself into a complete rage, lashing out at the furniture and sending it toppling.

Dancing out of range of a falling vase, Mrs Dolphin played with the white ruffle down the edge of her bodice, looking terrified and at a total loss, beseeching her husband to do something, but he too seemed unable to cope with the situation and turned to Algy for assistance, telling him to restrain the youth. Seeing the footman dive upon her obviously deranged brother, Miss Agnes started to cry. The two younger boys were equally at a loss until their father shouted at them to help Algy overpower the maniacal figure.

With no sign that his son was about to calm down, Mr Dolphin shouted, 'All right! All right, Tish, We'll allow Kit to stay!' Even then it took a long time to subdue the distraught young man, who was eventually led sobbing from the room with the firm promise that Kit would not be sacked.

Regarding their promise of reinstatement as an excuse to pacify their son, Kit retained her fear of dismissal, twisting the handkerchief into knots.

Her fears were well-founded, for the moment the door closed Mr Dolphin turned to the housekeeper. 'Mrs Grunter, I want this creature out of my house!'

'Husband!' Thankful that Tish was out of her sight, yet still afraid of the subsequent rage if he should find out he had been duped, a breathless Mrs Dolphin put forth a substitute idea. 'Much against my better judgement, I beg you not to go back on your word. Heaven knows what he will do –'

'He'll be locked in his room until he calms down!' Always averse to such treatment in the past, Geoffrey Dolphin was beginning to regret his former liberal attitude.

'It's too late to adopt such measures now,' replied his wife, with a hint of censure. 'After you have allowed him so much freedom, he may go completely . . .' She could not bring herself to utter the word insane. 'No, for his own safety we must keep our part of the bargain. Better we just move Kit into the laundry. At least she will have no need to come into the house –'

Mr Dolphin interrupted, wanting to know how Tish would know the difference between total dismissal and relegation to another building.

'Believe me, he will know,' said his wife. 'Our son may have many shortcomings, but he is not completely without reckoning. He will demand to see her to make sure we have not reneged.' At her husband's cognizant nod, she added helplessly, 'I'm afraid this is the best we can do for now.' Catching the look of vast relief that swept over Kit's face, her demeanour hardened. 'But do not be deceived that you are getting away scot-free! I have words yet to say to you. How *dare* you put the idea of marriage into that child's head?'

Any admonition that the mistress had to offer was of little consequence. Kit's mood had, in a matter of seconds, been elevated to one approaching euphoria. Indeed, had Mrs Dolphin wished to promote her she could not have thought of any better way, for the laundry, being a separate building, did not come under the housekeeper's jurisdiction; the women there were largely independent and could slip out into the garden whenever they liked – and a lover could come to pay suit without fear of reprisal.

12

Upon witnessing for himself the sight of Kit in her new role as laundress, Tish was pacified and, with her encouraging whisper that she would continue to help him and Myrtle whenever she could, he promised that he would give no further trouble.

Thrashing away with her posser, Kit was stirred by distant memory, but did not recognize her mother's shadow, for she had been too young when orphaned to recall this task they had shared. Besides, there were more urgent matters on which to contemplate. She had been exiled here amongst the steaming tubs and gushing mangles for two and a half days and already the constant immersion in hot water had played havoc with her hands. She must concoct some nourishment, for word had reached her ears that Thomas had arrived – at any time they might be reunited – and it would not do for her fingers to be caressed and be mistaken for sandpaper.

The fact that she was banned from the main house presented no problem in regard to her lover, for she had deposited a note in the grotto. Moreover, she had kept her old room, for there was none vacant in the laundry, and so there was legitimate reason for her to be in the servants' hall that evening. By this means she was able to gain access to a saucepan and all the ingredients she needed to make hand cream.

Only one small problem remained: she was still in possession of one of Mr Dolphin's books and must try to return it to the library without being caught.

This she attempted to do the following morning on her way to the laundry. There was some difficulty in that, early though it was, others were up and about their business. One of them being Ivy, who had just been to set the table in the breakfast room and was on her way back

195

through the house to the kitchen, when she happened upon Kit trying to sneak into the library.

Receiving Ivy's pointed warning that Mrs Grunter had asked staff to report any illegal sighting of Kit, the latter asked if that meant she should keep the master's book instead of trying to return it? Ivy retorted that she should not have taken it in the first place, adding that she hoped Kit would swiftly remove herself to another place and not put others in a compromising position.

'And talking of compromising positions,' she added before leaving, 'that Master Denaby has just asked me where you are when I took him his morning tea – seemed to have been expecting you, in fact. What mischief have you been up to?'

'None of your business.' Kit looked secretive.

Ivy shook her head accusingly. 'You're a disgrace to your family.'

Kit was highly offended, putting the comment down to jealousy and the fact that Ivy's former sweetheart had grown tired of her. 'How can it be a disgrace to marry someone above your own class?'

Donating something akin to a sneer, Ivy marched off towards the kitchen, muttering that chance would be a fine thing.

After replacing the book, Kit followed in the parlourmaid's wake. When she arrived in the kitchen for breakfast it was obvious that Ivy had repeated Kit's assertion, judging by the looks on the others' faces. It had been rash to divulge her relationship, but then apparently no one believed it anyway. Kit enjoyed an inward smile. She would soon show them.

The note Kit had left in the grotto instructed Thomas that she would be there at three. However, when she arrived that afternoon there was no one to greet her. Delving into the place where the missive was deposited, she was heartened to find another in its place. But her joy soon reverted to despair upon reading that Wyndham had forbidden his friend to have any contact with the maid whatsoever. The few scribbled lines went on to say Thomas was watched like a hawk and so they must recourse to meet some other way. He begged her to take heart for he had devised a brilliant plan. The note ended with the request that she try to be in the library tonight after the household had gone to bed.

Kit crumpled the note in her fist, cursing Wyndham for a jealous little brat. Wondering why Thomas had chosen the library, she pictured herself being intercepted there by a superior. Still, it was doubtful they would risk another tantrum from Tish by sacking her. She deemed the risk one worth taking. But for the next eight hours or so, mere dreams of passion must suffice. Faced with this agonizing wait, she wandered dolefully back to the laundry.

That night in her room, without aid of a timepiece, Kit had to rely on guesswork that the entire household had gone to bed. Luckily, her reckoning proved to be correct and she was able to make her surreptitious journey to the library unaccosted. She had expected Thomas to be already there but the library was empty and in complete darkness. There was not even the glow of a fire to light her path, for due to the unexpected burst of hot weather the only grate alight was in the kitchen. Unwilling to sit here alone in the dark, and familiar with the layout of the room, she groped along the wall until she found a bracket and thence laid hands upon a nearby silver matchbox, finally putting flame to a gas lamp. This done, she seated herself in Mr Dolphin's high-backed leather chair to wait.

She waited a long time, anticipation serving to keep her awake. Eventually, though, her eyelids began to droop, her chin sank further and further into her breast, and she fell asleep.

Something woke her – was it a shout? Had she been discovered? Kit sat bolt upright, listening. There was still no one else here. There it came again! A bloodcurdling scream – and another, and another! She jumped up and ran for the door, intending to make for the safety of her own room. The safest route was by the back stairs but to reach them she would have to dash all the way through the house until she reached the corridor that led to the kitchen, and there was the greater risk of discovery. Nearer by far was the main staircase. Kit took it – had almost reached the end of the landing and the back stairs when she was spotted.

Answering Mrs Grunter's command to stay where she was, Kit turned to watch the frantic activity which appeared to centre on Miss Agnes's room, servants rushing hither and thither with dustpans and brushes, towels and bowls of water. Curiosity getting the better of her, Kit wandered nearer, but immediately wished she hadn't, for there in the daughter's bedroom stood a beanpole figure covered from head to toe in soot. Mr Dolphin was demanding an explanation, which Thomas was trying to give, not very successfully.

'I beg you, sir, do not spring to the wrong conclusion –'

'There is only one possible conclusion I can draw upon finding a young man in my daughter's bedroom!'

'But I mistook the room!' Thomas suddenly noticed Kit and clammed up altogether. But Mr Dolphin had noticed his preoccupation and all of a sudden things fell into place.

Commanding one of the women to take the sobbing Miss Agnes to her mother's room, and the rest of them to clean up the soot that had fallen down the chimney with Thomas's descent, Mr Dolphin ordered both Kit and her suitor to follow him downstairs to his study.

Trembling with awe, and feeling a desperate urge to visit the privy, an incredulous Kit listened as young Denaby gave a fuller reason for his deed.

With his host now aware that it was Kit he had been attempting to meet, there seemed little point denying anything. He confessed to his love for her, adding that Wyndham's reluctance to share his friendship meant that he had no opportunity to meet her. Upon coming across a plan of the house he had noticed that the chimney from his room was directly connected to the library underneath – or so he had thought.

'But I must have taken a wrong turning because I ended up frightening the life out of Miss Agnes. Please believe me, sir, when I tell you how utterly ashamed I am to have done so!'

Mr Dolphin accepted the explanation but remained censorious. 'And what if you had found the correct room? How must I interpret your intentions?'

'Oh, I beg you, do not think ill of me, sir!' Brown eyes pleaded from a sooty face. 'My actions were undertaken purely from desperation. It is my full intention to marry Kit.'

Kit's breast surged with a mixture of love and pride, that he had broken his secrecy – and in front of his own kind!

Concerned that he could be blamed by the boy's parents for allowing such a relationship to get out of hand, Mr Dolphin spoke in measured tones. Kit watched his thick lips form every word. 'I appreciate that there was no dishonourable motive in your behaviour, Denaby, but you put me in an unenviable position. What am I to tell your parents? You are after all under my protection, it would reflect badly –'

'I implore you not to do so but to let me break the news,' said Thomas.

'You do appreciate that they expect you to marry someone of your own station?'

'I am quite aware of that, sir, but I believe when I tell them how very fond I am of Kit they will understand. Please, allow me to do so in my own time.' He and Kit shared a fond, nervous glance.

After a period of deep thought, Geoffrey Dolphin said wearily. 'Very well, we will not speak of this further tonight. Go and wash yourself now, then back to bed.'

Thomas thanked him, but showed concern for his paramour.

Dolphin was stern. 'I have no intention of wasting further time on either of you. Kit, you may go too. You will present yourself in the drawing room after breakfast.'

Naturally, Kit enjoyed very little sleep. Hour after hour she laid there, reliving the scene, unable to believe that Thomas had voiced his intention to marry her. But there was apprehension too, for the lovers were not out of the woods yet. The master would do his best to prevent the espousal.

In the morning, she deemed it pointless to go to the laundry for she was very likely going to be dismissed. Unable to stomach any breakfast, due to nervousness at facing Mr Dolphin, she sat at the table gazing sightlessly at her plate, until Algy dashed in with an announcement.

'Eh, have you heard?'

'Master Denaby got caught with his pants down in Miss Agnes' room,' said Lily without interest. 'Tell us summat we don't know.'

'He did not!' Kit came alive, furious at the assassination of her lover's reputation. 'He got the wrong room.'

'And I suppose he were looking for yours?' Lily's bulldog jaw protruded goadingly.

Kit obliged. 'He was looking for me, as a matter of fact – though we'd arranged to meet in the library.'

'Always comes down the chimney, does he?' sniffed Cook, over her teacup.

Others, too, were unimpressed. 'You're such a romancer,' accused Rosalind. 'My goodness, is there a man in this house who's not after you?'

'It's true!' protested Kit. 'And for your information we're going to be married. Tom told Mr Dolphin last night!'

'If you'll let me get a word in edgeways!' Algy interrupted further exchange. 'I'm not talking about last night's palaver, I'm on about Master Tish eloping with dopey Myrtle.' There was a united gasp of disbelief, then vociferous demands to hear the full story. Even Kit was agog.

Grinning with self-importance, Algy began to don his outdoor apparel whilst telling his captive audience that he couldn't tarry long as he had been ordered to fetch the police. It transpired that Ivy had just gone to take Tish's morning tea and found his bed had not been slept in. Having promptly alerted the master and mistress she had accompanied them back to Tish's room where a note was discovered telling them of his plans but not his whereabouts. 'Seems he must've escaped while all that kerfuffle was going on last night!'

'The little cat!' breathed Cook, referring to Myrtle. 'I wondered where she'd got to this morning. I just assumed she was poorly, she grumbled about feeling unwell last night. Why, she must have had it all planned!'

'God, you wouldn't think either of 'em could plan a walk to the gate,' offered Lily.

Ivy came rushing in then, saw Algy had beaten her to the revelation and cursed him. 'You're meant to be fetching the police!' Under pressure from the others for more information she turned instead to Kit whilst the footman left. 'The master wants to see you at once!'

All eyes upon her, Kit rose with a sense of impending doom.

In the drawing room there was no preamble. 'Are you aware what will happen if my son and this girl have children?' said Kit's employer when she was standing before him.

Numbed by events, she remained silent.

With the lack of response he gave bitter clarification. 'These people do breed, you know.'

How cruel, opined Kit, to refer to your child in such a manner.

'Well, speak up! You have had enough to say when persuading our son to go against us!'

To her horror Kit realized that she stood accused of being instrumental in the elopement. 'Sir, I had no idea Master Tish had even gone –'

'I don't believe you, and I doubt that the police will either!'

Kit's bowels turned to water. She begged her employer to believe she was not involved.

He was in no mood to listen. 'Was it not you who told my son that he could do as he liked when he was twenty-one?'

'Well –'

'Well, indeed! He has carried out your instruction to the letter, has he not?' Dolphin paced the room angrily. 'Do you deny that you encouraged this relationship?'

Kit tried to minimize the damage. 'Myrtle is a lovely girl, sir. She thinks the world of Master –'

'I dare say she does! For according to Ivy she is little more than an imbecile herself!'

Kit damned Ivy's unkindness, tendering nervously, 'Master Tish feels the same about her, sir.'

'Then, if this relationship was such a desirable one perhaps you would be so kind as to tell us why we, his parents, were the last to know? You stupid romantic fool! Did you never stop to ask yourself if either of them, barely capable of looking after themselves, is a fit person to look after a child? My son certainly is not, I am sure of that. He is little more than a child himself. Yet you encouraged him to think of himself as a man! Suppose they succeed in marrying before we find them? To what kind of life have you condemned their offspring? Or its parents, come to that? Where will they live? Eustace has no income. If the police are unable to trace him . . .' He paused as if to allow the maid to reveal where his son was.

Kit was contrite. 'I wish I knew where they were, sir, but I didn't even know they were going.'

Dolphin shook his head in dismay. 'I do not think you truly realize the consequences of your fanciful notions. Is it not enough that your aspirations to seduce a young gentleman have led him to dishonour his family?'

Kit tried to protest that she and Thomas were bespoke, but was given short shrift, and at this point her interrogation was interrupted by the entrance of Algy and a police sergeant from the village, who said he had already sent a constable to broadcast the alert to other stations for his colleagues to be on the look out for Master Eustace. Was there any further information that might be helpful in ascertaining his whereabouts?

Geoffrey Dolphin looked exhausted. 'This person is instrumental in my son's disappearance and may be persuaded to assist.'

Imagining herself being dragged off to prison, Kit began to weep. 'I don't know where he is! I'll swear on the bible if you want! Neither of 'em told me they were going!'

After putting her through a brief but harsh grilling, the police sergeant said that he had not been aware that the young couple concerned were both of age, and this being so there was no real crime involved and he could not reasonably detain Kit.

'No crime?' Dolphin spoke quietly, though his ire was great. 'Would you not term child abduction a crime? For that is what my son is. He may have the body of a man, but his mind is that of a child.'

Kit would liked to have argued that Tish was in no danger, that Myrtle was capable of looking after them both, that he deserved to be happy and to enjoy luncheon at his own table without being shoved behind a vase of flowers. But even had she dared she was not given the chance.

Mr Dolphin made one last announcement to Kit. 'You are dismissed. Collect your belongings forthwith. Charles has been instructed to remove you from the premises. Mrs Grunter will see to any outstanding pay.'

A distraught Kit had barely emerged from the drawing room when Thomas and Ossie Postgate descended upon her from a hiding place, having been eagerly waiting to hear the outcome of last night's debacle. When she did not stop, but hurried tearfully across the wide expanse of the great hall towards the servants' quarters, they rushed alongside her, continually entreating her for details. Lachrymosity forbidding speech, Kit bustled onwards between the suits of armour and rows of weaponry, twisting her handkerchief between her hands, trying to escape from her two escorts. She had burst through the dividing door and into the servants' section of the house before Thomas persuaded her to halt and tell him what on earth had occurred.

Out of range of the master's wrath, she now felt safe enough to fall into Thomas's arms. 'Oh, Tom, it's worse than you imagine! Mr Dolphin believes I'm responsible for Tish running away!' Asked if, indeed, she was, she blurted, 'No! But I'm the one being blamed – and now I'm being sent away! How will I get another job – and how will I see you?' She burst into fresh tears.

Aided by Postgate, Thomas tried to comfort her. 'Kit, you ninny! Why would you need to find work if we're to be married?'

'But you haven't completed your education!' came her muffled reminder.

'Stuff! I told you I've no wish to go to university.'

She lifted her tearful face from his shoulder. 'But if Mr Dolphin tells your parents, they might object –'

'Stop worrying, I implore you! My parents aren't such snobs. Besides, I doubt they'll hear anything. If I were Mr Dolphin I wouldn't want to broadcast last night's shenanigans.' He broke into a grin and described the moment he had tumbled down Agnes's chimney on a fall of soot. There followed a moment of laughter between the three, before Thomas made an invitation. 'I want you to come to luncheon on Monday. That gives me most of the weekend to prepare them.' Due to the rumpus he and Postgate were being packed off early.

'Will you tell them I'm a servant?' asked Kit, drying her eyes.

Thomas replied brightly that there was no need, as she was no longer a servant, and besides she didn't look like one.

Ossie Postgate regarded his feet for a moment, mulling over the idea that perhaps Denaby's parents would not feel the same way he did. 'If one may make a suggestion? I do feel in some part responsible for your dilemma, as it was I who encouraged you two to meet.' Staving off Denaby's cry of gratitude, he added. 'Supposing your parents object – you are after all only seventeen. It may be some time before you're allowed to marry and in the meantime Kit will have no livelihood. Have you thought of that?' He reproached his friend's guilty expression. 'No, I thought as much. It's hardly fair of you, old fellow.' Lifting his face to that of the tear-stained girl, he said, 'I can arrange employment for you if you wish.' Kit asked if he meant at his parents' house and with his nod she agreed gratefully. It would give her time to save for her wedding. Ossie seemed glad. 'I'll arrange it with my mother when I get home. I shall also write you an introduction which you can keep for the future, as a safeguard. Present it to the housekeeper. She's not such a dragon as Mrs Grunter.' He backed away, saying he would run and scribble a reference now and meet her outside in five minutes or so. 'Coming, Denaby?'

Telling his friend he would follow, Thomas took more intimate leave of Kit, confirming he loved her, giving her precise directions to his house and saying he would see her on Monday at noon, though perhaps they could save themselves an awful lot of trouble and just run away like Eustace and Myrtle. 'I never thought I'd see the day when I'd admire poor old Tish.'

Kit nodded. 'Me neither. At least he's happy.'

'And so will we be,' Thomas informed her kindly.

Kit dabbed away the last of her tears and smoothed her appearance to order, saying he had better go, for wouldn't Master Wyndham be objecting to his friend's abandonment.

'He's in his room, sulking,' smiled Thomas. 'I told him I won't kow-tow to his blackmail any more. I don't care if he never invites me again. If you're to be dismissed there's no further reason for me to come here.'

Fresh tears threatened. Kit gave his thin body one last hug. 'I'll see you on Monday then.'

With this they parted. Kit went up to her room to pack her box, enlisting Algy's help to drag it downstairs to the carriage in which Charles would drive her home. Whilst outside, she met Ossie Postgate who wished her luck and handed over the promised reference. Deeply grateful, Kit went back inside to collect her wage.

Though Algy gave her a cheeky squeeze and a kiss, no one else seemed particularly upset to see her go, apart from perhaps Beth Garbutt, who went against opinion and hobbled over to pat her hand. Others were less gracious, telling her she had only herself to blame and remarking that they didn't know how she had got away with it so long.

'Doesn't matter anyway,' came her sniffy response, the viscount's reference tucked safely in her bag. 'I never liked working here.'

Rosalind watched her haughty exit. 'Bloody Katherine of Arrogance – well, she certainly knows her place now.'

To avoid reprisal from her brother and sister-in-law, Kit decided to visit Amelia in Castleford, at whose home she could stow her box until she had something concrete to tell Monty and Sarah. The excuse she gave upon arrival was that she had been offered a better job but did not start for a week so had decided to pay her sister a visit. If all went according to plan on Monday there would be news of wedding bells. This part she divulged to Amelia, who had been somewhat put out at her pristine home being untidied by Kit's belongings and had to be coerced into letting her stay.

'You, getting married?'

'Well don't sound so surprised,' grumbled Kit.

'I didn't meant owt, I'm glad for you!' But not completely glad. With Kit married, Amelia envisaged herself as being left behind in the scheme of things, for as yet there was no sign of any babies.

'Well, come on, Kit, tell us where you met him!' Waiting to start his afternoon shift at the factory, Albert seemed as eager as his wife to hear Kit's revelation.

'At the Hall! We haven't been able to see much of each other, though, he only comes to visit once a year.'

'You don't mean he's gentry?' Amelia treated the relationship less seriously now. 'Well, don't get your hopes up. Some of these young men might seem polite but –'

'He'd hardly have invited me to meet his parents if he wasn't serious,' retorted Kit.

Amelia exchanged a shocked glance with her husband, then asked for more details, learning that Thomas's father was owner of the pickle factory where Kit had once worked. 'Oh, thank goodness. I thought for a minute you meant he was real gentry!' She let out a relieved breath. 'Even so, don't bank on getting a good reception, Kit. These trade folk want their sons to marry better than the likes of us.'

One could always rely on Amelia to burst one's balloon, thought Kit. 'The Dolphins made their millions from trade, yet you seemed to think they were gentry enough when you worked for them.'

Amelia crossed her arms under her aproned bosom. 'So, whatever happened to your ideal of only marrying someone for love?'

'I never said he had to be poor!' rejoined Kit. 'It's just a happy coincidence that the man I love happens to be rich as well. Anyway, I don't care about his background, nor he mine,' she finished rather tartly. Come Monday, they would all change their tune.

13

Mr and Mrs Denaby could tell at first glance that their guest was not the sort of girl they wanted their son to marry. Nevertheless out of politeness and not a little curiosity they underwent the charade of luncheon.

'We are very pleased to meet you, Katherine!' said her hostess, Thomas having deemed it wiser to introduce her as such to his mother. 'Do sit down. May I offer you a glass of sherry before luncheon?' It was obvious that this girl was much older than their son.

Awed by her situation, Kit answered in monosyllables, not wishing to embarrass her sweetheart by any rough speech. That she had been in such a grand house before had no bearing, for then she had been a servant and was expected to act a certain way. Now, without practice, she was expected to perform like gentry. Accepting the crystal glass, she sipped at it discreetly, managing to stifle a cough as the liquid burned her throat, then set the glass upon her lap, both gloved hands cupped around it to guard against spillage. Despite having worked in Mr Denaby's factory Kit had never seen him before. A surreptitious examination told her that Thomas resembled his mother, his father being of a rather less polished appearance, yet his attitude relayed the opinion that he was superior to his son's guest.

Inevitably there were questions as to her background. 'Thomas has told us a little about you,' smiled Mrs Denaby who was doing all the talking, her husband appearing bored. 'But we are eager to know much more. Perhaps we know your people?'

Kit was saved by Thomas who jumped in: 'I've told you, Mother, Kit lives several miles from here! You couldn't possibly know them.'

'Do excuse our son's rudeness.' Mrs Denaby continued to bestow her gracious smile. 'It is perhaps a good thing that he is going back to school this afternoon. The summer holidays always have a tendency to make him run wild.' It was as if she were pointing out to Kit that Thomas was only a boy.

Looking at her beloved, Kit was inclined to agree, for it was a very different Thomas who presented himself in his parents' house. Blushing under his mother's censure, he fell silent.

Spared from answering questions about her 'people' by the announcement that luncheon was ready, Kit put aside her unfinished glass of sherry and allowed herself to be escorted to the table.

Throughout the two years serving on her employer's table at Cragthorpe Hall, Kit had eagerly anticipated those rich tastes forbidden to her, and imagined that her first mouthful of red wine would sit upon her tongue like thick syrup and trickle slowly down the back of her throat. So, her rash gulp sent the thin but potent fluid cascading down her gullet, launching her into a bout of coughing.

'Goodness me!' Whilst Mrs Denaby showed amused concern for her guest, Thomas portrayed deep embarrassment, though his father seemed to find it hilarious to thump Kit on the back until she recovered.

If this were not enough, the green beans squeaked when she chewed them. Red-faced, Kit tried to eat them quickly, which only made the squeaking more pronounced, sounding to her like an army of mice.

In spite of impeccable table manners instilled by Sarah, and etiquette gleaned from Mrs Dolphin, Kit felt like an oaf, regarding the meeting with her future in-laws as a total disaster. How had everyone else foreseen this happening but Kit? Hating her hosts, hating even Thomas for landing her in this situation, she just wanted to go home.

Mrs Denaby seemed eager to comply with this requirement for not long after the meal was over she announced to Kit that Thomas must now prepare for his return to school and because of this they must say goodbye to their guest.

Kit looked at him anxiously. Not one word had been said about their being married or even engaged. Her eyes urged Thomas to do something.

It took a full thirty seconds for him to blurt it out. 'Father, will you grant us permission to marry?'

Mr Denaby raised one sardonic eyebrow at his wife who smiled – a rather treacly smile in Kit's opinion – and said, 'Ah now, dear, it is much too early to speak of marriage.'

'But you said you would consider it!' accused Thomas.

'And we shall, but you did not expect us to endorse your relationship with Katherine on one afternoon's acquaintance, surely?'

He made an attempt to stand up to them. 'But I've known her for ages!'

'You are so young.' The tone was kind but condescending.

'Nevertheless, I'm sure of my choice and so is Kit!' He stumbled over her shortened name.

'Yes, I'm sure she is,' said Mrs Denaby with the barest hint of accusation.

Kit stared back, guessing to her chagrin that she stood indicted of being an adventuress.

'But then if she loves you,' added Mrs Denaby, 'she will wait for you. I am certain Kit has no desire to ruin your education, have you, my dear?'

Kit bowed her head and said she had not.

'There! Your friend is possessed of more sense than you. Thomas, you have so much growing up to do before you can even think of choosing a wife. Now, say goodbye to Katherine, then run along and finish packing.'

And he went. Like a meek little lamb, thought a dismayed Kit, recalling the manner in which Tish had stood up for her against his parents, the power of his display forcing them to reinstate her. Would that Thomas possessed a little of Tish's backbone. There was a brief hesitation as he reached the door, whence he turned limpid brown eyes upon her. 'I shall wait for you, Kit.'

Upon the door closing behind him, Mrs Denaby explained, 'You do see that we have our son's best interest at heart?'

Kit nodded dully.

'Then you will retain that good sense and comply with our request that you have no further contact with him.'

Kit was honest. 'If he wants to see me I won't stop him.' Yet there was no sparkle to her eye. In the space of a few hours she had fallen totally out of love with Thomas, her only hurt stemming from wounded pride.

'I thought this might take a little more persuasion.' Mrs Denaby glanced tellingly at her husband, then drifted off to her chair whilst he took the floor, reaching into his wallet.

'Twenty pounds to leave our son alone!'

Kit's mouth fell open.

'Don't be hanging on for any more!' It was apparent that Mr Denaby regarded the girl as too insignificant to bother masking his rough origins. 'It's that or nowt – come on, take it and leave.'

Kit could scarcely breathe. It was a huge amount of money, more than a year's wages. Such a sum could be invested towards a life of future leisure. She had always envied the upper class their life of indolence and this cash would take her a long way towards such a goal. Yet, she hesitated, grappling with her conscience. How could one put such a price on lost love? And how could feelings change so quickly? By accepting the bribe she would confirm that the love affair was truly over. But then, what good would come of turning it down? Acceptance or nay, his parents would still forbid them to marry, there was no way she could fight against such power, and if Thomas truly loved her he would seek her out when he came of age. Sadly, though, she knew he would not.

Kit reached out slowly and took the money. The Denabys bade her good day.

Despite the rich lining of her pockets, there were tears on the way back to her sister's house, though these came more from self-pity than lost love. How could she confess to Amelia that there was to be no wedding? She would look such a fool. Determined not to be so regarded, she decided to explain away her bloodshot eyes by saying that Thomas's parents wished the couple to wait until they knew each other better.

Handing Kit a fresh handkerchief, Amelia was dubious. 'Are you sure that's all that happened? If he's asked to marry you and they've refused to give consent you might have a case for breach of promise. There was one in the paper the other day where a woman was awarded three hundred guineas.'

Kit almost collapsed. To add insult to injury they had duped her over the cash as well! But she waived Amelia's concern. 'I've told you, we're still engaged! We just have to wait a few years, that's all, until he comes of age . . . well, actually, we have to wait about four.'

'My God, he's only a bairn!' hissed Amelia. 'I don't know about you suing for breach of promise, it's a wonder his parents haven't had you arrested for kidnapping.'

'He seems a lot older than he is! He can't help it if they won't give permission. Now can we please stop talking about it?' Kit looked tearful.

'So what are you going to be doing with yourself this week, with no work to go to?' asked her sister, her sympathy short-lived. 'You needn't think you're moping about here all day, making the place look untidy.'

Kit remembered the cash in her pocket, the thought injecting her mood with optimism. 'I shall cheer meself up with a new dress!' Her good intentions of saving towards a better future all forgotten, she went out to buy the most expensive material she could lay her hands on.

Naturally, there were gasps of outrage at her exhibitionism when Kit turned up at Ralph Royd the following Sunday for the monthly get-together, the only compliments coming from Beata and the little girls, who thought their aunt looked truly resplendent in her peacock-blue merino wool, with matching feathers on her hat. Throughout the preceding week, stitching away at her gown, Kit had managed to suppress her melancholy over Thomas and now retorted to their objections in her usual jocular manner. She informed them that she was to start new employment – in an earl's household no less! And this meant she must dress accordingly. Sarah uttered the hope that others would share Kit's good fortune, at which Kit swiftly handed over a generous sum – her last wage from the Dolphins, plus more besides – which served to pacify.

It was one thing to be ridiculed over one's attire, quite another to be mocked for her aspirations to marry, and Kit had decided that if anyone should raise the subject she would act as if the engagement was still firm.

This was just as well, for Amelia had barely sat down before letting the cat out of the bag.

'Nothing to tell us this month?' asked Gwen, after Kit's new dress had been metaphorically torn to shreds.

Amelia flinched at the pointed reference to her own childlessness, and tried to avert discussion of her shortcomings by announcing, 'No, but our Kit has. She's bespoke.'

Beata, having been privy to the secret relationship, shared a fond smile with Kit, but there were screams of delight from the little red-haired girls, who clamoured to know if they could be bridesmaids. From the adults there was half congratulation and half disbelief, especially upon Amelia's further information that their sister had done very well for herself, her betrothed being the son of an industrial magnate.

'You're not in a pickle, are you, Kit?' joked Owen, who was censured by his brother for this innuendo.

'Well, show us your ring, then!' Even when Gwen projected friendship she remained bossy.

Kit was blushing. 'I haven't got it yet. We won't be married for a while. His parents want us to wait. This new job will give me a chance to save for my bottom drawer.' Milked for more information, she gave them a fictitious version of her afternoon at Thomas's house, wondering how she had managed to get herself into this mess.

''Ere, you wanna get cracking with that family of yours,' Gwen passed jocular warning to Amelia. 'Our Kit'll beat you to it – and Owen's catching up for all he's worth.' The latter now had two daughters in addition to his son.

'Enjoy it while you can, Amelia.' A world-weary Sarah patted her own distended abdomen. 'I wish I knew your secret.'

Taking this as some sort of indictment of his own failure, Monty lifted his son on to his knee as if seeking an ally.

Gwen persisted in tormenting her childless sister. 'You must be eating the wrong things or sommat.'

Dismayed that the topic of conversation had veered back to herself, Amelia grew redder and redder. How ironic, after all she had scoffed at Kit about no man wanting to marry her, all those references to her own childbearing hips, and now here she was incapable of conception. Listening to Gwen going on and on about her barren state every month, it was all too much. She started to cry.

Of course nobody had much to say then, just sat there gaping with acute embarrassment at this emotional display. From the corner of her eye, Kit examined them all. Charity hummed and ahhed and tried to change the subject. Flora, knowing what it was like to be the victim of their elder sister's bullying, looked as if she wanted to comfort Amelia but dared not go against Gwen for fear of attracting criticism. For the first time Kit noticed that Flora's dress was the same colour and style as the teapot cosy, and wondered if it was deliberately designed to make her blend into the drab surroundings. Sometimes, one hardly knew she was present. It wouldn't really matter if she never turned up at all, Kit doubted any of them would notice.

She gave Beata a nudge, and the pair slunk off to the farleymelow –

though this time it was not to share all her secrets. Beata's excitement over her aunt's wedding was so pronounced that Kit did not have the heart to tell her the truth. But she did relate the astounding episode about Thomas falling down the chimney, about Tish eloping with Myrtle, and about her friendship with Viscount Postgate who had recommended her for this exciting new post.

In their absence, a contrite Gwen was attempting to repair the damage she had inflicted by offering Amelia the comforting thought that there was still plenty of time for her to have children, a friend of hers had waited eleven years for her first. 'And I'd take Kit's engagement with a pinch of salt. I'll believe this fellow exists when I see him. Cheer up, my dear, you and Albert'll have a little baby soon.'

Then why did you have to say all those hurtful things? accused Amelia silently. But she dried her eyes and displayed pragmatism. 'Oh well, if we do we do, if we don't then it's no good sitting around waiting for it. Me and Albert are thinking of going back into service together – me as cook, him as a butler or something. I can't stand being on my own most of the day, and there doesn't seem much point in Albert slaving alone to pay off a mortgage on a house that isn't going to be filled.'

Upon return to Amelia's on Sunday night, Kit made arrangements with a carrier to transport her to her new place of employment on Monday, but as he was unable to do this until the afternoon, she told him just to take her box and she would travel ahead on foot.

Up before sunrise the next day, she shivered and quickly put aside her intended outfit for a warmer one. After the Indian summer it was a rude shock to find autumn was upon them at last. Knotting an extra shawl around her neck, Kit took a last sip of tea, grabbed some bread and cold meat, and set off. The morning was yet dark, but the pavement rang to the sound of clogs that led towards pottery, coal mine and factory. Lank-haired girls huddled into their plaid shawls, bundles of snap in hand. Exchanging the mean gas-lit streets for open countryside, Kit strode onwards, shawl muffled around her chin. Her goal led her north, taking a similar route as if to Cragthorpe, though just before reaching the latter she had been told to veer east.

The sun finally rose. She began to enjoy her journey. It was one of those bright blue autumn mornings when the amber and gold stood out in sharp relief and her breath hit the cold air, leaving droplets on the woollen shawl beneath her chin. During the miles ahead the sun began to make itself felt, allowing her to untie the extra garment from around her neck and scratch furiously at the irritation caused by the wool to her skin. Stopping only to breakfast on the lump of bread and cold meat, she lunged on, and finally arrived at her destination in time for lunch.

The three stone towers of Postgate Park straddled a gentle slope. Upon the central tower, through which was the main entrance, sat a coat of arms – this one genuine. In general, the whole building lacked Cragthorpe's artifice, and was somewhat smaller, its character Elizabethan. The parkland around it was thickly wooded, the gigantic spread of old cedars shielding its occupants from the industrial mayhem wreaked upon the otherwise picturesque landscape. A moment ago Kit had been in the presence of collieries, the road engrimed with coal dust, upon a ridge was the straggly outline of some industrial town, but these were soon to vanish, replaced by such rural tranquillity that she could have been in another world.

Originally there had been a moat but that was now filled in. Kit wandered across the square courtyard of the ancient building looking for a suitable way in. An archway led her only to the rear of the building where, spotting a gardener, she tripped across the still damp lawn to ask for directions. A fat old black labrador who had been lying nearby jumped up to sniff her, his eyes befuddled with sleep. Kit bent to pat him. He had bad breath.

The man who kneeled by the edge of an empty flower bed, squinted up at the robust young woman. The sun illuminated a typical raw-boned Yorkshire face, hacked from a limestone crag, though his manner was far from dour and he offered friendly advice on how to find the servants' entrance, in addition showing an inclination to extend their chat.

'How lucky you are to work out here instead of in a stuffy house.' Kit's gazed travelled up from his ragged tweed jacket to encompass the knife-edged lawns and hedges. Most of the herbaceous borders had been cut down, yet the garden was still resplendent in its autumn robes, scarlet fingers clinging to a wall, clusters of orange berries upon a backcloth of dark green. 'I suppose this'll be like the last place I worked at. They want to keep it all to themselves.'

Her informant surprised her. 'Not at all. It's for everyone's enjoyment.'

Kit brightened, then said she was not really surprised, having experienced Viscount Postgate's generosity before. 'I hope his father's as nice as he is. He's a grand lad, isn't he?'

'Most certainly.' Smiling, the gardener began to remove bedding plants from a box. Ignored, the old labrador flopped back on to the grass.

'I wonder why they don't have women gardeners? There seems no good reason.'

The man agreed with her. 'Is it your intention to apply?'

She laughed. 'I might do. Would it be bad-mannered to ask how much a gardener earns? I don't mean yourself!' she added quickly. Though his vowels were flat his overall accent was well-spoken and Kit thought he must have come down in the world, but was not so rude as to ask. 'I just mean an ordinary gardener.'

The man continued to arrange his winter bedding along the black soil. 'Oh, I believe the head man earns fifteen pounds a quarter.'

Kit reacted loudly. 'A *quarter*! I'm here after the wrong job. I doubt they'll be paying me that in a full year.' She paid closer interest to his behaviour. 'You're not the head gardener then?'

He looked amused and said he was not.

It was at this precise moment, that Kit realized she was talking to Lord Garborough. Oh, the embarrassment! She stumbled to apologize, trying to remember whether she had referred to his son as Ossie and feeling even worse at his gracious response.

'I'm not supposed to be here,' the Earl explained. 'Just trying to plant these out before the gardeners catch me and send me off with a flea in my ear. I so love the opportunity to get my hands in the soil, but they get so damned high-handed about it.'

Kit wondered why a curse from upper-class lips should make her blush when she was quite used to hearing it from her own kind, and said she had better remove herself to her proper place. It was an unfathomable mystery to her that the aristocracy could dress in rags and swear and grub about in the dirt and still maintain that noble manner.

Still trembling from her experience, she found the correct entrance and rang the bell, duly being escorted to the housekeeper's parlour where she presented her letter of introduction. Ossie had been right. This woman was much kinder than Mrs Grunter, not only personally escorting Kit around the servants' quarters and showing her to her room, but giving her a tour of the entire house. Besides being smaller than Cragthorpe and more ancient in character, with panelled chambers and carved oak fireplaces, it was much less ostentatious. Its furnishings were grand but battered and its shabby upholstery was in need of restoration. Every chamber harboured the smell of antiquity. There were no bathrooms and, from what Kit could see, no other form of heating than the huge fires. In keeping with these frugalities, she was informed that here, a parlourmaid received only fourteen pounds a year.

The housekeeper completed the tour by handing Kit an apron and cap and telling her that after lunch she could help the cook in the kitchen as there was to be a lavish dinner party tonight and all hands were required.

Rather miffed at this demotion, Kit nevertheless went to meet her new workmates in the kitchen, finding most of them more welcoming than at Cragthorpe. In fact, despite the brisk pace, the whole atmosphere was much friendlier here, imbuing Kit with the hope that she would find a niche within this new family. Even Mr Popplewell the cook, a rather crabby-looking person, voiced gratitude for her assistance, asking her whilst she waited to be given luncheon would she mind going to the game larder to fetch a neck of venison. Kit was directed towards a free-standing and decorative building in the kitchen courtyard. Having previously assumed it to be a gardener's cottage, she opined that she would be happy enough living in that, and went off to get the meat.

Upon her return to the kitchen with its great roaring fire, the nimble rolling pins and acres of pastry, she was about to hand over the venison when she detected an acrid odour and, in trying to decipher the origin of the smell she turned to see a stout, golden-haired woman enter the kitchen. A woman with a cigar in one hand and a parrot on her shoulder. It was obvious from the servants' deference that this was her ladyship, though there was not half as much bowing and scraping as in the industrialist's house, their mistress showing a friendly interest in how the preparations were going.

Seemingly excited by the busy atmosphere, the parrot danced up and down on her shoulder and let out a shout of, 'Oh, bugger!'

'Disgusting bird, be quiet,' ordered her ladyship without passion. 'I trust you're not going to mess about with that, Cook?' Her pale grey eyes inspected the venison.

Popplewell, a wavy-haired wisp of a man, just skin and bone and teeth, wore a fixed smile. 'No, indeed, ma'am, good plain food that's what his lordship likes, does he not?'

After a sociable chat, in which the blue and yellow parrot appeared to join, her ladyship departed, leaving a pall of tobacco smoke in her wake. Immediately, the cook dropped his rictal guise and began to waft violently at the air. 'The Countess and her blasted cigar smoke – it'll hang around for days! Good plain food, that's what his lordship wants and that's what his lordship will have, despite the fact that he's employed the finest cook in Yorkshire. But does he give a hoss's rectum for my feelings? No! Good plain boring old food – don't mess about with it indeed! Why doesn't he just go buy pie and peas from a barrow?' The man suffered constant frustration at not being allowed to give rein to his creativity. He almost threw the neck of venison at an underling. 'You might as well do it, for all I'm appreciated!'

Never having witnessed such a violent display at home, Kit was rather frightened and sought to appease him. 'Well, this looks delicious.' She sat down to the luncheon that had been provided, devouring a mouthful and closing her eyes in appreciation whilst a host of white pinafores hurried back and forth around her. 'I wish I could afford to employ you, Mr Popplewell. I hate cooking.'

'You obviously like eating though,' said one of the workers.

Popplewell noticed Kit's face redden. 'Nowt wrong with being well-built! I like a woman who enjoys her food. It's a real compliment to a cook. You could teach them upstairs a thing or two. Here, have one of these gooseberry tarts for afterwards!'

Kit licked her lips, glad to have made at least one friend, and formed an artless observation. 'You've got a lovely voice, Mr Popplewell.' His vowels were much broader than her own, his Es formed with great precision, as if elongated. No Ts were dropped at the end of his words, as in her own speech; this alphabetical letter emerging from his lips with a gentle tap at the air. 'Where do you come from?'

'Beautiful Barnsley,' he told her, somewhat calmer now, though his forehead remained knotted. 'And thank you for your kind compliment, my dear. It makes a refreshing change.'

After a few more mouthfuls, her face showed bemusement. 'Tell me, if her ladyship is a countess, why isn't he a count?'

'Mr Popplewell thinks he is,' quipped a passing footman to his colleague, and escaped before anyone could rebuke him.

Kit sighed. 'I don't understand all these different titles.'

'It's not our place to understand,' said the cook, vigorously beating an egg, 'just to serve – and what do we serve?'

'Good plain food!' chorused everyone.

Glad that the cook's temper was as quick to subside as it had been to erupt, Kit continued with her meal, during which she was asked by one of the numerous kitchen maids, Edith, 'So if you don't like cooking, what're you doing here then?'

Kit explained that she was normally a parlourmaid and hoped to continue in that role after today.

'Have you worked for nobility before?' asked another girl, Mary.

Kit's information about Cragthorpe Hall was not well received. 'Oh, self-made gentry,' sniffed Mary.

Popplewell jumped to Kit's aid. 'What's so special about the aristocracy? They go to the privy same as us, don't they?'

Mary conceded with a laugh that this was true. 'You never get any great beauties in the aristocracy, do you?' pondered another girl, Lizzie. 'Too much inbreeding. You need a bit of mongrel blood for a pretty face, that's what I say.'

Lips curled around her fork, Kit caught Popplewell's eye and both grinned, but her mousy, snub-nosed companion didn't seem to notice the irony in what she had just said. 'Have the Earl and Countess got a house in London?'

'They've got houses all over. Short o' nowt they've got. The only thing they lack is a recognition of talent.' Popplewell remained offended by his mistress's interference.

Another question was fired at her. 'So why did you leave your last job then?'

Kit had already decided not to repeat past mistakes and tried to sound humble, but could not help a certain amount of name dropping. 'Well, I wasn't very popular with Mr and Mrs Dolphin so Viscount Postgate offered me a job here – saved me bacon, he did.'

'Aye, he's a good lad is Ossie,' nodded Popplewell.

Others agreed, sparking off a bout of tales about the Viscount.

Finally, though, the conversation was cut short by the cook's directive that the dinner party was to be tonight not next week and could they all please get a move on? His orders continued non-stop throughout the afternoon, directed also at Kit now. Hard work or no, Kit decided that she owed gratitude to Ossie Postgate for changing her fortunes.

Routine here was much the same as at Cragthorpe Hall with daily prayers in the hall and bedtime cocoa, the only difference being that on Sundays the entire household would go across the park to the village church, the family walking alongside their servants in order that grooms and coachmen could be free to observe the Sabbath too. For the days in between, Kit was glad to find herself once more in the role of parlourmaid, this bringing her more into contact with the Earl and his wife. Far from expecting his servants to blend in with the woodwork, Lord Garborough would pause to enjoy a brief chat with his parlourmaid should they meet on the stairs. Even so, he remained something of a paradox to Kit. His raw-boned face would not have looked amiss under a layer of coal dust, and indeed his language often descended to that of the miners. The one difference being that instead of the miner's air of resignation, there was supreme confidence over who he was, this warning Kit to curb any attempt at familiarity.

There was no similar tendency with her ladyship. Despite her eccentricity, maybe because of it, it was quite obvious she was of the aristocracy. True, there were laughter lines set into her face, but these came from her ability to be nice to everyone whatever their station in life, yet the lines extended only from nose to chin, there were few around the eyes, and Kit had learned from past mistakes that a smile did not necessarily mean genuine friendship. However, she had no complaints about her treatment and much preferred the Countess's no-nonsense attitude to Mrs Dolphin's double standards.

Together, Lord and Lady Garborough were a devoted couple – although the Countess seemed similarly devoted to her parrot which accompanied her wherever she went, even at the dinner table, where it would wander at will up and down the linen cloth until it found something that took its fancy. Kit discovered that there were other offspring besides Viscount Postgate: fifteen-year-old twin daughters, Kerenza and Ursula – neither of them at all demure – followed by six other children whose names Kit had difficulty in remembering. All were to be seen careering around the house in total unrestraint. If there were rules then Kit failed to see them. Not that the Earl's children were ill-mannered, for they had very pleasant natures and were always very polite to the servants. Because of the younger offspring there had to be nursemaids and a governess, but these melted into the vast domestic army and Kit rarely saw them, other than to exchange a polite good morning, which was more often than not ignored. The Earl might address everyone as if they were equally important, but the servant hierarchy retained its airs and graces.

Amongst those who did give her the time of day, Kit had struck up a rapport with Mr Popplewell. Had she worked in the kitchen things might have been different, for his rages were very alarming. But because he only ever saw her at repast, and because she had nothing but praise for the meals he provided, he had taken her to his bosom and whenever she had occasion to visit the kitchen would summon her in the eager manner of a lovesick youth to taste his latest concoction, his insertion of a syrupy spoon between her lips taking on an almost erotic quality as she closed her eyes and murmured throaty appreciation.

Others were to benefit from Kit's new post, her brothers' children in particular, for at the beginning of December, the younger honourables were made to clear out their toy cupboard with Nanny and give their unwanted toys and books to those less fortunate. The Earl, knowing Kit's brothers were colliers and being a more paternalistic mine-owner than the one who employed the Kilmasters, instructed her to choose a small item for each of their offspring. These were duly wrapped, along with the sugar mice she herself had bought, and taken to Monty's house on her latest visit to Ralph Royd, for the one bad thing about Christmas at Postgate Park was that, with a houseful of guests, her services could not be spared and thus she would not be going home for the festive season.

News from Savile Row was mixed. Monty had been appointed check weighman by the miners, Sarah had recently given birth to a stillborn child and Beata was again racked by bronchitis. Other news went unsaid: Amelia had by now heard from Ivy, her old friend, about the mayhem brought about by Kit, but to her credit did not mention it to her elders, simply regarded her sister with disapproval. That there was somewhat more to the tale than anybody else was aware she did not doubt, for how could Kit afford such clothes on her budget? At any other time Amelia would have raised the question, but with Sarah still wan from her loss, today was not the time to cause such upset. Besides, every time one opened a topic there came a burst of coughing that made any talk inaudible.

Owen winced at the painful hacking from his niece's chest. 'Have you had this lass to a doctor?' He was informed that this was unnecessary as Beata got the same complaint every winter. 'If it's the one and six that's bothering you –'

Monty was offended 'There's no point in wasting Dr Ibbetson's time.'

'Ibbetson?' scoffed Owen, and mimicked the doctor's pat answer. '"There's a lot of it about – I've had it meself!"'

Monty would not have a word said against the physician. 'He knows well enough what ails Beata – he's seen enough of her. He makes up some special medicine for bronchitis that he keeps there all the time.'

'How does he know it's bronchitis if he han't even looked at her?' Owen had never cared for Dr Ibbetson, who always seemed to have something other than the patient on his mind.

'Why, he's a marvellous man – only has to hear the symptoms and he knows straight away!'

'Well, his medicine doesn't appear to be doing much good.' Owen grimaced at another bout of coughing and indicated the pan that simmered on the range, a mixture of linseed, vinegar and liquorice, raisins and brown sugar, which Sarah made every year against the common cold. 'You'd be as well giving Beat some o' that jollop rather than waste your brass. It sounds right dry to me. You want to try giving her inhalants so she can get some of that phlegm up.'

'We've tried it, nothing comes up!' An annoyed Sarah put tea on the table. 'The doctor's told us just to keep using the medicine – Probe, leave Beata alone, will you!' The little boy was clambering all over his sister's lap, swinging from her auburn hair. 'Monty, see to your son.'

Even illness could not suppress Beata's kind indulgence. 'He's not hurting, bless him.'

Despite this assurance Monty grasped a handful of the child's dress and swung Probyn on to his own lap, leaving Beata to clear her lungs without being pestered. Assailed by a less than festive spirit, he asked himself was this Sarah's only vision of his role? A bestower of punishment and wages.

Owen was scornful. 'Course he tells you to keep using it – it's paying for his holiday!'

'He must know what he's talking about, he's a doctor!' Sarah glared at him.

At Owen's persistence, his brother damned him as a blessed know-all and the matter was closed.

An umbraged Owen did not stay long after this. As he made to leave, Kit ran after him with her basket, whispering to avoid the children hearing. 'I've brought these little gifts for t'kids! Here, hide 'em under your jacket.'

'What, you've bought 'em?' Owen frowned in embarrassment. It was unusual for any of the Kilmasters to bestow gifts.

Kit told him that the donation came from the Earl. 'And there's a bit of pie here and some cake – go on, take it, it'd only get chucked out when they start their Christmas binge.'

Instead of benevolence, Owen regarding the toys and food as an illustration of the ruling class's wastefulness, and was appalled. Nevertheless, he took them. 'Some of us can't be so choosy. Thanks, Kit.' He turned to go, then wheeled to enlist Kit's help in another field. 'Eh, see if you can persuade our Monty to take Beata somewhere else. Lass needs to see a proper doctor. Go on, you can get round him, he waint listen to me.'

Kit promised to try, and wished him a merry Christmas before returning to the gathering. But her mind was on other things and not long after he had left she totally forgot Owen's request, spending much of the afternoon with only one ear on the family's conversation. Having still a good deal left of the twenty pounds from the Denabys, she had purchased another bolt of expensive cloth, for there was to be a servants' ball on Christmas Eve. This was hardly the news to give those who had just lost a child and so, upon leaving at the end of the afternoon, she merely told them that she would be sad not to join them at Christmas, and consequently made her eager return to Postgate Park.

Amid the excited planning came a vague hint of unease, for with Viscount Postgate soon to be in residence Kit wondered whether he would bring his friend Denaby to stay. She had tried to forget Thomas, but it was very hard not to be reminded when one was using his parents' bribe to purchase a ball gown, every stitch that went into it reminding her of her humiliation. Was she really so unappealing that

221

folk were prepared to hand over money so as not to acquire her as a daughter-in-law?

With only days left to go, Kit was having a difficult task in finishing the gown, an ambitious project in dark turquoise satin with flounced underskirts, twists and folds and pleats, and she had taken to sneaking the odd half-hour from her chores to work on it. With much more leniency shown at Christmas towards such digression, Kit was not alone, but was joined by two other parlourmaids, each of them stitching furiously in order that they might outshine each other at the coming ball.

'Shall we get to dance with Lord Bugger?' asked Kit drawing laughter from her companions over the nickname. 'Well, I've never heard anything like it! He swears more than any man I know. Our Monty'd never say half the things he does – especially not in front of women.'

Sophie told her that she would regret it if the Earl should choose to dance with her, as he might as well have two wooden legs for all the skill he showed. 'I hope to dance with Viscount Postgate – now, he *is* good!'

Kit smiled and said she was looking forward to seeing Ossie again. 'He got me this job, you know.'

The others shared an exasperated smile, for Kit must have told them a dozen times.

'You won't get to dance with him much if Mr Popplewell has his way,' grinned Lucy. 'He's right smitten with you.'

Kit gave a laugh of denial. 'Nay, he's old enough to be me father! We're just good pals.'

After exchanging another smile with Lucy, Sophie looked at the clock and said they had better get back to their work, it wouldn't do for them to take advantage of the housekeeper's generosity. Kit replied that she would just like to finish this bit and would follow on. Having packed their dresses carefully away, the others left the servants' hall. Kit delayed her exit for quite a while afterwards, sewing industriously away until the click of the door alerted her to the time. Thinking it was the housekeeper come to chivvy her, she issued, 'I'll be there at once!' But the smell of cigar smoke told her she was in more serious trouble.

Halfway along a hem, she started to rise with a look of alarm on her face and stuttered apology on her lips, but the mistress was too taken by the parlourmaid's nimble fingers to rebuke her, instead gesticulating for her to continue. Unsure of herself, Kit did as she was told, almost choking at the clouds of smoke that came wafting over her head as the Countess stooped to watch, the blue and yellow parrot perched unsteadily upon her shoulder.

'You're a fine needlewoman!'

'Thank you, ma'am!' Kit gave a nervous glance upwards as the bird performed a side-stepping jump from the Countess's shoulder on to her own auburn head. 'My sister-in-law taught me.' She winced as the sharp nails dug into her scalp. The Countess noticed this and chastized the bird, nudging him with a finger until he grasped it and was thus replaced on her shoulder. But still she bent over the maid to watch.

'The man's a bloody idiot,' said the parrot.

Wishing her ladyship would issue instructions for her to get on with her parlourmaiding, Kit was forced to proceed with her tiny stitches, and to endure the appalling stench of the cigar, knowing she would not be able to remove it from her hair and clothes for days.

'Hmm! I think we shall put you to better use. Go and tell my seamstress that you've come to help. You'll be much appreciated.'

Astounded by the sudden promotion, Kit was eager to escape, and folded away her gown, but was told by the Countess that she could take it with her and work on it once the main task was done.

Congratulating herself on this additional stroke of luck, Kit went off to the dressmaker's room, where her arrival was, in fact, greatly appreciated. Anticipating the glorious silks in need of her attention – perhaps a ball gown for one of the Earl's daughters – Kit was dismayed to be presented with a stack of gingham pieces. Not gowns for Ladies Kerenza and Ursula, but smocks for the poor children.

From morn to bedtime during those Advent days Kit stitched until her fingertips were raw, resigned to working on her own dress by candlelight in her room, the charitable Lady Garborough totally oblivious to the incongruity of this exploitation.

As it turned out, Kit would not have been able to get home for Christmas anyway, for with it came a violent snowstorm, the only stroke of luck being that it occurred after Viscount Postgate had arrived, for the entire household was now snowbound. She half hoped to avoid the Earl's son, for he would be aware by now of her humiliation at his friend's hands.

Though there was little time for reading in the busy days before

Christmas, Kit had discovered that Lord Garborough had an even more extensive library than Mr Dolphin and, encouraged by the rather lax atmosphere here, she had taken to repeating her previous skulduggery. Having been wholly occupied by the pile of gingham smocks, there had been no time for her to return the volume she had borrowed last week, secreting it under her bed. But now that the smocks had been delivered she sought to rectify this immediately. A feather duster tucked under her arm as explanation for her reason for being here if she was caught out, she peeked into the library, to her joy finding it unoccupied, for everyone was at breakfast.

Replacing the volume, Kit told herself she should make good her escape, but her enquiring nature would not allow her to leave the room empty-handed. To Kit the smell of old books had the bouquet of a wine cask, possessing the same inebriating effect. Outside, the world was white, but here in the cosiness of the library with its roaring log fire, the boughs of Christmas greenery, the rich oak panelling, and row upon row of leather-bound splendour, she was seduced into a mood of well-being. Sauntering along the perimeter of the carpet, trying to keep her eyes averted from the Bacchanalian prints upon the wall, her eyes perused the shelves, unable to make her choice for the selection was so vast. Curiosity exhorted her to stop and remove a volume from between its partners – but on opening the book she recoiled, for the illustrations within were outrageous. Shocked, she was about to put it straight back, then her inquisitive nature took over and she reopened the book to study its fantastic scenes of debauchery, turning the pages to discover more.

The door opened. An expert at subterfuge, Kit whipped the feather duster from under her arm and with two deft flicks of the leather volume had it replaced on the shelf before the intruder had realized what was amiss.

'Kit, how nice to see you again!' Ossie Postgate came forward, eyes performing their involuntary feline blink, his pleasure genuine.

Kit dropped a curtsy and returned his sentiment, thanking him once again for his help in attaining this post. Ossie replied that he was glad to assist and asked how she was getting along, receiving the reply that she was very happy. Kit answered all queries politely, pleaded silently for him not to make any mention of Thomas. To her relief, the young Viscount seemed instinctively to know the pain this would cause her, and on this issue remained silent. In addition to this kindness, he voiced hope that the road would soon be cleared of this wretched snow so as not to spoil the festivities – not that he was expecting any personal friends – thereby putting her mind at rest over the question of Thomas's appearance.

Ossie's eyes twinkled and he glanced at the bookshelves. 'I see you are still in possession of an enquiring mind.'

Remembering that he had been privy to her secret at Cragthorpe Hall, Kit looked guilty and admitted she had just returned a book, her flustered protestations about treating his lordship's library with respect receiving a magnanimous gesture.

'There's no need for such underhand measures here, Kit. One only has to ask.' Upon hearing that she did not like to, Ossie added, 'You'll find my father a generous man.' He reached for the volume she had obviously just replaced, for it protruded a quarter of an inch from the others. Too late to stop him, Kit was forced to watch as the Viscount opened the tome and raised his eyebrows. 'No wonder you didn't like to ask!'

She blushed furiously, her abashment made worse by his perpetual wink. 'That wasn't the one I borrowed, I was just dusting it when you came in!'

He beheld her as if she were a naughty child. 'Kit, really!' Then he started to laugh.

'I'm telling the truth!' Her fingers scrabbled along the shelves for the one she had genuinely borrowed but were unable to detect it. 'It was one about Africa!'

'I'm sure this one's far more stimulating.' Ossie continued to grin.

'It's disgusting! I've never seen anything like it.' Kit felt she might faint with the heat of embarrassment.

Ossie replaced the volume he held in his hand and, out of personal interest, took down another, the content of which proved to be even more lurid.

Kit covered her eyes as he held it out to show her. Laughing kindly, he made a gesture at the shelf. 'Then I beg you, stay away from this section completely.' He was obviously familiar with every volume in it.

Kit said indeed she would, wondering how a young aristocrat could behave in such a manner before the gentler sex.

She was about to leave, then thought to ask about a mutual acquaintance whose welfare often occupied her thoughts. 'Do you know if Master Tish has been found, sir?'

Ossie replied, 'Not to my knowledge.'

Kit looked satisfied that Tish and Myrtle had managed to evade capture. She hoped they were happy.

It was as well she left then, for not long afterwards the Earl came looking for his son.

Ossie chose not to report the amusing incident with Kit, but did put forth the request that she be allowed to borrow a book occasionally, adding that as she had been treated very shabbily by Denaby, it would be a charitable action.

The Earl granted his request. 'But she isn't to have free rein. Heaven knows what she'll choose.'

Ossie smiled to himself, having just witnessed Kit's amusing mistake.

However, he had misinterpreted his father's concern. 'The poor must not be allowed to think for themselves,' explained the Earl. 'It's our duty to guide them. I shall leave it to you to pick something suitable.'

Ossie promised to do so but, his company requisitioned by his father, he was forced to wait until later in the day, when he turned up in the servants' hall with a selection of reading matter. A blushing Kit expected that his favouritism would attract detrimental comments from her colleagues, but in fact there were none, for she was to discover that it was not favouritism at all. The Viscount treated everyone equally, seemingly a friend to each.

So it was that when his lordship's son was the first in line to ask her to dance at the servants' ball, Kit had learned enough to know that it was nothing more than an illustration of his noble lineage. There would be no dalliance with this young man.

However, there were plenty more fish in the sea and Kit was to dance with all of them that evening. Never had she had such an exhilarating time in her life, she announced to Mr Popplewell who now took his long-awaited turn, whisking her around the ballroom in a surprisingly sure-footed manner – even if the two of them were most unevenly matched, he being only five foot six, which in itself brought his face into line with the most appealing portion of Kit's voluptuous anatomy.

Lapping up his compliments about how absolutely ravishing she looked in her turquoise gown, with her auburn hair sculpted into a waterfall of ringlets, Kit had no inkling that her radiant response would be interpreted as encouragement. Not even when, at the end of his allotted time, Popplewell pressed her hand to his lips and thanked her for making him the happiest man in the world, did she guess, putting his enthusiasm down to his vast consumption of punch.

Not until the wonderful evening had ended, the band had played the National Anthem and the tired but jubilant servants went off to bed, did she discover the result of her performance.

After taking off her gown and caressing it lovingly for a second, Kit hung the garment on her clothes rail. With weary movements, she sat on the bed and pulled at the laces on her corsets, sagging with relief as her restricted flesh burst free.

A soft tap came at the door. Thinking it was one of the girls, Kit did not bother to hide her chemise and drawers, but upon opening the door to see Mr Popplewell she stifled a shriek and closed it in his face. Nothing happened. After a nervous moment, Kit opened the door a crack and peered round it. The skeletal, toothy apparition was still there.

'Can I come in?' He was still dressed as for the ball, though his tie was slightly askew and his eyes were glazed.

'No! Go to bed,' she hissed at him. But then he looked so forlorn that against her better judgement she opened the door wider and gave a rapid summons. 'What are you doing here? You'll get us dismissed!'

'Oh, Kit, you're that gorgeous!' He made an inebriated move to grab her but she staved him off with an outstretched arm. At which he looked confused. 'I thought – well, I thought there were summat between us . . .'

'Nowt like that!' said a horrified Kit, one arm still outstretched, the other trying vainly to cover her state of undress. 'We're friends, that's all. I never said I'd marry you.'

'Who said owt about marriage?' asked Popplewell, genuinely perplexed.

Kit gasped. 'What sort of girl do you think I am?'

He swayed, his lower lip caught under one protruding tooth. 'Well, I didn't mean – I just hoped –'

'Well, you hoped wrong! I must be bloomin' mad to let you in – will you please go?'

'Eh, Kit, I'm sorry if I've hurt your feelings. I'd never hurt you for

227

the world.' The skinny little man looked bitterly disappointed. 'I don't know what I thought really – I must've drunk too much punch.'

'I think you must! Now will you go?'

'Aye, of course I will.' He made no move to comply. 'If you want me to.'

'I do!'

He continued to stand there swaying. 'So, there's no chance –'

'None!'

He let forth a sigh. 'Won't you let me have just one good-night kiss? I promise it won't lead to anything else.'

'No! Please, Mr Popplewell, if anybody learns you've been in my room it isn't you who'll get the sack it's me. Parlourmaids are ten a penny. I'm not so talented as yourself.' Perhaps flattery would entice him to leave.

'You've always been lovely to me,' came the slurred but warm reply. 'I'd hate for this to get in t'way of our friendship. You will still be my friend, won't you?' When Kit said that of course she would he turned to go at last, but stopped short at the door. 'Then won't you just gimme a friendly little kiss? Just a weenie one.' He contorted his toothy face and held his finger and thumb apart. 'I promise I'll never bother you again – unless you want me to.'

Kit decided it was the only way she was going to get rid of him. Still hesitant, she bent her head, offering not her lips but her cheek. Popplewell delivered a chaste peck, then finally allowed himself to be ejected.

Kit allowed her trapped breath to escape, then fell upon her mattress, imagining what Beata's reaction would be when she heard this, and laughing fit to burst.

14

Any lasting damage that might have arisen from the incident was fore-stalled by Mr Popplewell, who took Kit aside the next morning and humbly apologized for his unpardonable intrusion. Although his feelings towards her were genuine, he said, his actions had been those of a bounder and he would understand if she wanted nothing further to do with him. However, he hoped very much that this would not spoil their friendship, for he valued it most highly.

Anyone other than Kit might have thrown up her hands in horror at the assault upon her person, but once over the initial embarrassment, the big-hearted girl replied that she wasn't aware of anything untoward happening, all that had occurred was a kiss between friends, and that was what they would always be.

The inclement weather was to become worse, causing a cancellation of the Boxing Day meet and other festive activities. The brief respite in which Ossie made his escape back to school was followed by even lower temperatures and January found Postgate Park under an eighteen-inch snowdrift, every beck and river in the area frozen solid. The Earl grumbled that the cold weather would play havoc with the foxes' breeding season and the hunt could expect a fall in the numbers this year. Others were more concerned with their own creature comforts. Rising to a thick layer of frost upon her window every morning, Kit grumbled constantly about the lack of heating in this ancient building, but was soon to find her heart warmed by different means.

The drudgery of sewing the smocks had produced dividends, the Countess deciding to promote her to the sewing room permanently. Initially there was opposition from the seamstress, Miss Martin – or Martinet, as Kit had quite fittingly dubbed her – who told this upstart that she was insufficiently trained to be let loose on good-quality materials. Yet, after a couple of weeks, Kit's likeable personality, added to her consistently neat sewing, forced the dressmaker to admit that the girl was in fact very adept, and therefore she graciously began to pass on her extensive knowledge, saying that when she retired Kit could take her place – though of course this would not be for a good while yet.

There were to be many more causes for celebration in 1876. In February Katherine Kilmaster came of age, receiving from her employer a little gold watch to pin upon her ample bosom. The following month Miss Martin suffered a stroke and consequently died – hardly cause for festivity for her bereaved relatives, but to Kit, who took her place, it was a godsend. There was to be some disappointment over the information that she would receive no extra pay, her ladyship obviously considering it enough of a privilege for Kit to have the position. However, towards the end of March came the news that as the countess's seamstress, Kit would be expected to accompany the family to London.

She could scarcely contain her jubilation, eager for the first Sunday of the month to arrive so that she could bear this news to her family. Alas, her vainglorious announcement was to receive short shrift in the Kilmaster household, everyone ready to warn her of the grave dangers in the capital that could befall those with a penchant for ostentatious display, Amelia compounding the detraction by telling Kit that she would be far too involved with her work to see many sights anyway.

'I'll be moving to different climes too, in a month or so,' announced the frizzy-haired Amelia. She and Albert had found positions with a family and were arranging to sell their house. 'Our employers are going to set up in York. I'm really looking forward to it.'

With everyone's attention riveted on the speaker, Kit wondered plaintively what was so much more enthralling about York than the capital. Naturally, had she herself been going there the others wouldn't be showing this amount of interest. 'Pity you couldn't get a family who was moving to London,' she said, in a tone that implied her destination was far superior.

'Eh, they're right posh in York, you know!' Charity informed her. 'It's a lovely place.'

Gwen was quick to spot the reason behind Kit's petty remark. 'Her just can't stand it if her's not the centre of attention!'

Kit looked stricken. 'I just meant we could have seen more of each other if she was in London.'

The accusing faces showed no one believed her.

'You're mean, that's what you are,' chastised Gwen. 'This poor girl's got to go back in service 'cause she can't have children and you even go and spoil that for her.'

It isn't me who's always harping on about Amelia being barren! I wouldn't be unkind enough to mention it, thought Kit. But not wishing to add to Gwen's thoughtless proclamation, and seeing Amelia's downcast face, she murmured that she would very much look forward to visiting her sister in York when the opportunity arose.

It was five-year-old Merry who saved the day. 'Will you take us for a picnic, Aunt?'

Others joined her plea, jumping up and down. Kit laughed and said it was a bit cool to sit around, but she would take them for a walk down to the woods before tea. 'Are you coming, Beat?'

Still recovering from her winter bout of bronchitis and looking wan, her eldest niece said that she didn't have the energy and would remain by the fire. Her siblings, grabbing their outdoor wear, were happy to escape the restrained Sunday atmosphere, the younger ones laughing and dancing along the street until they were ordered to show a little decorum by sixteen-year-old Ethel.

'Leave 'em alone,' censured Kit. 'They get enough of that from your dad.'

Out of the shadow of her own siblings, her mood lifted, though the thought did occur that there might be something odd in preferring the company of children. Monty's brood seemed to reflect her attachment, never far away from her side, running back to share a joke or ask a question. Away from the colliery, the muck stacks and railway lines, across a meadow and into a wood went the happy procession, Kit indicating plants along the oaken path for the children to take home for their mother's medicine chest. Amongst the canopy of newly budded branches they came to a small pond. Encouraged by the sun trap therein, she spread her shawl and sat upon it, exhorting the children to frolic at the water's edge. Ethel sat beside her, too old and dignified to romp.

Kit withdrew a handkerchief from her pocket – not to use, but to spread upon her knee and take delight from its colourful embroidery. Beata had given it to her for her twenty-first birthday, having worked every stitch herself, even whilst in the throes of bronchitis. Kit smiled and held it up for Ethel to admire. 'I can't bring meself to blow me nose on it. It's too pretty, isn't it?' Folding it carefully, she put it away.

It was not long before the youngsters came running back, Alice bearing a palmful of black-spotted jelly. Kit, lurching away in mock disgust, urged her to take it back to the pond immediately. Wyn stayed to question. 'Aunt, what's the difference between frogs and toads?'

Little Merry supplied the answer. 'Frogs come from frog spawn and toads come from toadstools.'

Rhoda howled with laughter.

Gently correcting the stocky-limbed child, Kit uttered a sound of discomfort as Probyn dived on to her lap and snuggled into her breast. 'I like you, Aunt Kit, you're like a giant cushion.'

Of all the children, Kit had come to gain a special fondness for the little boy, and now wrapped her arms around him and squeezed, pressing her lips to his pink cheek. 'Ooh, I like you too, Probe – I wish you were mine.'

He made a rapid decision. 'I'm going to marry you when I grow up.'

Kit thanked him, but said she would be an old lady when he was of age. He begged her not to marry anybody else. His aunt replied with another kiss to his auburn head and a hug. 'I shouldn't think anyone else will have me.'

Rhoda stepped in. 'All the lads I know think you're lovely, Aunt.' Her sister Ethel agreed.

Kit gave a little laugh and praised their kindness. In truth, she did seem to enjoy a good rapport with males. The trouble was that none of them seemed inclined to marry her . . .

Chasing Thomas Denaby from her mind, she dropped her chin and looked at the watch that was pinned to her breast, saying it would soon be time for tea.

Wyn pointed up into the sky and said that they could eat tea here, for weren't the fluffy clouds just like the cakes Aunt Kit had bought them? This evoked a medley of noisy chomping as the little ones pretended to claw at the meringue-filled sky and cram the supposed cakes into their mouths.

'By, you're that daft, you lot!' Rising, Kit picked up the damp shawl and led her singing entourage back to Savile Row and less agreeable company, who, as if they had never broken off, continued to lecture their irresponsible sister on how to behave in London.

Kit fought to recoup her buoyancy and by the time departure day arrived she was once again in high spirits. Why, even the train journey itself would be an adventure, for it would be her first. Up before the birds, she stood excitedly with others on the platform of the little station, waiting to board the Earl's private saloon carriage – though a different compartment to her employer, naturally.

Once the luggage and passengers were aboard, the railway carriage and a horsebox were shunted several miles along a private rail to the main line by one of the engines from the Earl's mine, then coupled to the rest of the southbound train. The journey then began in earnest.

Seated next to her friend Mr Popplewell, Kit thoroughly enjoyed every bit of the long but very scenic route, drinking in each morsel of geographical information, even enjoying the pauses for refreshment along the way at noisy, smoke-filled stations, for she could now include Doncaster, Grantham and Peterborough in her itinerary – in fact, a seasoned traveller – and would have much to tell Beata when she got home.

Hour after hour after hour, Kit gazed out of the window, always finding something of interest to see, only her aching bottom giving any indication of the duration of her journey.

When, in the early afternoon, the engine began to slow down again, Kit hoped it was just another stop for refreshment, for this grimy run-down approach could not possibly signify the capital. She was temporarily spared this abysmal view as the carriage was plunged into darkness, slowly negotiating a tunnel. When daylight returned and the train emerged into a station whose platform bore the name King's Cross, Kit enjoyed a moment of relief, but to her dismay her companions began to gather their belongings and Mr Popplewell told her this was indeed London. With a dreadful squeaking and grinding of wheels the train jolted to a stop. To loud clattering, doors were thrown open, spewing forth a crowd of humanity in which Kit was swallowed up and carried along involuntarily. The draughty smoke-filled building echoed to the whoosh of steam and the thud of people's feet all charging down the platform towards the exit.

Outside was mayhem with an army of hansom cabs, private carriages and horse-drawn omnibuses all competing to be nearest the kerb. En masse, the members of the crowd performed a sudden dash, each trying to be first in line for a cab. Though head and shoulders above the rest, Kit felt herself once again swept up on the human tidal wave and suffered a moment of panic, but she was easily spotted and rescued, the Earl's retinue making for a gleaming row of carriages with top-hatted coachmen, powdered footmen and railway porters who rushed to load the vast collection of trunks aboard.

It had obviously been raining heavily though the sun was trying to fight its way through the yellowish-grey pall that hung over the city, bringing a sparkle to the pavements. In a matter of only a few minutes Kit had found herself spirited from the interior of one carriage into another, this one pulled by horses. Only now, safe within its leather-scented confines and guarded by those who had been here before, was she able to draw breath and look around her as the Earl's carriage moved off with a procession following behind.

Bouncing gently up and down in the carriage that made a series of turns, her gaze followed a roofline comprised of ornamental spires and towers and cupolas. At one point the wide road was amassed with vehicles, the pavements with shoppers and clerks hurrying to their luncheon. Kit had never seen such magnitude of people and traffic, glad to be safe in here and not amongst that chaos. The immaculate greys who pulled the carriage trotted along the great shopping thoroughfare, with Kit craning her neck for a better view of the treasure trove that lay within those splendid bazaars and emporia, and thinking that the streets of London must surely go on for ever.

Constantly thrilled by new sights, she let out a little moan when the carriage made a sudden detour from Oxford Street into a quiet backwater, mayhem giving way to the genteel tranquillity of a square of tall four-storey houses in dark grey, red and yellow brick, a lawned garden at its centre. The carriage stopped. They had arrived.

For a moment of anticlimax, Kit sat there looking out at the almost rural scene. Around the perimeter of the iron fence that contained the garden stood broughams and saddle horses who tossed restless heads, jingling their harness. Others exited first, whilst she still idly gazed. At impatient behest, she eventually alighted into the damp atmosphere.

The road had been sprinkled with sand in order that the horses did not slip, its gritty texture collecting on the soles of her shoes as she moved away from the carriage to stand amongst the pile of trunks that were being unloaded. Through a gap between the houses she glimpsed the magnificent portico of a church, though the true charm of the vista was lost upon Kit, who had anticipated more. Where was the ornamented splendour that she had envisaged for an earl's London residence? Where were the landscaped grounds? The building, though huge, fronted directly on to the square and was in no way remarkable. Compared to some of the buildings she had seen on her journey it was extremely plain, with only a section of iron railing on either side of the door to separate it from the footpath, and judging by the small number of windows it would be equally unimpressive inside. The only indication that this house belonged to an earl was the brass plate on the door bearing the family name. Visibly uninspired by its simple Georgian elegance, Kit followed her companions across the threshold.

The interior was quite stunning. All disillusionment put aside, Kit allowed herself to be embraced by the deep red welcoming walls of the entrance hall, and wandered open-mouthed into the staircase hall with its magnificent vaulted ceiling, its elaborate wrought-iron staircase, its walls draped with plaster garlands, oil paintings, and niches containing busts of Greek gods. In contrast to the house in Yorkshire there was no peeling gilt, no threadbare upholstery, the whole effect one of ormolu splendour.

Revolving slowly, she came face to face – if that were the correct terminology – with an immense portrait of a naked woman and experienced a sharp thrill that ran the entirety of her body. It was not the nudity that so impressed Kit but that its subject was almost as amply endowed as herself. Fascinated, she studied every inch of that dimpled expanse, the shell-pink folds and blushing pleats. How, she debated, could she herself be classed as unattractive if an earl chose to hang such a portrait upon his wall?

Reproved by the steward for her blatant inspection and ordered to come to the servants' quarters, Kit did as she was told. Her own room was as one might expect for a minion, and she did not tarry long there before going to fill her rumbling stomach. Afterwards, given the afternoon off in which to settle in, she was invited to come on a tour of the area by one of the small number of housemaids who resided here permanently, and eagerly accepted. Escorted from the peaceful enclave, Kit found herself back on the busy thoroughfare and heading towards a giant monument which Dolly told her was called Marble Arch. Her companion's hard face reminded her of Rosalind and she was therefore somewhat wary of her, but this girl turned out to be much more fun, telling Kit she must accompany her to the theatre on their night off. Both showed amusement for each other's accent, Kit hiding a smile at the way Dolly pronounced the word as 'thee-etre', and Dolly teasing Kit for her flat vowels.

But there was soon more to occupy Kit's attention. There came a gasp as they turned into another road and she pointed to a magnificent palace that overlooked a park. 'Is that where the Queen lives?'

Dolly tittered. 'No! It's just some toff's house. Why, do you want to see Buckingham Palace, then?' At Kit's eager nod she injected a little more energy into her step, pulling the new girl after her. 'Come on, or we won't get back in time for tea!'

All the way along Park Lane, all manner of horse-drawn vehicles careering past her, Kit kept pointing to what she assumed were palaces, trying to guess which was the Queen's residence, each time receiving a no, until they reached the end when she felt sure that this magnificent edifice that looked like a Greek temple *must* be the one and pointed it out to her companion. Dolly, sick of repeating the answer that these were just the homes of the rich, told her to shut up and stop being so stupid.

Abashed, Kit began to realize what Amelia had meant about London being a very different place to home. Indeed, she was permanently agog with all that London had to offer, not the least of these marvels being the exotic-looking people it housed: black and brown and yellow; others who looked English but spoke in foreign tongue to each other. Kit found the whole experience wonderful, wishing she had made this visit long ago, and envying Dolly her birthplace.

Dolly said she was glad to have someone of Kit's enthusiasm and good dress sense to keep her company. The others were proper killjoys. 'By the way, I like your hat.'

Kit thanked her and returned the compliment.

'From what I could see,' added Dolly, 'you've really worked wonders on her ladyship too. She looked like a bag o' rags till you got hold of her.'

Kit laughed. 'She's not exactly what you'd call regal now, what with her cigars – and that wretched bird of hers!'

Dolly agreed. 'You look more the part than she does. Here, look, why don't you have some of these done?' From her bag she produced a calling card bearing her name and address in fancy copper plate. The one thing that stood out, however, was the prefix *Honourable*.

In awe, Kit grasped the card. How wonderful to be able to prove that she lived at such an illustrious address, but she doubted the fraudulent gesture. 'Wouldn't I get into trouble?'

'Why – you live there, don't you? And the other's just a bit o' fun.'

Kit grinned. 'The Honourable Katherine Kilmaster!'

Dolly nudged her. 'I'll show you where to have some done on the way back!'

After visiting Buckingham Palace, Kit being a little disappointed not to have seen the Queen at one of its windows, the girls made their return home to Mayfair via a grand arcade of glass and marble, its lofty arches more befitting a Venetian temple than a place of commerce. Gold lettering upon black glass pronounced a stationery shop where Kit was persuaded to put in an order for some calling cards, then allowed herself to be led, mesmerized, between the ranks of luxurious goods, gasping over the fantastic window displays, particularly those of jewellery. Indeed, as they moved on she was to gasp so much and so often that Dolly joked that she sounded as if she were having an asthmatic attack, whence Kit gasped again, this time with laughter, and pointed to a street sign that indicated Savile Row. 'Eh, that's where I live when I'm at home! Bit different to this, though.' Her mind was enticed back to Ralph Royd, causing a pang of homesickness. 'My, I'm worn out. London's a big place, isn't it?'

She was laughingly informed that she had seen but a portion of it. The constant clatter and the grind of wheels upon granite had begun to affect her senses. Suddenly weary and footsore from a surfeit of monuments and triumphal arches, her temples pounding from the noise of traffic and crowds, Kit was glad to learn they had not much further to walk. Dragging one foot after the other, unaware that a little of Yorkshire lay beneath her shoes in the form of stone flags, she shadowed her guide blindly until they came to the familiar sight of church steps guarded by two cast-iron dogs at the opening to a square, and then knew she had arrived.

*　　*　　*

Sunday was a day of rest with Kit accompanying the family to the nearby church and in the afternoon going for a stroll in Hyde Park with Dolly. It was to be the last of the outside world that Kit would see for a whole week, for on Monday she was put to work on a collection of new gowns for the Earl's eldest daughters to the end that they might be spotted by potential marriage partners, which Dolly told her was the main reason for them coming here. Kit's innate skill, her eye for the latest fashions and her consuming passion for such garb, made up for any lack of experience and the articles she produced equalled anything that might be purchased in the West End. With two young girls at her command, her enthusiasm knew no bounds and their sewing machines were rarely allowed to rest, whilst she herself laboured as never before, stitching from dawn to dusk.

During the following months, though, the constant rackety-rack of the mechanical needles became an irritation to Kit, who grumbled that she might as well be back in Yorkshire for all she had seen of the capital. The fancy calling cards, an extravagant purchase, lay unused in her bag. Whilst her employers enjoyed the constant round of garden parties, receptions, banquets and balls, Ascot and Henley Regatta, she was lucky to enjoy one night a week at the theatre and perhaps a walk in the park. Why shouldn't she be the one who benefited from all this hard work?

Why indeed? There were always scraps of material over when a gown was completed and already she claimed these as perks of her trade, but these were never large enough to provide anything more than an insert in a bodice. Would anyone notice if there were just a bit more fabric left over at the end, enough to make an overskirt or to provide a richer apron front for her own lesser-quality dress? It was doubtful the Countess would question her seamstress's estimation. A woman who classed fourteen pounds per annum as suitable recompense for such hard work obviously had no conception of value. It was not really stealing, Kit told herself, she was just taking what was due to her in another way, thereby conserving her 'Denaby money' for footwear and other necessities. Kit took a chance. At the next purchase of material, she ordered an extra yard.

Affixed to brocaded panels of an appropriate contrast, and hemmed by scraps of velvet, the green silk was transformed into an elegant mantle. Worn only on her day off, this addition to her dress might have gone unnoticed by her employer, but not by Dolly. The housemaid, who had now become her particular companion, made comment as soon as Kit met her for their visit to the theatre, offering a wink that told she knew exactly how the fabric had been acquired.

'You won't tell, will you?' begged Kit as they set off along Regent Street, one short, one tall, both wearing little plantpot-shaped hats festooned with ribbon.

'What do you take me for?' Dolly paused to examine the window display of a linen draper's where custom was still brisk, then walked on, her shoulders acquiring an arrogant swagger beneath her own gaudy shawl. 'Good luck to you, gel. Wish I could get me hands on some o' that.' She, like Kit, used every spare penny on clothes.

Kit ruminated. She had no wish to be outshone, but Dolly had been very generous with her company. 'I could get you a little bit of blue satin if you like.' It was only a scrap but would make an attractive insert. 'And I'll sew it in for you.'

Dolly gratefully accepted, linking arms with the taller girl. They strode on towards the Haymarket, joining the straggling band of theatregoers who were headed in the same direction. The evening breeze bore the scent of hot baked potatoes, coffee and ale. A man sauntered towards them clutching a bag of oysters in one hand. Blind to their nearness he tipped back his head, placed a shell to his mouth and allowed its occupant to slither down his throat. Kit shuddered and broke away from her friend to form a detour, each to either side of him, grumbling at his ignorance. Oblivious, he walked on.

Dolly rejoined her friend. 'I been thinking. Perhaps I can do you a favour in return.' Having come to know Kit well enough by now, she edged closer. 'Fancy a little part-time job, make a bit of extra cash?'

Kit laughed and said she was all for the cash but when would she get the time when she was glued to a sewing machine all day?

'This is something you can do of an evening,' whispered Dolly. 'You're not shy, are you?'

Kit gave a smiling frown and said she was not.

They had almost reached the theatre. Mingling amongst its six fluted columns was the usual bevy of painted women that Kit had come to expect. She recalled the chagrin she had suffered upon saying to Dolly on her third or fourth visit that these ladies seemed to be regular theatregoers. Her companion had sniggered and educated Kit in their true profession. It had not sunk in at first – she still did not really understand exactly what they did, but knew that it was lewd. The look she received now from one of the harlots, caught in the act of repairing her paintwork, confirmed that these were not ladies that would be found in the Earl's establishment.

Dolly caught the line of Kit's gaze. 'Good-looking gel like you could charge twice as much as them old trollops.'

It took a moment or two for Kit to put voice to her astonishment. 'Eh, just 'cause I talk like this doesn't mean I'm half-witted, you know!'

'Keep your hair on!' Dolly laughed. 'I wasn't saying you're thick. You need brains to be able to pick the right customer.'

At the hint of pride in the other's tone, Kit came to a terrible realization. 'You mean . . . ? Oh, how can you bring yourself to it? That's awful!'

It was Dolly's turn to take umbrage. 'Suit yourself! I just thought with you liking the fancy clobber there was some motive behind it. I mean, this is the nearest you'll come to snaring a gent.'

Tears of anger welled in Kit's eyes. 'Much as I want nice clothes I'd never ever contemplate such a way of getting them!'

'No, you'd just pinch 'em from your employer!' Dolly marched through the foyer clutching her ticket in an angry little fist. 'Bleedin' hypocrite.'

The friendship could have turned sour were it not for Kit's apology. 'I didn't mean to insult you,' she told Dolly some hours later, having missed a good part of the show due to much contemplation over the remark that she was a hypocrite and deciding that indeed she was. 'You just took me by surprise. You see, I'm saving myself for the man I'm going to marry.'

Dolly smiled at Kit's unworldliness. 'Well, I hope you find one that's worth it.'

After this, things went back to normal, Dolly never mentioning the incident again.

Kit's success in acquiring the extra yard of fabric without detection had led her to repeat the crime, her skilful use of the material making her appear almost as finely clad as the Countess herself. It was bound to invite jealous comment, even from those with whom she had got on well in Yorkshire.

'How did she get the money to buy that lot? It certainly wasn't earned in this house.'

'She's very good pals with Dolly, if you get my drift.'

'I reckon old Popplewell's giving her one an' all,' said a footman.

'Don't be so vulgar!' With a hiss of disgust the maids stalked off, leaving the men to their lewd gossip.

'I wouldn't mind giving her a length neither,' mused one. 'How much do you reckon she charges?'

Blithely oblivious to this slander, Kit continued to enjoy thoroughly all that London had to offer.

At the beginning of August, when the steward launched the well-practised move back to Yorkshire, commanding his army of servants with a precision worthy of Wellington, Kit said a reluctant farewell to Dolly, vowing to return to London next year.

Back at the Earl's country seat, Kit saw Ossie only briefly, for the Viscount was to spend the remainder of the summer at the Dolphin residence and would eventually be leaving for university. Her request for news of Tish and Myrtle received the reply that they were still at large.

From kitchen gossip Kit learned that there were more moves afoot to pair Ossie off with Miss Agnes Dolphin. The Earl was happy about this. As wily a bird as the industrialist, Lord Garborough saw the profit in such a union and, indeed, was hoping to extend the relationship between the two families by proposing Wyndham as a future son-in-law. A title for Agnes Dolphin, a well-needed influx of cash for the Earl's coffers and a facelift for Postgate Park. Unable to grasp this extraordinary symbiosis, Kit despaired of their lack of romance, still clinging to her ideal that her own union would be forged on love.

With the household back to normal, Kit was permitted to make a Sunday visit home before the shooting season began in earnest, for although her dressmaking services were not required, she might be called upon at short notice to help in other ways.

It was a depleted household that greeted her. Amelia was now in York, which was too far away from Ralph Royd to allow regular visits. Charity, too, was absent, having recently lost one of her children to scarlet fever, which drew a few tears from Kit. Adding to this misery, Beata was yet afflicted by her chest complaint, the dry cough which usually disappeared in summer refusing to budge at all this year. Kit heard that she had been unable to work for weeks, thus reducing the household budget, which of course made Sarah more bad-tempered. Even the younger members of the family had their complaints, saying that after the summer holiday they would be forced to go to school in Castleford – a walk of six miles there and back.

Kit looked to Monty for explanation. 'The authorities've closed Miss Ellerker down,' he told her.

'But they love that school!' Kit had gone there. It was not really a school but a private residence, its owner, the elderly Miss Ellerker, happy to comply with the parents' needs in return for a not unreasonable sum. Even babies were permitted to crawl around her classroom to give their mothers a rest, and those unfortunate enough to have to work to boost the family income were permitted part-time education.

'So do we, but apparently that doesn't matter,' said Monty. 'They say Miss Ellerker's not efficient enough to comply with the new regulations.'

What it boiled down to, he told Kit, was that Alice, who would, in the normal course of events, be leaving soon to work part-time at the glass factory would not be allowed to do so unless she attended a certified school – and the nearest of these was in Castleford. 'I don't know, a man can't educate his own children without others thinking they know better. The fellow says to me, it's compulsory and unless you want to go to gaol, they'm going to the school in Castleford!'

Owen chipped in with his usual rally against the ruling classes. 'And do they care that they've cut off Miss Ellerker's income? T'owd lass's had to go on Poor Relief.' There were not enough children of school age in the village for the parents to form an effective protest, he told Kit.

Kit sympathized with the children and, over a tea of pork pie, tried to raise spirits with amusing snippets about London, which were received with interest for a while before Gwen resurrected a problem.

Replete, she laid aside her crumb-laden plate and took a sip from her cup. 'You'll be looking forward to seeing that young fellow of yours again, I suppose.'

Kit started, burning her lips with the sudden gulp of tea. 'Oh – yes! Yes, I am.'

''Bout time we met him, ain't it?' Monty polished off the last of his pie and brushed the crumbs from his suit.

Kit realized she would have to do something eventually, but for now resorted to fabrication. 'I'd love to fetch him home, but,' here she donned a pathetic face, 'I won't see him for months. He's gone to the Continent with his family.' She had seized this idea from Ossie, who had told her that after university he would be off on a grand tour of Europe. 'I really miss him.'

Beata reached out to comfort her. Sarah did not share her empathy. 'Plenty of hard work, that's the cure for lovesickness. Flora, are you going to eat any of this pie or not?' Whilst everyone else had been wolfing enthusiastically, Flora showed reluctance even to touch the offering. Now, Sarah made as if to take it away. Owen grabbed another piece, Flora extended a tentative hand and the plate was proffered to another. 'Beata, have this last bit.'

'I can't face it.' Beata looked most unwell.

Her mother seemed annoyed, not a little of this inspired by the sight of Flora sniffing at her pork pie. 'There's no wonder you're ill if you don't eat!'

Beata sought to escape to the privy. Eager to impart her adventures, Kit rushed after her.

'Miss him, my eye!' muttered Gwen with a knowing smirk. 'He's a figment of her imagination.'

After a final sniff, Flora took the tiniest nibble of her pie. 'Do you think so?'

'I know so! If we see so much as a photograph of this paramour, I'll eat one of Kit's hats.'

Fortunately, Kit was too busy after this to worry much about conjuring up a suitor, for the daily shooting parties were to keep her out of Gwen's way for a time, the houseful of guests putting a great strain on the servants, and requiring that Kit adopt any role that was asked of her. After the latest flush of guests, however, came a lull and Kit was rewarded with two whole days off. To escape further interrogation from the rest of her family, she decided to call on Amelia in York and, coaxing one of the manservants into taking her by carriage to the nearest station, she caught a mid-morning train, thereby able to enjoy the whole of Saturday afternoon and most of Sunday in the company of her sister.

Amelia and Albert were cook and butler at an elegant stuccoed Regency house on the Mount. Kit was glad to find them both apparently well and happy, if still childless. Unlike Gwen, she made no mention of Amelia's infertility, which made it all the more galling when her sister raised the spectre of Thomas Denaby. Thinking it was done in all innocence, Kit gave a similar reply to the one she had used to Gwen and asked could they change the subject. Amelia was not to be fooled by the ruse. Knowing the truth about Kit's dismissal, but not having mentioned it before, she scolded the latter for her interference in Tish's life.

Kit turned defensive. 'What life? The poor lad didn't have much of one till I arrived.' At Amelia's further chastening, she added, 'Have they not found him and Myrtle yet?'

Amelia shook her head. 'No. Heaven knows what they're living on – and what about your Master Denaby?' she accused. 'Coming down the chimney in Miss Agnes's room!'

'That wasn't my fault! I didn't know what he had planned.'

'I should hope not! He hasn't tried to –?'

'No!'

'Good! Make sure you keep it that way.'

Kit asked what chance she would get for hanky-panky with the two of them separated by hundreds of miles, and used the question of distance to bring the subject round to London, though she reserved much of her enthusiasm about the place, not wishing to be accused, as before, of comparing the two cities unfavourably. In fact, she had been surprised to find such an architecturally pleasing city in Yorkshire, previously imagining York to be like others she had visited, marred by pit and foundry. This she told Amelia and Albert who, having been granted time off to enjoy their sister's visit, said they would be happy to show her round.

Despite much of that day being spent helping in the kitchen, Kit was happy for the change of scenery and to add York to her list of places visited, only really discovering its full beauty the next day during a tour of the ancient streets. Admittedly there were industrial chimneys here, the magnificent cathedral and other historical monuments blackened by their effluvia, and yes, the Georgian symmetry was interrupted by grimy medieval alleyways that stunk of urine and were littered with rubbish, but in all Kit found York a most pleasant interlude, and declared that she wouldn't mind living there herself.

After the initial frantic volley of enthusiasm to extinguish all signs of life from the grouse moors, and the lavish parties that accompanied such slaughter, the pace began to ease, allowing Kit to escape the chores she hated.

In the final burst of hot weather before autumn, on her next day off she decided to take her nieces and nephews on a long-awaited picnic, for this was the last they would enjoy until next year. Her announcement was not met with pleasure by all occupants of Savile Row, Sarah wanting to know who was going to supply the food for this. Kit held up her laden basket, filled with treats from the larder of Postgate Park, which engendered a whoop of amazement.

Sarah, replenishing the fireside boiler with water, voiced suspicion. 'I trust you didn't come by this dishonestly. Don't put that hurt face on with me, it has been known for you to take things without asking!'

Kit replied primly that her close ally Mr Popplewell had sanctioned every item. 'It's only stuff that would have gone to waste. Anyway, I'm sick of watching other folk shove it down their necks. Are you fit to come with us, Beat?'

Though pale of face, a smiling Beata dragged her body from the chair and helped Kit to organize the youngsters. Collecting Owen's eldest children along the way, they set off on their expedition.

Oh, what a joy it was to be with these little ones, thought Kit, revelling in their comical sayings, their hot breath on her ear, whispering secrets. Ensconced at their picnicking place, she stretched out on the grass, propping her chin on one elbow, to watch them scampering about the meadow and woodland. After a while, her arm beginning to ache, she lay back and narrowed her eyes against the cerulean glare of the sky. What on earth was she going to do about Thomas – or rather the lack of him? Even though she hadn't been in the house two minutes there were still questions – when was she going to bring her sweetheart to meet them? I shall just have to find someone else, thought Kit – but where and how?

'Come back,' said a plaintive voice.

Eyes still distant, Kit squinted at Beata, seated beside her. 'What?'

'You're always miles away these days. I haven't had two words out of you.'

Guilty of neglecting her niece of late, Kit became instantly affectionate. 'Aw, I'm sorry if it seems like I'm ignoring you, Beat! I were just thinking.'

'About Thomas?'

Kit could not bring herself to confess the original lie, and so glossed over the fictitious relationship. 'Oh, never mind about me! What have you been doing lately?'

Having been waiting for this opportunity, Beata turned coy. 'A lad smiled at me the other day.'

Kit pounced on her for every scrap of information. What did he look like? Did Beata know his name? By the time this had been exhausted an innocent smile had been converted into a full-blown love affair.

Those unattached grew tired of listening and begged Kit to perform their favourite impersonations. 'Do me mam, Aunt! Aw, go on, do me mam!'

And happy as ever to oblige, Kit launched into an exaggerated impression of Sarah's Welsh accent, drawing forth the usual merriment. Their shouts for encore giving her confidence, Kit went on to perform her entire repertoire, ending with a new impersonation of Mr Popplewell for which she had to pick almonds from the top of a fruit cake and insert them under her upper lip so that they looked like teeth, but in trying to speak she kept spitting them out all over the place and in the end the girls fell into hysterics, rolling on to their backs and kicking up their heels to reveal their drawers.

'Oh, I shouldn't make fun of him, he's lovely!' Exhausted with laughter, Kit fell back too, her breast rising and falling in mirth, eyes squeezed shut against the sun.

A little figure ran up, casting a shadow across her face. 'Look! I've found a dicky bird for your hat, Aunt!' And Kit opened her eyes to find a dead chaffinch thrust under her nose.

She screamed, and half rolled away, but the hurt in Probyn's blue-grey eyes made her sit up and examine his offering. The little boy studied the limp-necked chaffinch, trying to smooth its mangled feathers into place before offering it proudly for Kit's further inspection.

Gingerly, his aunt took possession of the bird, trying not to offend her nephew. 'Oh dear, a cat must have got him.'

Probyn leaned on his Aunt Charity's dictum. 'Never mind, it'll wash.'

Kit exchanged an amused smile with Beata, and delivered a loving hug, said it would make a remarkable decoration for the straw hat she had just purchased, then wrapped the none-too-sweet bird in a handkerchief and put it carefully aside, with the final announcement that it was time for tea.

Whilst the children consumed the treats she had brought them, Kit noticed a mark protruding from Alice's cuff and asked what it was. Drawing her sleeve further up her arm, Alice revealed an angry welt, about three inches long. 'I were on mornings at t'factory and I fell asleep in class. Teacher gimme a whack wi' t'cane – said it'd keep me awake.'

'The pizzock!' Kit recoiled, then seized Alice's wrist for a closer look. 'That needs attention – have you seen this, Beat?'

Beata frowned. 'Does Mother know about it?'

'Ooh, don't tell her! I'll get a whack off her an' all.'

'I don't think so!' Kit was furious, asking to know all about the culprit.

When the picnickers went home, she immediately informed Sarah of her outrage.

The girl's mother was angry too. 'Ach, that's nasty! Here, *cariad*, let me put some ointment on it for you. Why didn't you show me before? There, that'll make it better.'

Kit was amazed to find that this was the extent of her concern. 'Well, aren't you going to go and sort this teacher out?'

'I'll send a note,' replied Sarah, screwing the lid back on the jar of home-made ointment. At Kit's look of astonishment she demanded, 'What else can I do? I haven't got time to go swanning all the way to Castleford. And what can I say? The child wouldn't have been hit if she wasn't doing something wrong.' She turned on Alice. 'Just make sure you stay awake in future!'

Though Alice seemed to take this in her stride, Kit was far from satisfied and, on Monday morning when she was meant to be in the sewing room, cajoled a manservant to take her into Castleford. Clad in her best dress and the green silk mantle in order to make an impression, she was just about to climb into the brougham when a voice hailed her. It was Ossie, come to say farewell before going to university.

'I've been looking all over for you!' he told her, winking involuntarily. His intention to visit each and every servant personally ensured him a busy day ahead, and he was flushed from striding about the house and grounds. 'Where are you sneaking off to?'

'I'm not sneaking, milord!'

'Kit,' he scolded gently, 'you always sneak. Come now, tell me. Perhaps you are going to meet an admirer – why else would you look so very elegant?' His eyes perused her attire, as if with a hint of amused recognition.

Kit gave an exclamation to the contrary, then, with a desperate look at the man who had been going to drive her, she took her foot off the step and told Ossie about her niece's bruise.

The young gentleman seemed to treat it very lightly. 'Tell Alice to count herself lucky. At my school I was flogged until I bled!'

Kit remained obstinate. 'Well, begging your lordship's pardon, I don't think it's right.'

'And you were going to give this schoolmistress a piece of your mind when I caught you,' said Ossie. At her nodding sigh, he turned to the footman, ordering him to get down, and saying he could not allow him to be held responsible for Kit's venture. For a moment, she appeared thwarted – until Ossie sprang up into the driver's seat and invited Kit to sit alongside him. 'If there's to be any trouble, I'm going to enjoy it myself!' And with a flick of the reins he launched the vehicle towards Castleford.

Never, thought Kit, never have I had such a wonderful time in all my life! Basking in the illustrious company – such a handsome companion, who laughed and joked with her as an equal – she almost forgot the real reason for her visit until the carriage came to a halt outside a school.

'I'm a bit nervous now,' she confessed. Her companion laughed and, jumping down, said he would accompany her. 'Oh no! I can't let you get involved, milord.'

'You think I've brought you all this way not to get involved in the fun?' Ossie smoothed her ruffled state. 'Calm down! I won't come if you don't want me to. I'll wait here and then take you for an ice cream.' Kit could scarcely believe this was happening, her mind in a whirl. What had got into the Viscount today?

It took a while for her to find the right classroom and in doing so Kit began to reconsider her plan. Oh, she was still angry, but her rage had somewhat cooled overnight and the impetus of attack had been lost to her. However, the image of Alice's bruise prompted her to carry her plan through. She entered the classroom and made towards a large blackboard, in front of which was the teacher's desk, feeling not like a big strapping woman but a little girl. Thankfully, Alice was at work and not amongst the ranks of pupils who, one by one, lifted their eyes from ink-blotted exercise books to study the interloper.

Unsmiling, Kit stated her reason for being here. The schoolmistress listened to her complaint, but showed little remorse and said that should Alice fall asleep again she would receive similar punishment.

Irked by the officious little squit who was not much older than herself, Kit asked how she would feel if a bigger person inflicted such damage. 'If I were to shove you around you wouldn't like it, would you?' She nudged the teacher's arm, which received the instant command for a girl in the front row to fetch the headmaster.

'I hardly touched you!' protested Kit, and was still arguing with the woman when reinforcement came in the form of the headmaster. The mistress immediately burst into tears, and the headmaster told Kit that if she did not leave the building she would find herself arrested – he had already sent for the police.

Not realizing how intimidating she must appear to the much smaller man, Kit none the less continued to tower over him and protest over the conduct of his underlings, whilst the class looked on agog. It was to her misfortune that the police station happened to be close by and at that juncture a constable appeared, placing her under immediate arrest.

Shocked that it had all happened in the space of five minutes, Kit tried to protest that she was not the guilty one here, and enjoyed a flush of relief as Ossie burst into the classroom. 'Ask this gentleman, he'll tell you! He's Viscount Postgate!'

Seeing a member of the constabulary hurry into the school, Ossie had deduced that it might have something to do with Kit and had come to investigate.

The officer asked for confirmation of his identity, though there was little doubt that a person of note stood before him. Grave-faced, but privately rather enjoying the adventure, the Viscount endorsed Kit's announcement, gaining immediate respect from those involved. Asked if he knew the miscreant, Ossie said that Kit was an employee of his father and explained that this unfortunate incident had arisen from a sense of injustice; Kit felt that her niece had been dealt with too severely.

The headmaster obviously resented this interference but said that he would investigate the matter himself. Meantime, he would not have his teachers intimidated. He insisted that Kit be prosecuted.

'But I hardly touched her!' cried Kit.

With the tearful victim giving lie to this, the constable had no alternative but to lead Kit away.

Acute embarrassment followed. There were many to witness her humiliation in the moments it took to get to the police station for the streets were busy with workmen and shoppers. A host of unsavoury-looking people hung around the building, all seeming to eye her as she rushed through the door.

Inside, Ossie continued to support her as she was charged with assault, persuading the desk sergeant not to incarcerate her but to hand her instead to his custody and he would ensure that she appeared at the police court. His aristocratic demeanour lending sway, Kit found herself free to go for the time being – though with a thought as to the gauntlet of people outside, she refused the Viscount's offer of an ice cream to cheer her up, and instead begged to be taken directly home.

Miraculously, Kit was to find her exit unobserved. The layabouts had now organized themselves into a threatening knot, their attention focused on a police van that was emerging through a gate in the side of the building. In the noisy rush that followed, men and women hammering on the sides of the van, cursing and screaming, Kit and her escort were able to slip unnoticed back to the brougham. Still tense and increasingly frightened, she hurried to climb aboard, for the police van and its encircling mob were approaching the road and the Viscount's horses were in danger of bolting, all the while shying and chewing at their bits.

'Hang the bitch! Murdering bastard! Murderer, murderer!' The crowd continued to envelop the police van until its horse gathered speed and was able to pull away, though it was still pelted with rotten fruit and stones.

Only then did Kit glimpse the terrified face peering through the bars. Myrtle!

Trying to keep control of the horses, Ossie climbed up next to Kit, noting her astonishment. 'You know the person?' He grappled with the reins.

'It's Myrtle that ran off with Tish!' Kit's eyes were round, her own trouble forgotten for the moment. 'Oh, milord, I have to find out what's happened.'

Still having difficulty in controlling his horses, Ossie hailed a member of the mob, which was still hurling threats after the police van. 'You, fellow! What has that woman done?'

The man, his face twisted in fervour, stopped brandishing his fist and turned briefly to answer. 'Don't you read the papers? Her and that loony she married are up on charges of killing their baby. Put the poor little mite in boiling water, skinned it alive. They should flog 'em both to death! Hang her! Hang the bastard!' Enraged afresh, he resumed his vocal attack on the van though it was now too far away for the occupant to hear.

Kit retched. Words stifled by horror, her mind savaged by the appalling image, she could only blurt to her companion, 'Go, please go!', lurching back in her seat as the carriage sprang forward, one hand covering her mouth to contain the threatened vomit. That poor mite! Would Tish and Myrtle hang? They deserved it!

For a time, needing all his concentration to keep the horses from bolting, Viscount Postgate remained silent, as shocked as Kit. Not until they were two miles down the road did he utter an opinion. 'Good God, I can hardly believe it! It must just have happened – Dolphin never said a word – well, of course he wouldn't! Oh Lord, they must be absolutely beside themselves. It must surely have been an accident.'

'Oh, can you please stop, milord, I think I'm going to be sick!' Kit looked decidedly ill. Immediately he pulled on the reins, allowing her to get down. She rushed over to a hedge, putting as wide a distance as possible between her and the Viscount before bending double.

Respecting her feelings, Ossie remained in the carriage, wearing a perturbed expression. When she eventually stumbled back to the vehicle her face was ashen and tear-stained, her breast filled with guilt and self-abhorrence, for she had come to realize who was truly responsible for the death of that innocent babe. The one who had brought his parents together.

15

It was the nighttime that was worst. Through the day Kit had plenty of work to occupy her – though this did not prevent the awful spectre from dancing into her mind at unexpected moments. But the nights, the dreaded blackness, gave rise to such horror that she scarcely dared to close her eyes, knowing that the ghastly apparition would at once appear – a baby plunging into boiling water again and again and again. Toss and turn as she might, she could not put the child's suffering to rest – would she ever? No amount of tears would expunge her own guilt. Why, why had she not listened to Tish's parents, or old Beth Garbutt, they who knew him best? And between the awful visitations, Kit was goaded by the fortune teller's words to Myrtle: *A friend will help you achieve your aim, but you'll come to wish they hadn't.* It was all her fault.

Each morning her swollen eyes scoured the paper for news of the outcome of Tish and Myrtle's trial. As it unfolded, Ossie's prediction was confirmed – it was indeed a tragic accident. The mother had gone out to work and left the father, who was little more than an imbecile, in charge of the baby. The bath water had been too hot, the child had perished, this simple conclusion resulting in both parents being acquitted of murder. Stupid, stupid! Kit's mind raged against Tish and Myrtle. But in her heart she knew that for the rest of her life she would never be free of her own liability.

There was no one amongst her colleagues in whom she could confide – not even Mr Popplewell. She would have been too ashamed to admit her part. She knew that all were aware of it, though, for the case had incited much discussion in the servants' hall. One could not keep such things hidden. There had been no outright blame for her involvement, though she had overheard Mr Popplewell warning one of the maids not to cast the first stone, and knew he had been defending her, bless him.

Her own court appearance was less spectacular, though provoked similar gossip. To spare Viscount Postgate the indignity of appearing, Kit pleaded guilty to the charge of assault on the schoolmistress and was fined ten shillings, but this was as nothing compared to the guilt incurred over the greater tragedy. Neither the rebuke from her employer over the paragraph in the local newspaper – a lesser one than if the Earl had known his son was involved – nor a similar reprimand from her brother on her next day off, could make her feel any worse.

Even a month after it had happened Kit was still in desperate straits, and it was all she could do to prevent bursting into tears when, after lecturing her on her conviction, Monty resurrected Tish and Myrtle's trial. Having read about the case, he voiced the stern hope that his sister was not responsible for the couple's marriage. Ashamed, Kit lied and asked how could she be implicated when she had not worked for the Dolphins in ages?

But later, in the darkness of the farleymelow, she broke down and opened her heart to Beata, dear Beata who hugged and kissed her back to sanity and told her she was not to blame. Had she not simply acted out of humanity in bringing Tish and Myrtle together? God would surely forgive her.

And Kit sniffed and mopped her eyes and nodded, pretending Beata's words had helped, whilst in private screaming out. Was there no one who could understand? Kit was unable to forgive herself.

There were pangs of guilt to be experienced elsewhere too, though of lesser magnitude. The Earl having received his wife's drapery bill had deemed it excessive and so had put a brake on her spending until the following season. Ergo, the person who was partly responsible for the expense found herself demoted to mending and alteration. Thoroughly miserable, Kit tried to maintain her spirits with visits to the library or jaunts into the garden, though at this time of year there was little to inspire. Neither was there a handsome young aristocrat to poke his head into the servants' hall and spend a moment chatting, for Ossie had gone to university. Perhaps it was as well he had gone. Kit had no wish for a reminder of their last awful day together – she had enough to contemplate in the weeks following his absence.

Inevitably, though, she had to face him when yuletide came upon them. Try as she might to avoid him, he finally bumped into her on the garlanded stairs.

'I thought you might like to hear the news about Tish,' he told her, after offering seasonal greetings.

No, I don't, thought Kit, who had only just begun to feel better, fearing her nightmares would start all over again. But she reacted as if grateful.

'Mr Dolphin has taken him back into the fold – installed him and Myrtle in a cottage at Cragthorpe.'

Kit blanched, and could not help a cry of objection.

Ossie was quick to read her mind. 'Rest easy, Kit. There won't be any more accidents. Tish has undergone a surgical operation to ensure a similar tragedy can't happen again.'

Kit let out a sigh of relief. She had no idea what this involved, but Ossie's air of authority sufficed to calm her. But she did voice surprise that Geoffrey Dolphin had shown such charity towards Myrtle.

Ossie said that he had done it to pacify his son, to avoid the screaming fit that Tish would surely have thrown at being parted from his wife, and to bring the scandal to a close as quietly and painlessly as possible. 'I haven't seen the couple myself – Tish isn't allowed to leave the estate. But he's relatively contented, I think.'

Thanking Ossie for this revelation, Kit went on her way, hoping that this was the last she would hear on the matter, and resolving never to interfere in people's lives again. Her emotions over the news were mixed. She was not sure Tish deserved any happiness after what he had done – and how could Myrtle ever feel the same about him? She tried to picture herself in a similar situation, but could not envisage herself forgiving someone who had killed her child.

Pondering on the relationship between Tish and Myrtle, Kit reminded herself of the need to do something about her own lack of male companion, for the family would not be fobbed off for ever.

Christmas, New Year – no occasion passed without Kit being grilled by her siblings. The only reason she went home now was to see Beata and the children, and even that was not wholly pleasurable, for Beata's poor health forbade any kind of jaunt.

The situation was even more dire at Postgate Park now, in times of inactivity Kit having to double as a parlourmaid, her worst moment coming when Thomas Denaby's parents were invited to stay at the Earl's residence and Kit had to wait on them. They pretended they did not know her, of course, but she knew they did, all the upset flooding back to haunt her. There was some mischievous revenge to be had in ignoring their incessant rings for service, or allowing their morning tea to go cold before serving it. But, enjoyable though this was, it wouldn't bring Thomas back. She must make a concerted effort to find someone else.

'Have you got a young man?' she asked one of the younger girls as all were sitting in the servants' hall that Thursday evening after dinner. With the Garboroughs having finished their meal upstairs, those who served had been permitted to dine. Receiving an affirmative response, she quipped, 'Well, can you get one for me? Preferably by Sunday.'

Mr Popplewell was in jocular mood. 'I'd offer to step in, Kit, but I haven't got a ladder.'

Kit dealt the skinny little man a fond tap. Such remarks on her height were permissible between close friends.

'I wouldn't have thought you'd have any trouble procuring a man.' The speaker gave a sly smile at her neighbours.

Innocent to the sarcasm behind the comment, Kit smiled back, though was slightly puzzled that the others seemed to share a private joke. Leaving the table, she moved to one of the easy chairs, but found an obstacle in her way. A cup of tea in one hand, she had difficulty in moving the stool out of her path and made pathetic nudges with her knee.

Popplewell leaped up with a cry of mock exasperation, grabbing the stool with both hands and moving it aside. 'Eh, I don't know! Why not just use your initiative, lass?'

'I just did.' Kit smirked. 'I got you to move it.'

Popplewell was gracious enough to join the laughter engendered at his expense and made as if to chase the tall young woman around the room.

But this frivolity was curtailed by the appearance of the Earl. 'Hope I'm not interrupting?' His questioning gaze encompassed all in the room.

'No, my lord! We were just enjoying a bit of nonsense.' Popplewell grinned and smoothed back his mop of wavy hair.

'Don't want to put a damper on your fun, Cook,' continued the Earl, 'but I have to say those cutlets you served us were utterly frightful.'

There was an immediate change in the mood. The cook proceeded to bare his teeth, and nod benignly, though the others knew it for a dangerous grin and crouched in preparation for the storm to come.

'Who's our blasted butcher these days?' the Earl frowned, and when informed, said, 'Then change him. His meat's not fit to give to the hounds – well, that's all. Lecture over.' He rubbed his hands briskly and sought to lighten his rebuke with a chat. 'Speaking of hounds, we may have to shoot the blessed lot of them – no damned foxes to mention. Must have been that atrocious winter we had last year. Oh well, if there's nothing better to do I suppose it will compel me to visit the House more often.' His tone showed he found this a bore. With a final brisk rub of his hands he turned to go, then, remembering something else, he wheeled around. 'Ah, Kit, the Countess would like to see you in her boudoir.'

Upon the Earl's departure, Popplewell flew into a rage, throwing things about and saying that this was the final insult. 'Not fit to give the bloody hounds – well, stuff the bastard! I'm worth better than this!' Kicking aside a stool, he marched from the room.

Without waiting to learn the outcome of his tantrum, for such displays had become commonplace by now, Kit hurried off to the Countess's boudoir. Anticipating instructions for the coming season's new gowns, she was therefore unprepared for the interview that followed.

Lady Garborough looked up from her davenport and abandoned her letter-writing. There was an undercurrent to her address, a tone that somehow reflected the cool Chinese silk of the boudoir walls. 'Ah, Kit, you may recall some time ago I had recourse to enquire as to the amount of material you were ordering from the draper.'

Kit's heart leaped. One of her own dresses lay spread across a chair.

The Countess turned briefly to scold her parrot whose beak was ripping strips of mahogany from the edge of the desk. Replacing him on her shoulder, she proceeded to watch Kit like a hawk. 'I wonder if you might care to avail yourself of this opportunity to qualify the answer you gave at that time?'

Kit's skin prickled. On the previous confrontation she had sited inexperience as an excuse for her miscalculations, but now, with the damning evidence before her, she had no option but to own up. 'I'm ashamed to confess that I used the leftover bits of fabric to make myself a dress, ma'am.' She hung her head. 'I humbly beg your ladyship's pardon, but I thought nobody would want such small bits and —'

'And so you purloined them.' The Countess shook her head, looking stern, whilst the parrot muttered endearments in her ear, calling her his darling sweet lass. She glanced at the offending dress. 'One would hardly class them as small bits.'

'I'm deeply sorry for my incompetence, ma'am, but I swear there was no premeditated fraud! It just seemed an awful shame for such lovely material to go to waste.'

'Then might you not have consulted its owner so that she could make use of it?'

Kit's blue eyes projected apology.

'Was it that you thought I would not notice?' came the query. 'Despite what you may think, I do take an interest in my servants, Kit. I see what they are wearing on their days off. And it appears you have quite a collection at your disposal.' After a long pause, Lady Garborough demanded, 'So what am I to do now?'

'I could unpick it and make something for your ladyship, ma'am!'

'I am disinclined to wear my seamstress's second-hand clothing, Kit.' Lady Garborough stroked the parrot's breast with one finger. 'Besides, I referred not to the material but to you.'

Faced not just with dismissal but with a possible gaol sentence, Kit begged for leniency. 'I know I don't deserve it, ma'am, but I've never done this kind of thing before and I swear I'll never do it again.'

'Are you suggesting that I keep you on?'

'I'm not in a position to suggest anything, ma'am,' replied Kit with all the humility she could muster.

'Indeed you are not.' Lady Garborough had already given this deep consideration and had discussed it with her husband. Aware of the hardship that would befall Kit's family if she were dismissed without reference, and holding the opinion that one in her privileged position had a duty to those of lesser station, the Countess put Kit out of her misery. 'Very well, this is what the Earl and I have decided: the only way for you to make restitution for your misdemeanour is for you to remain at Postgate Park.'

Kit could scarcely believe that she had got away scot-free, and was soon to learn she had not.

'The cost of the material that you *stole*,' her ladyship laid heavy emphasis on the word in order that Kit might learn the true severity of her crime, 'shall be deducted from your wage in instalments. It is not my intention that your family should suffer for your wrongdoing. How much do you contribute per quarter?' Upon being told, the Countess proceeded, 'Very well, you shall still receive that amount – which I sincerely trust will reach its rightful owner.'

Kit gave an eager nod.

'But until the cost of the material has been recouped you will work for no reward, in whatever capacity you are required, be it seamstress, parlourmaid or chimney sweep. Should I require any new garments for the Season you will provide them before I go. You will not be accompanying us this year but will remain here to help spring clean the house. Another will be hired in your stead. I believe that you visit your family on the first Sunday of the month? Well, I am afraid that this must be restricted to once a quarter, when you will be allowed to take home your wages. Other than this you will be granted no freedom until I am sure you have earned it.'

Kit thanked the Countess for her leniency, and asked if a message could be sent to inform Monty of this for he might be worried over her non-arrival this Sunday. The lady relented and said that Kit could go herself tomorrow morning and confess to her crimes. As the miscreant turned to go, Lady Garborough called her back to collect the incriminating dress. 'Since this is of no earthly use to me, allow it to hang in your room as a reminder, and let us hope that it helps you to learn your lesson – though I should take a very dim view if I were to hear that you had been wearing it until it is paid for, Kit.'

'Oh, bugger,' said the parrot.

My feelings exactly, thought Kit. Thanking the Countess, she left the room with one small crumb of comfort. At least, visiting tomorrow, she would be spared all that cross-examination from Gwen on Sunday over the imaginary beau. After taking the dress to her room, she returned to the servants' quarters, wondering how long it would take the others to learn about the episode, but for now acting as if nothing had happened.

For a moment upon entry she thought the buzz of gossip was about her, for it stopped as she appeared but, on seeing her, one of the footmen announced laughingly, 'Eh, he's finally gone and done it, Kit!'

Still reeling from her own scrape, she looked confused.

'Old Poppy – he's gone!'

Kit was stunned. 'What – d'you mean for good?'

Their faces were still creased in laughter at the incident. 'Aye! Packed his bag, stuck his head in to say ta-ra and went!'

Kit was deeply hurt – she had always placed such value on Popplewell's friendship. How could he leave her without a word? It had been one thing after another lately.

'Aw, look, she's upset that he didn't wait to say goodbye to her,' teased a youth.

Oblivious to the implication, Kit disguised the extent of her injury by retorting. 'Why should he? I'm nowt to him. Anyroad, I'm up early tomorrow, I'm off to bed.' Feeling more wretched than ever, she went to prepare for the morrow's journey.

'Kit! What brings you here so early – Saint Friday, is it? Oh, you haven't got the sack have you?' Sarah's dark eyes were less than welcoming as her sister-in-law appeared in the doorway, interrupted her baking.

Kit asked cheekily how could she think such a thing, picked up her little nephew and gave him a kiss, then explained that as her services would be required on Sunday she had been allowed to come today. 'I set off at the crack of dawn to get here and this is the welcome I get!'

'Well, don't stand with that door open, come in if you're coming. It's freezing!' Sarah's bad-tempered face was temporarily hidden as she bent to take a loaf out of the oven and insert another tray of uncooked dough.

'Ooh, that smells lovely!' Kit set Probyn on his feet and unwrapped her shawl, face aglow from her brisk walk. Having expected to find only Sarah and Probyn in the house she was surprised to receive a greeting from Beata. 'Off work again?'

'She's never worked since last time you were here,' explained a harassed-looking Sarah, knocking the hot loaf out of its tin. 'Still, she earns her keep in other ways, looking after that terror – Probyn Kilmaster, just you wait till your father gets home!' He was attempting to scale the sideboard but, having once tasted paternal retribution, went to sit quietly next to Beata.

After some thought, he asked his mother, 'Will I go down t'pit when I grow up?'

'Not necessarily.' Sarah did not hold with the foregone conclusion that the coal owner's tenants would send their sons down the pit. 'If you work hard at school maybe you can get a better job.' She put her hands on her hips. 'Well, now! We were going to treat ourselves to a bacon sandwich for breakfast but I don't think I've got enough.'

'Kit can have mine,' said Beata, rubbing at her scrawny breast. 'I'm not right hungry.'

Her aunt objected. 'I don't want to take the food out of your mouth!' She apologized for not bringing her usual basket of goodies, adding that it was unlikely she would be so liberally endowed again after Mr Popplewell's sudden walkout.

'No, honestly, Kit. I couldn't stomach it.'

'No wonder you're all skin and bone, turning your nose up at good food!' The bad temper hid Sarah's concern. She tried to coax. 'Do try, Beat – half a rasher.'

Tears came to Beata's eyes and she begged to be excused from eating it.

Kit looked on, rather alarmed at this occurrence and also the change in her niece's appearance in the short time since they had last met. What little flesh she'd had previously had fallen from her, the bones in her wrists jutting like carbuncles, and her dark auburn hair lacked its sheen. Saying that the smell of bacon might tempt her niece, she began to lay rashers in a pan on the range. Turning to Sarah, she showed concern and asked if there was anything she could bring that would provide relief.

'I doubt it,' replied the girl's mother. 'I've tried everything. At least she's starting to cough some of that rubbish up now.' As the bacon sizzled, Sarah carved thick wedges from the new loaf, laying them upon four plates. The sight of Beata's constantly moving arm caught her eye. 'Why do you keep rubbing at your collarbone like that?'

'It hurts,' murmured the young woman.

'Some of this nice bread will take your mind off it.'

'I couldn't get it down, Mam,' came the weak protest.

'Well, you've got to eat something – here, I'll do you some pobs!' Sarah ripped the slice of bread into pieces and laid these into a bowl of milk to soak. 'Here, now eat this and no arguing!'

Whilst Kit, Probyn and Sarah devoured their bacon, Beata toyed half-heartedly with the bread and milk. When their plates were empty, hers was still three-quarters full. Finding her mother's constant reference to her poor appetite unbearable, she asked to be helped to the privy.

Kit was glad to do this for it gave her the opportunity to divulge the awful mess she had got herself into. It wouldn't really make much difference that she had been forbidden to make her home visits, she said, for she would normally have been away in London from spring until summer, so Sarah and Monty would suspect nothing. Just how she was going to explain her absence after that she had not yet worked out.

After Kit had made her confession, Beata revealed the true extent of her malady. 'I haven't had the curse again this month.' Seeing Kit's worried face she blurted, 'I haven't been doing owt wrong!'

'I wouldn't think that of you, love.' Seated on the wooden bench beside her, Kit pressed Beata's thin hand, feeling desperately sorry for her.

'I can't tell me mam.'

Kit said Sarah should be told. 'I'll tell her if you like.'

Beata thanked her. 'I hope she doesn't make me say owt to Dr Ibbetson. I'll go bright red.'

Kit echoed her feelings, then giggled. 'I can just see him saying, "There's a lot of it about – I've had it meself!"'

Beata broke into a fit of coughing. Having mislaid her handkerchief she was forced to hold her shawl over her face. This interrupted the conversation for a while. When talk resumed, the topic came around to men, and in particular Thomas, Beata wanting to know had Kit seen him lately. 'I'm so happy for you, Kit, you know. I'll never get a chap of my own but –'

'Of course you will!'

'Nay, you don't have to pretend.' Beata's eyes held a new maturity. 'Lads run a mile from me. But your happiness is as good as me own.'

Kit could have wept. They had always shared secrets before. Only pride had prevented her from revealing Thomas's abandonment; she could never give voice to the lie now. Telling Beata she had had a recent letter from him, she helped her fragile companion out into the fresh air.

It was cold, but with many private thoughts to share, they wrapped their shawls about them and tarried by the allotments for a while, watching the pigs and chickens. Anxious to make her niece feel better, Kit made Beata laugh time and again, plunging her into yet another paroxysm of coughing.

Kit looked on anxiously. Respiratory problems were a common feature of the mining village – Monty and his colleagues were always beffing to clear the coal dust from their lungs. The sound was commonplace in the Kilmaster household, but never had Kit seen her niece so severely afflicted. Alarm prickled her breast. People died from bronchitis.

Again, with no handkerchief at her disposal, Beata rid herself of the mucus as discreetly as possible over the allotment fence. Apologizing for her unladylike act, she rubbed her chest and said they had better be getting home.

Kit hovered assiduously, asking if Beata wanted a piggyback – only half joking – but her niece laughingly brushed these solicitations aside.

'Eh! I've just thought – if you're not allowed to come home you'll miss our Probe's breeching day.' Even in illness Beata's thoughts were for her aunt.

Kit made calculations. Probyn's birthday was not until summer. 'I might be in the good books again by then. Eh, I can't believe he'll be four! Time seems to fly after you're twenty-one. Anyway, one way or t'other I'll make it my duty to be here. I've been saving a brand-new sixpence to go in his trouser pocket.' She wrapped her arm around the invalid's waist, affecting a jocular air but really quite anxious. 'And I hope you're better by then, me lass. Or there'll be trouble!'

Kit's return to Postgate Park marked the start of a period of hard work which continued without abate, save for an interlude of prayer at Easter. Whilst the Earl and his family went off to London accompanied by their new cook and half the domestic staff, she was left behind with a band of skivvies and the housekeeper, who made sure that there was no escape. When the chimney sweeps had gone, Kit and the others went into battle against cobwebs, dust and grime. One huge room after another was stripped of its furnishings, which were beaten, shaken or laundered, gallons of water were dispensed over acres of paintwork, thirty-foot carpets were rolled aside, then rolled back again, feet ran up and down ladders, aching arms cleaned a thousand windowpanes – night after night an exhausted Kit fell into bed and woke minutes later, or so it seemed, ready to begin again. And still towards the end of May there were many rooms yet to go.

It was as she was cleaning the windows that overlooked the front drive that her horrified eyes saw the Earl's carriage coming down the drive and rushed to alert the housekeeper. 'It isn't July yet, is it? I must've lost a couple of months somewhere along the line.'

The housekeeper was as shocked as anybody and herded the servants to the staircase in order to greet their employer's arrival, moaning over their dishevelled state.

But when the Earl and his family arrived in the hall with his wife it was he who issued apologies, saying that he detested putting the staff to this inconvenience but he had received word that an elderly relative had died and the family had perforce come to pay last respects. They would only be staying for a day or two until after the funeral, he advised the housekeeper, and would avoid those rooms yet to be cleaned. He hoped it would not interfere with anyone's work.

Kit hoped it would, but was to be disappointed for her chores were as numerous as ever.

However, once the funeral was over, and the Garboroughs were preparing to return to London, she learned she was to be given respite. As the morrow would be Empire Day, and as a mark of his appreciation for his servants having coped so well with his impromptu return, the Earl had decided to grant them a day off. On top of this they would be transported to their homes in one of the Earl's own carriages. Unsure whether the treat extended to her, Kit tentatively consulted the housekeeper who, assenting, told her that the Countess was very pleased with her efforts and if she kept them up she might soon find her privileges restored.

The next morning, whilst the Earl's luggage was loaded for return to London, a delighted Kit stood in the courtyard with the rest of the home-going girls, awaiting their own promised vehicle. Teasing remarks were made upon the fact that she was more soberly dressed than usual – Kit had not dared to further provoke the Countess by wearing one of the offending garments and was clad in plain blue cotton. In the middle of jest, all bonneted heads turned expectantly at the sound of wheels, but the sight of a farm cart provoked laughter.

It was one of the Earl's neighbours, a more modest landowner, who pulled up alongside the waiting girls, his dour Yorkshire face bestowing a mere nod of acknowledgement before he jumped down. 'I heard his lordship were here. Thought he'd be glad to see these afore I take 'em to t'kennels.' Going to the rear of his cart he threw back a piece of hessian to reveal three cages of young fox cubs, fifteen animals in all.

There was a collective, 'Aw!' Whilst someone went to inform the master, Kit gathered round the cart with the others, looking at the terrified furry cubs that squirmed and cowered, each trying to hide behind the other. Farmer Alderson's face held no expression.

The Earl strode out, his fat old labrador plodding along behind. The scarcity of foxes had been the bane of his life of late and he treated this donation like a priceless gift, his craggy face examining the cages. 'Splendid, man! I was beginning to think it was going to be a year like the last – didn't have a kill in months.'

Without subservience, Farmer Alderson took off his hat. 'I thought your lordship'd be pleased. I do know how you like a chase.'

His beam seeming, to others, at odds with his mourning garb, the Earl heartily agreed. 'Mind you, there's no sport equal to shooting wild fowl with a punt and a big gun on water, I always say.'

'Fancy yourself as a poacher, milord, does tha?' The farmer's wry response held no disrespect.

'Hardly much fun on one's own land, old chap,' came the laugh.

'Oh, by the way, milord –' Farmer Alderson remembered something and pulled aside a piece of sacking to reveal a mangled badger – 'miners've been having sport down by your lordship's spinney agin last neet. I found it on t'way here still alive – it's deed now, mindst, I finished him off. Thought it might do to feed these little buggers.'

The Earl's attitude changed, he uttered a sound of disgust, condemning the working man's sport as brutal. 'It's bloody diabolical! I've warned my gamekeeper to keep his eyes open –' He broke off with a sigh of acceptance. 'But then he can't be everywhere I suppose. Anyway –' he started to back away, referring once again to his own superior class of butchery – 'I'm most grateful for these fellows, Alderson. You'll be rewarded.'

'Nay, I'm glad to get the buggers away from my lambs.' Responding to the Earl's instruction to take the cubs over to the kennels, Farmer Alderson threw a carpet back over them and climbed into his cart.

'You're not going to chase them tiny things, milord, are you?' tendered Kit.

'There'd be little sport in it,' came his reply. 'No, we'll feed them up then release them for future hunts – ah, your carriage awaits you, ladies!' A stately vehicle appeared from the mews. Kit's face lit up as the Earl himself helped her inside and waved his servants off. By the time it went through the gates all her sympathy for the cubs had been displaced by joy over the long-awaited visit home.

Her vigorous entry was to be somewhat tempered by the sight of her eldest niece in a makeshift bed by the fire. It had been impossible to imagine that Beata could lose more flesh, but the emaciation had progressed so far that it was as if a skeleton lay there – albeit a smiling one, for as ever Beata maintained her happy air. Though stunned, Kit hid it well and proceeded to acknowledge those gathered. It was a full house that greeted her, even Monty being allowed the day off to celebrate the glorious British Empire. In conjunction with this auspicious occasion it had been decided to bring Probyn's breeching day forward, partly to raise Beata's spirits. There he stood in his new trousers, jingling the coins in his pocket and waiting expectantly for his Aunt Kit to bestow another. Uncle Owen contributed too, he and his son having just arrived on their way back from a visit to the allotments. As much as Owen derided imperialism, the family noticed that he held his tongue when it came to a paid holiday.

The children as ever were delighted to see their aunt, the smaller ones hanging from her skirts in the hope that she might have a treat in her pocket.

Kit handed round a bag of conversation lozenges. 'Well, aren't we all lucky being given the day off to celebrate Her Majesty's birthday!'

'No, we're off because it's Empire Day,' corrected Wyn, waving her Union Jack.

'The Queen's birthday is Empire Day, dozy,' said Rhoda.

Wyn sulked and turned to Kit, 'It isn't, is it, Aunt?'

Kindly advising her that in fact it was, Kit led her over to the map on the wall and pointed out the large areas of red. 'See, the Queen is head of the Empire – which is a lot of foreign countries ruled by the British, because we're superior to the natives who live there and that gives us a responsibility to look after them.'

'Hang on!' exclaimed Sarah. 'Speaking of geography, I thought you were supposed to be in London?'

Kit had her answer prepared. 'The Earl had to come back early – he's had a death in the family. So he brought a few of us with him.'

There was muttered sympathy, then a concerned exclamation from Owen. 'Eh, we've just found that last bantie o' yours dead, Monty! Just like t'others, not a mark on it.'

'That's it then, all gone.' After an initial groan, Monty turned to Kit. 'You ain't been casting a spell on them, have 'ee? Thinking you'll have one on your bonnet for every day of the week.' He glanced at Beata and was satisfied to witness a grin spread across her wan face, which had been the joke's design.

Yet his quip masked a deep concern, and once Kit was installed, his attention and everyone else's for that matter, reverted to Beata in her fireside bed.

Somewhat ignored, Kit might have been glad that for once no interest was shown in her love life, had her niece not displayed such suffering. She seemed even too exhausted to indulge Probyn and begged him to go away.

'Ooh, I'll have to go again!' A sudden look of alarm on her face, Beata had to be helped from her bed by her father. Amidst an air of panic, Sarah thrust a wad of cut-up newspaper at Kit, who took over from Monty, she and Ethel half carrying their undernourished companion down to the privy on the corner of the street.

Sarah's black eyes showed anguish, demanding to know of Monty, 'How can she get so much diarrhoea? She doesn't eat enough to keep a worm alive. And she's been getting dreadful night sweats, her gowns are saturated. I'm forever washing.'

Discussion arose over what the malady might be, this being curtailed when Ethel and Kit returned the invalid to her bed, solemnly announcing that Beata had coughed up a lot of blood.

'Well, we don't need to ask what it is now,' murmured Owen through his teeth, though loud enough for his learned opinion to be heard. 'Consumption.'

'You don't know that!' In her fear, Sarah rebuked him.

'And neither will you if you don't have her to a proper doctor.' Owen was grim.

Monty defended Dr Ibbetson 'She's maybe just ruptured her throat with all that coughing,' he added. Turning his back on his brother, he attended the invalid, telling her everything would be all right, and wishing he believed it.

Unable to contain his frustration, Owen jumped up and told his son they were going home.

However, he was to reappear later that afternoon as Kit was preparing to leave, telling them that a doctor was on his way here from Methley and would appear any moment. 'He's just tethering his horse. Now, I don't want any argument, Monty! I'm paying for this out o' me own brass.'

Both Monty and his wife objected to the interference but their voices were stilled abruptly as the doctor poked his head around the door.

Monty became courteous. 'I beg pardon that you've been put to this trouble, Doctor. I wouldn't have sent –'

'I'm glad you did,' the younger man interrupted him, looking upon Beata with grave concern. 'Could we perhaps make a little room in here?'

Sarah packed the youngsters upstairs, she, her husband and a worried Kit attending the doctor whilst Owen went outside to lend Beata some privacy.

Showing kindness to his patient, the doctor asked numerous questions, then listened diligently to her chest for a few moments, before coming up with his verdict. 'I'm afraid it's phthisis.'

'Not bronchitis then?' asked Sarah. 'Only, Dr Ibbetson told us it was.'

'Did he?' The tone of the response told that this was nonsense.

Sarah went to open the door to re-admit Owen.

The latter whispered a request for the verdict, and was instructed that Beata was suffering from phthisis. He gave a jubilant exclamation. 'Told you!'

Sarah's face blackened and she hissed back at him, 'Well, there's no need to sound so blasted pleased about it!'

Subdued, he came into the room where Monty was asking if the rest of the family were in danger of catching it.

The physician felt unqualified to answer this, but liked to sound as if he was. 'There are different schools of thought on whether it's contagious or not. I rather doubt it myself. Some doctors say it's hereditary.'

Owen had been reading about the germ theory of disease and was keen to propound his knowledge, but the physician did not appreciate a layman telling him his job and said this was tripe. 'How could such an organism multiply so quickly? If that were so, all of mankind would be annihilated!'

Kit noticed Monty's satisfied glance at his wife, both enjoying Owen's comeuppance. How could they be so petty when Beata endured such suffering? She sat on the end of the bed and rubbed her niece's leg reassuringly.

The young doctor went on to list palliatives. 'Bismuth for the diarrhoea, and for the night sweats sponge her down at bedtime with tepid water and vinegar. If this fails I can prescribe something for that too, but I'd rather not give too much at the moment.'

Shaken by the verdict, Monty asked if they should keep giving her the medicine Dr Ibbetson had prescribed. The young man bit back an oath. 'Oh no, no, no! No medicine at all – unless the cough drives you up the wall.' Asked what else they could do to improve their daughter's health he instructed, 'Give her eggs –'

'All our chickens have died.' Monty looked decidedly forlorn. 'I can't understand it.'

Kit jumped in. 'I'll go buy some eggs from the farm now!'

'Good!' The doctor listed other commodities. 'Eggs, milk, mutton, and fat bacon.'

At the sight of her daughter near to vomiting, Sarah told him, 'She can't stand anything fatty, I'm afraid.'

There was no pandering. 'Make her eat it! Plenty of cocoa – and a glass of stout wouldn't go amiss.'

Monty and his wife shared a feeble joke that their daughter might become a drunkard. Beata was almost too weak to laugh, producing instead a sickly smile. Even that was wiped from her face by the sound of the continued prescription.

'Cod liver oil or extract of malt, half a pint of cream a day.' The doctor marked each off on his fingers. 'I'll give you a tonic too. As much fresh air as possible.'

Immediately Kit sprang up to open the window.

'For the pain in her chest, tincture of iodine must be painted over it. She must wear flannel – oh, she's already wearing it, good. Right, well, I think that's all I can do for the moment. Send for me if there's no improvement.' He was shown out by Owen, who left at the same time.

Upon their exit, Sarah pinched her brow, wondering where the money was going to come from to buy all these necessities, muttering that he had no idea of how other people lived.

'I don't want to be a drain,' tendered Beata.

Sarah affected brusqueness and rolled up her sleeves. 'If that's your way of trying to get out of eating this, my girl, you can think again!'

'Oh, please don't mention food,' came the barely audible request. 'Me poor bum feels like it's been passing nutmeg graters.'

Trying to appear jolly, though she was extremely upset, Kit went off to buy some eggs. Returning with them, she delivered a fond kiss to Beata's pale cheek, and said she would make an effort to get back to Ralph Royd as soon as possible. 'And when I come again I expect to see you looking like Humpty Dumpty!' But her joke hid an air of foreboding, and it was a wrench to leave, fearing Beata might not be here when she came again.

Noting Kit's sombre mood on her return, and on ascertaining the reason, the housekeeper took pity and decreed that if the maid continued to show similar industry as she had during previous months then she could go home again on Whit Monday.

Showing gratitude, and carrying a basket of eggs, butter and cream purchased out of her own reserves, Kit set off for Ralph Royd less than a week later to find the doctor thère again.

Far from the malady improving, Beata had been even more feverish, Sarah told her in the privacy of the scullery. They had even taken it in turns to maintain a nighttime vigil, she had been so ill. Both women watched anxiously whilst the doctor attended the emaciated waif in the fireside bed. Beata's face was almost grey and she had blue circles around her eyes.

From outside came the sound of children playing, the shouts of glee somehow emphasized by the quietude in here.

Upon completing his examination, the doctor was rather less cheerful than last time. 'I'm going to prescribe belladonna for the night sweats –'

269

A Welsh interjection: 'Isn't that dangerous, Doctor?'

He beheld the mother with compassion and said they must do every-thing to make Beata comfortable – a glass of brandy would not go amiss.

Even then, faced with the evidence in his eyes, Sarah would not allow herself to believe that her child was going to die. Little as she could afford the brandy she passed Kit a mug. 'Go down to the Well and fetch some, will you?'

The doctor made a joke to his patient. 'I wish I had that sort of well.'

From her pillow, Beata's grey face performed the feeblest of grins.

Anxious, Kit showed the physician out and afterwards set off for the Robin Hood's Well, mug in hand.

A procession was coming along the main street that was lined with villagers. The coal cart had been washed and scrubbed for Whitsuntide, its small occupants clad from head to toe in white, giddy with excite-ment. A batch of older boys and girls walked behind, clad in simi-lar garb.

'Aunt!' Alice waved. 'We're off to sing an hymn for our Beata!'

Kit waved back, yet the action lacked her normal enthusiasm and, upon observing her face, Alice and others broke free of the procession and ran up to her. 'What's up, Aunt?'

She scolded herself for alarming them. 'Nowt! I'm just running an errand for your mam – look out, they're going without you.'

But Alice, Merry and little Probyn insisted on tagging along, saying they would soon catch up with the procession, and all made their way to the whitewashed inn.

Peggo was on hand to serve Kit as she pushed her mug across the bar, for once free of his painful limp. 'Toothache, is it?' His lips barely twitched, though his blue eyes twinkled.

Kit found a smile and shook her head. 'No, but it is medicinal – yes, it really is today.'

Peggo continued to pretend disbelief, teasing the children who had accompanied Kit, until Alice piped up, 'Our Beata's badly.'

The creviced face altered. 'Eh, I'm reet sorry to hear that. Marion, fill this here cup wi' brandy for these young lasses!'

'I'm not a lass!' objected Probyn.

'I can see tha's not!' Peggo leaned over the bar to observe the child's white garb. 'Tha's wearing lad's breeks.'

Whilst Marion did as she was bidden, Peggo made further enquiries as to Beata's health. Kit formed a silent warning with her mouth, then bade the children run along or they would miss out on all the Whitsuntide fun. Only when they scampered out did she reveal to Peggo the true extent of Beata's suffering, her eyes filling up with moisture as she recounted her niece's appearance. He leaned on the counter, his coal-scarred hands clasped as if in prayer, periodically shaking his bald head and interjecting Kit's dialogue with a genuine, 'Eh dear, it's a bad do,' or other such sympathies.

When Kit asked how much she owed for the brandy he told her, 'Nay, it's on t'house, love – and tell my sweetheart I hope she's soon mended.'

As if his words were prophetic Beata did seem better when Kit was next permitted to visit, gabbling away to her aunt with great optimism about what she was going to do when she was fully recovered, saying she felt wonderful today.

Kit observed her still bed-ridden niece. She had gained no weight and remained exceedingly frail, but her cheeks were indeed pink and there was a brightness to her eye that had not been there before. Moreover, she had attended to her hair, the mirror and brush still at her side.

Kit gave a relieved exclamation. 'Oh, I'm right glad to see you looking so well! You look radiant – doesn't she, Sarah? Mindst, I don't know why I'm so pleased. I won't have any excuse to visit so often now.' She grinned. 'It must be Peggo's brandy that did the trick.'

Beata gave a weak chuckle. 'He brought me some more, you know. Me mam says he's trying to get me drunk so he can have his wicked way wi' me.' She shared a smile with Sarah, who stood at the table cutting up vegetables for tea. 'I told her, you'll have to put a bit more meat on me bones first.'

'I'd gladly give you some of this.' Kit jokingly indicated her own plump frame.

With a trembling arm, Beata held up the mirror and criticized her appearance. 'And I'd gladly swap this big conk – it looks even more like a beak with me face being so thin.'

'At least you're not the only one,' comforted Sarah. As each had grown it had become clear that all her daughters would share this disfigurement.

'Aye, it's like living in an aviary what with all them beaks.' But Beata's witticism was suffixed by a genuine complaint. 'The Lord must have an odd sense of humour, mun't He? Why else would all us lasses have got me dad's big sneck and the only lad among us has inherited me mam's little 'un.' Her mother said Probyn was too young for her to be able to tell yet. Asked where he was, she told Kit he now went to school with the others. He was in Baby Class.

'Well, at least you know who to blame.' Kit referred to her elder brother. 'I've no memory of my parents at all. I don't know which side your dad inherited his big nose from, nor Charity her thick hair.' A smirk began to play around her lips. 'Nor Gwen her thick neck.'

'Nor Amelia her thick skull!' Beata shook with laughter as she recalled some idiotic comment spouted by Amelia in the past. 'Ooh, help me up, I'm gonna wet meself.' She hauled herself out of the bed with Kit's aid and stood facing her hand in hand, tottering and swaying.

Sarah's thin lips broke into a smile as the auburn heads came together in girlish merriment. 'I'd hate to hear what you two say about me when my back's turned!'

Her daughter burst into fresh laughter, indicating guilt. Then, as if surprised, she drew back and half-coughed, half-vomited, and an array of bright scarlet drops peppered Kit's bodice. Brushing aside the voiceless, wide-eyed apology Kit lunged forth with a cry as the front of her niece's dress grew a crimson rose and Beata, missing the bed, fell to the floor. Sarah too came running to alleviate her daughter's suffering, praying that it would not last. It did not. Within moments Beata's eighteen years came to an end.

Whilst Sarah panicked, called out and grasped at lifeless limbs, Kit was rooted to the spot by shock, not knowing what to do. For the first time in her life she saw her brother's wife as a vulnerable human being. After the initial frenzy, the dreadful realization that there was nothing she could do, Sarah just kneeled on the floor at Beata's side, totally lost.

Kit began to sob. Deeply distressed, she wanted someone to hold and comfort her but Sarah had never been given to such displays, and Kit felt unable to offer succour in return now.

Pale with shock, she mopped her face, then, weaving her handkerchief in and out of her fingers, drew breath and muttered tearfully, 'I'd best fetch t'doctor.' The thought produced fresh sobs.

'What's the point of that?' Her mouth a bitter gash, her eyes black holes, Sarah stared at Beata, who remained sprawled upon the floor, her dead-weight impossible to lift even for the hefty Kit.

Incapable of answering at first, Kit shuddered and took a deep inhalation. 'I think you have to have someone qualified to tell you a person's . . . dead.' Her face crumpled again.

'I don't need a bloody quack for that,' spat the bereaved mother.

Oh, such bitterness! Hands clasped to her breast, Kit said she would go for Mrs Allen, and rushed to the neighbouring house. Her knocks and calls went unanswered, but aroused the neighbour on the other side.

'She's not in, pet!' Mrs Kelly's eyes took in Kit's distressed features. 'I just seen her pass my window.' On ascertaining what was amiss the Irishwoman became immensely kind, saying she would send her daughter for the doctor whilst she herself went back with Kit to wait with Sarah.

Even now her sister-in-law's emotions remained in limbo. How can she be so hard? Kit asked herself, her own eyes sore from tears.

Mrs Kelly had lost children of her own. At the sight of the forlorn figure kneeling by the body, she laid a hand on Sarah's shoulder.

'Would ye like me to help you shift her upstairs, darlin'?'

Sarah lifted blank eyes to the inquisitor.

'For the laying out,' came Mrs Kelly's soft explanation. 'She'll be better up there.'

Sarah appeared to have been hit with a sledgehammer. For a second she did not speak, then the look of horror was replaced by a tone of authority. 'Yes, yes, we can't expect the rest of the children to come home to a . . . with . . .' There was a long gap that signified acceptance, then she broke down sobbing and howling. Kit joined her grief, but at a distance.

Mrs Kelly put one arm around the bereaved mother and took charge of the situation. 'I can take two of the weans. They can spend the night at our house and I'll arrange for someone else to take the rest. I'll arrange the laying out too – you'll not be wanting to do it yourself, pet.' There was wisdom in her tone.

Sarah gulped. 'No, no! I couldn't bear it.'

'Then I'll whip out now and fetch Mrs Feather so's we can get your little girl more comfortable, and then I'll make you a cup of tea.'

Without speaking, Kit sniffed and indicated that she would do this, moving across to the range to attend the kettle. Before the tea was brewed, however, a grim-faced Mrs Feather and her team arrived carrying a board. Upon seeing it Sarah broke down again and, with Kit in tow, Mrs Kelly led the way to her own house.

'Come along, dear. Let the ladies get on with their task. It'll be a bit easier on you.'

After they had spent a period of time – Kit was unsure just how long – in Mrs Kelly's surprisingly clean house, being attended by this extremely kind and understanding woman, the doctor looked in.

Refusing the offer of tea, he seemed anxious to be on his way, just hovered awkwardly to deliver his opinion. 'Her heart gave out – I know what a dreadful shock it must have been for you, but, believe me, you must count it a blessing.' He had witnessed many an agonizing death from consumption, had watched the suffocation go on for days. 'It has spared her much pain.'

Mrs Feather popped her head in then to say all was done, giving the doctor the chance to escape. With obvious trepidation Sarah and Kit went home.

The living room was empty. Someone had been kind enough to remove the bloodstains too. Both steeling themselves against the ordeal, the bereaved women went upstairs. The children's room had been rearranged, a bed dragged into the middle with a gap to either side of it. Upon it lay Beata, washed and wrapped in a white sheet, a white lace-edged handkerchief covering her face, and a pillow on either side of her head. Hesitantly, Sarah ventured further to lift a corner of the handkerchief. Beata's jaw had been tied up with bandages which almost matched the whiteness of her skin. Little pads of damp cottonwool covered her eyes. All trace of blood had been washed away, but it would linger in Kit's memory for ever. She did not want to be here. Beata was gone.

'What about our Monty?' Her trembling voice seemed an intrusion in this place of rest.

'What about him?' Sarah knew it sounded callous but did not care.

Kit answered softly. 'Shall I go and meet him, let him know?'

'If you like.'

Kit pondered, the inside of her skull feeling one throbbing salty mass of mucus. 'Maybe I should go collect t'little uns from school first. If they find out from somebody else – aye, I will, then we'll go meet t'lasses from work and wait for our Monty.'

At Sarah's lack of interest she hovered for a while, feeling excluded, overwhelmed by grief and shock over the suddenness of it all. Then she grabbed her shawl and left. Not until she was outside did she realize that for the second time today she had omitted to count to five. Ever after, she would never feel the need to do it again.

Owen had spent his entire day sloshing around in water. His boots were drenched, his whole body ached. He had added half an hour to his day by standing at the pithead after work trying to get men to join the union and he was now ready for his tea. But when he reached the end of Pit Lane and saw the long-faced group awaiting his brother who walked alongside him, all thoughts of his own discomfort vanished. It could only signify one thing.

Instead of going home, he joined the sad procession, one coal-black hand on a child's auburn head. At his brother's abode, both he and Kit showed surprise that Monty underwent his usual ritual, stripping off his jacket and shirt and bending over the enamel bowl in the yard. Catching the accusation on their faces, Monty challenged them, his eyes red and anguished. 'Beata's not going anywhere, is she? The least I can do for her is wash myself.' He plunged his hands time and again into the water, sluicing it over his head, experiencing an impotent rage at not being able to prevent his daughter's death, thinking that this was all his life would ever amount to, and that however hard he worked it would never restore that brief loving relationship he had once shared with Sarah. Their only bond was the children. And now the sweetest of those was gone.

Inside, the clock had been stopped, the mirror and pictures covered, the curtains drawn. From that moment until their child was buried they dwelled in darkness. With their bedroom a chapel of rest and no space downstairs, the younger children stayed with neighbours, their siblings taking turns to maintain the vigil whilst their parents dozed. A mundane consideration shortened the viewing period: the weather was hot, speeding up decomposition, the funeral must take place within the next day or so. Throughout the duration there was a constant flow of friends and neighbours come to view the departed, though no one came from Wales; it was too far.

In death as well as life, Mrs Feather saw to all the arrangements, organizing the food and the women who would serve it. A photographer came too. Sarah had never been one for likenesses but now in her grief she realized that the lock of Beata's hair encased in a brooch was insufficient memento and bade him capture her daughter's spirit.

Kit thought it macabre. How could he portray Beata as she had been in life?

As if affected by this same thought, on this, the day of the funeral, Sarah clutched the deathbed photo in her hand, deeming it unsuitable. 'I'm going to use it to have a portrait made of her, but the artist will need to know her colouring.' Her voice came out of the gloom, surrounded by a tide of ebony crepe. Lined up on a bench, her daughters with their prominent beaks and black garb looked like little crows upon a branch. Holding the face of each of her children in turn, she sought similarities. 'Alice's eyes are the nearest in colour to Beata's – the shape of Rhoda's face – Ethel's chin –'

Wanting desperately to give part of herself to Beata, Kit said, 'My ears are just like Beat's.'

Sarah beheld her witheringly, as if Kit were trying to be amusing. 'I hardly think you've anything to contribute that her sisters can't.'

Feeling that her heart would break, Kit lowered her tear-filled eyes to her lap, where her hands played with a black-bordered handkerchief. Black, black, everything was black.

Monty stood in silence, wearing only a hint of his private pain.

His wife gazed blindly into mid-air. 'I got quite a shock at that Mrs Kelly's house. It was remarkably clean, considering. And she was actually quite nice.' There had been little contact between the two women since that day, but Sarah was not quite so swift to condemn now.

Probyn, confused over his sister's death, looked from one face to another, seeking answer, but finding none.

'They're all here.' A grave billy-goat face inserted itself into the crowded room.

At Owen's utterance, Kit risked a glance through the window. Almost every inhabitant of Ralph Royd appeared to be gathered outside. She and everyone in the room rose as one. The Minister entered, offered a prayer and a hymn was sung.

Owen, regarding the Minister as a boss's man, stepped forth to voice his own contribution. 'Well, Beata lass, tha's off to a better world than this, to sup with the Lord and enjoy His everlasting love. I know He'll be as pleased to see thee as we that are left behind are sorry to lose thee. You'll be the bonniest and best angel in His heaven. Amen.'

Monty stood with bowed head and gritted teeth, hating Owen for his ability to speak at such a time. Anger filled his every pore: anger that Owen could take it upon himself to perform what should have been a father's speech, anger that his brother's words moved him to tears, tears that he had so far valiantly managed to suppress.

After a respectable interval, a man came forward with a screwdriver and secured the coffin lid, whilst Mrs Feather supervised the passing round of glasses of port and funeral biscuits to those who waited outside.

Although a non-smoker himself Monty handed round clay pipes and tobacco to those he knew partook of the weed. Peggo reached out and took a plug of tobacco from the black plate, filling his own pipe, afterwards helping to position two chairs on the footpath. The coffin was then carried out and placed on them.

Flora, the last out, attempted to close the door behind her but Gwen quickly threw it open. 'How will her soul escape? Dope!'

'Eh, they've done the lass proud,' murmured a neighbour, admiring the casket that had been provided by the insurance payments. Everyone agreed.

Peggo puffed on his pipe and spoke thoughtfully to the coffin. 'Well, you're on your way now, honey. God speed.'

Eyes shone. When the glasses of port had been drained, the villagers united in a hymn and Beata's remains were borne along Savile Row, past the allotments and onwards down the slope to the chapel. Behind, in their black hats and white crocheted shawls walked Mrs Feather and her team, then the Minister, the bereaved family and the rest of the mourners.

After the service, Mrs Feather and her helpers escaped as inconspicuously as they could in order to prepare the funeral tea whilst the coffin was carried to the graveyard where they all sang 'Gather at the River'. The clink of blacksmith's tools, echoing across the field from the mine, was both a death knell and a sign that life went on.

Reluctant to look down into the hole, Kit read each of the epitaphs around her on those slabs of weathered stone, many of them bearing the names of miners, then lifted her eyes to stare across the field at the loathsome structure that had put these men in their graves. Such an uninspiring view for Beata's last resting place.

Afterwards, all retired to the Sunday school room for a meal of ham and fruit cake.

When the family went home, Sarah removed the covers from the mirror and the picture and life continued as it always had. Just one person less.

Hating Gwen's stupid platitudes – 'Life must go on, I zuppose,' – and listening to Amelia talk about the important people who came to dinner at her employer's house, Kit yearned to get away, but was forced to spend a respectful time amongst them, knowing that none of her siblings, except perhaps Monty, could feel the loss as deeply as she.

With shattered heart she eventually managed to depart for Postgate Park, mind railing at the injustice of her loved one's premature demise – poor, dear Beata, never so much as a boyish kiss to touch those lips!

Her boots felt like lead, dragging her dispirited form along the coal-dusted track. Was spinsterhood to be Kit's lot in life too? She recalled the gypsy's prediction: *I see no marriage. I see no children.* The woman had been right about Myrtle; must Kit, then, accept her words as truth?

Casting her eyes ahead, Kit saw her future unfurl before her, a long and empty road. When the tears came again, they were not entirely for her dead niece.

16

The devastation Kit experienced over Beata's death stayed with her a long time. It was said that hard labour took one's mind off one's troubles but even in her overworked role of general dogsbody there were still pauses for reflection, at which point Beata's lovely face would manifest itself. A very different face to the one which hung on the wall of Savile Row.

True to her intention, Sarah had taken her remaining daughters to an artist's studio in Castleford and, presenting him with these models, the lock of hair and the deathbed photograph, had instructed him to create a pastiche of the dearly departed and thus bring her back to life.

Kit thoroughly detested the finished portrait, not because she was excluded from participation, but because it had no soul. This was not the Beata she had loved.

It had been hard enough to come back here at all after the funeral, but to be faced with that awful picture was more than Kit could bear. Receiving a good report about Kit from the housekeeper on her return from London, the Countess had reinstated her seamstress and restored her days off, but perversely this seemed not to please Kit, her visits to Ralph Royd so subdued that others could not fail to comment on her mood.

'If her don't buck her ideas up I'm going to give her what for!' Kit heard a familiar voice as she came up the incline on her latest visit. 'Why, the face on her, you'd think it was her child who'd died. I mean, we're all sad, but really she always milks a situation for all it's worth, does our Kit.'

Rounding the corner, she came across Gwen and Flora, two black beetles moving up the street, the latter agreeing with her sister's every word as they made their way to their brother's house. Her mind raged against such unfeeling comment. Did they not appreciate that Kit had been especially close to her niece, having grown up alongside her? She had only been four when Beata was born, it had been like having a baby sister.

Hearing a footfall to her rear, Gwen looked round and her expression turned to one of command. 'Here! I want a word with you, my girl, before you go in.' Waiting for her youngest sister to catch up, she took hold of Kit's mourning dress. 'You can get rid of that miserable face for a start! We're all feeling the loss but it don't do Sarah any good to have you moping around all the time. If the girl's mother can carry on, then so can you.'

Chastened, Kit saw that Gwen was right in part. Promising she would do her best to contain her grief – though just how, she could not tell – she accompanied her sisters along the row.

Gwen was kinder then, patting her arm. 'There's a good lass. It'll make you feel a whole lot better too. And I know you're only being respectful but don't let it be too long afore you go back to wearing your normal clothes, outlandish though they might be. Well, we gotta have sommat to laugh at, ain't we?'

Kit was forced to smile.

'That's better!' The portly middle-aged Gwen reached up to chuck her much taller sister's chin. 'I'm sure your young man don't want to look at a misery guts either, does he?'

Kit's heart leaped. Courtship being the last thing on her mind, she had totally forgotten Thomas. Even presented with this opportunity, she could not force herself to admit that someone had paid her to stay away from their son. The only admittance she was prepared to make was that she had not seen anything of him in ages.

'Why, you must be sick and tired of us old busybodies going on at you,' Gwen told her as they arrived at their destination. 'I won't utter another word about it.' But she enjoyed a self-satisfied glance at Flora, one that said: Didn't I tell you he was only a figment of her imagination?

By the following spring, Kit had managed to struggle free of her mental fetters and Mothering Sunday found her dressed to the nines. Most of the servants had been given leave to take daffodils home from the park. Kit would not be taking any, not from any sense of malice but because she did not want to outdo the children, who would be going out to pick

280

their own. As a further treat and to help those whose homes were at a distance, the Earl and Countess had provided transport – no mother should be deprived a visit on this special day.

Hence she arrived in style at Ralph Royd. Being the last of the servants to be dropped off, it appeared that she alighted from her very own carriage. Children came to gather in the street, Probyn amongst them.

Immediately spotting the colourful bird on her new hat, he asked, 'Is that the one I gave you, Aunt?'

Kit lied and said it was, adding didn't it look splendid? The little boy looked proud, and ran into the house ahead of her, shouting to his parents that he was the one responsible for his aunt's wondrous attire.

Sarah passed a disparaging glance at Kit's apparel, she herself still in mourning dress. 'I wondered how long it would be.'

Inferring that she was being accused of an uncaring attitude, Kit looked stricken. There was an awkward silence in the room, broken only by the younger children's fidgeting. Her own siblings were not here, having visited only a few weeks ago. There was no reason for Kit herself to be here either; Sarah was not her mother. Though, physically, Sarah had looked after her well, there was a dearth of affection between them. Never more so than now. Look at that big healthy lump, Sarah's attitude seemed to say, when my own daughter lies in her grave.

Kit inhaled and tried to sound cheerful. 'Well, who's coming for a walk?'

'We can't yet we've got to bury t'bird,' Wyn told her.

A look at Monty produced the answer that they had found the canary dead in its cage this morning. The children said they would like to have a funeral and Kit agreed to help them, saying they needed a little box to put him in.

Sarah looked as if she might explode with anger. 'Haven't we had enough funerals in this house?'

Knowing that it was more than the death of a canary which made her thus, Kit glanced at Monty. The air of friction that was always there between these two seemed to have intensified since Beata's death.

'I'll walk with you up to the allotment.' Monty looked grim. 'Georgie Smith said he'd sort me out a new bird.' Taking the empty cage, he went up the street alongside Kit, the children spread out in front, bearing the feathered corpse wrapped in cloth.

When Kit asked if anything was wrong between Monty and Sarah, he replied, 'No more than usual.' How could a man tell his sister that his wife would not let him near her – had never let him near her since Beata had died? He was not yet forty years old and life might as well be over.

Reaching the allotments, he asked, 'D'you want to come with me for the bird, Probe?' But the little boy preferred to attend the funeral. Feeling a childish sense of resentment towards his son for rebuffing this offer, Monty stalked off to his friend's aviary.

Kit performed the funeral, suggesting that the children needed some lolly sticks to form a cross. A search ensued, providing two sticks, which were bound together with some cotton from Kit's pocket. Afterwards she and the children went off to pick flowers.

Upon the way back, his cage bearing a new occupant, Monty noticed the miniature cross with 'RIP' written on it in pencil. The children were still out when he got back. Not wishing to be in the house alone with Sarah, he stayed in the yard for a while, examining his feathered companion. The young canary was nervous and kept leaping around its bars in a panic. Reaching into the cage, Monty cupped the bird in his hand and began to stroke its yellow feathers gently, talking to it in a low murmur in order to calm it. 'Young chap like you shouldn't be trapped in a cage,' he told it, all too aware of the analogy. 'But 'twouldn't do to set you free. You wouldn't survive a minute out there on your own.' Having calmed the bird slightly he put it back in the cage, then reluctantly carried it indoors to show to his wife.

A great awkwardness remained between them until eventually the children spilled in, each bearing an armful of flowers.

Their mother showed little gratitude. 'Good grief, is there anything left standing in the meadow? We haven't got room for all those in here. Go and put some of them on your sister's grave.'

Kit wondered if that suggestion was for her benefit. Did Sarah truly think she had forgotten Beata? Steering the disappointed children back outside, she murmured that she would not stop for tea but had to get back to Postgate Park, adding that she would not see the family for a while as she was due to go to London tomorrow. With his wife apparently unaffected by the news, and Kit obviously upset, Monty was kind enough to accompany his sister along the street.

Only when they had all left her did Sarah weep.

Kit wept too on her way home. Too early to meet the Earl's coachman at the arranged point, she made her return to Postgate Park on foot, this lending much time for contemplation. Poor dear Beata, how Kit missed her. Try as she might to drive that gaunt image from her mind, mile after mile Beata was to accompany her. What if she too were to die before she had known a man's love? It was all too much. Along that lonely stretch of road, each step was accompanied by a sob.

The sound of a horse's hoofs came clopping up behind her, the rider passing her a glance as he went by. Upon noting her ladylike attire he raised his hat. For once Kit did not appreciate the attention, but kept her head lowered so that he would not see her mottled face.

She was in the act of blowing her nose when the rider pulled in his reins and steered the horse back towards her.

'May I be of any assistance, ma'am?'

Half of Kit wished for him to go away, the other part of her desperately needing friendship. 'I am unwell . . .'

He was off his horse in seconds and, leaving it to graze on the verge, came to her side. Simultaneously, he removed his top hat, revealing dark hair to match his eyes, and offered a handkerchief. Kit shoved her own drenched piece of linen into her pocket and accepted his, thanking him sincerely.

Dismissing it as of no consequence, he told her to keep it, adding, 'I should very much like to be of further assistance, if I may?' Without his hat, he did not appear so tall now.

Badly in need of company, Kit asked if he would escort her home. It was not very far away.

This he agreed to, and walked alongside her, leading his horse. Introductions were made, the young man giving his name as Ninian Latimer. Kit provided explanation for her tearfulness, telling him that she had lost someone dear to her. He offered his sympathy, then seemed content to remain quiet until they arrived at Postgate Park, where his next comment was to surprise her. 'You must have only been visiting Cragthorpe Hall the last time we met.' The ensuing look of puzzlement caused a grin. 'You don't remember me, do you?'

Kit studied him as closely as politeness would allow. How could she have forgotten meeting such a finely dressed fellow? He was quite good-looking too. 'How very rude you must think me.' Instinctively, she found herself reacting in ladylike manner, and this in itself caused a pang of guilt. What manner of woman showed such artifice when purporting to grieve?

His laugh was kind. 'Not at all! I'm afraid my comment was a bit of a sham, for we were never introduced. I merely saw you walking by and before I could summon the courage to do anything more than raise my hat you had gone through the gates of Cragthorpe Hall. I should add that it was some years ago when I was but a callow youth. Yet I remember you very well.' Fleetingly, his eyes took in her Junoesque figure.

Through the haze of teary confusion, Kit received a sudden vision of the time she had borrowed Mrs Dolphin's clothes. Recognition appeared on her puffy face.

He seemed glad that she had at last remembered. 'I've been hoping we would meet ever since.'

'Have you?' She was utterly taken aback.

'What a great pity that it had to be my intrusion into your distress which brought us together.'

'Your compassion does you honour, Mr Latimer.'

'Without wishing to impose upon your grief further, could I hope that we might meet again in happier times? Perhaps I could come to call upon you soon?'

'I'm afraid I'll be going up to London tomorrow and shall be there until the end of July.'

He was unfazed. 'Then could I arrange to call upon you when you return?'

Still recovering from her tears, Kit was in a quandary. There had been no intention to mislead him at first – she had referred to Postgate Park as home quite naturally. But would he wish to meet her if he knew of her humbler origins? Presented with such a chance of happiness she could not allow it to slip. Beata would want her to be happy. 'I should love to make your further acquaintance,' she told him. 'But although I am of age to make my own decisions, my brother, who is my guardian, is very strict and doesn't care for me to receive gentleman callers.' It was not an actual lie. She had not said that Monty lived here. 'Could we meet somewhere else? One afternoon or evening, perhaps.'

He was eager to arrange such a meeting. There was an inn, the White Hart, in the nearby village of Aldwaldwyke; across the road from this was a stone memorial cross. If she cared to wait there on the first of August at noon he would come with his carriage to whisk her off for a picnic luncheon. Inclining her head at his bow, Kit turned and walked up the drive, doubting very much whether she would ever see him again, for the first of August was a very long way off.

Upon arrival in London, Kit was disappointed to be told that her friend Dolly was no longer there. She had caught scarlet fever.

Still raw from her own bereavement, she was concerned. 'Our Charity's bairn died from that!'

'Dozy!' Her informant enlightened her. 'I mean she fell for a soldier – gone off to India with him, she has.'

Kit envied her friend's romance, but was also a little lost, for it soon transpired that none of the other servants was keen to be seen out with her, Dolly's reputation having rubbed off. Even the ones who had been agreeable in Yorkshire were now showing reticence about talking to her, lest they too be sullied by association – though Kit herself remained innocent as to their true reason.

Hence, she who had been primarily bowled over by London, awed by its historic buildings, dashing cavalry officers in their brilliant tunics and their glossy black steeds, the expansive parks and spectacular fashions, was now in the awful position of having to spend her free time unaccompanied. And this vast metropolis was no place to be alone.

Kit fought the cowardly urge to stay home, and a week after her arrival set off on her first solo outing. Almost immediately she discovered it was a mistake. London was crammed with humanity, all of whom appeared to know exactly where they were going, unlike Kit, who had always relied on others to guide her. She marched along with purpose in her step, fearing that any hesitance, any sign of vulnerability would invite attack from the criminal element who were never far away in the big city. Constantly glancing up for street names, she found herself in New Bond Street where she paused to draw breath and take stock, pondering over a display of mourning jewellery. Perhaps she should buy something in memory of Beata. But when she enquired as to the price of an elaborate jet brooch she found herself unable to afford it, and hurried red-faced from the shop.

Embarrassment caused her to rush headlong without consideration for her route. The streets suddenly became narrower, and she realized that she was lost. The rubbish-filled lane terminated in a small market. Wondering frantically how to get back to familiar ground, she instead went deeper. The cacophony of vendors cries made her scowl and hurry onwards with a muttered curse for them to shut up. Passing three down-at-heel characters who loafed against a wall, she threw an anxious sideways glance and noticed that they were paying close attention to her smart dress.

'Carry your bag, ma'am?' The scruffy, unshaven speaker laughed with his companions as the young woman shrank from his impudent offer and hurried on, eyes upon the pavement. A wink and a mutter passing between them, the three set off after her, causing her to increase her speed, which amused them all the more.

Trapped within a maze of ancient archways and narrow insalubrious lanes, the three ruffians still on her tail, Kit began to panic, looking wildly about her. Then, out of an alley came a procession of tiny-shaven headed waifs from an orphanage – obviously girls for they wore pinafores. Noting authority in the orphans' course, Kit fell into line behind them, praying fervently that they would lead her back to civilization, all the while casting terrified glances over her shoulder.

The loud clip–clop and jingle of heavy traffic and the sight of a green sward brought a sigh of relief to Kit's lips. There was Piccadilly, a place she knew! Hurrying forth, she performed one last turn of her head and to her further relief saw that the laughing ruffians had changed course, disappearing into another street with a cheeky wave that told her they had merely been pulling her leg.

Kit slunk away, taking the familiar route home, thinking how pitiable a creature was she, forced to rely on infants to guide her.

Safe in the comforting arms of a chair in the servants' hall, Kit found herself in the company of a new maid, with whom she struck up a conversation, for with the rest of the household hard at work they were the only two in the room. Gladys had just arrived from the country. She was to work in the kitchen, after being allowed this first hour to settle in. Even to one as unsophisticated as Kit, Gladys appeared very green and ill at ease. The former sought to warn the new girl that under no circumstances should she go out alone, telling her of the dreadful fright she herself had just had, and asking would Gladys like to accompany her on their next day off. Eager to make friends, Gladys said she would, telling Kit that she was awfully kind and allowing personal information to flow. Seduced by the other's friendly open manner, Kit too shared intimacies, stretching out her legs beneath her ruched skirts to voice sadness over Beata, then going on to boast of the young man who waited for her back in Yorkshire.

Gladys was agog at the other's expensive appearance, and the fact that one so superior could stoop to chat with a kitchen maid. She listened with reverence until another maid entered, at which juncture Kit gave a final stretch, smiled at the new girl and rose. 'Well, I think I'll go and wash before tea. Remember now, you must tell me when your day off is and we'll arrange to go to the theatre or something.'

After Kit had left the room, the maid who had entered now pounced on Gladys with a warning. 'Here, you want to stay away from that one. She's a bad lot!'

A look of alarm washed over the new girl's face as she listened to the other's further defamation of one she had thought so nice. In a matter of moments Kit was demoted from benefactress to harlot. 'Oh, my goodness – is that how she can afford those lovely clothes?'

The other gave a curt nod. 'So just watch yourself, don't go out with her or you'll end up the same way.'

'Why, she were just telling me all about this fella she's met,' breathed Gladys. 'I wonder if he knows what she's at?'

'Ooh, I haven't heard about him!' Eager to hear more, the other girl sat down beside Gladys.

Upstairs, Kit enjoyed a leisurely toilet, unaware that her confidences to the new girl were already doing the rounds of the house.

Finding it hard to comprehend the new girl's sudden reluctance to take up her offer of an outing, Kit shrugged and said perhaps some other time. But Gladys, although still pleasant enough and happy to listen to Kit's woes, made one excuse after the other, saying she had mending to be done or other such chores, so over the next four months Kit grew accustomed to going out alone.

Yet even by July she had not become acclimatized to the big city, and still she restricted her course to the main thoroughfares – a walk in one of the parks, a saunter along Oxford Street to look at things she could not afford, a mouth-watering tour of Fortnum's. Despite these wonderful venues, and the distant glamour of the glittering balls that took place in the Earl's drawing room, life was terribly lonely and she yearned for the sight of a friendly face. Today her prayer was answered, though only fleetingly. Going down to the hall on this, her Monday morning off, she encountered Ossie Postgate, who bestowed a much warmer greeting than she would receive from a member of her own family. Since he had been at university she had seen little of him, his holidays spent in one country house after the other – which was exemplified in the surrounding paraphernalia of guns and fishing tackle, rods, rackets and suitcases that he had brought with him. Kit returned his greeting with polite warmth, then a brief chat and he was gone, leaving Kit to her solitary walk. She sighed – two and a half weeks to go before she could escape to Yorkshire and meet Ninian Latimer. Though in truth she held no illusions here either, for in her absence he could well have met someone else, even have forgotten the rendezvous.

It was very hot. The air smelt of horse dung and leather harness. Taking as direct a line as possible she made for Hyde Park. Immediately upon entering she felt more lonely than ever – an insignificant dot on the vast acreage beneath a wide open sky – and struck out across the green towards other signs of life. The park was more sparsely populated than on a Sunday – a boy walking a dog, a tramp with filthy nails picking up cigar butts – though there were still plenty of the idle rich in evidence, parading their ravishing gowns to lesser folk's envy. Spotting two young ladies in riding habits, each upon an immaculately groomed bay with only a servant for escort, Kit recognized the Earl's twin daughters, and inclined her head deferentially as they greeted her. Did they know that she was here for the same reasons as they, each hoping to attract a man? They would have more luck than her if the fortune-teller had spoken the truth – but Kit was determined to prove the gypsy wrong. For a while she strolled amongst the riders and those who sauntered, enjoying a smile at gambolling children and wondering what little Probyn was up to at this moment.

Meandering amongst the shade of ancient trees, their bark a mass of whorls and knots and hollows, and twiggy offshoots where branches had been lopped, Kit suddenly found herself isolated. Overcome by unease, she glanced around her but saw nothing to invoke concern. Still, the feeling persisted. She began to hear rustling in the bushes and looked round sharply, but saw no one. Increasing her pace, she hurried towards the sound of children playing – when a sudden cry caused her to break into a trot. Rounding a clump of greenery, she saw a lady and her female servant being accosted by a man with an upraised cane.

Kit's involuntary yell of, 'Murder!' startled the attacker, and immediately he ran off.

The silken-clad victim, though possessed of a rather stout constitution, was extremely flustered and was helped to a bench by her maid and Kit. 'Oh, how fortuitous that you happened along at this moment, my dear!' She praised her saviour, grasping Kit's plump arm in gratitude. 'Heaven knows what would have happened – the vagabond!' There was a slightly foreign note to her voice.

Kit had recovered some of her own decorum and tried to match the lady's manner. 'He was dressed like such a gentleman too.'

'Be not deceived by his appearance, my dear!' The lady made rapid attempts to cool herself with an ostrich feather fan. 'Good breeding extends far beyond apparel.'

Inferring accusation, Kit blushed. But the lady did not seem to intend any slur for she continued to address the young woman as one of her own class, even bidding Kit to sit beside her, the lilac and mauve silk rustling as she made room on the bench, and the maid standing by.

'You should not be out alone, my dear! '

Kit said that sometimes she preferred solitude. The lady agreed and said that, anyway, a maid was not much use if one was attacked. With a disparaging glance at her servant, she asked, 'Is there anything, *anything* at all, I can do to repay your bravery?'

Kit eyed the other's jewelled brooch with a hopeful pause, but her hint went undetected and she was forced to give some flippant response. 'That which I most desire is impossible for you to give. I should like very much to be married.'

'Ah! You and all the other young beauties in the park, I imagine.' The lady beamed, her white cheeks crinkling. 'But, my dear, your wish is so simple to answer! A handsome young woman like yourself –'

'I fear I am too tall.'

'*Mais non* – statuesque!' The lady began to question her. With whom was she acquainted?

Suddenly remembering the calling cards in her beaded bag, Kit snatched this first opportunity to use one, embroidering its presentation by adding that she was a companion to the Countess of Garborough.

This was met with faint astonishment. 'I cannot believe you have found no eligible bachelor amongst such distinguished company!'

'I confess there are many I've admired,' sighed Kit, 'but sadly my feelings are not reciprocated.' Whilst not forgetful of Ninian, she began to see in this lady an opportunity to hedge her bets.

'Tosh! They must be blind. I know a dozen perfectly charming young men who would leap at your company.' The lady produced her own card. 'This is my address. Call there tomorrow afternoon and I shall be most happy to make introductions.'

At the inscription 'Baroness Cazalet', Kit became flustered and tried to remember which day she would be off next week. 'I'm afraid I shall be unavailable tomorrow – but I should dearly love to call upon you Tuesday week if that would be acceptable?'

The Baroness was most gracious and said that would be fine.

After making sure that the lady was fully recovered from her ordeal, Kit went on her way, unable to believe the opportunity that had arisen from a mere walk in the park.

Seven nerve-racking days later, Kit set out for Baroness Cazalet's residence, to reach it being required to take a hansom cab across London. Arriving in her best attire at a leafy terrace, she took the six steps up to the front door of the three-storeyed residence and rang the bell. Beset by terror that her lack of social graces might give her away, her heart had not stopped thudding since she had set out. The door was being opened. Kit galvanized herself.

A footman escorted her through the black and white tiled hall, with no indication that he beheld Kit as anything other than a lady. She had never been shown such deference in her life. However, the main test would come from another direction.

Double doors were thrown open, revealing a sparkling scene of young ladies and gentlemen, all smiling politely as the latest guest was announced. Accustomed to grand interiors, Kit gave no thought to her surroundings, concentrating instead on her own role and the roomful of people she would have to hoodwink. Maintaining her posture, she glided straight across the carpet to be received by her hostess.

'My dear Miss Kilmaster!' Baroness Cazalet's round face lit up. 'How wonderful that you could come. Let me introduce you to my other guests.'

One by one, the guests were introduced. A glass of sherry in her hand, a smile upon her lips, Kit found herself fully accepted by this noble circle. From the moment she entered the drawing room until the time came to leave, she was shown not one hint that she was any less than they. Moreover, she found herself surrounded by young men, every one of whom treated her like royalty.

At the end of the afternoon, the Baroness took her aside and whispered that one gentleman was particularly taken with her and would very much like to meet her again in Hyde Park on Sunday. 'I should be happy to act as chaperone, should you so wish.'

Kit tried to curb her eagerness and asked which one might it be. Upon him being indicated, her heart sank, for if anyone was out of place here it had to be the foppish young man with the monocle, his loud laughter and his 'don't-cher-know' being most off-putting, even for one as lacking in suitors as Kit. The Baroness noted her reluctance and said that of all the gentlemen, Mr William Sinclair was most eligible. 'He is extremely kind and generous.' She spoke the following word behind her fan. 'And rich. And he is most taken with you. I beg you, do not disappoint him. Should you feel oppressed in any way, I will be in the carriage behind.'

Not wishing to be ostracized, Kit agreed to join the Sunday parade in Hyde Park. After all, she could always ask the Baroness to make other introductions.

Sunday was another glorious day – not a cloud in the sky – and the whole of London seemed to be out enjoying it – the gentleman in his top hat, frock coat and kid gloves, the urchin in his rags. Hurrying towards Rotten Row, where she had been told to meet the Baroness's entourage, Kit felt that the whole of high society must be arrayed before her, a vast multicoloured tide of silk and quivering plumage. Mingling with the parade, head above the crowd, she felt at once dowdy, though she was clad in the very best material. The scent of flowers teased her nostrils, their vendor extending a fragrant posy. Kit ignored her. Having the vantage of height she was quick to spot the Baroness's landau with its four occupants and another besides, the latter containing her admirer. Bracing herself, she made her approach.

A smile on his monocled face, William Sinclair passed the Baroness an envelope, then rushed forward to greet his companion. She was helped into his carriage and, with the other vehicle travelling behind, joined the magnificent parade along the sandy track towards Kensington Palace. The day was one of shimmering blue and green. Upon the Serpentine bobbed a flotilla of rowing boats, swans and ducks. Bathers frolicked at the water's edge, children in sailor suits chased toy boats, dogs ran alongside carriages, pink tongues lolling.

Despite all of this, the rendezvous was turning out to be as bad as Kit had expected, her companion's affected behaviour provoking intense irritation, though she was careful not to show it.

Conversely, he seemed to find her quite charming and begged that they might become more closely acquainted. Swaying gently to the movement of the carriage, Kit forced herself to suffer his breath on her cheek, and with a smile asked if he did not think they were quite close enough at present. Regarding her comment as a jest, he uttered an uproarious laugh, and asked her to marry him.

Kit was flabbergasted. 'Mr Sinclair, I climbed into your carriage less than two minutes ago! How can you know I'd make a suitable wife?'

He scooped her hand in his, uttering overtures and saying he had known she was the woman for him the moment he set eyes on her.

Under his amorous attentions Kit looked wildly over her shoulder at the Baroness, who merely waved. 'Sir, I cannot marry you!'

'Oh, but why?' His face implored her.

Kit opened and shut her mouth like a goldfish, searching the air for an answer. 'Because I don't love you!'

'Can you not come to love me?' He sounded desperate.

Having been rejected herself, Kit donned a compassionate expression. 'Given time, perhaps I could –'

'Then let us marry!' Sinclair was almost on his knees.

She was about to refuse again, when a band of men came pouring from every direction, surrounding both this carriage and that of the Baroness, grappling with the occupants and hauling them from the vehicle. Finding herself manhandled, Kit gave a cry of terror and tried to beat off her assailants – until she noticed to her further horror that some of them wore police uniform. Thence, respectful of the law though frightened out of her wits, she permitted herself to be bundled rudely from the carriage, heart and lungs pumping as if they would explode.

The Baroness was, to Kit's astonishment, uttering oaths and beating the officers over the head with her parasol as she too was apprehended, all eventually being taken in order and given the same proclamation.

'I'm arresting you for conspiracy to obtain money by false pretences!' Kit almost fainted as the words were directed at her.

'There's been a mistake!' she interrupted, aghast at the gentrified audience who had gathered to watch. 'I don't know anything about a conspiracy.'

The police officer ignored her plea.

'Ask my employer, the Countess of Garborough!' implored Kit. 'I'm her seamstress!'

'Why, you conniving witch!' William Sinclair lunged forward. 'Officer, I have been duped! I was led to believe this woman was an heiress!'

'I never told him that!' shrieked Kit, and looked to the Baroness for help, but the lady averted her face in dispassionate manner.

'You can all have your say down at the station,' said the officer in charge, trying to avoid a mêlée as others joined the argument. Then those under arrest were bundled into horse drawn vans and taken to a police station where Kit was pushed into line behind others.

One after the other they gave their names and addresses to the desk sergeant, each to witness the others' ignominy – but none could be as mortified as Kit, whose rash confession of her true position in life had suddenly made her into a pariah.

The desk sergeant tipped out the contents of Kit's velvet bag, scrutinizing one of the calling cards therein. 'The Honourable Katherine Kilmaster,' he read aloud, raising an eyebrow.

Eyes downcast and trembling, she felt his mocking glance.

William Sinclair was still claiming to know nothing of any conspiracy and said he was only at the scene of the arrest by accident. His sole reason for being there was to make a proposal of marriage and he now knew that false pretences had been used to trick him into making that offer. He demanded that the police take action.

Kit defended herself. 'I never misled him!'

'I demand that you retrieve the money I paid!' persisted the fop.

'I never took his money!'

'No, but the Baroness did!' Sinclair pointed an accusing finger.

The desk sergeant was unmoved, merely passing a cynical glance at the accused. 'Baroness this week are we, Sylvia?'

The self-styled noblewoman shrugged and moved up to give her details, her automatic monotone conveying that she had had much practice.

'You mean she isn't who she claims to be?' Squinting through his monocle, the fop looked her up and down. 'Well, who is she then? Dammit, man, I've paid her five hundred pounds! She told me she'd get me an heiress, don't-cher-know. If I'd wanted a wretched seamstress I could have had one for five shillings!'

'Not me you couldn't!' Of all the humiliations heaped on Kit, this must be the worst. The spell of captivity had given her time to consider her position. There was only one person she could turn to. 'Please, will you send someone to that address and ask for Viscount Postgate. He'll tell you who I am.'

'You trollop, leading me on like that!' Sinclair proceeded to dish insults upon Kit until, almost mercifully, she was led away and pushed into a cell to await questioning.

It was useless to deny her involvement, the detective told Kit hours later. The calling cards in her bag were proof enough that she was part of the self-styled Baroness's gang.

Kit was thoroughly browbeaten, her fingertips gripping the edge of the bare wooden table between them. 'They weren't meant to deceive! It was just a bit of fun. Has Lord Postgate arrived yet?'

'I believe so.'

Her plump shoulders sagged with relief. 'He'll tell you the same as I did, that I'm his mother's seamstress.'

The detective said he did not doubt her identity, just her denial of involvement. 'This Lord Postgate, he wouldn't happen to be another acquaintance of Sylvia's, would he?'

'No! He's a real viscount.' Kit realized she had made a terrible error in involving her employer's son. 'You've got to believe me! If I didn't know the Baroness wasn't a baroness how can I be involved?'

She wrung her hands. 'I don't even know what I'm supposed to have done.'

The detective's only response was to continue with the interrogation. 'Tell me again how you met Sylvia.'

Kit was forced to repeat the degrading tale of how she had imitated a person of note in order to find a marriage partner. 'But I had no intention of duping anyone!' she protested, wet-eyed and earnest, before venturing to ask, 'Who is that woman if she isn't really who she claims?'

'She's a crook. A very nasty one. In between robberies she makes a living out of fleecing avaricious young men, promising to find them a wealthy partner.' Giving Kit pause for thought, he added, 'She runs what you might call a stable of young women who help her achieve her aims. They attract the target, who hands over the money, which is never to be seen again and neither is their "bride". We've had our eye on her activities for weeks.'

Casting her mind back to her first encounter with the woman, Kit saw now that the supposed attacker had merely been another of those duped. She covered her face in despair of her own naivety. 'Oh, please believe me, I had no idea!' Keen to unburden herself of any guilt, she repeated everything that had occurred since the day she had met the 'Baroness'.

At the end of a very long interview, the detective smiled at his colleague. 'Makes a change for someone to pull the wool over Sylvia's eyes, don't it?'

'You mean, you believe me?' Kit's handkerchief was almost in tatters. 'Can I go?'

'For now,' came the discouraging answer.

When Kit emerged from the interrogation room it was to see a very annoyed Ossie Postgate seated on a bench, tapping his heels. Upon seeing her he jumped up. 'I don't appreciate being detained in a police station for half an hour, Kit!'

Apologizing profusely, she allowed him to take her elbow and steer her briskly outside. 'I had no intention of getting your lordship involved in this! I just didn't know who else to turn to.'

'This is a very different situation to the one with which I helped you before. A rumpus with a schoolteacher is one thing, involving your employer in a charge of conspiracy is quite another!'

The vehemence in his attitude made her stomach roll over. 'Do the Earl and Countess know?'

Ossie gave brusque response. 'No, and I've no desire that they should! That is the only reason why I waited for you, to say that you must say absolutely nothing to any of the servants –'

'Oh, I wouldn't, milord!'

'– for if this gets out I shall never forgive you. Though none of that will be relevant if this appears in the newspapers! How could you be so damned stupid?'

Utterly subjugated, Kit bowed her head and followed him to his carriage. Nothing more was said between them. Kit felt she had lost his friendship – if any had been there in the first place.

Ossie drove his carriage into the mews and ordered Kit to go ahead whilst her superior dealt with the stable lad. She hurried in, bypassing the servants' hall, and went straight to her room where she capsized upon her bed. Oh, what a fool she had been! The enormity of the afternoon's events revisited her. She began to sob.

A tap at the door caused her to draw in her breath, but her visitor was only Gladys.

'I was just passing your door and heard you crying! Are you ill?'

Swollen-eyed, Kit said she wished that it were so. 'It's much worse than that – oh you won't tell any of the others, will you? I'll just have to get it off my chest.' She told of her involvement with the gang of crooks, of her subsequent arrest and of Viscount Postgate coming to save her. Gladys's eyes grew wider every second. 'If it hadn't been for him I doubt they would ever have let me go! But I promised him I wouldn't tell a soul so you won't –'

'Not I!' swore Gladys, and laid a comforting hand on the victim's shoulder.

'Bless you!' Kit inhaled deeply. 'Honestly, I don't know how I manage to get myself into such things! But I've definitely learned my lesson. I can only hope and pray now that it all blows over.'

Before bedtime, however, Kit was to find that far from blowing over, her scrape with the law had been blown into such proportions as to reach the Countess's ears. Ossie Postgate, summoned to appear before his parents, tried to make light of the matter but this was ineffectual. Horrified that a servant had involved their son in such a shameful occurrence, the Earl and Countess demanded to see Kit. It was not, however, to hear any explanation.

Summarily dismissed, Kit tried to offer apology, especially to Ossie who had been such a champion in the past. But his eyes were cold, as were those of his parents. The Earl told this ungrateful chit she would leave immediately without reference. Never before had such perfidy been wreaked upon this household. His only concession would be to give her the fare back to Yorkshire. She would leave forthwith.

Thoroughly shamed – what explanation would she give those at home? – Kit slunk from the room.

Whilst a footman was sent to bring her box to the servants' hall, Kit fidgeted awkwardly under the furtive looks of her peers. Gladys bustled in, saw Kit and immediately stopped in her tracks, cheeks reddening. Having guessed the source of the leak before this, Kit had been seeking the culprit and now beheld her with hurt accusation. Awaiting retribution, Gladys nibbled her lip.

Kit glanced away momentarily as the footman informed her that her box had been put in the waiting cab. Summoning every ounce of dignity, she rose and moved to the doorway, issuing solemn goodbyes to those who cared to listen, and offering a parting shot to Gladys, whose trepidation had increased with her nearness. 'Don't worry, I'm not going to slap your face – but only because I can't decide which one of them to slap.'

17

One small mercy accompanied Kit on her train journey home. At least she still had the letter of introduction written by Ossie Postgate almost three years ago. Guarded within her bible, it was the only thing that would assure her another position. Wiser by far, she resolved never again to pretend to be anything other than what she was. If this meant admitting to Ninian that she was more humble than he had assumed, then so be it.

Unable to bring herself to go home, for her box would give her away, she went instead to the White Hart at Aldwaldwyke where she had arranged to meet him on the first of August. That she was rather earlier than expected would only grant her time to reflect on her situation, and she possessed enough money to cover the room and board.

Paying a man threepence to carry her wooden box upstairs, she ordered something to eat, then spent the rest of the afternoon mulling over her predicament. At least she could honestly say she was no longer a servant – though she still had to confess she was not the tenant of Postgate Park.

But how silly this all was. He might not even turn up at all. After spending a restless night at the inn, Kit decided she could not sit here for three whole days and expect to retain her sanity. Instead, after breakfast, she went down to the proprietor and asked him to store her box until she came to collect it. Then, armed with suitable explanation, she set off for Ralph Royd.

Unlike her own tumultuous life, everything here was as it had been before she had left. Neither Sarah nor Monty saw anything odd about Kit's impromptu appearance, for she always turned up to see them whenever she got back from London. Telling them she had been granted a few days' holiday before going back to work, Kit voiced her desire to stay amongst her family. The children were delighted as ever to see her, and made room in one of the beds for their aunt. After all the turmoil, it came as such a comfort to snuggle down amongst them, squashed and hot or no. Yet, her mood remained tinged by sadness for the loved one who was missing.

On the last day of July, she travelled back to the White Hart, not really believing that Ninian would turn up, but intending to be there in good time to prepare her appearance – just in case. Despite all this, by nighttime she had talked herself into the belief that he too would leave her in the lurch.

At noon the following day, still half expecting him not to be there, Kit's mood underwent a rapid elevation at the sight of him in an open carriage rolling into place at the stone cross before she herself had even bothered to leave her room. Having been dressed and ready for hours, she rushed downstairs and hurried across the road to meet him.

'You remembered!' Her face was one large beam.

'But of course!' Jumping down only to assist his guest, Ninian sprang back into the gig and in a moment the pair of them were spinning along a country lane. Aside from his primary greeting, her companion seemed disinclined to talk, but he was obviously pleased that she had come and Kit was quite happy to jog along in silence, enjoying the male presence.

After a while, Ninian steered the horse into a gateway that opened on to a farm track and then put on its nosebag. 'Not fair for us to have lunch and him to starve!' Taking the picnic hamper from the carriage, he helped Kit through the gate and escorted her across a sunny meadow towards a chestnut tree. Beneath its sweeping skirts, Ninian laid a rug and both sat down, shaded from the brilliant August sunshine.

Kit took off her straw hat, noting her companion's look of admiration for her auburn hair.

'Would you like to eat now?' He indicated the hamper. At Kit's smiling nod he unbuckled the leather straps and began to investigate its contents.

Their shared enjoyment of the rather exotic food inspired a conversation, Ninian saying that he had acquired a fondness for such fare after a three-year tour of the world. Intrigued, Kit begged to hear all about his travels. Before the meal was over they were chatting like old friends.

The sun moved slowly across the sky, occasionally piercing their leafy canopy. Over his initial shyness now, Ninian waited upon Kit's every whim, displaying sweetmeats for her delectation, tempting her with wine, even becoming so bold as to pop imported fruits into her mouth. Without objection, she allowed him to cosset her, reclining on one elbow and parting her lips for one treat after another.

'You look even more beautiful than the first day I saw you, Kit,' he said at last.

Surprised, she did not know what to say.

'I remember exactly what you were wearing.' Reposing next to her now, he held another grape to her lips.

'You've a better memory than me, then.' Seeing that her words had invoked a look of sadness, she rushed to correct her impression. 'I only meant I don't recall my clothes! I remember you very well. I thought you were very handsome.' He possessed the dark looks she found attractive.

Ninian chuckled and said there was no need for flattery.

'It's not flattery! I really do think you're handsome.'

'It's wonderful that you say so.' Eyes rarely leaving her face, he plied her with more grapes and more compliments, telling her eventually, 'I've never met anyone who makes me feel like you do, Kit.' His voice was as warm as the sun on her face.

'I've never met anyone like you either.' So pampered did he make Kit feel, that when her lips experienced not a sweetmeat but a human mouth, she did not flinch, but returned its soft pressure, closing her eyes and laying back in order to invite more.

With the barest interval between kisses, Ninian shuffled his body closer, each kiss becoming more ardent, his hand caressing her shoulder, sliding down her arm, moving up again, along the sweep of her neck and around her cheek, then sweeping in one long caress to the mountainous rise of her breast –

Kit squeaked and pushed him away. He stopped immediately.

'Dear Kit, forgive me! You're just so beautiful I got carried away. I swear to wait until we're married – but oh, it will be such torture!' At her look of astonishment, he shook his head at his own tardiness. 'I fully intended to make a formal proposal at the end of this afternoon, if passion had not taken me by surprise – but you will marry me, won't you? Say you will?' He seized her entreatingly.

300

Kit felt as if she had undertaken a ride on the helter-skelter, so quickly had the romance developed. She could not truly say she loved him with a passion, but his genuine interest in her was a wonderful compliment – and a poke in the eye for the fortune teller. She had always sworn she would only marry for love, but she had been in love before and had been let down. Besides, who was to say that this attachment would not grow into something deeper? She must allow herself time to get to know him. This was what she tried to convey to her suitor.

'Ninian, I'm deeply honoured, but we know nothing about each other.'

'I know everything I need to know! It is all displayed in those wondrous eyes. And as to myself, there is little to know. I have an excellent allowance – my father is chairman of the Ralph Royd Coal Company and is a most generous man.'

Not in my brothers' opinion, thought Kit, startled to learn of her companion's full identity. What would Owen have to say if she brought Ninian home? Her resolve to be truthful was quickly evaporating. The mention of an allowance also provoked unease – Ninian was not, then, of independent means.

Sensing her reserve, he pleaded for her to give his proposal deeper thought. Never had Kit anticipated being faced with the decision of whether to marry or not! Heart thudding, she stared into his brown eyes. It was quite obvious to her that his affections were not fabricated.

Overwhelmed, she took a deep breath. 'I beg you to wait a six month.'

'But why?' His cry was agonized.

'Or at least until Christmas! My brother will insist upon it, and even though I am of age I am respectful of his wishes. If you are still so sure of your heart then ... I would very much like to accept your proposal.' The thought did cross her mind that the time would come for her to confess she was only a servant – not even that currently – but by then he would be too smitten for it to matter. It also occurred that she would have to be presented to his family, but she would meet that when she came to it. At least this one was too mature for them to be of any influence, allowance or no. She was determined there would be no re-enactment of her doomed relationship with Thomas Denaby. And how could there be? Ninian showed none of Thomas's boyish indecision. Here was a man who was in command.

She allowed him to kiss her again. This time, equipped with a promise of matrimony, she was not so coy and permitted his hands to linger in places hitherto forbidden – though was not so foolish as to completely abandon her morals.

At the end of the afternoon, Ninian showed great reluctance to let her go, saying that they must meet as often as they could both get away, but that his heart would break at the thought of leaving her.

Highly excited by the contact with his body, Kit promised to meet him the next day, hardly able to believe her own luck.

For many days to come, Ninian Latimer whisked Kit off in his carriage to reiterate his passion. That he had promised to marry her – even providing her with a jewelled ring as proof – counted for little after what had gone before, and Kit decided to insure herself against penury by finding another job, albeit temporary.

Impressed by the aristocratic reference, the elderly lady who required a general servant hired Kit without delay and, generous to a fault, allowed her not one but two afternoons off per week, whence Kit would scurry off to meet her lover. She did not reveal her new and more humble position to her family, of course, nor indeed to Ninian, allowing the latter to uphold his belief that she was of private means. This being accomplished without actually having to lie, Kit overlooked her previous resolve and saw no wrong in it.

When after several weeks, Ninian grew sick of being kept at arm's length and asked to be taken to meet her brother in order for the proposed marriage to gain approval and thus end his own suffering, Kit stalled him with the lie that Montague would need much gentle persuasion before this happened.

Ninian's obsession with her burgeoned to the point of explosion. Kit too fell victim to his ever increasing ardour, though she had as yet managed to withhold the ultimate prize. September was upon them. It was becoming too cool to meet out in the open air, yet where else could they assuage their passion? Tired of this situation and of being fobbed off, Ninian asked her yet again today whether he might accompany her on her Sunday visit to her brother's house to put his case.

Again she put him off.

'Are you absolutely certain you wouldn't prefer to elope this very minute instead of hanging on your brother's permission?' he begged her, his face suffused with craving, both his and Kit's garments in disarray.

'Most definitely I'd prefer it.' She smiled and kissed his tousled head, their bodies entwined upon the rug. So why did she not simply do as he asked? Kit herself did not know. Perhaps it was the niggling thought that around the next corner she might just meet the man of her dreams – not that there was anything disagreeable about Ninian, he was a splendid catch. And she undoubtedly experienced something when she kissed him. She kissed him now, grinding her mouth over his, enjoying the feeling it produced deep in her abdomen.

Ninian was obviously enjoying the feeling too, launching into it with gusto. He straddled her and buried his face in the huge bosom she had willingly exposed for him, mouthing rosy tips, rubbing his groin against her wherever it made contact. At his point Kit would normally have pushed him off, but today something new occurred. Quite what got into her she did not know, but when Ninian's hands pushed her skirts up to her thighs she made no objection. Nor did she shove away the hand that crept around the white tender flesh of her inner thigh. The sudden waft of cool spring breeze, replaced by human warmth that strained to be inside her, none of these drew complaint. Unable to resist her own desire, Kit opened herself to him, amazed at the act this engendered – why, men were just like the beasts of the field, came the wondrous thought as he moved up and down inside her! That which had been such taboo was in reality nothing more than the same she had witnessed between dogs in the street. At once the image came of Sarah rushing out to throw a bucket of water over them and it was all Kit could do to keep from bursting into laughter. Oh, wouldn't Beata laugh when she . . . but no, her dear soulmate was dead.

Plunged back to stark reality, all desire vanished, Kit tried to push him off, but only succeeded in making his movements more frantic. Hurting, she called his name, to no effect. There was little for her to do but to wait until it was over.

Ninian gave a series of frenzied lunges, one last shuddering sigh, and relaxed on top of her, his face concealed in her shoulder. When he raised his head his expression was one of shame. She had asked him to stop and he had ignored her – 'It's just that I love you so much!'

She adopted blame. 'I should have stopped you sooner.'

'And you forgive me?'

When she nodded he looked relieved and permitted her to rearrange her clothing.

'I never meant it to go so far.' Kit stretched the edges of her bodice to contain her marshmallow flesh and began to fasten the buttons. 'You don't think any less of me, do you?'

He showed amused fondness and threw himself flat on his back. 'Kit, my dearest, I adore you!'

'D'you think I could . . . I mean is this what starts babies?'

Ninian said it wouldn't happen to her.

For a moment, Kit pictured herself cradling a baby. 'I wouldn't mind if it did.'

'Even if it does, it won't matter as we're to be married. I've been investigating how one goes about putting up the banns – in the hope that you'd change your mind about keeping me waiting. Apparently, one has to live in that parish for a certain amount of time in order to be able to wed there. You'll obviously want to marry in your own parish, so should I move my place of residence?'

The time had come to tell. Even so, Kit was hesitant. 'I think you might be under a misapprehension about me. I'm not . . . I'm not a tenant of Postgate Park.'

This brought laughter to his brown eyes. 'I didn't imagine you were Lady Garborough!'

She smiled too, but uncertainly. 'I was nothing grander than an employee there.'

'Oh.' He frowned at her attire. 'But you must have a superior position.'

'As a matter of fact, I'm no longer employed there at all. I handed in my notice.' Even now, she could not quite bring herself to tell the whole truth.

'So, you don't actually reside in that parish?'

'No, I am companion to an elderly gentlewoman in Castleford.' Kit fought her nerves; she would have to go the whole hog. 'But my true place of abode is Ralph Royd.'

His face lit up. 'Then we're from the same parish!' When she failed to share his immediate joy, his brow became furrowed by confusion.

Kit sought to explain. 'My brothers work at your father's mine.'

'I see.' His face underwent the slightest change, before creasing into its usual kind smile, and he nudged her fondly. 'But what difference does that make?'

'I didn't intend to mislead you!'

'Of course you didn't! I told you it's of no consequence.' He grabbed her and began to lark, tickling her until she fell into relieved laughter.

Their antics gave rise to another bout of lovemaking. This time Kit was to concentrate on the matter in hand, doing everything in her power to keep his mind from what she had just told him. Indeed, her powers were such that Ninian repeated his intention to marry her when they parted that evening.

Nevertheless, Kit could not help wondering as she went off to her brother's house for the usual monthly get-together if he would still be keen to see her when she got back.

Kit arrived at Ralph Royd bursting to show someone her ring, though she managed to rein in her enthusiasm, for they would doubtless accuse her of showing off.

As it turned out, Rhoda spotted it immediately, pointing it out to everyone. 'Aunt Kit's engaged!'

The whole family gathered round her to admire the jewelled band. Probyn wanted to see too but as usual the smallest child was pushed out by his elder sisters and was left to sulk on the outskirts.

Gwen was as surprised as any of them. 'And it's about time! How many years is it since you met him? I were beginning to think you'd made this chap up.'

Amelia, here on a rare visit and still childless, spoke in her sister's favour. 'Well, Kit did tell us his parents wanted them to wait four years.'

Alarmed that they assumed her suitor to be the young man whose father owned the pickle factory, Kit did not know what to tell her family. If she corrected them, she would have to reveal that she had been bought off by the Denabys and had kept up the pretence all these years. Would they remember his name? She could not risk having them call him Thomas, but neither could she admit to being made a fool of. 'As a matter of fact, my feelings towards Thomas cooled. I decided he wasn't the right one for me.'

Gwen looked knowing, and made a pointed exclamation: 'But he were such a good catch!'

'Aye, we could've had a lifetime of free pickles,' said Owen.

Kit wondered if he would be so jocular when he knew of Ninian's background. 'Anyway, I met Ninian –' She shot an accusatory glare at the little girls who sniggered over her fiancé's name. 'If you don't mind! I met him quite recently and he asked me to marry him almost at once. I think you'll like him.'

'I should hope we do!' said Sarah. 'Throwing up a well-heeled chap like that – you must be mad, girl!'

'So when do we get to see this one, then?' asked Monty. 'After all, we want to make sure he's the right sort.'

'Of course he is!' objected Kit.

'I don't know about that. I would've thought it were manners to ask a girl's father for her hand – yes, I know you haven't got a father,' he forestalled her objection. 'But I'm responsible for your safety. Bring him home next time you come – no arguments.'

Kit said she would see if she could persuade him to come.

Probyn emerged from his sulk. 'Can you tie me bootlace, Uncle Owen?'

An amicable Owen complied. 'Eh dear, hasn't tha learned how to do it for thissen?'

Probyn watched fascinated as the man's hands worked on his laces. 'Uncle Owen, why have you only got two fingers and a thumb on that hand?'

'I've told you that,' interjected his father. 'Your uncle lost them down the pit.'

'But how?'

'Crocodile,' said Owen, and having tied the laces, sat up.

Probyn's eyes widened. He knew that one day he would have to go down the pit too. But before he could ask for further information the adults resumed their conversation.

'So what does this one do for a living, then?' asked Amelia, perching on the edge of her chair.

Kit brushed an imaginary speck from her skirt and tried not to sound as if she were bragging. 'He doesn't do anything. He's a gentleman.'

There was an exchange of looks between those assembled.

'He must've got his brass from somewhere,' opined Owen. 'What's lad's surname anyroad?'

'Latimer.' Kit waited for it to make an impact, which it did.

Owen was stuck for a response. 'Thou doesn't mean . . . He's not one o' that lot?' He jabbed his thumb in the direction of the hill whereby lay the coal king's mansion, his mien turning black.

'He's a lovely lad! He can't help what his father does.'

'No, but you can!' accused Owen. 'I'm telling you now, our Kit, if you marry him I'll never talk to thee again!'

'Don't then!' she retorted.

'Monty, are you going to let her bring that devil's spawn into thy house?'

His brother cocked his head uncertainly. 'Well, if she's determined to marry him –'

Owen shot from his chair. 'I'm off home! And don't expect me to be here when he comes! In fact, I don't know if I'll ever set foot over this threshold again!'

If only Owen had kept his word, thought Kit, her stomach lurching at the sight of him here today when she entered with Ninian. It was hard enough for her beau to present himself to her family at all, without the addition of this antagonistic figure. The afternoon was bound to be fraught.

Awkward introductions were made between Ninian and Kit's elder brother, though the younger one chose not to proffer his hand, standing back as if a mere spectator. Sarah showed the least discomfort, asking the visitor to take a seat at the table, which had been spread with her best lace cloth. All stops had been pulled out for the provision of tea, the table barely visible under its selection of platters. Everyone gathered round then, Sarah being careful not to put Owen next to their guest – indeed, she had warned him beforehand that if he intended to give trouble he could go home.

Beneath the table, Ninian's hands fidgeted, his every move watched like a hawk by five young girls – not to mention the older women who appeared just as fascinated. Kit groped for his fingers, squeezing them reassuringly.

Tea was undertaken in reticence, broken only by the chink of cups and saucers, a polite smile from the hostess and the query, 'I hope everything meets with your satisfaction, Mr Latimer?'

'Indubitably, Mrs Kilmaster!' Ninian beamed and gently hoisted a piece of sponge cake as evidence.

'My mother used to make an excellent sponge.' Gwen pondered on the slice in her hand, apparently reluctant to taste it.

Ever smiling, Sarah directed hard eyes at her.

Amelia, trying to help her younger sister, sought to impress Ninian. 'I cooked dinner for the Foreign Secretary last week. He said it was the finest meal he'd ever tasted.'

'I'm afraid to say our Kit didn't inherit that talent, sir.' Gwen sounded apologetic. 'But then, I suppose you'll have servants to look after you.'

Ninian inclined his head, and tried to uphold his friendly air, though in truth he was feeling very uncomfortable. This was worse than he could have imagined.

Flora was sniffing at the morsel in her hand. Sarah tried to kick her under the table but someone else cried out and upset their cup of tea all over the pristine cloth. Trying to make light of the episode Sarah mopped feverishly at the brown patch, throwing a sideways glare at Charity who calmly resorted to her homespun remedy.

'Never mind, it'll wash.'

Upset dealt with, the meal continued. Five-year-old Probyn, never having enjoyed so large a spread, was about to take advantage of this by reaching for another wedge of cake when a deft hand drew the plate away. Below the angelic sandy red curl, the little boy's face took on a determined set and he muttered to the person seated next to him. 'Can I have another piece o' cake, Father?'

Monty ignored him.

'Our Ethel waint let me have another bit o' cake.'

Monty maintained his dignified air. 'Hush now, boy.'

Probyn sat quiet for a time, but the sight of others munching away whilst the plate lay inaccessible to him proved too much to bear, and he grumbled at the sister to his other side. ''Snot fair that I can't have any while she's sat shoving cake in her 'oile.'

There was a tinkle of embarrassed laughter.

'Whoever taught you to speak like that?' Sarah was smiling but those familiar knew her amusement to be artificial. 'Speak properly, child.'

'My friend Jim says you talk funny.' Probyn intended no slur, was just repeating others.

Unable to inflict corporal punishment whilst her guest was present, Sarah simply uttered another strained laugh and inflicted a more subtle revenge, asking Ninian if he would care for the last piece of cake. He tried to refuse, but it was rather forced upon him. Hence he spent the next five minutes with the eyes of an envious little boy glued upon him, trying to dispose of the unwanted and rather dry cake by periodically washing it down with mouthfuls of tea.

Kit had been dreading the end of the meal, for now would come questions. She did not know how Owen had managed to contain himself for so long. Indeed, neither did Owen, who barely allowed Ninian to lay cup upon saucer before firing his first volley.

'So, what's your opinion on sliding scales, Mr Latimer?' Having shoved tobacco into a clay pipe, he lit a taper from the fire and began to puff.

Ninian was taken aback but smiled politely. 'I beg your pardon?'

Owen puffed away. 'Do you think it's justified for owners to extract their profits at the miners' expense?'

'I don't see –'

'Ninian isn't part of his father's business.' Kit jumped in to save her betrothed.

Through the cloud of tobacco smoke, Owen's thick black eyebrows formed a V. 'But surely he takes an interest in where the money comes from that keeps him in the manner to which he's accustomed?'

Ninian remained polite. 'Naturally, I –'

'Sithee, we've been trying to get a sliding scale agreement with your father's company for the past three years but he won't budge an inch. It's not an ideal situation, by any means – in my opinion, we should be paid a regular amount for the coal we hew regardless of the market price – but at least with a sliding scale we'd feel the benefit when prices rise.'

Ninian found it hard to argue with this opinion. 'I confess I am totally ignorant when it comes to the economics of the mine –'

'So long as the money keeps coming, eh?' Owen narrowed his eyes, puffing long and hard on the pipe.

'Times have not always been so good for my family, Mr Kilmaster,' defended Ninian.

Owen appeared to sympathize. 'Aye, it's a hard life when a man has to go without his crate of port wine.'

Too much of a gentleman to respond to this sarcasm, Ninian merely looked at the tablecloth. Amelia blushed crimson, Flora simpered, Gwen and Charity exchanged raised eyebrows over their teacups, whilst the host of youngsters stared from one to the other, not quite understanding the tension.

Monty ran a finger around his starched collar, trying to warn Owen with his eyes, but to little avail.

'I mean, it's not as if your father's company can't take the losses, is it? Whereas, we that do the dangerous work often have to go without basic commodities when times are bad. Does that seem just to you?'

Still his victim refused to be baited, trying instead to assume a dignified air for the benefit of all those eyes that were upon him.

Kit's eyes displayed unusual venom for her brother, but she had no wish to pursue the issue.

'You and your politics, Owen!' Sarah tried to lighten the atmosphere with a gay laugh but the look she gave her brother-in-law held a warning. 'I'm sure our guest doesn't want to listen to that – more tea, Mr Latimer?'

Ninian smiled at her but refused. 'Delightful though it was, I really must depart, Mrs Kilmaster.' He rose and offered his hand to Kit, who took her own leave, telling them she would see them in a month.

The moment the couple had left, everyone relaxed with a unified sigh, then immediately began to discuss Kit's fiancé. After rebuking Owen, Monty hauled his five-year-old son off the chair and delivered a smack to his bottom that was so hefty it almost lifted the child off his feet. 'And that, my lad, is for being disrespectful to your mother!'

Ninian was very subdued as he drove Kit back to their meeting place. The afternoon had been so much worse than he had feared, that he saw it was impossible for this relationship to continue. Though his infatuation for Kit remained undimmed, knowing what he did now, it was socially unthinkable for him to marry her. But how did he tell her? Could he indeed tell her at all?

Watching him from the corner of her eye as they jogged along in the gig, Kit detected a new reticence to his mood, and thus began a battle to keep him, snuggling up to murmur eroticisms in his ear, caressing his inner thigh until, inflamed, he stopped the carriage there and then and, behind cover of a hedge, made urgent love to her.

I can't give this up, he told himself, thrusting deep inside her, gripped by warm moist muscle. I can't, I *won't*.

And why indeed should he have to? The answer came as he lay atop the fleshy cushion, recovering his breath. Where was the need to marry when this lovely young woman gave herself so freely?

Worried at first, that Ninian had been put off by the awful afternoon at her brother's house, Kit was rather relieved to find that in a matter of hours he had quite recovered and his ardour appeared uncooled. If anything his lovemaking seemed even more intense.

Not until December, when she had to remind him that, if they were to be married, she had yet to meet his parents, did she begin to suspect that all was not well. He began to show a marked reluctance to present her to his kin, saying that with their vastly different backgrounds he detested having to put his beloved through the torture he had suffered at her family's hands. Could she not spare herself the ordeal at least until the festive season was over?

For the moment, she accepted this, but Kit began to fear that he was merely using her. With this in mind, she designed to test him, by forbidding him to sate his lusty appetite, pretending to be unwell or some other excuse, until his waning interest finally revealed the truth. The affair was over.

Both knew it, but neither knew what to do; Kit because she could not bear another rejection; Ninian, because he was too soft-hearted to tell her outright. Instead, he simply arranged to see her less often, their meetings dwindling, until the moment Kit had dreaded finally arrived. He failed to turn up at all.

Enraged and wounded, Kit hovered outside the White Hart on this bright blue January day, allowing him another fifteen minutes, but knowing in her heart that it was a waste of time. A flash of colour and the sound of hoofs caused her to turn, but it was only the local hunt, its members come to slake their thirst after the morning's chase.

Dispassionately, Kit watched the victorious approach of the Earl of Garborough and his group of bright-eyed, top-hatted men, jingling up the lane between bare twiggy hedgerows – a vivid host of scarlet, grey, chestnut and bay – who now gathered noisily outside the inn, a cloud rising from their foam-flecked steeds. Unnoticed, she continued to stare as Ossie Postgate, his face glowing pink, jumped down from his saddle, brandished the mask and brush and called for a clean bowl to be filled with whisky. The vessel was brought. Kit watched with revulsion as the dripping tail was dipped in, turning the whisky into a revolting bloody concoction with bits of hair floating in it. It was then seized and handed round the vociferous crowd to drink. His triumphant face emerging from the bloody bowl, Ossie caught sight of Kit then – must surely have seen the look of disgust with which she regarded him, but he showed no hesitation in coming over to greet her.

The words were laced with whisky fumes. 'Kit! How nice to see you looking so well.' His smile seemed genuine. In fact it was as if nothing untoward had passed between them – though his next words showed that he had not forgotten and he expressed regret that things had turned out the way they had. 'I trust you have found other employment?'

Would it matter to you if I hadn't? thought Kit, staring at his blood-stained cheeks, but answered merely with a nod. When all was said and done it was her own actions that had landed her in trouble. She could not blame him.

Responding to habit, Ossie scrunched up his eyes. 'Good, good – well, I must dash!' and he left her, to return to his own kind.

Examining her watch with a bad-tempered eye, Kit decided then that she was sick and tired of people casting her off like an unwanted garment. The time had come to put her experiences to good use.

A lengthy walk ahead of her, she struck out with a determined gait, heading for the coal king's mansion near Ralph Royd.

Ninian was in the drawing room with his mother and various siblings when the footman came in to tell him that a young lady was here to see him. Immediately he reddened and told the minion to convey his apologies but to say that he was too ill to receive the visitor.

'One moment!' Mrs Latimer prevented the footman from carrying out the order, telling him instead to bid the young lady to wait and she would receive attention. When the man had gone she turned to her son and demanded to know what this was about, though she already had an inkling. 'You cannot expect a servant to do your dirty work, Ninian. Come now, tell me quickly what is amiss.'

'Not in front of them.' He indicated his siblings, and they were asked to leave.

In their absence, he told his mother – a dignified and gentle lady of slender proportions, soft features and compassionate eye – of the mess that he had got into, though not in its entirety. 'I was truly misled! Though not purposely, I hasten to add. Kit's manner and her clothes induced me to believe that she was a suitable match and so I pursued her – indeed, I thought most highly of her – until I found out that her family was more humble than I had been led to expect.'

Mrs Latimer frowned upon this streak of snobbishness. 'A good match does not necessarily mean that both parties should be possessed of equal funds, Ninian. If you love this young lady –'

'Mother,' the young man spoke with a slightly impatient, haunted look, 'her family lives in one of Father's houses.'

'You mean they are colliers?' The situation underwent a rapid change. Mrs Latimer matched his expression of dismay. 'Then we must seek to extricate you from this mess before your father gets to hear of it!'

Notwithstanding this intention, Kit was received quite warmly into the coal king's luxurious drawing room, Ninian's mother gliding forth to greet this rather Amazonian young woman, whilst he himself took pains to assure her that only the very worst of maladies had kept him from her side. To illustrate this, he fell back upon the sofa immediately after issuing his greeting and put a hand to his brow.

Kit did not take the offered seat for a moment, but held him with her clear blue eyes, asking silently how he could sit there and lie to her after all he had promised, all she had given? Into her mind came the fortune teller's prediction – *I see no marriage, I see no children.* Kit had often wondered during the last five months why all those reckless couplings with Ninian had produced nothing. Could it be that she was barren like Amelia? Who would want a barren wife? And who would look after her in her old age?

With a newly acquired cynicism, Kit decided that if Ninian could play games, then so could she. A hand went up to her brow, a puzzled expression spreading slowly across her face. 'Oh dear, I fear I am unwell too. In fact, I feel quite bilious. I think I'm going to . . .' Her words dispersing on a moan, she appeared to faint.

Mrs Latimer gave an exclamation of panic. Whilst her son kneeled at Kit's side, patting her face in an attempt to bring her round, she moved across the room with the intention of tugging on the bell rope, but Kit's half-conscious moan stopped her.

'You shouldn't have done it to me, Nin – what if I have a baby?'

The victim 'came round' to shocked faces. Indeed, thought Kit, Ninian looked a picture as he was bundled from the room by his mother.

'I shall deal with this!' Mrs Latimer closed the door on her son and came back to tend to the young woman who was now sitting on the carpet wearing a look of disorientation.

'Miss Kilmaster, is it true?' The lady appeared deeply concerned.

'Is what true?' Kit maintained a befuddled expression.

'When you were coming round just then, you said . . . you gave indications that some indiscretion had taken place between you and my son.'

Kit allowed her expression to show that she knew what Mrs Latimer meant. 'But please don't blame Ninian! He has promised to marry me.'

'Then, you *are* in a certain condition?' There was a urgent edge to Mrs Latimer's query.

'I fear it could be so.'

Mrs Latimer wrung her hands, and wheeled away from Kit to pace the room, swishing back and forth in her grey silk gown.

Rising slowly, Kit transferred herself to a sofa and waited.

The lady spoke without turning. 'I believe that when my son promised to marry you he meant it.'

'You mean he has changed his mind?' Kit sounded shocked.

The mother paused, then turned and nodded with a commiserating expression.

'That cannot be! He must marry me, he must! How shall I live with this shame?'

Mrs Latimer resumed her agitated pacing. 'There is little I can do about it if he has made up his mind! He is a man –'

'I heard,' Kit jumped in, 'that a lady in Wakefield was awarded five hundred pounds for breach of promise.'

Mrs Latimer whirled and stared at this young woman, whose attitude

314

left her in no doubt that she would carry out her implied threat. 'That is a huge amount of money!'

'It is a terrible deed that was done to her,' murmured Kit. 'She must have been in anguish to lay herself open to a court of law in order to defend her good name. And to think it could all have been settled quite amicably. Had the young man been gallant enough to offer her suitable recompense, he too could have remained anonymous.'

There was no equivocation.

Deeming it beneath her to haggle, Mrs Latimer went straight to her davenport and scribbled upon a piece of paper, handing it to Kit along with a look of reprehension.

Miraculously recovered, Kit did not hesitate, but took it and left forthwith, armed not simply with the cheque but with the strong conviction that nevermore was a man going to misuse her. She knew what men wanted now. Her romantic tendencies had merely attracted abuse. Instead, she would grasp what was offered, devote her energies not to finding a husband but to a hedonistic future. And if marriage was a consequence of these lucrative dalliances, then all to the good.

PART 3

Womanhood

1880–1890

18

Kit's first act had been to hand in her notice to her elderly employer; under no circumstances would she ever be press-ganged into domestic service again. Naturally this meant she needed a place to live, and with such funds at her disposal as she'd received from Mrs Latimer, she could have chosen anywhere she liked, but she had come to think that perhaps the place to be was near her family. It was the only one she was likely to have. So, she bought a cottage on Main Street, close to the Robin Hood's Well. Even with the addition of furniture, the sum this deducted from her bank account was but a drop in the ocean. Nevertheless, she had matured enough to see that the remaining balance, though large, would not last for ever in the hands of such a spendthrift and she intended to open her premises for business, for there would always be the need for a good seamstress. Armed with this fait accompli and a collection of gifts, she had attended the family get-together to deliver her news.

This time there was no possible way for Kit to avoid the humiliating confession that she had been jilted, but the acquisition of five hundred pounds had been an enormous influence on the family's reaction. With or without the money, she had immediately gained Owen's support, her brother being of the opinion that Latimer's son treated his females in the same callous manner that his father treated his employees and Kit was well shut of him. Glad of the endorsement, Kit chose not to mention that she had obtained this payment by slightly false pretences.

That had been over eighteen months ago, since when Kit's business had flourished. Though few of the villagers could afford the fashionable styles she offered, there was bread and butter to be earned from the creation of a simple dress or various alterations, whilst the advertisements she inserted in the newspaper attracted custom from the more affluent gentry who had become regular clients.

One thing marred her life. Kit was lonely. Her days, filled with industry, passed happily enough, but she had no wish to continue working right up to bedtime, for that would defeat the whole object of her new-found independence. Nevertheless, this was what she had found herself doing in order to fill her lonesome evenings after her visiting nieces and nephews had gone home to bed. Even her fine collection of books was a poor substitute for human companionship. The sojourns with her brothers could hardly be classed as inspiring, and there was no form of entertainment in the village other than the odd magic lantern show on the evils of drink, and the chapel social meeting on Saturday night with Blind Man's Buff being the most exciting thing on offer. True, Kit had enjoyed the occasional liaison since becoming an independent woman, and with a new carrier service in the village she was able to make frequent trips into Leeds for the music hall, and every other event that a big city had to offer, but once the fun was over she still had to return to an empty house. With the nights already drawing in, Kit was dreading another winter here.

As if to emphasize her solitary state, the first of her nieces had married and moved away. Whilst Kit had been more than happy to create Rhoda's wedding gown, she held mixed feelings upon seeing one much younger than herself walk down the aisle. Only four and half years to go and she would be thirty. Ethel seemed not to be affected by the fact that her younger sister had married before her, nor by the jokes bandied by Owen that every young man was probably frightened to death of her. Only Amelia seemed to empathize with Kit, probably because she knew what it felt like to be unfulfilled – but at least she had Albert, sighed Kit, and the two of them had become even more devoted over their seven childless years of marriage. Kit had no one at all.

Chivvying herself over another such bout of discontentment, she reminded herself that she had no real cause for complaint. Her thriving business had helped to restore most of the money she had paid for this cottage, and even with her penchant for shopping her bank balance remained at a healthy level. She was her own mistress, who could afford anything she wanted, and today, she decided, she would have some new corsets. Donning a kingfisher-blue paletot, with a little kingfisher on her hat to match, she set off for the Robin Hood's Well, where the carrier would pick up his passengers and take them to Castleford.

The autumn breeze threatening to destroy her equipoise, she escaped into the public house to chat with Peggo whilst awaiting the omnibus. Living nearby, they often shared fond reminiscences about Beata. Today, the barmaid joined in. Marion had become a frequent customer, and indeed a friend, grateful for the tips and improvements Kit had made to her appearance. For herself, Kit had matured enough not to give away any of Marion's intimate secrets, had almost forgotten that she was a man, though on the odd occasion during a fitting Beata would spring to mind, and Kit would smile and wonder if her beloved niece was up there laughing at all this.

The horse-drawn omnibus arrived, interrupting her discourse. Kit braved the elements, inwardly swearing at the gust of wind that assaulted her twixt pub and omnibus. With nothing of interest to see from the windows during a journey made many times before, she chatted amiably with her fellow passengers, Mrs Feather the midwife and Mrs Kelly. By the time the omnibus reached Castleford she had acquired an order from both.

After going to be measured for her corsets, Kit had hours to wait until the omnibus made its return. Averse to walking home in this wind, she went into a restaurant, took a seat by the window and ordered a luncheon of sausage, mashed potato and peas. It was whilst she waited for her meal to arrive, idly watching passers-by that she spotted a familiar face and her own lit up in recognition.

At first, Mr Popplewell did not heed the banging on the window. Only upon hearing the faint voice that accompanied it did he turn and see Kit gesticulating wildly behind the glass. Baring his unattractive teeth, he immediately went inside to join her, sweeping off his bowler hat.

'Kit! You're looking very windswept and interesting.'

She affected a shiver. 'Aye, it's right back-endish, isn't it? Oh, it's lovely to hear your beautiful Barnsley voice again!' She clasped the hand he offered, endowing him with a wide smile. 'What have you been doing with yourself. Eh, I shouldn't really be talking to you!' She dealt him a tap of reproach. 'Going off like that and never saying goodbye to me.'

'Aw, I'm sorry about that, me dear!' The man in the tweed ulster retained her hand. 'I just couldn't stand another minute. I would've been up for murder. Eh, but I hear you're not at Postgate Park any more. I saw one of your advertisements in the newspaper. I'm so pleased you're doing well.' He eyed the plate of sausage and mash that had just arrived. 'Or at least I thought you were – what did you call that when it was alive?' This last was directed at the waiter.

Kit muttered hurriedly, 'Don't upset him, I'm starving!' She thanked the offended man, who stalked off.

'You must be to even contemplate putting that anywhere near your mouth.' Popplewell beheld the charcoal-coloured sausages with distaste. 'You can get me a cup o' tea!' he called to the waiter, then put his bowler hat on a nearby table and sat down opposite Kit, wincing as she began to eat.

'So, what are you doing with yourself these days?' She rolled a portion of hot sausage around her mouth, trying not to smirk at his brown wavy hair which stood on end and looked as if it were about to take flight. 'Where are you living?'

Through a row of irregular teeth, Popplewell told her that he no longer suffered the whims of a single employer but worked on a freelance basis, serving anyone who required his expertise for an extra special dinner party or banquet. There were plenty of moneyed folk round these parts to keep him busy. He had taken lodgings in Castleford, which was in a position to suit his needs, having numerous country mansions within its vicinity. The life suited him well, lending him more time to do as he pleased.

Kit replied that she enjoyed a similar life. 'The only thing I miss about Postgate Park is the Christmas ball and your lovely cooking. I hate having to see to meself.'

There came instant invitation to dinner. It would be a pleasure to cook for one so appreciative, he said.

Kit beamed. 'I'd love to if it wouldn't put anyone out. Are you married yet, Mr Popplewell?'

'No, still single. Mindst, that's not to say I live like a monk.' He noted a look of dubiety flicker across her face. 'Oh, you've no need to worry on that score, Kit. There'll be no funny business.' He smiled as she relaxed. 'No, it's simply that I haven't the time to devote to a wife. It wouldn't be fair.'

During the next half-hour they caught up with each other's news before Popplewell had to leave for an appointment. Scribbling his address down on a scrap of paper, he asked her to come next Monday evening when his services would be at her complete disposal – that was if he had not been evicted. He had already had numerous altercations with his landlady over his violin practice.

She portrayed surprise. 'I didn't know you were musical.'

'My landlady would complain I'm not.' Popplewell gave brief explanation that he had formed a quartet. 'I'm not professional, it's purely for my own enjoyment. I do so like a spot of torture.'

Saying she would love to hear it, Kit allowed him to leave, both of them looking forward to their next meeting.

After enjoying a superb meal at Mr Popplewell's lodgings, Kit returned his invitation, saying that she could not offer the same excellence, but he would be more than welcome to visit as she did not wish to lose touch again. This was accepted, Mr Popplewell adding that she must come and listen to his quartet. He would be playing at a soiree next week at a friend's house. No one would mind if Kit came along, she would be an asset to any party.

Thus she found herself introduced to a new circle of friends and dancing partners, all of whom were invited back to Ralph Royd for games of cards or charades or whatever home-made amusement Kit, a popular hostess, could muster. This sparked off a regular routine, with Kit going to Castleford to participate in dancing to music provided by Mr Popplewell's quartet, and the following week Mr Popplewell and his friends – most of whom were men – coming to her house. All agreed that Kit was tremendous fun with her impersonations and the rude songs she had learned in London.

Though nothing particularly untoward went on at these parties, the succession of men who visited Kit's house week after week, month after month, was bound to provoke gossip. Naturally, Kit was intelligent enough to realize this, but held the opinion that it was her own business, she worked hard, and would continue to reward herself in this manner as long as she chose. Not once did it occur to her that others might be sullied by the reputation she was fast earning for herself.

On Kit's twenty-sixth birthday Mr Popplewell arranged a celebration, for which he provided both food and musical entertainment. Some months later, she in turn made him a splendid waistcoat for his fiftieth. They became even firmer friends. Yet, even after months of shared tomfoolery, she chose to ignore his insistence that she call him by his first name of George, unable to show such disrespect to one old enough to be her father. However, Kit had to agree that for one so decrepit, her friend had remarkable stamina and was more than able to keep up with this young woman, the noise from their get-togethers driving his long-suffering landlady into a fury.

Which was the reason why, when Kit arrived at his house one summer evening, expecting to be wined and dined, she found Popplewell, crimson with rage, standing on the pavement surrounded by a collection of shattered belongings.

'The old – she's chucked me out!' came his spluttered explanation to Kit. 'I wasn't away an hour and she's nipped in, had the lock changed and thrown all my stuff out of the window, didn't even have the decency to carry it down the stairs. I should sue you, you old sow!' Verging on apoplexy, he brandished his fist at the door that remained barred to him.

Kit had grown used to his tantrums, though still abhorred such unseemly displays. 'Well, it's no good standing here. Away, I'll help you to pick your stuff up.'

'And put it where?' Saliva flew at his demand.

Kit tried to calm the little man by remaining composed herself. 'Can you fit this in your dogcart? Well, go and get it and we'll take it back to my house.'

He stopped ranting, though the veins in his temple still pulsated and his face remained flushed. 'You mean, move in with you?'

'Why not? I'd like a cook but I can't afford one – at least, not one of your calibre. I'll provide free shelter and buy the food in return for you cooking it.'

'Hm, not daft, are you?' Popplewell began to see the mutual beneficence. He studied her for a moment, then put out his hand and the deal was struck.

With his belongings heaped upon the dogcart, Popplewell drove them and his new landlady to Ralph Royd where he was given a pleasant room and the kitchen put at his disposal. Thereafter, whilst Kit spent her days at her sewing machine, catering for the gentry's sartorial requirements, he provided for their other appetites, setting out with his dogcart heaped with culinary masterpieces for some stately home or other – but always, noted the village gossips, always returning here to spend his nights with Kit.

'Father, where's Sin?' asked eight-year-old Probyn, trying unsuccessfully to flatten the unruly curl at the front of his head by plastering it with water.

Monty's scrubbed face shot up from his newspaper, noting that his daughters had suddenly become ill at ease, only Meredith still young enough not to grasp the risqué situation. Somewhat tentatively, he asked what his son meant.

Without aid of a mirror, Probyn felt blindly to see if the auburn curl was still sticking up. 'I heard Mrs Kelly say Aunt Kit was living in Sin – but I only saw her t'other day so she can't have moved.'

Monty exchanged a brief but telling glance with Sarah, who was washing the pots after their evening meal. This was not the first such reference to Kit. Owen had suggested their sister be taken in hand, her brothers had a duty to protect her from herself, but neither seemed eager for confrontation, hoping the situation would go away. In fact, since hearing that Kit had invested a lodger neither of them had visited at all. Monty asked his son to relate the full details of the episode.

Probyn continued to press the heel of his palm against his head, his attitude one of innocence. 'Well, I were talking to Tommy Kelly and –'

'Haven't I told you about consorting with those ruffians?' interjected his mother. She might be more polite to Mrs Kelly since Beata's death but she still viewed the family as undesirable company for her offspring.

'– And his mam came out and told him to get inside and I heard her say he hadn't got to play wi' me cause Aunty Kit was living in Sin.'

Sarah gasped at the irony of it – the Kellys looking down on *them*! 'I told you, didn't I?' she snapped at her husband, her Welsh accent becoming more pronounced with her excitement. 'You'll have to tackle her. It's all round the village.'

'What is?' asked Probyn.

'Coal dust!' evaded his mother and wiped her hands on a towel, leaving Wyn to dry and put away the pots. 'Where's that Alice got to? I told her to be in before I set off for Mothers' Night.' She was inspecting her agitated appearance in the mirror over the hearth when Alice came in. 'Where have you been, young lady?'

Alice flushed. 'You said it was all right for me to go to Eddie's house if his mam was there.' Eddie was her young man – a clerk at the glass factory. They had in fact not been at his house where there were too many prying eyes, but in the woods. 'Sorry, if I'm a bit late. I just popped in at Aunty Kit's on me way back.'

'Yes, well, I think we'll have to stop all this popping in,' said Sarah firmly, ready to go.

'Why?'

'Never you mind! Monty, I'm off, see you at half-past eight.' Her tone implied that there would be something to discuss when she got back from chapel.

And there was. His wife expected him to go round and confront his wayward sister that very same evening.

The objection that Kit might be in bed cut no ice. Sarah pointed out that to delay might result in his own daughters being polluted. He must order Kit to change her ways or else.

It was still light as Monty travelled down the incline and along Main Street, the pleasant summer's evening jarred slightly by the sound of ranting from the wooden mission hall. Yet, his brother's voice had a certain eloquence as it overrode the blackbird's evensong, a mixture of politics and prayer.

'We asked the Lord for a check weighman to stop the bosses cheating us, and did He give us it? He did, bless Him. I'll serve Him till the day I die. We asked Him to make our Yorkshire brethren see sense and join us in our fight against oppression, and He sent His guiding light to steer us together in the Yorkshire Miners Association. By His blessed mercy our number now stands at three thousand!' There came gruff shouts of support. 'Three thousand, mindst – but there are sixty thousand hearts out there still to conquer. Men who grab the benefits we've won for them without lifting a finger, nor parting with a penny. Lord, we're not expecting Thee to do this all on Thy own, we're just humbly asking Thee to fill their ignorant hearts with Tha' compassionate love. Give us t'soldiers and we'll provide the battle. And united in Thy glorious cause we're going to get that minimum wage and an eight-hour day, let them bosses see if we don't!'

Owen's voice fading behind him, Monty plodded on to his sister's cottage, wondering just how he was going to broach such an indelicate topic.

Kit was surprised to see him at such an hour, for although it was light Monty would normally be in bed by nine. Guessing his visit must mark something of import, she made an excited assumption. 'Has she had it?' Rhoda's baby was expected at any time. Monty had been pleased as punch to learn that he was to become a grandfather; Kit too was delighted at the prospect of becoming a great-aunt. 'What did she get?'

'It's not about that,' said Monty.

Kit sensed then that he was troubled. 'Oh, you'd best come in then.'

He refused. 'I'm not stopping, I just came to tell 'ee –' He broke off, looking uncomfortable, then almost vomited his frustration in an ill-considered rush of words. 'We don't think you're a good influence on the girls, spending all that money on fripperies and whatnot. Besides, there could be anything going on here, they could walk in and see things – so I just came to tell 'ee that we're not cutting you off, you're still welcome to call at our house but, well, you're not to expect any more visits from us.' He ended with an abrupt nod.

Kit appeared stunned. 'But what have I done?'

Monty made furtive glances round his sister's outline as if to see into the room behind her, as if someone else might be lurking. 'Do you honestly not know? Are you deaf to all the talk that's going round the village about the man you got living here?'

Kit laughed. 'Mr Popplewell? For goodness' sake, he's my cook!'

'A male cook,' corrected Monty. 'Kit, an unmarried girl can't bring a man into her house and expect nobody to say aught – and if it's so innocent, why didn't you mention anything about it to us?'

'If you'd bothered to visit me once in a while I'd have introduced you. Come and meet him now. I'll call him down, he's only just gone to bed.'

Monty reddened and muttered, 'Don't mention such a word. It ain't proper.'

Hurt by his attitude, Kit urged her brother to come in and he would find everything was above board. She was to be further bruised by his refusal.

'And what about all the other men who come here?' he continued. 'What reason are we to give our neighbours for their visits?'

Anger joined the hurt. 'You can tell them that if I choose to entertain my gentleman friends it's none of anyone else's business.'

'It is if you're bringing our good name into disrepute.' Monty did not raise his voice, his anger as ever restrained, but Kit was left in no doubt as to his feelings.

'How can anybody object to a game of charades and a few songs?' she demanded.

'Are the gossips to know that? All they see is a load o' men going into your cottage and they make their own minds up.'

'Then they've got mucky minds,' retorted Kit.

'Have you never given a thought to what your family has had to put up with because of you? Now, I'm not telling 'ee how to live your life – much as I detest the path you've chosen – but I won't have my children subjected to such behaviour. Right, I've said my piece, I'm going home.' In dignified manner, he turned and walk off.

Shocked, Kit paused to watch his tall retreating figure for a moment before closing the door. When she turned back into the room a fully dressed Mr Popplewell had come downstairs.

He looked sympathetic. 'I'm sorry, I couldn't help hearing it all, your voices came drifting up through my bedroom window. Do you want me to leave?'

'No, of course I don't.' In low spirits, she parked her wide beam on a chair and sighed. 'I should have known I couldn't enjoy meself round here without some nosy devil putting their oar in.'

Popplewell showed his maturity. 'You're young, Kit, but an old fellow like me should have given a bit more thought for your reputation. I don't want to upset your family. I'll leave.'

'No, you won't,' insisted Kit. 'I'm blowed if I'm cooking for meself just because they've got dirty minds. You're staying put and so am I.'

At first, Kit was able to maintain her resolve, for even though she was denied the children's company at her own house she was still permitted to see them at Monty's so there was little hardship involved. But with the announcement that Probyn had been taunted by some older boys about his aunt running a knocking shop, and the consequent enquiry over what this might be, Kit decided that it would be best for all if she temporarily removed herself from the gossips.

Hence, she went to visit Amelia in York, whom she had not seen since Christmas.

Forewarned of Kit's arrival by a letter, though as yet ignorant of the true reason behind her appearance, Amelia already had a little room prepared in her own quarter of her employers' house. Escorting Kit to it, she bustled about in her maid's uniform, smoothing and tugging at covers and curtains, taking over her sister's unpacking.

'Sorry about the awful stink!' she said. 'They haven't been to water the roads in ages and we've had no rain to speak of to clear the drains. Come on then, let's go see if Albert's made that cup of tea and you can tell us all the news from home. I know our Rhoda had a little boy! Have you seen him?' All the way down the stairs they discussed the new arrival.

Then, seated affectionately next to her husband, Amelia was given a report of recent happenings at Ralph Royd, Kit beginning with the least devastating snippet. 'Our Ethel's got a new job in Leeds. You'll never guess what it is – well, you might, 'cause she's had it written all over her since she was a bairn.' Kit looked impish. When both sister and Albert failed to get the correct answer she blurted, 'Prison wardress!' And broke into giggles.

Amelia laughed heartily too, then, name by name, went on to ask after almost every person in the village. 'How's Mrs Feather? 'Cause she were poorly last time I heard.'

'Gone for a slow walk and a cup o' tea.' Kit sampled her own beverage. 'Went last Friday. Just on her way to deliver Mrs Kelly's forty-ninth bairn – or whatever – and she dropped dead in t'street.'

Amelia looked at Albert and voiced sadness. 'I'd've gone to pay me respects if I'd known. Was it a nice do?'

Kit wrinkled her nose. 'I've been to better. Ham were a bit dry, I thought. It's a pity she wasn't there to organize her own do.'

Amelia nodded. 'She always put on a good funeral tea, did Mrs Feather.' She looked down at her hands, and extended a digit. 'Eh, look at this horrible wart. Don't know how I got it, but I can't get rid of it. Tried all sorts but it won't disappear.'

Kit took this as an opening to confess. 'I bet that's what our Monty's saying about me.' Immediately interpreting that tone as a forecast of trouble, Amelia pointed out to her husband that it was time for him to bring the carriage round for their mistress's afternoon outing. Not until he had gone did she ask for an explanation. Upon hearing it all, she shook her frizzy ginger head at her wayward sibling. 'Eh, Kit!'

'There's nothing going on between us. I simply give him board in exchange for him cooking my dinner. Where's the harm in that?'

'But you can't blame folk for thinking – I mean, even if you didn't intend anything, what if he crept into your bedroom and took advantage of you?' When Kit objected that she trusted Mr Popplewell, Amelia threw up her haunted blue eyes. 'Eh, you're that innocent!' Acting the part of the old married woman, she explained, 'You don't have to be wed to have a baby, you know.'

Kit gave a sad little smile. 'Chance would be a fine thing.'

Her sister's voice was stern. 'It's nowt to joke about.'

'I'm not joking. I can't have any.'

'How can you possibly know that?'

'A fortune-teller once told me I'd never marry nor never have children.' At the other's scoffing response, Kit hesitated, then told her sister about her intimate relationship with Ninian Latimer. Gazing into Amelia's scandalized expression, she murmured. 'So, I'm not likely ever to get married, am I? Nobody wants a –' She broke off but too late.

'A barren wife,' finished Amelia. 'Oh, don't worry, I'm used to people going on about it now.' A gleam of tears gave lie to the brave remark.

'Aw, I didn't mean to upset you!' Kit grabbed her hand. 'I know how you feel, truly I do. It's all I've ever wanted, is bairns.'

Amelia blew her nose, fighting an embarrassing display of emotion. 'Well, there's nothing we can do about it. It's the Lord's decision – anyway, what are you going to do about your other problem? It'll still be there when you get back, you know.'

Kit sighed. 'Maybe I should move away altogether.'

For her brother's sake, Amelia agreed, deciding then that it was her duty to relieve Monty of his problem, even if it meant landing herself with one of her own. 'York's a nice place to live.' And there was more chance of anonymity here than in the parochial Ralph Royd.

Kit agreed, saying how impressed she had been on her first visit. 'You've certainly got more to do on your doorstep – the theatre and concerts and suchlike. Mm, that's a good idea of yours. I might just have a look round while I'm here.'

*　　*　　*

Amelia was to be amazed when her sister returned from her afternoon jaunt with the announcement that she had bought a house. Kit laughed and said she did not let the grass grow under her feet, though she couldn't move in until the contract was signed, of course, which would be in approximately a month's time, so she would have to suffer the village gossips until then – what would they find to talk about when she left?

After spending a week at her sister's, Kit returned to Ralph Royd to give others the news, telling Mr Popplewell that once she had finished her outstanding orders she would be off.

Expecting him to be equally delighted, she was surprised to see his bony face drop and was quick to remove this obvious misapprehension. 'Naturally, I'm expecting you to go with me.'

Popplewell looked apologetic. 'I'd love to, honey, but you know all my custom is around here.'

'Well, so is mine! People as talented as us can soon get a new lot.'

'There's folk depending on me, Kit. I can't let them down, and what with the shooting season upon us – no, I'm sorry, I can't come.'

'You mean I'll have to cook for meself?' responded Kit.

'Aw! You'll get somebody else. And a word to the wise –' he gripped her hand – 'get a female, she'll be less trouble for you. But I'd love to come and visit you in the future. Until then, I suppose I'd better start looking for new lodgings.'

'Aw no, I won't be chucking you out,' said Kit. 'You might as well stay here. They'll have nowt to gossip about once I'm gone. I don't want t'place to stand empty. Stay as long as you like, I won't be coming back.'

Within a month the transfer of ownership of the house in York was completed, and after making swift purchase of carpets, curtains and basic pieces of furniture, Kit was able to move in. In common with many of her previous purchases it had been rash. City dwellings being a lot more expensive than in rural areas, its procurement almost halved her bank balance, but the notice in her window advertising the occupant's dressmaking skills would soon restore it to health. In addition, Mr Popplewell had insisted upon paying rent for the use of her cottage. Kit found it rather amusing to think of herself as a woman of property.

The fact that her new dwelling was antiquated with jutting upper storey and crumbling stucco, was squashed between shops and public houses, and had the smell of an incontinent old lady, mattered not at all to Kit. It was in the centre of town, and had been chosen for its lively surroundings. From its window, should she have time to lift her eyes from her sewing machine, she could watch all the activity in the marketplace, or if she so chose, could have an afternoon off to mingle with the shoppers. With the employment of a maid of all work there was no need to attend to anything other than herself – though Lizzie's cooking left a lot to be desired after Mr Popplewell's culinary expertise.

During that first year Popplewell came to visit quite often, bringing the occasional bunch of flowers to brighten Kit's sparsely furnished parlour, taking her to the races, boating on the Ouse or for walks around the ancient Bar Walls – though Kit made sure he always wrote to say when he would be coming. It wouldn't do for him to bump into one of her other callers – for with her flamboyant dress and magnificent proportions it hadn't taken her long to find another circle of admirers.

No longer the innocent maid courted by schoolboys, Kit had come to realize what an impression she made on men, knew very well what deeper yearnings ran behind those admiring expressions, and played them for all she was worth. Her open smile luring them into introduction, men queued to court her. Sometimes, to test her own power, Kit had the audacity to invite them to her house four at a time, pretending innocence when they found themselves amongst rivals and offering consolation by organizing a game of cards or charades. By the end of the evening her sparkling banter and her ability to flirt with all at the same time had erased any insult and they came to enjoy a sort of brotherhood – though each hung back when the time came to leave, hoping that he would be the one who was asked to stay behind and sample her pleasures. But, of these there were few, for Kit had resolved never to sell herself cheaply. The rest were merely diversions until someone better came along.

However, these acquaintances had their uses, for they introduced Kit to a new batch of customers, and she was very soon inundated with orders. Hence, with such a full life, she had no chance to visit her relatives – though she frequently corresponded. The first chance she had to visit Ralph Royd was at Christmas when, all garments completed, she hurriedly shut up shop and caught a train, bearing gifts for her nephews and nieces. She genuinely missed not seeing them on a regular basis, but most of them were grown up now and, if not married, were occupied in work. They were not the little people she had taken on picnics – though Probyn could still be relied upon to supply unwitting entertainment.

With Mr Popplewell gone to spend the festive season with relatives, Kit found herself alone in the cottage. Naturally she was invited to take dinner with Monty's family, and on Boxing Day Owen played host. But as Christmas in the Kilmaster household was little different to the rest of the year, plus the fact that Kit was seated opposite the portrait of Beata that she had always loathed, so that it watched her throughout the meal, it was not long before she was packing her bag to return to York.

After a miserable yuletide, the New Year celebrations proved to be more uplifting, with gentlemen aplenty to take her dancing, and a constant flow of admiration over her evening gown, which in turn produced a flurry of orders. In all respects, Kit announced that 1882 was going to be an exceptionally good year – though just how good she was yet to find out.

One day in January an impromptu visit to her sister's place of residence on the Mount coincided with the arrival of a guest. The tall, mustachioed, very distinguished looking man in black overcoat, striped trousers and a top hat, was alighting from his carriage as Kit crossed the road towards, it trying to negotiate a width of frosty cobblestones without damaging the heels of her kidskin boots before reaching the footpath. Accustomed to men being struck by her appearance, she reacted with a dignified smile at his open admiration, at which he swept off his top hat to reveal dark, closely cut hair. Noting that they were heading for the same residence he stepped back with a slight bow and allowed her to pass through the iron gateway first.

Hovering at her window to catch the guest's arrival, Amelia looked most put out and embarrassed to see her sister arrive at the same time, and rushed out of her own entrance to intercept her whilst a fleet-footed Albert sped to the front door to greet his employer's visitor.

Kit was rather disgruntled to be hauled through the tradesmen's entrance. 'Do I gather I've come at an inopportune moment? I just thought you'd like this as soon as possible.' From a brown paper parcel she produced the dress that Amelia had ordered last week.

'That was quick!' Amelia's anxiety-ridden blue eyes examined the seams, further offending its maker.

Kit took off her gloves and replied with dignified restraint, 'That's because I put it before all my other orders.'

Chastened, Amelia thanked her and asked how much she owed.

'You don't think I'm charging my sister, do you?' Kit unbuttoned her coat. 'Though a smile and a cup of tea would be nice – that is, if I'm allowed to stop.'

Realizing how shabbily she had behaved, Amelia bade Kit take a seat by the range. 'I'm sorry, if I'd known you were coming I'd have told you not to.' At Kit's outraged laugh she smiled apologetically. 'I mean, I won't be able to spend as much time as I'd like with you. We've got an important guest for high tea. He's a member of the cabinet.'

Returning from the drawing room where he had deposited the visitor, Albert told his wife he would see to matters if she wanted to chat with Kit. With the sandwiches and dainties already prepared it was only a matter of serving them. But in devoted fashion she insisted on helping him and left Kit to her own devices for fifteen minutes or so, after which she finally had time to relax.

In her sister's absence Kit had helped herself to a cup of tea and a big slab of fruit cake loaded with cheese, but now accepted a refill. 'I see you've got rid of that wart you had on your finger.'

Amelia put down the teapot and extended the unblemished digit. 'The laundry woman fixed it for me. She rubbed a pea on it – fancy, that's all it took!'

The listener was aghast. 'The mucky cat! How could you let her?'

Amelia was puzzled. 'She rubbed it on the wart, then wrapped it in paper and burned it.'

After a confused pause Kit burst out laughing. 'Oh a *pea*! I thought you said her pee.'

'Our Kit, you're that daft. Trust you to come up with summat vulgar.' But Amelia laughed too, as did her husband.

Kit felt someone watching her then and turned towards the doorway to see the visiting politician. Her lack of discomfiture upon being studied so closely obviously intrigued him for he seemed loath to tear his eyes away, though politeness forced him to do so. He lingered in the stone-paved corridor.

'I'm sorry to intrude but I appear to have taken a wrong turning.' In actual fact, upon hearing Kit's hearty laughter he had done so deliberately. 'I should be grateful if you could direct me to the convenience.'

Whilst Albert complied immediately and his wide-beamed wife shot from her seat to bustle around red-faced, Kit paid close heed to the politician before he disappeared, having instantly recognized the look he gave her. So, when Albert was later summoned to show their guest out, Kit decided it was time for her to depart also.

Their exits coinciding, Kit and the politician smiled through the fading light in acknowledgement of each other, the latter once again standing aside for her to pass through the gateway.

Equine breath emerged as a cloud on the wintry air, as did his own as he indicated the carriage and asked, 'Could I perhaps offer you a lift, Miss –?'

'Kilmaster.' She studied the blue eyes that were on a level with hers, the dark hair streaked with the faintest hint of grey at the temples, the waxed moustache, the gentrified air. 'If it wouldn't take you out of your way. I live in St Sampson's Square.'

He assisted her into the closed carriage. 'I'm afraid I do not know York very well, but no place is very far from another in such a small city – at least compared to London.' Upon establishing that his driver knew where to go, he climbed inside and sat beside her. 'I do beg your pardon, I should introduce myself.' He gave his name as Valentine Kitchingham, then tapped on the roof with his silver-topped cane for the driver to move off.

Kit rested her gloved hands in her lap. The air in here was little warmer than outside and she noticed that her breath eddied around his face as she asked, 'You hail from London then, Mr Kitchingham?'

'I reside there for most of the year, yes, but only by nature of my work.' He told her what she already knew – that he was a Liberal MP. 'I'm a Yorkshire lad by birth. My constituency is here too.'

With not the slightest hint of Yorkshire in his accent, it occurred to her that he was only trying to ingratiate himself, but she made no disparaging remark and charmingly told him how she had so enjoyed her visits to the capital and hoped to go again some day. 'As a matter of fact I'm quite new to York myself. It's a very quaint place, isn't it? I love its antiquities. And there are such varied social occasions. It has so much more to offer than my own small village.'

335

Ascertaining that this was in a mining community, Kitchingham said he had many colliers in his own constituency and that he deeply sympathized with their struggle against the coal masters. He hoped to be able bring in legislation to help them.

The carriage advanced upon the turreted tower of Micklegate Bar, and negotiated its limestone arch. Kit said that whenever she passed through one of these ancient entries to the city she imagined the decapitated heads of traitors looking down at her. To which Kitchingham chuckled and said that although he shared her love of history he was glad that, being a politician, he had been born into more enlightened times. As the iron wheels rolled down a hill characterized by old-world charm and across the bridge over the Ouse, they exchanged desultory chitchat. All too soon, though, they arrived in the marketplace where the stallholders were packing up their depleted stocks, the greasy road beneath littered with squashed fruit and vegetables, feathers and bits of paper.

The carriage proceeded to the end of the wide street, heading towards the towers of the Minster that projected far above the roofline, its stupendous presence dwarfing everything around. Finally the vehicle slowed, its driver calling to enquire where to pull up. Kit said there outside the Golden Lion would do. Turning to her escort, she invited him in for refreshment. But after looking at his watch on the end of its gold chain he regretfully declined, saying that he had to catch a train in half an hour back to London.

'I wish I were going with you,' said Kit without artistry.

'Who knows, perhaps we can arrange it some time.' Her suave companion emerged from the carriage to help her alight. The way he looked at her left her in no uncertain terms as to his desires.

Kit smiled in similar fashion to show that she understood, then pointed. 'That's my little house there. You're most welcome to call the next time you're in York, Mr Kitchingham.'

She was encouraged that he made a point of scribbling her address down in his notebook, telling her, 'I should be honoured, Miss Kilmaster.'

Thanking him for the lift, she waited on the pavement for his carriage to move off, shivering slightly, before waving and going inside, a smile playing about her lips.

The next time Kit saw Amelia she received an admonishment. 'I thought you'd come to visit me, not arrange assignations – don't bother to fib, I saw you get into his carriage! You'll get me dismissed, you will.'

There was to be even more outrage when Kit showed her the violet-strewn card that had arrived on Valentine's Day, bearing a London postmark and an inked message beneath the printed verse that proclaimed, 'My heart's desire is to be your Valentine'. 'A romantic soul, isn't he?'

Amelia snorted, 'Romantic, my foot. Have you thought that a man of his age must be married?'

Kit was amused as she perched on a chair and studied the Valentine. 'Well, it had crossed my mind.'

'And you're still prepared to consort with him?' Amelia slammed the brown glazed teapot on the table between them, rattling cups against saucers before sitting down opposite, her face prim beneath the frizzy ginger fringe. 'He won't leave his wife, if that's what you think.'

'Who said I want him to?' retorted Kit.

'What sort of a thing is that to say?' Amelia paused abruptly in the pouring of tea. 'How would you feel if someone did it to you?' The Kilmasters had always been made to heed their brother's philosophy: do unto others as you would have them do unto you.

'What she doesn't know can't harm her,' said Kit irresponsibly.

'Well, that's a very Christian attitude, I must say! Just because you can't find a husband doesn't give you the right to steal someone else's. I know how I'd feel if anyone took Albert. Oh, Kit!' Annoyance melted into matronly concern. 'Are you sure you know what you're getting into? Have you thought that you might get yourself a bad reputation?'

Amelia had always annoyed Kit by the way she allied herself with the senior members of the family, treating her sister like a child when she herself was only three years older, questioning Kit's every deed or word.

'Will you shut up with your *are you sure*s and *have you thought*s – of course I've bloomin' thought!' snapped Kit. 'Stop acting like me granny. It's only a blessed Valentine, not an invitation to Sodom and Gomorrah!'

'There's time yet,' concluded her disapproving sister, and with pursed lips handed over a cup of tea.

Two months after the arrival of the Valentine, the sender himself turned up on her doorstep, apologizing that it had taken him so long to act on her invitation to visit but an important bill had kept him a prisoner in London.

Dismissing Lizzie, who had brought him into the cosy parlour, Kit made him welcome, thanking him for the charming card. 'It was from you, wasn't it?'

'Miss Kilmaster, I cannot tell a lie.'

'A rare breed of politician, my brother would say.' She smiled. 'Do call me Kit.' Over glasses of sherry, she tried to glean more information, asking what exactly he did in his role of cabinet minister. He appeared hesitant to answer, saying that he was sure she had much more interesting topics of conversation. Kit insisted this was not so and pressed him to be less modest. 'Tell me, where exactly is your constituency?'

He remained pleasantly evasive, taking a sip of sherry before replying with a smile, 'Oh, here and there.'

'So you're addressed in the Commons as the Honourable Member for Here and There, are you?' Kit gave a knowing smile. 'If you're afraid of me finding out you're married, it had already occurred to me, you know.'

He seemed relieved by her attitude. 'You are a most understanding woman, my dear,' and he came to sit nearer to her on the sturdy red sofa.

Sufficiently informed as to where she stood, Kit allowed the conversation to become more intimate, but before it got out of hand, she arose and produced a generous tea of assorted sandwiches, cakes and trifle.

'I was hoping that you'd accompany me to dinner at my hotel later,' said Valentine, mopping his moustache on a napkin afterwards. 'But after such hospitality I don't know if I'll be able to move from my chair. You are a most generous hostess, Kit.'

Kit said she would like to come with him, but would it not be a little indiscreet?

He did not appear to think so, and some hours later, when their tea had been digested, Kit enlisted Lizzie to haul on the laces of her stays, changed into a pale blue satin evening dress festooned with lace and ribbon, and elbow-length white gloves, and fastened her coiled auburn tresses with pearly combs. Whereupon, Valentine whistled for a hansom to take them to his hotel.

Aside from those places in which she had been a domestic servant, Kit had never enjoyed such opulent surroundings. Fittingly, the meal was splendid, undertaken to a background of orchestral music – though her unnatural wasp waist prevented her from eating much of it. Apart from this self-inflicted torment, everything else was perfect, for Kit was to discover that the music came from a ballroom and, upon learning of her favourite pastime, her escort whisked her off for an evening of extended dance.

Tired but happy, as the orchestra packed away their instruments, Kit proclaimed that she had never enjoyed such a good time. 'You're such an accomplished dancer!' She unhooked the loop of her silken train from her wrist and allowed it to fall. 'I feel as if I could go on and on all night – but I suppose I should go home, more's the pity.'

He bowed over her hand, allowing his eyes to linger on her frothy lace décolletage, and agreeing that it was a shame she had to go. 'Could I not persuade you to share a nightcap?'

Understanding that he was inviting her to his room, Kit smiled reprovingly and, though she was more than a little attracted to him, said that would not be wise. Besides the poor maid would be waiting up for her mistress.

Signalling for a cab to be brought to the door Valentine accepted the rebuttal in urbane manner and took her home, though when it looked as if he was not to be allowed any chance of intimacy here either he offered a plaintive rebuke. 'I had hoped you might show a little more compassion, Kit.'

Consequently, she sent Lizzie off to bed and invited him in, but said that after one glass of brandy he must leave.

Finding himself drinking alone, Valentine urged her to join him. She declined the liquor but, during its leisurely consumption, was happy enough to sit beside him on the sofa, even allowing his hand to pat her silken thigh once or twice, finding him very seductive.

Head back and deeply relaxed, he remarked how homely she had made this room feel – he could almost fall asleep. 'But, it's back to dirty old London for me tomorrow,' he sighed.

'Don't speak about it like that!' Kit scolded. 'It's a wonderful place.

I'd love to go there again.' Maybe he would take her? 'Though I have to agree that London is no place to be alone.'

'You don't have to be alone.' Valentine put the brandy glass aside. 'You could come and be with me.'

Kit tried to sound concerned. 'But your wife –'

'Lives in Yorkshire,' he finished, taking hold of her hand. 'When Parliament is in session I live alone in rooms – but if I had someone to come home to, life would be infinitely more agreeable.' He became more earnest. 'Kit, you are aware how deeply I am attracted to you. No – more than that. I find myself thinking about you all the time. Forgive me if I'm wrong, but I suspect that it is only your natural modesty that prevents you from admitting that you share my feelings. I should say here and now that it would be dishonest of me to promise marriage – indeed, you already know I cannot do that – but my feelings for you are so strong that I can deny them no longer. I have the wherewithal to provide a fine house, a carriage, servants – anything that you desire. The fun that we've enjoyed tonight we could enjoy any night of the year!'

With Kit struck dumb by the generosity of his offer, he made a practised move, throwing her back on to the sofa and running his hands over the intimate parts of her body, bestowing her lips with so masterly a kiss that for several moments she allowed herself to enjoy it.

Fighting her natural attraction, Kit eventually pushed him off – though her smiling face negated any offence. 'If you're serious –'

'I am!' Eyes suffused with lust, he made as if to leap on her again but she held him at bay.

'Then I should like to see evidence of this house before I agree one way or another.' Her hand remained resting on his chest that rose and fell with ungratified passion. Even watching this display caused a ripple of excitement in her own belly, though she would continue to fight it until satisfied that she was not being duped again.

Seeing that he would get nowhere, Valentine Kitchingham moaned and gave up, telling her how cruel she was to make him wait. Kit retorted pleasantly that the length of time he waited depended entirely on him. Straightening her dress, she rose and piloted him to the door. Upon closing it, she leaned against the wood, wondering whether she had acted correctly in making him wait.

Four days later she was to find out, when an envelope arrived bearing a London postmark. Inside was a railway ticket to King's Cross, a scrap of paper bearing an address in St John's Wood, and a key. Kit gave a whoop of triumph and ran off to pack.

19

It transpired that the key was totally unnecessary. Whilst Kit was still alighting from the cab at the gate of the white detached villa, with its garden of daffodils, forsythia and flowering currant, the black front door opened and a manservant came to relieve her of her luggage, and a maid bade her welcome. Overlooking the fact that it was an aloof kind of welcome, Kit gave smiling response and, excitement mingling with apprehension, she went up the path and stepped inside to wander along the tiled hallway, her eyes following the gentle rise of the blue carpeted stairs to an arched window on the landing.

Comparison with her own little house provoked brief thought of Lizzie who had lost her job through Kit's departure. She hoped that with the excellent reference she had given her, the maid had found another post by now. As for her house, that would remain empty for the time being. Kit was reluctant to put it up for let; not knowing how long this would last, she might need a bolthole.

'Fred'll bring your luggage up, ma'am.' Bustling ahead of Kit, the slim-hipped maid in black and white directed her up to her room, whilst the footman struggled behind. Whilst she was of similar age to Kit, the man with greying hair was fifteen years her senior, though it was obvious who gave the orders. 'You'll obviously want to refresh yourself. Oh, by the way, I'm Cara.' Accompanying the rather inanimate freckled face, blue eyes and light brown hair, was an Irish accent.

Kit pursued her, her own expression showing that she was obviously thrilled to bits with the house. She asked Cara to inform Cook that she'd like luncheon once she had freshened up. It was two o'clock and her stomach was rumbling like thunder.

'Ah, there's no cook, ma'am, just me and Fred and Dilly, the scullerymaid – but don't worry now, you'll get your luncheon. Though I'm afraid 'twill be a cold one. We weren't sure when to expect ye, see.'

'So you do just about everything yourself?' Kit sounded impressed. 'Well, I appreciate the hard work you must've had in such a short time.' Noting the puzzled stare that was flung over the maid's shoulder, she added, 'Well, you can't have been here long. It must have been a mammoth job getting the place into this order.'

'Ah no, I've been here six years.'

It was Kit's turn to be puzzled. 'But I thought Mr Kitchingham only acquired the house recently?'

A look of understanding hit Cara's face as they reached the large square landing, and even before the negative reply this smirking expression alerted Kit to the truth – how naive of her to assume herself to be the first he had brought here. For a moment, a little of the glitter was tarnished. But then she told herself not to be so silly: had she not known what he wanted from her at the outset? Reminding herself that she too was guilty of manipulation, and determined not to let Cara's supercilious attitude cloud her enjoyment, she maintained her smile and swept into one of the bedrooms.

'This one's yours, ma'am.'

Kit ignored the maid's instruction, inspecting both this room and its view of the walled back garden before eventually responding.

Cara and the footman waited patiently whilst their mistress made critical examination of her surroundings. Two walls of the room were lined in a light wooden panelling that included all manner of drawers and cupboards, a section of this being devoted to a writing desk with little compartments for envelopes. The fact that there was no flame in the cast-iron fireplace seemed not to matter for the room's furnishings lent it ample cosiness. The floor was clothed in a thick flower-patterned carpet. From the canopy above the brass bedstead descended the same deep green velvet as embellished the windows, there were tasselled and braided pelmets, a heavy counterpane and an abundance of tapestry cushions and pillows. Upon the shelves were pink glass ornaments and a collection of books. There was a dressing table and stool, a plump upholstered armchair, and upon those walls which were unpanelled was a light-coloured paper with an elegant scrolled pattern, this air of refinement being enhanced by the white bell-like shades of the gas lamps.

343

Deciding it would be pointless to argue that, as mistress, she would choose her own room, for the allotted one was far superior, Kit gave her approval, told Fred where to deposit her luggage, then sat at the dressing table and looked in the mirror. Removing her hat, she wiped the specks of soot from her face, and asked for hot water to be brought up.

Cara replied politely, 'It'll be here in two shakes, ma'am – and luncheon will be waiting when ye get down.' With this she and the footman promptly departed.

Unpacking her cases, Kit frowned to herself. She had no valid reason to complain about the quality of service, it was just that the servants appeared to be so much more at home here than she was, and knew much more than she did about the man with whom she had come to live.

However, after recovering from the tedious railway journey and partaking of a three-course luncheon, albeit a cold one, she was more amiably disposed towards Cara, telling her that she provided excellent fare and that she looked forward to sampling more of her meals, though after such a late luncheon she would only just have recovered from its effects by supper time.

'By the way, at what time does Mr Kitchingham usually take supper?'

'We're not expecting the master tonight, ma'am. Is he aware that you'd be coming?'

'Well, I just assumed –' Kit prevented any further indiscretion, unwilling to reveal the insecurity of the relationship.

It was as if Cara guessed. 'See, as you'll know, he doesn't actually live here, ma'am. He just comes and goes as he pleases. It pays to be flexible with Mr Kitchingham. Will there be anything else, ma'am?'

Kit wanted to slap that punctilious expression from the maid's face, but instead thanked her and said that would be all.

The next few minutes were given to investigating the lower storey of the house, which consisted of a drawing room, a dining room and a study, plus the kitchen and servants' rooms, which she chose to avoid for the time being. Having already seen the bedrooms earlier, this left Kit with nothing to do for the rest of the afternoon but listen to her thoughts.

When Kit had told her sister that she would be going away for a while, but prevaricated upon being asked where she was going and for how long, Amelia could not help but guess.

'You're going to London with him, aren't you? Oh, Kit don't do it – there'll be a duck in t'hedge somewhere, you're bound to get hurt – and what of his poor wife and children?'

Kit had made light of this. 'I'm not taking him away. He'll see as much of them as he does now. No one need be any the wiser. We're not out to harm anyone, we're just enjoying ourselves.'

'Your idea of enjoyment and his might be two different things! And I don't know what our Monty will have to say when he finds out – and as for our Owen! He'll have a few things to say about your Mr Kitchingham – a cabinet minister, for heaven's sake. Couldn't you find any more of a public figure?'

'I might just be able to do a bit of good in that area,' Kit had argued. 'Explain to Val just what it's like to be a miner. Anyway, he's already very philanthropic towards his constituents.'

Philanthropic, my eye!' had said an irate Amelia. 'He just wants to get into your drawers!'

Kit had been surprised at such crudity from her sister, and had immediately gone home in a huff. But privately she had to admit that it was true – though just when he would arrive to claim his prize was anyone's guess.

Going to the large bay window, she peered out into the quiet street, then wandered around the room picking up various objets d'art, and feeling at a loose end. Having always envied the upper class their indolent lifestyle, she now felt a prickle of panic at the thought of having nothing to do. It was all very well for those with acquaintances of a similar ilk with whom they could enjoy morning rides in the park or make one afternoon visit after another. But what chance of that was there for Kit, who knew no one in London? And in the impulsive rush to get here she had cancelled all business orders – she had had quite enough of sewing for a while – though now she decided it might be a good idea to install another machine here, if only to help occupy such idle moments.

She tapped her lips with a finger, trying to conjure up something to do until Valentine made an appearance. A carriage! He had promised her a carriage – she would ask Fred to take her for a drive. That way she could safely acclimatize herself to her surroundings without fear of violation. It would also serve to use up the rest of the afternoon.

Squaring her shoulders, Kit marched into the kitchen.

The servants had obviously been talking about her for they clammed up at her entry. Cara was grinding something deliciously aromatic with a pestle and mortar and fourteen-year-old Dilly was washing up the crockery used at luncheon. Unlike Myrtle, this flaxen haired youngster appeared to have her wits about her and responded to Kit's hello with a bright smile.

'Yes, he's picked himself a biggun this time!' Fred was in a separate little cubbyhole polishing silver and was unaware of Kit's entry. 'Still, if you have to have one, have a biggun, that's what I always say.' At Cara's warning cough, he poked his head out to witness Kit's towering presence and immediately rectified the comment by adding, 'I don't see any point in skimping on something as important as a mattress – do you, ma'am?'

Not entirely at ease, Kit agreed, then said that if he was too busy she would understand but she'd appreciate it if he could take her out in the carriage. Cara's expression showed that she wasn't pleased but Fred seemed happy to oblige, and whipped off his apron.

Asked where she would like to be taken, Kit admitted that she did not know. Fred, metamorphosed to coachman in a black plush top hat with a cockade on the side, and dark green caped overcoat piped with yellow, replied that he would take her around Regent's Park, which should provide a pleasant excursion before tea. If she cared to go any further afield tomorrow he would be at her disposal. Still, there was a jaded air about him when Kit tried to involve him in conversation, making her wonder to just how many of Mr Kitchingham's mistresses he had been forced to offer similar services?

When she got back from the park, Kit had a cup of tea, then decided to read a book until Valentine turned up. It was so enjoyable that she lost all inkling of time, until Cara came in to light the gas lamps and said that supper was ready. Disappointed to be eating alone, Kit rushed through the meal and went straight back to her enthralling tale. Before she knew it, the clock struck nine. It was doubtful he would come now. Hoping the friendliness of her voice disguised her forlorn mood, Kit bade the servants goodnight, said she was going to bed, and took the book with her.

The rest of the week was to take on a similar pattern, Kit despairing that Valentine would ever turn up at all. Though used to living alone, her surroundings then had been familiar and amongst her own kind, this place was totally alien. There was a limit to how much time one could give to admiring one's new acquisitions before becoming bored.

Kit had almost reached that limit when, to her delight, Valentine arrived on Friday evening. His pleasure at seeing her there totally made up for the long wait which, he explained, was due to pressures of work and the simple fact that he had not expected her to arrive so swiftly. He had merely come tonight on the off chance that she might be here.

'Had I realized, I would have been here like shot!' He kissed her hand and led her to the sofa where he sat very close, looking like a boy who has just received the promised train set in his Christmas stocking. 'Oh dear, poor Kitty, sitting here all on your own with nothing to do.'

'I was under the impression that you'd be living here all the time,' she told him somewhat reproachfully.

'I shall, now that I know you're here – at least as much of the time as I can possibly manage. Though sometimes I will have to stay at my dreary little flat in Westminster – the House often keeps me until midnight.'

Kit said she understood that he had an important job, and asked him to tell her all that he had been doing. Replying that she would find most of it boring, he related instead a number of amusing incidents that had taken place in the House during his time there, causing her to laugh and he in turn to tell her how much he loved the unselfconscious way she displayed her merriment. They talked and laughed non-stop until supper, after which he asked if she would mind very much if he went to change out of these formal clothes. With her permission, he returned in a maroon quilted smoking jacket with an open necked shirt and corduroy trousers, though the waxed moustache helped maintain his suave demeanour.

'Ah, that's much better!' He fell on to the velvet sofa beside her, resting his head on her shoulder for a moment, before lifting it to ask, 'Kit, be a sweetheart and pour me a brandy.' He favoured her with a warm smile as she acceded – 'Oh, God bless you!' – then took a grateful sip and ordered her to sit beside him again. 'Now!' He performed a deft tweak of both ends of his moustache. 'You must tell me what you want to do tomorrow – and Sunday. We have the entire weekend to ourselves.'

Kit snuggled up and told him that the choice was his, she would be happy just to escape the house. He voiced the realization that he had no idea as to her preferences – apart from dancing that was. There would be plenty of opportunity for the latter on an evening, with many a colourful ball to attend, but what about the daytime? He listed the things which he himself enjoyed – museums, art galleries, boating in summer, skating in winter, horse racing, the theatre – to every one of them Kit acquiesced, her shining eyes telling him that a wonderful partnership lay ahead.

'There is, of course, one thing that I enjoy above all,' said Valentine, his lazy smile and his hooded eye informing her just what this might be. Finding the invitation he sought in Kit's face, he put his glass aside, took her in his arms and delivered a long kiss.

With its increasing ardour, Kit broke free.

He misinterpreted her look of concern and murmured seductively, 'You need have no fear, Kit. I'll be very careful.'

It was not the right time to say he need not be concerned, for she was barren. Kit explained that her cautious attitude was merely inspired by the thought that a servant might walk in on them. Should they not find somewhere more private? Granting her a little time in which to prepare herself, Valentine said he would finish his brandy and send the servants to bed, before coming to join her.

Delivering a lingering kiss, Kit left him.

Once upstairs in the yellow glow of the gas-lit bedroom, her attitude became more hurried, her fingers scrabbling over the twenty-four buttons down the front of her bodice, the complicated laces of her stays, the layers and layers of petticoats, until finally she stood, panting slightly, in chemise and drawers. Freed, her great breasts rolled like the waves beneath their thin layer of cambric as she hurried to the dressing table stool and sat down to pull off her shoes and stockings. A nightgown replaced the chemise and drawers. One by one a dozen hairpins were ferreted out by impatient fingertips and dropped with a succession of pinging noises into a china dish. Finally, with rivulets of auburn hair about her shoulders, she felt ready to meet him – though an afterthought sent her wobbling rapidly across the room to pull down one side of the bed linen.

When Valentine entered, Kit was brushing her hair with gentle strokes, the tranquillity of the scene belying her previous activity, only the pink flush to her cheeks giving her away. She put down the brush and rose, heart racing. Instead of approaching, he sat on the bed as if staggered by what he saw.

As she came towards him smiling, he rose to meet her, ripping off his smoking jacket and wrapping his arms around her pliant flesh, kneading and moulding it to his own body. Kit responded to his kisses with gusto, her feet inching with his towards the bed. Once there he lifted her nightgown over her head so that she stood naked before him, then pressed his lips to the warm gigantic swell of her breasts, his face disappearing into soft flesh, his fingers sliding underneath her buttocks. Deeply aroused, she gave a little cry of objection as he dropped to his knees, his lips travelling down her belly. She urged him to take off his own clothes which he did, returning to her, naked and engorged. Falling on to the bed, Kit spread herself eagerly, pulled him into her, rejoicing in the contrast between their two bodies that merged into one writhing unit, rolling, arching, crashing like waves against rock . . .

And afterwards, as their sated, sweat-drenched bodies lay panting, each of them agreed that this association was going to be of great mutual benefit.

The pattern set, on Sunday morning Kit awoke to find a hand clamped between her thighs, and wriggled her buttocks invitingly at the warm, rigid presence to her rear, thereby sparking another sensual alliance.

Afterwards, the aroma of fried bacon filtering up from the kitchen, Valentine rose and put on his dressing gown, instructing Kit to do the same and they would go down to breakfast. Kit admitted self-consciously that she did not own a dressing gown. At which, as if seized with a burst of inspiration he rushed off, telling her to stay where she was. When he returned he was carrying a large tray bearing tea and toast, bacon, eggs and sausages, which he balanced precariously whilst slipping into bed beside her, and told Kit to dig in.

'Though you're not to expect this every morning, mind!' A loaded fork disappeared into his mustachioed grin. 'At least not from me. Cara will serve you well.'

Kit wanted to issue a scold – 'Don't speak with your mouth full' – but thought better of it.

The meal consumed with relish, they leaned back on the pillows, taking time over their cups of tea, Valentine telling Kit that he had instructed the maid to bring up a bath for her. Alarmed at the thought of being discovered in such circumstances, Kit started to leap out of bed, but he laughed and told her to calm herself, Cara would only come when summoned by the bell. 'When she's on her way you can hide in one of the other rooms if you so wish.'

When they had emptied their cups, Valentine rang for the maid and Kit retired to another room. Upon hearing the uneven thud of feet coming up the stairs – which meant Cara and Dilly were arriving with the bath – she peeped around the door to watch them deliver it, finally to emerge, one of them carrying the breakfast tray. Only when she was sure they had gone did she return.

Seated in the armchair, one leg crossed over the other, Valentine smiled at her prudishness and said he hardly dared to make his suggestion now.

'Suggest what?' Kit hovered by the bath.

'That I sit here and watch you bathe.'

Kit was astounded – a bath was such a private thing.

'Why, Kit, such modesty! It's hardly as if we don't know one another.' He made no move to leave the chair, issuing a smile of encouragement. 'Come, don't be a spoilsport. I have always been fascinated to learn what's involved in a woman's toilet. Having never been allowed to do so, I took you for one more liberated. You've always displayed such generosity in other spheres.'

Reluctantly, she agreed to let him stay, praying that the hip bath would contain her grand proportions and that the water would not overflow when she got in. Fortunately, though the water came to within an inch of the brim, no spillage occurred. Unwilling to perform more intimate ablutions, she merely lay there enveloped in steam, stroking the sponge up and down her arms, feeling self-conscious under his gaze.

'I thought we might do the Row this morning.'

Kit flinched. 'D'you mean in Hyde Park?' An unpleasant memory sprang to mind of the last time she had been on Rotten Row when she had suffered the humiliation of being arrested.

'Where else? Parade with the nobs. Then, after luncheon – well, who knows what we will do after luncheon? It rather depends on who we meet in the park.'

With Kit's acquiescence, he urged her to get out of the bath whilst he stripped off and took her place. Even then, he insisted on watching her movements, lying back in the suds to watch as one after another item of clothing was donned: drawers and chemise, stockings and petticoats.

Postponing further accoutrement, Kit decided to brush her hair, wrapping each lock around her finger and securing it with a pin, allowing others to fall free while he watched in fascination.

But Kit was to draw the line at putting on her corsets in front of him – it was something no man should witness. Saying that if they were to go out should he not make a move to go and get dressed, she was able to acquire the privacy she desired and hurriedly completed her outfit.

On their way to Hyde Park in the open carriage, he told her that apart from everything else at her disposal she could expect a personal allowance. He understood that she would be lonely and thus wanted to provide the means for her to enjoy a shopping spree. During the conversation she was to discover that he came from a privileged family, and Kit was therefore spared from any guilt about taking money that should have been spent on his children. With a large house in Yorkshire, the one in London, a cottage in Cornwall and – remarkably – a villa in Spain, it was unlikely that he would ever be strapped for cash.

Happy in this knowledge, Kit smiled to herself as the carriage rolled sedately along.

Sunday Parade in Hyde Park was just as she remembered it, a regiment of toppers and morning coats, an intermingling tide of silken, multicoloured hats bobbing graciously to right and left; a colourful pride of peacocks. Somewhat nervously, she glanced around as the carriage turned into the Row to join others on the sandy track. Kit could have held her own with anyone, in her green braided costume and matching ostrich-plumed hat – the feather alone costing her a staggering five shillings – yet, she remained ill at ease, fearing that someone might spring from the bushes and label her a fake, thus ending her magical charade.

Valentine was quick to spot her tension and asked what was amiss, receiving the answer that she was afraid they might bump into someone he knew. In response, he laughed and said that this was the whole idea – and at this point he directed his cane at a group of people on foot who were looking in his direction and waved in recognition, telling Fred to stop the carriage alongside them.

Kit warily extended her gloved hand over the side of the carriage as she was introduced to the two men and women, who were presumably acquainted with Valentine's wife. She was therefore stunned to receive only warmth from all four people who, at Valentine's invitation, climbed into the carriage to join her for a spin to Kensington Palace, during which they treated Kit as if she were an old friend.

'My dear, you must come to luncheon!' insisted one of the women, an artificially pretty creature, much slimmer than Kit but of a similar age, with a southern accent, a ready smile and hennaed hair. 'Unless of course you have anything arranged.'

'Today?' Kit decided she liked the speaker and mirrored her smile. 'Won't it be short notice for your cook?'

'Not at all!' At the young woman's denial, a feather quivered on her aquamarine hat. 'She's a marvellous creature, always prepared to feed an army.'

Kit looked enquiringly at Valentine, who sat with his gloved hands resting on the cane between his legs, and who answered for her. 'We'd love to come, Angela, thank you. How fortunate that we bumped into you, particularly as Kit knows no one in London.'

'Oh, we'll soon remedy that!' Angela consulted the other woman, Frances, who gave an encouraging nod at Kit. 'First thing tomorrow I'll endeavour to arrange a get-together of all my friends for the afternoon – to welcome you into the fold.'

'You're very kind,' said Kit, and extended her smile to the menfolk, who seemed similarly disposed towards her, one of them flashing an admiring glance at Valentine for his choice.

Kit was to repeat this opinion some hours later when, after a corset-threatening luncheon, the ladies withdrew for coffee and private chatter, leaving the menfolk to their claret and cigars.

Her thanks was accompanied by an embarrassed confession as she spread her skirts upon Angela's sofa, surrounded by lacy antimacassars and a menagerie of stuffed animals under glass. 'When I first saw you in the park, I wasn't sure what reception I'd get.' She took a sip of coffee from a tiny oriental cup, then put it back on the mahogany side table.

'But why would we wish to spurn anyone so charming as our new friend?' asked her bemused hostess.

Fearing that the women might be ignorant of her escort's marital status, Kit said tentatively, 'Well, I wasn't sure if either you or your husbands were acquainted with Mrs Kitchingham.'

Angela and Frances shared a kind but hearty laugh, the latter giving her an affectionate tap with her painted fan. 'Kit, we're all in the same boat!'

Kit touched her lips, feeling at once relieved yet slightly decadent, the other two mistresses somehow emphasizing her own sordid status.

She tentatively asked if they had known Valentine long, a roundabout way of finding out what had happened to his previous consorts. Angela seemed to guess this and, without going into too much detail, said that in the three years she had been acquainted with him, Valentine had only had one other 'friend' and they had parted amicably some time ago when the woman had gone off to France – so there was no danger of Kit bumping into her. She had been very popular amongst their circle, said Angela, but Kit need have no worries about petty resentments, she would be welcomed into their little club.

Kit felt slightly grubby over her membership, but this was soon alleviated by the announcement that Angela and Frances were going to take her on a shopping trip on Tuesday morning. Added to the various other activities they were listing on their fingers, this eagerness to take care of her convinced Kit that there was nothing lewd or rude about either of them. Putting her qualms finally to rest, she hoisted her coffee cup in the manner of a toast and smiled her gratitude, deciding that in the bosom of such very good friends, life in London was going to be just as she had always dreamed it.

20

For Kit, the remainder of 1882 was a constant round of shopping expeditions, soirees and high jinks, during which she became rather fond of her illicit provider. Apart from being a generous man, Valentine shared her thirst for enjoyment, and their time together was never dull, nor was he shy of parading his mistress before London society. The only place she was not allowed to go was Westminster, as he said this might be regarded as a little too blatant. He had invested a great deal of money in getting himself elected, and would risk his position for no one.

Sometimes, if the politician was able to free himself from duties of office, they would go to the races, or boating on the Thames. At night there was the theatre or an opera – every week provided a new experience. Even if she sometimes failed to see him for days on end there was no lack of comfort, food and wine being in copious supply. Nor was Kit ever lonely, her wide circle of female friends making sure of that. At certain times, she was even pleased that he did not turn up, for Val's idea of enjoyment tended towards the physical rather than a witty tête-à-tête, and he could be very demanding, not to mention adventurous. Kit was now thoroughly familiarized with those erotic volumes she had seen on Lord Garborough's bookshelf.

He had never volunteered any information about his wife and children, and Kit had never asked, the only reminder of their existence coming at holiday periods when he would vanish for weeks at a time. Kit tried not to picture the scene of domesticity that his homecoming would engender – the loving wife rushing out to greet her husband, children scrambling on to father's knee – preferring to concentrate instead on the good life that Valentine had brought her. It was difficult, though, for one who yearned for children not to supplant the loving wife's image with that of her own.

This was especially true in the week approaching Christmas when, faced with his absence, and overwhelmed by a tide of homesickness, Kit decided to make a trip up to Yorkshire where the lights might not be as bright as Regent Street, but she would be assured of a warm welcome.

With her impulsive decision, came the urgent need to buy gifts. Fred dropped her off outside Swan and Edgar, where she pondered over the eye-catching window display of foreign dolls and little fir trees amongst artificial snow, before deciding with a hint of nostalgia that all her nieces were too old for these now. Instead, she fought her way through the army of top hats and frock coats, capricious ladies and their parcel-laden servants, and amongst the festoons of brightly coloured decorations she made purchases of silken shawls, lace-edged handkerchiefs, and scented bath salts. Similar frivolous items, including jewellery, were provided for Gwen, Sarah and the rest of the womenfolk, leaving only her brothers and nephews to buy for. These were more difficult, and their purchase was made even more so by the fact that it had begun to snow heavily, though a hectic glance at the sky provided the answer to one of her problems when Kit noticed the opaque globe of a gaslight bearing the word 'Cigars', and immediately rushed along to the tobacconist's to acquire a tin of the dreaded weed. For Probyn and her other nephews she bought boxes of toy soldiers. Only Monty posed a problem. He neither smoked nor drank. With her hat and the shoulders of her overcoat accumulating a layer of snow, Kit hurried back to where she had left the carriage, hoping to find something along the way, but all she managed to buy was some wrapping paper and labels.

Fred had been sheltering in a shop doorway whilst waiting for his mistress to return, but the poor horse was covered in snow and kept shaking his miserable head to dislodge it. Pitying the animal, Kit threw her large collection of gifts into the carriage and was just about to climb in when she had a burst of inspiration and hurried along the crowded street to a watchmaker's where she purchased a silver timepiece for her elder brother. All accounted for, she made her happy return to St John's Wood.

It continued to snow well into the night. When Valentine left her after their early morning bout of love-play, saying he would be thinking of her whilst they were apart, the thick flakes were still descending. Fearing that this might mean a cancellation in the train service if she left it any

355

longer, Kit wrapped up warmly and set out with her portmanteau and bags full of gifts. Just what sort of reception she would have from the Kilmasters remained to be seen. They were aware of her circumstances, for at the outset she had thought it best to inform them by letter of her whereabouts. Since then she had written regularly to Monty and Sarah and each time had received a reply, though none of their correspondence disclosed any opinions, and were simply designed to keep her up to date with the family news.

Luckily, the train managed to carry her all the way to Yorkshire without mishap. When she arrived in York six hours later it was evident that the north had received a more severe pummelling from the elements, immense walls of ice in place of hedgerows where the roads had been cleared, leaving Kit in some doubt as to whether she would be able to reach Ralph Royd after all. Instead of going to her own house, she decided instead to visit Amelia first, and hailed a cab.

Despite the nature of their parting, Amelia was pleased to see her sister and said she too was hoping to make a visit to Ralph Royd for Christmas, if the snow would allow it. They would travel together. She was pleased, also, to receive Kit's gift, though when any mention was made of London she seemed purposefully to steer the conversation away, as if reluctant to discuss anything that might cast the shadow of Valentine Kitchingham. Realizing it embarrassed her sister, Kit did not mention him either, though it was difficult to relate all her news without his name arising once or twice.

Later, Kit went to check on the state of her own residence. Finding it secure and in good repair, albeit a little musty through lack of occupancy, she returned to spend the rest of the night with Amelia and Albert.

The next day, Christmas Eve, Albert got out the horse and trap and drove his wife and her sister to the station, joking that he did not mind in the least being left behind to cope with the hard work, so long as his darling wife returned before midnight when he would turn into a pumpkin. Kit smiled at their parting kiss, envying their closeness.

The countryside was a blanket of unrelenting white, but, with the line remaining clear of snow, the sisters arrived in Ralph Royd by late morning. The mining village was somewhat prettified today, though the well-trodden snow on the footpaths was made grey from the ubiquitous layer of coal dust. As anticipated, there were no decorations in her brother's residence. Yet, Kit was somewhat taken aback by the disparity between this and the house in which she herself resided. Even whilst working at stately mansions she had not noticed quite so drastic a contrast, for to her it had just been home. But now, after a year's absence, and the months of gracious living, it came as quite a shock to see how she had formerly existed. That which she had once considered normal appeared most poverty-stricken. Kit thanked goodness for the blazing heat of the Yorkshire range, coal being one thing that was never skimped on, and went straight to it, presenting her hands to its radiance, the much shorter Amelia coming to hover alongside.

Unexpectedly, Gwen's barrel-like figure was seated in a fireside chair, though apart from Sarah she was the only occupant, everyone else at work or out playing in the snow. There was no great drama attached to Kit's homecoming, each treating her as if they had only met last week.

'Give us your hat and coat,' ordered Amelia, still playing the mother to her younger sister.

After handing over her garb, Kit continued to rub her body as if to induce some warmth.

'You shouldn't be cold with all that fat on 'ee,' said Gwen.

Such remarks had always irritated Kit. 'Well, I am!' She sat down and began to sort through her bag of gifts.

'What's she rooting about at in there?' asked Sarah, busy rolling out pastry for mince pies.

'I'm trying to find Gwen's present,' Kit's face remained hidden as she continued to rummage through the bag. 'Though heaven knows why,' came the private mutter.

'Presents?' barked Sarah. 'Well, you needn't expect anything in return. We haven't got the money you have.'

'We don't need to ask where it comes from, neither.' Fat arms crossed beneath her even fatter bosom, Gwen's exaggerated pose resembled a malevolent Toby jug.

Kit ignored both slights. 'Ah, here it is!' She handed it over. 'Gwen, you might as well have yours today as you won't be here tomorrow. The rest of you will have to wait till the proper time to get yours. A shame Charity and Flora aren't here, but I'll nip over and see them before I go back, weather permitting.' She perched on the edge of the chair in confident expectation, her face still pink from the wintry journey.

Sour-faced, Gwen had ripped the paper and now examined the extravagant gift inside, holding the paisley shawl by its hem as if it were contaminated.

Kit's smile faltered, 'If you don't like it . . .'

Gwen was tart. 'There's nothing wrong with the shawl. I just don't think it's right you coming here flaunting the proceeds of your wanton behaviour – and if I accept it, then that makes me as bad as you are.'

Amelia turned red.

Kit was deeply hurt that her gift had not been accepted in the spirit that it had been given. She might have known it would be Gwen who voiced what the rest of them were thinking. Not knowing what to say, she said naught for fear of crying. Her offering rejected, she suffered rejection too. For, starved of physical affection in her childhood, this was the only way she knew how to show she cared.

'Still . . .' Gwen had noticed the glimmer of tears and now draped the shawl round her shoulders, examining her reflection in the mirror over the hearth – 'seeing as you've brought it . . .'

But her change of attitude was too late for Kit, who swore to herself that this was the last time she would tramp about getting sore feet just to have the gift thrown back at her. From now on she would only buy for the children. Averting her face, she looked at the wall, and was immediately assailed by that awful portrait of Beata.

'I suppose you'll be staying with that other fancy man o' yours while you're here,' opined Gwen, folding up the shawl.

Kit tried to avoid looking at the portrait but it was impossible to look away with its eyes boring into her. Why, why had she come? 'If you mean my friend Mr Popplewell, yes I had intended to. In fact, I'll go there now and tell him to expect me.' Anxious to escape, she jumped up and put on her coat, leaving before she had even fastened it.

'Well, it's good to see she ain't lost all sense of shame,' announced Gwen as her youngest sister exited with a chastened expression. 'There's chance yet she might be redeemed.'

Kit found to her great disappointment that Mr Popplewell was not there, his missing clothes telling her that he had gone away for Christmas. But she remained in the cottage for a couple of hours until she saw Gwen pass the window on her way home, accompanied by Amelia. Only then did she return to Savile Row. What a miserable Christmas this was going to be.

But there was to be more pleasant reception to her kindness the next day when the girls and Probyn came down on Christmas morning to find that a gift accompanied the usual bequest of fruit and nuts. Having witnessed Kit's distress at Gwen's belittlement yesterday, Sarah had decided to display a more Christian attitude – yet even so she was astounded to receive a brooch studded with tiny rubies.

'That's real gold – and real jewels, if I'm not mistaken!' Her exclamation drew forth a cough and she covered her mouth with the back of her hand, staring at the gift in astonishment.

Kit explained. 'Well, you always said there was no point in having jewellery if it wasn't genuine.'

'It must have cost a fortune!'

'I bought it out of my own savings,' said Kit. Please, *please* don't you throw it back at me too.

But Sarah was already pinning it on to her clothes, her Welsh voice lilting up and down in excitement. 'Look, Monty! Look, girls! Isn't it lovely? Oh, pity you didn't bring me a new dress too, Kit! It makes this one look really shabby. Thank you very much.'

Vastly relieved, Kit laughingly promised to bring one next time.

The young women were similarly pleased with their gifts. Upon receipt of his own, Probyn yelled his delight and taking each of the metal soldiers from their box proceeded to set out his miniature army on the hearth, setting a tiny bayonet at a leaden throat, making crashing and whooshing noises to simulate the sounds of battle. 'Eh, Father! Look at this – look! Dad, you're not looking!'

A thoughtful Monty broke off from examining his watch to nod benignly. 'Yes, yes, I can see – Probe, keep the noise down, will 'ee? War's not really a fitting thing for Christmas Day.'

'Eh, Dad! I'm going to be a soldier when I'm old enough.'

Monty grew annoyed then and shoved the watch in his pocket. 'You're not, you know! You think Mr Latimer lets you live in one of his houses out o' kindness? You're off down the pit like your father.'

'But me mam said if I work hard at school I'll get a better job!'

'A better job, yes!' Sarah shared her husband's aversion. 'The army's for riffraff who can't get anything else.'

'Now, put those blessed things away, 'tis time for chapel,' Monty told the sulking child, and ordered everyone else to get ready.

'I haven't time to breathe, let alone go to chapel,' said Sarah, and began to set out the things she would need for their Christmas dinner.

Though unused to domestic routine now, Kit said she would help, her offer echoed by others. Sarah said she didn't need everyone and it was only their excuse to avoid chapel. Appointing Ethel, who had been allowed time off from her job as prison wardress, to help her too, she packed the rest off to chapel. She and Kit got on with preparation, their chores lightened by Ethel's exciting anecdotes about the criminals in her care.

In the afternoon, after a plain but delicious meal, Kit walked with the others to Owen's house where they had tea. Her gifts receiving similar gratitude in this household and, no mention made of her way of life, she was able to return to London a few days later in much better spirits than she had arrived.

The contrast she had experienced at her brother's house assailed her once again on her arrival home. Feeling a tinge of guilt that those she had left behind could not experience similar pampering, Kit handed over her filthy shoes for Fred to clean, then ordered Cara to set a hot bath in front of the fire in her bedroom, and when it came, she sank her shoulders beneath the steaming surface, extremities tingling as her circulation was gradually restored, and lay there luxuriating in the perfumed water, wondering when she would see Val again.

But the thought was in no way melancholy, for until their reunion she would have Angela and Frances and others to keep her company. In their role as mistresses, they had become a sort of family, and Kit could exchange far more intimate secrets than with her own sisters, knowing they would never condemn, would always welcome her honesty.

In this confidence, the following morning, she decided to call upon Angela and invite her back for luncheon. Even with her friend only living streets away, Kit gave orders for Fred to hitch up the carriage, for the snow had turned to slush and a wintry mist hung over the streets, making them appear as if coated in brown soup. The hem of her skirts would be filthy within seconds if she went on foot.

The drive lasted but two minutes. Kit alighted, giving orders to Fred to wait there. Then, skirts hoisted, she picked her way over a carpet of greasy leaves up to Angela's front door. A sharp rap on the brass knocker produced a maid, who gave apologies but said that her mistress was indisposed and could see no one. Slightly disconcerted, Kit left her best wishes, hoping that her friend would soon be recovered, then returned along the slimy pathway to her carriage.

Undeterred, she decided to call upon Frances who lived slightly further away, hoping that it would not be a wasted journey.

Thankfully, at this residence, she received invitation to enter and was soon graced by Frances's benevolent smile. Kit exchanged kisses – something she would never have contemplated within her own family but which seemed normal down here. Besides, in a strange sort of way Frances reminded Kit a little of Beata, not in looks, but in the overall warmth of her smile. Perhaps that was why she had become so attached.

Upon hearing that Kit had been turned away from Angela's, Frances looked grave. 'Oh, the things that have happened in the short time you've been away, Kit. Poor Angela, she discovered she was *enceinte* and when she –'

Kit interrupted to ask for translation of this foreign word.

'What a girl fears most!' said an agitated Frances. 'You know – oh, Kit, she was having a child, for heaven's sake! And she's been so careful to avoid it.'

Kit's lower jaw descended in shock.

'The poor girl – I mean, George was very good about it, gave her the money and everything, but it was still such an ordeal to go through. I went with her yesterday. Oh, it was horrible!' Frances put her palms to the sides of her head as if to shut out the memory. 'She was screaming so loudly I thought the police would surely come . . .' She broke off her anguished chatter at Kit's look of total incomprehension, and was forced to explain.

When this finally sank in, Kit felt a wave of nausea rush to her throat. Tears sprang to her eyes. 'You mean, she's killed her baby?'

At the accusing tone, Frances became defensive. 'Kit, you'd do just the same.'

'No, I would not!' Oh, the dreadful injustice, raged Kit, that she can murder a child so callously when I, who would love it, can never hope to bear one.

'And just see how long your friends would stick by you with a bastard in tow,' said Frances, peeved at the lack of support for their friend.

Still Kit shook her head in torment. Even the idea was totally abhorrent. 'But I'd have stood by Angela, if only she'd told me – and so would you.'

'Yes, but we are not the ones who support her financially, nor socially. She would be utterly destroyed.'

In whose eyes? Kit wanted to ask. But it was pointless to argue the point further. However horrible, what was done was done.

'I said I would wait until later this afternoon before going to see how she is,' added Frances. 'You can come with me if you wish.'

There was a challenge in the request. Though Angela had plummeted in Kit's estimation, she fought her personal revulsion of the act and agreed to accompany Frances after luncheon. Remembering that she had left poor Fred out in the cold, she made hurried invitation for Frances to dine with her, and the pair left for St John's Wood.

Later in the afternoon the two women, dressed against the cold in fur-trimmed paletots, took the short journey to Angela's house where, Frances being expected, they were admitted and shown up to the invalid's room.

Prepared to offer coolness, Kit was totally shocked at Angela's pallor. The last time she had seen a complexion as grey as this had been that of her beloved niece not long before her death. Whilst Frances donned a tentative smile and took the invalid's hand, making silly little noises of reassurance, Kit overcame her natural repugnance of Angela's deed to come straight to the point.

'This lass needs a doctor!'

Too frail to respond, Angela made weak movement of her head, but had to rely on Frances to put her argument. 'We can't do that. He'd call the police!'

Kit dragged Frances aside and spoke through gritted teeth. 'I'm telling you, she needs a doctor! Look at the colour of her!'

Though wringing her hands with worry, Frances decided, 'Let's just wait a while and see how she is when we get some beef tea into her.' So saying, she went to haul on the bell pull. 'That'll put the colour back in her cheeks. It's obvious the maid hasn't been looking after her.'

When the maid arrived she was taken to task by Frances for allowing her mistress to get into such a state. Any argument to the contrary was ignored. Kit, watching Angela sink deeper and deeper into oblivion, sided with the maid and said that it would take more than beef tea to restore her. 'Go fetch a doctor. I'm not arguing – go fetch one, now!'

'Kit, she'll never forgive me for doing this!' hissed Frances as the maid left. 'And I'll be implicated too.'

'You should have thought of that.' Angry at such wanton butchery, Kit was not inclined to spare anyone's feelings. 'Now, let's see what we can do to make her more comfy.' So saying, she pulled back the covers.

But a horrified gasp from Frances told that it was probably too late to save her. Angela's mattress was a pool of red.

Kit stood there for a moment, riveted by shock. Then, only slightly recovered and still trembling, she made frantic gestures at the distressed Frances to leave. 'I'll stay with her. I can honestly say I came here and found her like this.'

Tearful, Frances looked hesitant to depart, but Kit pushed her at the door. 'You're not in a fit state to answer questions! You'll only get yourself into trouble – now go!'

Kit paid brief attention to the other's exit, then flopped on to a chair at Angela's blood-soaked bedside, and watched helplessly as, before the doctor could arrive, the pretty young life seeped away.

21

What was so doubly awful about Angela's needless death was that it brought back the memory of Beata's demise. Kit supposed it was the sight of all that blood which provoked the nightmares. Whatever the reason, it totally spoiled her reunion with Valentine who, though sympathetic when she awoke crying in the middle of the night, could not fully understand the depth of her melancholy. Snuggled against his chest, Kit tried to explain that part of the reason was that she could not have children. It was the first time she had broached the subject, her vulnerable state causing her to confide in him more than usual – but he was to show complete insensitivity by responding that at least she must be relieved at never having to suffer a similar ordeal as poor Angela.

From then on, Kit retained her confidences for female ears, gradually recovering from her melancholy to be once again the consort Val had so admired – though privately, amongst all the cavorting, she could never rid herself of that sombre reminder of mortality, and the wasted life of a child that she could never bear.

To compensate, as he saw it, for that past gloomy period, Valentine arranged a party to celebrate Kit's twenty-eighth birthday, hiring a ballroom and an orchestra and an army of caterers. Kit, who had assumed they were just going dancing when he told her to put on her best gown, was completely overwhelmed to find that she was the guest of honour, and her eyes filled with tears at his thoughtful act – though these were soon wiped away and she found herself dancing with almost every man in the room.

Breathless from her latest frenetic circuit of the ballroom, she sought time to recover before taking up another offer, and joined Frances and a group of other female companions to chat for a while. Valentine was standing some distance from her, occupied in conversation with another man. Kit watched him fondly, waiting to catch his eye, at which point she would wave. Already aware that her provider had the ability to listen to two conversations at once – his right ear able to detect some relevant comment whilst the left was apparently listening assiduously to another voice – from her vantage point now she had time to detect another of Valentine's traits. His intelligent nods and eager expression made out he was paying homage to the speaker, as if he deemed this man the most important person in the world. But Kit's keen examination noted that his eyes were constantly flitting around the room, surreptitiously looking for someone more interesting, someone more useful, and a sudden doubt arose in her breast.

But whilst she was still wondering if he used the same ploy with her, Valentine caught her eye and dealt her a warm gaze, thereby quashing her qualm. So much warmth did he bestow, in fact, that at that precise moment Kit found herself musing over the possibility that he would leave his wife and marry her. The thought was just as soon dismissed. It was obvious now that the fortune-teller's prediction had been accurate – no marriage, no children. Kit must be thankful for the time he spent with her, for the generous gifts he had bestowed, for the wonderful life she had.

The politician's generosity was to continue throughout another year, during which Kit alternated her place of residence between London and York where, in his absences, she often went to ensure that her property was secure, to visit friends and to see her sister. There were also brief visits to Ralph Royd. A far more exciting destination, though, was Valentine's house in Spain where he took her for a short holiday that autumn, unwittingly presenting Kit with her first glimpse of the sea and laughing at her childlike enjoyment of what was to him commonplace. Despite the awful bout of seasickness that accompanied the voyage, Kit was soon to recover, especially upon laying eyes on the white, sun-washed villa set at the edge of a cliff with its own private little beach where she could bathe unobserved. Her only tinge of regret was that she could not share this with her loved ones.

Yet, Valentine's continued benevolence did allow Kit in turn to show other forms of generosity to her kin. The following summer it was Alice's turn to be married, her aunt rising to the occasion by making the most wondrous ivory gown that Ralph Royd had ever seen. The brief visit home for the wedding was made more enjoyable by the discovery that at last she found Mr Popplewell in residence, her old friend providing an excellent distraction from her own family's lack of gaiety, the latter seeming even more pronounced after her wild life in the capital.

She had received quite a shock on meeting her siblings again. In the long gap since she had last been home their appearance had deteriorated considerably, the elder ones showing signs of middle age, those with dark hair bearing large tracts of grey. Though thinning, Monty's auburn hair retained its brightness, but his tall frame had adopted a definite stoop, and there were lines of hardship around his mouth and nose. Older herself now, and blessed with more intuition, Kit wondered if these had been etched as much by marital discord than by hard work – for Sarah too had those same lines of embitterment. Only a fool could misread those expressions as ones of wedded bliss.

They managed to put aside their discontentment for Alice's wedding though, and the bride herself was overjoyed at her aunt's handiwork.

Owen was quite the jester too, his union having recently managed to acquire a ten per cent wage rise for its members, and he teased Kit about the latest parliamentary bill to enfranchise women being defeated, saying that with her contacts he would have thought she could have held some influence. Such mention of her provider would have been unthinkable a year ago. Kit wondered if this was an indication that the family's disapproval of her chosen life had been relaxed, but one look at their collective faces showed her this was an illusion. Despite the lack of condemnation, they remained embarrassed at her presence in the village.

Nevertheless, this did not spoil her enjoyment of Alice's wedding, and she was thrilled to see Rhoda's little boy again. Like her sister, Alice had married someone with a cleaner occupation – much to her mother's pleasure – and would be moving away after the ceremony. Being the only two daughters left at home, Wyn and Meredith finally got the opportunity to be bridesmaids – Kit having made their dresses too. But it was eleven-year-old Probyn who drew her deepest affection, looking most grown-up in the collar and tie and new suit that his aunt had brought him from London. It seemed like only yesterday he had been born, yet here he was, almost ready for work.

366

Thoroughly exhilarated at seeing him again, and anxious to make the most of his last years of childhood, Kit asked Monty if she might take his son for a few days' visit to her house in York before she returned to the capital. 'I give you my word that there won't be anyone else there, not even a cook.' Her residence in York being only temporary, she had not bothered to hire a servant. 'He won't come under any bad influence.'

'You won't be there yourself, then?' came his cynical enquiry.

'You cheeky monkey!' Recognizing that behind the straight expression was a joke, she punched him lightly, then turned to Probyn, who was waiting with bated breath. 'Eh, he's that cheeky is your dad!'

'Aw go on, Father, let us go!' begged the boy. 'Mother, can I?'

'With pleasure,' said Sarah, though not with malice. She was in light-hearted mood, having seen another of her daughters improve their lot.

Wyn and Merry asked if they could come too, but were reminded by their mother that they had work to go to.

Monty turned back to study his sister, holding her with his blue eyes so that she was left under no misapprehension. 'No newspapers, no introducing him to any of your friends, male or female – and no dancing.'

'I promise,' vowed Kit.

'So I can go?' Probyn leaped into the air with a whoop, then set about preparing for his expedition. 'Can I take me soldiers, Aunt?'

A smiling Kit replied that he could, then noticed that one of the lead figures had its head swathed in what appeared to be a bandage and its body wrapped in a blanket. 'Eh, I don't know if he'll travel very well if he's wounded.'

Probyn sighed. 'He's not wounded! That's the Mad Mahdi – that's his turban and robes.'

'Oh, of course I recognize him now!' Kit's exclamation gave rise to a brief discussion about General Gordon's outrageous comment in the press that if the Government refused to send a relief expedition to help him in the Khartoum, he was going to adopt the Muslim faith and resign as British Envoy.

This in turn led to a condemnation of all foreigners including the Fenians, who had recently set off bombs in London, killing one person and injuring half a dozen. Monty showed concern for his sister's safety but Kit laughed and said he did not realize how big London was – the bombs had been miles away from where she lived. Giving Monty her thanks for allowing Probyn to go to York, she said that she would have the boy back safe and sound in three or four days.

When they arrived at York station, instead of taking Probyn to her own home, Kit took him to Amelia's, saying they would get a better class of luncheon there. But there was ulterior motive, as Probyn was to discover when, upon driving away from Aunt Amelia's in a hansom, Kit directed it not to her house but back to the railway station.

Before his aunt had time to explain, the boy objected, 'Aw, you said we could see the soldiers!' Aunt Kit had told him they might be lucky enough to witness a military parade, York being a garrison town.

'Aye, but I know where we could see them for sure,' grinned Kit. 'I bet you'd much rather go see the Changing of the Guard at Buckingham Palace!'

Probyn looked at first astounded, then a smile of awareness spread across his face. 'You mean, we're off to London?'

'Aye! It'll be much more exciting than your aunt's boring little house – but don't tell your dad, else he won't let you come again!' Kit looked gleeful, knowing her nephew was adept at keeping such secrets, having been weaned from infancy on his aunt's escapades. 'I know all these train journeys are a bit of a chew, but if we go now that'll get you there in time for a good night's sleep and you'll have the whole of tomorrow for sightseeing.'

Imbued with his aunt's sense of adventure, an eager Probyn replied that he didn't mind how many trains he had to go on, he was having a right grand time.

Laughing conspiratorially, they alighted from the cab and went to the ticket office, where Kit purchased two return tickets to London. She would have Probyn back in a few days as promised and nobody would be any the wiser.

But Kit had reckoned without the fact that Valentine might not appreciate a third presence in the drawing room when he came to see his mistress. When, upon his homecoming that evening, Valentine found the usual lusty interlude denied him, and discovered the reason behind this to be a small ginger-haired boy who was watching agog from his seat by the fire, he was none too impressed. In fact, Kit considered his surly greeting to her nephew to be down-right rude.

'Oh dear, Probe, Mr Kitchingham seems to be in bad humour tonight. Perhaps he'll be a little more amenable after supper.' With a telling expression, she rang the bell to summon Cara and told her to serve the meal.

Valentine disliked the flippant tone, and stalked ahead of her into the dining room – though he did pull out a chair and made sure she was comfortably seated before going around to the other side of the table.

Looking awkward in this totally foreign environment, Probyn waited to be asked to sit down. Showing great kindness, and wishing Valentine would be as good-hearted, Kit pulled out the chair beside her and patted its moquette seat, telling the youngster to come and sit there. Throughout the meal she continued to pay him such court, asking him what he liked best about the food, offering second helpings of beef and gravy, and whilst not completely ignoring Valentine, making sure he knew she was annoyed at his treatment of her loved one.

After a heavy dessert, noting that Probyn was almost falling asleep at the table, Kit took him up to his room, attending to him per-sonally, tucking him into bed and saying they would have a lovely day together tomorrow, listing the places they would visit – Mad-ame Tussaud's, the Horse Guards, the Tower of London, Buckingham Palace.

'Will Mr Kitchingham be going with us?' asked the sleepy boy, in a tone denoting aversion.

Kit smoothed back his curly forelock and delivered a kiss to his brow, wiping away a smudge of soot. 'No, he'll be busy at his work. It'll be just thee and me.' With this she patted him, wished him goodnight and left the room.

Downstairs, she was about to tackle Valentine about his behaviour when he jumped in first.

'Could you not have warned me that your nephew would here?' His face was cross.

'Oh, I do beg your pardon!' said Kit mockingly. 'I thought this was my home. I didn't realize I had to seek your permission before inviting members of my family here.'

The reply from behind the waxed moustache was terse. 'It would

369

simply have been nice to be consulted.' He made no move to touch her, his attitude unbending. 'How long do you intend for him to stay?'

'I haven't decided yet.' Though accustomed to controlling her emotions, Kit had a struggle to contain her rising anger. A red tide crept over her cheeks.

Holding his frame erect, Valentine rose and strode to the door, speaking as he went. 'Then when you do, perhaps you'd be good enough to inform me so that when I next come here I can be sure to expect what I've paid for.'

Kit's mouth flew open, her eyes looked for something to throw at him, but before she had chance to retaliate the door to the hall had slammed, followed by the sound of the front door.

Lips pressed together in a bloodless line, she fumed for a while longer, pacing up and down to try and calm herself – how *dare* he? The wretch, she did not care if she ever saw him again!

But three days later, when Kit was making the long return journey to London following the delivery of her nephew back to Ralph Royd after his brief but exciting sojourn in the capital, she decided she *did* care whether she saw Valentine again. How could she not, after sharing over two years of intimacy? Life would be so much duller without him. More pertinently, she had grown fond of her mode of living and had no wish to jeopardize it, but was none the less disinclined to have him tell her who she could and could not see. She had sworn long ago to let no man misuse her again. Trying to picture what she would do if he were to sever their contract, Kit swayed in time to the kitty-come-home of the train's wheels, hoping, praying, that she had not made a grievous error.

When she arrived at St John's Wood that evening, being charged the earth for her transport from the station by growler, but not having the energy to argue with its seedy-looking coachman, Kit's mood was to descend even further upon entry to the house.

Met by Cara in the gaslit hall, she asked had Mr Kitchingham visited in her absence.

'No, ma'am,' returned the Irish maid, with her usual air of assuredness. 'I dare say he was afraid Master Probyn was still here. Himself's not too fond of children. Well, I'm sure he's fond of his own o' course, but that's a different matter. And Master Probyn was a bit rowdy with his games of soldiers an' all.'

Kit was offended, not least by Cara's perpetually familiar attitude, and almost thrust her coat at the maid. 'No rowdier than any normal boy.'

Cara waited to receive her mistress's hat. 'Well now, I wouldn't know, not having any boys of my own – all I meant was, Mr Kitchingham's not coming here to play with children, is he?'

'Just what are you implying?' Kit regretted asking almost immediately, for the maid's expression told it all.

But, despite the insolent slant to her eye, Cara's civil reply bore an air of innocence. 'I didn't mean nothing, ma'am. Just quoting a fact.'

From her lofty position, Kit had the advantage and, looking down her nose at the maid, said, 'You don't like me, do you?'

Unintimidated, Cara replied, ''Tis not for me to like nor dislike, ma'am.'

'You're right, it isn't.' Eyes still fixed to her adversary, the taller woman gave a curt nod. 'So I suggest you alter your tone when speaking to me, because if you don't buck your ideas up you'll find yourself looking for another post.'

'Sure, I'm not the only one,' muttered Cara on her way to the kitchen.

Overhearing her, Kit spun and demanded that the maid repeat herself.

'I said, shall I put the kettle on, ma'am?' lied Cara, a cocky air about her, her whole attitude telling Kit just how low a rung of the ladder she occupied in the maid's estimation.

Kit glared down at Cara for a second, then turned her back and began to walk away, instructing her to fetch something to eat to the dining room, whilst she herself went up to her room to freshen her appearance.

In the pretty panelled bedroom, her annoyance turned once again to concern. What on earth was she going to do about Valentine? He had said she should treat this house as her own but when she had done he didn't like it. Well, she would just have to wait and see what happened. Because Kit was damned if she was going to apologize.

But during supper, she recalled Valentine's instruction for her to tell him when Probyn had gone, and decided to do just that. After finishing her meal, she told Cara to send Fred to her, and in the hiatus she scribbled a note and was putting it into an envelope when the manservant came in.

'Do you know the whereabouts of Mr Kitchingham's flat in Westminster?' she asked. When he replied that he did, she handed him the envelope and asked him to deliver it.

'What – now?'

Kit had been about to express regret for sending him out so late, but decided now that he was getting as uppity as Cara and she did not like it. 'Well, I don't mean next week! It'll make a change for you to earn your brass. Go on then!'

With an undisguised sigh the footman left.

Hours later, wondering where he had got to, Kit visited the kitchen to find him half asleep by the fire, Cara knitting nearby and the scullerymaid getting things ready for morning.

'What you doing lozzocking here?' she demanded crossly. 'I've been waiting for a reply.'

'There wasn't one.' Fred stretched and rubbed his eyes.

'I think you're forgetting something.' Kit eyed him threateningly.

'There wasn't one, ma'am.'

Though miffed at the information, Kit inclined her head, and said that as she would be retiring, they could go to bed too.

'How long d'ye give her?' asked Cara, thinking their mistress had gone.

Kit lingered in her passage to witness Fred's reply. 'A week,' he said.

Cara emitted a musical titter. 'Ah, come on now! Much as I can't stand her myself, I'd give her at least until Christmas.'

'You didn't see his face when I gave him her note,' said Fred.

Kit's heart sank.

'Come on now, Fred, make a sensible bet.'

'All right, I'll say she'll be gone within a month.'

'And I say Christmas – how much?'

'Two bob.'

'You're on!'

With a grim expression, Kit marched up to bed, though her anger was to keep her awake for hours.

* * *

372

When Valentine did not respond to her message the following day, nor the one after that, Kit began to suspect that perhaps the servants were right. He intended to end the affair.

Disallowing this to concern her, for it was not as if she was without money or property of her own, Kit passed the time amongst her female friends, and the evenings with her face buried in a book – though she was forced to admit to some degree of tension over being kept in ignorance of his plans.

It came as a total surprise when he turned up on Friday evening as if nothing untoward had happened, greeting her as charmingly as ever and explaining his absence as being due to nothing more sinister than pressures of work. The House of Lords had rejected the Liberal Government's Franchise Bill which would have extended the vote to thousands of small property holders, thereby plunging the country into political crisis. So crucial was the issue that there was a suggestion of Lord Randolph Churchill crossing the House to join the Liberals because of it – so could he please rely on Kit's understanding if he had to rush away suddenly?

Moreover, there was to be apology over another issue. 'I'm sorry for that silly little episode over your nephew.' Genuinely remorseful, he sandwiched her hand between his, embellishing it with a ticklish kiss, before leading her to the sofa. 'But you see, Kit, I so look forward to our times together that I detest anything to spoil it. I'm sorry if that sounds callous, I know how much you care for your family.' Their names had become familiar over the years. 'I really don't mind if you bring the whole tribe of them here – just so long as you warn me first. Please believe me, it was purely disappointment that caused such a childish display. Am I forgiven?'

Kit gave immediate absolution, plus an energetic embrace that had him instantly aroused, drawing forth the request that they postpone supper until his more important appetite had been placated.

In the aftermath of a vigorous bout of sexual capers, Kit enquired if he really meant it about her bringing members of her family here. She would not, of course, include all of them, for most disapproved of her way of life. But she would like perhaps to invite the younger ones occasionally. With his affirmative reply, she asked if this extended to his villa in Spain too. 'Our Probe'd love it there.'

373

Valentine rolled his happy mustachioed face across the pillow to kiss her. 'My dear, at this moment I would grant you anything. Just so long as you let me know when you wish to go.'

Kit tested the water. 'Well, I wouldn't be able to take him till next year – in the school holiday.'

He nodded his agreement. 'August would be convenient from my point of view.'

'So you're not going to get rid of me yet, then?' asked Kit.

He showed surprise. 'How could you even ask such a thing?'

'The servants have been taking bets on it,' she told him, her tone one of relieved amusement.

He chuckled and snuggled up to her. 'Ah, but they don't know how much pleasure you give me.'

Experiencing his fresh arousal, Kit laughed and held him at bay. 'How can you be ready again so quickly? Wouldn't you like supper first?'

'After supper, then.' He scissored his legs, ejecting himself from the bed, and in cheerful fashion began to dress.

Kit too arose and was to copy his less formal mode of dress, donning first a nightgown and then a peignoir – in part, as illustration to the servants that it was she who made the rules here and not them.

If there was going to be anyone leaving by Christmas then it would not be Kit.

Notwithstanding the political crisis that enforced several absences, the relationship between Kit and Valentine continued to bring mutual pleasure – though it was easy to tell from Cara's expression that she still held on to her original wager. Kit had wanted to sack her, but Valentine said she had not really committed any misdemeanour, servants were wont to play these silly games, and he would have such trouble to find another general maid who could cook so well. Kit had to agree that the Irish girl was very efficient, but prayed for Christmas to arrive so that the silly wager could finally be laid to rest.

During the interim, she wrote a letter to her brother in Yorkshire, telling him to expect her in December as usual, including a little note for Probyn in which, knowing his deep interest in all things military, she sought to allay his fears about General Gordon by saying she had learned that a relief expedition was being sent to Egypt and that would

374

put paid to the Mad Mahdi once and for all. She also included a message that told him he could expect another holiday next year if he was good.

In preparation of her trip, she went into town to buy presents – though only for the younger members of the family. After that first year Monty had suggested that, however grateful they were, it wasn't fitting for her to buy such things as they could not return the gesture.

Unusually, she was to get a reply from Monty, telling her that though she would be welcome he was not sure how much hospitality he could show her, for today a notice had been posted at the pit-head saying that the company intended to change the rates. It was all a bit complicated for her to understand as she did not work down the pit, but in essence it would seem that the colliers' wages were to be cut. That didn't directly affect him, for as weighman he was paid by the miners, but it affected the miners themselves. Owen and his union were trying to do something about it, but Kit knew what the Ralph Royd Coal Company was like for digging its heels in. So – Monty ended – she was welcome to come but it might be a lean time and he would understand if she chose not to sacrifice her usual comfortable lifestyle.

Kit showed the letter to Valentine, asking if he could do anything about her brothers' plight. To which he shook his head and said he was up to his eyes in legislation at the moment.

She nodded. 'I read in the paper that the Tories are going to introduce another bill allowing women the vote after the Christmas recess – is that true?'

'Yes, that old chestnut again,' sighed Valentine. 'It hasn't a cat in hell's chance of getting through.'

'But you're going to vote for it, aren't you?' prompted Kit. When younger, she had shown little interest in politics, but now, especially as a property owner, she felt more need to have a say.

'But of course!' He reacted in his usual charming manner. 'That is, if I'm still here. Did you read of today's explosion?' When Kit said she had not read the evening paper yet, he sought out the article. 'Those odious Fenians tried to blow up London Bridge – two minutes after I'd crossed it!'

'My God!' Kit's arms reached out to him.

He donated a little chuckle, patting her hand. 'It's wonderful that you

375

care, my dearest, but I'm still here, am I not? No, it was another of their usual botched efforts, just a little damage to one of the arches.'

Kit exhaled with a look of relief. 'Even so, I'm going to worry about you all the time I'm away!'

Kissing her, Val said he would be thinking of her too, and looked forward with pleasure to their reunion.

Forewarned about her brothers' situation, in addition to the gifts Kit packed several large parcels of food into her bags, then with last instructions to the staff, she left for Yorkshire.

As ever, she went first to York to see Amelia. Then, upon hearing that her sister had already paid a recent visit to Ralph Royd, as had Gwen and the others, she travelled on alone, arriving on Christmas Eve just as the miners were finishing their day's toil, a moving mass of shadows in the dusk.

Despite the bleak aspect, the naked trees dotted with redundant crows' nests, the winter was very mild compared to previous years, and Kit found herself perspiring under her heavy baggage as she staggered along Main Street. Ahead of her, one by one, she saw the gaslights come on as the lamplighter moved about the village. Depositing part of her cumbersome load at her own cottage, where there was disappointment over Mr Popplewell's absence, she rejoined the procession of home-going miners and advanced up the incline to Monty's house. Normally, in their safe return home, there would be light-hearted banter from the colliers, especially in view of the festive holiday, but Kit sensed an air of hostility, and there was sombre response to her good-humoured greetings.

Spotting her brothers just ahead of her, along with Owen's son, who had lately joined his father down the pit, she broke into a heavy trot and caught up with them just as Monty was turning into Savile Row. About to proceed to his own street, Owen stopped abruptly under a gaslight to inform his sister what had occurred, his mood as black as the layer of coal dust on his face.

'You heard what's going on, then?' he asked Kit.

'Our Monty said they wanted to cut your rates.'

'Oh nay!' The billy goat face made instant repudiation, his exaggerated response giving lie to his words. 'Nay, we'll be getting exactly t'same as we got before – I mean, it must be reet if manager's told us, mun't it?'

He recited a list of facts and figures which Kit failed to understand, but it was evident that beneath his airy tone he was furious. 'Apparently it's all down to bad sorting and filling – we haven't been doing it reet, sithee, mixing too much little coal with t'big stuff and they've got all this coal piled sky high, but they can't sell it 'cause the stingy merchants won't pay 'em enough. Company's had a reet bad year, poor lambs. Eh, I do feel sorry for 'em – an' it's all the silly miners' faults. But, manager sez, if we do it this new road we'll earn exactly t'same money – so we'll all be laughing, won't we?' He made a grand gesture at the stream of colliers who passed him. 'Eh, it's grand to see such smiling faces, in't it?' In mock jollity, Owen concluded by relating the manager's parting words. '"Anyroad," he sez, "I wish you all a Merry Christmas an' a prosperous New Year and I'll be happy to discuss the new proposals at any time."'

'So, how did it end?' asked his concerned sister.

'We told him to shove it up his bum,' said Owen, then suddenly reverting to his weary pose, started to back away towards home with his son, telling them he would see them both tomorrow.

Kit proceeded along Savile Row with Monty. 'What a terrible do. Will there be a strike?'

He gave a grim nod. 'It's highly likely. What they're proposing is tantamount to a thirty per cent cut in wages, whatever the flowery terms they might like to use. Owen's trying to avoid that by asking for arbitration but the company won't allow it – won't have any outside interference.' They reached home, whereupon Monty sighed as he imagined his wife's reaction. 'Now for the difficult part. I'll bet you're glad you came.'

In a way, Kit was glad she had come, for at least it meant she could offer support. After the Christmas period, instead of returning to London, she sent a letter to inform the servants that she may be forced to extend her stay in Yorkshire for a week or so, instructing them to let Mr Kitchingham know if he happened to turn up in her absence. Her life suitably organized, she joined the rest of the village womenfolk in attending the daily outdoor meetings that were held in the field by the colliery, and prayed for a happy outcome.

Mr Popplewell had now returned from his break, as delighted to see Kit as she was to see him. It was so good to know that at least she could rely on one person to provide a light hearted distraction in this anxious period – though even now the village gossips remained a nuisance.

Despite the return to work after Christmas the situation intensified. Letters flew back and forth to the newspapers: complaints from miners over inaccurate reporting, responses from the coal owners saying that the fall in profits gave them every right to expect the miners to pull together. After all, it had been the ten per cent pay rise they had won which was partly responsible for this as the high wage bill meant that other pits could undercut them. As usual the colliers had brought this on themselves.

A strike loomed, though even Owen questioned the wisdom of this for with such plentiful stocks, all the owners had to do was sit tight and empty bellies would soon force the miners back to work. However there was principle involved. Supported by a resolution by the Executive Committee, the Ralph Royd Lodge formerly rejected the proposed change and the men went on strike on the last day of the year.

Comparatively little hardship was suffered during those first few weeks of the strike, for the colliers received payment from their union. The thirteen shillings a married couple received, plus a shilling for every child under twelve – which in Monty's case only included Probyn – might be a drastic reduction on the usual wage, but was supplemented by gifts of food from local tradesmen, plus financial aid from a neighbouring pit. The Christmas food parcels Kit had intended for her own family had, as was usually the way in times of trouble, been shared amongst the strikers. Being spread so far these had not lasted long, but Kit intended to provide more. They would not starve.

However, Owen reported inevitable discord over the fact that non-union members were receiving funds and, after great debate, and the threatened withdrawal of support from the neighbouring pit if this continued, such payments were withdrawn, immediately plunging families into distress. Seizing on his, the employers resorted to every underhand method in order to get the miners back to work: the privies were left unemptied and were in a dreadful state. To compound matters, the village was now ravaged by an epidemic of measles; several children had died.

Kit and the rest of her family were lucky enough to escape with heavy colds, presenting a picture of misery with their bloodshot eyes and red-raw noses. She tried her best not to moan, though others did not share her fortitude. Having experienced previous hard times in the village, a bad-tempered Sarah announced that this must surely be the worst.

Owen, similarly afflicted, issued a scold. 'Count yourself lucky. Our poor Chairman's had to cut short his stay in Switzerland because of us, poor lad.'

Blowing her nose for the umpteenth time, Kit reproved him. 'Rotten hounds, spoiling Mr Latimer's holiday.'

'Are you having a good time here, Kit, that's what I'd like to know?' quipped Owen, wiping his own proboscis. When she rolled her eyes, he added, 'Well, you might not have much to eat here but at least you're out of t'way o' them Fenian bombs in London.' Unable to afford a newspaper he had gleaned this information from the rather tattered copy that Peggo provided for his customers. 'Tried to blow the whole Government up this time.'

Kit felt her stomach turn over and put a hand to her mouth. 'Are you just kidding me?'

'Nay!' Owen hunched over the fire and rubbed his hands. 'There were two dynamite explosions at Houses of Parliament and another one at Tower o' London.'

Kit's heart was thudding. 'Was anybody hurt?'

'Aye, I think so – don't know how many.' Owen noted her concern now and guessed the reason.

'I'm sorry, I'll have to go and see –' Kit rushed about like a headless chicken, not knowing which way to turn, picturing Val in the carnage.

The others watched her fretful antics, the Fenian bomb also exploding any myth that Kit was with the MP simply for the luxurious lifestyle he could offer. It was obvious she really cared for him.

Sarah took charge then, helping Kit into her coat and passing her hat. Kit said she would leave her luggage at the cottage for she would be coming back here, hopefully with more financial assistance. Owen abandoned his seat by Monty's hearth, saying he would accompany Kit to the station.

Frantic with worry, Kit tossed brief thanks over her shoulder, then made for the door. 'I'll be back as soon as I can!'

When she arrived in London it was dark, although only early evening. Kit would have gone straight to Westminster, but Valentine had always

379

been adamant in prohibiting this intrusion. Snatching at the improbable hope that he might be at the house in St John's Wood, she decided to go there first before resorting to drastic measures.

Hardly surprised to find that Kitchingham was not there, Kit first enquired if the servants had seen him at all since Christmas. With their negative reply she ordered Fred to bring the carriage round and set off back across the great city, in growing panic.

There were still thousands on the nighttime streets, rich and poor alike – gents sauntering to their clubs, beggars around a hot chestnut vendor's brazier, pickpockets, harlots, Salvationists and jaded clerks – the taverns, theatres and eating houses bulging. Shops too, were yet a-brim with customers, but their illuminated windows held no joy for Kit tonight, her mind on one person.

Eventually, the carriage reached Westminster. There was a strong police presence in the area. After a moment's hesitation, during which she blew her streaming nose, Kit alighted from the carriage. Following the manservant's instructions, she approached the large building and went through the front door into a communal hallway. The yellow flicker of gaslight shed lustre on a flight of marble stairs. Throat tickling, she coughed, the sound reverberating off the hard surface.

Kit was halfway up the first flight of steps when the sound of descending voices caused her to lift her face. A young boy and girl rounded the corner ahead of their mother, chattering to each other about their day in London with Father. Travelling slightly behind, the father adopted a look of horror, this expression frozen for three seconds as he waited for Kit to betray him. Open-mouthed, Kit stalled for the briefest of moments, before tossing an anxious smile at the woman and rushing onwards up the stairs. Without a backwards glance she hurried to be around the corner and out of sight before collapsing against a wall, heart beating as if it would leap out of her breast, whilst the family continued its chattering descent.

Only slightly recovered, she moved up to a landing and waited, unsure what to do. Through the thudding of her arteries she heard a man's footsteps take the stairs two at a time, and swallowed nervously, sensing the anger in his tread.

Yet, she had not gauged the full extent of it. Accosting her on the landing, his face as white as the marble stair, Valentine grabbed hold of

Kit's upper arms and delivered a violent shake, hissing like a serpent. 'What the devil are you doing here?'

However robust, Kit flinched like a child, protesting her concern. 'I thought you were injured! I heard about the Fenian bomb and came here straight away – I was so worried!'

'I warned you never to come here!'

'But I've told you I was –'

'Keep your voice down!' His fingers dug into her plump flesh. 'Didn't you stop to consider that my wife would think exactly the same and come rushing up here too?'

'I'm sorry, I didn't think of –'

'No! You didn't, you stupid – my God, if she'd realized who you were!' Abruptly he pushed her from him and began to walk along the landing. 'Oh, go home!'

Through the tears that had sprung to her eyes Kit watched his retreating back and all of a sudden her shock turned to anger. She had come two hundred miles nursing a streaming cold and this was how the wretch treated her! 'My family's at starvation's door! I should be with them, but I came rushing here because I thought you were injured!'

Kitchingham came striding back to hiss at her. 'Stop screeching like a fishwife before someone calls the police. Do as you're told and go home!' These his final words, he marched off, wrenched on a door handle and disappeared.

Kit had been taught since childhood never to lose her temper. A placid soul, she had suffered all kinds of insults with stoicism, until now. Blood pounding in her temples, she rushed headlong down the stairs, out to the waiting carriage and almost threw herself inside, too consumed by rage to form an instruction for the manservant to take her home. Fred, however, had seen Kitchingham's family emerge and could not wait to tell Cara about it. With a cheery flick of the whip he steered the horse into motion.

Kit had never understood the term blind fury until now, and it was terrifying. She felt physically sick, her head throbbed and on top of everything her nose was red raw. Tense with anger, she pressed her body into the dark interior, clenching her fists at the memory, replaying it over and over in her mind all the way to St John's Wood.

When Fred pulled up outside the white detached villa she rushed straight inside, ignoring Cara, who waited to receive her coat, ripping off her gloves and hat, oblivious to the handful of hair that came off with it. Following her in, the manservant waited for Kit to rush into the drawing room before whispering to Cara what had happened – but Kit heard the tinkle of Irish laughter and came storming back to remonstrate.

'You!' She stabbed a finger at the maid. 'You can pack your bags and leave in the morning!'

'What?'

'You heard! Bloody Irish, planting your bloody bombs all over the place – you're sacked!'

'You can't do that to me!' But faced with Kit's anger the maid was not so cocksure now.

'I'll throw you out this minute if you don't get out of my sight!' Kit towered over her.

Cara flinched and hurried away, Fred making himself scarce too. Almost hysterical, Kit charged up the stairs, throwing herself on to her bed and bursting into floods of tears.

Naturally, there was no breakfast in the morning, though Cara was still in the house, waiting in the kitchen with her bags all packed when a puffy-eyed Kit came down.

Far from rescinding her impetuous dismissal, Kit showed cool surprise that the maid had not yet gone. Upon hearing that the girl was waiting for a reference, she scribbled a most basic one, then showed her the door. At the last moment Cara turned defiantly and shouted, 'Home rule for Ireland! Three cheers for the Mahdi!' before making a swift exit.

Kit shook her head. Even now she remained angry at Valentine's treatment, which, added to the lack of sleep and the heavy cold, made her head throb. Placing a hand to her forehead, she stared at Dilly, the only one of her servants she genuinely liked.

'Can you cook, Dilly?'

The sixteen-year-old was eager to return her mistress's favour – Miss Kilmaster had taken the trouble to improve her reading and writing. 'I can do good plain food, ma'am!'

Reminded of Popplewell's rage over that same phrase, Kit could almost have laughed. Telling Dilly she was now in charge of the kitchen, she ordered just tea and toast for breakfast, then added that she would be going back to Yorkshire for a while. Catching sight of Fred's expression she warned him not to waste his money on wagers, for she would be returning when her family no longer needed her. Though whether she actually would, Kit had not yet decided.

22

Kit's return to Ralph Royd coincided with an outbreak of smallpox. In the damp and dismal weeks that followed there were many deaths, both from this and from another wave of measles. Owen's children fell victim to the latter and for a time were badly afflicted, but through luck or through the villagers' fervent prayers, they recovered. Kit's thirtieth birthday passed without celebration.

The coal company's stance had not altered, the owners sitting pretty in their comfortable homes. Some of the miners, weakened by poverty, had sought work at other pits but this had been denied them, the coalmasters sticking together. Owen regarded the act of these miners as betrayal and consequently refused all aid to the traitors. There was little enough food to go round as it was, without taking it out of the mouths of brave men. His children recuperated, he was now able to devote all his energy to rallying the stalwarts – they were fighting for all of Yorkshire he told them. If the masters won at this pit it would lead to a reduction in wages for all. They must stand united.

The dispute extended to the beginning of March when, seeing an advantage in the miners' acute distress, the masters offered to reopen the pit, saying police protection would be given to all those who wanted to return to work. Henceforth, Owen and his union were embroiled in constant battle to prevent the strike from crumbling, his ranting speeches likening the village of Ralph Royd to that of Khartoum where treacherous Egyptian soldiers under Gordon's command had opened the gates and let the Mahdi's troops in to murder the general. For the most part the miners stood firm, receiving support throughout the county as other pits went on strike. But noble words were poor fodder for those who were literally starving, and a few caved in, willing to suffer the insults and the cuts from flying stones in return for a full belly.

Privately Owen himself wondered just how long they could hold out, for after three months union funds were now almost dry.

Thank goodness, thought Kit, that she was here to help, her ill-gotten gains gratefully accepted now in the form of nourishment. Would that it were so easy to remedy another matter, for, added to the hardship of the strike, something far graver had occurred in Monty's house. Whilst the rest of the family had long since recovered from their chest colds, Sarah's persisted even into April. No comment had been made as to its nature, and no diagnosis had been sought, for even the youngest child knew what that dreadful hacking sound meant.

There might be no love lost between Kit and her sister-in-law, but she would never wish such a dreadful affliction on anyone, and her heart went out to the youngsters who would have to watch their mother suffer the slow cruel death that had claimed Beata. Kit would do her utmost to fend that moment off for as long as she could.

On her way back from Castleford with another basket of wholesome food to combat her sister-in-law's tuberculosis, she paused briefly to talk to a group of rough-coated pit ponies, granted a respite from their grim underground existence, the only ones to benefit from this strike. After patting each inquisitive nose, she walked on.

A notice was being posted on to the side of the Robin Hood's Well. Kit looked over the shoulders of the gathered crowd to read it, instantly adding her voice to the angry rumble. Without wasting time, she hurried on to Monty's, glad to find Owen there too.

She planted her heavy basket on the table. 'They're going to evict you!'

Both men flew out of their chairs and demanded more information; Sarah, too.

'Everyone who lives in houses owned by the colliery is going to be evicted if they don't go back to work!' panted Kit.

A pale-faced Sarah threw up her hands, then clutched her head. 'Where are we supposed to go, damn them?' Rhoda and Alice lived miles away, the latter was expecting a baby, and, besides, neither of them would want their nice neat homes invaded by a host of refugees.

'You can come and stay at my house,' came the immediate offer. Kit performed a brief head count. There were five at Monty's and the same at Owen's, but she had suffered such overcrowding before.

'What, with your fancy man?' asked Sarah unkindly, her face gaunt with worry and illness.

Weary from such petty remarks, Kit did not know how she managed to bite her tongue, but with great restraint said she would ask Mr Popplewell to leave, the family came first. But they should wait until they were actually thrown out, that would give him time to find somewhere else.

Owen said she could play an even bigger part by enlisting the help of her politician friend. Inwardly Kit balked at this but listened to his plea. 'Tell him to use his influence to get more working men elected – which is what his lot promised when they were after our votes! Get rid of all them Pharisees. How can t'House o' Commons represent nation unless folk of all classes are allowed a say?' He pointed a finger at his sister. 'Just tell him to think o' the voters he'll lose if he doesn't help us. It was working men who gave him his power, they can just as easily take it away.'

Though reluctant to lose face in approaching Valentine first, Kit recognized the sacrifice she must make for her family who was in such dire straits, and agreed to help. Going straight home, she gave Mr Popplewell the bad news about his tenancy, and to make amends, spent the next few days helping him find new lodgings.

With her friend successfully rehoused, she caught a train to London.

First, she decided upon arrival at her house in the capital, there would have to be apology. Much as it choked her, she dispatched a letter to Valentine via Fred, telling him how sorry she was and that she hoped to be able to deliver her regrets in person if he would grant her the opportunity.

It came as some surprise when the politician returned with the man-servant that very same night, behaving as nice as pie, telling her he understood the reason that she had disobeyed his warning not to come to Westminster and indeed was touched by her concern. 'But really, my sweet, you must never do it again.' The dapper man sat beside her on the sofa and kissed her hand. 'It almost gave me an apoplexy seeing you there.'

'Did your wife suspect?' Kit displayed concern. 'Oh, Val, I never meant –'

'Not a thing!' He pacified her with a hug. 'But promise me you will keep to the rules we set ourselves at the outset.'

'I was just so worried!' She returned his embrace.

'I know, I know. I felt wretched afterwards at being so harsh. But what could you have done if I were injured? Nothing at all.'

Kit gave a nod of understanding, vowing she would never endanger his marriage again. Negating her own remarkable appearance in a tea gown that ranged from pale cream to dark chestnut and paid glorious compliment to her hair, her breast rose in a sigh as she remarked of his wife, 'She's very pretty.'

Valentine agreed, adding that his wife's nature matched her sweet countenance. 'But there are other things a wife just cannot provide. Dear Kit, how I've missed you.' Admiring her voluptuous form for a second, he ground her lips with his own, then led her to the stairs.

Kit was weary from her journey and would have much preferred to curl up and go to sleep. But to deny him this would be to destroy his receptive mood and she had come here to seek help. Meeting his sensual gaze, she allowed him to lead her upstairs.

Permitting a respectable period to elapse between their lovemaking and the question of the striking miners, Kit went all the way through supper without mentioning a word, asking instead what he had done in her three-month absence. Had they caught the person responsible for the bombing?

Picking at his meal, Valentine said blame had been put on O'Donovan Rossa who had already caused a series of explosions in London and carried out a similar attempt to destroy Parliament in Quebec. 'Someone – a British nurse by all accounts, God bless her – managed to get five shots into him in New York, but unfortunately he survived.'

Kit said she would liked to have put five shots into Cara, then begged pardon for the poor meal but she hadn't had time to hire anyone else. 'So there've been no more explosions?'

He laid his knife and fork together, mopping at his moustache before replying. 'About a month ago we were sitting in the House when there was an almighty bang – shook the entire building. Turned out it was caused by gas in the Palace Yard.' He took a sip of wine and grinned. 'Probably all the hot air spouted by that windbag Churchill. Gave us a frightful shock though.'

'I heard Mr Gladstone was going to retire.' Kit tried to work the conversation round to the striking miners.

'He's been persuaded that it's his duty to stay in office for the moment. There'll be an election at the end of the year anyway.' Valentine savoured the last of his wine and gazed thoughtfully into mid-air. 'What else have I done? Ah, a memorial service at St Paul's for General Gordon, tried to avert a war with Russia –'

Kit broke in to ask if the threat was real.

'Indubitably. The hostilities have sent the Stock Exchange into a total panic. Fortunately, I managed to sell my shares before they plunged too far. Anyway, that's quite enough of me.' He rose and led the way to the drawing room. 'Come sit by me and reveal what you've been doing in Yorkshire.'

At last Kit had an opening. With a great sigh, she leaned against him to relate everything that had taken place during the last three months, concluding her sad tale with news of the threatened evictions. 'They might be out on the streets by the time I get back.'

'But that's truly awful,' responded Valentine. 'So you don't plan to stay in London?'

Kit shook her head. 'I didn't like to leave them at all.' There came a brief hesitation. 'But I thought you might be able to lend a sense of direction to their plight.'

Valentine gave a futile shrug. 'My sympathies go out to the colliers, naturally, but from what I'm told it appears that the only answer is for them to go back to work. A reduction in wages is better than no wage at all. There's a general depression in the entire coal trade. In all fairness, one can't expect the owners to shoulder the burden.'

'Why not?' was her simple question. 'They're the ones with all the money.'

'I know it seems unfair –'

'Because it is unfair! I was expecting more from an intelligent man like yourself. When I mentioned a sense of direction, I referred to your capacity as a politician.'

He retained his helpless air. 'I can't intervene in private battles.'

'It's not private, the whole of Yorkshire's involved – probably your constituents too, as far as I know. And if they're typical of the men in our village they feel they're being let down by the Government – the

388

Government they helped to elect.' Kit stared him in the eye, making sure he knew exactly what she meant. 'I have to tell you, Val, you won't be able to rely on the working men's vote again if you stand by and let them be evicted.'

He cocked his head and offered smiling rebuke. 'Kit! Can it be that you are trying to blackmail me? If so, it's not a very clever ruse. If the miners have no homes they'd be effectively disenfranchized anyway.'

Feeling she was being patronized, Kit moved three inches along on the sofa, replying coolly, 'So you only care about the men with votes. Seem to have lost your philanthropic edge, Mr Kitchingham – or was that just to get into my good books?'

He did not rise to the bait, wagging a finger as if to a naughty child. 'If there's anyone being mercenary here, Kit, it's you. I'm rather hurt – you only came back to curry favour, didn't you?'

'No.' She remained firm in her lie. 'But if that's what you think, then I'll bid you good night.'

In a remarkably good mood due to their earlier lovemaking, Valentine began to tease her, picking away at the cool edifice until she was forced to laugh. Thence, he told her he would speak to other members of the cabinet and see what could be done – but she must expect no miracles. This said, he coaxed her into remaining in the capital for a few days longer than she had planned. In truth, Kit needed little enticement. It would be a wonderful release after the three grim months in Yorkshire. And she hoped by the time she got back her reason for coming here would have borne fruit.

April showers interspersed a bitterly cold north-east wind as Kit arrived back in Ralph Royd a week later. Hunched into her coat and fur boa after what seemed like an endless walk from the nearest station, she was grateful to reach Main Street at last – but upon seeing the mob gathered outside the Robin Hood's Well and the vast array of police uniforms, she faltered in her step. Surely the evictions had not begun already?

Hurrying onwards through the crowd to her brother's house, she saw the steep road ahead crammed with people and furniture, her first glimpse of Savile Row producing a similar scene. Yet there was no violence, the police merely being there to observe, those evicted standing amongst their belongings and wide-eyed children, unsure of where to go.

Mingling with the crowd, her eyes searched for Monty but not for long for his red hair shone like a beacon on this bitterly cold afternoon. Helping to pile his household goods on to one of the many handcarts provided by local tradespeople, she went with the family to deposit their furniture in the mission hall. Then, whilst Monty went off to find Owen, who was organizing accommodation for the rest of the evicted strikers, she went ahead to prepare her cottage for the influx of bodies.

By nightfall the streets were almost deserted, but the chapel and mission hall, barns and sheds were stuffed with dispossessed families, and the pasture looked like a gypsy encampment. Peggo's upstairs room which normally held union meetings had been given over to more of the evicted. Almost every person in the village with a roof over their head gave succour to the unfortunate.

Squashed into the cottage with her two brothers and their wives, and their six large offspring, Kit apologized and said she had tried her best with Valentine, telling them word for word what the politician had said. Owen replied that he had not really expected anything to come of it. There was no glory in it for Kitchingham. But the time would come, he promised, when the working man would have his say.

During the week that followed there was plenty of opportunity for Owen to have his say in the daily open-air meetings that took place in the field near the colliery, hundreds in attendance, men, women and children.

'Let me tell thee just what sort o' man we're dealing with!' His voice rang across the misty pasture to accuse those who had evicted them. 'Latimer doesn't just use the miners but uses miners' womenfolk as well!'

Kit was aghast. He couldn't be going to tell them that!

'I have it on very good authority that he threatened a young woman to prevent her marrying his son! That's how highly he thinks of us! And that's not all. When she showed a bit of spirit and said she'd take the lad to court for breach of promise, the old man bribed her with five hundred pounds!'

Trying to reduce her height, Kit felt the blush rise up her throat and across her cheeks. Even though he did not mention her name everyone in the village would have heard the gossip, but she could do naught to prevent her brother from continuing.

A colliery official who had come to observe shouted out, 'Slander!'

Owen turned on him, as did the crowd. 'Then tell Latimer to sue me! How much brass d'you reckon he'd get?' With great drama he displayed his empty pockets. 'I've got a witness to testify in court that all I've just said is true! And now he thinks he'll have his money back by taking it out of miner's wages. Well, I've got news for him – he won't!'

The angry crowd cheered. Kit just wanted to die.

Later, in her overcrowded parlour, she reproached Owen for his words. 'I could've flattened you! What if I have to go to court?'

He showed disdain. 'You won't! He doesn't want that sort o' publicity. Anyroad, it were all true what I said, wan't it?'

'Yes, but it was Mrs Latimer who gave me the money!'

'You can't tell me he didn't know about it.'

Fearing that her actions could be construed as obtaining money by false pretences – for she had intimated to Mrs Latimer she had been expecting a child – she appealed to her brother not to raise the matter again. 'Whether he did or he didn't, it's not something I care to be reminded of, and I'm sure Monty and Sarah don't either.' She glanced at them for support and received it by way of their tart expressions. 'Just be thankful the Latimers did give me all that money and I'm able to help you now.'

Fortunately, Owen conceded that his words had been thoughtless – he had just been attempting to rally the miners in any manner he could. 'Aye, you're right. Just because he's stooped to underhanded means to fight us, doesn't mean we have to sink to his level.'

Kit thanked him and offered her total support for as long as the strike continued. Whilst her money lasted her family would never have to go begging for food as had befallen others less fortunate.

Owen detested having to rely on his sister's benevolence, as did his brother – especially knowing the source of the funds that kept them alive. But charity or no, it gave him the strength he needed to maintain the struggle, to rally those who would have caved in to Latimer's demands.

It was now almost the end of April. Through the miners valiant efforts and public support the strike had been the longest on record, though it had crippled the whole village, and the grocers and butchers so previously supportive were now refusing to put anything further on tick. Worse still, word had come that colliery agents had been recruiting men in other parts of the country. If the strike persisted, these would be brought in by the trainload.

Kit's cottage being located on the edge of the village, its occupants were the first to see a band of such outsiders arriving at the sidings and marching to the pit, accompanied by a dozen police officers. Owen took immediate action, instructing his wife and Kit, Sarah and the youngsters to run and summon the strikers, whilst he and his son and Monty hurried after the immigrants.

Within minutes a crowd had gathered and was tearing after the intruders, showering them with stones and earth and anything else the strikers could lay their hands on, shouting abuse, fighting to get past the wall of police who, because the mob was so disorganized, eventually beat its members back, allowing the foreigners to enter the shaft to cries of 'Black sheep!'

Though allying herself with their cause, Kit chose not to mimic the band of jeering women, some with babies on their hips, alarmed at their violent antics. However noble the objective it was not right to indoctrinate tiny children with such hatred.

'They'll have to come out some time!' panted Owen to the crowd. 'And when they do, we'll be ready for 'em!'

Upon the cheer of agreement, he led the angry strikers back to the village to co-ordinate their next move.

That afternoon, when the foreigners emerged warily from the shaft they were met by a hail of abuse and a shower of accurately aimed stones. Only by the aid of police truncheons did they manage to escape, but even then the mob broke apart and its separate factions began to pursue the frightened interlopers, men women and children calling for blood. This time Kit watched from a distance, concerned that members of her family might be hurt, especially Probyn.

With insufficient police to control such a large number, the foreigners found themselves surrounded and blows began to rain upon their crouching backs. Before the violence got out of hand, however, Owen appealed to the mob to stand back and give the incomers a chance to hear their case, for they surely would not have broken a strike intentionally. Protesting their ignorance, the foreigners said they had been duped into coming here, their Cornish spokesman announcing that they would refuse to go down the pit tomorrow and would back the strikers. There was a spontaneous cheer

392

from the crowd. To a shrill burst on a tin whistle, the spokesman and others were hoisted on to shoulders, now the best of friends, and the mob of men, women and children paraded round and round the muddy field in a state of triumph, banging pan lids, waving handkerchiefs to show the police and colliery officials that they had won.

Next morning, true to their word, the foreigners joined with strikers at the colliery gates in a display of solidarity, a victorious Owen leading the crowd in hymn and prayer, thanking God for His help in their fight against evil.

The battle might have been won, but the war was to continue into the summer. For every foreigner who was persuaded to go home another took his place, thereby enabling the Ralph Royd Coal Company to keep the pit open. However small an amount of coal they turned out, its production was an arrogant sign to the strikers that they could never hope to win.

With new men arriving by the trainload, the strikers became more desperate to persuade them to go home, bombarding them with stones and heavy missiles, their confrontations becoming more and more fraught, the violence coming to a head when one of the new men fired a revolver at his assailants, injuring two miners. Had the police not charged the crowd and arrested the man, the strikers would have torn him apart.

At the next gathering outside the colliery Owen tried to calm matters by using shock tactics of his own, hurling a bucketful of pig's blood at the colliery gates and saying that this was the only blood he wanted to see spilt. The coalmasters had set miner against miner, but they must not allow the likes of Latimer to destroy them. But as if in a show of contempt his voice was drowned out by the colliery engines, telling him exactly who would win.

One by one, throughout the Yorkshire coalfield, miners on the brink of starvation were forced to capitulate, conceding the ten per cent reduction and drifting back to work. A few of the Ralph Royd miners began to return – though the vast majority had yet been persuaded to stay out and their daily attendance at the pit-head was merely to pour scorn on those who broke the strike. Owen, still determined that those who had perished in the smallpox and measles epidemics – occasioned by the cold-hearted evictions – should not have died in vain. He formed a deputation to put new resolutions that would at least allow his union members to return with dignity.

Sensing triumph, the company refused all demands. Furtherto, it became even harder, threatening to close the pit for an indefinite period unless sufficient miners resumed work on their terms of five shillings and sixpence a day.

The tension that had been building up in Kit's house over the last two months in particular was now threatening to overwhelm her. Her brothers and indeed their wives were so very different, it was inevitable that there would be petty disagreements. The house no longer felt like hers. She felt totally trapped and helpless. Staring out of the window on this sunny June morning, the only ones getting ready for work being Wyn and Merry, the others sitting despondently round the breakfast table, she noticed the little speckled thrush who came regularly to feed in her garden. The sight of him perched at the top of a hawthorn bush trilling his heart out struck a sudden chord in her heart. Never once whilst feeding him crumbs had she recognized the incongruity before, only now equating him with the lifeless creatures who served as decoration for her hats.

'Father, what's the age of consent?' Probyn was tucking exercise books into his school bag.

This drew everyone's attention, even interrupting his mother's bout of coughing. 'Where did you learn such a phrase?' demanded Sarah.

'As if we didn't know!' Failing to prevent Kit from buying her *News of the World*, Monty had pleaded for her at least to keep the filthy journal hidden. Not well enough by the sounds of it. 'It's how old you have to be before you can get married,' he explained to Probyn, at the same time gesturing to his daughters. 'You're all going to be late if 'ee don't get going! We're relying on you, remember.'

Once the younger element had been removed from the house, Owen's fifteen-year-old son being considered adult enough to hear this, Monty threw an accusation at his sister.

'I hide the paper as best I can!' replied Kit. 'It's not my fault if he goes rooting round and finds it.'

'If it wasn't there in the first place, he wouldn't be able to find it.' A pained Sarah coughed again into her handkerchief. 'I don't know why you waste your money on the filthy thing when others can't even afford food.'

394

Unusually, Kit flared. 'I don't see you going without – and I'll spend my money the way I like, thank you very much.'

'It's all very well for those with money to spend!'

'This is my house and I'll do as I please!'

'You're absolutely right! And I shall do as I please too.' Her black hair scraped unflatteringly from her haggard face, Sarah shoved the handkerchief into her apron pocket and gathered the breakfast pots noisily. 'Monty, you're going back to work.'

'How can he go back?' Owen's black eyebrows formed a line of dissent in his high pale forehead. 'He's paid by us miners.' His wife, Meg, supported him.

'Nobody says he has to be check weighman. He can go back underground,' wheezed Sarah. 'God knows, there are plenty of jobs going. I can't stand any more of this – and if you've any sense, Meg, you'll do the same. I don't know how we let ourselves be talked into it in the first place!' As always in a strike it was the women who suffered. Monty and Owen could go out and play in their allotments, enjoy their stupid games – but they still expected to be fed, and it was the women who had to make ends meet.

'Are you going to stand there and let your wife tell thee what to do?' Owen demanded of his brother.

Monty responded with bitterness. 'Well, I've let 'ee tell me what to do for long enough, ain't I? Listened to all your claptrap – and what good has it done me? I've got no house, no food, no money save for the few bob the girls earn. What sort of a man is it relies on his sister to house him?'

Owen tightened his lips over the implied insult. Meg stood at his shoulder, where in her opinion a wife should be, not running him down.

Kit relented over her previous outburst. 'I don't mind, honestly.'

'But I do,' insisted Monty. 'So we'll be going home as soon as I can arrange it. Thank 'ee for your help, Kit, we're most grateful.'

Owen offered grave warning. 'If you break this strike, that'll be the end of thee and me.'

Monty looked his brother in the eye. You ungrateful little sod, came his thought. It was my sweat that earned you the luxury of being able to pick and choose, my toil that put you through school. But all he said was, 'Do as you must.'

*   *   *

That same day, Kit's elder brother walked up to the manager's office and asked for a job. It was immediately granted. He also received the key to his old house. By nightfall he and his family were out from under Kit's feet.

Whilst Owen remained stubborn, he had been rankled enough by Monty's remark to tell Kit he would leave too if she wanted. He had no wish to impose further. His sister told him not to be proud, he could stay here as long as he wished, though she feared Monty might view this as an indication of where her loyalty lay. Accordingly, she made sure to visit her elder brother regularly, even if it did make her unpopular with others.

The preponderance of dwellings in Savile Row now housed the new men, providing company for those like Monty who had chosen to fight his way through the jeering mob that attended the pit-head every morning. Yet he still found it a dreadful ordeal to run the gauntlet of erstwhile friends, the hardest part to bear being his brother's contempt.

Whilst the rest of the mob threw punches and sneered and sang

> 'Ba ba black sheep have you any pride?
> No sir, no sir, I'd lick t'master's backside!'

and

> 'Old King Coal was a stingy arsehole
> and a stingy arsehole was he!'

Owen simply moved back to allow his brother to pass, offering none of the violence he bestowed on others, that vitriolic glare being even more efficient than blows, his black eyes following Monty's every move until he disappeared from sight.

Day in, day out, the strikers continued to intimidate the black sheep, undaunted by the summonses brought by the owners. Owen was amongst those dragged before the court, bound over in a sum of ten pounds to keep the peace for three months.

Faced with the thought that the strike could last that long, Kit felt she would go mad, both from lack of privacy and the burden of divided loyalty. The village where nothing ever happened had now become a political battlefield, foreigners took the place of friends, the Kilmasters just one of many families split by the lockout.

And then all at once it appeared to be over. The sight of some miners going back to work seemed to infect others. The trickle became a stream, the stream a river, until one morning Owen and his stalwarts found themselves outnumbered and were no longer regarded as a threat.

Inasmuch as she felt desperately sorry for her younger brother who had fought so long and hard against injustice – and it was terribly unjust – Kit felt a wave of relief upon seeing the tents dismantled from the pasture, the houses once again inhabited, most of the foreigners being sent home. Yet, her own troubles were far from over, for though Owen resigned himself to accepting the ten per cent drop in wages, the masters had other ideas. Regarded as troublemakers, he and his ten staunchest allies, including his son, were blackballed. Unable to get a job anywhere, he was forced to throw himself on Kit's mercy.

Thoroughly exhausted by the turmoil, Kit had been so looking forward to having the house to herself once more, that when Owen asked if his family might stay until he or his lad found work, she was hard put to prevent a scream of frustration.

But how could she deny her brother a roof over his head, especially with other property at her disposal? This sparked a sudden decision. No longer needed here, she would go back to her comfortable home in London.

Telling Owen he could stay as long as he wanted, she added one proviso: 'By the time I return, I expect to see you and Monty back on speaking terms.'

'If your decision to let us stay hangs on that,' announced Owen gravely, 'I'll say ta-ra now.'

She saw that he was deeply serious. 'You can't not talk to him – he's your brother, he brought you up, for heaven's sake.'

'He's a traitor,' said Owen. 'I'll never talk to him again.'

Reflecting on this conversation during her train journey, Kit decided that it was purely through lack of work and lost pride that Owen had made this bitter utterance. Once he had found a job, he would be better disposed. Kit hoped she would be able to help in this field – though for the moment she could not prevent her mind wandering back to her own personal woes. In defiance of all efforts to fight it, she was plagued by the niggling thought that she might have contacted tuberculosis from living cheek to cheek with Sarah. Reading up on the subject, she had found opinion to be that it was after all contagious – but then why had no one else caught it when Beata had died? Still, one could never be sure, and in Kit's weakened state of mind the idea had found fertile ground. Despite the lack of a cough, her chest felt tight, in fact her whole body felt run down and exhausted.

Perhaps, Kit told herself, she just needed to get away for a rest – though the thought occurred that she was going to the wrong place for that. The moment Valentine heard she was in residence he would be pressuring her for favours. Maybe she would not let him know she was there, not for a while anyway. Though he really needed to be told if she did have consumption.

Even after a few days' rest, during which she cosseted herself with perfumed baths, boxes of chocolates and good books, Kit remained out of sorts, but still she decided to send word to Valentine. He had a right to know.

A mere day after Fred's delivery of the note, the politician appeared in Kit's hallway, somewhat earlier than usual, pleased as ever to see her and enquiring straight away as to the health of her family.

'I don't ever recall a strike lasting as long as this!' Most attentive, he escorted her into the drawing room where they sat down. 'You must have suffered dreadful hardship. I tried my utmost to help negotiations along but was virtually told to mind my own business. Anyway, it's over now, thank goodness, and you're back. I'm so glad to see you.'

Kit returned the compliment, wondering how on earth she could introduce the subject of tuberculosis into the conversation.

'It's such a happy coincidence that you chose to return at this time as I've been bidden to attend a party this evening – by a very important host. I assumed I would be forced into going alone but now you're here –'

'Oh, Val, I don't know if I've got the energy.' Kit looked plaintive.

'Of course you have!' came his bright reply. 'Plenty of time to get ready – and I've brought you something to wear.' He produced a box and from it took out a silver dog collar from which dangled a large pearl.

'Is this all I'm to wear?' joked Kit.

He laughed and said later, maybe.

'It's lovely, thank you, but do I have to parade it this evening? I'd much rather stay in and catch up with all your news.'

'Stay in? What happened to the woman I used to know?'

She allowed her auburn head to fall to her shoulder. 'I just feel exhausted.'

He sighed and looked decidedly put out. 'How fearfully boring. I suppose I shall have to go alone.'

'Do you have to go at all? I'd like to talk to you.'

'Yes, I have to go. I told you, I'm expected by important people.'

Kit fought her negativity. Normally she would have jumped at the chance of such a party. Maybe this was just what she needed to lift her spirits. She gave a smile of surrender and rose in a manner that instantly restored his good humour. 'All right, scallywag, you've persuaded me! I expect we'll have plenty of time to talk later.'

For a moment, whilst Dilly heaved and hauled and grimaced over the laces of her mistress's stays, Kit felt like abandoning the whole idea, grunting and gasping as her waist was reduced almost to life-threatening proportions. Once arrived at the glittering venue, however, her favourite satin ball gown drawing looks of admiration, she was glad to have made the effort – and was particularly so upon discovering that one of the guests was most familiar to her.

Ossie Postgate saw her the instant she entered the ballroom. How could anyone not notice Kit – especially sporting such a dress? A squadron of turquoise butterflies adorned its eau-de-Nil skirt, whilst another perched atop one magnificent shoulder as if about to take flight.

After allowing his host sufficient time in which to greet the statuesque woman and her companion, he came forward smiling to reacquaint himself. 'Kit, what a pleasure!' He still possessed that uncontrollable blink.

Recovered from the moment of startlement, Kit returned Ossie's greeting, smiling too at the young lady on his arm – Agnes Dolphin, though the glimmer of gold upon her finger signified that she was no longer Miss Dolphin.

'You know my dear wife, of course.' Ossie looked fondly at his partner who also hailed Kit in genuine fashion, as if she had totally forgotten that the last time they had been in the same room she herself had been screaming blue murder over Thomas Denaby's sooty apparition.

399

Smiling up at her, Agnes asked, 'And do you reside in the capital permanently now, Kit?'

'Much of the time, though I've been in Yorkshire for several months.'

Ossie guessed immediately. 'Ah yes, the strike – a terrible business. Thank God it's over.'

Kit noticed Agnes's quick glance at her former servant's hand. Having adopted the fashion frowned upon by older ladies of going without gloves she was made conscious of her own lack of a wedding ring, and this in turn caused her to remember Valentine's presence. Realizing that he was not similarly acquainted, she quickly remedied this, introducing him as her friend. Once familiarized he seemed very keen to strike up a conversation and managed to maintain it for a while until Ossie politely withdrew and said he should just go and talk to someone else. Kit was rather annoyed at Valentine's monopoly, for the warmth of Ossie's greeting had inspired in her a sudden urge to atone for her disgraceful behaviour whilst in his father's employ. Inclining her head towards Viscount Postgate and his wife, she expressed the hope that they would be able to speak again later.

Valentine seemed most impressed that his companion knew such illustrious people, and asked Kit how she had met them. She told him quite honestly that she had been in service at both their households, thereby spoiling the effect a little. During her account of life below stairs, she noticed that his eyes strayed away from her face and across the room to look at a pretty girl. Kit was surprised to find she did not care. Indeed, there were times during the evening when her own attention was to wander away from the social chatter, preoccupied with thoughts of her divided family and her suspected illness.

Seated at a long supper table at one end of the ballroom, awaiting the next course, she became mesmerized by the decorative vase of flowers before her and was instantly transported to the past, to Tish Dolphin, and consequently his dead baby. Startled to recall such awful images, Kit tore her eyes away, the arrival of another course helping to take her mind off such unwanted thoughts, but just as soon she was presented with another dilemma. Upon the large white plate in front of her lay a tiny bird that reminded her of the thrush who came to feed at her windowsill. How on earth could she eat such an object? Fingering the silver dog collar at her throat, overwhelmed with revulsion, she came to decide that there was only one way to avoid this without offending anyone. She pretended to swoon, a murmur of alarm going up from others seated nearby as she toppled sideways into Valentine, who caught her deftly before she slipped from her chair.

Faking unconsciousness, Kit heard the scraping of a chair and a man's voice saying, 'Let me help you, old chap.' And, lifting a befuddled face she found herself supported between Valentine and Viscount Postgate.

Her apology brushed aside, Kit was helped from her seat by the two men and taken to an anteroom where, at her insistence, the pair left her and returned to their meals.

Once certain they had gone, Kit relaxed as much as her corsets would allow, then sat there thinking for a long time until she could be sure the meal was over. Valentine's appearance confirming this, she allowed herself to be escorted back to the ballroom.

'You're beginning to worry me,' he told her, patting the arm that was linked with his. 'I think we'll have the doctor in tomorrow.'

Standing beside one of the marble pillars that supported the edge of the room, Kit nodded, wafting her Honiton lace fan. 'I haven't felt well for weeks. That's what I wanted to talk to you about. I'm afraid I might have something serious.' She was about to tell him the extent of her fears when she noticed his eyes were flickering again. Though he responded in a perfectly solicitous manner, saying she should not worry until the physician had had a look at her, she knew she had lost her hold on him. Standing back from the gathering now, watching them perform the Lancers, she noticed how ridiculous they appeared with their strutting and cavorting. How could she ever have envied their life of extravagance and indolence? All it produced in her now was a sense of unfulfilment.

The dance finished and the orchestra changed to a waltz. Automatically, Valentine took her hand and attempted to lead her on to the floor, but Kit refused, saying she would sit this one out. As Kitchingham was escorting her to a seat, Ossie Postgate waylaid them and asked if Kit had recovered.

She smiled at him, saying it was most kind of his lordship and that she was fully recuperated.

'In that case,' said the fair-haired man, with an assured little bow, 'I should be honoured if you'd consent to dance with me.'

Noting Valentine's look of surprise when Kit accepted, Ossie sought to explain. 'I trust you don't think me impertinent to steal Kit away, but, as you see, my wife has deserted me.' He indicated the floor where Agnes was dancing with their host.

'Not at all.' Valentine inclined his head, yet was, Kit realized, rather put out.

Enjoying his discomposure, Kit placed a light hand on the shoulder that was slightly lower than her own, then followed Ossie's lead into the waltz, smiling at him.

Ossie held her gaze, blinking occasionally. With the plumpness of youth drained from her face, Kit seemed almost beautiful tonight. 'It really was a pleasure to find you here,' he told her, one hand upon her waist as they swayed from side to side. 'I'm not just saying it. I've often wondered about you over the years.'

Moving quite gracefully for one so large, Kit said she had thought about him too. 'It's for that reason I've been waiting to speak to you all evening, to apologize for my thoughtless attitude towards you and your parents after you'd been so kind as to give me a position.' Seeing his face begin to negate this she deterred him from speech. 'No, I acted abominably, and I'm truly sorry.'

'You are pardoned, madam.' Ossie wore that teasing smile she remembered from his boyhood.

'I hope to extend my apology to Lady Agnes too,' said Kit, 'but if I don't get the opportunity, will you pass on my regrets? Dare I ask how Tish is, these days? Are he and Myrtle still together?'

The Viscount's air remained merry. 'Yes, they're doing splendidly! Have their own little cottage on the estate with chickens and rabbits and whatnot. Agnes and I call upon them occasionally. They seem contented enough, all things considered.'

Still burdened with guilt over her part in the affair, Kit wondered if Myrtle shared her own emptiness over the absence of children. But to the Viscount she voiced only gladness that they were happy.

They went on to chat about mutual acquaintances, including Mr Popplewell, the Earl's cook, enjoying a chuckle over his tantrums, Kit telling Ossie that she had seen him quite recently and he was much mellowed.

'It must be your influence, Kit.' Ossie glanced at Valentine then. 'And Mr Kitchingham, is he a special friend?'

Kit gave a wry smile, enjoying herself now more than at any point in the evening. 'He was. He's fast falling out of favour, I can tell you.' The tune was three-quarters of the way through, she wished it could last longer.

'And what of your family? Did they suffer much hardship during the strike?'

She threw up her eyes and said it had been awful, adding that her younger brother, Owen, and his son had been blacklisted and were unable to gain re-entry to the pit. None of the local collieries would employ them either. Hence, they would have to remain under her roof for the foreseeable future. 'That's why I've come back to London. Much as I care for him, it's difficult to have your house overrun.'

'Tell him to come to the Garborough mine,' instructed Ossie.

For once it had not been Kit's intention to curry favour and she gave a cynical laugh. 'If you thought I was trouble –'

'He'll have his chance. Tell him to mention our conversation to the colliery manager.'

She studied his face as they moved from side to side. 'You mean it? Will he be able to get accommodation too?'

Her partner gave a nod. 'Father's just had another row of houses erected at Garborough Junction.'

Kit showed gratitude. 'Well, I'll not refuse your kind offer, but you should be warned: Owen's a strong union man – and I can tell you now he won't accept a job if his friends aren't granted the same favour.'

'The colliery manager's a fellow of principle. Your brother will get a fair hearing, the others too, though you should warn them we won't tolerate any rabble-rousing.'

The music was at an end. Kit breathed her gratitude and said she would write to Owen tomorrow. Allowing Ossie to escort her back to Valentine, she thanked the Viscount again, then watched him go back to his wife.

'A charming man,' muttered Valentine, watching Ossie's easy manner as he moved amongst the guests.

Kit agreed. 'And generous too. He's offered to help my brother out of trouble.'

Valentine construed this as some kind of slur over his own lack of assistance. 'Obviously he has more influence than some.'

'I meant no slander. I know you did your best –'

'Legislation has its limits, Kit. The working man can only hope to better himself by his own efforts – unless of course he has a charitable aristocrat at his beck and call.'

She clamped her jaws together, setting her lips in a hard line.

'As a former member of his staff you appeared to be very at ease with Viscount Postgate.'

'Take me home,' said Kit.

'Very well, but are you certain you wouldn't like to stay and dance with your – friend?'

Kit turned and walked to the door. Valentine followed at a sauntering pace, and paused to issue smiling apology to his host for being forced to leave by reason that Miss Kilmaster was unwell.

'You didn't *have* to leave with me,' she told him in the darkness of the carriage as it made its way across London.

He did not reply. In fact the journey was undertaken in complete silence after this.

When they reached St John's Wood, upset at his behaviour, Kit went straight upstairs. Valentine did not accompany her but went into the drawing room and poured himself a drink from a crystal decanter.

Struggling over the laces on her corset, and all the layers of clothing, it took Kit a long time to undress. She was still not ready for bed when the door opened and Valentine came in wearing a somewhat hangdog expression, though he made no apology for his boorishness. Instead he took off his patent shoes, white waistcoat and dinner suit, then, still clad in his underwear, he came to stand behind her as she brushed her auburn hair, bending over to kiss her neck. Kit allowed this, but when his hand slipped under her chemise she shrugged him off.

Offended, he straightened and looked at her reflection in the mirror. 'What's the matter with you these days? You used to be such fun.'

'I've told you I don't feel well.'

'Well enough to dance with an aristocrat – and I'm not surprised you feel so unwell, you're always stuffing your face with those.' He indicated the half-empty boxes of chocolates on the bedside table. 'Do you really want to become any fatter?'

Kit was deeply offended. 'Some folk choose not to judge by physique.'

'Like your winsome viscount? If you must know you looked ridiculous dancing with him.'

404

Kit gasped. He could stand there in his woollen combinations and tell her she looked ridiculous! She rose majestically. 'Then if I'm obviously so unattractive you'll want to sleep elsewhere!'

Under her imposing glare he grabbed his discarded suit and retired to another room – or so Kit imagined, but moments later she was to hear the front door slam.

In bed now, she turned on her side, though the incident had upset her too much to allow sleep. Desperate for peace, she decided that tomorrow she would go to York, where a period of solitude might help her to decide what to do. But it was obvious now that Valentine could not care less if she lived or died.

23

Drained from her long journey, and thoroughly miserable, Kit arrived in York on a sultry Saturday night – which was quite the wrong time to arrive for anyone desirous of peace and quiet. The rather musty, oven-like interior of her house dictated that she should open every window, but then sleep was impossible with all the noise going on. Yet, rowdy as the marketplace might be with its boisterous drunken revellers, at least they were on the outside, and their disturbance of Kit's repose was not personal. And all alone in her bed she would have the whole of Sunday morning to recover.

Anticipating a leisurely snooze, Kit was therefore greatly displeased to be roused by a Salvation Army band at eight o'clock in the morning. There had been trouble from these religious zealots prior to her leaving, but then their music had not greatly bothered her. Now, though, her calm shattered, she groaned and shoved her head under the pillow, pressing it to the side of her face in the vain hope of eliminating the din of the big bass drum.

'*Onward, Christian so-oldiers! Marching as to war . . .*'

'I'll give you bloody war in a minute.' Kit added another pillow to the one already in situ, but got no relief, the resonating clash of cymbal and drum piercing every defence.

On and on and on played the band, until Kit could stand it no longer and hurled herself out of bed, opened the sash window and bawled into the glorious summer's morning, 'For pity's sake, shut up!'

Her plea was to no avail, the Salvationists banging, singing, trumpeting as if to wake the dead.

A crowd had gathered in the sunny market square, made up of the people who lived above shops and public houses, who now started to make grabs at the band's instruments. For a moment the din became even worse – the strangled hoots of trumpets as they were wrenched from their owners' mouths, the hammering of instruments against the wall until the brass was full of dents, tambourines bashed over heads. Kit cheered as the police arrived and threatened to charge every Salvationist with breach of the peace if they continued. As the hullabaloo died down, she closed the window and fell back into bed with a thankful groan – but her peace was to be short-lived, ruined by the sound of a lone voice in accompaniment to a tambourine.

'*Onward, Christian so-oldiers! Marching as to war . . .*'

Rushing back to the window she shouted at the black-bonneted stalwart to have some consideration, but the thump of the tambourine and the reedy voice persisted. Driven to distraction, Kit grabbed the chamber pot from under the bed and hurled the contents with great accuracy – but alas, after the briefest of interruptions the drenched Salvationist continued to praise the Lord, urine dripping from the brim of her bonnet. Only when a policeman came to arrest the nuisance did Kit gain the peace she so desired.

But she was now too angry to go back to bed, and instead decided to have breakfast. Preparing the frying pan to receive three rashers of bacon, she recalled Valentine's insult, and decided that she was perhaps getting too fat and instead had only tea and toast.

Wondering what to do for the rest of the day, she decided to visit Amelia in the hope of receiving luncheon. Relating the tale of this morning's rumpus, and drawing laughter from her sister, Kit had to admit that it did have its amusing side but complained that such incidents were all that she needed with her worries.

Amelia, beating a Yorkshire pudding mixture, assumed her to be referring to the family. 'Have you still got Owen's lot under your roof, then?'

Kit gave an exclamation. 'Oh good heavens, that reminds me! I must write a letter straight away – Ossie Postgate offered him a job.' Agreeing with Amelia that it was wonderful, she added that it would put some distance between the two brothers which might make them come to their senses. 'They still weren't speaking when I left last week. It's made me feel really ill being stuck between the pair of 'em.'

She became grave and pulled at the neck of her summer dress in the heat of the range. 'But it's not just them. Oh, I'll have to tell somebody – I think I might have got consumption off our Sarah. I've been right worried.'

'You look as fit as a lop!' exclaimed Amelia. 'You've got no cough or anything.'

Kit looked awkward. 'I know, but there's other things, and I feel rotten.'

Still beating away at the earthenware bowl, Amelia asked what other things. Kit blushed and studied her fingernails. 'Well, when our Beata got really bad her whatsits stopped. I haven't had anything for three months. I just know I've got it.'

When Amelia realized that Kit referred to menstruation, she looked aghast and deposited her mixing bowl on the table. 'You soft cat!' Flopping on to the chair opposite Kit's she clamped both hands to her head and stared at her. 'It's not consumption that ails thee!'

Still Kit did not understand for a moment. Then a flood of colour washed over her face, as the revelation hit her. 'I can't be!' At her sister's insistence that indeed she could be, Kit's shocked expression slowly turned to one of joy. A baby! Oh dear Lord, a baby. It was incredible – after all these years!

'I don't know what you're looking so happy for!' accused Amelia, her own eyes wide in apprehension. 'What's our Monty going to say? He's got enough on his plate.'

Dazed, Kit shook her head, overwhelmed with thoughts of the new life within, totally oblivious to anyone else's discomfort including her sister's.

Amelia rested her elbows on the table and dropped her head into her hands, suffering a conflict of emotions, on the one hand worried for her sister, on the other overcome with jealousy. Why was it not her who was having this child? She, who had never committed a sin in her life – at least not a serious one – and here was Kit, a total embarrassment to her family, being blessed in such a fashion with the child that should have been Amelia's. It wasn't fair. Somewhat peeved that Kit presented no sign of shame, she offered accusingly, 'Your politician friend'll run a mile now!'

Kit did not care, for that moment totally engulfed in happiness. But Amelia had planted uncertainty in her mind, one she must put right without delay.

After luncheon with her sister, she went back to St Sampson's Square and packed a bag in preparation of the morrow's return to London.

The next day, as the city of York erupted into violence over a Salvation Army procession in support of their arrested member, with windows smashed and fireworks hurled, their soldiers punched and kicked, their banners and clothing torn by the mob, a jubilant Kit travelled southwards, blissfully unmoved, lulled by the motion of the carriage into a state of euphoria. She was wise enough, though, to see that Valentine would probably not share her happiness, and was therefore somewhat nervous whilst awaiting his response to the note she dispatched to him on her arrival at St John's Wood.

This time, there was some delay in his arrival – the Liberal Government was once again in crisis and was being forced to resign over defeat of its Budget proposals. Notwithstanding his concern over losing his position, Valentine seemed courteous enough, though there was a definite lack of cordiality to his greeting, confirming to Kit that the affair had finally reached its end. All the more reason for her to divulge her news.

'I must confess I was rather surprised to get your note,' he told her, casually dropping his gloves into his top hat, then setting the latter on a table. 'Pleasantly so, of course.'

Kit had intended to entertain him first, but now decided to shock him with her announcement. 'I'm expecting a child.'

Kitchingham went white. For a moment he was unable to speak. When he did his tone held accusation. 'But you said you were barren!'

She retained a dignified stance. 'Obviously, I was mistaken.'

Kitchingham puffed out his chest then exhaled noisily, a sound of despair. 'God!' This was all he could say for a time, gazing into mid-air, rubbing a finger and thumb over his chin. At last he spoke again. 'How can I be sure –'

'It's yours.' She saved him the bother of finishing. 'You know it is.'

'Do I?' The distinguished face suddenly resembled that of a weasel. 'You seemed very intimate with that chap Postgate. Perhaps it is he who should pay for this dangerous laxity.'

How could I ever have liked you? thought Kit. But she continued to look him in the eye, and spoke with dignity. 'Viscount Postgate is a gentleman. If he were the father of my child I am certain he'd own up

409

to it, but unfortunately he is not, you are, and I'd be willing to announce it in court if needs be.'

He knew her of old, could tell straight away she was bluffing. 'What good would that do but to denounce you as a woman of loose virtue?'

'And denounce you in turn as a cad.' She tried to keep her voice and eyes level. 'Make no mistake, I've got my child's future to think about. I'll do anything I have to.'

He bemoaned loudly, 'How you've misled me! Did I mean nothing to you but money? I always believed you were the kindest and softest creature on earth.'

'Soft, yes, but not soft in the head. You've been using me. I know it, you know it, everyone knows it. The least you can do is pay for your fun.'

He uttered a laughing gasp, sweeping an arm around the sumptuous room. 'And what do you call this? In three years you've wanted for nothing. You have servants, a carriage, beautiful gowns –'

'I'd prefer a father for my child and a husband who loves me!' Her calm exterior was beginning to crack.

'Come now, Kit, you knew it wasn't that kind of arrangement.'

She fought the urge to cry. 'Yes, I did – but I never expected this to happen in a million years.' Face brimming with emotion that he could deny the life they had created, she laid a hand over her abdomen as if to protect her baby. 'And I certainly didn't think I was living with the sort of man who'd denounce his own child.'

He threw up his arms in surrender. 'Very well! You win. I accept it's mine. But you must understand that I can never offer you anything other than financial support.'

Kit nodded sadly.

'Now, you'll obviously want to return to Yorkshire.' There was a businesslike tone to his voice. 'I'm prepared to give you three hundred pounds to buy a house.'

'I've got a house – I've got two houses!'

He uttered a noise of despair. 'Then what are you complaining about, woman? Three hundred pounds is more than ample to bring up a child.'

'It's not *a* child it's *your* child! I'll bet your other two don't have to fight you for every penny. I want a thousand at least, and I also want you to pay the *accouchement* fees – I'll be staying here till it's born.'

'Impossible! I can't have you being seen with a belly out to here. People will talk.'

Kit barked with false amusement. 'That didn't seem to concern you when you brought me here!'

'That's entirely different. It's common knowledge that a man needs a companion when he's away from home. People turn a blind eye, wives expect it – but if that companion is so careless as to get herself into a delicate condition the neighbours miraculously recover their sight.' Kitchingham turned and walked to the door. 'This is ridiculous, I refuse to stand here and argue. Let me know when you're in a less hysterical state of mind and we'll talk sensibly – but I can tell you now to expect no more than I've offered.'

'I'll let you know, all right!' yelled Kit, losing all sense of decorum now. 'From the public gallery for all to hear!' She formed a tight smile as he stopped in his tracks. 'And don't say I wouldn't 'cause I would.'

The threat made him even more angry. 'I've been perfectly fair with you and this is how you repay me. It's disgraceful!' He stabbed a finger at her. 'Well, you can threaten as much as you like, but you won't get a penny more than three hundred. And I should be grateful if you can be packed and ready to leave when I return in three days' time!' He slammed the door after him.

Kit had never visited the Houses of Parliament before, and her approach to this majestic building the following day was less than confident. Having worn her most flamboyant attire to add a touch of bravado, she found it sadly lacking, her normally sturdy legs trembling like an invalid's even before she had entered. Almost nauseated by her sense of awe, and overtly conscious of the child within, she tiptoed uncertainly through the hallowed portal, weaving her way through the mass of officials and ordinary members of the public, following directions to a steeply-terraced gallery where she eventually took a front seat and waited for Valentine to arrive. Dismayed to find her view obscured by a grille, she feared that her threat might be in vain, that he might not see her. Would she have the courage to draw attention to herself?

Occasionally during her wait, Kit became so frightened that she almost answered the urge to leave, to let things be, to go home to her family. But that would be to let him get away with it. And so, clinging to her important reason for being here, she continued to wait, gazing down through the grille on to the scene beneath.

In the midst of the theatre formed by rich panels of wood and green leather benches was a huge sturdy desk, its area as large as a miner's parlour. It was laden with manuals, piles of documents and brass-handled boxes which to the imaginative mind might have contained treasure. Also upon it lay a gold-coloured ornamental mace. At intervals, groups of men would slip into the benches to one side or the other of the desk, at the far end of which sat a number of men in wigs, one of them apparently overlooking the proceedings from a throne.

Gradually, the entire chamber became packed for, unbeknown to Kit, Mr Gladstone was to make his resignation speech. Never having seen the Prime Minister, she was ignorant as to his identity at first, but, spotting Valentine, she sat up like a ramrod.

Amongst the ranks of morning coats, top hats, winged collars and striped trousers, seated at the end of a green leather bench, he looked exceptionally splendid today, one leg crossed over the other in relaxed, rather arrogant pose, whilst the Prime Minister made his speech. Others beside him appeared similarly comfortable, a few of them even apparently asleep. Far from being soothed by their calm demeanour, Kit found her tension increasing. Pressing her face to the grille, she willed him with all her might to look up.

His arms crossed, Kitchingham's neatly trimmed head remained at the same interested tilt for some time as if listening assiduously to the Prime Minister's oration, only a sporadic twitch of his polished shoe interrupting his pose. But as he rolled his head to nod at his neighbour at some pertinent point in Gladstone's speech, his thoughtful gaze turned upwards, and that was when he saw a movement in the Ladies' Gallery. How could he not recognize that hat?

Kit gulped at the sudden vehemence that overcame his gaze – but noting that his confident air had been involuntarily sapped, she gained strength from this and maintained her determined expression. Slowly, she unbent her trembling legs and rose to her feet.

She had hoped it would be enough to frighten him, but he was made of sterner stuff. With the utmost insolence he turned his head away and proceeded to ignore her. Someone to her rear expressed irritation. Unnerved, Kit sat down, heart thudding, not knowing what to do now.

And then, she noticed the involuntary movement of his hand as it fidgeted with the handkerchief in his breast pocket, caught his surreptitious glance – saw that he was bluffing too – and knew that she had him cornered. Sustained by this revelation, but aware that this was not the time, she continued to attend the Prime Minister's speech, gaining patience from the knowledge that under Valentine's cool facade he was as riddled with nerves as she was.

A sudden commotion on one of the front benches drew her attention away momentarily. An elderly Member appeared to be having a fit. His speech interrupted, Mr Gladstone shared others' concern – until it was discovered that the old man had simply been dreaming. A titter ran through the chamber. Kit took her chance. She stood again.

'Excuse me!' All eyes turned aloft. A look of sheer panic rippled Valentine's face and he shook his head rapidly as if to plead with her not to proceed, his look of capitulation telling Kit that he would grant her anything she asked. Feeling a glow of triumph, she apologized to the waiting assembly. 'I beg your pardon, I was addressing this lady here.' She redirected her enquiry to the person sitting beside her, indicating her intention to leave, drawing huffs and grumbles over her interruption of the dignified proceedings as she edged along the row.

On her way back to St John's Wood in a cab, drunk on victory, Kit took issue with her conscience: she really shouldn't have frightened him like that, after he had looked after her all these years. But the memory of his insulting words the night before soon helped remove a little of her compassion. She had her child to think of now: the child that he had denied. Under no circumstances would she allow it to become some despised outcast living on poor relief.

When Valentine arrived that evening he was cool but polite, agreeing to every demand she made. She would remain here until after the birth, have the assistance of the best doctor, would continue to have use of the servants and carriage and would receive a lump sum of seven hundred and fifty pounds. She would also, for this year only, have the use of his villa in Spain. In exchange for this most generous of settlements she would be as discreet as she could in her dress, would not flaunt her state before the neighbours, would remain indoors during the period in which her girth

413

was too large to conceal and would leave London within a fortnight of being delivered, never to return and never to approach him again.

Her future wealth confirmed, Kit felt safe enough to leave behind the constitutional crisis that had begun to build in London and return to York for a while. It might be deemed contrary, when she had fought so hard to remain here, but in the knowledge that he would not dare evict her she felt able to come and go as she pleased. Besides, she had another trip to organize.

Upon arrival in York she went to see Amelia and asked if she had divulged the news to anyone else. Her somewhat enraged sister asked what Kit took her for – she had no wish to be the subject of pointing fingers and gossip. Kit would have to tell the family herself.

Kit replied that she would leave them in ignorance for a while, for she would be staying in London until the child was born. But she wanted Amelia to do her a favour. She would be inviting Probyn to come and spend the school holiday with her in York – ostensibly. In truth, said Kit, they would be enjoying a vacation in Spain. The youngster had had such a rotten time of it with the strike, she added hurriedly at the sight of her sister's dismay, and Kit needed somebody to accompany her on the voyage. He would come to no harm. She just needed to forewarn Amelia, in case Monty should ask if she had seen the lad.

Amelia pointed out that upon sight of Probyn's sunburned face his father would immediately guess something was amiss, but Kit replied that the weather here had been glorious of late, no one would know the difference, and anyway, how could he possibly guess the lad had been to Spain.

So, with Amelia's co-operation, Kit had been able to arrange the illicit voyage to Spain, endowing her overawed nephew with an everlasting memory of a sunlit beach, an azure sea and sky, and the sight of his Aunt Kit discarding her blue velvet cloak at the water's edge to reveal the most immodest costume he had ever laid eyes on.

Now, four months later, all Kit had to remind her of that wonderful time was the memory of a boy's happy face and a silver thimble bearing the name Villa Garcia. The latter wedged on her finger, she immersed herself in the creation of an expansive layette, for there was little else to do on these foggy November days in London, trapped as she was by her elephantine proportions. Still, she had managed to conceal her pregnancy for a long time, allowing her life to continue as normal. None of her friends knew even now, for they took her absence to be due to the yellow-brown fog that was so thick as to prevent one seeing further than three feet ahead, providing valid reason not to venture out. Any intrepid visitor was to be told by the maid that her mistress was in York where she went quite often. Kit had no wish to share this precious secret with any of them for, nice as they were, they would undoubtedly consider her mad for wanting to keep her baby and try to talk her out of it. Whatever the personal cost, she would allow no one to spoil this longed-for occasion.

With the birth imminent, Kit had thought it best to inform her family of the situation by letter. They had not as yet responded. Even the servants had only recently become aware of her condition; Kit knew this to be so by eavesdropping on their gossip, their ignorance stemming from the fact that Miss Kilmaster was normally robust, an extra stone in weight making no great impression. Naturally they had made no mention of this to her, though she would have to broach the subject with Dilly, who would be required to fetch the doctor when it was time.

That time came on Christmas Night. Had Kit's girth not prevented her from venturing into the outside world the severe winter most certainly would have. There was only one place to be on a night such as this. After her loneliest festive period ever, Kit had just heaved her massive body into bed, when to her horror she began to wet herself. Unwilling to cry out for assistance, she rolled out of bed and with great difficulty perched on a chamber pot until the trickle eased. Afterwards, though not entirely comfortable, she dragged the bottom sheet with its sodden patch from the mattress and replaced it with fresh linen, finally crawling back into bed.

However, she still felt most restless and when, in addition to her leaking bladder, she began to develop backache, she got out of bed and spent much of the night pacing about her room trying to relieve the discomfort. From time to time the pain would ebb, allowing her to get back into bed, but just when she was falling asleep the niggling ache would prod her into wakefulness again. By the early hours, she was so exhausted that she eventually drifted off, pain or no.

Accustomed to bringing her mistress a cup of tea in the mornings,

Dilly found Kit already out of bed, standing with one hand pressed to her arched back, her face contorted in torment. By now, its intensity increasing, Kit had understood the significance of the backache and after this latest spasm waned she ceased to groan, puffed out her cheeks in temporary relief and told Dilly to go and fetch the doctor straight away. She was feeling very frightened.

In view of the adequate reward he had been promised, the doctor and an accompanying midwife arrived quite promptly, his calm manner as he examined her and his advice that the birth would be an easy one if she had got this far on her own, helping to reduce Kit's terror.

So confident was he that the birth would pass without incident, that he went off to finish his breakfast leaving the still anxious mother-to-be in the midwife's capable hands, saying he would be back in ample time for the delivery.

Emitting one deep-throated growl after another, in accompaniment to the waves of torment that continued to grip her throughout the morning and well into the afternoon, Kit cursed him for a lying toad, cursed him and all men alike, her pain gradually building to the point where she feared she might be ripped apart, and she let out one agonized yell – at which she heard her baby cry.

In a rush of splitting flesh and blood and mucus, Beata Kilmaster was separated from the womb, seized by the ankles, smacked rudely on the bottom, then wrapped up in a parcel and given to her anxious weeping mother to hold.

Blinking back tears, overwhelmed by joy and relief, Kit fixed loving eyes to the perplexed navy-blue ones of her new-born, and hugged the tiny creature to her breast. At last, came her inward sigh of happiness. Bless the Lord, at last.

24

Being cooped up so long had made it something of an ordeal to re-enter the outside world. A fortnight after giving birth, feeling odd and vulnerable – in fact a different person altogether – Kit had watched through the open front door as Fred loaded her baggage into the carriage. Then, with Dilly's assistance, she had braced herself against the bitter cold and ice, and tottered down the path bearing her precious load.

A final kiss for the little maid who had been so supportive, and Kit was off, bound for King's Cross and home.

But where exactly was home? Kit stood in her cold and empty house in York, shushing her crying infant, surrounded by baggage and unsure what to do. The most sensible thing would be to light a fire, but Beata was famished and demanded feeding now. Wrapped in her tasselled carrying cape of deep blue wool, she was warm as toast, but her mother shivered upon bearing her breast to the frigid air and rocked back and forth as much to keep warm as to lull her baby.

After the child had gorged and had fallen asleep, a trickle of milk oozing from one corner of her rosebud mouth, Kit laid her down and went about setting a fire in the hearth. Yet even with the coal ignited and a cup of tea in her hand there was a miserable air about the room. Beneath her smart velvet outfit she felt isolated and somewhat frightened. There had been curious looks from her neighbours upon her arrival carrying a child. Questions would be asked, ones which Kit was not yet prepared for. She needed to be around people she knew. After finishing her tea, she put her hat and coat back on, scooped up her sleeping child and braved the elements to visit her sister.

Amelia, in her usual uniform of black dress, white apron and frilled cap, stood at the open door, staring at the dark blue bundle in her unmarried sister's arms for an extended moment before shaking herself from her trance, blushing furiously, and letting her in.

Greeting Albert and moving to the fire, Kit made comment on the terrible weather. Both her sister and brother-in-law replied in similar vein, then Amelia put the kettle on and told Kit to sit down.

When after a some minutes no comment had been made on her baby – not even to enquire over her name – Kit said, 'Well, this is Beata. Do you want to hold her?'

Acting self-consciously, hoping her employer would not come in, Amelia wiped her hands down her apron and came forward to peep inside the quilted silk hood with its feather trimming, before accepting the package.

Kit watched her sister's expression to try to gauge her feelings. Amelia's pale lips formed a smile as she presented the babe to her husband, yet there was a hint of disapproval, resentment even, and it was not long before she was returning Beata to her mother. Even with no actual statement that she should not have come here, this was the feeling conveyed.

For a second, tears burned Kit's eyes. So consumed was she with love for her child that she had hoped others would feel this way too. Was she to be made an outcast by her own? To take her mind off this hurt, she asked for news of the family. Were their brothers speaking to each other yet? Amelia answered in the negative. Owen never attended the monthly family get-togethers now. But then neither did she.

'I was going to ask you about that,' said Kit, shifting the babe in her arms. 'Will they all be there this Sunday, d'you know? It would be good if I could catch them together, save me having to pay them separate visits.'

Amelia looked at Albert, both thinking that it would have been kinder not to visit them at all – discretion had never been one of Kit's traits – but each found it rather embarrassing to say so. She told her sister that Gwen, Charity and Flora would probably be there.

'I thought I might stay for a while,' mused Kit. 'Just till I get used to being a mother.'

Amelia suffered a fresh shock of embarrassment. How could her sister have such blatant disregard for others' sensibilities?

'It's nice to have family nearby.' The instant she had said it, Kit wondered if she might have erred by this thoughtless implication that Amelia was not sufficient reason for her to stay in York.

But surprisingly there was no outburst. It appeared that Amelia was actually discouraging her from coming here. As confirmation of this, there was no invitation to tea and Kit was forced to visit the shops on her way home, for there was nothing at all in the house. Plus, there were more strange looks when she arrived home with her baby. After a disconsolate evening, Kit decided to lock up her premises and go to Ralph Royd the very next day, hoping for a better reception than the one she had had here.

On Saturday night, she made no big fuss of arriving, preferring to install herself at her own cottage before going to visit her family. As had been the case in York, the uninhabited cottage held no welcome, but there was plenty of coal and the thought of her kin nearby helped to warm the atmosphere.

Of course, news of her arrival had already been broadcast by the village gossips, and there was no hint of surprise when she turned at her brother's house on Sunday afternoon. There was, however, a great deal of discomfort on all sides as room was made for the unmarried mother and child to enter. It was almost like having to meet one of Owen's union deputations, so grim were the faces. Having been afraid of exposing her baby to tuberculosis, Kit was relieved when Sarah did not ask to hold her, but was hurt that none of the others did either, only her nieces and Probyn showing any form of gladness that Kit was home.

Once settled into a chair, she smiled around the gathering, taking in each face, noting the differences, especially in Sarah whose appearance had deteriorated rapidly, the glint gone from her hair and eyes.

Gwen, though, was still as dominant. 'I hope you've been churched, my girl?'

Kit replied that there had been no time for this – she had only been out and about for a couple of days.

Her eldest sister was firm. 'Well, make time, if you don't want to lose what little support you got.'

Sarah added to this, 'Heavens, my mother would never have allowed you over the threshold!'

Kit looked meek. 'I'll go to chapel tonight.'

'What, here?' Monty was not unpleasant, merely uneasy. 'How long do you intend to stay then, Kit?'

She replied that she hoped to remain in the village for a while, which produced disapproving mutters all round.

In the awkward silence, Kit caressed her precious burden and asked, 'Have you seen anything of our Owen?'

There were more black looks and murmurings to the effect that he no longer enjoyed contact with Monty's family. Monty himself looked none too happy at having to work underground again. Since being deposed from the respected role of check weighman he had endured much victimization for his part in breaking the strike. His tubs had been sent back down by the master's weighman as being made up by the addition of stones. Unable to prove sabotage, Monty had put his objection to the new check weighman who was meant to protect him, but had got nowhere. Only by stoicism in the face of such malevolence could he hope to emerge from this. Meanwhile, the price of coal was still depressed, he told Kit, and the money he brought home was set accordingly. Thank goodness there were not so many mouths to feed now.

Taking this as a hint, Kit said she would be happy to contribute. 'I've brought a nice bit of ham for tea, and some fruit and stuff.' She reached over with one arm and delved into her basket.

Monty cleared his lungs and spat on the fire. 'Well, just don't go throwing your money around expecting others to look after 'ee when it's all gone. You got a child to care for now.'

'She's extremely well provided for,' said Kit, thereby informing the listeners to her baby's sex.

'Well, that's one thing, I suppose,' replied Gwen. 'Poor thing ain't got much else going for her.'

Kit bowed her head.

'Eh, it's a queer do,' exclaimed Charity. 'Come on then, let's have a hold!' She almost seized the baby out of Kit's arms and hefted her as if to guess her weight, commenting that she was nowhere near as big as her mother had been.

Relieved that someone was at last taking notice, Kit gave a little laugh and said thank goodness.

'Oh, you're a canny little thing, aren't you?' Charity bestowed a welcoming smile on the baby. 'And look at all that red hair! Eh, who could hurt 'em?'

Tentatively, others joined the examination of Kit's child, Flora enquiring her name. Upon being told that she was called Beata, there were nods of remembrance for her namesake's untimely departure. Kit had feared Sarah might object, but she did not appear to mind this so much as that the child had been born at all, this coinciding with others' feelings.

After suitable inspection had been made of the babe, Monty was the one to make the announcement: 'Well now, Kit, you've done wrong, there's no pretending we're happy about it because we're not. But as we see it, it's no good taking it out on the child. What's done is done, and it's our duty to rally round.'

Gwen offered her own opinion. 'And I hope you know how lucky you are. Most in your position would find themselves on the street.'

Kit showed suitable gratitude. 'I'm sorry for all the trouble I've caused.'

Gwen was appeased. 'Well, at least having this little one has stopped you gadding round with all them fellas. Reckon they'll steer well clear of 'ee now. Right, we going to have our tea then?' She made as if to take charge.

'I can do it, thank you very much!' Frail as she looked, Sarah ordered Gwen out of the way, and sought to conclude the affair by a warning: 'Just don't expect others to be so tolerant, Kit. This place isn't the same as it used to be.'

Kit was to recognize this quite quickly during the following week. There were new faces in the community since the strike, many of the old ones having been exiled with Owen, others gone of their own accord. The former camaraderie that had pervaded the mining village, in which she herself had been embraced, was now thinly spread. Bad feeling persisted amongst the old order against those who had broken the strike and between their families. Unacquainted with Kit, all the newcomers saw was a brazen unmarried hussy with a child, and accordingly she was to suffer gross insults.

Upsetting as this was, Kit refused to let it drive her out until she was ready to go, disregarding the fact that the insults were extended to the family who supported her, thus demeaning them in the eyes of their neighbours. It had been bad enough when Kit had attracted gossip over her men friends. Now with a child as evidence of her lack of morals, the Kilmasters were a magnet for contempt.

But Monty refused to be bullied, saying that he had fought to keep this family together and would continue to do so, conveniently forgetting that one of its number had chosen to defect.

Whilst Monty never spoke about his younger brother at all, Kit had made an effort to visit Owen to see how he fared under his new employer. She found he and his family well and grateful for her intervention on his behalf, but he seemed most despondent about the plight of the union, which had lost much of its gains since the strike.

'And we all know who to blame for that!' he told Kit – though he refused even to mention Monty's name and warned his sister not to mention him either.

It was impossible, therefore, for Owen to attend his new niece's baptism. Sad though this made Kit, there was no lack of candidates when it came to choosing godparents, for despite their aversion to her illegitimacy everyone had come to love the little red-headed baby. Kit herself doted on the child, though she jokingly admitted that Beata had brought terrible weather with her. Three months after her birth, when the daffodils should have been in bloom, the earth was still invisible under a layer of snow and ice.

Another visiting day came around. Kit donned her fur-trimmed winter coat and hat, a sealskin boa and boots, and set off for her brother's house, pushing her new perambulator. Upon passing the Robin Hood's Well, she saw Peggo come out for a breath of fresh air and smiled a greeting, knowing it would not be rebuffed as had often been the case with others.

She caught his wince. 'Leg troubling you again, Mr Wilcox?'

He hid his discomfort to wander up close. 'It would if I let it. How's that there bairn o' yours?'

'She's a bit genny today.'

Though not really interested in babies, Peggo engaged Kit in conversation for a while, before allowing her to go on her way. 'Well, you'll be genny if tha doesn't watch that path round theer!' He nodded towards the incline. 'It's treacherous.'

Kit found this to be true and tried to stick to the route that was covered in ashes, but almost lost her footing several times before reaching the corner. There were a couple of women waiting outside the privy at the end of the street. Kit did not know them, but inclined her head in polite fashion as she tottered passed. Despite the fact that she was respectably dressed and pushed an expensive perambulator, the pair looked at her as though she were contaminated.

Accustomed as she was to this, Kit still found it hard to ignore and was glad to reach Monty's house, steering the vehicle inside too, for there was more room these days.

'Here, don't you be mucking up our Sarah's clean floor,' warned Gwen.

Provided with an old newspaper, Kit laid it under the ice-encrusted wheels. 'Where is she?'

'In the farleymelow.' Charity was frowning and rubbing her arms. 'Eh, put wood in t'oile, lass, we're nithered here.'

Kit shut the door. 'I didn't know if you'd make it today. Weather doesn't let up, does it?'

Gwen's miserable visage provided agreement. 'Wouldn't have bothered coming at all if I'd known I were gonna be offered shop bread for my tea – no, I'm only kidding, clot!' She made a pacific gesture at her brother. 'Monty were just telling us how Sarah ain't got the energy to bake her own now. Can't say I blame her really. She looks bad, don't she? I'd make some myself, but I know how uppity that'd make her.'

Catching Probyn's sullen disapproval which he shared with his sisters, Kit said the shop bread was quite nice. Gwen said Kit would think so, seeing as she bought it too – and she didn't even have the excuse of being ill.

'I don't know what's wrong with folk today,' sighed Gwen. 'The whole country's going to rack and ruin, what with all this unemployment and whatnot – still, it's not surprising with no leadership. One minute we're told it's the Liberals, next it's the Tories.' Amid great economic depression the Salisbury Government had resigned, Gladstone was once more at the helm. 'How can you expect folk to know how to behave when the politicians are behaving so badly. Speaking of which, how is that little girl o' yours today?'

As if in response a cry went up from the perambulator. Kit went to rock the handle in an attempt to calm Beata.

'I were just telling Peggo, she's been genny all morning.'

'What's genny?' Probyn was seated on the fender with one hand clamped to his sandy forelock in the hope that permanent pressure would eventually make it lay down.

'You should know that,' said his shivering mother, entering upon an icy blast. 'Considering you were the genniest baby of the lot.'

Charity answered her nephew. 'It's a bit like maungy.'

'Well, I've lived round here all me life,' remarked the youngster, 'and I've never heard that word.'

'Maungy, genny, or just downright miserable,' said Monty, 'can 'ee do sommat about that child o' yours, Kit?'

'She wants feeding,' said Flora, hovering in her annoyingly earnest fashion.

'She can't be hungry, I've just fed her.' Kit bent over the perambulator. 'She's usually so good – oh!' She jumped back as a fountain of vomit just missed her.

'That's right, all over the rug,' said Monty. 'It'll stink us out till Whitsun now.'

At their father's behest Wyn and Meredith rolled the soiled rug up and carried it to the scullery. But still the floor was spattered and Sarah went to fetch a mop and bucket. Monty lifted his feet off the ground for the mop to pass beneath, but otherwise did nothing to help.

For the first time Probyn really looked at his parents, and discovered that it irked him to watch his sick mother running around while his father never lifted a finger.

'I'll do it, Mam!' In manly fashion, he jumped up and took over the cleaning, resolving never to let his own wife carry such a burden.

Beata was screaming now. Dabbing at the baby's sticky clothes, an anxious Kit picked her up and held her at arm's length.

'She'll be all right now she's got rid of whatever it was,' soothed an unconcerned Gwen, barely shifting in her chair. 'You new mothers always worry too much.'

'But she looks as if she's in such pain,' breathed Kit, her troubled eyes running all over the grimacing child before cradling her gingerly.

Flora agreed. 'Poor mite, it's probably colic – that can be very painful. Give her some dill water.'

This was done, but with the baby continuing to scream, upsetting everyone around her, Kit decided to take her home. Sarah agreed with this decision, adding that Beata would probably want feeding again after vomiting all her last meal away. When the door closed on Kit a sigh of relief went up.

Normally, the motion of the perambulator would soothe the child immediately, but today Beata screamed and screamed all the way down the frozen street. Upset and flustered by the people who came to their windows to see what all the noise was about, Kit hurried as fast as the slippery surface would allow towards home.

Once there, she put the distressed child to her breast. Beata immediately suckled, moaning as she did so – but almost instantly she vomited again, and started to scream and twist about in agony. Panicking, Kit scrabbled to remove the pin from the child's napkin – perhaps it had mistakenly pierced flesh. But no. Laying a concerned hand upon the small white abdomen Kit found it as hard as a rock, and the napkin was clean. Perhaps that was the problem. She delivered another teaspoon of dill water, knocking the bottle over in her panic, but ignored it to pace up and down, the babe in her arms, trying to soothe her, shushing and rocking. Eventually, after long desperate minutes, the dill water appeared to work, the screaming died down and Beata went to sleep.

Relieved, but hardly daring to move for fear of waking her, Kit sat down gingerly, the babe still in her arms, and found that she was trembling.

A while later, though, Beata woke and instantaneously emitted a bloodcurdling screech. Kit tried to feed her, but again the same thing happened, the child violently regurgitating all she had swallowed, as if suddenly allergic to her mother. And the dreadful screams began all over again.

Terrified, Kit wrapped her up, laid her in the perambulator and rushed back to Savile Row. Her sisters were just making ready to leave, swathed in coats and mufflers. All gathered round at her entry, trying to calm her and tell her it was nothing serious – things always seemed worse than they were with babies.

On being told about the clean napkin, Gwen gave a knowing nod. 'Why, that'll be it then! Give her some liquorice powder and she'll be right as rain by morning.'

With Kit too upset to carry this out, Sarah administered the dose. Then, with the baby still making an awful din, the three elder sisters walked back along the icy path with Kit, waiting with her at home for a while until the crying ceased.

'There you are,' said Gwen with a comforting pat of Kit's arm. 'Told you that'd work. No time at all you'll have a stinky old nappy – and don't say we never give you aught.'

Concluding with a reassuring laugh, Gwen, Charity and Flora went on their way.

But before they were out of sight, the terrifying screams began again.

After a dreadful night in which the paroxysms of pain reappeared at frequent intervals, Beata's little face was by now haggard and pale, her belly tense and distended. All that had appeared in the napkin was bloodstained mucus. Knowing that something was seriously wrong, Kit wrapped the whimpering infant in a thick blanket, and hurried down to the doctor's vine-clad house, slipping and skidding on the icy road.

There were others in the waiting room as Kit and her wailing bundle came in and sat on one of the rush-bottomed chairs. Before long, mutters joined the coughs and sneezes.

'Listen to the poor little soul. It wants feeding. Why isn't she doing owt?'

Kit tried to ignore them, kissing and lulling her baby as best she could, her heart pounding.

Angered by the baby's pathetic cries a women took it upon herself to approach Kit. 'That bairn wants feeding!'

'She's been fed!' protested Kit, desperation in her voice, but was informed in no uncertain terms that her child was starving – one only had to look at her.

'You'd think with the size o' them udders she could feed an army,' announced the complainer to another.

'She's been fed! She's ill!' Near to tears, Kit turned her rage inwards, condemning herself for not coming sooner and urging the doctor to hurry.

Finally, Dr Ibbetson peered into the waiting room. Without waiting for permission Kit rushed past him into the surgery, where she unwrapped her pathetic bundle for his inspection.

'She can't keep anything down, Doctor! She hasn't had any nourishment since yesterday morning!'

As soon as he set eyes on the child, the doctor became grave, and

426

warned Kit not to administer any more purgatives. It would only intensify the child's agony.

'But she hasn't done her number twos!' Kit was frantic.

He rubbed his face, looking almost as tormented as she was. 'I'd say that's because of a mechanical fault, Kit,' he replied in sombre tone, unwilling to meet her eye. 'There's only one way to remedy this and that would be to open her up.'

Kit flinched. 'Can you do it then?'

He shook his head sadly. 'I've never attempted it on one so young. It would require a very skilled ma –'

'Get the best!' interrupted an agitated Kit. 'I can pay whatever he asks!'

Dr Ibbetson looked regretful, and said in the kindest tone that he could muster that Beata was now so weak that she would not survive such an operation even if it could be done. 'All I can do is give her something to ease her pain. I'd say it'll only be a matter of hours.'

Aghast, Kit collapsed against the back of the chair and stared into space, great breasts bursting with milk, her mind trying to cope with the nightmarish thought: that having endured the agony of labour, the months of waiting – the years of longing – there could surely be no greater cruelty than to watch one's beloved child starve to death.

25

'My breasts hurt,' murmured Kit, staring into empty space, but in a perverse kind of way enjoying the pain.

There was silence from those gathered in her cottage. Despite the merry flame in the hearth, the atmosphere was one of the utmost sadness. Receiving word via her brother, Charity had immediately come to offer comfort. Sarah, too, knew what it was like to lose a child and had chosen to sit with Kit through the day. Amelia had merely arrived for an impromptu visit and stumbled across the tragedy. The rest would be here for the funeral, but first there would have to be an inquest, to check that Beata had not been unlawfully killed, prolonging Kit's ordeal.

'I noticed someone advertising in the paper for a wet nurse in York,' Amelia gave quiet utterance. 'Maybe that would help – I mean, not just for the discomfort but to help you get over Beata, knowing you're helping another little baby.'

Kit said nothing.

'I suppose everything happens for a reason,' came the sighed addition.

This inane comment was one too many. 'What possible reason could there be for the death of a baby?'

Having never seen Kit so angry, they were shocked at her vehemence, Charity as usual acting as mediator. 'She were only trying to offer comfort, love.'

'I can do without that sort of comfort!'

Amelia tried to make amends. 'No, it was daft of me. I know how you feel –'

'How could you possibly know how I feel?' cried Kit.

'Taking it out on other people isn't going to help,' came Charity's sad response.

This made Kit even more furious. 'Don't you *ever* get angry at *anything*?'

Charity said nothing, just got up and brewed another pot of tea. Kit wrenched her furious eyes back to the fire.

'Don't pour one for me,' whispered a teary-eyed Amelia. 'I'll get off.' With a hesitant look at her younger sister, she murmured, 'I'll be back in a few days, Kit. Sorry.' Saying goodbye to the others, she swathed herself against the cold and left.

Kit was silent for a long time before apologizing to Charity. 'I didn't mean to take it out on you. It was just Amelia going on, when she doesn't know – can't know.'

Charity's sallow face gave gentle reproof. 'Then pity her rather than be angry, love. It isn't her fault. It isn't anybody's fault. Sometimes, there is no rhyme nor reason.'

This was not what Kit wanted to hear either. During another long silence, she continued to gaze into mid-air.

'My arms feel so empty.'

What could they say to that? Sarah and Charity exchanged cognitive glances, but remained silent.

There was the clip-clop of hoofs outside. Then a knock came at the door. Charity went to answer it. There had been many callers during the last twenty-four hours. This one, though, looked surprised upon finding her there.

Mr Popplewell had come to visit Kit, not knowing of her bereavement. When Charity showed him in, he was at a loss as to what to say, his toothy smile deserting him.

'I'll be off now.' Charity picked up her coat and told Kit she would return.

Sarah, too, began to rise from her fireside chair. An anxious Popplewell told them not to go on his account – for what on earth would he find to say to a bereft mother? The sick-looking individual wrapped a shawl round her head and answered that she had to go and get her husband's tea ready anyway. With that, Popplewell found himself alone with Kit.

'I'll just take t'hoss up to t'stables!' He disappeared for a time.

When he came back he was no more equipped to cope. 'I brought some scones for tea.'

'Grand,' murmured Kit. 'Is the weather still as bad out there?'

'Aye.' Popplewell came to sit near the fire, rubbing his hands and looking ill at ease. 'Roads are clear, though.'

'Good.' Kit stared into the fire. 'Shall I put kettle on?'

Popplewell sprang up. 'I'll do it.'

He buttered some scones too, but Kit didn't eat any of them.

'I don't know what to say, love,' he offered lamely.

'You can't say owt,' came the dull reply. 'Just sit there with me.'

It grew dark. The two figures by the fire hardly moved nor said a word, until finally Popplewell straightened his back and said, 'I suppose I'd better be off.'

Kit didn't take her eyes from the fire. 'Will you stay wi' me?'

'Aye, course I will,' he answered, and reverted to his former pose.

In the morning a note came through the door. Seated by the fire in her lifeless position, Kit ignored it, in her mind performing the daily ritual: bathing her baby, dressing and feeding her. Popplewell finished buttering the toast and handed a plate to Kit before going to pick the note up.

Unfolding the piece of paper, he found one word – 'Murderer'.

Startled, he screwed the letter up and threw it on the fire. 'Only rubbish,' he told her, then sat down to eat his breakfast.

Afterwards he told Kit that he would stay on for the inquest, which would be tomorrow, followed by the funeral in the afternoon, though he would have to leave her briefly to cook dinner for a client this evening. Seeing she had not touched her toast he tried to encourage her to eat but to no avail.

'Come and have a little walk and get some fresh air then,' he coaxed. 'It'll make time pass a bit quicker.'

In agreement, Kit cast her glazed eyes around for outdoor wear that was appropriate to mourning. She being partial to much brighter colours, the black bombazine dress she wore now had hung in her wardrobe for years and smelled of mothballs. Rummaging around, Popplewell found a dark coloured cape and, reaching up, laid it around her shoulders. Aptly enrobed against the icy air, she allowed him to escort her, not knowing or caring where they were going, allowing him to lead the way.

Popplewell chose the route that led through the village and towards the bridge over the Calder. A woman on Main Street had defied the cold to scrub her front doorstep, her hands red raw. Hearing the sound of their boots crunching against the remnants of ice on the path, she lifted her head to greet the passers-by, but on seeing Kit her expression changed and she returned her attention to the step, scrubbing more vigorously. Two more women emerged from a shop, chatting, but broke off their conversation as Kit and her shorter male companion walked past.

Popplewell overheard one of them whisper, 'Eh, she's got a nerve!' And he looked back sharply, but the culprit averted her face. Wondering whether Kit had heard, he glanced at her, but she showed no sign of having done so.

Feeling desperately sorry for her, he cracked a feeble joke. Wanting to feel normal, Kit gave an inappropriately loud laugh in response to something that was only slightly amusing.

'Listen to her!' accused one of the gossips. 'The cold-hearted cat. Can't even wait till the poor little mite's buried and she's gallivanting with fellas.'

'It's plain to see why t'poor bairn died! Her mother – if you can call her a mother – were too bothered about getting dolled up and enjoying herself to feed it. She wants hanging!'

There were further such comments as Kit and Popplewell returned later, having walked for miles. Again, he looked up to try and measure the effect they had on her, but Kit appeared to be in a daze.

She was to remain in such a stupor throughout the day, refusing all efforts to feed her, but existing on copious amounts of tea. At mid-afternoon, Mr Popplewell said he would have to go and prepare his ingredients for this evening's dinner party, but he would be back in order to see she did not spend the night alone.

Monty looked in on his way home from the pit and asked if she would like to come and eat tea with his family. Kit refused.

When darkness fell around five o'clock, she summoned enough energy to draw her curtains, then returned to her chair by the fire.

For hours there was only silence, and the occasional hiss of gas from a lump of coal.

Then came a voice from outside. At first Kit assumed it was Mr Popplewell and did not move from her chair.

'Come out, bitch!'

Her skin prickled. She cocked her head to listen, but still did not rise.

431

'Out! Out! Out!'

Stumbling from her chair she pulled aside the curtains and peered out into the darkness. There was no streetlamp nearby. Initially she could see nothing but the glow of a lantern, but eventually she could just make out the shape of several figures. Immediately she dropped the curtain in fear. What did they want of her?

'Come out here!' A series of bangs on her door made her jump.

Stricken with anger as well as fear, she hurried to open it. There were about a dozen men and women present, one of them holding a straw effigy on a pole.

'What do you want? Go away!'

A lump of ice hit her in the face. Thinking it was glass, for it hurt as much, Kit gave a cry and examined her hands for signs of blood.

'That's for the babby!'

'Burn her!'

With this, someone set light to the effigy. Kit saw to her horror that it was meant to represent her, its hair fashioned from red wool and its chest puffed out like her own bosom. Terrified, she slammed the door and pulled the bolt across, leaning against it, fearing they might try to break it down. A roar went up from outside, the glare from the fire visible through her curtains. There was chanting, people marching up and down outside her door, hurling insults through her letterbox. Pressing her hands over her ears Kit sank to the floor, cowering.

Then came the sound of a horse and trap and another voice – Mr Popplewell!

'Leave her alone! You frigging bastards, I'll –'

Kit heard his voice cut off by a blow. There were scuffles and thuds and grunts of pain.

Jumping up, Kit looked out of the window to see her friend being attacked from several fronts. Without thought, she hauled back the bolt and dashed outside to help him – but immediately someone grabbed her hair and pulled her back and forth, hands groped her body, nipping, ripping, scratching, a man grasped her round the waist and pretended to copulate with her. In a hail of blows Popplewell dropped to the floor and fell victim to his attackers' boots. In the flickering light of the burning effigy Kit saw the vicious kick being aimed at him and let out a scream as it made sickening contact. She screamed and screamed.

Then, amid the pandemonium, others came running, dragging the attackers aside and raining blows upon them. Kit saw Peggo's crutch make impact with someone's head and fell him like an ox before, in the confusion, she was knocked over, still screaming and crying as the attackers were routed and those still conscious disappeared into the night.

Kinder hands took charge then, steered Kit into her cottage, carried the bleeding Popplewell in after her. Deeply distressed and sobbing, Kit could hardly catch her breath.

''Sall right, flower, it's all right!' came Marion's deep voice. 'They've gone, the buggers.' She grabbed a dishcloth and went to tend Popplewell, who was just coming round, though his face was discoloured and gashed. 'Look, your friend's waking up. He'll soon mend.'

Peggo went outside to pick up his crutch on the floor, having only brought it to use as a weapon. 'The drunken sods, I heard 'em chuntering about thee earlier. If I'd known what they were up to . . . !' He hovered over Kit, looking disturbed, for she was obviously in no fit state to be left.

Popplewell was sitting up now, wavy hair awry. Suddenly aware who it was that was tending him, he took the cloth from Marion and held it to his own head whilst at the same time enquiring after his friend.

Well equipped to cope with physical violence but not a woman's grief, the three faces adopted a look of uncertainty over the banshee wails that now rent the air. Kit had just come to realize that her baby was truly dead.

How ironic thought Kit, when indeed she was capable of any rational thought, that the agony of grief was just like that of giving birth; swamping her in great uncontrollable waves, pushing her to the very brink of the precipice, before mercifully subsiding into a bearable numbness.

After the inquest at the Robin Hood's Well, the village gossips had been silenced by the awful truth and were ashamed, though it was inevitable that a few of the groundless rumours would persist, the more wicked among them holding the view that Kit had brought it on herself. Paradoxically, the family that had gathered round to shield her from these calumnies were now driving her insane with their own well-meant platitudes – not to mention their squabbles. Owen had turned up at the funeral, but all

433

attempts at conciliation between the two brothers failed. Kit was angered that they extended such childish nonsense to her child's entombment, was seized by the urgent need to get away – but where? Wherever she went, nothing could take her mind off this terrible sadness. The mere glimpse of a baby drew tears, and to hear its cry was veritable torture. She who had always derived joy from the news that another great-nephew or -niece was expected, now received it like a slap in the face upon hearing about Rhoda's latest addition. Never a slave to melancholy, Kit found her grief so intense that it threatened to destroy her. Finally she understood how Mrs Dolphin could try to kill herself.

Irony was everywhere, in the way that the same mob who attacked her could tolerate being served their ale by a man in a dress; in the new-born lambs that were dug unharmed from twenty feet of snow. She must get away.

Swept up on another wave of desolation, and temporarily robbed of her wits, Kit found herself on a late-night train to London. Though quite how she had got there she was not sure. She had no luggage, not even a brush and comb, and carried only one thought: Valentine should be told that their baby had died.

The train journeyed through darkness. By the time Kit arrived in the metropolis it was morning. Wandering out of the station into a cold and filthy mist, she stared at the row of cabs. Through the fog of grief, a moment of sentience prevailed. What foolhardiness had brought her here? It had been a stupid notion to think that he would care.

But what was she to do now? Overwhelmed by heartache, she rearranged her black fur boa under her chin, ignored the offered transport and wandered along the damp road.

Never had she seen London so quiet, just the swish of bristles from a street-cleaner's brush and the sporadic call of 'Milko!' Few others were about, and most of them vagrants. One of the forlorn creatures approached her, the fingers of his outstretched hand blue with cold, as was his nose. Frightened, Kit reached into her pocket and gave him threepence, then walked on.

There was another call of 'Milko!' A man in a shabby coat, scuffed boots and a felt hat emerged from a side street pushing a handcart with two large wheels at the back, a small one at the front and his name emblazoned on the side. Balanced on the cart was a big metal churn with a scoop dangling from the side of it, that clanked as he jarred over the cobbles.

Wandering aimlessly, Kit felt a rush of acid burn her stomach, and for the first time made a conscious effort to take care of herself. Wishing she had stopped the milkman, she made do with a cup of tea from a shabby cafe, warming her hands around the steaming vessel and gazing out of the window as the streets slowly began to come alive.

She would have sat there all day had the owner not broken her trance by attempting to make friendly conversation. Then, reluctant to answer questions, Kit drained her cup and went out into the cold.

Shop shutters came up in a clattering of iron bars. The traffic began to increase, with cabs and carriages, omnibuses taking folk to work. Porters rushed to and fro with loaded barrows. Kit had no idea where her feet were taking her. Sometimes, upon recognizing her surroundings, she would make a detour, wandering in and out of shops, before becoming lost again.

The sun broke through the pall. By late morning the temperature had risen considerably, though it did nothing to clear the fog in Kit's mind. Travelling in and out of awareness, she meandered along Regent Street amid bakers, stationers, opticians, grocers, music shops, shawl shops, jewellers, French glove shops, perfumiers, confectioners, milliners and parasol makers. Shaken momentarily from her trance by the sight of a funeral warehouse all draped in black, the accompanying monument shop displaying urns and marble tablets and obelisks, she turned away and hurried into a drapers, adhering to this less upsetting route for a while, finally to emerge into Piccadilly.

The clock above Fortnum and Mason struck twelve, the mechanical Mr Fortnum turning to perform a bow to his partner. Outside a bookshop, footmen and carriages waited for their masters. Crossing the road, Kit walked on.

Along the railings of Green Park a lone artist exhibited his paintings. Behind him, dirty sheep grazed, intermingling with knots of unemployed men. Kit entered the park and wandered along a path lined with black cast-iron lamp standards. Eventually, though, having reached the other side, she became conscious that she was drifting too far and made a conscious decision to follow the road back round into Piccadilly.

435

The artist was still there, seated on a piece of matting on the pavement, his back against the railings. Kit stood for a moment gazing at his exhibits.

'Weather's pickin' up,' he said, in an accent that was familiar.

'Beautiful Barnsley,' murmured Kit, unsmiling.

'It is indeed.' The shabby young man nodded and squinted up at her from beneath a lock of dark hair. 'From there yourself, are you?'

She shook her head.

Intrigued by this tall and rather hefty but splendidly attired woman, the artist's eyes ran her entire length. Her sable toque bore three erect feathers of a similar hue, adding to her statuesque appearance. Her disconsolate blue eyes and the black mourning garb forbade the need to ask what was amiss, yet he felt the urge to know more. 'Is there anything I can do?'

Kit hoisted her shoulders.

He studied the woman for a moment longer, then, still curious, he stood with an announcement: 'I'm off for some dinner – do you want to join me? That's if you've nowt better to do.'

Kit sighed. 'I don't know what I'm doing, really. I came to see someone, but it was a mistake.'

'Then come home wi' me!' He started to gather his paintings. 'I've had enough for today. I'm Philip, by the way.'

Ignoring the fact that he was a total stranger, Kit went with him.

He took her to a red-brick tenement, six storeys high and one of four such buildings that enclosed a square of grass. Despite it being not far from Mayfair, there was a working class atmosphere about the area, though the construction was modern.

Noticing a lavatory at the end of the hallway, Kit asked if she could use it. Philip told her he would go ahead and gave her the number of his flat on the third floor.

When, moments later, she tapped at his door, Kit noticed the one across the hallway was ajar and a middle-aged woman was scowling at her.

'Take no notice of her,' said Philip as he let her in. 'She just likes to keep tally – now, give us your hat and coat. There's some bread and cheese, sit yourself down and tuck in.'

The room smelled of artist's materials. It might have spoiled Kit's appetite had she possessed one in the first place. Forcing herself to eat, she asked how long he had been in London and in turn gave information about herself, though nothing too personal.

'Were you thinking of staying?' he enquired.

Kit found it hard to answer. 'I don't know.'

His dark brown eyes showed concern. 'Have you got anywhere to stay?'

Kit shook her head. It was a lie. Any one of a dozen people would have put her up – Frances would have welcomed her with open arms. But she did not want to see any of them. She had come here to lose herself.

At this point, a woman entered without knocking. Crust in hand, Kit blushed and looked at her companion, hoping that he could explain her presence to his wife.

'You're early,' was all he said.

The woman – now obviously not his wife after all – apologized for spoiling his lunch.

'That's all right.' Philip polished off the last of his bread and cheese, washing it down with a mouthful of tea. 'You get ready and I'll be with you in a minute.'

Turning to Kit, he asked, 'You don't mind, do you?'

Bewildered, Kit shook her head, not knowing what it was that she was meant to be granting permission to.

'You can sit and talk to me while I work.' He went to the window where stood an easel and began to prepare his palette. Only then did Kit understand that he was going to paint the woman and, cup in hand, changed her seat for one that gave a better vantage point of the artist.

'Kit, this is Julia.' Philip introduced the sitter, who had just emerged from the bedroom wearing a robe.

The two women exchanged smiling nods, then Julia took off her robe and lay naked on a couch. At one time Kit would have been shocked, now she simply watched dispassionately.

For the next couple of hours she sat in quiet observation, responding to the occasional question from artist or sitter, but otherwise volunteering nothing. The sadness ebbed and flowed.

Eventually Julia put on her clothes and went home. Philip told Kit to put the kettle on whilst he cleaned his brushes.

'I got you here under false pretences. I were going to ask you before Julia came in. Will you let me paint you?'

Kit dealt him a quick glance. 'Oh, no.'

'I don't mean with nowt on.' He smiled and rubbed a pungent-smelling rag up and down his fingers. 'It's just – well, I've never in me life seen anybody look as sad as you do.'

Her lips parted – but just then a banging came at the door, making her start.

Philip went to answer it.

It was the caretaker. 'I've got a complaint from the lady across the landing!'

'Well, that's what you get from consorting with loose women,' said Philip. 'I hear there's ointment that'll clear it up.'

'Don't get clever! She says there's funny goings-on here – lots of women rolling up at all times of the day. I just thought to warn you I'm going to report it to the landlord.' He stalked off.

'The nosy old witch, what's it got to do with her?' Philip noticed the women's door was open a crack and shouted at her. 'Mind your own business!'

The woman scuttled like a spider across the landing, glimpsed Kit through the open door and shouted down the stairs to the caretaker, 'He's got one in there now!'

'If I have twenty in here it's nowt to do with thee! I pay my rent.'

'From immoral earnings!' screeched the woman.

'I'm not standing for this!' Philip grabbed a pot containing paint and before the woman could run away he upturned it over her head.

Kit broke into hysterical laughter – then almost instantaneously burst into tears. Slamming the door, Philip hurried over to console her, knowing that something terrible must have happened to this woman.

Finally, the awful sobbing stopped. Philip would have let her go, but Kit held fast to him, pressing him more tightly than ever to her aching bosom. How could he deny her the comfort she sought?

26

'She hasn't long to go, God love her,' said Mrs Kelly, walking up the street alongside another neighbour towards Sarah, who sat outside her front door, imbibing the sunshine. After the long harsh winter Yorkshire was enjoying a heat wave.

'Aye, she looks like death warmed up,' came the muttered agreement. 'Hasn't cleaned her step for ages.'

Upon drawing closer, their mouths converted to smiles. 'Lovely day, Mrs Kilmaster! You're looking better.'

Handkerchief in hand, Sarah replied that she wasn't so bad and passed a few moments in conversation until Mrs Kelly went inside her own house and the other woman walked on, allowing her to return to her thoughts.

Sarah had found herself thinking a lot about Kit lately. It wasn't simply because she had disappeared four months ago without telling anyone where she was going. She thought about her all the time, even in her sleep. No morning dawned without a nightmare going before it – not that her waking moments were any easier – filled with images of Kit as a little girl who had just lost her parents, yearning affection from her brother's wife who dealt her naught but unkindness.

Her thoughts were interrupted as Mrs Kelly's youngest came out to play in the street. The infant crouched in the gutter and began to gather tiny stones which he meticulously inserted one by one through a hole in a drain cover. Sarah watched him play, comparing him to her own youngest. With a shock she realized that Probyn was almost a man. A rush of mortality overcame her. What had happened to her own youth? She was forty-seven, she was dying, and she had never had a youth. Tears pricked her eyes.

439

But the tears were not merely for herself. Through the mist she reviewed her past life. She had been thinking about that a lot lately too. Things she had done. People she had hurt. If only she could meet those people now and make amends.

For no apparent reason, the little boy jumped to his feet and galloped indoors. Squinting, Sarah's eyes followed him and in doing so glimpsed another figure coming up the street, seeing not a tall robust young woman but a vulnerable three-year-old child.

For the first time in her life, Kit saw her sister-in-law's face light up in a smile of welcome. It rather took her by surprise. She continued along the row, waiting for the smile to fade, but it didn't.

'Kit, it's good to see you back – and you're looking a lot better, *cariad*.'

Wishing she could return the compliment, Kit smiled back. 'I feel it. Sorry I didn't let you know where I was. I just had to get away.'

Sarah reached out and patted the other's arm that was still encased in mourning garb, this gesture telling Kit that she had no need to explain, Sarah knew that feeling well. Nor was there any need to say Kit would never get over the death of her child, would just learn to survive the best she could, to get on with life. The glance they exchanged was sufficient to convey this knowledge.

Kit thought then how much worse it must have been for Sarah to lose her adult daughter, having steered Beata through the dangerous years of childhood, only to suffer the cruellest of partings.

Aghast at how ill the other looked, Kit asked if she could get her anything.

'Yes, you can make a pot of tea and bring it out here with another chair. It's a shame to waste the sunshine. Doing my old bones a world of good, it is. Pity there's nothing more to look at than that wall though.' She indicated the boundary of the graveyard, wherein lay both their daughters. Before her sister-in-law disappeared, she added, 'Hang on, Kit. While you're waiting for the kettle to boil, there's a bottle on the sideboard, fetch that too, will you? And a spoon.'

Kit went to put the kettle on and waited for it to boil, in the meantime placing another chair besides that of Sarah, then going to fetch the required spoon and bottle, which she found contained a laudanum mixture. 'Is the pain very bad?' she asked softly.

'Bearable, with this.' Sarah pulled the spoon from her mouth and handed it back to Kit, thanking her.

In time Kit sat down, handing her sister-in-law one of the cups she carried. Acceptance was delayed by a bout of coughing.

'Roland died while you were away.' Sarah dabbed at her lips with a rag and took possession of the cup, referring to Flora's husband. 'An aneurysm, it was – he collapsed at work.'

'Oh, God!' Kit's brow puckered. 'I'll have to go and visit t'poor lass.'

'Don't bother, she'll be here on Sunday.'

Kit nodded. 'How's she coping?'

'Well, you just get on with it, don't you?' Her sister-in-law balanced the cup of tea on her lap and tilted her pallid face to the sun. 'So, where've you been all this while?'

'London.' Kit did likewise with her cup and saucer, waiting for the tea to cool.

'With . . . ?'

'No, he's not interested in me any more. No, I just stayed with a friend.' Kit sipped at the tea. It was too hot. She stared thoughtfully at the churchyard wall that was blackened by coal dust, recalling the months she had spent with Philip, wondering who had bought his various depictions of her. 'Well, a sort of friend. But after a while I decided it was time to come home.' She threw a guarded glance at Sarah. 'You're not going to be too pleased when I tell you.'

Sarah turned her emaciated head. The look in Kit's eyes told all. 'Oh, Kit, you're not . . . again?'

Kit gave a guilty nod.

Sarah gasped, then coughed into her rag. 'Is it something they put in the water down there? Every time you go down to London you come back in an interesting condition. Oh well, it's no use me ranting on, there's nothing we can do about it now. Your brother will be none too pleased though.'

The lack of condemnation from this quarter was totally unexpected. 'I thought you'd be really furious.'

Sarah gave a weak shrug. ''Twould be a waste of breath, wouldn't it?' She swallowed a mouthful of tea, then sat for a while thinking. After a long silence, she asked pensively, 'Did you love either of them?'

Taken aback, Kit confessed. 'No, not really. It just happened.'

'It must be wonderful mustn't it? To have had one great love in your life. What I'd give to have a mad passionate affair before I die.' Sarah's black eyes burned intensely.

Kit blushed, amazed, not least because Sarah's comment related to her own brother. How would Monty feel if he knew this?

'If I had my time again I might choose to be irresponsible once in a while.' One side of Sarah's mouth was tweaked into a wistful smile. 'But there's not much chance of that, is there?'

Kit looked at the haggard face with its blue circles beneath the eyes, and was imbued with deep guilt for ruining this woman's life.

'Don't look so glum,' teased Sarah. 'It's not your fault.'

'Well, it is in a way. If you hadn't had us to look after —'

'I might have been run over by a train. Who knows what might have been? There's no one to blame.' There was once, came the private thought, but not any more. There came a time when one had to stop blaming others. 'As you said yourself, it just happened.' She finished her tea. 'So, what do you intend to do?'

Kit said she was not entirely sure, it all depended on the family's reaction. 'I'd like to have the baby here, but I don't want to be a constant embarrassment to you.'

Sarah gave a snort. 'I couldn't care less what people say. Stay if you want.'

Though thankful for this unexpected ally, Kit said she would wait until Monty had been consulted. He might feel very differently.

Monty did feel differently. One mistake was allowable; two, it seemed, were unforgivable. He had also been nurturing another complaint in Kit's absence. Probyn had let slip that his aunt had taken him to Spain. Had Kit not sprung this on them now, Monty would not have been so hard on her for she had suffered greatly, but exasperated beyond endurance he subjected her to a vociferous scolding, not only for endangering his son on such a voyage but for showing Probyn a life that he could never hope to emulate. 'And now this! Isn't it enough that 'ee shamed us once? My God, girl, 'ee'd better do some praying 'cause you'll never be redeemed.'

Gwen seized her turn. 'I've no sympathy for you either, Kit!' She mopped her perspiring brow. 'It's downright irresponsible. Don't you ever think of anybody but yourself?'

'I didn't do it on purpose.' With the younger family members out enjoying the sunshine, Kit suffered the full brunt of her siblings' disapproval.

'Is that right? Then why wouldn't you let us get rid of all those baby things after Beata died? You knew exactly what you were going to do.'

'If you mean I'm trying to replace her, that's just cruel and plain silly!' Gone were the days when Kit would sit and listen to such nonsense. 'I'm going home.' This she did, before they caught the glint of tears. How could anyone imagine that she could substitute one child for another? As if to illustrate the anathema of this, she did not go directly home but went instead to the graveyard where she laid flowers upon her baby's resting place, silently weeping in the bright afternoon.

Back at Savile Row, Gwen was unrepentant. 'Bain't no good pretending we're glad about her behaviour else she'll think we condone it.'

Monty shook his head. 'Oh, don't mistake my silence for approval! I'm just beaten for words.'

Flora never disagreed with Gwen, her contribution emerging from a black mourning bonnet. 'You'd think she would've known better after the first time. Hasn't she ever heard of the word no?'

Normally so benevolent, Charity sided with the popular view. 'And there's poor Amelia and Albert would love a child, and our Kit churning them out like sausages.'

'Well, I reckon it's time we intervened,' decided Gwen.

'In what way?' Sarah coughed with great effort into a handkerchief. 'Show her the door?'

'My goodness, no! Every time she goes out of it she comes back expecting. No, I'd as soon lock her up. I just mean we have to make her see sense. What sort of a life is this baby going to have? You saw the way folk treated Kit when they thought she'd let the first one die. It's not fair on anybody, least of all the child.'

'Well, things have calmed down now,' said Sarah, wiping her pale lips. 'I doubt she'll have to face that sort of violence again – not that folk will be any kinder.'

'Exactly, which is why I think we ought to persuade Kit to hand the baby over to Amelia,' said Gwen, looking pleased with herself. 'That'd solve everyone's problem.'

Sarah looked at Monty, both showing doubt. 'I don't think Kit would be amenable to that.'

'Maybe not at the moment. But, as I said, if we can talk some sense into her, make her see what she's doing is wicked and it would be in the interests of the child to give it two parents . . .'

Monty gave a thoughtful nod. 'Mm, you got a point.'

'She won't budge,' replied his wife with certainty.

'Why're you sticking up for her all of a sudden?' asked Monty. 'She never did anything right in your eyes before.'

Sarah's magnanimity did not extend to her husband, who seemed intent on irritating her more than ever these days. 'I'm not saying she's right or wrong. I'm just saying you'll have your work cut out, and don't expect me to waste my breath persuading her. Now, is there anybody else's life you'd like to put to rights before we have tea?'

'Sit there,' commanded Gwen, 'I'll make it.'

'No, you won't.' Gravely ill as she felt, Sarah dragged herself from the chair. 'Long as I'm alive, home rule still applies in this house.'

'Oh, don't get our Gwen on that subject,' wailed Charity. 'She bent my ear all the way here.' Parliament had been dissolved over the issue, making its sitting one of the shortest in Victoria's reign.

'I can't see why they don't just give it to 'em,' said Gwen, referring to the Irish, 'they're nothing but trouble anyway. We'd be better off without them.'

Monty opposed this view. 'Do that, start breaking Britain up into bits, and where will it stop? They'd all want their little corner of earth then. Next thing you know, that'd be the end of our Empire.'

Gwen said she supposed her brother was right. 'I wonder what Her Majesty makes of it all. Our newspaper said they're trying to persuade her to come out of hiding for her Golden Jubilee next year, says it'll help all these unemployed that're going round causing trouble and ruining the country. I don't see how. Can't say I blame her for staying indoors, I don't know what the world's coming to.'

'I wonder if she'll get up to Leeds,' mused Charity. 'I'd love to go and see her.'

'There's one thing certain,' added Gwen, 'I'll bet she don't have so much trouble from her family as we have. Wonder what Amelia will say when she hears about Kit?'

'It's not a good idea to tell her about your plan just yet,' advised Charity, the others agreeing. 'Don't want to give poor lass false hope.'

Gwen was blasé. 'Won't be false hope. We got five whole months before it's born. I'm sure if we all band together we can make Kit see sense.'

Nothing made sense to Kit at the moment. She had two houses and over a thousand pounds in the bank, but with no idea of direction she might as well be a pauper. The knowledge that most of her confusion stemmed from losing Beata did nothing to make the way ahead any easier. To be sure the new child would restore some stability to her life, but robbed of such purpose once, and taunted by the fortune-teller's prophecy, she had no reason to doubt that it could happen again. How could she make plans when she did not know how long her baby would live? With such funds at her disposal she had no need to work, yet how else was she to make time pass? One thing was sure: her days of dalliance were over. Her only bout of socializing took place with Mr Popplewell or within her own family. Kit feared she would never recoup her zest for fun, though she tried to present herself as the same old Aunt Kit to her nephews and nieces, disallowing them to glimpse the fear and uncertainty in her heart.

During the school holidays, she was to organize the kind of trips and picnics that had thrilled in the past, though with only three of her brothers' children still of school age, the picnics were quieter affairs than in the old days, and at thirteen, Probyn showed signs that he would much rather be mixing with his peers.

He had even turned down his aunt's most recent invitation to accompany her to Castleford that morning, which rather hurt her – though she did not say.

However, conscience must have got the better of him, for when Kit returned from her trip he was waiting in the sunshine outside the Robin Hood's Well to meet the omnibus, an inflated pig's bladder in his hands. Accepting her invitation to a cup of tea and a bun, he walked alongside her, dribbling the pig's bladder with his boots.

'Will you be going to your house in York again soon, Aunt?' came his casual enquiry. 'Only, if you like, I could come with you.'

Kit smiled, fully aware that it was not her house that so attracted him but the fact that York was a garrison town. 'Well, I was thinking of putting it up for let.' Sensing his disappointment, she added, 'But it'll want a good bottoming first.'

'I'll help you! Can we go tomorrow?'

Even in the knowledge that there was ulterior motive for his voluntary services, Kit was pleased to have his company. Under that manly facade there remained the little boy who had gained her lasting affection. 'Tomorrow? That's a bit sooner than I intended. Not much fun cleaning – are you sure you wouldn't rather be with your pals?'

'Oh, they're off to Leeds tomo–' he broke off, looking guilty.

Kit laughed and said tomorrow would be suitable for her. She had been plucking up the courage to go and visit Amelia anyway, to let her know about the baby.

As luck would have it, their arrival at York station coincided with that of a contingent of soldiers, the platform a mass of scarlet uniforms. Though inconvenienced herself, Kit smiled fondly at her nephew's awe-struck face and suggested they sit on a bench and watch for a while as they wouldn't be able to fight their way through till the soldiers had departed.

Probyn was happy to do so, his mouth agape and his eyes taking in every detail.

After a while, he said thoughtfully, 'You know me father?'

'Is it that fella with the ginger hair?' asked Kit. 'I think I've met him.'

'D'you think you can persuade him to let me go in t'army?'

'Your dad never places great value on anything I have to say, love.' Kit had tried to intervene before. Monty had replied that no son of his was joining the army. 'But he's not an ogre. I know he won't force you to go down the pit if you can get something better.'

'Where else is there to work round our way? Apart from shops.' Probyn heaved a sigh – then was suddenly alert as the soldiers were mustered. 'Eh, they're off! Come on, Aunt.' He jumped up and dragged at her arm.

'You're not expecting me to march alongside them?' At her nephew's eager straining face she fished into her bag and gave him a key. 'Here, you go on ahead! I'll call in on your Aunt Amelia and see you at home later.' Making use of this opportunity to visit her sister alone, she smiled to herself at the sight of Probyn marching out of the station after the colourful troop, then took a hansom cab to the Mount.

As yet ignorant of Kit's expectant state, Amelia treated her kindly, though made no reference to her sister's recent loss lest it be construed as a thoughtless remark, but allowed the sympathy to show in her eyes. The current hot weather had forced Kit to emerge from her heavy mourning attire. The grey cotton dress was subtle enough, but Amelia deemed the straw hat too flamboyant, piled with huge loops of ribbon and white daisies that spilled over from the brim and dangled in a strand down the back. Still, at least she could be grateful it was flowers and not a vulture or one of Kit's usual monstrosities.

Accepting a glass of lemonade, Kit sat at the table and said she had brought their nephew with her but had left him following the soldiers through town. 'He only wanted me to march alongside! I've been accused of being many things, but never a camp follower.' She smiled. 'Poor lad, he's desperate to go in the army.'

'Is he coming here afterwards?' Amelia sat opposite.

'No, I'll bring him to see you after we've done our cleaning. I'm putting the house up for let. I don't want to sell it, but it seems daft allowing it to stand empty.'

'Why don't you come and live in it, then? Isn't that what you bought it for?'

'Yes, but things have changed since then.' Kit sighed and gazed into her glass. 'Truth is, I don't really know where I want to be at the moment.'

Amelia gave an understanding nod, in a similar quandary herself. Her employers were planning to move to America early next year and had asked their butler and cook to accompany them, but it was a big move. Amelia's initial reaction had been to turn it down. She was about to convey this to her sister but was prevented by the appearance of Albert.

Kit looked up as her brother-in-law came in and smiled a greeting. 'Hello, Albert. Is she still giving you a regular beating?'

'Eeh, she's a tyrant,' he joked, then handed over the letter that had arrived with the afternoon post, and leaned on the table. 'Have you told Kit our news?'

Amelia said she had just been going to. She looked at the writing on the envelope. 'Oh, it's from our Gwen.' She began to tear it open.

Kit forestalled her. 'I think she's writing to tell you about me.'

Amelia paused and dealt her sister an inquisitive glance.

Kit glanced ruefully at Albert. 'I'm having another.'

Whilst her husband merely whistled through his teeth, it was all Amelia could do to prevent herself from crying out. She simply stared at Kit, the letter unopened in her hand.

'That's why I didn't bring Probe. I wanted to let you know, and he's such an earwig, nothing gets by him.'

Somewhat dazed, Amelia merely nodded, then stared thoughtfully at the letter without making any move to open it, running finger and thumb around the edge of the envelope.

'I'll be staying at Ralph Royd for the birth. Sarah's been marvellous about it. I expected her to go mad.'

'Yes, well, I suppose she's got enough to worry her,' murmured Amelia, her own news totally forgotten.

Feeling uncomfortable, Kit drained her glass and began to rise. Albert moved back – she always made him feel like a dwarf. 'Well, I'd better go see if Probe got home all right. I'll fetch him to see you before we go back.' Saying goodbye, she left Amelia seated at the table.

When Albert returned from seeing Kit to the door, his wife was able to vent her fury. 'I could throttle her! I really could. It's not fair, Bertie. There's us who'd give that child all our devotion and our Kit just has 'em willy-nilly. I mean, what does she want with a baby when all she wants to do is go gallivanting? She doesn't deserve it.' And her face crumpled in torment.

Albert pulled a handkerchief from his butler's suit and used it to dab at her tears. 'Aw, don't, love. Don't let it upset you.'

'It does upset me!'

'I know.' He bent over to put his arm round her shoulders and squeezed. 'It does me an' all.'

'Aw, I knew you minded more than you let on!' Amelia bawled.

'No – I only meant it upsets me that she upsets you!' Looking aggrieved, Albert tried to comfort his wife. 'You're the most important person in the world to me. I'm not bothered that we don't have children, I just feel sorry that you can't have what you want.'

'I have got what I want, I've got you. It's just – oh, what does she have to come here telling us for? As if we're interested.' Amelia gave a huge sniff, then wiped her red eyes and finally blew her nose. 'I suppose I'll have to hear about it all over again in this.' She brandished the letter.

Albert patted her. 'You open it and I'll make a pot of tea.'

Sniffing, Amelia tore open the letter and immediately let out a humourless laugh. 'I knew it! The whole of the first page is devoted to Kit.' Tossing aside the offending page, she read on, and slowly her expression changed to one of interest.

Aware of her metamorphosis, Albert did not question her but proceeded to set out the cups and saucers, patiently awaiting his own curiosity to be assuaged.

Amelia's blue eyes finally looked up. They were wide with excitement. 'She says they're all going to try and persuade Kit to let us adopt the baby!'

Faced with that starry gaze, Albert very quickly told his wife not to pin her hopes on this – after all, Kit had mentioned nothing.

'No, but if it were possible, what would you say?'

Albert frowned and rubbed his hands together, not a sign of indecision but a gesture of annoyance that Gwen had put this idea into his wife's head. 'If it would make you happy, I'd say yes, of course – but even if Kit does agree she could change her mind.'

'Don't mention the move to America – not to any of them!'

He guessed what was in her mind. 'Please, dear, don't bank on it before you hear it from the horse's mouth.'

Amelia nodded and bit her lip, but could not quite manage to chase that gleam of excitement from her eye. And now that the idea had been planted, she began to make rapid plans of her own.

Kit was to remain in total ignorance of these machinations, unaware too that her only ally against the conspirators was the person who had always seemed to resent her most.

'Leave the poor girl alone!' Sarah railed at them after listening to another Sunday afternoon of plotting before their victim arrived. 'Hasn't she suffered enough?'

'We're only trying to do what's best,' challenged Gwen.

'Well, I'm sick of bloody hearing it!' In agonizing pain, Sarah broke into a fit of coughing, and stabbed a finger at the sideboard, indicating that she needed relief. Monty jumped up and poured out the laudanum, though even after this was administered it did not ease her temper. 'You're always trying to run people's lives,' she told Gwen, once able to speak. 'And you're not doing it in my kitchen, so don't let me hear another word.'

Gwen opened her mouth to object, but just then Kit came in and all reference to her pregnancy ceased. Sarah gave warm if breathless greeting, her pain subsiding.

Bemused by her sister-in-law's change of attitude, Kit was nevertheless grateful for it and in a rush of compassion said: 'I've been thinking on my way here: you've never been back to Wales have you? Would you like to? For a holiday?'

There followed a snort of derision, showing a glimpse of the old Sarah. 'If I had the money for a holiday, I wouldn't waste it on going to see them!'

'No, I meant I'd pay for you to go,' said Kit.

The refusal was pleasant. 'Oh, don't go throwing your money around on me, you might need it!'

'I've more than enough. Let me give you a holiday. It'll do you a power of good.' Kit knew as well as anyone in the room that nothing could bring about a cure.

Reclining against a pile of cushions, Sarah voiced what the rest of them were thinking. 'I doubt I even have the energy to get on a train.' Her haggard face turned pensive. 'I wouldn't mind a day trip to the seaside, though.'

Kit seized on the idea. 'Aye! Whilst this lovely weather lasts – where do you want to go, Scarborough? I'll go and book the tickets for next Saturday. We'll all go!'

Sarah raised a weak laugh. 'Sometimes, I really admire you, Kit.'

Gwen rolled her eyes at Charity as Kit warmed to her theme. 'I'll get the carrier to take us to the station and then it'll be straight on a train so you don't have to walk anywhere – I'll even hire a donkey to take you along the sands!'

Probyn shared a grin with his sisters. Monty sighed at Kit's impetuous gesture, but he too was secretly pleased.

Kit turned to her sisters. 'Are you coming with us? My treat.'

After brief discussion they agreed, and thanked her for the kind offer.

'It's very generous of you, Kit,' concluded Sarah, then gave an oblique glance at her other sisters-in-law. 'Though I can't help but think some people don't deserve it.'

The tone of her voice puzzled Kit, who looked around for evidence of some previous bad feeling but found none. Though looking back on the afternoon that evening she decided there had been a definite air of tension.

There was no such feeling on the trip to Scarborough, everyone seemingly eager to make it a day to remember for poor Sarah. Kit had made her sister-in-law a new dress for her outing and had bought her a matching parasol. Beneath its shade, Sarah reclined on a rug on the sand, eating ice cream with her grown-up children, chatting amicably to Gwen and bestowing smiles on the husband who had become almost a stranger over the past years, the result being that Monty appeared to shed a decade off his age. Kit, too, had not felt so good in a long time, revelling in the sun and the sky and the sea, and the baby who wriggled full of life inside her. Never had the Kilmasters enjoyed such a harmonious day.

For the rest of the country, tension was to remain high throughout the summer as groups of unemployed converged on London, gathering in its parks and squares, holding huge demonstrations, the continuing heat wave adding to the stress. Still crippled from the strike, Ralph Royd was relatively unaffected, though the monotonously high temperature had a similar affect on its inhabitants, provoking more bad tempers, more arguments, more fights than usual.

The claustrophobic weather played havoc with the invalid, stealing into her tubercular lungs and threatening asphyxiation. Sarah felt as if her windpipe had been crammed with towels, each breath a massive effort. To alleviate her suffocating, sweat-drenched nights, she had taken to imbibing a concoction of brandy, ether and laudanum. But her face belied the effectiveness of this. She had refused the attention of a doctor, asking what was the point. But, unable to stand by any longer and watch her sister-in-law wasting away – not least because it brought back memories of another such death – Kit paid for the physician to come, begging him to show compassion and hasten this long, lingering expiry. Morphine was administered. Merciful sleep came. Prayers were said. The family was prepared for death. Yet, Sarah tarried . . .

The days dragged by, the high temperature continuing until finally, mercifully, the explosive atmosphere was dissipated in an overnight thunderstorm.

Thankful for the purified air, Kit was none the less at a loss as to how to stem the torrent that greeted her as she came down to the kitchen that morning. The spouting had overflowed, sending rain cascading down her walls and under the back door. She was making futile attempts to mop up the puddle when a drenched Probyn arrived, bringing yet more water into her cottage.

'Oh, thank goodness!' She clutched her swollen abdomen. 'Grab those towels and help me get this water under control, it's like Niagara Falls.'

Oddly subdued, Probyn did as he was told and launched into a vigorous mopping-up operation, telling his aunt to stand aside and taking complete charge until every drop of water was transferred to the towels which were thrown in the sink, and then going outside to rectify the blockage and prevent any more coming in.

Having achieved this, he stood in his aunt's kitchen, breathing heavily and red in the face.

'What would I do without you?' Kit praised him. 'Get your wet jacket off and sit down.'

This he did, leaning on his knees and staring at the floor, whilst rubbing his hands in an agitated manner.

'Have you had your breakfast? I'll get you some.'

'Me mam's died,' said Probyn, not lifting his head.

'Aw, love . . .' Kit reached out but the boy held up an outstretched hand to stave off any gesture that might make him cry.

Resting her hands on the bulge under her dress, Kit asked softly, 'Was it in the night?'

He nodded, still not looking at her. 'Me dad doesn't know what to do. Can you come?'

Kit said that of course she would. Without so much as a glass of water passing her lips, she grabbed her umbrella and escorted Probyn back to Savile Row.

Monty wondered as his youngest sister delivered her misty-eyed con-dolence, what she would think of him if she could read his mind. What sort of a man was he to feel relief at his wife's death? Oh yes, he felt anguish – and guilt that whilst his wife had drowned on her own blood he had slept on – and all the other more fitting emotions, but these were overridden by an overwhelming surge of freedom. Ashamed, he flayed himself with an index of her qualities – Sarah had been a good woman, her children were devastated by her death, he was devastated too, but underlying his genuine display of sorrow was a glimmer of hope. His miserable marriage was at an end. He was glad to replace the burden of melancholy with that of grief, however painful, for at least the grief would be finite.

One would think that Gwen had been waiting for this moment all her life, thought Kit watching her sister take over Sarah's kitchen after the funeral, telling everyone what to do and how to do it. Monty didn't say much, but then he never did. The house was crammed with black figures, spouses and offspring lurking in every corner like spiders. Owen and his family were conspicuous by their absence, having sneaked in at the back of the chapel but slipped out again and were on their way back to Garborough Junction before anyone could invite them to the house.

Having made sure that everyone had a cup of tea, Gwen sat down herself – in Sarah's chair. 'Well, that's three gone this year. Wonder who'll be next?'

Flora gave a heavy sigh, as did her daughters.

'I hope it'll be a wedding that brings us together next,' opined Charity. 'Set a date yet, Wyn?' The latter had been courting for some months.

'She's only nineteen,' intervened Monty.

'Our Alice was only nineteen when she wed,' objected a puffy-eyed Wyn, who had indeed been contemplating her nuptials. 'So was Rhoda.'

'Things were different then,' argued her father. 'You can't leave poor Merry to look after us on her own.'

Noting the look of alarm that passed between Merry and Wyn, Kit fully understood their concern. With Ethel devoted to her career of prison wardress, and Rhoda and Alice married, the others were going to be trapped as their father's slaves if they didn't receive help. 'It's not really fair to penalize either of them. Young lasses –'

'What?' Her brother was abnormally pugnacious. 'Have a right to go running about all over the place having children willy-nilly?'

Kit blushed – everyone else looked embarrassed too. Though the youngsters were aware of their aunt's pregnancy now it was never mentioned in front of them. 'I only meant they're entitled to get married if they want to be,' she said quietly.

'Some of us aren't so lucky to have a choice.' retorted Monty. 'Some of us put duty first.'

Kit had never argued with her brother. She fell silent.

Seizing this opening, Gwen said, 'Maybe you should take a leaf out of Monty's book, Kit. Ever considered how it might feel to be the child of an unwed mother?'

Thoroughly shocked by this unexpected question, Kit was unable to answer.

'Can't be very nice, can it, being called all sorts o' names? Well, you should know all about that, but then it's different for an adult than for a child. An adult chooses their path, a child doesn't.'

Kit found her voice, made a sad little protest. 'I didn't choose –'

'I know, you said, it just happened.' Gwen's face was cynical. 'Wouldn't it be nice to make a conscious decision for once in your life, Kit? I mean, given the chance, would you knowingly subject a little child to the sort of thing you suffered at the hands of that mob?'

'No, but –'

'Would any of us here put a child through that?'

Wearing a mask of incomprehension – how could Gwen be so cruel, and at such a time? – Kit looked around the assemblage, heard the murmurs of agreement as all sided with her elder sister. 'But that was because they thought –'

'You know what Thought did? Followed a muck cart and thought it were a wedding. It was a dreadful incident! And who's to say it won't happen again? You know what folk round here are like. Wouldn't you prefer to make a fresh start somewhere else and give your child a fresh start too?'

Kit was even more affected. 'You want me to go away?'

'Not for the reasons you think! Not because you're an embarrassment. I think we all genuinely want you to be happy, Kit, and we want that poor child to be happy too. When I say give it a fresh start, I mean with a proper family – somebody who's married.'

Kit felt as if someone had stabbed her. 'Have it adopted? Never! It's all I ever wan–' She broke off in tears.

Though the atmosphere was uncomfortable, especially amongst Probyn and the other young ones, who felt sorry for their favourite aunt, there were some who thought to comfort her, Charity for one. But Kit was to suffer additional shock upon discovering that Charity held the same view. 'We're not saying it to be cruel, love, but we want you to consider it very carefully. Think of the baby.'

'I am! I can't! Who's to say it would have any better life with strangers?'

'Kit, we're not talking about a stranger,' warbled Flora. 'It'll be with your own flesh and blood.'

At first bewildered, Kit noticed the look of eager expectancy on Amelia's face, the way she was gripping Albert's hand, the look of urgency in his own eyes as he willed Kit to say yes. She knew then that they had all been plotting this behind her back.

'You couldn't hope for a better mother than your sister,' coaxed Charity. 'And the beauty of it is you'd still be able to see the baby whenever you want.'

Amelia dared not blink.

'It was very remiss of us not to persuade you to do the sensible thing with Beata,' said Gwen. 'Looking back, we could have saved you a lot of pain.'

'I wanted her!' wept Kit.

'We all know that.' Gwen was genuinely sympathetic. 'But, Kit, you can't always have what you want, especially if it's going to make others suffer.'

'It's the kindest thing to do, lass,' urged Charity.

Her own fate hanging by this umbilical thread, Amelia still dared not say a word.

Kit sobbed for a while, then blew her nose and sat gripping her handkerchief in her hands, looking around at the doleful gathering, only then remembering that they were at a funeral. It was obvious that Gwen was the ringleader but equally obvious from others' expressions that she had support. Kit locked bloodshot eyes with Monty, trying to assess his view of all this. Her brother's affection had always been important to her, if he was looking at her like this she must take it seriously. Without a word being said between them she read his opinion: he had always forfeited his own needs in favour of his siblings, had done everything to keep the family together at the price of his own happiness. Sarah too had made tremendous sacrifices of her own and had paid for it with premature death. Kit had only ever considered herself. Now she must behave with maturity and think what was best for the child.

Her face a picture of anguish, she rose suddenly and made for the door. 'I have to have time to think!'

Gwen opened her mouth to offer more persuasion but Amelia's hand shot out and grabbed her wrist, urging her to leave well alone. She looked worriedly at Albert, thankful that they had not revealed their plans about going to America, for that would surely have jeopardized the outcome.

As the door closed on Kit, the atmosphere relaxed. In the burst of animated conversation that followed, an annoyed Probyn had to remind others that his mother had just died. What irked him most was that his father seemed to have forgotten too.

Even by Christmas they had still not managed to solicit a positive response from Kit, though they continued their gentle persuasion. Gwen's bullying might be disguised in a velvet glove, but Kit felt under extreme pressure, most of it from a personal source. One moment she had thought to conquer her selfishness and hand over her baby to Amelia, the next she was filled with an unbearable ache to keep it. She was vulnerable and weepy, thoroughly divest of any festive spirit as every day brought her closer to that terrible decision.

Bumping into Probyn this Saturday on the corner by the post office, she felt the urgent need for young company, and asked if he would like to come and have a cup of tea with her.

His nose red from cold, Probyn gave anxious apology and backed away as he spoke, in a hurry it seemed. 'I'd love to Aunt, but I have to go watch 'em kill Smirthwaite's pig.'

'Oh well, you'll have to go then.' There was sadness in her smile.

Probyn continued his backwards walk, the sound of porcine squeals making him even more hasty. 'I'll come and see you later, though!'

Kit gave a smiling nod as her nephew pelted away, but knew there would be something more important to occupy him later.

Snow fell. The grocery windows were decorated with Valencias, muscatels, currants, lemon peel and angelica. Confectioners vied with each other for the best plum cakes and sweets. Butchers displayed gigantic sides of beef and pork and birds galore. In total contrast to previous years Kit spent the period in quiet contemplation, deriving what little joy she could from the child whilst it was still safe inside her. Yet its playful kicking served only to remind her of the trial to come.

The year of political controversy and personal tragedy came to an end. January brought firm resolution – Kit would do right by everyone, would give her baby up and start afresh – then just as quickly she reneged. How could she bear to part with it? You'll be able see it, they persuaded. Yes, but in someone else's arms.

The snow continued to pile up. At least it kept them from her door. Not that it really mattered; with or without them the argument went on inside her head.

Hoping she still had weeks left to go, Kit was shocked to awake one winter morning to experience birth pangs. Her first instinct was to ignore them, pretend this wasn't happening. Rising, she went about the business of the day.

Alas, within three hours the pains had become intense enough to make her groan. Prodded by fear, panic, but most of all anguish, she went outside and looked for someone to act as messenger. Catching sight of a boy shifting snow, she called out and dispatched him to the midwife's house. There was no point in sending him to inform Monty; Sarah was no longer there and neither of his girls was qualified to attend a birth. Kit would just have to cope on her own.

The birth was quick. A mere five hours later Kit held her baby, another daughter, in her arms. Mrs Carlton, the midwife, asked if she would like anyone informed. It seemed callous to leave this newly delivered mother alone with nothing more than a cup of tea. Propped up with pillows, Kit gazed down at the black-haired baby, such a serene little thing. 'Not for now,' she murmured. 'Somebody'll be round soon enough.'

Left alone, she lowered her face to inhale the new-born's scent, pressing gentle lips to its cheek, luxuriating in the sense of creation.

Too soon, her reverie was disturbed. The babe was not an hour old when a knock came at the door. To ignore it was to achieve nothing, for the person entered unbidden and called from the foot of the stairs, 'You up there, Kit?'

Loath to reply, Kit nevertheless allowed her brother to come up.

Cap in hand, his face red from the cold, Monty approached her bed, showing no surprise at the new-born. 'Somebody saw Mrs Carlton with her bag.' He stood for a while looking down.

Kit sighed, 'I suppose they'll all have to know now.'

Monty sat on the edge of the bed. 'It'll be a while afore they come – the roads are blocked.' Noting the flicker of relief, he sought to deter her from complacency. 'Have you decided what you're going to do, then?'

Kit shook her head, her mouth trembling.

'Bain't wise to leave it too long, Kit, nor to get too attached to her. The decision will have to be made eventually.'

'But not now,' said Kit firmly.

Monty did not push the matter. 'Shall I send Wyn over to stay and look after you?'

Kit said if he could manage without Wyn then she would appreciate the help. After he had gone, she settled back down to enjoy these precious moments.

A week was to pass before news reached the outside world. A week filled with joy and sorrow and indecision, during which Kit had wept at the drop of a hat. She was still feeling depressed and unsafe when Gwen and Amelia descended on her, the former having made it her duty to inform the other.

Initially they made great play of asking how she was, and paying only scant notice of the baby. Low as she felt, Kit knew where their priority lay.

'I've called her Serena.'

Amelia looked as if she had been slapped over the face. She turned to Gwen who, for once in her life, was speechless.

'I think it suits her,' added Kit. 'She's such a quiet little thing – ever so good.' She bestowed a lingering kiss to the sleeping babe in her arms.

Then without further warning she held out the bundle to Amelia.

Nonplussed, her sister took possession, still unsure whether this would only be temporary.

Immediately, Kit wanted to rescind the gesture, but fought the urge. Never before had she bowed to popular opinion, had always done as she wanted without a thought of the consequences for others, but at last looking at life through her daughter's eyes she knew that the sacrifice must be made.

'There's a cheque for five hundred pounds on the sideboard,' stammered Kit. 'It's for her schooling and to give her as good a life as possible – don't argue, I want the best for her. Take all her things with you when you go, the pram, everything. I couldn't stand seeing it here.' Her voice cracked. 'I don't know how I'm going to bear it, hearing her call you Mother.'

Amelia did not notice Gwen's triumphant smile, aware only of the weight of her own responsibility, the child in her arms. 'You won't have to.' Trembling both with excitement and for her sister's pain, she tried to convey the news in as kind a manner as possible. 'Our employers are moving to America and they want us to go too. It'll be a new start for all of us.'

Kit stared at Gwen, who obviously knew nothing about this either.

'It's all been very rushed.' Amelia blushed at the lie. 'But I think it'll be better all round, don't you?'

Gwen was quick to recover from her shock and sought to persuade Kit of the benefits. 'Wounds heal a lot better if it's a clean cut – better if it's over quick.' She steered Amelia towards the door. 'Best go now. We don't want to prolong it for Kit, I'll get the rest of the stuff.'

It wasn't meant to be like this! The mother's hands reached out as if to retrieve her child, but after a hasty word of thanks Amelia spirited the bundle from the room, from the house, from Kit's life.

27

Perhaps they were right about a new beginning, thought Kit when the crying stopped. Perhaps she should sell up and move to another place. But to what effect? Wherever she lived, every morning when she opened her eyes her first thought would be for her lost babies.

This morning was just the same. Kit lay there for a moment, trying to gather the enthusiasm to get out of bed. Serena was in America now and had been for almost three months. Kit had not held her baby since the day she had handed her over to Amelia, though she had received a photograph of Serena with her adoptive parents marking the start of their new life. Since the parting she had tried to continue as normal, occupying herself with sewing and had coped quite well considering. But it was very difficult to rub shoulders with the kin who had made her give Serena up. Perhaps it would be a good idea to minimize contact with them and start afresh where no one knew her.

A knock came at the door, forcing her to rise and go downstairs. Accepting a couple of letters from the postman, she saw that neither of them came from America and left them unopened on the table whilst she dressed.

After breakfast she examined the contents of the envelopes, one of which was from Mr Popplewell, inviting her to come for dinner next week; Kit gave a tight little smile then laid it aside and opened the other which came from the Local Vaccination Officer, asking why she had not yet protected the child whose birth had been registered three months ago.

The pain welled up as fresh as ever. Kit screwed the letter into a ball and threw it on the fire, then burst into tears. Still sobbing, she reached for her coat and went outside. The snow had gone and the spring was comparatively mild, though it had been raining overnight and the bare brown hedgerows were draped in jewelled gossamer.

She set off at a brisk pace, without direction, just walking, walking, walking for miles. Heading north, she tramped for a couple of hours, came to a village she had not visited before and, without stopping, came out at the other side. It began to drizzle. Without a hat her auburn hair turned to frizz. Her legs and feet ached.

Across field and ford, she stumbled. The muscles in her thighs throbbed at the uphill journey. The rain eased. The sun came out, dazzling her. Finally, exhausted, she paused on a hillside and stared out across a deep ravine at the town clustered on the limestone ridge opposite. In the sunlight, the wet roofs of the houses glistened like ruby and agate. A renovated church tower glowed as butter. One would never guess that the earth beneath was honeycombed with mines. From here, the vernal landscape resembled the face of a sleeping baby.

Staggering, slithering and sliding, her skirts covered in mud, Kit descended towards the valley and came to rest against a wooden fence, clinging to its upper rail as if her life depended on it.

Unaware of time, she stood in a trance looking across the lower valley. Just then, a fox ran across her view, mouth panting. Without stirring, Kit watched it hasten across the field and disappear beneath a hedge. Shortly afterwards, a pack of baying hounds came streaming over a wall and onwards after the scent, followed by the hunt resplendent in pink and black. Kit gazed dispassionately at the scene.

'It's a grand sight.'

Startled, she turned to find a man at her side, admiring the same view. Unusually, she had to look up at the speaker. He was much taller than herself, a huge man of heavy build with a wide leather belt emphasizing his girth.

Too consumed by grief to pay much heed to his appearance, she reverted her gaze to the field, only now actually seeing what was taking place before her, acutely aware of how the fox, the pursued, the victim, must feel. She, who had tasted the savagery of the human animal now began to question the rights of man over lesser beings.

'Would you care to be hounded so cruelly?' Though her blue eyes were directed straight ahead she felt him look at her sharply.

His reply was dismissive. 'They don't feel fear like we do,' he said with the supreme arrogance of man.

'How do you know? Have you ever been a fox?'

'Well, I never looked at it like that. You can't invest a dumb animal with human emotions.'

'What are human emotions?' she demanded, still without looking at him.

He could not answer.

'I thought man was meant to be kind to his fellow creatures.'

His expression was not so friendly now. 'You wouldn't be so sentimental if you'd seen a chicken coop after old Reynard's paid a visit.'

'Then you should take better care of guarding your chickens.'

The man said huffily that his chickens were his business and strode away. Kit stood there for a while watching the pursuit, thinking back to Lord Garborough's treatment of his hounds, which was no better than that of the fox they hunted. Once they had outlived their usefulness they were dispatched. A bit like the servants. On consideration, that was not quite fair. She could find no complaint as to the way she had been treated, with courtesy and kindness, but now she recognized that they were only being good to her because it was the duty of superior beings to be charitable to those beneath them. She began to share Owen's view of the ruling class. Just because they were richer or of nobler birth, should they be granted the power of life and death over others?

The hunt vanished into the distance. Coming to her senses, Kit looked around, somewhat bewildered. She had no idea where she was. Had she not upset the man he could have set her on the right road. Retracing her steps, she paused at the top of the rise to take another look at the encircling countryside. It was undoubtedly beautiful. Now that the air no longer held the baying of hounds it was very peaceful too. The warm red roofs of the village held invitation. In that instant Kit made up her mind to sell up and move here – though she would rent rather than buy, for if she had learned anything from past impulsive purchases it was that she could not seem to stay in one place for long. Returning to the highway, she consulted a signpost, then took the road home.

One thing bothered her about leaving Ralph Royd: her widowed brother's welfare.

462

But, to her great surprise, when she divulged her news on the following Sunday morning after chapel, Monty seemed unconcerned. He even went so far as to say it was a good idea – they must all make new lives for themselves some time. Noting the look of slight disapproval that passed between the two young women and Probyn, Kit felt that there was something much deeper to this last remark, but was too apathetic to try to guess what it might be. Grateful for the lack of obstacle, she began to make plans for her future.

Remembering only that her journey had taken her northwards, Kit set off one Saturday morning to look for the place she had found so appealing. Alas, she had not guessed it was so far away. When, hours later, she came to the ridge where she had rested before and spotted the village across the ravine, she saw that there were many more miles yet to travel. Dispirited, she sat down to rest. Then to her great good fortune she saw a cart rolling along towards her. Hurrying back to the road, she hailed its driver who agreed to give her a lift to her destination.

However, on its way there, the cart was to pass through another village, one too secluded for her to have seen it before, a most picturesque and charming place surrounded by undulated wooded slopes, its walls softened by moss and lichen. A place of peace. Along the main street a beck tumbled over a bed of pebbles; as the cart followed its gurgling course Kit was to see that it emptied into a pond where ducks and water-hens dabbled. Nearby was an ancient inn and a small green. At the end of the street, just as the cart was about to leave the village, it passed a stone house, solid and square, its front garden crammed with spring flowers and a board that said 'To Let'.

It was as if this was meant to be. Acting on impulse, Kit asked the man to stop and, thanking him, got down from the cart.

Whilst the prospective tenant was still at the gate running her gaze over the roof and walls, a gentleman appeared at the door and came to meet her. Finding him most polite, Kit accepted his invitation to enter. It took but two minutes to examine the interior to know that she would like to live here. Kit tentatively enquired the rent, which was rather steep but, too embarrassed to haggle and fearful that someone else would beat her to it, she agreed to a twelve-month contract. Over a pot of tea she learned that the lessor and his wife would be going abroad in June which, Kit told them, would give her ample time to sell her own property. The fact that they were leaving behind their furniture caused no problem, for this house would easily accommodate her own belongings too.

After shaking hands on the contract, she made ready to embark on the long journey home. Discovering that his well-dressed tenant was about to set off on foot, the man said he could not allow such a thing and went to fetch his horse and trap.

When he proposed to convey her all the way home, Kit made only feeble argument and was secretly glad that he chose not to heed it. Given more time in which to stare, she drew quiet pleasure from the journey. Leaves were beginning to burst from the stark branches that formed a network over the lane, the verges to either side yielding a predominance of gold.

Another vehicle was trundling up the lane towards them. The man driving Kit steered his more nimble horse and trap to one side to allow the other to advance, crushing daffodils and dandelions in the process. As the heavy cart horse clip-clopped past, its driver raised his hat and called a greeting to the other.

'Good afternoon, Mr Langley – much obliged!'

'Good afternoon to you, Farmer Treasure!'

With this brief exchange the vehicles went their separate ways. Kit thought she recognized the farmer from somewhere but it was not until she was well on the way home that she remembered him as the man who had watched the hunt with her.

The landscape began to change, pocked-marked by industry. Upon reaching Ralph Royd in the late afternoon Kit thanked the man who had brought her and asked him in for a cup of tea. However, to her acute embarrassment she found that the caddie was empty – she had become rather absent-minded of late. Chuckling, Mr Langley told her not to worry and said he hoped they would be in touch soon apropos the house. Feeling silly, Kit waved him off, then instead of going inside, went to the grocer's to purchase some tea, intending also to visit Monty and give him the news.

As luck would have it, she caught sight of her brother's red hair through the grocery store window and so was able to tackle two things at once.

There was no one but Monty in the shop apart from Mrs Carr a miner's widow who stood in for the owner a few hours every day. Kit's brother was leaning on the counter when she opened the door, engaged in some intimate chat with the widow, but at the jingle of the bell he sprang upright as if caught out. Upon seeing his sister he blushed scarlet.

'Oh, hello, Kit! We were just taking about this new substitute for butter that's come on the market – what was it you called it, Mrs Carr?'

'Oleomargarine.' The widow seemed similarly perturbed at being interrupted, or so it appeared to Kit. A neat and attractive dark-eyed woman, she was picking stuff up and laying it down as if affecting to tidy up. 'I had a taste of it when I went to Leeds – dreadful stuff! Like putting axle grease on your bread.'

Monty gave a nervous laugh, his face appearing even more red in contrast to his white starched collar. 'Well, I'll be sticking to butter thank you very much. What about you, Kit?'

Pretending not to have noticed their odd behaviour, nor the fact that her brother was wearing his best suit, Kit fumbled in her purse. 'I'll never remember the name of it. I can't even remember to keep my tea caddie stocked.' She told them of her recent embarrassment of inviting someone in for tea and finding none.

Mrs Carr was charitable as she weighed the tea, its scent permeating the shop. 'Well, you've had a bad time of it lately, dear, haven't you?'

In subdued tone, Kit agreed but voiced the hope that she was in line for improvement as she had rented a house in the lovely village of Soke. 'I was just coming to tell you all about it, as a matter of fact,' she told her brother.

Monty said he was pleased for her, though he would be sorry to see her go.

The tea weighed, Mrs Carr handed it over and took the money. Kit smiled at each in turn. 'Well, I'll be off. Have you got what you came in for, Mont?'

Monty seemed reluctant to accompany her, but with his bag already filled with groceries he had no excuse to remain. He opened the door for his sister. Even in her preoccupied frame of mind, Kit noticed the fleeting smile he dealt Mrs Carr on his way out.

Nothing much was said at first as the two tall figures made their way along Main Street. Then Monty blurted, 'There's nothing going on!'

'I never said there was,' replied Kit.

'I just wanted a bit of company.'

'She's a nice woman,' said Kit.

'I know Sarah's been gone less than a year. I'd never do anything –'

'Monty, it's your business,' interrupted his sister.

'There's no business to speak of! I was just talking, that's all.'

Kit shrugged and, to save her brother further embarrassment, changed the subject to her new home. 'Well, anyway, I've got a proposition for you. Don't say no before you've thought about it. To save me the bother of selling my cottage,' it had to sound as if he would be doing her a favour, 'could I sign the deeds over to you?'

Monty was astonished. 'But, you'll need the money to buy another house!'

'No, I won't.' Kit's voice held no excitement for the subject. 'I've got a house in York if I want it, and more than enough money in the bank. I'm too confused to bother with any of it at the moment. You've got children, I haven't. There doesn't seem any point in a spinster having all this property – and you'd no longer be beholden to the coal company for your living accommodation.'

Monty was interested. 'I'd pay you rent!'

'Why? I've told you, I don't need it.' Kit looked weary. 'I just want to get rid of the place. It holds too many memories for me. Please, I haven't got the strength for an argument.'

Her brother, though obviously taken aback by the offer, finally agreed. 'Won't I have something to tell them at home! You've really taken me by surprise, Kit.'

In more ways than one, thought his sister, who now understood the look that had passed between Wyn, Merry and Probyn. They knew of Mrs Carr and disapproved.

Family politics were of no further concern to Kit. Within six weeks she had moved into her new abode, far from Ralph Royd and its slag heaps. For a time the hard work of making the place into a home, sewing curtains and painting walls took her mind off her loss, though every night when she closed her eyes the memories came back and every morning she awoke to her babies' faces.

Once the work was done there followed a period of deep unrest. Kit neither knew nor cared what lay ahead. She had considered offering her talents as a seamstress to the inhabitants of her new village but as yet had done nothing about it, too apathetic to do anything but sit in her back garden and ponder. The summer garden was a sight to behold with roses in abundance, an explosion of pink and scarlet and yellow, but it held no real joy. Kit wondered as she sat here this afternoon, dolefully staring at nothing in particular, if she would ever be happy again.

Through the perimeter hedge came the sound of amateur musicians and children's laughter; there were celebrations for the Queen's Golden Jubilee. It would have been the perfect opportunity to meet her neighbours, but then they would ask questions which Kit had no inclination to answer.

All of a sudden, something fell out of a bush and plopped to the ground next to her bench. Looking down, Kit saw that it was a fledgeling sparrow. Hardly able to keep its balance, it looked up at her, cheeping plaintively. From the depths of her despair Kit summoned a smile that this tiny wild creature ventured so close to her foot. Yet she was to marvel even more when the fledgeling spread its wings and jumped on to her lap, hopping from one knee to the other whilst maintaining its pitiful cheep as if trying to communicate. For seconds it kept up this strange behaviour, looking into her face and cheeping, before eventually flying back into its bush. Moved, Kit sat there pondering for a time, her spirits gradually lifting and imbuing her with the knowledge that however bad her experience had been she would come through this eventually.

'Ah, here she is!'

Probyn's voice made her jump. She clutched her chest, laughing and showing pleasure at seeing her nephew who, due to distance, did not get to visit as often as both would like. Unusually, he was accompanied by one of his sisters.

'Wyn, this is a bonus!' Kit rose from the bench. 'You've just arrived at the right time. I was sitting here feeling sorry for meself.' She beckoned them indoors. 'Come on, it's a bit hot out here now. How did you get here? Have you had your dinner?'

Wyn said yes they had packed sandwiches and had been lucky enough to cadge a lift for part of the way.

'I'll give you some lemonade then.' Her aunt led the way.

Probyn, his face like a tomato, said they would appreciate that as they had still had to walk miles. Allowing both women to enter the kitchen first, he stumbled over the threshold after them, complaining that he could not see in the dimmer indoor light.

The cool stone floor provided much needed relief to the travellers who collapsed on to kitchen chairs whilst their aunt took a jug of lemonade from the pantry.

'There's a party on t'green – we thought you might be there.' When Kit said she wasn't in a fitting mood, Probyn added, 'Well, you haven't missed owt. They haven't even got a proper band. Our Jubilee do was miles better. Mr Wilcox were dressed as Neptune and he kept chasing folk wi' his pitchfork – got me dad a right good jab up bum!'

'I've never heard of a Neptune with a wooden leg.' Feeling much better from their company, Kit laughed and handed out glasses of lemonade. Once this was consumed and her guests were somewhat cooler, she suggested they move into the parlour which was just as shady and more comfortable.

'Do you want a chocolate?' Kit went to fetch a bowl. 'Oh, sorry, there's only one left.'

'Probe can have it,' said Wyn.

Kit and Probyn shared a look of astonishment. It was unheard of for Wyn voluntarily to share anything with her brother, let alone surrender all rights.

Probyn rolled the chocolate round his mouth and wandered about the room, this treat being only one of many reasons that he loved to visit his aunt. Kit had mirrors that he could actually see into. Even on tiptoe he was only able to glimpse the top half of his head in the one above his own fireplace. At the first sight of his reflection today he was shocked at how much it had changed from his previous visit and went for a closer look, exploring his nose between finger and thumb as if he had only just discovered he had one – which in fact was not far from the truth. Since the last time he looked it had grown from a tiny insignificant blob to a real man's nose and seemed to fill his entire face.

Kit laughed at Wyn, who looked rather preoccupied. 'When I used to do that I was accused of being vain.'

Disturbed from her thoughts, Wyn grinned at her aunt, though in truth had not heard the joke.

The young man was unabashed, continuing to examine his appearance, muttering about the childish curl that persistently fell over his brow. 'Have you got any scissors, Aunt? Can you just chop this off for me?'

468

'I will not! It's lovely. Takes me hours with tongs to make mine as good.' Kit touched her fringe of auburn curls.

Probyn sighed and, spitting on to his hand, tried to plaster his hair into shape. 'They'll never take me in t'army looking like this.' Stretching to his full height he continued to inspect himself in the mirror, wishing his voice would remain steady at its new lower level and would not keep emerging in the occasional silly little squeak. 'How tall do you have to be to go in t'army?' It was of some concern that he had not even caught up with his youngest sister as regards to height.

Kit felt sorry for him. It must be hard to be a man. 'I don't know, love, but you're only fourteen, you've plenty of time to grow. Will you both be staying for tea?'

'Thanks all the same, but the man who brought us said if we wait in the same place at half-past four he'll give us a lift back. Anyroad, we're having tripe and onions at home and it's me favourite.' When his aunt displayed surprise, Probyn explained, 'I like fish.'

An amused Kit was about to correct her nephew's misassumption when Wyn butted in to ask if she could see the upper storey of the house. When they were up there, she whispered to her aunt, 'We've never told him what it really is or he won't eat it.'

Kit laughed and said she would keep their secret, then commented on Wyn's peculiar mood. 'You don't seem yourself today.'

Her niece blushed. 'I'm not.' She bit her lips and looked at Kit but said nothing more.

Kit remained ignorant. 'What ails thee?'

Wyn was obviously hesitant to say what it was. 'I thought you'd know.'

'I wouldn't be asking if I did,' answered her favourite aunt.

'It's something that happened to you,' said Wyn.

Kit spread her hands. 'Nay, that could be any . . .' In that same breath she interpreted her niece's meaning. 'You're not expecting?' It came out as an amazed whisper.

Wyn gave a quick nod, half agitated, half triumphant. 'So me father'll have to let me get married now, won't he?'

Her aunt gave a groan of despair and paced the carpet for a moment as the news sank in. Probyn shouted up to ask what they were doing and could he come up but Kit said they would be down in a moment and for him to stay where he was. She turned back to Wyn and asked, 'And is the young man responsible for this willing to stand by you?'

Wyn brightened. 'Oh, yes. We were going to get married anyway, if only me dad would find another slave to look after him. Mean old toad won't let me go.'

'Eh, don't talk about your father like that,' Kit rebuked her. 'Have some respect.'

'You should be saying that to him,' sulked Wyn. 'Me mother hasn't been dead a year and he's flirting with another woman.'

'He's lonely,' explained her aunt. 'He just needs somebody to talk to.'

Wyn was intransigent. 'Well, he needn't think we're accepting Mrs Carr as our new mother.'

'You could do worse. Anyway, it's daft to discuss such hypothetical matters when there's a more immediate problem. What did your dad have to say about all this then?'

Wyn flushed. 'I haven't told him yet. I wondered –'

'Oh, no!' Kit was annoyed at being so used. 'If you're old enough to have a baby, you're old enough to face the consequences. I'm not getting the blame for leading you astray. I'm sorry, Wyn, no; you'll have to tell him yourself.'

Wyn burst into tears, which almost had the effect of changing the soft-hearted Kit's mind but she thought better of it, having no desire to get involved in their family disputes ever again. Trying to comfort her niece she said kindly that although Monty would be angry she was sure he would get over it. There would be no question of him throwing Wyn out on to the street as might happen to some other poor girl. Monty was a good man and would do what was right by his daughter. Having mopped at her niece's eyes, Kit shoved her handkerchief back into her pocket and led the way downstairs.

Probyn frowned at the red eyes. 'Have you been blubbing?'

'Mind your own business,' snapped Wyn, who had always harboured resentment for him.

'Eh, eh, less of that,' scolded Kit. 'Come on, we'll have a cup of tea and some date and walnut cake, then afterwards I'll walk you to the end of the lane to meet your Good Samaritan.'

* * *

470

Having seen her nephew and niece safely aboard the wagon, Kit gave a final wave as they disappeared around the bend, then embarked on her return journey. The news about Wyn's baby could have set her back months had she allowed it to do so, but this afternoon Kit had determined to make an effort to regain her vitality – even if she would never quite be the same person again. Refusing to slip back into despondency, she began to hum as she went up the lane. Hearing the clatter of hoofs behind her she automatically moved to one side, then turned as the horse and cart came alongside her. The person in charge of it hauled on the reins, doffed his felt hat to expose a receding hairline and asked rather gruffly if he could give her a lift.

Accepting his kind offer, Kit watched him jump down. Even when his feet touched the ground she had to squint up at him. His size made him unmistakable. It was the man who had voiced opinion on the hunt that day. 'Oh, I think we've met before. You're –' She broke off.

'Worthy Treasure,' he told her, and helped her up as if she were but a slip of a girl.

'That's right, Farmer Treasure.' She remembered the man from whom she had rented the house addressing him as such as their paths coincided. 'You're very kind.'

Still somewhat gruff, Worthy climbed back on to the seat beside her and flicked the reins. The cart resumed its leisurely passage up the lane.

Inhaling the smell of horse, leather harness and honest sweat, Kit introduced herself, then said, 'I think I owe you an apology. I was a bit rude at our former meeting.'

Shadowed by the brim of the soft felt hat, his eyes passed her a quizzical glance. They were the very bright blue possessed by many northern folk.

'When you said the hunt was a grand sight,' explained Kit.

'Oh, that!' Worthy nodded. 'I'd forgotten all about it.' That was untrue. He had thought about the incident quite often, or more accurately the woman.

'You were right, it was a splendid sight.' Kit turned thoughtful. 'Isn't it an enigma that something so violent can be so beautiful at the same time?'

Farmer Treasure seemed to take a lot of thought over his answer, at the end of which all he said was, 'That's very true.'

Whilst addressing him, Kit had been taking in his physical appearance, having previously put his height at about six foot eight. He was as heavily built as she was, the pair of them taking up the whole of the seat, though there was no hint of the gentle giant about him, his profile showing a harsh line on his brow that could denote a quick temper. His thinning hair was dark brown, his complexion healthy. His head was quite large but he was not meant to carry quite so much weight judging by his facial features – the narrow pointed nose and rather patrician mouth. Kit's private assessment was confirmed by the incongruously delicate hands that held the reins. But for the rough clothes one would not immediately guess he worked on the land.

The horse clip-clopped steadily along, passing the end of an upwards sloping lane. 'I live up there,' Worthy nodded.

'Oh, you must drop me here then!' exclaimed Kit. 'Don't go out of your way, I haven't much further to walk.'

But he insisted on taking her to her door. 'Won't take us five minutes to get back.'

'Have you always lived round here?' she asked.

'All my life.'

She guessed that would be about forty years. 'It's lovely. I never knew it existed till I came that day.' Not wanting him to ask what had brought her there in the first place she began to ramble. 'I come from Ralph Royd – well, I was originally from Somerset but a long time ago. My parents died when I was young and my brother brought me up – there were five more of us besides. Monty's a coal miner. His wife was from Wales – she died last year. We lived in Wales for a time but then he couldn't get work so we came up to Yorkshire and we've been here ever since – although I lived in London for a time too.'

Looking straight ahead over the horse's rump, Worthy shook his tanned head. 'London's too big for me.'

'You've been then?' Kit looked interested.

'No, and I never would. I like a quiet life.'

Kit smiled and looked around at her bucolic surroundings. 'Just lately I've begun to prefer it too.'

'Can't get much more peaceful than round here,' said Worthy. 'Though I've heard some awful caterwauling coming from the village.'

Kit smiled and asked why he was not attending the Jubilee celebrations.

472

He replied that with no disrespect to Her Majesty he had other more important things to do.

An interval of silence followed, eventually broken by a rare question from Farmer Treasure. 'So, er, did your brother move here too, Miss Kilmaster?'

Kit's smile faded. 'No, we've had a bit of a falling out – I won't go into the details. I just wanted to be on my own.'

Worthy gave no response but took note of her solitary status.

'He's still at Ralph Royd. As a matter of fact, I've just set my nephew and niece back on the road there – they came to visit me this afternoon. Poor Wyn, she's got herself into a bit of trouble, if you get my meaning.' Seeing that he did she went on, 'Wanted me to tell her father, but I said, "You're old enough now you'll have to tell him yourself."' Suddenly realizing that in the space of five minutes she had told him a good part of her life story and more intimate details besides, Kit covered her mouth. 'Hark at me! I'm sure you don't want to hear all about our troubles.' She berated her own talkativeness and sat quiet for a time, hands resting in the lap of her summer dress. But her interest got the better of her. 'Have you any brothers or sisters, Mr Treasure?'

'One brother and three sisters. I'm t'eldest. Two of t'girls are away and married, the youngest helps out at home.'

'And your brother?'

'Abel's married too and lives in a cottage on the farm – that'll go to me when my parents die, sithee, but it seems a shame when I've no children to hand it on to. My brother's always been a bit resentful about that, but I suppose his sons'll get it in t'end.'

'You're not wed, then?' Kit thought him rather old to have never been married – especially as he was so eligible, being in line to inherit a farm.

'Never found anyone I'd care to marry.' A shadow passed over his face.

From the way he said it Kit recognized a man who had been hurt – one whose wounds took a long time to heal – and wondered over the circumstances.

Worthy felt her eyes on him – wanted to tell her that at sixteen he had been cruelly hurt by a beautiful girl with whom he had been infatuated and had sworn never to have any truck with women again; but instead he said nothing.

473

For some strange reason Kit felt sorry for him. In an attempt to remove his frown, she repeated her opinion that it was a lovely place to live and, finding herself at ease with him, began to tell him all about her travels – though she made no mention of the men in her life nor of the children she had lost.

His gruff manner having shown gradual improvement during the journey, Worthy displayed interest in her tale, but at the end of it said that he had never been out of Yorkshire and had no wish to. It was not meant to be an insult, he said, others could go where they chose. It was just that he himself could think of no better place to be.

'So you enjoy being a farmer?' enquired Kit.

'I was born to it.'

Kit asked what sort of farm he had, and though that kind of life held little personal interest, she paid attention as he told her it was partly arable, partly livestock. 'Oats, barley, peas, beans, taties, carrots, turnips, wurzels for the beasts. We used to grow more grain but we stopped bothering. Weren't much point in face of all these cheap American imports. Fifty breeding ewes, half a dozen sows, four cows . . .' His voice trailed away.

'I should like to see it,' she said at his conclusion.

He became momentarily awkward.

Kit reddened. 'I beg your pardon, that seemed as if I were inviting myself!'

'No, no you'd be quite welcome.' Fearing that he must appear to her like a bumbling youth, Worthy scolded himself into order and perversely readopted his gruff pose. 'You must come up to the farm and take tea with us one day.' Damn! It had emerged as an order.

But his attractive companion bestowed him with a smile. 'That's most neighbourly. I don't know many folk round here yet.'

'My mother knows everyone worth knowing,' said Worthy, wishing he could study those clear blue eyes without appearing too bold. 'I'll ask her to introduce you.'

Kit felt as if she might have made a mistake, was not yet ready to return to society – though she had enjoyed talking to this man. His slow, quiet speech was a comfort.

Their journey was almost over. On the village green celebrations were still going on, the pinafored children in paper hats sitting down to a tea

474

of buns and jelly. Kit responded to their merry waves and noted that her companion did too. When he asked where to take her, she pointed the way to her house and, upon climbing down from the cart, asked, 'Would you like to come in for a cup of tea?'

'I'm sure you've had enough of my company for one day.' Worthy made as if to gee up his horse.

Though reluctant to face the solitude of the house, Kit remembered his comment that he had better things to do, and let him go. 'I've enjoyed your company very much, Mr Treasure. Thank you for the ride and I hope we meet again soon.'

Worthy seemed to want to say something, then simply nodded and clicked his tongue at the horse, turned the cart around and drove away.

Expecting nothing further of him, Kit steeled herself for another evening alone.

28

During the next few days other things were to occupy Kit's mind. Thinking that perhaps she had been too harsh on Wyn, and knowing what a frightening situation it was to find oneself unmarried and with child, she travelled over to her old cottage – now her brother's – to offer support. However, she was to find that Wyn had broken the news and moreover Kit found herself accused by Monty as a prime constituent in his daughter's downfall – as she had known would happen. Telling them they could sort out their own battles, she immediately returned home to Soke, wishing she had never gone in the first place.

She had not been home long when someone knocked at her door. Still annoyed at Monty's accusation, she answered the door with a look on her face that was less than gracious to her visitor – a woman of mature proportions whose face seemed rather familiar.

The visitor was taken aback. 'Perhaps I'm come at the wrong moment . . .'

Realizing that she must have been frowning, Kit immediately banished her mood and gave rapid explanation. 'I do beg your pardon. I've just had an altercation with my brother and – oh, well, you don't want to hear all my family troubles, I'm sure!'

The elderly woman in the print frock and straw hat introduced herself. 'I'm Phoebe Treasure. I believe –'

'Oh yes, come in!' Eager to make amends, Kit summoned Worthy's mother over the threshold. 'Let me fetch you some lemonade.'

Mrs Treasure's miraculously unlined face performed the same non-committal twitch as her son, displaying friendliness without actually smiling. 'Thank you kindly. It's a long walk down that hill – though even longer going back. My son mentioned you were new to the village so I just came down to introduce myself and ask if you'd like to come for tea.' When Kit said she would, Mrs Treasure added, 'Perhaps if you've nothing better to do you'd like to accompany me right now? I could introduce you to a few folk on the way.'

Kit replied that she would appreciate this and once her visitor had finished her lemonade the pair made their way through the village, stopping here and there along the way for Kit to be introduced to her new neighbours.

Mrs Treasure had been right, it was a long walk up the hill to the farm but Kit proclaimed that it was well worth it – the view from up here was stunning. Gazing out across the fields of cows and sheep one could see for miles on this clear day. Nearer to home, the long grass in the meadow had been cut and exposure to the hot sun had turned it into hay, its sweet scent filling the air.

Her companion pointed out several figures who, with wooden implements, were raking the hay and tossing it up on to a cart. Three of them were much larger than the rest. 'There's Worthy and his father and brother. They won't be home for a while – it'll give us time to chat.' Turning back to the farmhouse, she took off her hat to reveal a bun of dark hair barely touched by grey.

Accepting an invitation to enter, Kit found herself in an expansive kitchen with a stone-paved floor, oak furniture and a large cooking range from whence came the aroma of onion gravy. Here she was introduced to Worthy's sister, Ettie, and, finding both women pleasant company she chatted happily to them until, some time later, Worthy's large frame appeared in the doorway. Though his face lacked exuberance, his blue eyes told that he was glad to see her.

Upon first meeting his mother Kit had noted the marked similarity, and it was true that Worthy did have her colouring, but now that she was introduced to his father, she found a resemblance here too – although George Treasure was six inches shorter and many pounds lighter and had the rather grizzled appearance of an elderly badger. She was not to meet his brother, Abel, yet; he had apparently gone home to his own cottage. The rest were just hired hands. Flanked by people of a similar height to herself – and Worthy even taller – Kit did not feel so out of place, and thoroughly enjoyed tea which, to the Treasures was a gigantic meal of Yorkshire Pudding, stewed beef and vegetables, with rhubarb tart to follow.

Afterwards, when the hired men had gone to their quarters, she offered to help wash the pots but Mrs Treasure said she would not dream of it and told Worthy to show their guest around the farm. Upon the couple's exit, Phoebe's unwrinkled face became more animated as she told her husband and family, 'I never thought I'd live to see that boy make such a perfect match – and judging by her house she's very well set up too!'

George Treasure was as laconic as his son. 'Must be summat wrong with her if she's never been wed at her age.'

Spying from behind the curtain, his daughter scolded him. 'She can't be much older than me!'

'That's what I said, there must be summat wrong with her.' Mr Treasure's dour expression did not alter, but there was hidden amusement in his eyes.

His wife took him to task, then unable to resist, crept up to join Ettie at the window.

Outside, the land was still bathed in golden sunlight. Kit shot a quick look over her shoulder at the farmhouse, smiling as her action created a flash of movement that betrayed the presence of spies – they were bound to be interested, she supposed. Of more interest to her were the ancient stone jambs of the farmhouse door, which she asked about now. Worthy told her that its builder had employed some of the old relics his ancestors had unearthed in their fields – Roman and Saxon monuments.

'I'm forever ploughing old coins up too – here's one I found today.' He delved into his pocket and after rubbing at the dark brown disc displayed it on his palm. 'I think you'll find it's Roman when it's cleaned up.'

Kit bent over to look, noticing again how tapered were his fingers. 'That's fascinating! My nephew would love it.'

'Take it,' said the big man. 'I can get plenty more.'

Kit showed gratitude and studied the coin closely for some time.

He seemed to warm to his subject. 'I can show you the old Ermine Street, if you'd like.'

'That was the old Roman road, wasn't it?' Kit had read about this. 'You mean it's still there?'

Worthy gave a nod and bade her come further up the hill, using the arduous climb as an excuse to offer his arm. Grabbing a handful of pink candy-striped dress and petticoat, she laid her free hand upon his forearm and hauled herself up the slope. Once atop the limestone summit

478

he indicated an expanse of moorland where a panting Kit could make out an arrow-like ridge that marked the great Roman road.

Her voice was filled with wonder. 'I never knew such things were on my own doorstep.'

'Better than seeing it in any museum, I reckon,' said Worthy.

She cast her eyes wider. 'The Lord was certainly in a good mood when He created this.'

Worthy murmured agreement and the two of them stood gazing at the vista for a long time.

'I might be cursed with a poor imagination,' said her burly companion eventually, 'but I find it impossible to grasp the concept of nothingness – what was there before God created this? Just blackness? But blackness has substance, doesn't it? I can't understand what there could be before the Beginning – do you see what I mean?'

Kit nodded. 'What was the Lord doing before He created the earth and everything in it? Where did He come from – everything has to come from somewhere – and what about time? I mean, time can't just start out of nowhere, can it? And as for the notion of eternity – well, it's totally beyond my comprehension.'

His words were sombre. 'If you think about it too deeply it scares you, doesn't it?'

Not I, thought Kit, picturing the two Beatas in Heaven, and the joy of her reunion with them.

Worthy uttered a rare laugh to lighten the atmosphere. 'Bet you never thought you'd get this when you were invited to tea – a total stranger discussing the meaning of life – and a sober one at that.'

He could not possibly know what memories his conversation had invoked, how she pined for her babies. Fighting the inclination to wallow in grief, Kit shared his amusement, then said, 'I don't feel as if you are a stranger.'

Worthy seemed pleased at this. 'Mm, funny that, I don't neither. I hope you'll visit us again, Miss Kilmaster.'

With this latter statement appearing as a hint that she should be leaving, Kit had no choice but to suggest they make their way back down the hill.

Halfway down the grassy incline, Worthy performed a quick stoop, picked up a bit of earthenware and examined it. 'Here's a piece of Roman pottery.'

479

Still walking, Kit leaned over for a closer look and asked how he could tell.

'You can just make out this writing here.' He peered at it as if trying to decipher the marks.

'What does it say?' She showed keen interest.

He squinted at it closely. 'Made by – Julius Caesar.'

'Does it rea–' She broke off as she saw he was pulling her leg, and laughed with him as he tossed the bit of modern pottery over his shoulder.

Back at the farmhouse Mrs Treasure asked if Kit would like a cup of tea before she left. Not wanting to outstay her welcome the guest refused, but was glad when Worthy said he would take her home on the cart.

After he had helped her up, Kit noticed Mrs Treasure nudge her son and hiss at him, 'Now, don't you dare come back here and say you forgot!' But Kit merely straightened her candy-striped skirts, pretending she had not overheard. It obviously embarrassed him to be treated so by his mother.

Upon reaching home, however, she was to guess that Mrs Treasure had instructed her son to keep in touch for, prior to taking his leave, Worthy asked, 'Would you consider it an intrusion if I were to call on you some time, Miss Kilmaster?'

'I'd be delighted, and please call me Kit – or Katherine, if you prefer.'

'Might I see you at chapel on Sunday, Katherine?' When she answered in the affirmative Worthy added, 'Then maybe we could go for a walk afterwards?'

Kit agreed and said he must come to luncheon too. With that, she waved him off and went indoors.

On Sunday Kit was to meet Worthy's brother when the Treasure family's arrival at chapel coincided with hers, and they invited her to share their pew. After joining in a series of rollicking hymns, and prayers punctuated by shouts of 'Hallelujah' and a final amen, Mrs Treasure was to introduce Kit to the minister, his wife, more villagers and local tradespeople, making great play of telling them that although she and Kit had only just met they had so much in common that she regarded her almost as a member of the family.

It was obviously of deep embarrassment to Worthy, who, once they were alone and strolling along the lane, apologized to Kit. The starched Sunday collar and clothes seemed to add to his discomfort, making him less relaxed than on their previous meeting. 'I hope you'll pardon Mother. She's that desperate to see me wed she'd have me take any old wife.'

Kit laughed.

Blind to the fact that he had insulted her, Worthy went on, 'At least I'm not alone, she does it to my sister Ettie too.'

Kit said she liked his family. Though they were as undemonstrative as her own they had made her feel welcome.

'The way you told it the other day, you don't get on very well with your own,' ventured Worthy.

Kit replied that it was not so much that – though they were all very different – it was more that she had never really fitted in. 'They always wanted me to be like them and I'm just not. I know chapel folk are not meant to dance but I could never understand what was so sinful about it. I like dancing – at least I did in my younger days. I like nice clothes too.'

Worthy said rather admiringly that he had noticed this. 'I lead a simple life meself, but I'd never condemn others for wanting something different. You must do as you must do, that's my philosophy. Mother's a bit strict on that kind o' thing, wouldn't let any of my sisters go the village dance – doesn't like Father creeping off to have a glass of ale neither, but I don't see any harm in it. Like a drink meself, as a matter of fact, in moderation.' He looked down at her, bestowing that twitch of a smile.

Kit returned it more widely.

'I think you mentioned your brother was a miner.'

'I have two brothers,' Kit informed him, 'both miners. Owen used to live in the same village but after the last strike he was blackballed – he was a strong union man, you see – and he had to move to another mine. They don't speak to each other now. Owen thinks Monty betrayed him by being one of the first to go back to work, Monty feels he's been betrayed by Owen, whom he brought up.' She suddenly glimpsed the anomaly here: if her brothers were humble miners how was it that she could afford to rent such an impressive house and wear such finery?

481

Paradoxically, it was Worthy who provided the opening for her explanation. 'How is it that a presentable woman like yourself has never married?'

'I was close to it once, but he jilted me.' Remembering Ninian Latimer, she did not look at Worthy but heard his murmur of contempt for this bounder. 'I received quite substantial compensation, but money's no substitute for being treated in so vile a manner, is it?'

'No, indeed.' Worthy had turned pensive. 'An experience like that turns your mind against marriage.'

Kit tried to imagine what was causing that furrowed brow, then righted his assumption. 'It was bad, yes, but its effect was only temporary. I would have accepted another proposal had I been given the chance, but no one asked.' She went on to tell him that after that painful episode she had invested the money in business, adding that she had carried out her skills as seamstress to the gentry until recently. 'I'm considering reopening for trade here, once I become acclimatized.'

Worthy made no comment on this. They walked on, enjoying desultory conversation, until Kit said perhaps they should return to the house as the joint of beef must be almost done by now. Up until today she had eschewed the help of a servant, but the fact that she was starting once again to entertain guests meant that someone had to tend the cooking. 'I've left a little girl in charge but I wouldn't trust her to prepare the whole meal – not with such an important guest.' She smiled. 'I shouldn't be mean, she's a nice lass. I'll be glad of her help if I do reopen for business.'

Worthy was not to comment on her future plans until Sunday luncheon had been consumed and they had chatted about a whole range of subjects throughout the afternoon.

Directing the conversation from the world in general to more pertinent issues, Worthy spread his graceful fingers upon his great big thighs and studied them thoughtfully. 'What you were saying before about opening your business – wouldn't you rather be married and have children?'

Sitting opposite, Kit flinched at the mention of children but maintained the gay air that their former dialogue had engendered. It was a long time since she'd chatted so easily to someone, and certainly never to a man, except Mr Popplewell. 'I'm a bit long in the tooth for anyone to ask me now!'

'There's one here who would ask.'

She was nonplussed. 'Is that – a proposal?'

He nodded his ox-like head. The starched collar bit into his neck and carved white lines in his tan.

Kit found it impossible to answer. Always quick to spot the irony of a situation she saw it in bucketsful now. Why could he not have come along a year ago when she was carrying Serena? Instead of having the baby wrenched from her she could have passed it off as his. She studied his face. Would she have been able to commit such deception against this honest simple man? Perhaps, if it meant she could keep her longed for baby. But she would never know now. The chance had gone.

He took her silence as refusal and began to rise as if to leave, muttering apologies, but she bade him wait. 'Worthy, I genuinely appreciate your offer – but you know absolutely nothing about me!'

He was not a man to guffaw out loud, confining his laughter to his eyes, but he emitted an uncommon laugh now and listed everything she had told him in the last few days, making her objection look ridiculous.

She allowed him that, but insisted, 'It's not really the same as living with a person, is it?'

'I've seen all I need to see to know you'll be more than capable. The woman who bears my children will have to be big and strong – like you.' He showed not the slightest recognition that he'd made her sound like a prize cow.

Kit was offended, but gave this her serious consideration. Even in such unglorified terms it was a tremendous proposal. After giving up Serena, on top of Beata's death, there had seemed no reason to her life, now he was offering Kit what she had always wanted: a husband and children – as many as she liked. Even if they would never replace those lost to her, she had not dared to envisage such consolation.

Yet still she faltered. 'It's come as a shock. I took you for a confirmed bachelor.'

'And so I was until I met you.' It was hardly an impulsive gesture. Worthy had been thinking very hard about this since the day he had met her. He hoped she would not ask him to enlarge on what it was that attracted him, for he could not put into words that which he drew from her clear blue eyes – purity and intelligence, an honest and upright woman in whom, at last, he could place his trust, one to share his dreams, to bear his children. In silence, he waited for her response, trying not to show how much it would bother him if she said no.

'It must have been something very bad to turn you against women.' Though it was not a direct question, her eyes asked that he enlighten her.

There arose a hint of his former gruff manner. 'I suppose you've a right to know. When I was sixteen I gave my heart to a girl – asked her to marry me. She laughed at me.' His gaze came up briefly from the floor. 'It sounds very paltry now, I know –'

'No it doesn't,' she interrupted kindly.

'It was just the cruel way she did it – in front of an audience. And all the time she was leading me on, she was going with another chap.'

'Don't say any more,' begged Kit. Though his confession had lent a touch of humanity to the proposal, she had no wish to prolong his discomfort.

'Oh, it doesn't bother me now.' He was surprised to find that this was true. 'I've found someone much better, someone of integrity.'

Looking into his expectant, weather-beaten face, Kit wondered whether it was too late to furnish this unwitting suitor with the whole truth. But then why should she? One child was dead, the other as good as – why risk losing the only genuine proposal of marriage she had had – for at her age it would be her last? No, Kit had come here to start a new life, she could not take a backward step now. Wondering just what she was letting herself in for by marriage to this stranger, she gave her considered reply.

'Thank you for asking me, Worthy. I'd be honoured to become your wife.'

Mrs Treasure was beside herself with happiness at the prospect of such a match and, disallowing Kit any chance of escape, launched herself into preparations for the wedding, even suggesting that there was no need for the couple to wait for the banns to be called, they could get married by licence. Already swept up by the suddenness of it all, Kit answered kindly that three weeks would be quite soon enough – she had never been married before and this one and only occasion required a special gown; she must be allowed time to create it. Of even more importance

484

was where she and Worthy were going to live. Mrs Treasure put a stop to this objection, informing her that it had all been decided long ago: when Worthy married he would have the farmhouse and his parents and sister would move into smaller premises. This large house was meant to contain children and Mrs Treasure hoped her son and his wife would be blessed with many of them.

So, all the problems appeared to have been solved – at least in Mrs Treasure's eyes. Little did she know what lay beneath the veneer of her future daughter-in-law's honest smile. Unsure what to do about the house in York, for the sale of it would mean a complicated explanation to Worthy, Kit decided to continue letting it out. An agent already collected the rent for her and sent her a monthly cheque, which she paid into her bank account. Even allowing for the money she had given Amelia, such an enormous accrual in her bank book would still be a shock to her new husband were he to know of it, but she had told Worthy about the compensation she had received for being jilted, and had not quoted an exact figure so that provided no difficulties – but the receipt of regular instalments would do.

In a quandary, she decided to open a separate account. As currently happened – for she had not yet bothered to alter the arrangement – the cheques would still be sent to Ralph Royd where she could pick them up from time to time and take them to the bank. It was no good asking her brother to attend to this matter – he never went into town and Kit doubted he had ever entered a bank in his life. With no one else competent she would have to deal with this herself. Others would tell her that she was making life very complicated for herself, but Kit saw no other way out.

Apart from any other reason, Kit deemed herself most fortunate only to have rented her present abode. The fact that there were still several months to run on her tenancy and this would incur needless expense was not without hidden benefits: if the wedding fell through she would still have a roof over her head. It might appear cynical to others but Kit had learned not to set too much store by people's promises. If the marriage went ahead she would count herself most fortunate, if it did not – well, just wait and see what the day brought.

During the interim, whilst stitching and sewing at every opportunity, Kit grew to like her intended even more. In contrast to many of the men she had known he was totally without artifice. If he said he was going to do something he did it. He was a blunt man who uttered the first thing that came into his head and, though it was sometimes hurtful, Kit preferred it to lies. It was a comforting thought to know she could always expect the truth, though this in itself spawned guilt that he could not expect the same from her. Telling herself what was past was past, she relegated all signs of bereavement to her solitary moments, outwardly appearing calm and committed, whilst underneath experiencing the awful fear that she might burst into inexplicable tears.

Thankfully, her betrothed interpreted any unusual signs as nervousness over the wedding. He was nervous too and had been putting off something which should have taken priority, but this evening when he visited his bride-to-be he raised the subject. 'I suppose by rights I should ask your brother for your hand – as he's your guardian.'

Kit had been forced to hide her half-finished wedding gown at his arrival and already looked flustered but was now even more so. 'I've been thinking of that too – not about asking permission – I'm a bit mature for that, but whether I really want any of them at my wedding.' She showed a marked lack of inclination, especially after her last visit, when Monty had accused her of leading Wyn astray – and thereby lay the main reason for her reluctance. What if they should reveal her secret? Still reeling from Worthy's unexpected proposal the last thing she had thought about was that someone else could report her colourful past, but now she had to face the serious possibility. How could she risk taking him to Ralph Royd where everyone knew her?

'What – have no member of your family attend your special day?' The big man portrayed surprise.

'It's for that very reason I don't want them here,' explained Kit, 'because it is my special day. I don't want any of them to spoil it with their silly comments.' She sighed and made a face. 'I suppose it would look a bit odd, wouldn't it?'

Worthy had placed her silver thimble on his fingertip and was reading the name, Villa Garcia, though he did not need to ask about it for Katherine had told him she had been to Spain with the family she had once worked for. In fact she must have told him just about everything about herself, such was the volume of her conversation. Finding it impossible to remember every detail, he intended to ask her to recite

486

her exciting tales again when winter came upon them, to while away the dark nights. It was still something of a miracle to Worthy that one so widely educated could choose to marry him.

Kit decided. 'Very well, I'll go over and tell them tomorrow.'

'If you wait until evening, I can take you,' he offered.

That would not do at all. 'No, I'd rather prepare them for the shock.' Kit smiled, then grabbed the thimble from his fingertip and shooed him from the house. 'Now, Mr Treasure, would you please take yourself off or I'll have nothing to wear for this wedding!'

It was a mixed blessing that she happened to be visiting her brother on the first Sabbath of the month, thus finding all her siblings – what was left of them – gathered in the parlour of her old cottage. With Amelia in America, Owen in self-imposed exile, Sarah dead and most of the young ones married, it was a poor gathering nowadays. Wyn had been quickly marched down the aisle and was living with her husband's parents, leaving Merry the only girl at home. It was disappointing to find Probyn absent too; gone on an outing with his pals.

Gwen was as vociferous as ever, being the first to comment on her youngest sister's appearance. 'My word, to what do we owe this honour?' Her rather miffed attitude sprung from the fact that two of her siblings had benefited from Kit's generosity whilst she had received not a bean – nor had she yet been invited to Kit's new home. 'Must be months since I saw you last.'

Kit sat down, unperturbed now by the dead-eyed stare of Beata's portrait, glancing instead at her brother to check what sort of mood he was in, wondering how to begin her news.

Gwen did not give her time to answer. 'You haven't noticed, have you?' At Kit's blank look, she exclaimed, 'There's one missing!'

'There always somebody missing.' Kit received a brief mental vision of Amelia with Serena in her arms. It was rare for her to think of her sister as a separate unit now; she was always holding a baby. Kit's baby.

'I'm talking about Flora!' At Kit's modicum of interest Gwen dealt her trump card. 'She's only run off with another woman's husband, that's all!'

Kit gaped and looked at the others for confirmation.

Charity smirked. 'It's right! Never mentioned a word about him before.

Last Saturday morning she packs her bags and gets on a boat for America – seems he's a bigwig on the White Star Line. Loaded by all accounts.'

'It's always the quiet ones that are the worst,' opined Gwen, then gave a sideways look at Kit and added, 'with a few exceptions that is.'

Kit demanded more details, inwardly scolding herself for being as bad as the rest of them, though she just could not help but be astounded. Flora of all people!

Gwen concluded the information with a laugh. 'He can't ever have taken tea with her, all that sniffing every morsel of food. If he ain't mad enough for taking her on she'll drive him mad!'

Kit had to join the laughter. Then, still with a twinkle in her eye though a note of apprehension in her voice, she admitted, 'There's another madman on the loose – one who's promised to marry me.'

She had everyone's full attention now. Gwen could not speak for many seconds. 'You're joking!' she stuttered at last.

After receiving astonished congratulations from all, Kit told them briefly about her great good fortune in meeting Worthy and the speed of his proposal.

Gwen had recovered somewhat. 'It goes without saying that he's not from round here – must be desperate too, or ugly as sin.'

'Now, Gwen, there's no need to spoil the girl's good tidings,' warned Monty, trying to make amends for his previous slander: with Wyn safely wed everything had settled down now.

Kit was grateful for this unspoken forgiveness. 'He's a lovely man,' she told her sister firmly. 'And he's looking forward to seeing you all at our wedding – though if you carry on like that you won't get an invitation.'

'Sorry, Kit, I was only joking.' Gwen gave her a fond tap. 'I'm genuinely glad you landed a bit of luck – mind you don't let this one get away.'

'I don't intend to,' replied Kit. 'That's why I wanted to have a private word with you all before you meet him. Worthy doesn't know anything about what went on in the past.'

Gwen gave a nod of recognition at Charity. 'I didn't think he'd have the full story.'

'And I don't want him to have it,' said Kit, her expression becoming pleading. 'This is my last chance – I know that. I didn't tell him at first because, well, I just didn't – and now it's too late.' She wrung her hands. 'I can't risk losing him.'

488

'So you want us to keep mum,' guessed Monty. 'Well, that's not too much to ask, is it?' he enquired of the others, Gwen in particular.

The latter shoved out her chest. 'I don't know why you're looking at me, Monty Kilmaster! I never yet advertised the fact that my sister is a woman of loose morals and I don't intend to start now – though I can't speak for the rest of the community.'

Kit said she was well aware of that risk. 'We're having the wedding in Worthy's parish. You're all welcome.' She told them exactly when the ceremony would be.

Afterwards there was a lot of superficial chatter and genuine compliment from Kit's relatives. When she departed at the end of the afternoon it was with a much lighter heart than when she'd arrived.

'Well, that be a turn up for the books,' remarked Monty to his sisters, who had stayed behind to gossip. 'I feel really happy for the girl. She seems to have found a decent man at last.'

Charity echoed this, though Gwen's final comment held a note of caution. 'But she's carving a difficult path for herself by lying to him. You can't keep things like that hidden for ever.'

Encouraged by the reception from her other siblings, Kit decided to visit Owen that same week and invite him to the wedding. The long summer days meant that she could arrive when he finished work and still be home before dark.

A note of apprehension accompanied her journey, for her route took her close to Postgate Park. Remembering her last meeting with Ossie at the dance, she pondered over the amount of water that had passed under the bridge since then, and wondered whether he and his wife had had children, and whether or not she would bump into him.

But she was not to see the Viscount nor any other member of the Earl's family today, her brother's being the first familiar face she set eyes on.

As expected there were jokes on the competence of her groom. 'Will they let him out unattended?' came Owen's deadpan enquiry, before he elaborated, 'Well, I can't see any man in his right mind taking thee on.'

Being scolded by both his sister and his wife, Owen said genuinely, 'Nay, I'm right glad for you, Kit! Congratulations, lass.' He bade his sister sit down and did likewise. 'We could do with a bit o' good news round here, couldn't we, Meg?'

Standing at the table brewing a pot of tea, she agreed, but knowing what was to come said that Kit didn't want to hear all his woes.

Ignoring her, Owen said despondently, 'I don't know what's matter wi' folk round here. I can't seem to get anybody interested in t'union.' Throughout the county, membership had plummeted since the strike.

Kit frowned. 'But do you really need a union?' Her brother enjoyed much better living conditions than he had at Ralph Royd, the Earl providing medical treatment for his colliers, a variety of recreational facilities, plus a splendid library. 'I thought his lordship was a good master.'

Owen beheld her as if she had learned nothing. 'Aye, a bit too good if you ask me! It's made the men who work for him too apathetic to fight for their rights – and I'll tell you what we need a union for –'

'Owen!' warned his wife. 'She doesn't want to hear it.'

'I don't want to rely on paternalism! I want to know for definite that I've got a job to go to every day, that I don't have a two-hour walk underground before I can start to earn me living, and I want a fixed rate of – eh!' He broke off as his wife, grabbed the knitted tea-cosy, slipped it over his head and pretended to suffocate him.

'Think yourself lucky you can go home, Kit!' said Meg, struggling to contain him. 'I have to put up with this every day of the year.' She refused to liberate Owen until he promised not to mention another word about the union. Then came a muffled shout of surrender and instant release.

'Aw, you've messed all me hair up, woman!' Red-faced from his tussle, Owen smoothed his tousled black hair. 'Lord, she's got a grip on her like a navvy.'

Laughing with them, Kit was glad that her brother and his wife still enjoyed a happy marriage, and uttered the jocular hope that they would not fight like this at her wedding.

Owen turned sombre. 'I suppose yon fella'll be there?' He had never referred to Monty by name since their rift. His sister knew who he meant and nodded. 'Then I'm surprised you even bothered coming over to invite us.'

Kit looked to Meg for help but knew it was a waste of time, Owen's wife would always back him. 'I'd really like all my family to be there.'

'But they won't be, will they?' Owen pointed out. 'Sarah's dead, Amelia's gone –'

'Flora's sailed away with somebody else's husband,' provided Kit, and smiled half-heartedly as her brother came to life. After waiting for Owen and Meg to end their scandalized discussion, she went on, 'There's nothing I can do about those who are far away, but can't you and Monty put aside your differences for one day?'

'Not differences, Kit – principles. At least they are on my part, and if I could put them aside so easily they wouldn't be principles, would they? I'll never forgive what he did, never.' The determined set to Owen's billy-goat chin told Kit that there was no point in arguing. 'But I wish you and your man every happiness, and you'll both be welcome to visit any time.'

'Bring him for his tea,' urged Meg. 'I can't wait to meet him, he sounds a nice chap.'

'Worthy Treasure,' mused Owen, reaching for his pipe and tobacco, 'I hope he lives up to his name.'

Kit smiled and said she was sure he would. She told them a little bit more about her intended, though added that there was much she had to discover about him herself.

Owen raised one thick black eyebrow and asked, 'Does he know about . . . ?' He deliberately made no mention of a name, ending his question with a sideways jab of his pipe stem. Meg had explained just how difficult it must have been for his sister to give up her baby, though he could not put himself in her shoes, of course.

Kit shook her head. Owen nodded and reinserted the pipe stem between his teeth, puffing thoughtfully and glancing briefly at his wife. 'Well, nobody's likely to say owt, are they?'

His sister thoroughly hoped not. However cynical her experiences had made her, she could not quite bring herself to abandon the notion that people were fundamentally decent.

Against all fears, Kit's wedding day passed without a hitch. She stood there as a married woman, surrounded by guests, inebriated by all the compliments on her gown – which was the most stunning of all her creations, made of pale gold satin with an embroidered bodice, a labyrinth of ruching, braid and ribbon and artificial pearls, and a train that stretched for yards and was almost in danger of being severed from the rest with little girls hanging on the end, fighting over who should hold it. Hardly able to believe that she was married at last, she continually examined the gold ring on her finger, alternately sharing smiles with her family and her groom.

The fact that she did not love Worthy had no bearing on her happiness, for he was a good kind man and as eager to start a family of his own as she was. Despite being unaccustomed to life on a farm, she was determined to give it her wholehearted devotion, and was equally certain that Worthy would make an excellent father to her children.

For all she did not love him – indeed there had been no mention of love from either side – Kit found herself becoming physically attracted to the big man who stood beside her now, shaking hands with their guests, his face a picture of confidence. He looked different in his newly tailored wedding attire – quite handsome, in fact. It would not be so difficult to lay in his bed. She wondered whether he had ever slept with a woman, but doubted it. It also crossed her mind if he would be able to tell that she was not so pure as he imagined, and it rather worried her. She had no wish to hurt him.

She had also suffered qualms about inviting Mr Popplewell to the wedding. It was not simply that she would have to explain this male friend to her husband but that Popplewell might be hurt by her marriage. Nevertheless, she felt unable to neglect the friend who had been through so much with her, and was now glad that she had written to him, for he stood there chatting quite amiably with Worthy, who assumed him to be an old friend of all the Kilmaster family and not just Kit.

Amongst the wedding presents was one she would rather not have. Monty had donated the portrait of Beata, telling Kit that, before the end, Sarah had expressed the wish that he should pass it on to his youngest sister when he died. '"I want Kit to have it," she said. So, I thought this was a more fitting occasion to pass it on.' So poignant was his gesture that Kit did not have the heart to burn it as she would have liked to have done for years, and told him it would take pride of place in her new home.

After the reception in the village hall, Kit and her groom departed for the farmhouse. Upon arrival she was touched to learn that Worthy had planted a root of honeysuckle on either side of the door, especially for her coming. Its perfume, he said, would enhance their evenings in years to come. He further astounded his bride by carrying her over the threshold. Now that they were alone she expected him to be as nervous as herself, but he did not appear to be so, the only emotion written on his face was happiness.

In that moment Kit felt desperately sorry for him – wished she could salvage her own innocence.

Misreading the glint of tears he rushed to hold her begging her not to be afraid. Wrapped in his embrace Kit enjoyed a moment of wonder – no man before had had the arms to totally envelop her, the ability to make her feel like a little girl.

Then he held her from him slightly and looked deep into her face, his blue eyes never blinking as he told her in his simple honest manner, 'You look most beautiful, Katherine,' and he kissed his bride for the first time.

The sweetest warmest kiss, thought Kit.

Finally, stepping away from her, Worthy cleared his throat and asked would she like to go upstairs before him? He had no animals to attend tonight for his father and brother had promised to see to these but, said Worthy, he usually liked to go to bed after everyone else.

Kit asked if he would undo all the pearl buttons down the back of her dress, this taking quite a time.

Then, whilst her new husband went outside into the warm summer eve, Kit hoisted the skirts of her gold satin gown and made her careful way up the staircase. The sight that greeted her brought another wave of emotion. Her rather taciturn, unsophisticated groom had covered the bed in flowers. Not an inch of mattress showed beneath the floral counterpane. Flowers of the meadow, garden and woodland, whose pungent scent filled her head and her heart.

She did not remove them but let them lay, taking off the dress she would never wear again. A shower of rice hit the floorboards, having gathered in the draped satin pouches of her skirts. Shaking more rice out, she laid the dress aside and replaced it with a nightgown, then smiled at the creak of Worthy's foot upon the stair, and waited with open arms.

29

Even after months had gone by Kit was still giddy. How could her life have changed so dramatically in so short a period? Just when had she made the transition from grieving mother to loving wife? For she did love Worthy, intensely. His tenderness and passion had aroused in her feelings that no other man had achieved. That he was a romantic soul had nothing to do with it, nor did the gratitude and duty that had previously coloured her resolution to make him a good wife. She loved Worthy for no other reason than himself, was glad to have been through every stab of pain for it had carved a path to him.

There was little to perturb Kit during those glorious dog days on the farm, far removed from hurtful gossip. Encouraged to do so, she had taken to addressing the elder Mrs Treasure as Mother. Having no inkling of her daughter-in-law's past, Phoebe had taken Kit to her heart as surely as if she had been her own daughter. Similarly accepted by all the Treasures, Kit had never been so involved in family life and felt as if she were perpetually wrapped in warm blankets – even if her duties were more strenuous than she was used to.

The lack of modern amenities was no deterrent to her happiness – Kit accepted it as normal to draw water from a pump instead of from a tap, and a paraffin lamp was just as efficient as gas. Her own bodily comforts overcome by love for her husband, she was quite content to rise at four thirty, learning how to milk the cows, then drive them to pasture, to deal with the poultry and pigs and to assist at harvest, toiling alongside Worthy as if she had been born to it. Long after the pigeons had come home to roost on the beams of the fold yard shed, Kit was still busy, cooking and tending to her husband's needs, finally retiring at an hour when in her previous existence she would just have been setting out for

494

a ball. The satin gowns and elaborate hats were shut away; Kit doubted, without a twinge of regret, that she would ever wear them again.

Not that this meant she could never get dressed up, for there were opportunities to wear less ostentatious garb. Monday was market day when she would accompany Worthy and his brother to the nearest town. Whilst they attended auctions or bought supplies she would go off alone, ostensibly to attend to what she jokingly referred to as women's business, but in fact to visit the bank to pay in her secret cheques. Probyn had agreed to fetch these over from time to time, to spare her the journey, and also because he liked to come to the farm where his Uncle Worthy allowed him to watch the gruesome tasks that interested boys, such as castrating the piglets. Kit was glad for this assistance. The less she had to visit her old village the better, for Worthy might ask to go with her and overhear some gossip. She had not been there in months.

Far removed from her old haunts, there was no danger of Worthy learning of her past. The only danger was that Amelia might make reference to it in her letters, but upon her marriage Kit had written to her sister and warned her not to make any mention of Serena's parentage – though she hoped she would still be kind enough to contribute news from time to time.

As yet, Kit had not been fortunate enough to conceive, which rather surprised her, for her husband was a passionate and attentive man – seemingly making up for lost time. Worthy's obvious longing for a child made her yearn even more deeply to bear fruit, but even as November came upon them she remained barren.

'I told you there must be summat wrong with her,' George Treasure opined to his wife as they discussed Kit in her absence over afternoon tea. 'Married four months and not a sign.'

'How do you know?' Phoebe defended Kit. 'She might be having one and be too shy to say anything.'

'Don't try and kid me. You'd know if she was in that condition.'

'Plenty of time yet,' argued Phoebe, then upon hearing the lowing of cattle, warned her husband to hold his tongue. 'Hark! Here they are back from market.'

Worthy and his brother had been to purchase store cattle, which would be fattened up and sold for slaughter. Kit, who had accompanied them, was first to show her face, unsurprised at finding Worthy's parents and sister in her kitchen. Accustomed to Phoebe invading her home – for it had been Mother's home until late and the habit would be hard to break – Kit made no grumble, and was happy to accept a scone and a cup of tea as if she were a guest instead of mistress.

'You've got a letter from your niece in Leeds.' Phoebe went across the paved floor to collect it from the mantel. 'The one who's a prison wardress.'

Kit beamed, wondering how Mrs Treasure senior had recognized Ethel's handwriting, before realizing it would be the postmark that had informed her.

'She's got promotion.' Phoebe handed over the letter. 'Doing really well for herself by all accounts.'

Kit wondered how her mother-in-law could possibly know this from an envelope – until she saw that it had been opened. Her lips parted and she faltered slightly before unfolding the letter, hardly able to read it from indignation.

Phoebe was still singing Ethel's praises, saying what a worthwhile occupation it was for an unmarried woman and showing so much interest that Kit did not have the heart to take her to task.

But later, when Phoebe and her daughter had gone home and George was inspecting the store cattle with his other son, she asked Worthy if he might have a discreet word with his mother about opening other people's mail.

He cocked his head on one side. 'I don't think she meant any harm, Katherine. She's just treating you like one o' t'family.'

Kit did not want it to seem as if she were making a fuss about nothing, but said she would never dream of opening her mother-in-law's letters, nor her husband's come to that. She would be obliged if others would bestow the same courtesy.

Worthy's smiling reaction showed he thought she was odd – his mother had always opened everyone's letters – but he promised Kit he would have a word with her if it would keep his dear wife happy. Katherine meant the world to him. Though he was not the kind of man to tell her this, the least he could do was to show it by deed.

It was glaringly apparent the next morning in the dairy that Phoebe did not take kindly to Kit's instruction, though her displeasure was couched in an apology.

'Seems I've overestimated the strength of our friendship,' she told her daughter-in-law curtly, tipping a bucketful of milk into the separator. 'I never for a moment meant to pry into your secrets, I just –'

'Oh, I know you wouldn't!' Kit felt dreadful at treating Phoebe thus after receiving so much hospitality from her. 'It wasn't that there was anything secret –'

'You must have something to hide if you don't want us to see.' There was a slight note of petulance.

'Mother, I don't mind you reading any of my letters – after I've read them.' Her attitude one of defence, Kit tried to coax back the other's respect, her blue eyes holding Mrs Treasure affectionately. 'That's all it was. I get so few letters that it's such a joy to open them and it's just so disappointing if someone else has opened them first. I don't want to fall out about it.'

'I've never fallen out with anyone.' Still rather cool, Phoebe concentrated on turning the handle of the separator where the milk sloshed round and round. 'And if that's your wish I'll respect it, of course. I suppose we've just got to get used to each other's ways.'

This settled, the two of them got on with their work, but Kit could not help thinking that she had fallen out of favour.

'I wish I'd never said anything,' she told Worthy when they met up again mid-morning in the kitchen, taking the opportunity to mention it whilst they were not yet joined by others.

Seated at the table, her husband gave his support. 'No, you had every right to speak up if that sort of thing offends you.'

Kit saw from his face that he did not set a great deal of store by the incident, and had to smile at this attitude, 'You're just like our Charity,' she teased him, setting a plate of bread before him. 'Even if there was a landslide I don't think it'd bother her – she'd just say, "Oh, it'll wash!"'

Worthy liked the way his wife performed these impersonations. He felt he knew her family well though he had only ever met them once. 'You haven't seen any of them since our wedding, have you? Except for Probe. Wouldst like me to take thee over one Sunday?'

Kit tried not to sound too alarmed. 'Oh, we've too much to do round here – at Christmas maybe.'

Worthy laughed and said Christmas was an even busier time on the farm, what with pigs and fowl having to be butchered – but he would make time to take his dear wife to see her kin.

Kit smiled. Christmas was weeks away. She would find some excuse by then. She leaned over his chair to enjoy a quick embrace before others disturbed them, kissing the top of his balding head. 'I hope when we do go it's to take some good news.'

'About a babby, you mean?' He caressed the arms that imprisoned his shoulders. 'Aye, well, can't say we're not trying.'

They did pay a visit to Ralph Royd at Christmas, though all the while she and her husband were there Kit was on tenterhooks and she was glad to have the excuse that there was lots of work to be done on the farm, thereby rendering her stay brief. Her relief at getting away was two-fold, for Wyn had had a stillborn baby, and besides feeling sorry for her niece, Kit did not wish to be reminded of her own past hurts nor to dwell on her present infertility.

Making a January resolution to stop bewailing the absence of a baby, Kit threw herself into another year of hard work. It was tremendously difficult for her, though, when spring came to see the mares producing foals and the ewes their lambs – especially so when the orphans and weaklings were brought into the kitchen for her to rear. Once a piglet, too, was given to her care, nestling in Kit's arms like a little pink baby. Her devastation when it died brought ridicule from her father-in-law, who told her she was too soft to be a farmer's wife, and even Phoebe with whom she got on so well began to think that Kit was overly sentimental.

Whitsuntide came. Little girls and boys dressed in white marched in procession round the village. The hawthorn hedges were amassed with creamy blossom. In the pasture the daisies grew so thickly that one could hardly see the grass beneath. But still there was no wriggle of life within her womb.

Kit began to despair that the fortune-teller had been right after all: she was destined to remain childless. And if she could not give Worthy the child he longed for, then he might conclude there was no point in remaining married to her, so fulfilling the gypsy's entire reading. His words and actions denied this, he was as loving as ever towards Kit, but watching him give piggyback rides to his small nephews and nieces, seeing the warmth upon his face as he spoke to them, she found it impossible to ignore this blight upon her otherwise happy marriage.

Worthy thought she might be homesick and, as they waited for others to join them for a cup of tea one sunny morning, said, 'You haven't seen tha kin since Christmas – we mun go over this Sunday!'

Kit thought about this. It would be the first Sabbath in the month and the family – or what was left of it – would be gathered in one place. But any contact with her old village brought risk and she did not want to expose herself. 'It won't be much of a pleasure for you, dearest. They're an odd lot.' She concentrated on pouring the tea.

'They're all right to me.' Having come to read his wife's face well, Worthy noticed that she seemed reluctant for him to accompany her. It rather hurt him. 'Have I done something to offend you?' He tried to think of some inadvertent blunder he might have committed.

'No!' She had finished pouring the tea, though had not yet sat down, setting more cups on the table, pretending to busy herself. 'It's just an old tradition that our family gathers at Monty's house on the first Sabbath of the month.' That, at least, was the truth.

Worthy was baffled as to why she would want to leave him out. 'But aren't I part of your family now?'

'Of course! But none of them bring their spouses –' Kit broke off as her mother-in-law appeared in the doorway. 'Oh, the devil take tradition! You can come if you like.'

Her family was pleased to see Worthy again, for all had taken to Kit's giant of a husband, deeming him a good sensible chap – just the sort their sister needed to keep her in line. Kit was mortified when Gwen voiced this to Worthy, but upon realizing her mistake Gwen qualified her statement by saying that her youngest sister had never been particularly keen on housework nor cooking and she hoped he wasn't suffering too much at his wife's hands. Worthy merely laughed and, pointing to his expansive girth, replied that he had not had to tighten his belt yet but if he did it might not be a bad thing.

Excusing herself, Kit said she was just going to the farleymelow. Gwen thought to explain the word to Worthy but he already knew what it meant – Kit had told him all about the funny things her nephews and nieces had said when they were little. He could tell from the way she spoke about

499

them how much she loved children. It was a crying shame, he said in his wife's absence, that Katherine did not have a baby of her own. She would make such a wonderful mother.

Charity glanced at Gwen and said, 'Well, there's plenty of time yet.'

Gwen made a joke and said, 'She's maybe building up all her energy – it'll be a big un when it comes, looking at the pair of 'ee.'

Worthy said it was a wonder his mother had had any more after him. 'I were a huge babby – sixteen pounds, Mother said.'

There were gasps. 'We thought Kit were big!' laughed Monty. 'You make her look like Thumbelina.'

As if their conversation had been transmitted, Kit was thinking about babies too. Kneeling by her daughter's grave, she plucked handfuls of grass away from the stone in an attempt to tidy it up. Deep in thought, she jumped at the sound of a voice.

'Sorry, Aunt.' Probyn dropped to his knees beside her, and gripped her arm – she looked as if she were going to faint. 'I saw you coming in here and came to say hello.'

'I'll swing for you one of these days.' Slightly recovered, Kit brushed the dirt from her hands and rose. 'I'm supposed to be in the privy.' The closet at the end of her garden backed on to the allotments; after answering the call of nature she had sneaked through the hedge and across to the graveyard. 'I just thought I'd pop in and see her – and your mam and your sister – I get so little chance.'

Probyn nodded, fully aware that his Uncle Worthy knew nothing of this.

Kit studied him. Over the past year he had shot up but it seemed doubtful he would exceed his current height of five foot five. With the demise of his mother, he remained the smallest in the family. In fond manner, she made to take his arm. 'Come on, we'd best shift.'

Asked where he had been, Probyn said he had visited the pit to look down an old shaft before the watchman had chased him off. He had often peered down into the blackness, dropping pebbles and waiting for the responding sound, trying to picture himself at the bottom. He inhaled, looking nervous. 'I start tomorrow.'

Kit felt sorry for him, but said she was glad that he had resigned himself to the fact.

He corrected her. 'I still want to go in t'army.'

500

The trees in the graveyard sagged under a froth of blossom, its pungency tickling her nostrils. When she spoke her voice had a nasal tone. 'Well, maybe you can when you're older. Just keep your dad happy for the time being.'

Her nephew was terse as he opened the gate for her. 'He's happy as a pig in shi– in muck, making a fool of himself with that Mrs Carr. Everybody in t'village is talking about 'em.'

'That lot are never happy lest they're talking about somebody,' retorted Kit. 'It makes a change for it not to be me!' She tightened her grip on his arm and said in kind tone, 'I know you loved your mam but she's been gone two years now. You shouldn't begrudge your dad some happiness.'

Probyn distorted his mouth and remained stubborn. After escorting his aunt back across the allotments to the end of her garden he said he had promised to visit one of his pals and would have to leave her. Kit returned to the cottage alone.

'We were just going to send out a search party,' said Gwen.

Kit groped for an excuse. 'I saw our Probe over t'fence in t'allotment and got chatting to him. What's all this about you and Mrs Carr?' she asked her brother, and thought how quaint it was to see a fifty-year-old man turn as red as his hair.

Her sisters obviously knew nothing about it either. Merry, who kept house for her father, pursed her lips and looked at the floor.

As Monty was pounced on by his womenfolk, Worthy looked from one to the other, without a clue as to what was going on.

'You've no need to justify yourself to me,' said Kit as her brother started to do so. 'I like Mrs Carr – but I think it's about time you made an honest woman of her.'

Still crimson, Monty looked at his other sisters, who seemed to be in accordance with this. In fact he was the only person in the room to voice contrariety. 'People might say it's too soon,' he mumbled.

'From what our Probe says it's not soon enough,' said Kit.

Monty banged his fist on the chair arm. 'Dang that little – what's he been saying? If he's slandered that fine woman I'll –'

'He hasn't!' Kit soothed him.

Monty brought his bad-tempered frown under control and glanced at his brother-in-law, who was looking bemused. 'I'm sorry, Worthy.'

'No need to apologize to me,' came the big man's reply.

Kit turned to her seventeen-year-old niece. 'Merry, you'd like to see your dad happy, wouldn't you?'

Meredith held the same grudge as her brother – did not want Mrs Carr coming in here taking over as if she were their mother. It was bad enough when Aunt Gwen came in and bossed her about. She gave an unenthusiastic, 'Yes.'

'There you are!' Kit told her brother. 'There's nothing to stand in the way of a proposal.' She was surprised to see Monty cringe again. His reply was sheepish. 'I've already asked her. She agreed.'

There was laughter, congratulations and pleas for him to waste no more time. Infected by their pleasure, Monty grew more animated and told them that he and his lady friend had talked about marrying next month – he hoped they would all attend.

Kit said she for one would be there and gave a happy sigh. 'Eh, I don't know – we're all embarking on our new lives: Probe down the pit, Monty getting wed, me with my fine husband.' With a warm smile she told Worthy they should be on their way home. 'It's been a grand day.'

Worthy asked if he could take the ladies anywhere – the trap had room for four. To Kit's annoyance, Gwen was swift to acquire a lift home, taking them miles out of their way. Charity as usual was more thoughtful, alighting at the same time as her sister and saying she had not much further to walk.

Before the trap pulled away, Gwen said: 'I been thinking. This wedding might be an ideal time to bring those two brothers of ours together. They've been acting like schoolboys long enough.'

'I don't think that's such a good idea,' said Kit.

'No, well you might not,' replied Gwen. 'But I feel sorry for Monty. He did so much to keep his family together and I know it hurts him to see it fallen apart. There's only us two make the effort now.'

Charity excused their younger sister. 'Kit has further to travel than we do, Gwen.'

Worthy jumped in. 'I don't mind bringing her more often.'

This was not what Kit wanted. 'You've enough to do!'

'Anyway, never mind that,' said Gwen. 'I think we should hatch a plan to get Owen to come to his brother's wedding.'

'It's a waste of time,' said Kit, her other sister agreeing. 'Once Owen has his mind set against something it's impossible to shift him.' He was not alone. There were other families in the area that had been torn apart by the strike and had not shared one word for the past three years.

Gwen thought she knew best. 'I've been around longer than you have. Sometimes people need a good shove.'

'What are you going to tell him?' asked Kit.

'Oh, he'll know I'm up to something,' said Gwen, abdicating her role. 'Better if you do it – you're the only one to see him anyway.'

Kit frowned. 'I don't know whether I can lie to him.'

'It's never stopped you before,' retorted Gwen – then at her sister's blush realized she had put her foot in it and added quickly, 'It's for a noble cause. We got to get these two silly boys back together, Kit. What do you say? Worthy, you wouldn't want to be exiled from your brother, would you?'

He shook his head, but said that as he did not know Owen he could not say how he would react. 'I abhor lies myself, but then if it's for a good cause . . .'

Kit pondered over the matter. It would be nice to see her brothers reunited. 'Shouldn't we consult Mrs Carr?'

'What's it got to do with her?' demanded Gwen.

Kit emitted a laughing gasp. 'Well, it's her wedding too!' Then, she sighed. 'This is daft. Owen won't come within a mile of Ralph Royd and we can't get Monty to change the venue without raising his suspicion.'

Gwen didn't care to be told her plan was silly, and was determined to see it through. Charity came up with a solution. 'Your Donald comes of age soon, doesn't he? You'll be throwing a bit of a do I expect – well, invite Owen and Monty to that.'

Though not as dramatic as the wedding idea, Gwen agreed that it was the only way to do this. She pressed Kit for support.

Kit sighed again. 'Well, I still say it's a waste of time, but I'll do it.' At the others' thanks she allowed her husband to drive off. 'Now all we have to do is think of a convincing excuse for Owen,' she told Worthy.

He sighed, 'Well, rather you than me. I can't lie to save my life.'

It was sad that Monty's wedding took place without his brother present, but in retrospect Gwen had to agree that it had not been a good idea. Had anything gone wrong the event would have been ruined. As it was, the day turned out to be a very happy one, even Probyn and Merry discarding their misgivings.

As ever, Kit was worried that Worthy might overhear some snippet of gossip, but that did not happen, the occasion spawning only good things. She and her sisters were able to use this get-together to devise a plan to bring their brothers into the same room.

Speaking to his brother-in-law, Monty indicated the three sisters who huddled in conference in a corner of the reception hall. 'Like witches round a cauldron – I wonder what they're at.'

Worthy hoped he would not receive a direct enquiry, for then he could not pretend ignorance. 'In forty-odd years I've never come to know what goes on in a woman's head.'

You'll certainly have your work cut out with Kit, thought Monty, suffering a pang of guilt that he himself was party to deceiving this good man. But he smiled at Worthy and said, 'It's better not to know.'

On the way home from the wedding, Kit asked her husband if they might make a slight detour and visit Owen to save her going back another time. When they arrived at Garborough Junction, it was to an unusually warm reception. Owen was alone, mending his boots but, presented with visitors, he put these aside.

'Why, look at this!' His dark eyes sparkled at their fine attire. 'I'm honoured – but you didn't have to get dressed up for me tha knows.'

Entering the cool shade of his pit cottage, a smiling Kit revealed the truth. 'As a matter of fact we've been at Monty's wedding. He married Mrs Carr who works at the shop.'

Owen maintained his happy edifice, though brushed over Kit's information by asking if they would like a cup of tea – Meg was out somewhere, gasbagging he suspected. Seeing his guests were about to sit on the shabby sofa he told them to hang on whilst he shoved a newspaper underneath them. 'I don't want you muckying my furniture.'

To the crumpling of paper, Kit sat down next to her husband, telling Owen. 'It would've been nice if you'd been there.'

Owen gave a nonchalant shrug, then reached for the teapot. 'Do you want a biscuit with this? Oh aye, we can afford such things now tha knows – we're nobbut posh.'

Pleased at his jovial air, Kit thought she knew the reason. 'Our Monty's just got a ten per cent rise – did you get it too?'

Owen looked momentarily distracted and tapped his chest. 'He got it because I fought for it!' Then, swallowing the brief taste of bitterness, he sat down with his sister and brother-in-law to explain the reason for the increase and all the work that had gone into acquiring it. Coal prices had shot up lately, thereby lending him bargaining power. Since seeing her last year he had made great inroads towards increasing membership – which was now even higher than it had been before the lockout. The Yorkshire miners had formed an alliance with Lancashire and the Midlands, so strengthening their cause. 'I thought we might have another strike on our hands but the masters backed down – even them stingy blighters at Ralph Royd!' He rubbed his hands in uncharacteristic glee. 'Can you believe it? We're out for a rise every year now – and an eight-hour day if we maintain this unity.'

Kit said she hoped he would get it. Owen confidently predicted he would, then seeing that glazed expression come over their eyes which indicated he had spoken too long on the union, he asked what other family events there had been.

Kit took a deep breath. 'Well, that's the reason we're here really. It's Donald's coming of age next Saturday. Gwen's having a little tea party and asked me to extend an invitation to you and Meg and the kids.'

'Too idle to come herself.' Owen cleared his lungs, then dipped a biscuit into his tea. 'I never see her now.'

'There's nowt to stop you going there,' Kit accused him. 'Why should folk have to come to you?'

He was unresponsive. 'I'm not right bothered about seeing any of 'em, especially Donald – he's turned into a right jessie – and I never got a do for my twenty-first.' The Kilmasters had always eschewed such frivolity.

'We're off, aren't we, Worthy?' Kit turned to her husband, who nodded his balding head though he was unable to participate in his wife's machinations and could not look Owen in the eye, paying more attention to his teacup.

'I suppose t'other fella will be goin' an' all,' said Owen. 'Well, I won't.'

Kit's lie was delivered in a casual straight-faced manner. 'Oh, Monty won't be there. He's promised to take Mrs Carr somewhere – or Mrs Kilmaster I should say. They've had it arranged for ages apparently.' She raised her cup to her lips.

Owen studied her. One could never tell if Kit were being truthful. 'You're sure? Well, we might just stick our heads in then.'

Kit grinned and said she was sure the others would be glad to see him again. Her mission accomplished, she finished her tea, then told Worthy it was about time they were getting along. 'Tell Meg we were sorry to miss her.'

Owen said they might see her on the way home. Rolling down his shirtsleeves to make himself decent, he lighted his pipe and accompanied them to the ostler's in the village of Aldwaldwyke – only a matter of minutes away across a field – where Worthy had left the horse and trap. 'I wish I hadn't come,' he muttered at the looks that were directed at Kit and Worthy in their best clothes. 'You're showing me up in them rags.'

Passing the ancient cross outside the White Hart, Kit had the fleeting picture of Ninian Latimer, but did not dwell on it. Whilst Worthy went into the stable to collect his horse, she chatted to her brother in the evening sunshine.

A rider came trotting down the lane that led to Postgate Park. Kit knew him immediately and, with a prick of alarm, moved surreptitiously into the shadows, affecting to be dazzled by the sun, hoping he would not see her. Of all days, she must bump into him now, without a chance to warn him of her marriage.

It was to no avail. Spotting one of his workers, the Viscount turned to make brief address as he rode by. 'Kilmaster.'

Owen tugged at his cap and murmured a response.

Almost past, Ossie recognized the tall, finely dressed woman beside Owen Kilmaster and immediately hauled in his reins. 'Kit!' Kneeing his mount to perform a half-turn, he came back to where they were standing. 'How are you?'

'Very well, my lord.' She smiled, but cast a glance over her shoulder to see if Worthy was within earshot – what if Ossie should ask about Valentine?

'I'm most pleased to hear it!' Viscount Postgate sensed that his presence was not wholly welcome. Knowing Kilmaster to be a surly chap, he assumed Kit's nervousness to be caused by her brother's presence, but just then a huge man came out of the stables leading a horse in harness.

Turning quickly, Kit exclaimed with a blush, 'Ah, this is my husband,

Worthy Treasure! Worthy, this is Viscount Postgate whose family I used to work for.'

The two men appraised each other, Worthy raising his hat. Pipe in mouth, Owen watched the interplay, an idea forming in his mind. Did this nobleman number amongst Kit's lovers? He seemed unduly friendly for a former employer.

It turned out that Worthy was already acquainted with the other, and they had brief exchange. Then, looking down from his horse, Ossie gave congratulations on Kit's marriage and said he sincerely hoped they would be as happy as he and his wife, adding that he had been blessed with two fine boys and hoped they would be too.

Worthy wondered why his wife was so flustered but put it down to shyness at being addressed by an aristocrat. Thanking the Viscount for his interest, he watched him ride away, then backed his own horse between the shafts of his trap.

'Hang on, love, I'll give you a hand.' Owen stuck the pipe between his teeth and went to help his brother-in-law. 'Know his lordship then, do you?'

Worthy nodded. 'Father bought some land off the Earl not so long ago.'

This caused amusement. 'Eh, Kit,' exclaimed her brother. 'this lad o'yours must have a few bob.'

Breathing a little easier, Kit formed a smile. Worthy showed under-stated mirth too and said he had heard that the Earl was not doing too well from his tenants, many of whom were feeling the pinch from the agricultural slump, which the Treasures had so far managed to avoid. Owen said he hoped that did not mean a cut in wages for him, then smiled to himself over Worthy's fine handling of his sister as he helped her up into the trap, making it appear that she was a featherweight.

Kit said she would see Owen next Saturday, then took her leave. Waving them off, he went home.

There was much mumbling going on, opined Monty to his wife, the following Saturday when they attended his nephew's coming-of-age tea party. 'There's zommat queer going on here. Don't normally see Gwen skulking in a corner; she's too busy bossing everybody about. It's more like a meeting of some secret society than a birthday party.' Whilst the rest of the family – aunts, uncles, nephews, nieces – were crammed into Gwen's modestly furnished living room, Monty's sisters connived in the scullery.

Uninvolved, his wife simply smiled and shrugged. Aside from Kit, Monty's sisters were a clannish lot and hardly ever included her in anything.

'Are you sure he'll come?' Gwen was whispering to Kit, whilst pretending to be loading the sandwiches on to plates whilst Charity buttered more alongside.

'Well, he said he would,' answered an anxious Kit. 'But have you reckoned how to keep him here long enough for a reconciliation? The minute he sees Monty he'll be off.'

Gwen had thought of this. Her husband would keep one section of guests in the back room – Monty amongst them – whilst Owen would be shown into the front parlour with another section. Once he was seen to be relaxing, they could bring the two together. 'You get on with these sandwiches,' she ordered her sisters, 'And I'll go into the front and keep a lookout for him.'

'I always fall for it,' complained Charity to Kit, and waded into another pile of bread with her butter knife.

Some time later, Owen, Meg and their adult children arrived. Following the plan, Gwen spirited them into the front parlour and for a time everything went well. Kit wrung her hands and murmured to her husband that she hoped things would not misfire, then mouthed a query to Gwen, asking if it were time to bring the two together.

Gwen straightened her back. 'Monty, can you give me a hand to clear up some of the pots from the parlour? We're running short of cups.'

This was just the sort of thing to make Monty suspicious, hissed Kit to Charity. Their brother was never expected to help around the house. However odd he might consider it, Monty made no comment. Guessing that he did not want to appear a sluggard in front of his new wife, Gwen enlarged on this idea – if his wife were there it might prevent a scene between him and Owen. 'Ann, can you help too?'

Glad to be included, Monty's attractive wife followed him to the parlour. Taking Charity's example, Kit summoned her husband to come too, all crowding into the doorway of the front room to prevent either of the brothers escaping.

The moment Monty's auburn head appeared Owen knew he had been duped. Glaring around for the culprit he spotted Kit in the passageway and stabbed an accusing finger at her. 'You, you lying –' He tried to make his way to the door but was held back.

'Isn't it time you stopped all this daft carryon?' reproved Gwen. 'Come and sit down with your brother. You haven't seen him for years.'

Owen still struggled, followed by his wife and family, who obviously held his view for their faces were as dark as his. 'I don't waste me breath on blacklegs!'

Monty was equally furious, a red tide emerging from his starched collar and flooding across his cheeks. 'You pompous little shit!' The fact that he hardly ever swore lent more impact to his oath.

To cries of 'Language!' Owen stopped trying to carve an escape route to the door and offered retaliation. 'You've got the first letter right – only it's not P for pompous, it's P for principle! But you'd know nowt about that, you bloody turncoat.'

In an instant Monty's hands were around his brother's throat. With a lot of hair-pulling the women eventually managed to haul him off and he was dragged along the passage into the back room, his new wife clearly horrified.

Red in the face, Owen ignored Kit's plaintive apology and, shoving Meg before him, he barged out of the house.

There was a moment of shocked silence, then mumbled disapproval of the outrageous display.

Unhappy, Kit linked arms with Worthy for support and shook her head at Gwen. 'I told you he wouldn't have it.'

'The stubborn little –' Gwen was flustered at having her son's celebration spoiled. She marched into the back room to confront her elder brother, but Monty was to jump in first.

'I wish you'd all mind your own damned business!' After years of practice at suppressing his temper, he was livid at his sisters for making him lose it now. Without apology, he too strode from the house, pursued by his worried wife.

'Men!' snorted the eldest sister. 'Well, I wash my hands of both of them.'

Kit glanced at Worthy to see what he made of it all, performing a comical grimace as their eyes met.

It was difficult to restore the same light-hearted atmosphere after such violence. Kit did her best to salvage Donald's party with a few jokes, but she was glad when the afternoon was over, and commented to her husband as they drove home, 'What a rum lot families are.'

30

Kit thought it best to wait a few months before going to apologize to her brothers for her part in the deception. In fact, she told Worthy, she felt no great desire to see any of her family again after that shameful episode. What must he think of them?

Christmas was to pass without her usual visit to Ralph Royd, although she did send gifts of food with Probyn when he came to deliver the latest cheque. He was one relative she was always pleased to see and she felt great sympathy for her nephew who had not yet grown used to working underground. She was pleased to learn, though, that his disgruntlement was only for the work itself; the camaraderie of men was a great delight to one raised in a houseful of women.

To coincide with his visit a letter came from Amelia in America. After eighteen months of marriage to Worthy Kit had stopped being nervous about him reading such missives, for although they were filled with Serena's accomplishments there was no reference to her natural mother.

Amelia's letters were to mark each quarter of the following year, one arriving at Easter with the gambolling lambs, another to mark hay-making – which Kit was additionally pleased to receive for she was laid low at the time from some nauseating complaint – and yet another to celebrate Harvest Thanksgiving.

Reading the latest correspondence, after a back-breaking day of pulling wurzels, Worthy's heart went out to his wife. Her sister must surely be a thoughtless person, rambling on about her own little girl when she knew Katherine was childless. Perhaps he should write and ask her to reduce the exuberant tone of her letters. He had been secretly concerned about Kit of late. She was much quieter than usual – distracted.

Seated on the other side of the hearth, her face cast in firelight as she mended a torn hem, Kit glanced up to smile, but caught his frown and immediately asked what was amiss, fearing that she might have overlooked some detail that pertained to Serena being hers.

Worthy put the letter aside and stretched his long body. 'Oh, nothing, I were just thinking.'

She guessed what the subject might be. With the sewing resting on her lap, she nibbled her lip and beheld him almost shyly. 'I didn't want to tell you yet, till I was sure, but . . .'

His expression became alert, and his mouth began to turn up at the corners.

'Don't get your hopes up, it's too soon!' Kit made an entreating gesture, but found herself suffocated in a bear-like embrace and laughed at his sounds of delight, all the while begging him not to set too great store on this, she might be mistaken, but even as she said it she knew her feelings to be true; she was carrying Worthy's child.

The joy was all consuming – though this was not to devalue her grief over her lost babies, which would be for ever part of her – but with the grief impossible to share with Worthy, she chose to share his joy instead.

Her entreaties for him to make no announcement yet were useless. Within an hour of his rising the next morning every member of his family was acquainted with her condition and were offering their applause. Worthy even wanted to transmit the news to her own family but she prevented this, saying she would rather wait for medical confirmation first. Even so, Kit could not help a twinge of smugness at proving the fortune-teller wrong. What a ninny she had been to let such nonsense rule her life.

Once her fecundity had been established, Kit allowed Worthy to take her over to Ralph Royd to announce their glad tidings and from there to Owen's house – though here she was to find her announcement overshadowed by his own triumphant crowing: the miners had just won another ten per cent pay increase. Since last year's reward the new Federation had acquired even more members – their number now totalled almost a hundred thousand! His prediction had been right, boasted Owen: with such widespread support they could expect ten per cent every year now.

By now, October, he had forgiven her interference, but despite being in such a good mood he made it plain that he and his brother would never be reconciled. Kit accepted his wishes. She had her own family to think of now.

Everyone, it seemed, shared the couple's gladness over this long-awaited child. At every turn came more congratulations. Kit had never been so happy and contented in her life. Yet, beneath her euphoria lurked an element of worry. Having already given birth to two babies her labour would probably be short – too short for a first child. How could she explain this? Weary of subterfuge, and having come to know her husband intimately, Kit teetered on the brink of revelation, of stepping down from the pedestal upon which he had so obviously placed her. Worthy loved her – surely this Christian man would forgive her sins, accept her for what she was? Over and over in her mind she practised her confession, almost reached the point of divulgence, until at the last nerve-racking moment the risk would present itself as too great and she would retreat into secrecy.

Confined by this worry, the memory of her lost children and her steadily increasing girth, Kit felt it impossible to carry out her chores around the farm and, with the aim of conserving her energy, spent her days sewing or reading, awaiting the springtime birth of her child. Whilst her besotted husband might be happy to pamper her, others were not. Ignorant of how precious this baby was to its mother, Phoebe thought it scandalous that Kit had chosen to neglect her duties – but was even more amazed when Kit's lack of industry extended to the home.

'Doesn't take much stamina to sweep the floor!' she complained privately to her own daughter. 'I just went in now and there's crumbs and muck everywhere. There'll be rats in before she knows it. It breaks my heart to see that house go to ruin. I never had Kit down as a slattern but she's certainly heading that way. I mean, she's hardly five months gone. I'd better not find she's neglecting my boy or there will be trouble.'

Unable to bear the squalor, Phoebe took it upon herself to keep the farmhouse up to its former standard of cleanliness, hardly bothering to conceal her disapproval and not even waiting for Kit to leave the house before she started sweeping and dusting around her.

Far from being shamed by this Kit was rather annoyed for, in her opinion, the house was tidy enough – though she voiced no complaint to the culprit, instead lamenting to her husband.

'Let her do it if she's daft enough,' said Worthy, ever the peacekeeper. 'Nobody's blaming you for looking after yourself.'

'It's not from selfishness that I do this but for the baby!' protested Kit. 'I'm so fearful of losing –'

'I know!' The big man pushed her gently into a chair. 'I've waited a long time for this baby too. Take no notice of Mother. If she comes in interfering, just leave her to it, get your coat on and come up to the fields and have a natter to me.'

This Kit took to doing, further devaluing herself in Phoebe's estimation – for what wife with any respect would leave her mother-in-law to do her work!

Returning after her latest escape Kit found the house spotless and her red-faced mother-in-law preparing lumps of bread and butter for the afternoon tea-break. Soon after, on a draught of wintry air, a tired-looking Worthy, his father and a bunch of hired men came in from the fields, rubbing their hands before the fire. Everyone, it seemed, had earned their rest except Kit.

There was little talk whilst appetites were being slaked, each concentrating on the matter in hand. Only when the level of tea in his large mug had been considerably reduced did George Treasure utter words. 'Suppose you men'll be wanting a week off then.' It was Martinmas, when the hired workers received their wages. 'Be coming back for another year, will tha?' The young men said they were willing, if he would have them. 'You'll do,' he told them.

'Don't tease the lads,' said Phoebe. 'They work a lot harder than some we've had.' Her comment was not a slur on Kit but she took it as one and, after the tea was drunk, she was the one to collect the pots and carry them to the sink.

The men, including Worthy and his father, lumbered back to the stubbled fields, some to plough, and some to sow. Phoebe called out to Kit that she would see her later and left. Kit breathed a sigh of relief at being left alone, and collapsed into an armchair, lovingly stroking her abdomen.

'Worthy!' Hearing his name, the big man stopped and waited for his mother to catch up with him.

'You go on!' Phoebe flicked a hand at the other men who had also looked round. 'It's this one I want.'

The elderly Mr Treasure rolled his eyes and departed. His wife was wearing that look of intrigue which could only spell trouble.

'I was dusting the top of the rafters and I found this!' With a quick glance to check that Kit was not watching from the window, Phoebe pulled a small book from her apron pocket.

Worthy looked amused at the lengths to which his mother had gone. 'Dusting the top of the rafters?'

'Look at it!' she urged him. 'It's a bank book – and it's got Kit's name in.'

Worthy's earth-stained thumb flicked the pages. The balance therein was insignificant compared to the funds Kit had brought to the marriage, but he noticed that it comprised regular instalments.

When her son's face remained passive Phoebe prompted him. 'Did you know about it?'

He closed the book. 'It's neither summat nor nowt.'

'So you didn't know?' She seized on his answer.

'Katherine's entitled to her privacy –'

'She's your wife!'

'Everyone has their little secret, Mother,' said Worthy, remembering a childhood incident in which he had set fire to the barn and someone else had got the blame.

'I haven't, nor have you.'

He wasn't about to confess now. 'The point is –'

'The point is that Kit reckons to have nothing to hide yet she won't let anyone read her letters and keeps her bank book hidden!' Mrs Treasure had a habit of turning away when she made a comment, then returning with a 'so there' kind of nod; she made such a gesture now.

'She doesn't hide her normal bank book, she's just kept this one separate for some reason. I've always known exactly how much she's got in the bank – Oh, I'm that daft!' Worthy smote his head. 'I remember now, Katherine told me she's been putting money away for the babby. I didn't take much interest what she said about it then, but that's what this will be.' He tapped the book. 'Now tell me exactly where you found it. I don't want her to think my mother's been prying, do I? When informed, he pocketed the

515

item. 'Well, I'm going to put it back, and don't you dare go bothering Katherine about it.'

'If you know about it, all well and good.' Phoebe shrugged and crossed her arms. 'I just thought it was a funny sort of place to keep a bank book.'

'Katherine's got things all over the house –'

'Don't I know it!' came the disgusted exclamation.

'– in case robbers come!' finished Worthy. 'Now, you're clear about what I said? I won't have her upset with the babby expected so soon.' Receiving his mother's promise, he went back to work.

Though curious and a little upset that his wife had chosen to hide this from him, Worthy never mentioned the incident. Hence, Kit had no idea that anyone had discovered one of her secrets. The fact that Phoebe had started to treat her in a different manner held no relevance for Kit, other than to show she was annoyed about her daughter-in-law's laziness. The latter was determined not to risk losing another child by tackling strenuous farm work, though Phoebe's attitude did concern her, for they had been such good friends before, and she resolved to pull her weight again after the baby was safely born. Worthy understood this without being told, but how could Kit explain it to his mother without disclosing the reason?

Another month went by. Kit tried to show willing by helping to pluck the Christmas fowl but got little praise for her contribution. Thank goodness there was something she could do sitting down, Phoebe muttered to her daughter, wrenching feathers out by the handful as if she would like to do the same to Kit. Nothing, it seemed, would repair this fall from grace.

The Advent days were mild, allowing Kit to make one last visit to her relatives before the birth of her child in spring. Contentment with her husband had added a great deal of weight to her frame of late, thus disguising her pregnancy and allowing her to travel without fear of inviting offence.

Alas, bad news awaited her at Ralph Royd. Kit and Worthy did not proceed beyond the outer door. The only member of the family still on her feet, Ann Kilmaster told Kit that Monty and his children had gone down with influenza. Half the colliery village had succumbed to this scourge, which had affected the whole country. Gwen had caught

516

it too and was blaming Ethel for fetching it from Leeds. They were all very ill.

Kit's primary instinct was to protect her baby and run, but instead of turning tail she forced herself to ask if there was any way she could help. Monty's wife thanked her, but said she and Worthy would be well advised to isolate themselves on the farm until the danger of contagion was over.

'I'll drop you a line to tell you when it's safe to come,' concluded the weary-looking Ann, and shepherded them towards their trap.

Worthy went ahead to untie the reins from a post. Whilst waiting for him, Kit felt a nudge. Turning to Ann she glanced down and, responding to the urgent, secretive gesture, quickly took possession of the latest cheque. It was to remain in her pocket until the following day.

The pigeons who roosted in the rafters of the shed were becoming a nuisance. The next morning before breakfast, Worthy picked up a lantern and his gun and went to reduce their numbers. In his absence, Kit dragged herself up on to a chair, then on to the oak table which was directly beneath a beam that ran the width of the kitchen. Sides of bacon, legs of ham and bunches of dried herbs were suspended from the beam, but to Kit it had other uses. The sporadic noise of Worthy's gun confirming his whereabouts, she reached up and felt along the upper surface of the beam for her bank book. It was not there. Alarm fluttered in her breast. She was certain this was not just a slip of memory – someone had taken it. Threatened by panic, more concerned that Worthy might have found it than a thief, she waddled gingerly along the table, her fingers creeping a good way along the beam before accidentally dislodging the book and knocking it to the floor. With a sigh of relief mixed with impatience, she took a tentative step from table to chair, tottering slightly before reaching the ground and eventually bending with great difficulty to pick up the book. After a quick look inside it, she inserted the cheque between its pages and shoved it into the pocket of her tartan flannel dress, with the intention of taking it to the bank later that morning. Worthy was transporting a last consignment of geese and chickens to the Christmas market and she intended to go with him.

After breakfast, Worthy loaded the cart with live fowl, helped his pregnant wife aboard and took her to market.

At this busy time of year, the usual crowd was swelled threefold, extra stalls laden with mistletoe, holly and other greenery, and a virtual forest of Christmas trees, the scent of which plunged Kit into brief nostalgia for the yuletide ball at Postgate Park. Above a cacophony of animal ululations, Kit told Worthy as usual that she would meet him later after performing her business, but today Worthy objected, saying that as there were only the two of them why didn't she stay and keep him company. It was a lovely day and she was well wrapped up. 'I shan't be long selling these and we can have a look round the shops together and have some dinner.'

Unable to use the excuse that she wanted to purchase a Christmas gift for him, for she had used this before, Kit remained at her husband's side as he unloaded the crates of fowl, and sat by him on a bench whilst he proceeded to sell them.

The fowl went quickly. Within an hour there were only a couple left. However, discomforted by her full bladder, Kit said she really would have to leave him on his own for a minute and go find somewhere to relieve herself.

She had fully intended to leave the cheque in her pocket, to save it for another day, but on the way back from emptying her bladder her route took her directly past the bank and she decided not to waste this opportunity. Brushing her way through the crowds, she went inside.

Worthy had sold his last bird. Upon stacking the empty crates on the back of the cart, his eyes followed the direction his wife had taken some minutes ago, expecting to see her head and shoulders above the crowd, but there was no sign of her blue feathered hat. After a moment of contemplation, he decided to go to meet her.

The bank was full. Kit swayed impatiently whilst her turn came, was debating whether to wait at all, when finally a space appeared at the counter. It took only moments to deposit the cheque. Deposit book in hand, she hurried from the bank – and encountered her husband.

She gave a little cry of exclamation, her face turning a deep red. 'I was just passing the bank and I thought I'd kill two birds with one stone – oh, that makes it sound as if I had a widdle in there!' She hid an embarrassed laugh behind her glove.

After his initial flicker of surprise, Worthy did not appear in any way indignant, and made no move to confront his wife. Though his eyes glanced at the book in her hand, he did not ask what it was, making

Kit think that perhaps he already knew, that he was the one who had moved it from its hiding place. So why had he not said anything?

Unable to think quickly, she said with another sheepish laugh, 'Don't worry, I wasn't trying to spend all your money! This is just a little account I keep separate – I told you about once living in York, didn't I?'

The big man nodded, his eyes fixed to her face. Streams of shoppers meandered round them.

'Yes, I thought I had.' Kit tried to make light of the bank book in her hand. 'Did I say I put my house up for let? Oh, I couldn't remember if I told you – probably because it wasn't worth mentioning – well, anyway, when I get the rent every month I just pop it in here. It's hardly worth the bother, but I had difficulty in selling the place so I decided to put it up for let. The regular payments will make a nice little nest egg for the baby.' She held out the book to show him she had nothing to hide.

He wanted to believe her, but in the face of such obvious fabrication, Worthy could not help feeling saddened. Nevertheless, he did not mention that he already knew about the sum enclosed, and made perfunctory examination of the bank book. 'I could have saved you the bother of trailing into town and done it for you.'

Relieved to have one secret out in the open, Kit told him she would be glad of his help in the future and told him to keep the book in his pocket. 'Much as I like coming into town, I don't think I'll be able to drag myself here much longer.' Taking his arm, she gave it a loving squeeze and asked if they could find a restaurant, for she was absolutely famished.

Skilfully concealing his woe at her lies, Worthy said that as it would probably be their last outing together before the baby, he would take her to the best one in town. His wife issued a gay laugh and joked that the owner would probably take one look at the hefty couple and bar them from the place, fearing they would clear him out. Worthy laughed too, desperately trying not to succumb to the darker side of his nature, yet underneath a little of his respect for her had died.

Thereafter, apart from an occasional outing to market, Kit was confined to the farm. Visitors were few, though there was a letter from Ann to say that, thankfully, all had recovered from their influenza. In addition there was correspondence from her nieces and from Amelia to help her while away her long days up to spring.

The time of birth crawled nearer. From the nucleus of dormant primrose leaves, came tiny bright green shoots. Impatient to hold her baby, fearful that something would go wrong, Kit was glad of anything to take her mind off it and was even more glad if this was a visit from her nephew.

This Friday afternoon, her joy at seeing him was especially pronounced, for Phoebe had been driving her mad, rushing about cleaning things that did not have to be cleaned. 'Probe!' Kit greeted him with open arms but, encumbered by her pregnancy, was slow to reach him. 'Is the pit playing today?' Kit wished her mother-in-law would go away and leave her to enjoy this visit in peace but there seemed little chance of that, Phoebe had put the kettle on and was laying out three cups and saucers.

Cap in hand, he looked somewhat concerned. 'Nay, we're on strike. You know t'union was hoping for a ten per cent rise every year?' Similarly worried, his aunt nodded as she lowered herself back into a chair. 'Well, masters've ganged up on us this year. I hear some pits've been offered what they want – Uncle Owen's done all right by all accounts – but union says they're not allowed to accept it unless everybody in t'Federation gets it, so notice went up t'other week and we're all out.'

Kit asked how Probyn's father was coping.

'Oh, we're all right – at least we can't get evicted this time thanks to you giving us your house.' At his aunt's sudden look of alarm, he blushed. It was so difficult to know what one could mention in this house. He tried to cover his slip. 'Anyroad, I'm not bothered when we go back! I'm having a grand time going rabbiting and whatnot.' He rambled on for a while, then came to the real reason for his visit, ineptitude taking over. 'As a matter of fact, I've got some bad news. Aunt Charity's died.'

Kit gave a little cry of shock – then began to weep.

Probyn shifted uncomfortably in his chair, telling his youngest aunt that her sister had had an apoplectic stroke yesterday. 'Funeral's on Monday – they're not expecting you to go, o' course. Me father said he'll represent you.'

Kit was still weeping for her easygoing sister, Charity's favourite saying echoing in her mind – Never mind, it'll wash. 'I can't believe it. She was only forty-three.'

Mrs Treasure senior made commiserating noises. 'It's no age, is it?'

Probyn sat for a while, playing with his cap, whilst his aunt intermittently wept and voiced her disbelief. He was glad when Kit changed the subject. He wished Mrs Treasure would give them some privacy, but she obviously found his chat so interesting that she had no wish to miss anything.

All too soon, it was time for Probe to leave. Voicing the hope that the next time he visited she would have a new cousin for him, Kit accompanied him to the gate, her eyes still red from weeping. With his uncle too busy with spring lambs to transport him home, Probyn was having to travel on foot. Before taking his leave, however, he slipped the latest cheque into her hand.

'I thought I were going to have to take it back home with me,' he whispered, 'with Mrs Treasure being there.'

Sniffing, Kit waylaid his fears and said he no longer had to maintain the subterfuge. 'Your Uncle Worthy knows about it now.'

Probyn looked most relieved. 'Oh good. Does he know everything?'

Kit shook her head quickly. 'No, it'll only hurt him.'

Probyn murmured agreement. 'I'm sorry about letting slip that you gave us your house – d'you think she noticed?'

Kit said she did not think so, although privately she too had been very concerned about this.

Holding his cap by its peak, Probyn flicked it on to his head and, with a final wave, embarked on his homewards journey.

One hand pressed to her side, Kit waddled back to the farmhouse. To her relief Phoebe had gone, allowing her to sit and wallow in grief over her sister's death, until it was time to put her husband's meal on the table.

It was dark when, lantern in hand, Worthy plodded across the yard, hungry both for food and for his wife's company. The beasts whose gentle lowing could be heard from the shippon were warm and secure, but there would be no such comfort for him. Once fed, he would have to brave the night again, for a predator had been mauling his lambs. A quick movement from the nearby cottage caught his eye. Silhouetted in her doorway by lamplight, his mother was summoning him. With a sigh for this delay, he traipsed through the darkness to see what she wanted.

Phoebe's urgent whisper joined the faint clucking of the hens as they settled down for the night – it was never silent on the farm. 'Did you know your wife used to own a house before she came here?'

'Yes, of course I did, Mother.' Worthy ached all over. A tethered sheepdog had jumped up to greet him but fell back, subdued by his lack of response.

Phoebe made a sound of disapproval. 'She must think we're a charity or something – I mean, she shouldn't rely on you to keep her. By rights anything she owns is yours now.'

Worthy rubbed his head – he had been plagued by a splitting headache all day. 'No, they changed all that, Mother. A married woman can keep her own property. Anyway, I do get the benefit of it, from the rent Katherine's tenants pay.'

His mother frowned. 'You mean she charges her brother rent? Oh well, that's not so bad then.'

He was baffled and impatient. 'Where does her brother come into this?'

She clicked her tongue. 'He lives in the house she used to own at Ralph Royd.'

Worthy shook his head, wishing he had not, for it felt as if it might drop off. 'No, you're getting mixed up –'

'No, I'm not!' Phoebe was adamant. 'Young Probe was here this afternoon; he let something out about her giving them her house.'

Worthy stared at his mother for a second, then turned his back on her. 'Well, what does it matter if she wants to give it away? It's nowt to do with us.'

'By the way, her sister Charity's died,' Phoebe called after him.

With curt acknowledgement, he went home. Kit met him with a sad smile and made to help him off with his coat. He groaned as if was removed from his aching body, drawing sounds of sympathy from his wife, who held the towel for him whilst he washed. His evening meal was on the table. There was a cheque lying there too.

'Mother's just told me about your sister. I'm sorry, lass.'

Kit nodded and fought back tears.

'Probe all right, is he?' He began to wolf down his meal, afraid to reveal his annoyance over yet another conundrum.

Kit gave a worried smile and told him about the strike. 'I hope it's not as drawn out as the last time. They were locked out for about five months.'

'Yes, I know. I read about the evictions.' Another large forkful was inserted.

Kit studied him. The words were not delivered in any peculiar way, nor did he come right out and ask her, but she feared that Worthy's mother had not confined her gossip to news of Charity's death. Alarm prickled her skin. If he did not question her directly what was she to say: 'Oh, by the way, I owned another house besides the one in York that you've only just found out about'? How many more did she own? he would want to know. And what other secrets?

But he seemed his usual self, ploughing through his meal until the plate was empty. Coming to stand beside him, she said of their child, 'He's been very quiet today.'

Without speaking, Worthy put his arm around his wife and pulled her close so that her bulging abdomen came level with his face, then rested his head against it, closing his eyes. Looking down at him, Kit was filled with love.

Then she felt his head. 'Oh, you're red hot!'

Worthy retained his position. 'I'm dead beat.'

She tried to bend over and kiss him but the bulge under her apron prevented it. 'I hope it's not that influenza. You should have an early night.'

'Can't.' Eyes closed, he felt her pulse beneath his cheek. 'It's my turn to sit with the lambs.'

Groaning, she tried to coax him into relinquishing this chore, but he said it was his duty. Shortly afterwards, with a lantern and a gun, he went out into the night.

Thinking about him in the cold dark night, worrying that he might have influenza, Kit did not sleep very well. People had died from this. With news of her sister's death fresh in her mind, Kit was terrified she was going to lose her husband too. She rolled over with difficulty, trying not to think of it, but could gain no comfort. Hours passed. She must have eventually drifted off, for the sound of a weapon going off jolted her back to wakefulness. After this, she could not sleep at all.

When her husband's weary figure appeared through the early morning mist, Kit was waiting with a hot breakfast. Looking exhausted, he laid his weapon aside and sat at the table, muttering disappointment at having missed his target. Kit stood behind him whilst he ate, rubbing his shoulders, pleading for him to climb into the still-warm bed.

Ignoring his objections that he could not leave others to do his work, she went across the yard. There was no one in George and Phoebe's kitchen, but the glow of a lantern in the milking shed told where they were. Waddling there, Kit conveyed her suspicions that their son had been stricken with influenza. Knowing there was no point in sending for the doctor, for it would have to run its course, she told them she would try and tackle a few of Worthy's chores, though she doubted she would be much use.

For once, Phoebe made no averse remark and said that of course Worthy must come first. Sending Kit back to the farmhouse, she said she would be over later to help.

He was still at the table when she entered, refusing all attempts to get him to bed, though he accepted another mug of tea, hunched over it in forlorn manner.

Some time later, Phoebe came across to see how her son was and to bring the mail. She beheld him worriedly and said she had never seen him look so ill. 'Kit's right, you should be in bed.'

Worthy listed the things to be done, and to draw attention from his illness, held out his hand for the letters.

'There's one with funny writing on the front for Kit – looks important.' Though dying to open it, Phoebe had never done so since her daughter-in-law's objection. However, she hovered for information.

Kit was staring at the typed envelope in concerned manner and hurriedly tore it open, primarily frowning at the address on the front page, then sifting through the pages to the final one when she saw that it was signed by Flora, whence she gave a sound of relief.

'Ah, it's only from my sister in America! Not Amelia, another one.' Breathing a little easier, she groped for a chair and lowered herself on to it. 'I don't suppose either of them knows about Charity yet.' After a sigh, she began to read the letter. 'Fancy that – she's learned how to type – acts as secretary to this man she ran off with. What a dark horse she is. She's been in touch with Amelia, that's how she got our address.' Kit read on, making sporadic remarks. It was a lovely long letter. She had not reached the end of it before the sound of cartwheels came grinding into the yard and Phoebe interrupted, saying that would be Abel. She would have to go and tell him Worthy was ill.

Knowing she would be interrupted again, Kit broke off from reading her letter and hoisted her body off the chair to go and pour a cup of tea for Abel. Leaning on one elbow, his head resting on one hand, a feverish-looking Worthy rotated the letter on the table and began to peruse it half-heartedly.

Though the reams of information about Flora's offspring held little personal interest, he continued to browse, page by page, finally coming to the end when Flora reiterated her pleasure upon learning the news that Kit was having a baby. *I am so very pleased for you. I always felt guilty that I was instrumental in you having to give Serena up, but you can be assured –* Worthy's gut lurched. He went back to make sure he had not misread.

Turning to check on her husband's health, Kit saw that his face had become white. She opened her mouth to donate concern, but when he held out the letter, her heart almost stopped.

'Is it true?' He watched her as she took the page, saw the tremble in her hands.

Kit felt ready to faint. Her eyes searched for the damning passage, and finally there it was. *I always felt guilty that I was instrumental in you having to give Serena up, but you can be assured that your daughter has a good life. Amelia has been a wonderful mother to her . . .*

She read no more. Worthy dragged himself to his feet, leaning on the table for support. 'Katherine, I asked if it was true. Did you give birth to that child?'

She closed her eyes and nodded, her lip trembling with emotion. When she dared to look at him she saw that he was devastated.

Outside, Phoebe and her younger son were making their way to the farmhouse when they heard a cry.

'Please, Worthy – oh God, don't!'

The urgency of that yell increased their pace. Abel threw open the door to see Worthy directing his shotgun at Kit, who cowered behind a chair. Leaping forward he knocked the barrel upwards, the gun went off, blasting a hole in the ceiling above Kit's head. She screamed and, terrified both for herself and the baby, lumbered as fast as she could for the door.

'For God's sake, man, what are you doing?' Having foiled the murder, Abel stepped back, clutching his head and beholding his brother as if he were mad. His mistake was to not keep possession of the gun.

Repelled by his own actions, debilitated by illness and an uncontrollable heartbreak, Worthy turned the weapon on himself. Again, his brother fought to disarm him.

Appalled, Phoebe grabbed Kit's arm as she tried to escape, screaming at her, 'It's that letter, isn't it? What is it? What have you done to him?'

Trying to wriggle free, Kit returned the scream: 'I had another baby!'

With a frantic glance at her sons, who were still locked in turmoil, Phoebe damned Kit and urged her from the room and into the yard. At the first explosion George had come running towards the open door and now almost collided with his wife and hysterical daughter-in-law. Ettie too had run outside. All stood momentarily pinned by horror to watch the struggle between the brothers, Kit sobbing and cowering behind George before he rushed to help his younger son disarm the other, leaving her vulnerable.

But before he reached his goal the gun roared again. Kit saw the blood spout, saw Worthy fall, saw him die.

Stunned beyond comprehension, through a veil of semiconsciousness she heard angry voices, orders being given, felt herself shoved from one to another – and then in the next instant her skirt was drenched and a dull ache was creeping from the small of her back into every muscle of her abdomen. In the confusion, she heard someone mention doctor, then Phoebe screeched that she never wanted to see her again, and she felt men's hands grab her and shove her into the back of a cart.

With an urgent thrash of his reins Abel set the horse into motion, steered it out of the yard and down a long stony track towards the road. Jolted and jarred, on the point of fainting, Kit hugged her abdomen to protect the child, tossed this way and that, her bouncing buttocks colliding time after time with the unforgiving surface. Too shocked to complain, she swayed from side to side, at the mercy of the driver and of the unstoppable pain that heralded labour.

The cart reached the road. It was all downhill from there and the horse set off at a brisk pace, encouraged by an anxious Abel, who seemed oblivious to his human cargo, intent only on reaching the village. The pains increased – merged into one constant bout of suffering – would her journey never end?

Finally, it did. Groggy and disorientated, Kit stumbled blindly as Abel and a woman helped her from the cart and into a house. Then all at once Abel was gone and she was alone with the woman. The pain was much stronger now. The woman made soothing noises as she piloted her charge towards a bed. Moaning, Kit felt the clothes being stripped from her, fell upon the mattress and allowed rude hands to poke and pry, begged for the Lord to take her, for her beloved husband was dead and, even as it was born, she knew instinctively that her child was dead too.

31

'No wonder you had such a hard time!' Nurse Fenton scooped a last handful of water over the baby boy, then lifted him, dripping, from the small enamel bath by the fire and on to a towel on her lap, the umbilical cord still protruding from his pink belly like the stem of an apple. 'He must weigh a stone – if not a ton.'

Watching the scene from her bed, Kit gave a wan smile, still hardly able to believe after two days that those lusty cries were real. Upon his entry to the world she had gasped and laughed and cried at the same time, but throughout that joyful moment had come intense despair. For her little boy's father would never see him. That same sorrow still throbbed within her now.

Nurse Fenton ignored the baby's protests and rubbed him with the towel. Fearing that she was going to grate his skin right off, an anxious Kit said she thought she had heard someone at the door. The nurse said they could wait, but at least she finished her rough handling of Kit's baby and dressed him in clothes she had made herself that were normally reserved for destitute mothers. After wrapping him up in a tight bundle, she passed him over to be fed.

In the nurse's absence, Kit put her baby to her breast, and gazed down at him whilst he suckled, her mind a conflict of emotions. At last she had a legitimate child that no one except the Lord could take away – but how was she going to care for him? Everything she owned was at the farm. She could not even pay the nurse.

The latter came back grumbling that there had been no one at the door. Kit apologized and said she must have been hearing things, then thanked the nurse for her devoted care over these last two days.

'You've already thanked me,' said Nurse Fenton.

'Have I?' Kit looked dazed. 'I can't remember much at all.' Did not want to remember.

'That's hardly surprising after what you've been through.' The nurse stood and watched the baby feeding, her face overtaken by a munificent smile.

'I shall get up after he's finished,' said Kit, 'and be out of your hair.'

'You'll do no such thing!'

'But I can't pay you – at least not yet.'

'Then pay me when you can,' said the nurse. 'You'll get up when I say you can.'

Kit responded with a sickly smile. 'I don't know what I'm going to wear. I've only the clothes I came in.' And they would be ruined.

'Your dress and petticoats are on the line. I can lend you a pair of my drawers whilst yours are in the wash.' Nurse Fenton went to empty the bath water, telling Kit not to worry her head about what lay ahead, but to get some rest.

But Kit did worry. Where was she to go? The house in York was occupied at the moment. She would have to write to the agent and ask him to remove the tenant, but that would take weeks. She could not stay here that long. She would have to fall back on one of her siblings. Thoughts of Charity brought the glint of tears. Discounting Gwen, Kit decided that it had to be one of her brothers; she had housed both in times of trouble. But they were on strike. How could she expect them to feed her? Well, they would just have to, for she had no one else. But then she remembered Mr Popplewell, and decided to throw herself on his mercy. Changing her baby to the other breast, she began to form a letter in her mind.

The baby, still unnamed, was over a week old and still Kit's letter had gone unanswered. She had stated how urgent it was that Mr Popplewell come at once but no word had arrived. The nurse had been very good, but Kit felt dreadful at having to accept her charity. There was only one thing for it: she must rely on her family. It had always been Monty to whom she had turned in the past, and the house in which he lived had been bequeathed by her, but it did not seem fair somehow to keep doing this to him – especially not to his wife, Ann, who had struggle enough in trying to make herself accepted by his children. Owen's house was nearer.

He was living on strike pay too, and would not thank Kit for landing him with this, but there was no other way.

Feeling decidedly grubby, having only the clothes she stood up in, Kit thanked Nurse Fenton but said she could not impose on her any longer. Asking one last favour – that the woman conjure up some transport to Garborough Junction – she made ready to depart.

Expecting to meet with desperate faces at her brother's house, Kit was surprised to be made most welcome. So soon after losing one sister, Owen was shocked to hear of his brother-in-law's death – and by such terrible means. He told his distraught sister she could stay as long as she wanted. Meg was similarly disposed, taking charge of the baby so that Kit could sit and drink her tea in peace.

Wiping her eyes, Kit told them, 'I hate being such a burden during the strike but –'

'Aw nay!' Owen was quick to respond. 'It's all but over. Aye! It's right. The master's have caved in – except for one pit. I'll give you three guesses where that is.'

Kit knew. 'Ralph Royd.' She frowned. 'But Probe said nobody was allowed to go back unless every pit got the reward.'

'That's reet.' Owen did not seem in the least worried, in fact he was most cheerful. 'But they won't be able to hold out this time, not if they want to keep face with the other coalmasters. In fact, we're expecting to get word any day that they've knuckled under.'

Kit was relieved that she was not going to be such a burden as she had feared, and said that as soon as she got word that her house in York was vacated she would leave.

Owen studied her glazed eyes, felt sorry that she had had such transient happiness with Worthy. 'You stay here as long as you want, Kit.'

'I feel terrible at not being able to contribute anything, but everything I own is at the farm, including my bank book.'

'I'll go for it if you like,' offered Owen. 'Not just 'cause I want paying, mind.' He addressed Meg who seemed to be enjoying holding the baby. 'You'd think Worthy's family would've brought poor lass's stuff, wouldn't you?'

Kit said they had probably burned it, the way they felt about her.

Owen dealt a brief pat to her shoulder and said he would go tomorrow.

However, long before then news arrived to say that the Ralph Royd Coal Company had made similar compromise to the rest of the Yorkshire coalfield – the ten per cent rise had been conceded and the strike was effectively over. Bringing his hands together in a loud smack that jerked Kit's baby from the breast and set him crying, Owen praised the Lord, then rushed off to help with the organization of the return to work – for this was going to be the most spectacular return that Yorkshire had ever seen.

Indeed it was. Within hours of the news, the village was resounding to the tunes of a brass band. Whilst her baby slept through all the din Kit joined her sister-in-law and others who lined the streets to watch the triumphant procession of miners, their colourful banners held high, marching to the clash of cymbal and drum, and singing songs of glory.

With the restoration of employment, Owen was unable to spare any time to organize a cart in which to go and collect his sister's property. Kit gave lacklustre reply that this was of no import, though she would appreciate the recovery of her bank book so that she could at least make a contribution and buy some underwear in order to return Nurse Fenton's drawers and the borrowed baby clothes. In that case, Owen told her, he would go on Sunday morning before chapel. When his sister said she hoped he would not be given any trouble, he replied that she had a right to her money, which Kit thought was something of an anomaly from Owen's lips.

Sunday came. Owen was about to set off, having got as far as the passage, when someone rapped at the door. Returning to the kitchen, he told Kit, 'You've got a visitor.'

'Kit, I'm that sorry I haven't come before this!' A manifestation of teeth and hair and skin and bone came at her and seated itself beside her on the sofa, grabbing her arm. 'I only just got back from Malvern last night – oh, I'll tell you about that later – and when I opened your letter I couldn't believe it. The minute I got up this morning I went straight round to that nurse's address and she told me you were here. I'm ever so sorry I wasn't there to help.'

Tears in her eyes, Kit told Mr Popplewell that she was well looked after here, but said she was pleased to see him. Shown the baby, he murmured that its father would have been proud of such a grand lad, setting Kit off crying again, at which point Owen cleared his throat and said he would be away to collect the bank book.

Mr Popplewell accepted a cup of tea from Meg, who went about the business of preparing Sunday lunch whilst Kit spoke intimately to her guest.

An hour or so after this Owen returned, both his wife and sister showing surprise.

'You didn't take long!' exclaimed Meg. 'Did you get the bank book?'

Owen wore an odd expression. 'No, I brought summat else instead.'

Seated next to Mr Popplewell on the sofa, Kit almost swooned as Worthy came in.

There were exclamations from others, but Kit could say nothing, just sat there staring at her husband who filled the room with his large, living, presence.

Making no move to approach her, Worthy allowed his brother-in-law to give a few words of explanation. 'He were on his way over here when we met halfway,' said Owen, then jerked his head at the front parlour. 'Take him in t'front, Kit.' And as she passed, still speechless with shock, he dealt her a reproachful tap and muttered, 'You daft cat.'

Alone with Worthy in the front parlour, Kit found it hard to meet his eyes, ecstatically happy that he was alive, yet sorrowful that his love for her had been destroyed.

Worthy spoke first. 'Owen says you thought I were dead.' At her lip-trembling nod, he turned his head to reveal his disfigurement. 'Just took the top of my ear off, and a bit of scalp. Deafened me, an' all.'

Kit broke her silence. 'I saw all the blood . . .' She pressed a hand over her mouth, her eyes filling with tears.

He stopped all the pretence then, strode forward and held her, telling her how much she had hurt him, crushing her so tightly she could hardly breathe. Yet there was a gruffness, a reservation in his attitude, as if he were unsure whether to make the ultimate step to forgiveness.

'I tried a hundred times to tell you!' she wept. 'But how could I when you thought you were married to the perfect woman?'

Hugging her to him, Worthy admitted that his ideals had been far too high. He would not expect such perfection in the future – all he would demand of her was the truth.

She lifted her wet face from his shoulder and sniffed. 'You mean, you'll take me back?'

'You're my wife, Katherine. Nothing can change that.'

They stood embracing for long emotional moments. Then Kit heaved a sigh, wiped her eyes and said he must come and meet his son.

The big man looked uncomfortable. 'I'll pay more heed to him later – when there's no other folk about. Come, I'll take you home.'

She hesitated. 'Do your mother and father know you're here?'

His eyes would not look at her – an indication that he was fully aware his parents would not be pleased. 'No. While they were in chapel I went to Nurse Fenton's. She told me where you were.'

Kit projected disbelief. 'I truly thought you were dead. Oh, Worthy, I can't tell you how glad I am, how sorry, how miserable I was, how –' She broke off, not knowing what else to say.

'I was bad for the best part of a week. Not just with the wound, but from influenza. That was what saved me in a way. When Abel and me were fighting over the gun I felt so dizzy I collapsed, pressing the trigger as I fell, but it didn't do as much harm as it might.'

'Enough.' With rueful expression and tender fingers, she examined the damage that the stray pellets had done to his ear. There was only a raggy little piece of it left – the side of his head a mass of scabs and dried blood. 'Your mother isn't going to thank you for taking me back.'

'It's my choice, not hers.' Unsmiling, he guided her to the door.

First thanking Owen and his wife for their kindness, and refusing the offer to stay for dinner, Kit told Mr Popplewell that she was sorry their meeting had been brief, but she was now going home.

Outside the row of miners' cottages a patient old mare waited in the spring sunshine. Worthy helped his wife and child aboard the cart, then drove them home.

During the journey, Kit took the opportunity to be totally honest with her husband. He would not like what he heard, she told Worthy, and if he found it unbearable then she would ask only that he help her remove all her belongings from the farm and take them elsewhere, and she would disappear for ever. 'But first,' she added, her voice heavy with emotion, 'I want you to know that you are the only man I have every truly loved – more than my own life. Indeed, that life will be worthless if you abandon me.'

'Tell me now,' he said in a manner that urged her to get it over with. 'I won't abandon you.'

Kit bit her lip. 'You may despise me.'

There was hesitation. Worthy looked at the sleeping baby in his wife's arms. 'Are you trying to say he isn't mine?'

Tears of horror sprang to her eyes. 'Of course he's yours! How could you think it?'

Worthy became stalwart. 'Then nothing you say can hurt me.'

Abruptly he pulled on the reins and stopped the cart in the middle of a quiet lane, turning to her, but concentrating on the child, his eyes running over every inch of it. 'He's a big lad. Have you named him yet?' Before the birth they had debated many options.

Kit shook her head, smiling through her tears at the slumbering infant. 'I didn't have the heart. Let his father name him.'

Worthy pulled the shawl gently from the baby's face and gazed upon him. 'Tobias Treasure.'

And that was that. With a flick of the reins the cart was once more in motion.

Worthy encouraged his wife to proceed with her confession. Nothing she could tell him would be a revelation. During his recuperation, his mother had gone over to Ralph Royd and made enquiries of the local gossips. The resulting information had appalled his entire family. However, he did not tell her this. It must come from Katherine's lips.

'I don't like to think of it, but I'm not stupid enough to believe that a woman conceives without the help of a man. Was he the one who jilted you?'

With no lessening of tension, Kit took a deep breath and exhaled. 'More than one.' She rushed to explain, 'I wasn't one of those women – you know, one of *those*. It was just that I tended to get myself entangled without proper thought. I believed I was going to be married but the other parties had a different idea. How could I have ever imagined they'd really be interested in me – a servant? They were from good backgrounds.' She shook her head at her own gullibility. 'Then, I must confess I went rather astray, fooled myself into thinking that the only happiness I would achieve was from dancing and parties and other gay pursuits. So I allowed myself to act as consort to rich men.' She stopped in time to prevent it sounding as if there had been an army of them. 'I didn't set out to be an embarrassment to my family – all I ever wanted was a family of my own and a husband such as you. But people didn't seem to want me as a wife.' She shrugged sadly, her plump shoulder occasionally colliding with his from the motion of the cart. 'So I just let life roll along, doing as I pleased, until I had Beata.'

Worthy affected a frown, though he already knew there had been more than one birth out of wedlock.

'She was the first of my babies,' explained Kit. 'When she died I was so crazed with grief I fell into the first pair of comforting arms that came along – but they weren't really comforting, they were using me as all the rest. My family was furious – quite rightly. That's when I realized I had to stop thinking only of myself, to put my child first. Serena's much better off with Amelia, I'm sure.' The pained expression on her face denied this. 'She was desperate for babies – loved Serena to bits.' So caught up had she become that she didn't realize how tightly she was squeezing her son, who now let forth a wail. Issuing apology, Kit pressed her lips to the soft cheek and shushed the infant, rocking him back to sleep.

'You must have given birth to her just before you met me.' Her husband's voice brought forth more explanation.

Kit nodded. 'When, at first, you and I couldn't have babies of our own I thought it was God's punishment. I wanted to tell you, I truly did, but couldn't bear the thought that I might lose you – you're the best thing that ever happened to me, Worthy.'

'Compared with those men of high standing?' He looked straight ahead between the horse's ears. 'I hardly think –'

'High standing? They might have thought so but none of them could hold a candle to you, none of them treated me as you do.'

Worthy looked rueful. 'You mean they didn't try to kill you.' How could he make such a jest when his heart weighed so heavily?

She objected. 'You didn't try to kill me!'

'Oh, but I did!' His face contorted at the memory.

Kit returned to her subdued mood. 'Well, any man would have done the same – and you didn't succeed. You blew more holes in yourself than in me.'

Worthy fought with himself, his face a picture of incomprehension. 'I'm still angry with you, Katherine, for not telling me any of this before.'

'You have a right to be. I should have told you.' Her arms occupied with her son, she pressed herself against Worthy in an attitude of contrition.

'I'm sure I don't deserve your forgiveness.' When he didn't answer she felt a pang of fear that their marriage might never be mended.

But then he looked her in the face and said, 'What's done is done. I can't say I like the thought of – Well, I've said enough on that score. We'll not speak of it again.'

Phoebe could not believe her eyes upon seeing the cart pull up in the yard, bearing not only her elder son but his estranged wife. Dropping the rolling pin in her hands, she rushed out, hands covered in flour and pastry and shouted above the lowing of the beasts and the clucking of hens. 'I hope you've only brought her to collect her rubbish!'

'No, Mother, I've brought my wife and child home.' Worthy helped Kit down from the cart. A row of inquisitive bovine faces watched from behind a stone wall, jaws chewing in unison.

There was disbelief. 'After all I told you? You don't even know that bairn is yours!'

'I do,' came his dignified reply. He began to escort Kit towards the farmhouse.

Phoebe stood in his way. 'I won't have her here!'

'Might I remind you this is my home,' said Worthy. 'Mine and Katherine's and Toby's.'

'Your father worked all his life for this farm! He won't let it go to a slut.'

'I'll thank you to take that back, Mother!'

'I won't! That's what she is and don't you try to deny it, for there's a whole village of witnesses at Ralph Royd to prove what a fool you're making of yourself.'

George and Abel Treasure had heard the noise and came to lend Phoebe their backing. 'That woman's brought shame on all of us! You heard what she's like yet you brought her back here to drag us down further.' When his elder son took a step forward George blocked his path.

Worthy fixed his father and brother with determined eyes. 'I intend to go into that house and let no man here stop me.'

'See! She's got father against son, brother against brother,' cried Phoebe to her daughter who had also appeared on the scene. Then she turned back to Worthy. 'That house was given to you by your father and me.'

'I've worked as hard as anyone here to earn it,' insisted Worthy. 'And

536

I won't be denied entry. Now, I don't want to fight with any of thee, but I'm going in and so is Katherine.'

George Treasure gritted his teeth and stood aside. 'Very well! Take it. I might be no longer strong enough to throw you out – but, by God, let me tell you this: that square of land beneath those walls is the only bit of this farm you'll occupy. I don't intend to see all I've worked for going to a child who could be anybody's. If that woman goes through that door it's Abel who'll inherit the lot.'

Worthy stood there glaring at his father. Kit watched the indecision play upon her husband's face. This farm was his life. How could she, who had committed so great a trespass on his goodness, expect him to choose it over her?

Dull of eye, she simply gathered her baby's shawl more tightly around his little body and began to walk away, unable to endure any more.

Worthy turned a bad-tempered face and called after her, 'Katherine! Stand your ground.'

Kit turned only briefly. 'I'd be obliged if you'd send all my belongings to Owen's. Excuse me, I must go!'

'Let her go, son!' warned George. There was a pause while no one moved. Then – 'I'm warning thee! You'll get nowt!'

For one wonderful moment, upon hearing those words, Kit pictured Worthy running after her, telling her not to leave. But as she reached the track that led to the road, she found herself alone. And no one followed.

The baby was amazingly heavy. Kit's arms ached from supporting him – though this was nothing compared to the pain in her heart.

She had travelled almost a mile before she heard the cart behind her, but did not look round, just moved on to the verge for it to pass.

Worthy was angry. 'Don't you think my wife and bairn's worth more to me than any bit o' dirt?'

Kit was astonished to see her belongings hastily piled on the cart behind him, Beata's portrait atop everything. 'Worthy, you can't sacrifice your farm for me. You love this place!'

Worthy had jumped down. 'It's no sacrifice – now get up there!' He made an impatient gesture and shoved her bottom from behind.

The baby in one arm, she struggled into the seat and watched him stride round the horse who shied at his bad humour. 'But you've worked for this all your life.'

'I've waited for you all my life, and compared to how I feel about you and our little lad the farm's nowt. Nowt!' He sat down angrily beside her and lashed the reins. The horse stepped out along the lane. 'How dare they bloody tell me who I can love?'

Kit seemed to have done nothing but cry lately. Upon hearing this statement of affection she burst into fresh tears – for never once had he told her he loved her. Still, she argued through a quagmire of salty mucus. 'But –'

'But nowt!' Worthy glared at her, swaying along with the cart. 'You'll stay as my wife and be damned to them!' Yet after a moment, he calmed down and made hasty addendum. 'If you don't mind being a labourer's wife with naught to your name, that is.'

And as the horse clip-clopped onwards, Kit smiled back over their child's head and gave her fond reply. 'Dearest, all I ever wanted is right here on this cart.'